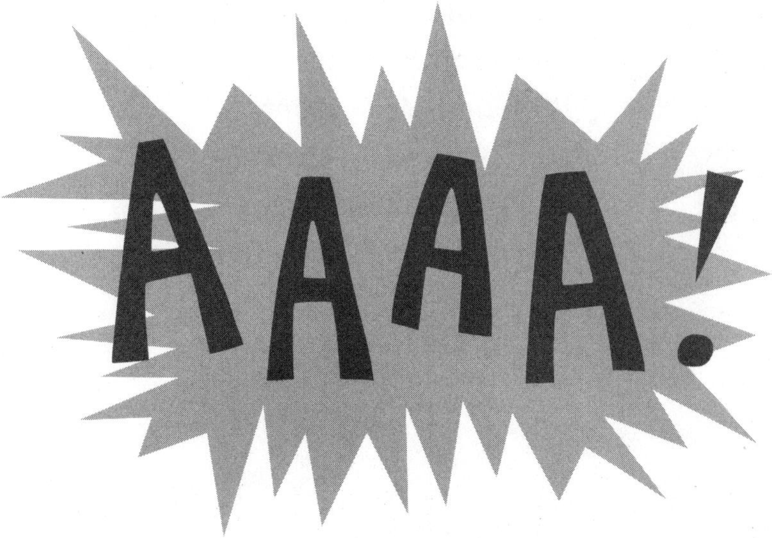
AAAA!

Recent *FoxTrot* books by Bill Amend

Jasotron: 2012

FoxTrot Sundaes

Wrapped-Up FoxTrot

Jam-Packed FoxTrot

FoxTrotius Maximus

FoxTrot: Assembled with Care

A FoxTrot Kids Edition

by Bill Amend

Andrews McMeel
Publishing, LLC

Kansas City • Sydney • London

FoxTrot is distributed internationally by Universal Uclick.

Andrews McMeel Publishing, LLC
an Andrews McMeel Universal company
1130 Walnut Street, Kansas City, Missouri 64106

www.andrewsmcmeel.com

12 13 14 15 16 RR2 10 9 8 7 6 5 4 3 2 1

ISBN: 978-1-4494-2305-6

Library of Congress Control Number: 2012936749

ATTENTION: SCHOOLS AND BUSINESSES

Andrews McMeel books are available at quantity discounts with bulk purchase for educational, business, or sales promotional use. For information, please e-mail the Andrews McMeel Publishing Special Sales Department:
specialsales@amuniversal.com

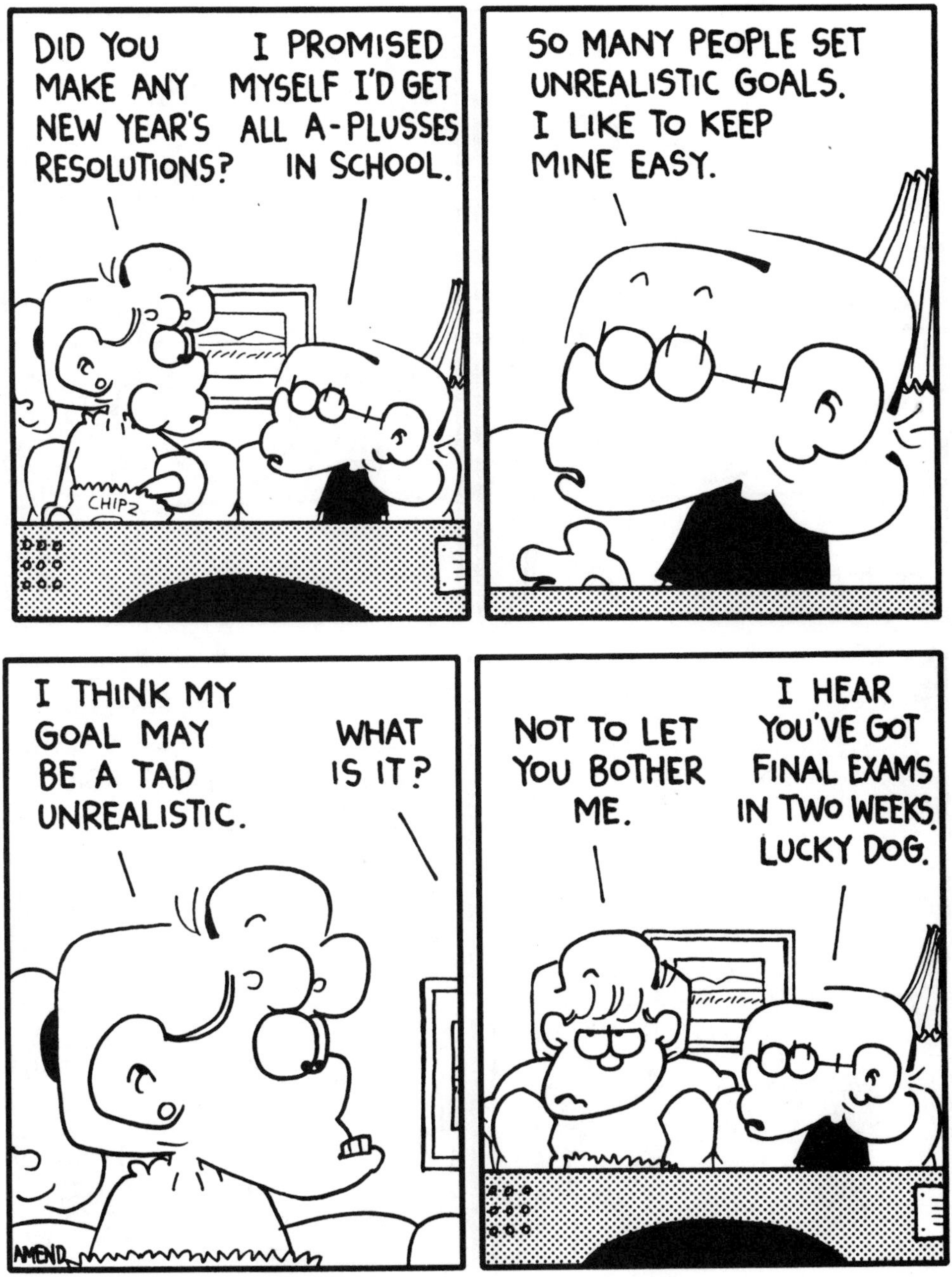
DID YOU MAKE ANY NEW YEAR'S RESOLUTIONS?
I PROMISED MYSELF I'D GET ALL A-PLUSSES IN SCHOOL.
CHIPZ
SO MANY PEOPLE SET UNREALISTIC GOALS. I LIKE TO KEEP MINE EASY.
I THINK MY GOAL MAY BE A TAD UNREALISTIC.
WHAT IS IT?
AMEND
I HEAR YOU'VE GOT FINAL EXAMS IN TWO WEEKS. LUCKY DOG.
NOT TO LET YOU BOTHER ME.

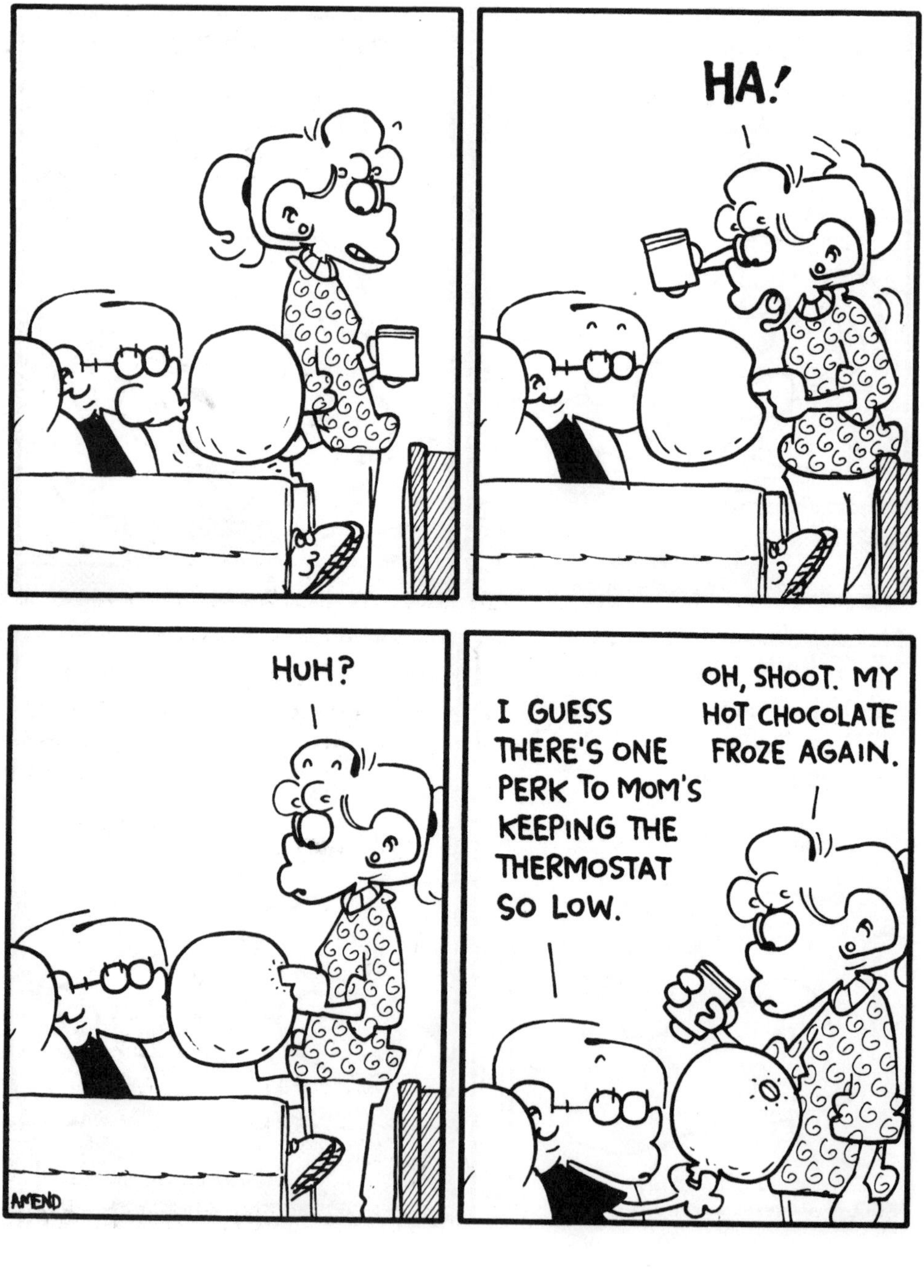
HA!
HUH?
OH, SHOOT. MY HOT CHOCOLATE FROZE AGAIN.
I GUESS THERE'S ONE PERK TO MOM'S KEEPING THE THERMOSTAT SO LOW.
AMEND

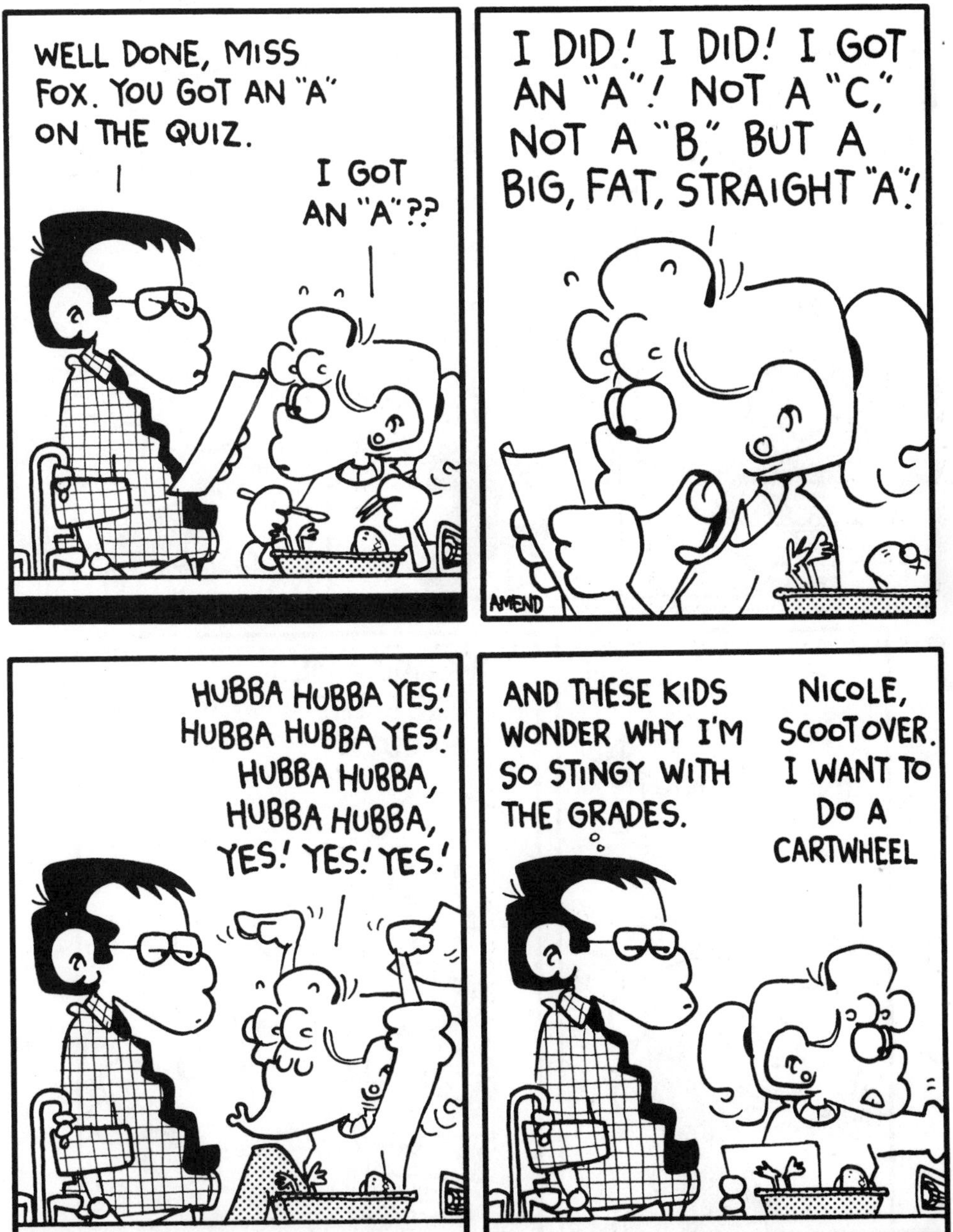
WELL DONE, MISS FOX. YOU GOT AN "A" ON THE QUIZ.
I GOT AN "A"??
I DID! I DID! I GOT AN "A"! NOT A "C," NOT A "B," BUT A BIG, FAT, STRAIGHT "A"!
AMEND
HUBBA HUBBA YES! HUBBA HUBBA YES! HUBBA HUBBA, HUBBA HUBBA, YES! YES! YES!
AND THESE KIDS WONDER WHY I'M SO STINGY WITH THE GRADES.
NICOLE, SCOOT OVER. I WANT TO DO A CARTWHEEL

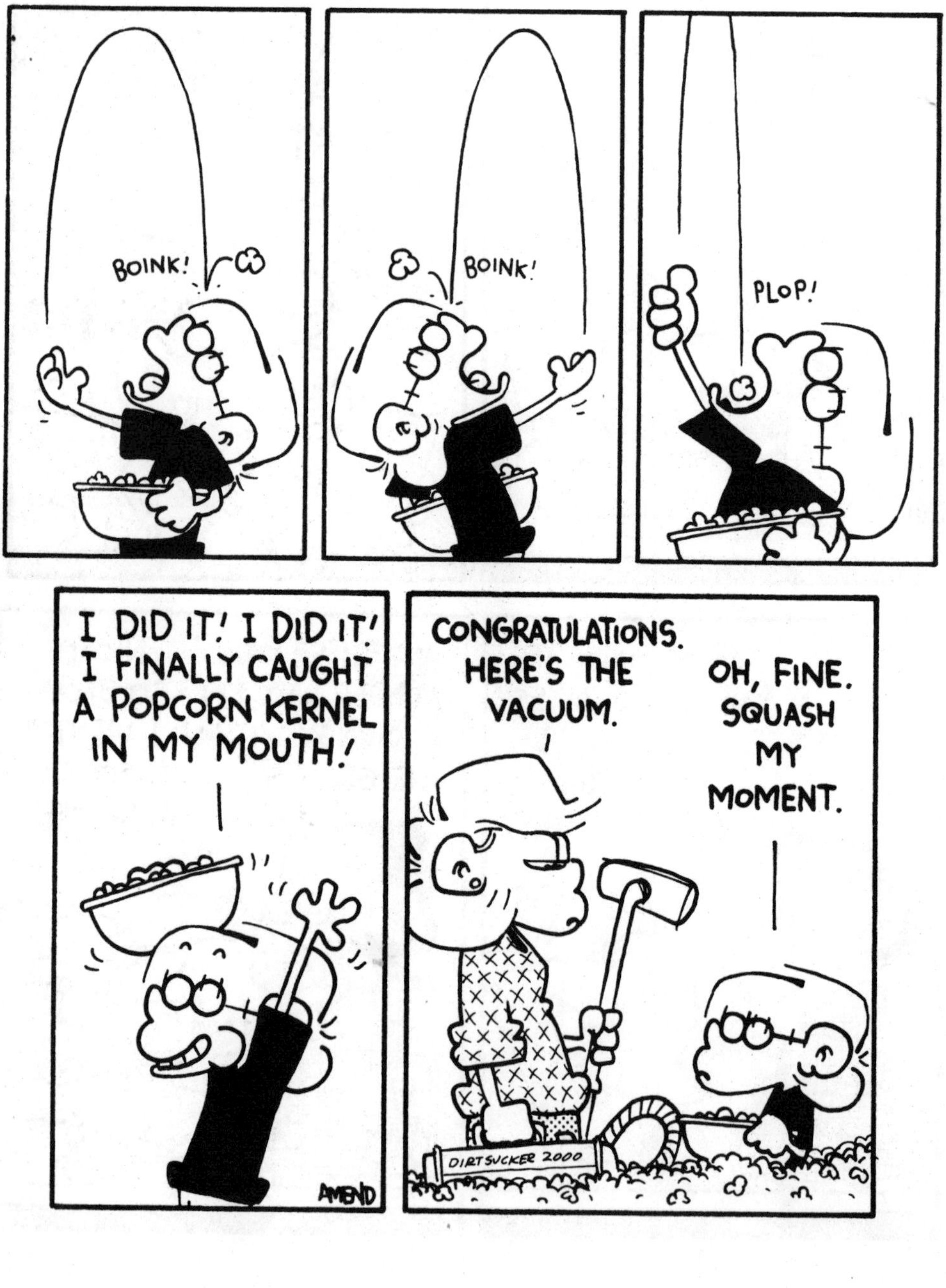
BOINK!
BOINK!
PLOP!
I DID IT! I DID IT! I FINALLY CAUGHT A POPCORN KERNEL IN MY MOUTH!
AMEND
CONGRATULATIONS. HERE'S THE VACUUM.
OH, FINE. SQUASH MY MOMENT.
DIRTSUCKER 2000

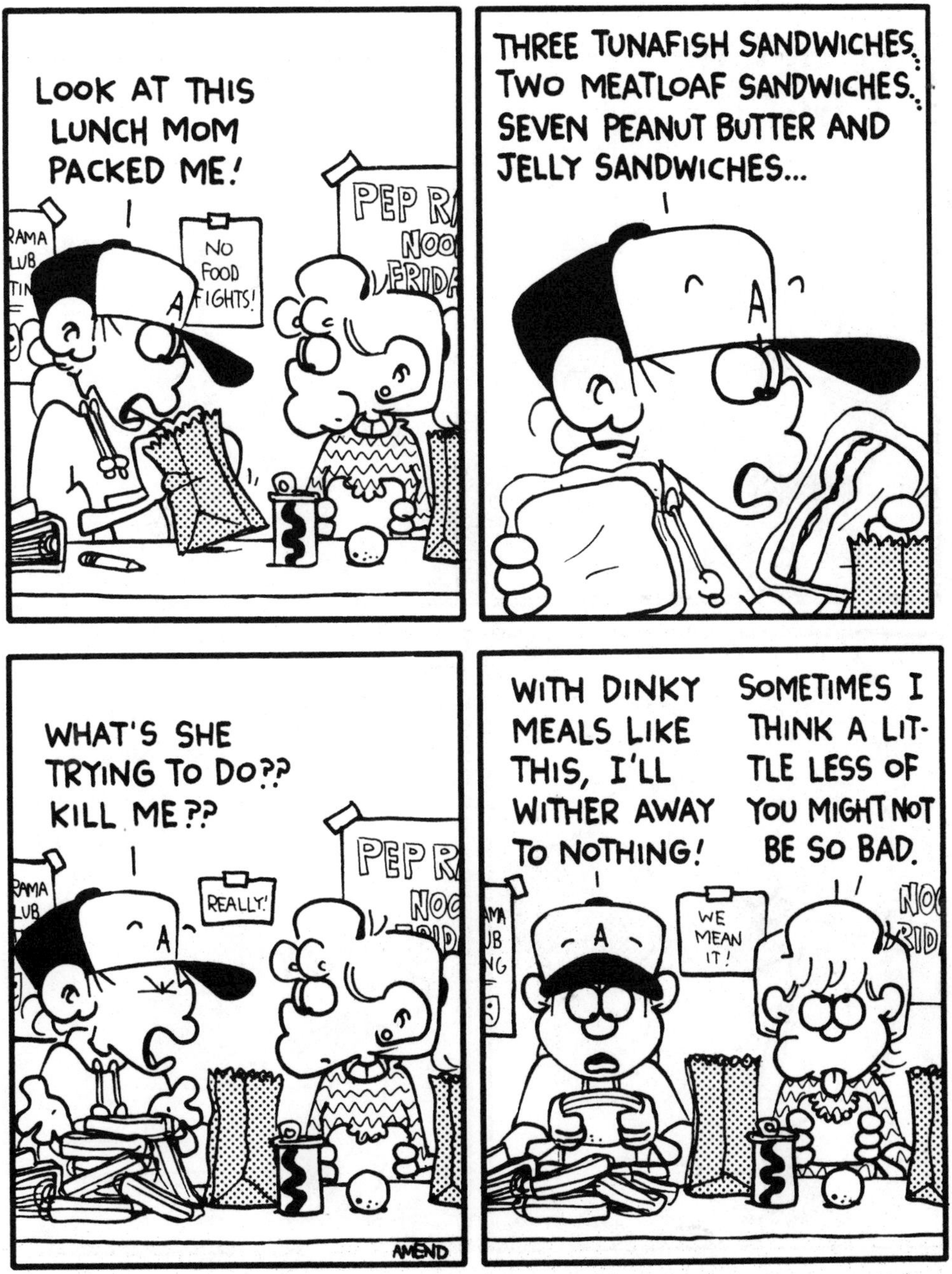
LOOK AT THIS LUNCH MOM PACKED ME!
NO FOOD FIGHTS!
THREE TUNAFISH SANDWICHES... TWO MEATLOAF SANDWICHES... SEVEN PEANUT BUTTER AND JELLY SANDWICHES...
WHAT'S SHE TRYING TO DO?? KILL ME??
REALLY!
WITH DINKY MEALS LIKE THIS, I'LL WITHER AWAY TO NOTHING!
SOMETIMES I THINK A LITTLE LESS OF YOU MIGHT NOT BE SO BAD.
WE MEAN IT!
AMEND

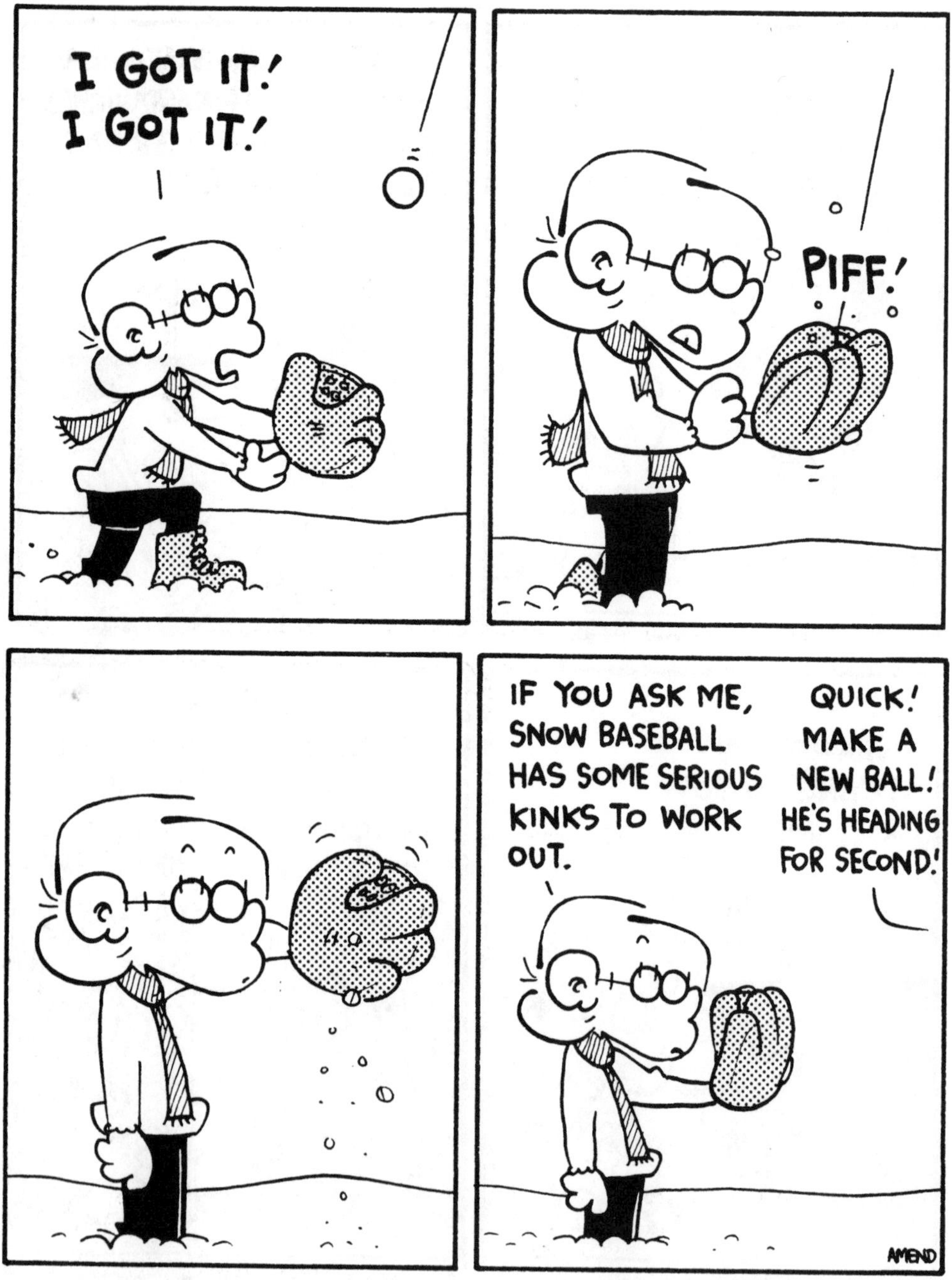
I GOT IT! I GOT IT!
PIFF!
IF YOU ASK ME, SNOW BASEBALL HAS SOME SERIOUS KINKS TO WORK OUT.
QUICK! MAKE A NEW BALL! HE'S HEADING FOR SECOND!
AMEND

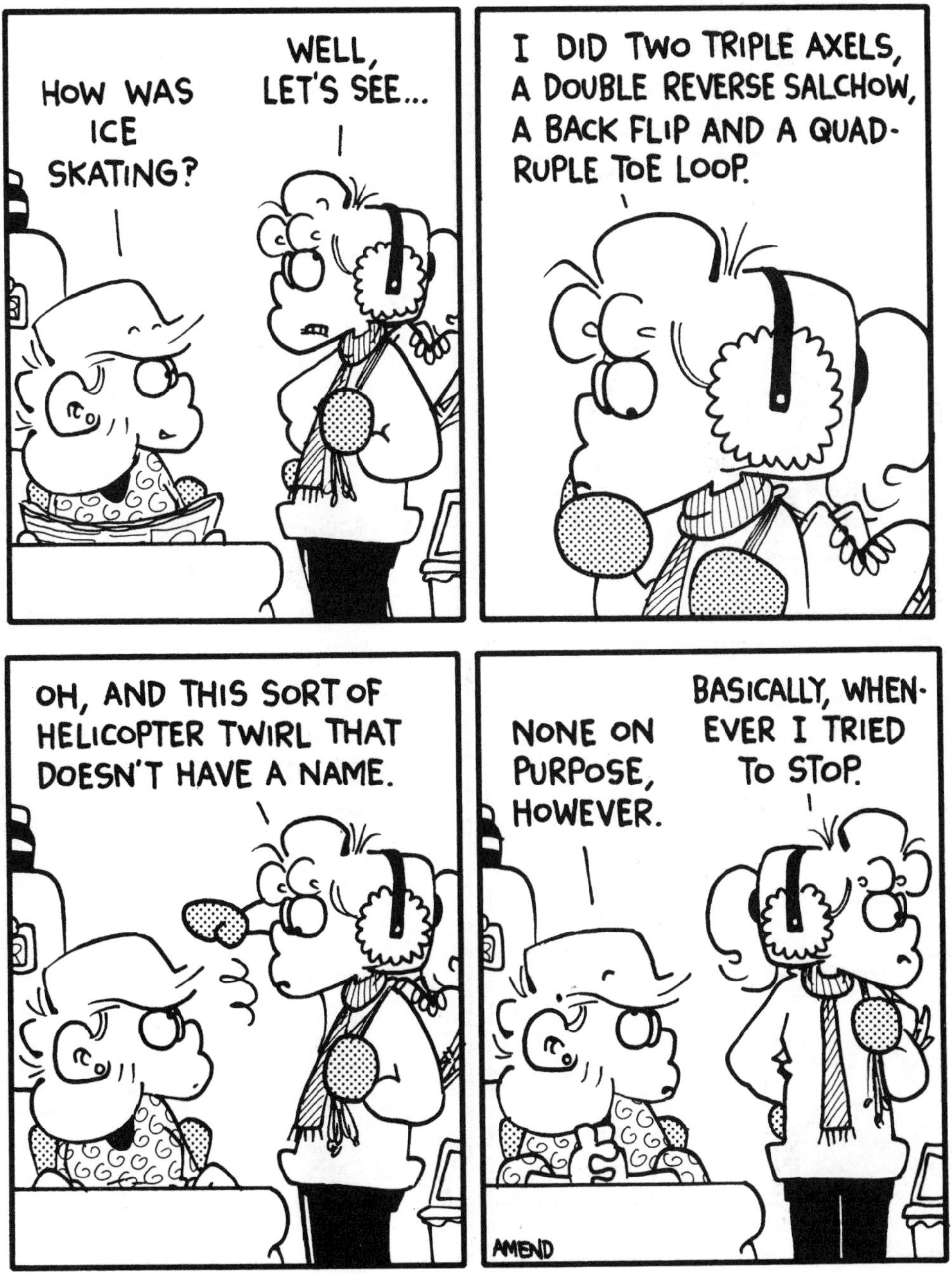
HOW WAS ICE SKATING?
WELL, LET'S SEE...
I DID TWO TRIPLE AXELS, A DOUBLE REVERSE SALCHOW, A BACK FLIP AND A QUAD-RUPLE TOE LOOP.
OH, AND THIS SORT OF HELICOPTER TWIRL THAT DOESN'T HAVE A NAME.
NONE ON PURPOSE, HOWEVER.
BASICALLY, WHEN-EVER I TRIED TO STOP.
AMEND

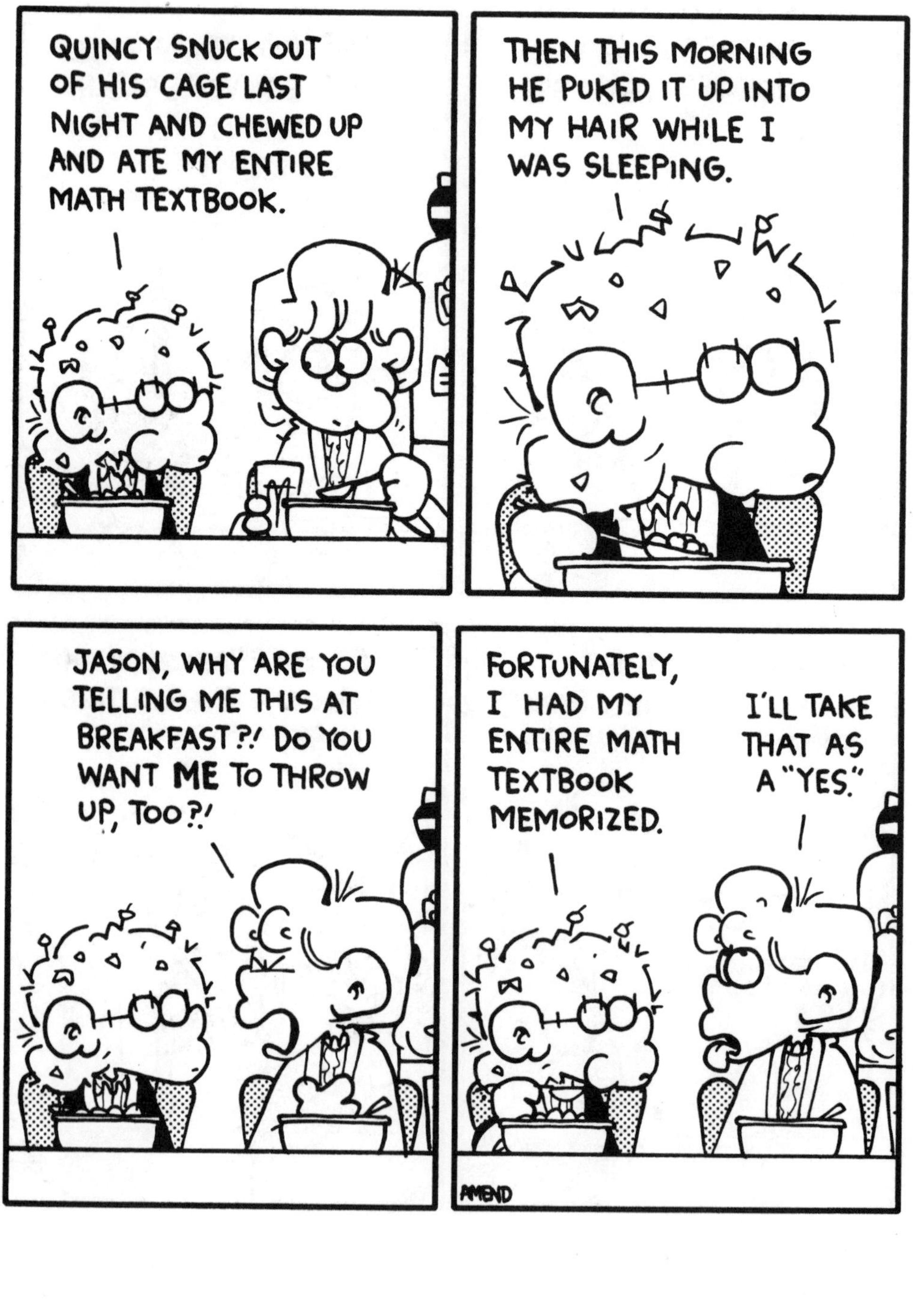
QUINCY SNUCK OUT OF HIS CAGE LAST NIGHT AND CHEWED UP AND ATE MY ENTIRE MATH TEXTBOOK.
THEN THIS MORNING HE PUKED IT UP INTO MY HAIR WHILE I WAS SLEEPING.
JASON, WHY ARE YOU TELLING ME THIS AT BREAKFAST?! DO YOU WANT **ME** TO THROW UP, TOO?!
FORTUNATELY, I HAD MY ENTIRE MATH TEXTBOOK MEMORIZED.
I'LL TAKE THAT AS A "YES."
AMEND

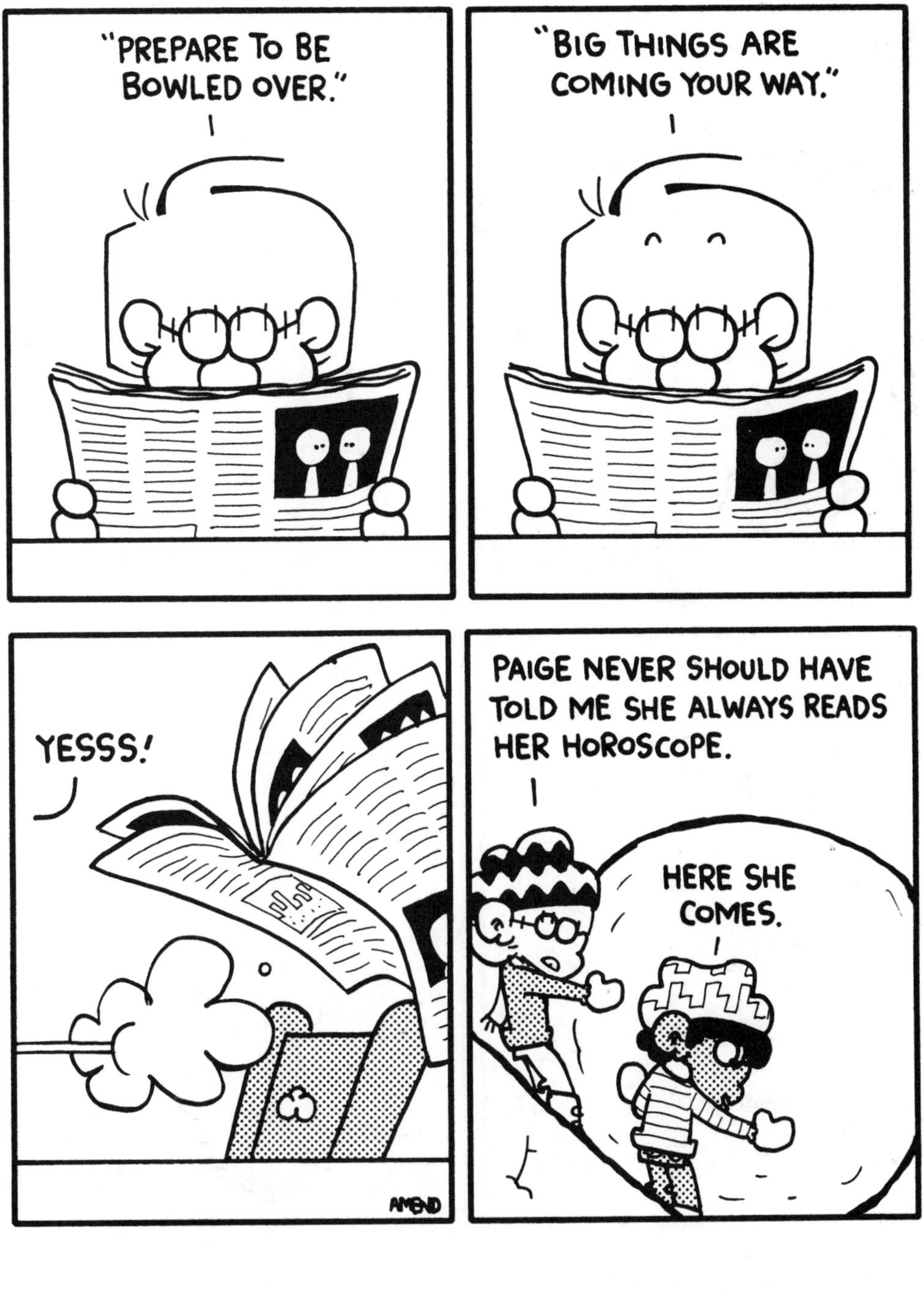
"PREPARE TO BE BOWLED OVER."
"BIG THINGS ARE COMING YOUR WAY."
YESSS!
AMEND
PAIGE NEVER SHOULD HAVE TOLD ME SHE ALWAYS READS HER HOROSCOPE.
HERE SHE COMES.

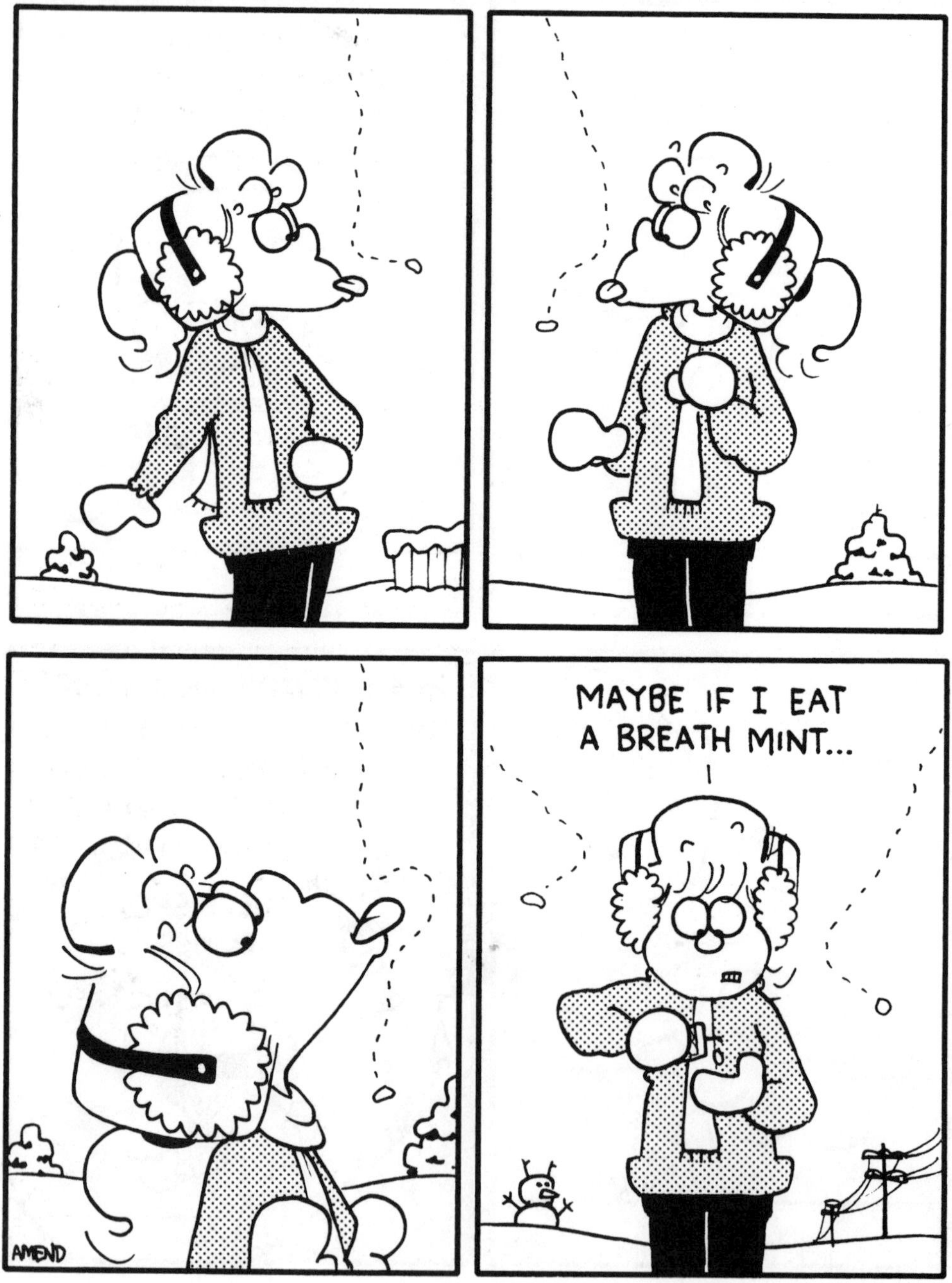

AMEND
MAYBE IF I EAT A BREATH MINT...

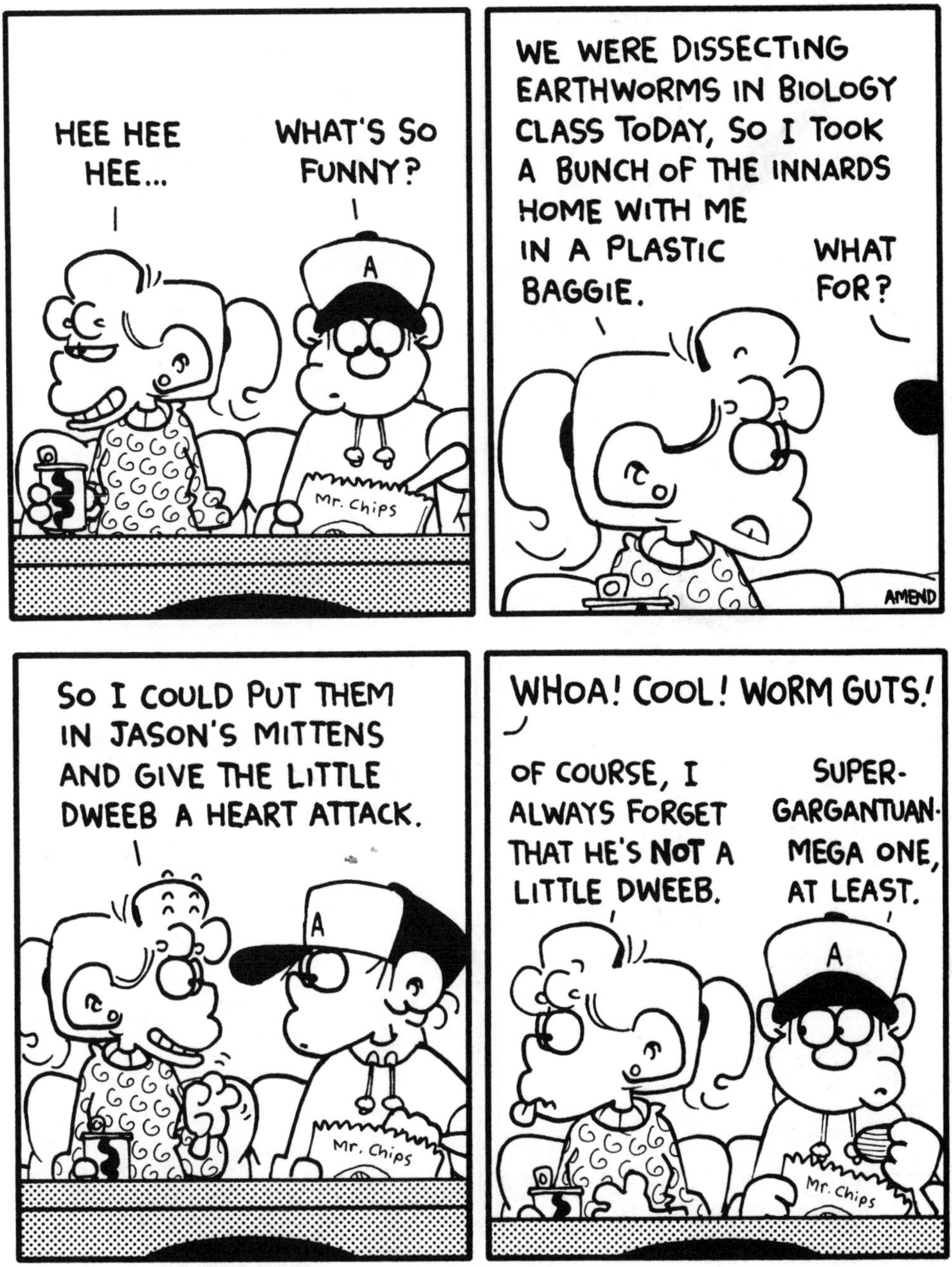
HEE HEE HEE...
WHAT'S SO FUNNY?
WE WERE DISSECTING EARTHWORMS IN BIOLOGY CLASS TODAY, SO I TOOK A BUNCH OF THE INNARDS HOME WITH ME IN A PLASTIC BAGGIE.
WHAT FOR?
AMEND
SO I COULD PUT THEM IN JASON'S MITTENS AND GIVE THE LITTLE DWEEB A HEART ATTACK.
WHOA! COOL! WORM GUTS!
OF COURSE, I ALWAYS FORGET THAT HE'S NOT A LITTLE DWEEB.
SUPER-GARGANTUAN-MEGA ONE, AT LEAST.

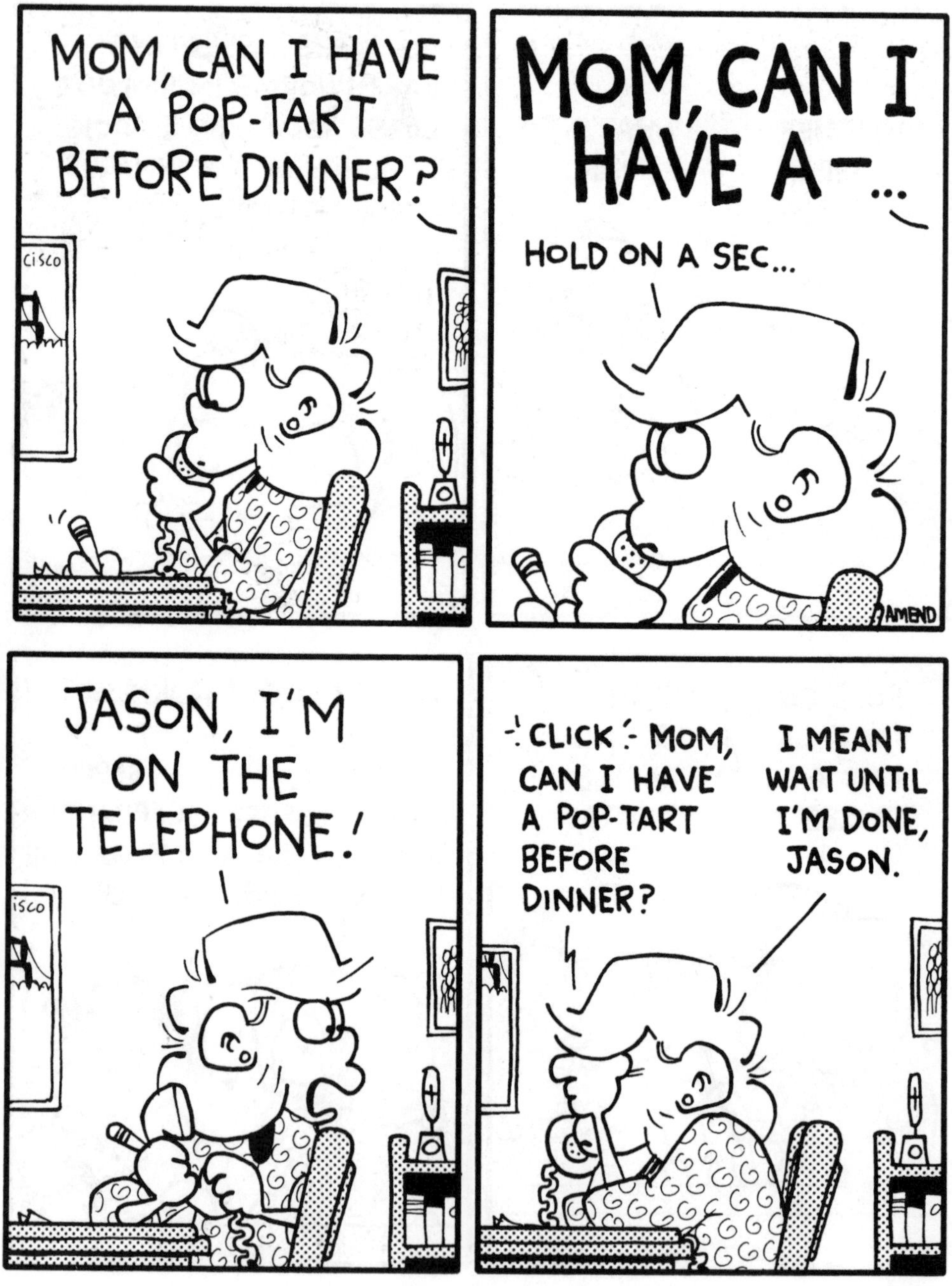
MOM, CAN I HAVE A POP-TART BEFORE DINNER?
CISCO
MOM, CAN I HAVE A–...
HOLD ON A SEC...
AMEND
JASON, I'M ON THE TELEPHONE!
ISCO
-!- CLICK -!- MOM, CAN I HAVE A POP-TART BEFORE DINNER?
I MEANT WAIT UNTIL I'M DONE, JASON.

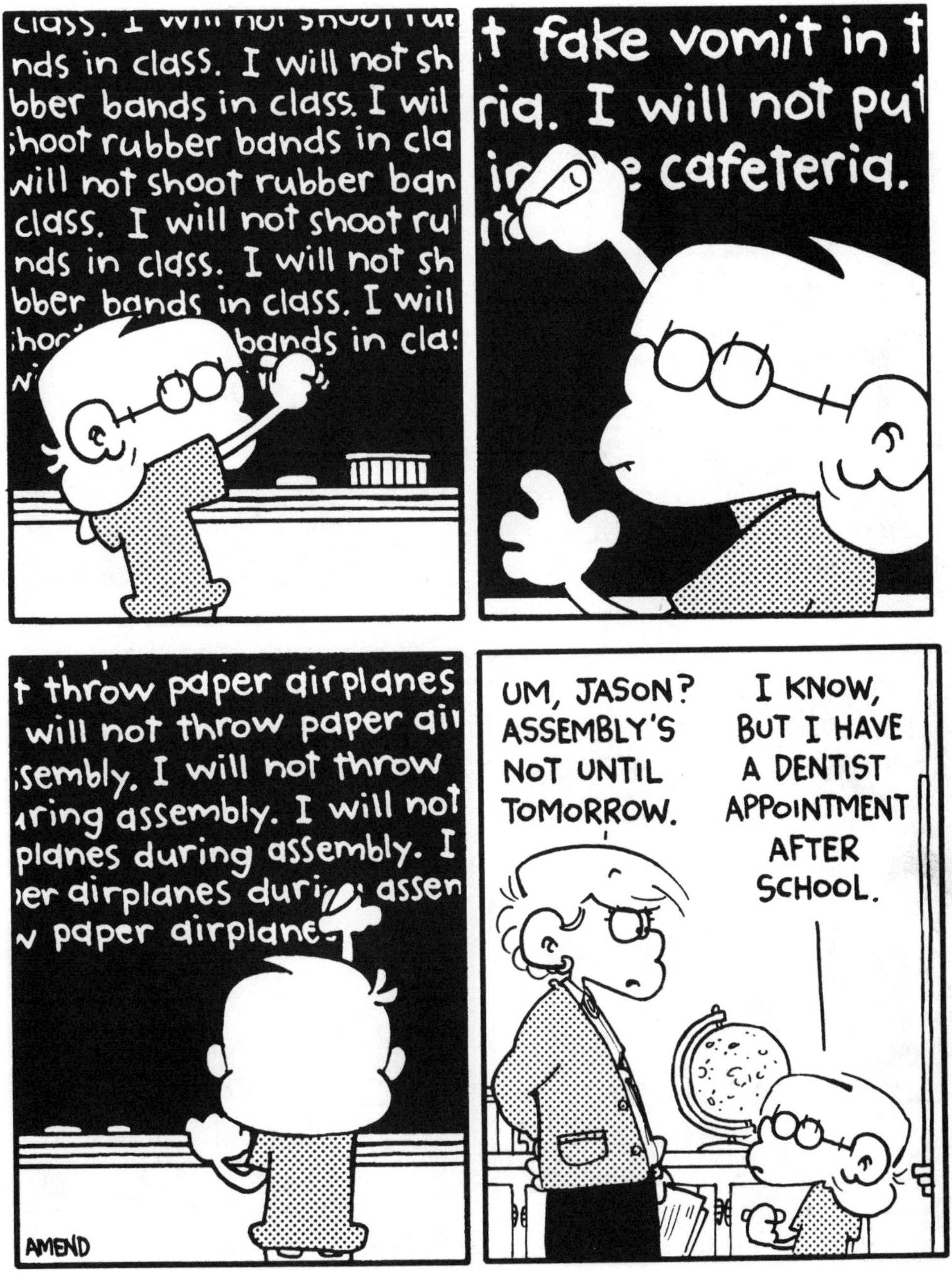
nds in class. I will not sh
bber bands in class. I wil
hoot rubber bands in cla
will not shoot rubber ban
class. I will not shoot ru
nds in class. I will not sh
bber bands in class. I will
bands in cla
t fake vomit in t
ria. I will not pu
cafeteria.
t throw paper airplanes
will not throw paper ai
sembly. I will not throw
ring assembly. I will not
planes during assembly. I
er airplanes duri assen
paper airplane
AMEND
UM, JASON? ASSEMBLY'S NOT UNTIL TOMORROW.
I KNOW, BUT I HAVE A DENTIST APPOINTMENT AFTER SCHOOL.

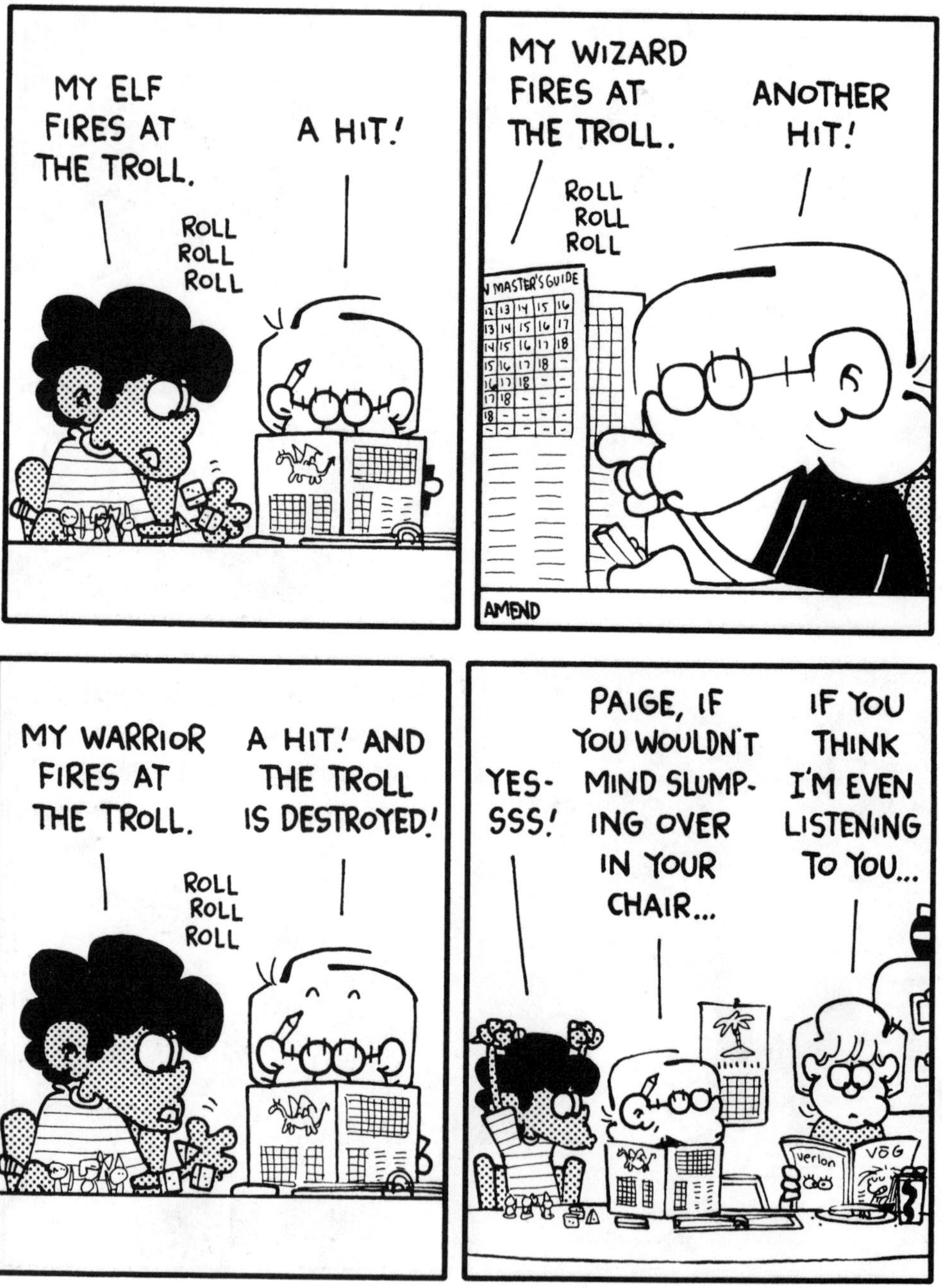
MY ELF FIRES AT THE TROLL.
ROLL ROLL ROLL
A HIT!
MY WIZARD FIRES AT THE TROLL.
ROLL ROLL ROLL
MASTER'S GUIDE
ANOTHER HIT!
AMEND
MY WARRIOR FIRES AT THE TROLL.
ROLL ROLL ROLL
A HIT! AND THE TROLL IS DESTROYED!
YES-SSS!
PAIGE, IF YOU WOULDN'T MIND SLUMP-ING OVER IN YOUR CHAIR...
IF YOU THINK I'M EVEN LISTENING TO YOU...
verlon
VŌG

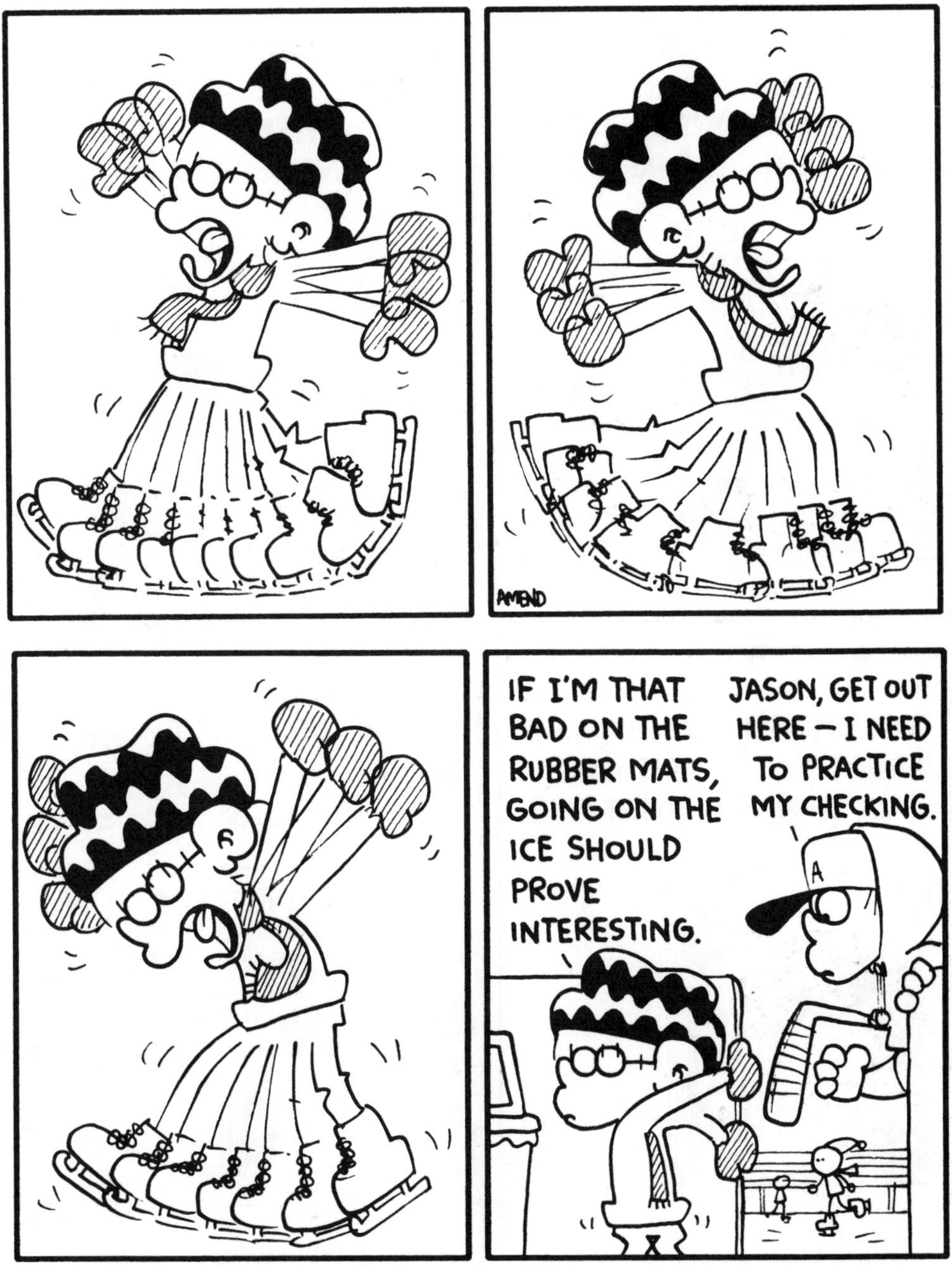

AMEND
IF I'M THAT BAD ON THE RUBBER MATS, GOING ON THE ICE SHOULD PROVE INTERESTING.
JASON, GET OUT HERE – I NEED TO PRACTICE MY CHECKING.
A

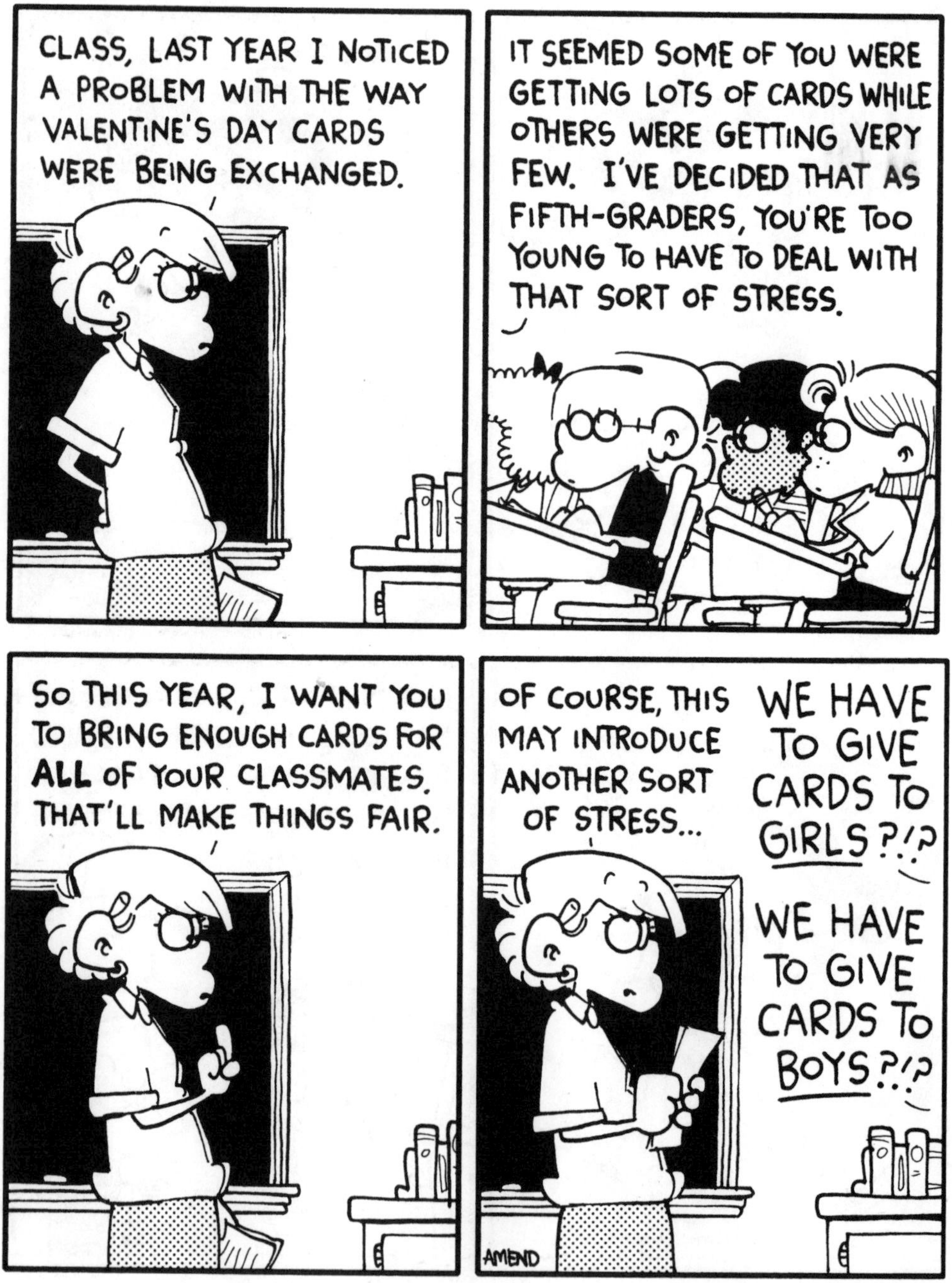
CLASS, LAST YEAR I NOTICED A PROBLEM WITH THE WAY VALENTINE'S DAY CARDS WERE BEING EXCHANGED.
IT SEEMED SOME OF YOU WERE GETTING LOTS OF CARDS WHILE OTHERS WERE GETTING VERY FEW. I'VE DECIDED THAT AS FIFTH-GRADERS, YOU'RE TOO YOUNG TO HAVE TO DEAL WITH THAT SORT OF STRESS.
SO THIS YEAR, I WANT YOU TO BRING ENOUGH CARDS FOR ALL OF YOUR CLASSMATES. THAT'LL MAKE THINGS FAIR.
OF COURSE, THIS MAY INTRODUCE ANOTHER SORT OF STRESS...
WE HAVE TO GIVE CARDS TO GIRLS?!?
WE HAVE TO GIVE CARDS TO BOYS?!?
AMEND

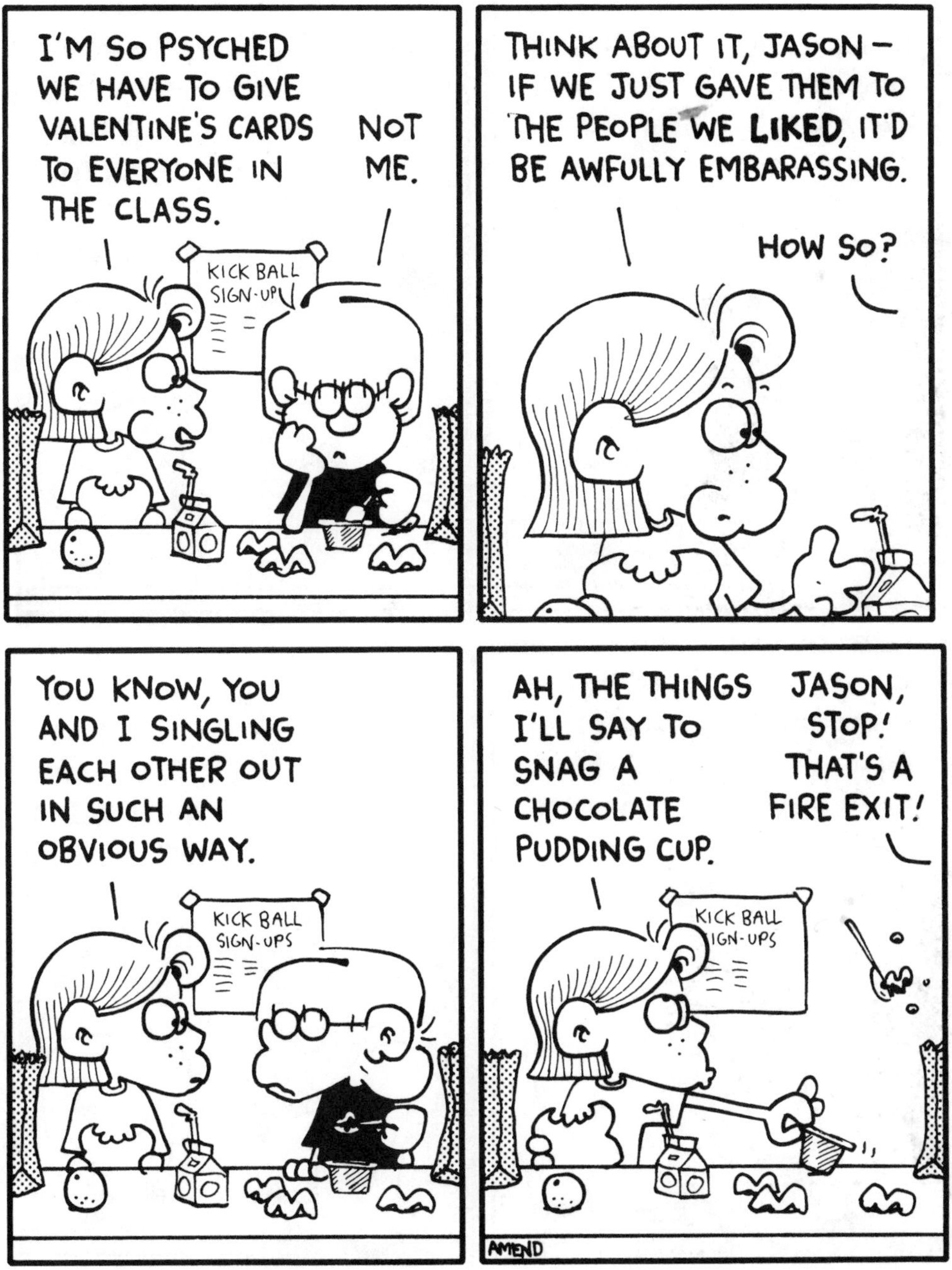
I'M SO PSYCHED WE HAVE TO GIVE VALENTINE'S CARDS TO EVERYONE IN THE CLASS.
NOT ME.
KICK BALL SIGN-UPS
THINK ABOUT IT, JASON - IF WE JUST GAVE THEM TO THE PEOPLE WE LIKED, IT'D BE AWFULLY EMBARASSING.
HOW SO?
YOU KNOW, YOU AND I SINGLING EACH OTHER OUT IN SUCH AN OBVIOUS WAY.
KICK BALL SIGN-UPS
AH, THE THINGS I'LL SAY TO SNAG A CHOCOLATE PUDDING CUP.
JASON, STOP! THAT'S A FIRE EXIT!
KICK BALL SIGN-UPS
AMEND

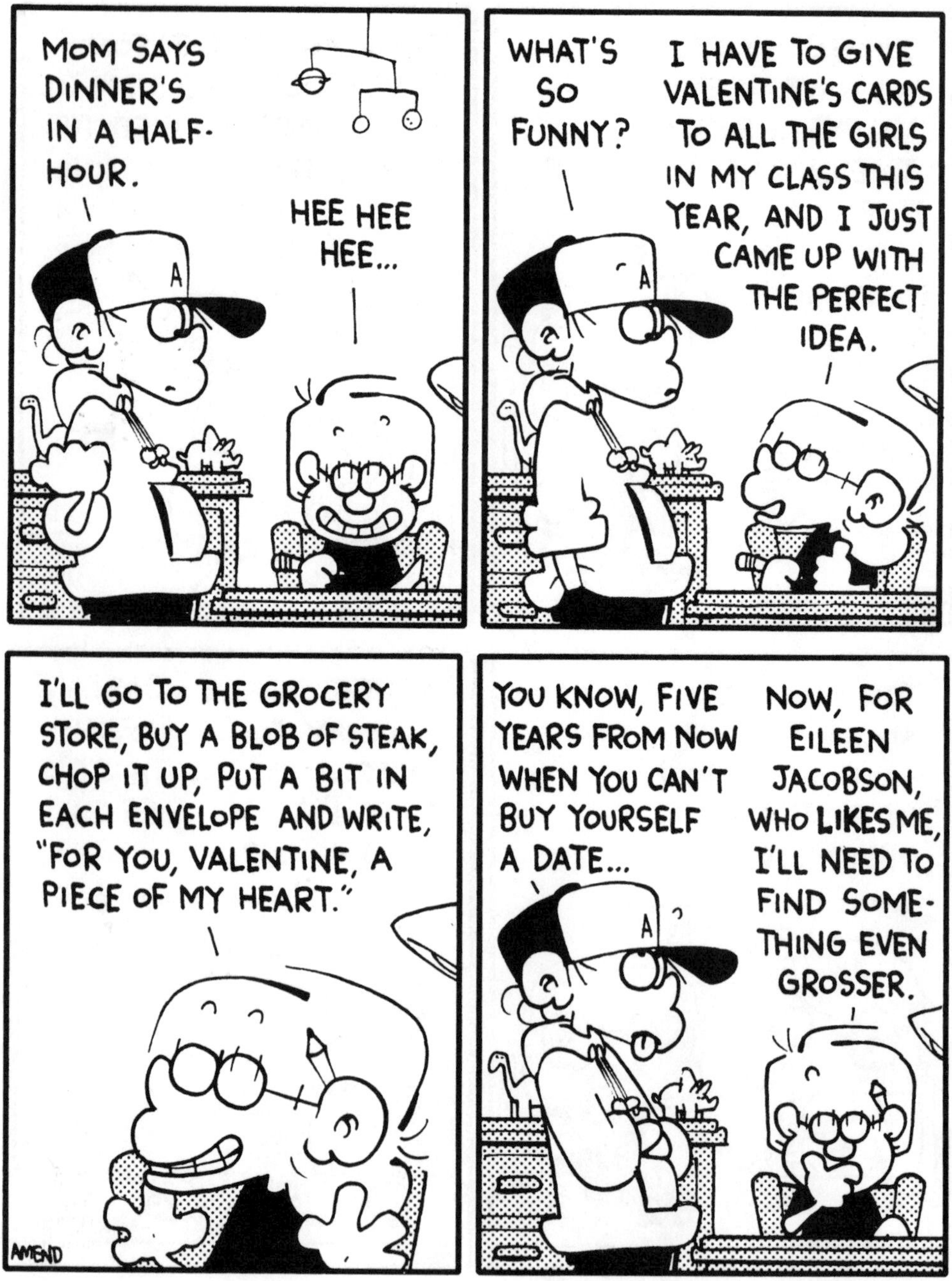
MOM SAYS DINNER'S IN A HALF-HOUR.
HEE HEE HEE...
WHAT'S SO FUNNY?
I HAVE TO GIVE VALENTINE'S CARDS TO ALL THE GIRLS IN MY CLASS THIS YEAR, AND I JUST CAME UP WITH THE PERFECT IDEA.
I'LL GO TO THE GROCERY STORE, BUY A BLOB OF STEAK, CHOP IT UP, PUT A BIT IN EACH ENVELOPE AND WRITE, "FOR YOU, VALENTINE, A PIECE OF MY HEART."
YOU KNOW, FIVE YEARS FROM NOW WHEN YOU CAN'T BUY YOURSELF A DATE...
NOW, FOR EILEEN JACOBSON, WHO LIKES ME, I'LL NEED TO FIND SOME-THING EVEN GROSSER.
AMEND

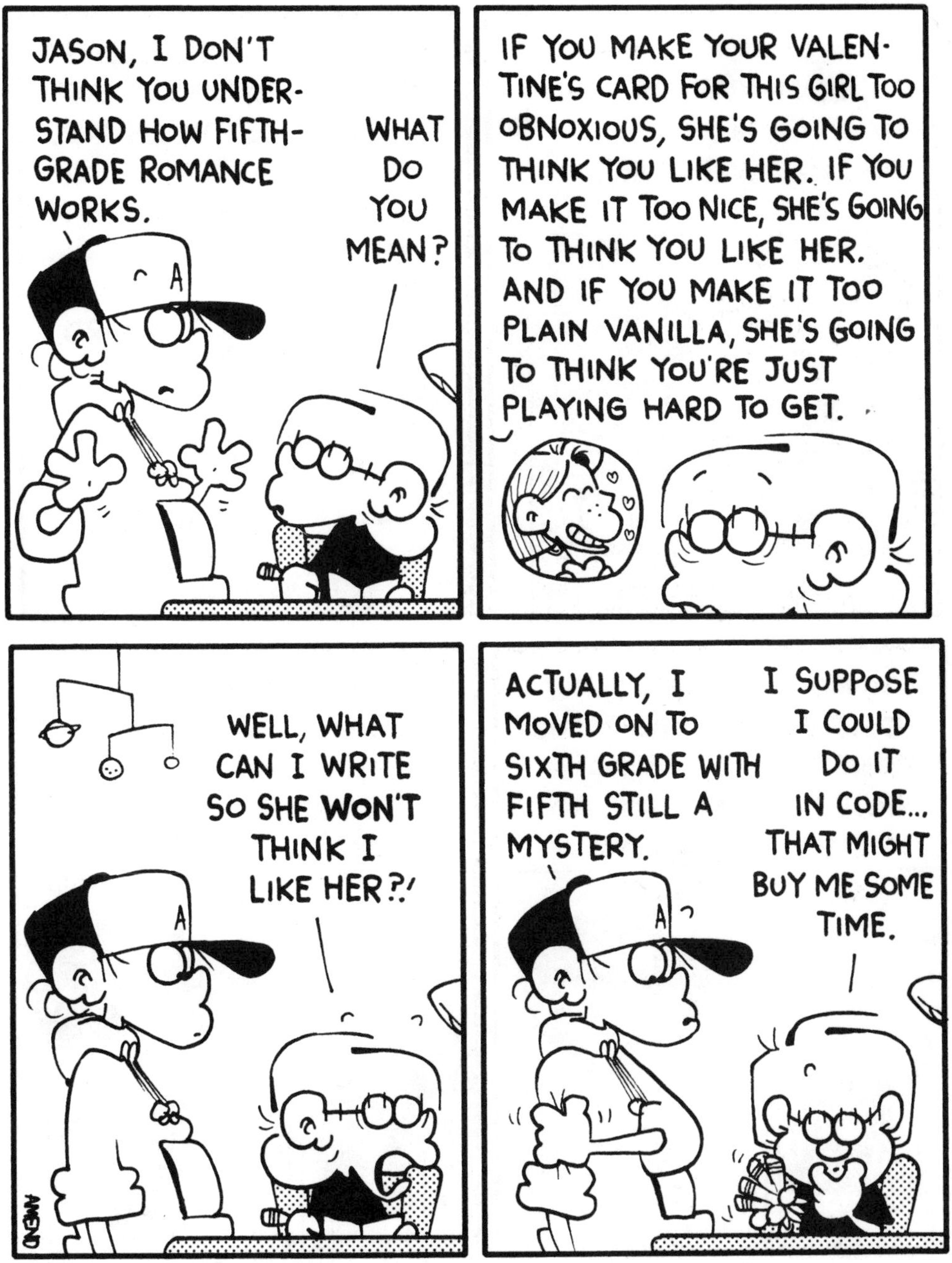
JASON, I DON'T THINK YOU UNDERSTAND HOW FIFTH-GRADE ROMANCE WORKS.
WHAT DO YOU MEAN?
IF YOU MAKE YOUR VALENTINE'S CARD FOR THIS GIRL TOO OBNOXIOUS, SHE'S GOING TO THINK YOU LIKE HER. IF YOU MAKE IT TOO NICE, SHE'S GOING TO THINK YOU LIKE HER. AND IF YOU MAKE IT TOO PLAIN VANILLA, SHE'S GOING TO THINK YOU'RE JUST PLAYING HARD TO GET.
WELL, WHAT CAN I WRITE SO SHE WON'T THINK I LIKE HER?!
AMEND
ACTUALLY, I MOVED ON TO SIXTH GRADE WITH FIFTH STILL A MYSTERY.
I SUPPOSE I COULD DO IT IN CODE... THAT MIGHT BUY ME SOME TIME.

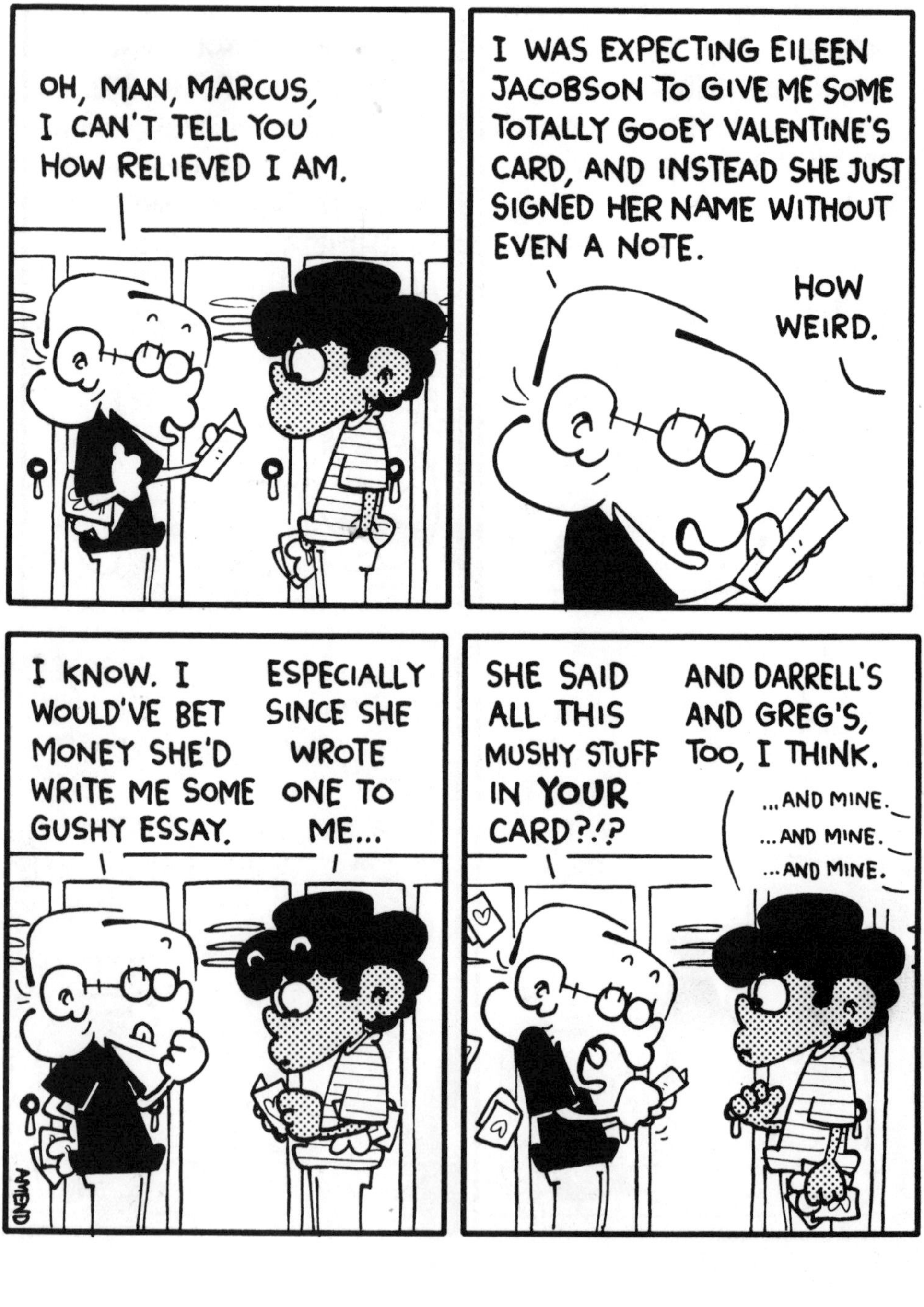
OH, MAN, MARCUS, I CAN'T TELL YOU HOW RELIEVED I AM.
I WAS EXPECTING EILEEN JACOBSON TO GIVE ME SOME TOTALLY GOOEY VALENTINE'S CARD, AND INSTEAD SHE JUST SIGNED HER NAME WITHOUT EVEN A NOTE.
HOW WEIRD.
I KNOW. I WOULD'VE BET MONEY SHE'D WRITE ME SOME GUSHY ESSAY.
ESPECIALLY SINCE SHE WROTE ONE TO ME...
SHE SAID ALL THIS MUSHY STUFF IN YOUR CARD?!?
AND DARRELL'S AND GREG'S, TOO, I THINK.
...AND MINE.
...AND MINE.
...AND MINE.
AMEND

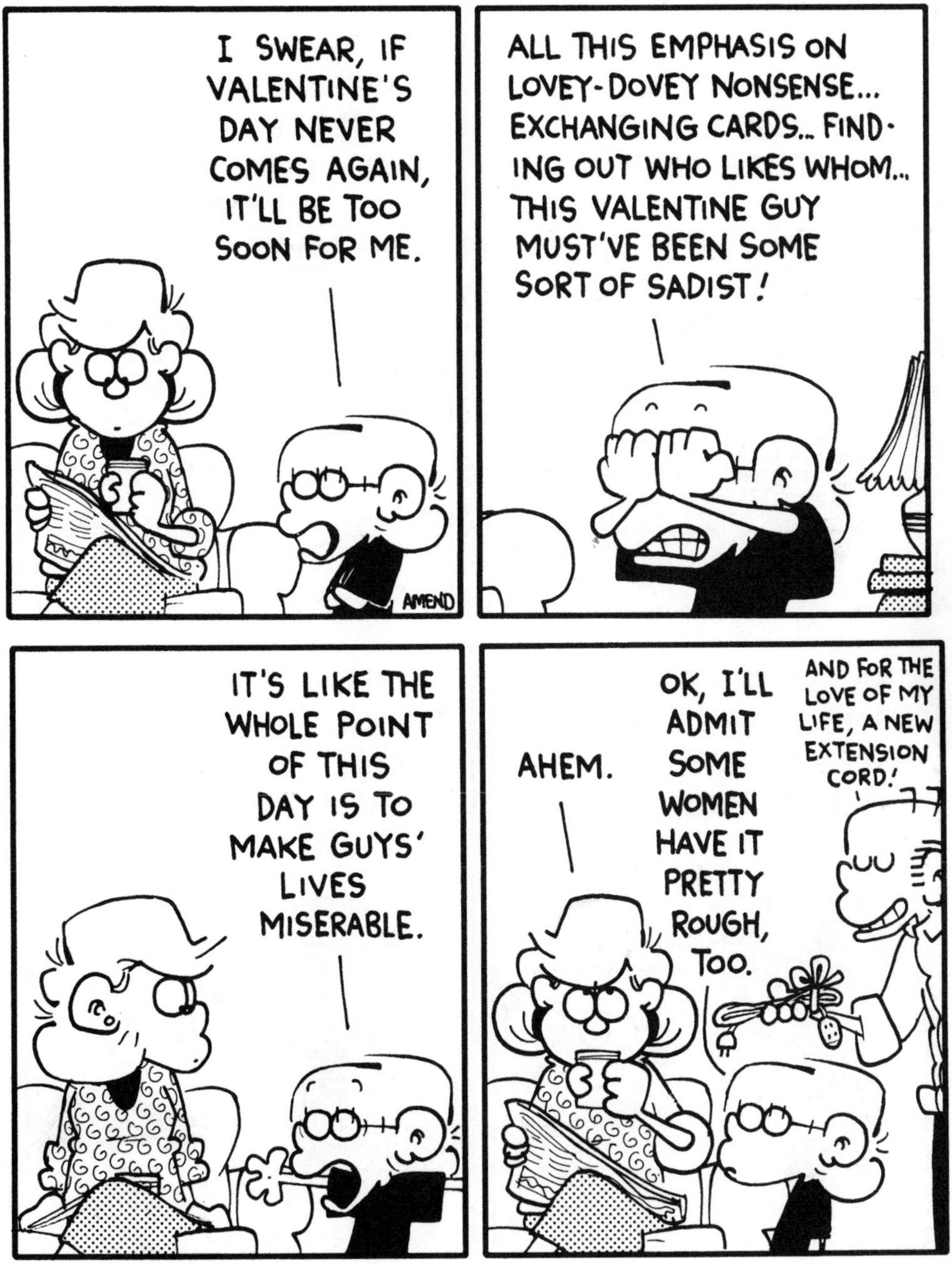
I SWEAR, IF VALENTINE'S DAY NEVER COMES AGAIN, IT'LL BE TOO SOON FOR ME.
AMEND
ALL THIS EMPHASIS ON LOVEY-DOVEY NONSENSE... EXCHANGING CARDS... FINDING OUT WHO LIKES WHOM... THIS VALENTINE GUY MUST'VE BEEN SOME SORT OF SADIST!
IT'S LIKE THE WHOLE POINT OF THIS DAY IS TO MAKE GUYS' LIVES MISERABLE.
AHEM.
OK, I'LL ADMIT SOME WOMEN HAVE IT PRETTY ROUGH, TOO.
AND FOR THE LOVE OF MY LIFE, A NEW EXTENSION CORD!

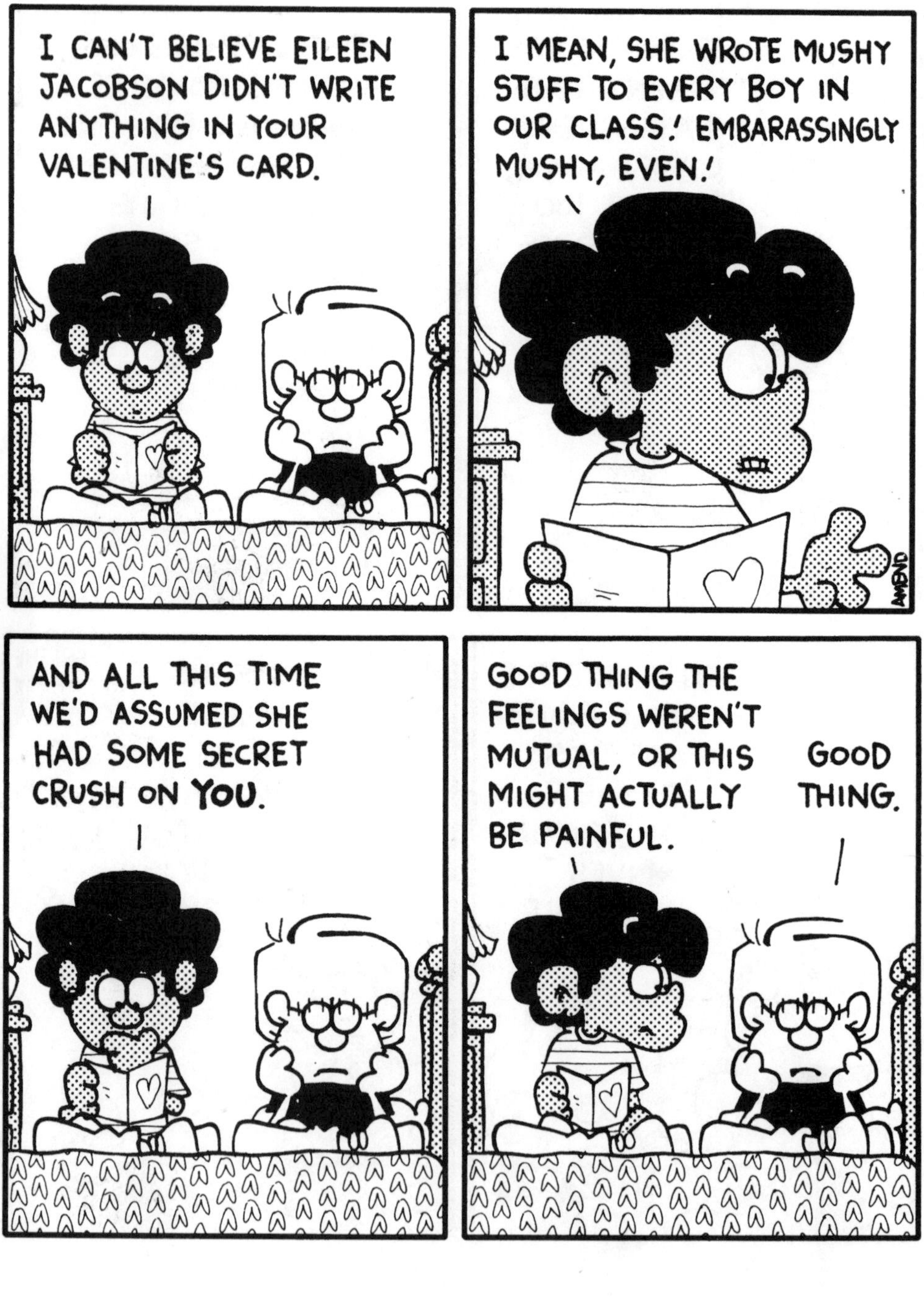
I CAN'T BELIEVE EILEEN JACOBSON DIDN'T WRITE ANYTHING IN YOUR VALENTINE'S CARD.
I MEAN, SHE WROTE MUSHY STUFF TO EVERY BOY IN OUR CLASS! EMBARASSINGLY MUSHY, EVEN!
AMEND
AND ALL THIS TIME WE'D ASSUMED SHE HAD SOME SECRET CRUSH ON YOU.
GOOD THING THE FEELINGS WEREN'T MUTUAL, OR THIS MIGHT ACTUALLY BE PAINFUL.
GOOD THING.

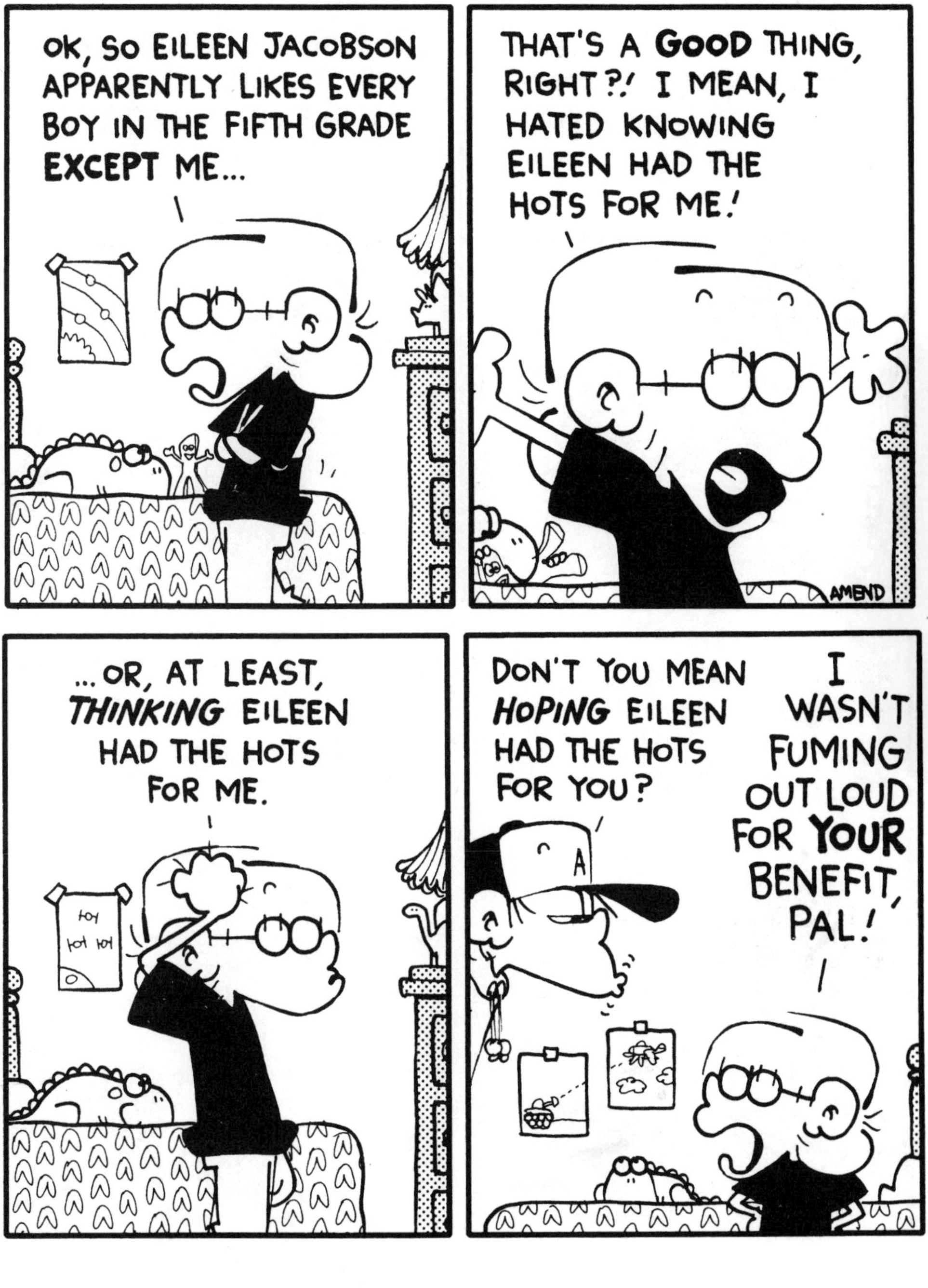
OK, SO EILEEN JACOBSON APPARENTLY LIKES EVERY BOY IN THE FIFTH GRADE **EXCEPT** ME...
THAT'S A **GOOD** THING, RIGHT?! I MEAN, I HATED KNOWING EILEEN HAD THE HOTS FOR ME!
AMEND
...OR, AT LEAST, ***THINKING*** EILEEN HAD THE HOTS FOR ME.
DON'T YOU MEAN ***HOPING*** EILEEN HAD THE HOTS FOR YOU?
I WASN'T FUMING OUT LOUD FOR **YOUR** BENEFIT, PAL!

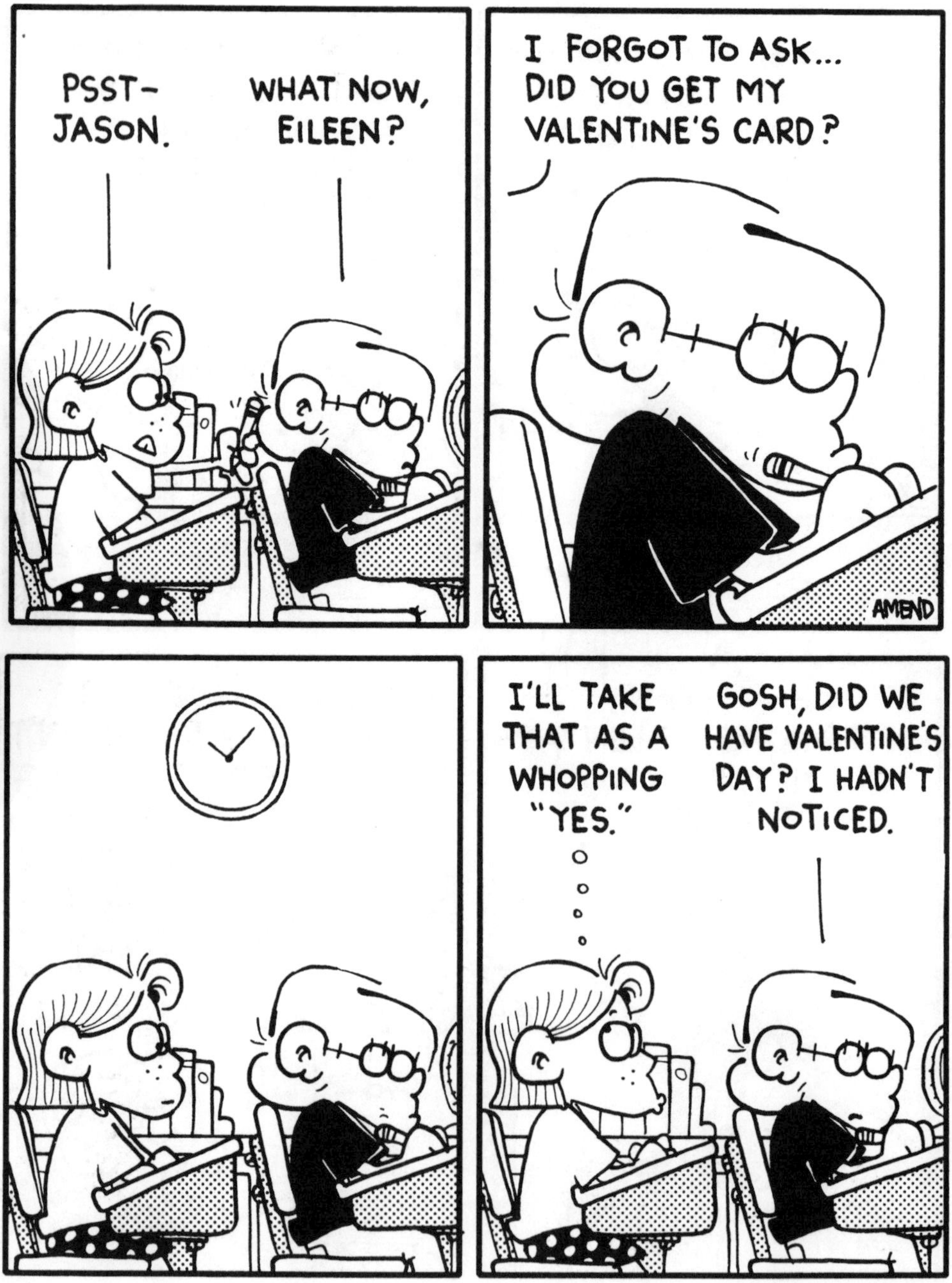
PSST-
JASON.
WHAT NOW,
EILEEN?
I FORGOT TO ASK...
DID YOU GET MY
VALENTINE'S CARD?
AMEND
I'LL TAKE
THAT AS A
WHOPPING
"YES."
GOSH, DID WE
HAVE VALENTINE'S
DAY? I HADN'T
NOTICED.

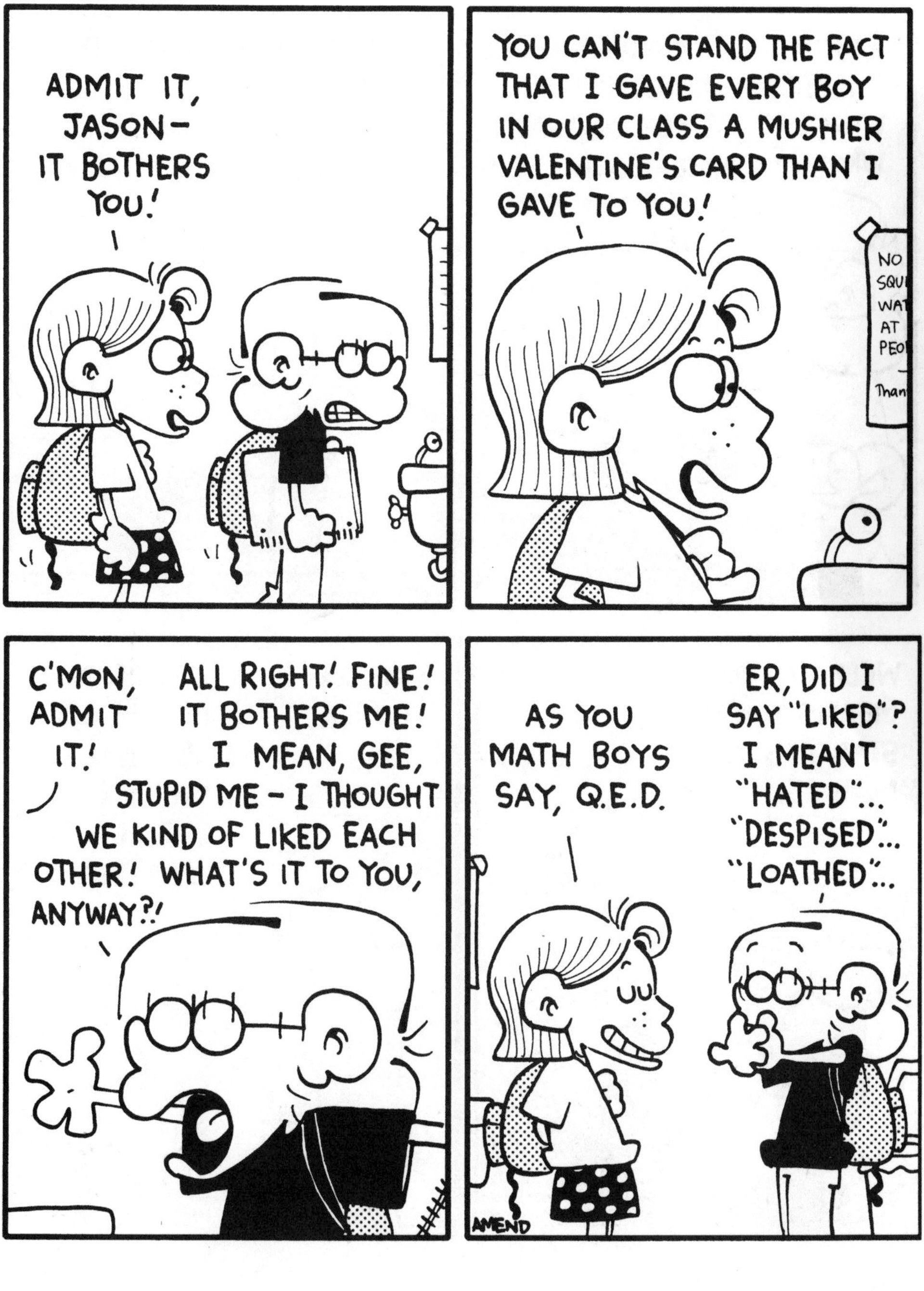
ADMIT IT, JASON— IT BOTHERS YOU!
YOU CAN'T STAND THE FACT THAT I GAVE EVERY BOY IN OUR CLASS A MUSHIER VALENTINE'S CARD THAN I GAVE TO YOU!
NO SQU WAT AT PEO — Than
C'MON, ADMIT IT!
ALL RIGHT! FINE! IT BOTHERS ME! I MEAN, GEE, STUPID ME – I THOUGHT WE KIND OF LIKED EACH OTHER! WHAT'S IT TO YOU, ANYWAY?!
AS YOU MATH BOYS SAY, Q.E.D.
ER, DID I SAY "LIKED"? I MEANT "HATED"... "DESPISED"... "LOATHED"...
AMEND

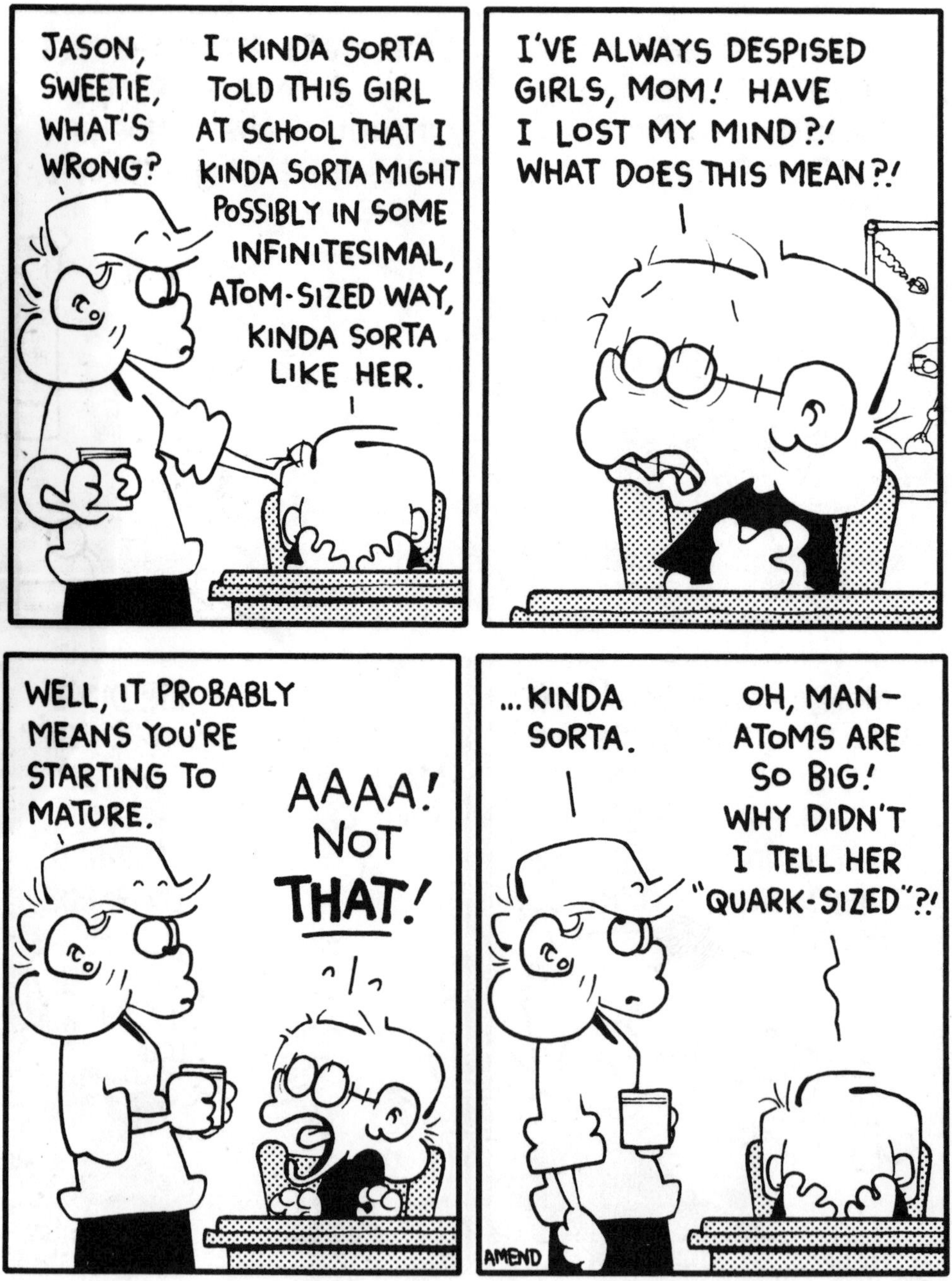
JASON, SWEETIE, WHAT'S WRONG?
I KINDA SORTA TOLD THIS GIRL AT SCHOOL THAT I KINDA SORTA MIGHT POSSIBLY IN SOME INFINITESIMAL, ATOM-SIZED WAY, KINDA SORTA LIKE HER.
I'VE ALWAYS DESPISED GIRLS, MOM! HAVE I LOST MY MIND?! WHAT DOES THIS MEAN?!
WELL, IT PROBABLY MEANS YOU'RE STARTING TO MATURE.
AAAA! NOT THAT!
...KINDA SORTA.
OH, MAN— ATOMS ARE SO BIG! WHY DIDN'T I TELL HER "QUARK-SIZED"?!
AMEND

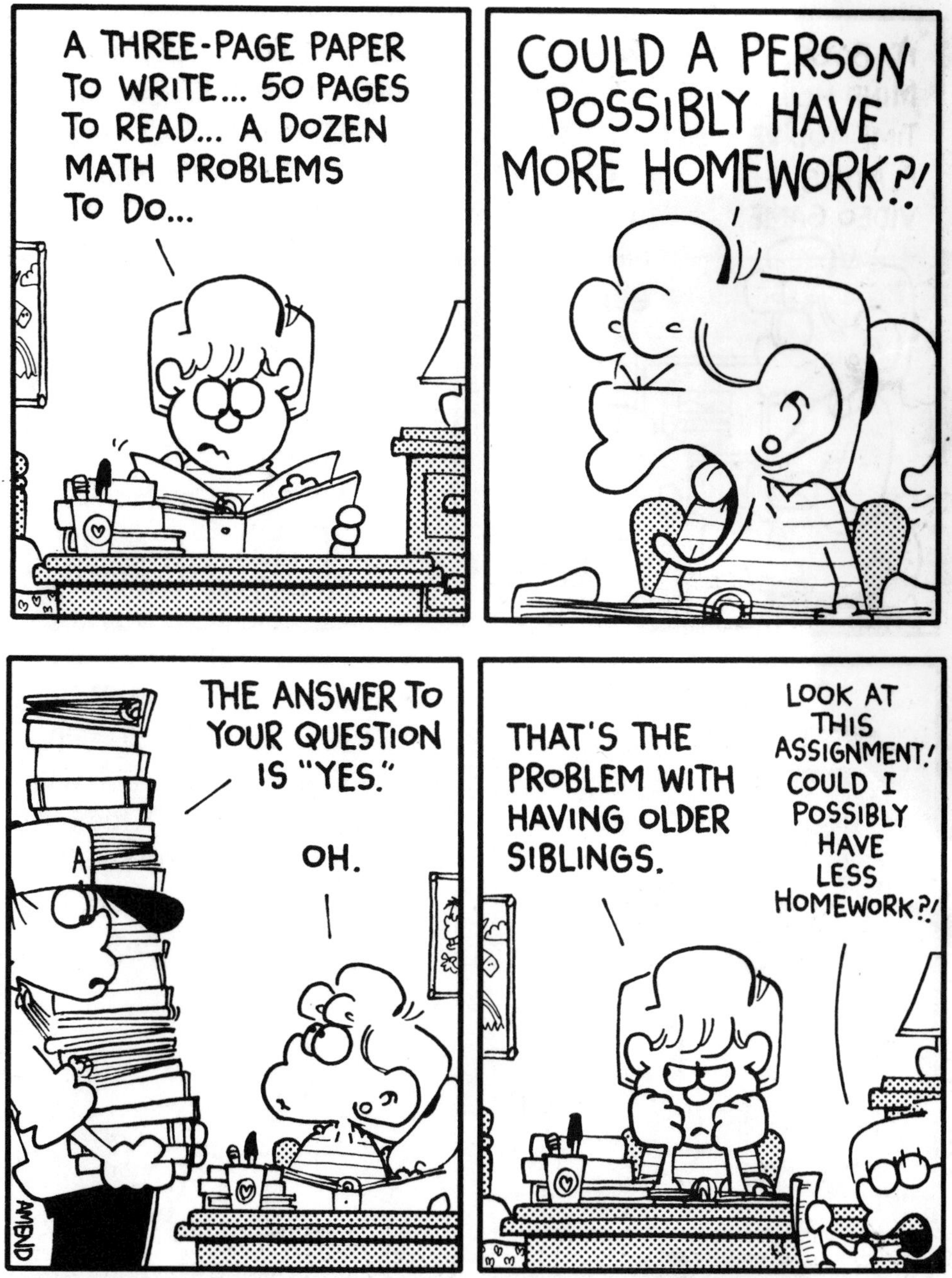
A THREE-PAGE PAPER TO WRITE... 50 PAGES TO READ... A DOZEN MATH PROBLEMS TO DO...
COULD A PERSON POSSIBLY HAVE MORE HOMEWORK?!
THE ANSWER TO YOUR QUESTION IS "YES."
OH.
AMEND
THAT'S THE PROBLEM WITH HAVING OLDER SIBLINGS.
LOOK AT THIS ASSIGNMENT! COULD I POSSIBLY HAVE LESS HOMEWORK?!

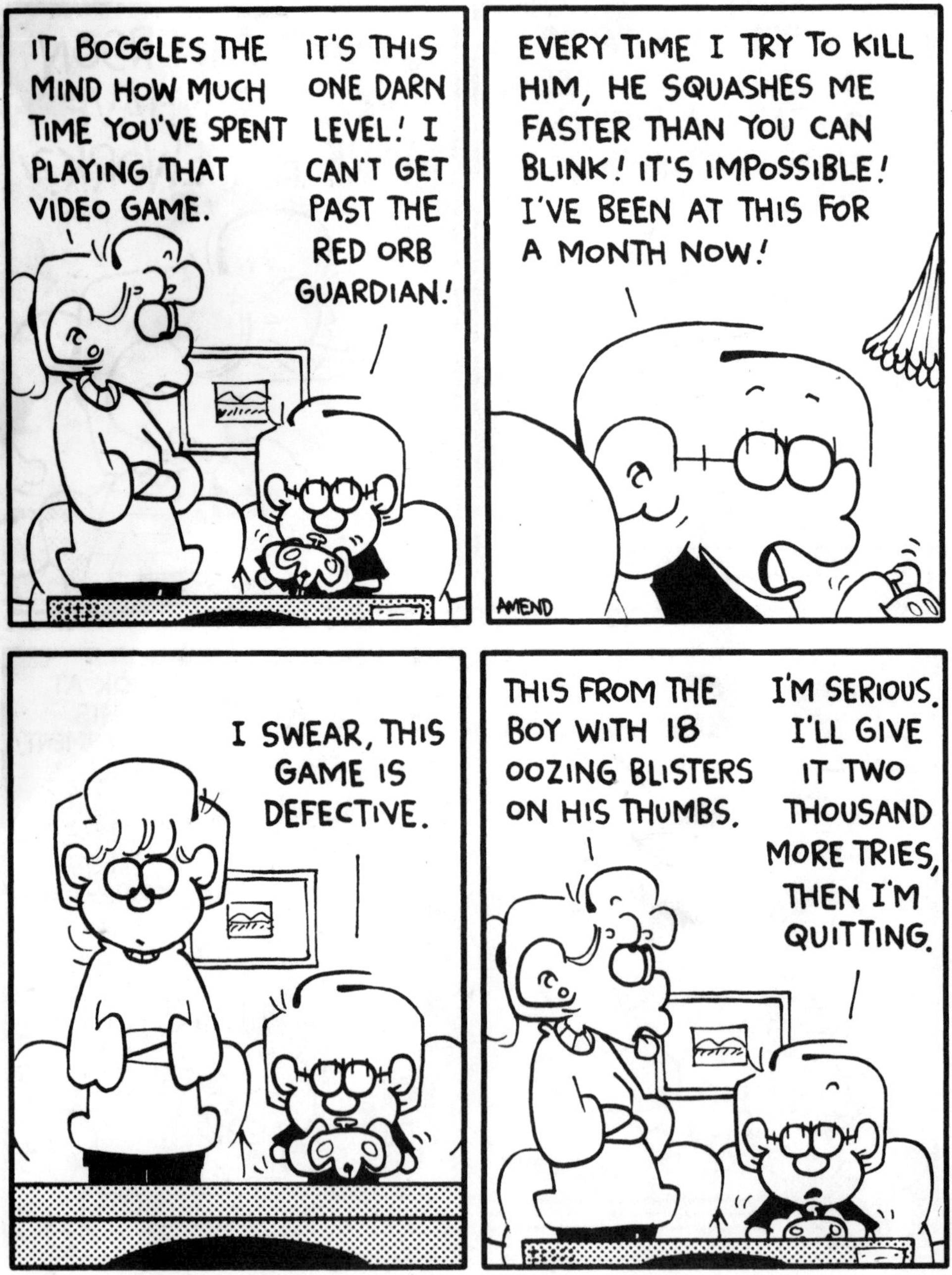
IT BOGGLES THE MIND HOW MUCH TIME YOU'VE SPENT PLAYING THAT VIDEO GAME.
IT'S THIS ONE DARN LEVEL! I CAN'T GET PAST THE RED ORB GUARDIAN!
EVERY TIME I TRY TO KILL HIM, HE SQUASHES ME FASTER THAN YOU CAN BLINK! IT'S IMPOSSIBLE! I'VE BEEN AT THIS FOR A MONTH NOW!
AMEND
I SWEAR, THIS GAME IS DEFECTIVE.
THIS FROM THE BOY WITH 18 OOZING BLISTERS ON HIS THUMBS.
I'M SERIOUS. I'LL GIVE IT TWO THOUSAND MORE TRIES, THEN I'M QUITTING.

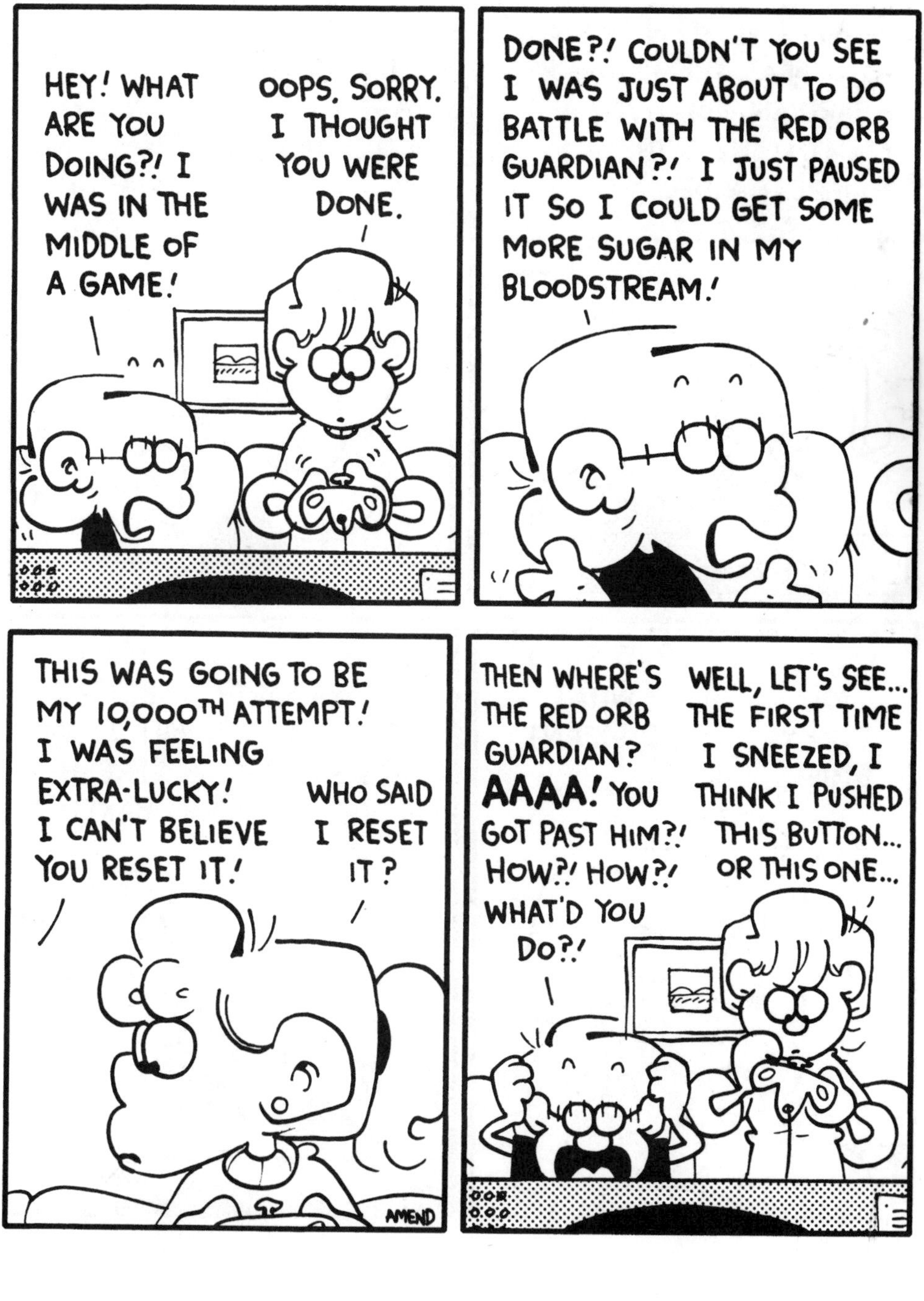
HEY! WHAT ARE YOU DOING?! I WAS IN THE MIDDLE OF A GAME!
OOPS. SORRY. I THOUGHT YOU WERE DONE.
DONE?! COULDN'T YOU SEE I WAS JUST ABOUT TO DO BATTLE WITH THE RED ORB GUARDIAN?! I JUST PAUSED IT SO I COULD GET SOME MORE SUGAR IN MY BLOODSTREAM!
THIS WAS GOING TO BE MY 10,000TH ATTEMPT! I WAS FEELING EXTRA-LUCKY! I CAN'T BELIEVE YOU RESET IT!
WHO SAID I RESET IT?
AMEND
THEN WHERE'S THE RED ORB GUARDIAN? AAAA! YOU GOT PAST HIM?! HOW?! HOW?! WHAT'D YOU DO?!
WELL, LET'S SEE... THE FIRST TIME I SNEEZED, I THINK I PUSHED THIS BUTTON... OR THIS ONE...

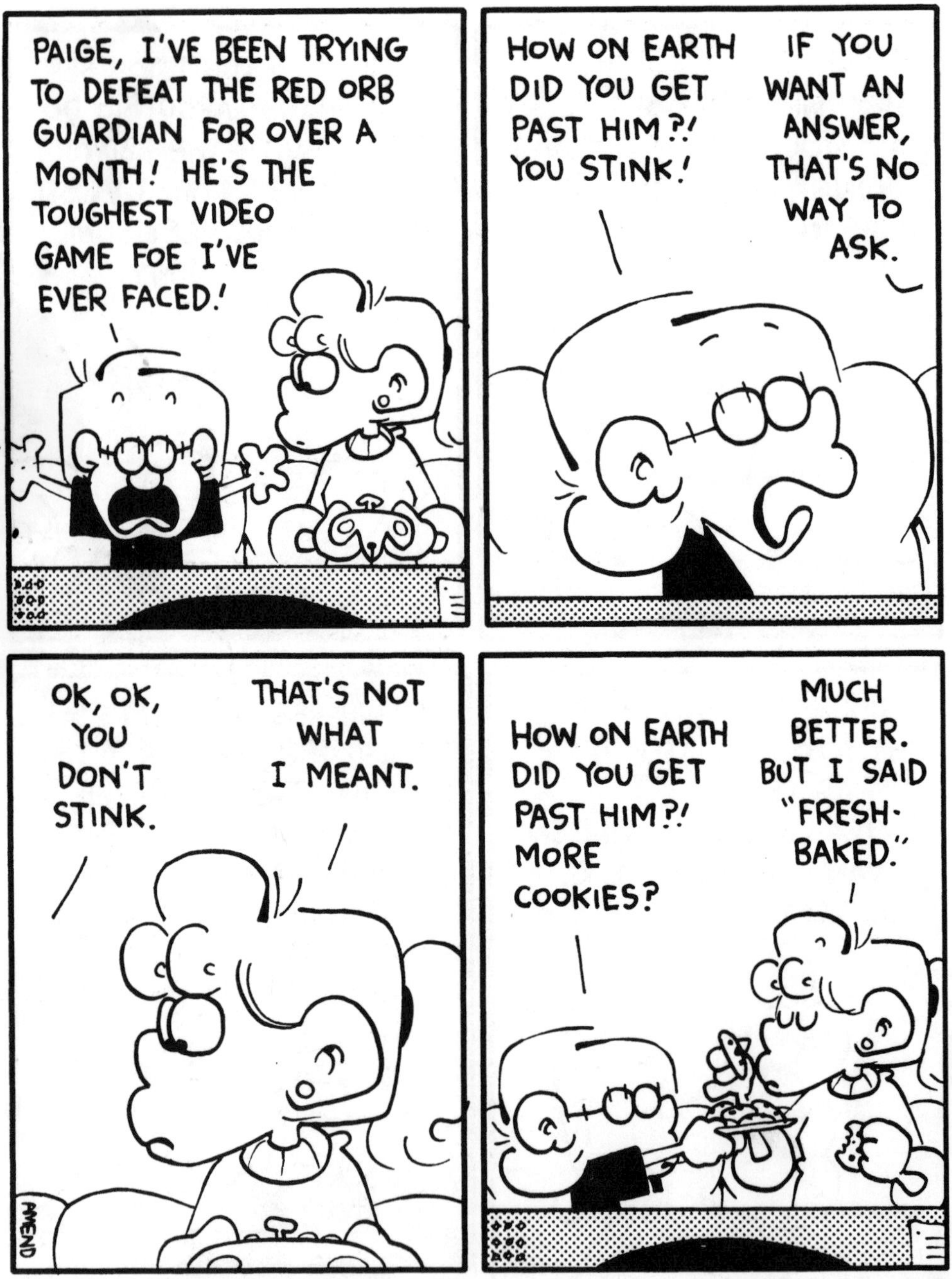
PAIGE, I'VE BEEN TRYING TO DEFEAT THE RED ORB GUARDIAN FOR OVER A MONTH! HE'S THE TOUGHEST VIDEO GAME FOE I'VE EVER FACED!
HOW ON EARTH DID YOU GET PAST HIM?! YOU STINK!
IF YOU WANT AN ANSWER, THAT'S NO WAY TO ASK.
OK, OK, YOU DON'T STINK.
THAT'S NOT WHAT I MEANT.
AMEND
HOW ON EARTH DID YOU GET PAST HIM?! MORE COOKIES?
MUCH BETTER. BUT I SAID "FRESH-BAKED."

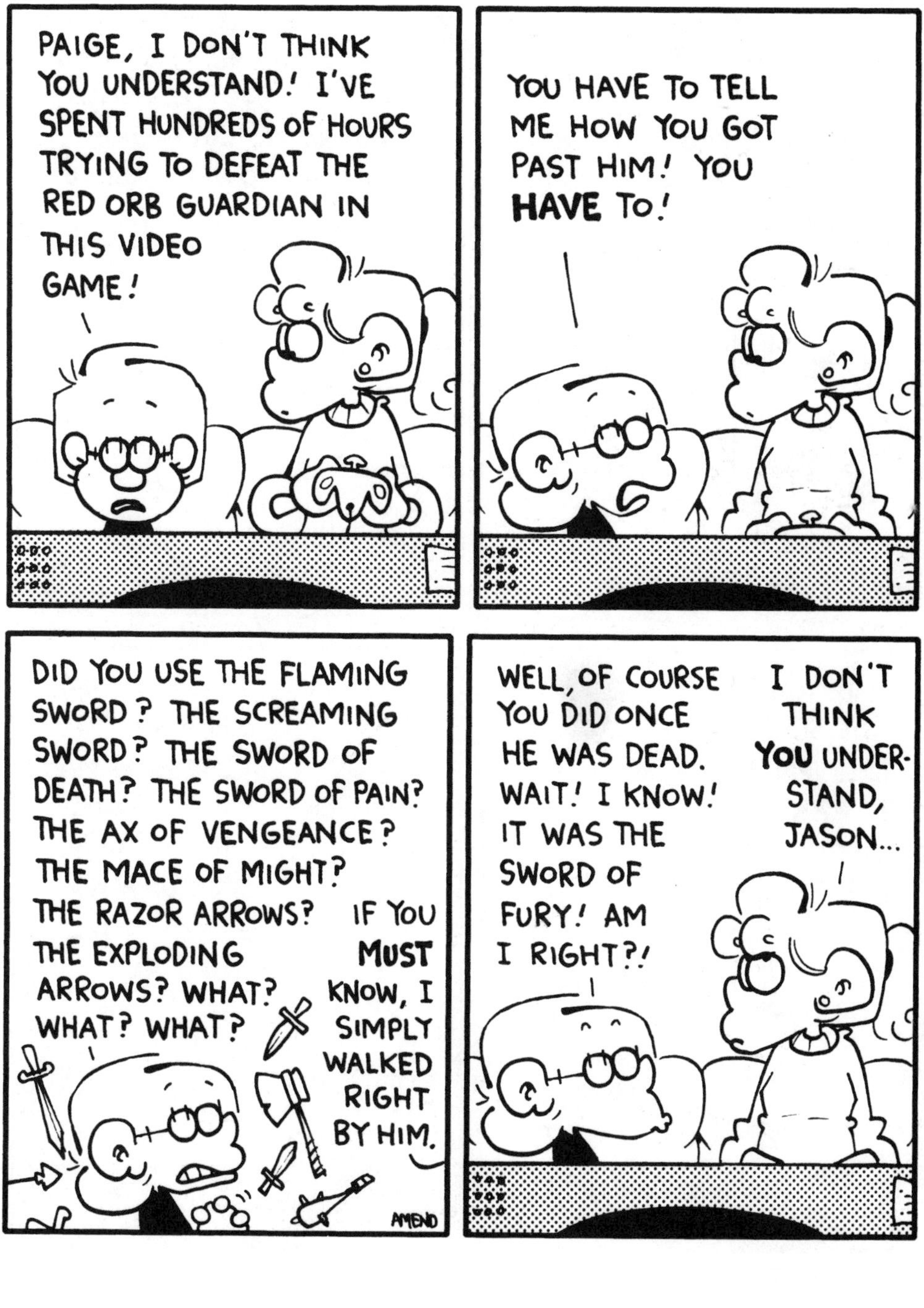
PAIGE, I DON'T THINK YOU UNDERSTAND! I'VE SPENT HUNDREDS OF HOURS TRYING TO DEFEAT THE RED ORB GUARDIAN IN THIS VIDEO GAME!
YOU HAVE TO TELL ME HOW YOU GOT PAST HIM! YOU **HAVE** TO!
DID YOU USE THE FLAMING SWORD? THE SCREAMING SWORD? THE SWORD OF DEATH? THE SWORD OF PAIN? THE AX OF VENGEANCE? THE MACE OF MIGHT? THE RAZOR ARROWS? THE EXPLODING ARROWS? WHAT? WHAT? WHAT?
IF YOU **MUST** KNOW, I SIMPLY WALKED RIGHT BY HIM.
AMEND
WELL, OF COURSE YOU DID ONCE HE WAS DEAD. WAIT! I KNOW! IT WAS THE SWORD OF FURY! AM I RIGHT?!
I DON'T THINK **YOU** UNDERSTAND, JASON...

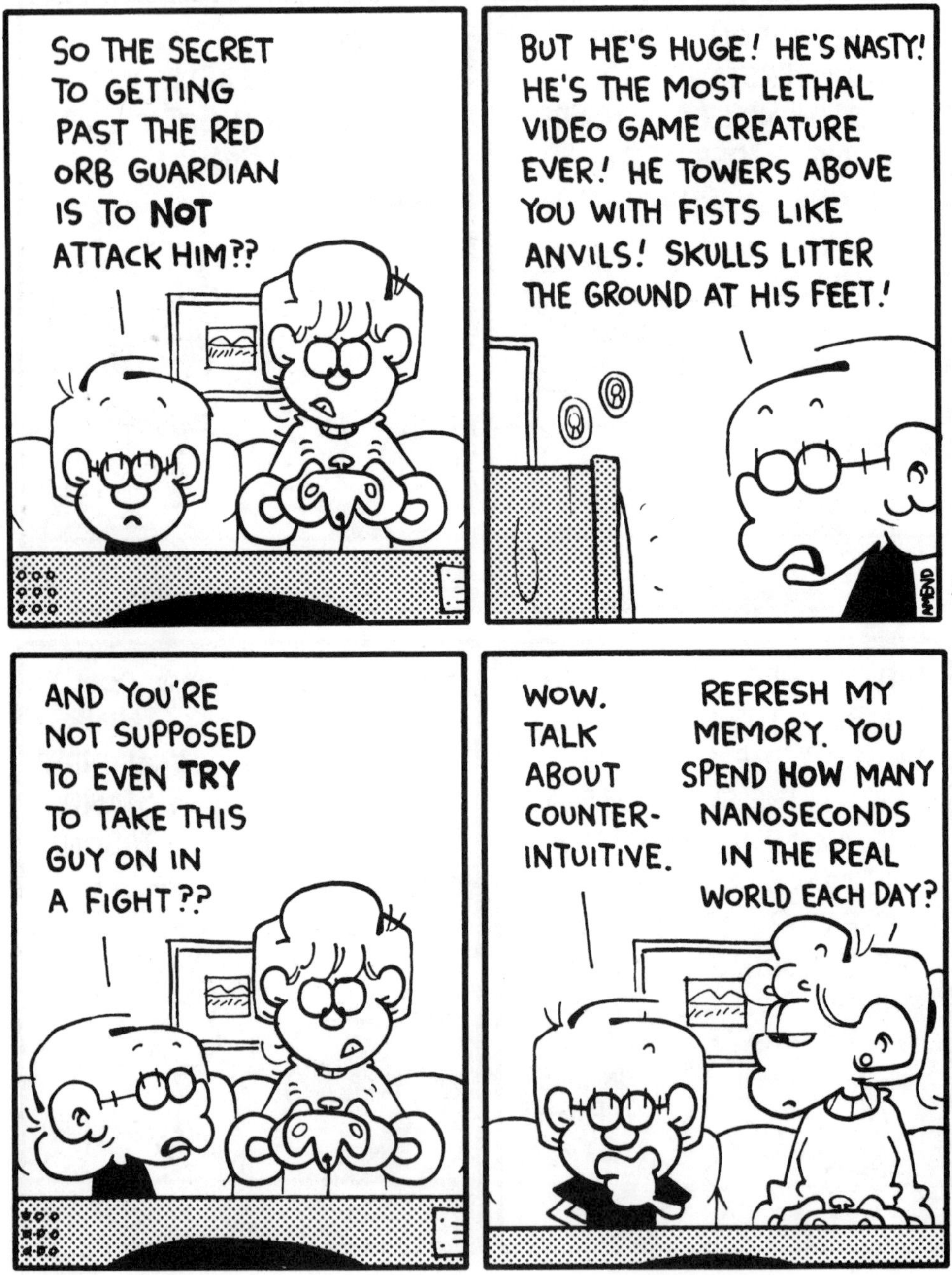
SO THE SECRET TO GETTING PAST THE RED ORB GUARDIAN IS TO NOT ATTACK HIM??
BUT HE'S HUGE! HE'S NASTY! HE'S THE MOST LETHAL VIDEO GAME CREATURE EVER! HE TOWERS ABOVE YOU WITH FISTS LIKE ANVILS! SKULLS LITTER THE GROUND AT HIS FEET!
AMEND
AND YOU'RE NOT SUPPOSED TO EVEN TRY TO TAKE THIS GUY ON IN A FIGHT??
WOW. TALK ABOUT COUNTER-INTUITIVE.
REFRESH MY MEMORY. YOU SPEND HOW MANY NANOSECONDS IN THE REAL WORLD EACH DAY?

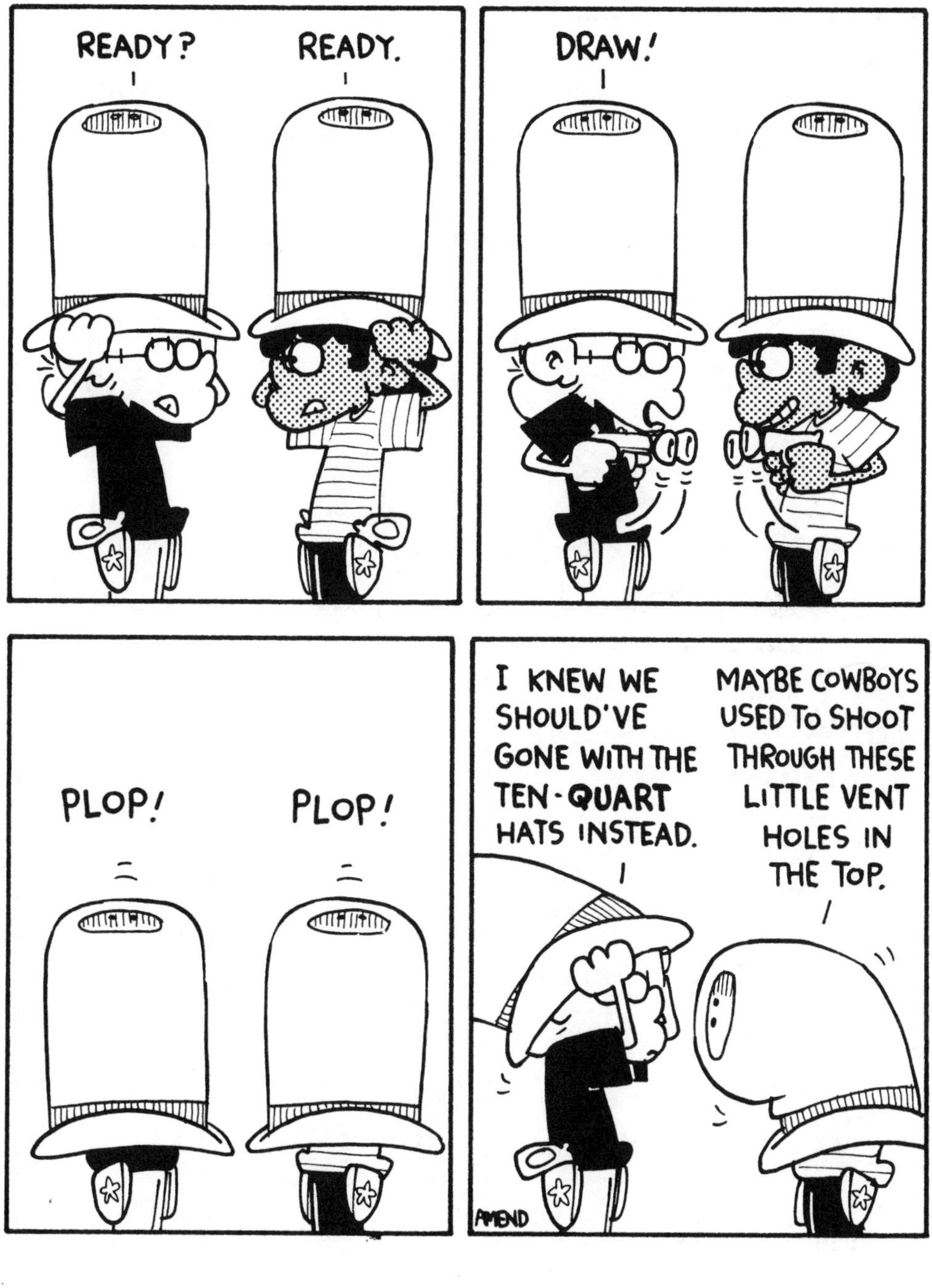
READY?
READY.
DRAW!
PLOP!
PLOP!
I KNEW WE SHOULD'VE GONE WITH THE TEN-QUART HATS INSTEAD.
MAYBE COWBOYS USED TO SHOOT THROUGH THESE LITTLE VENT HOLES IN THE TOP.
AMEND

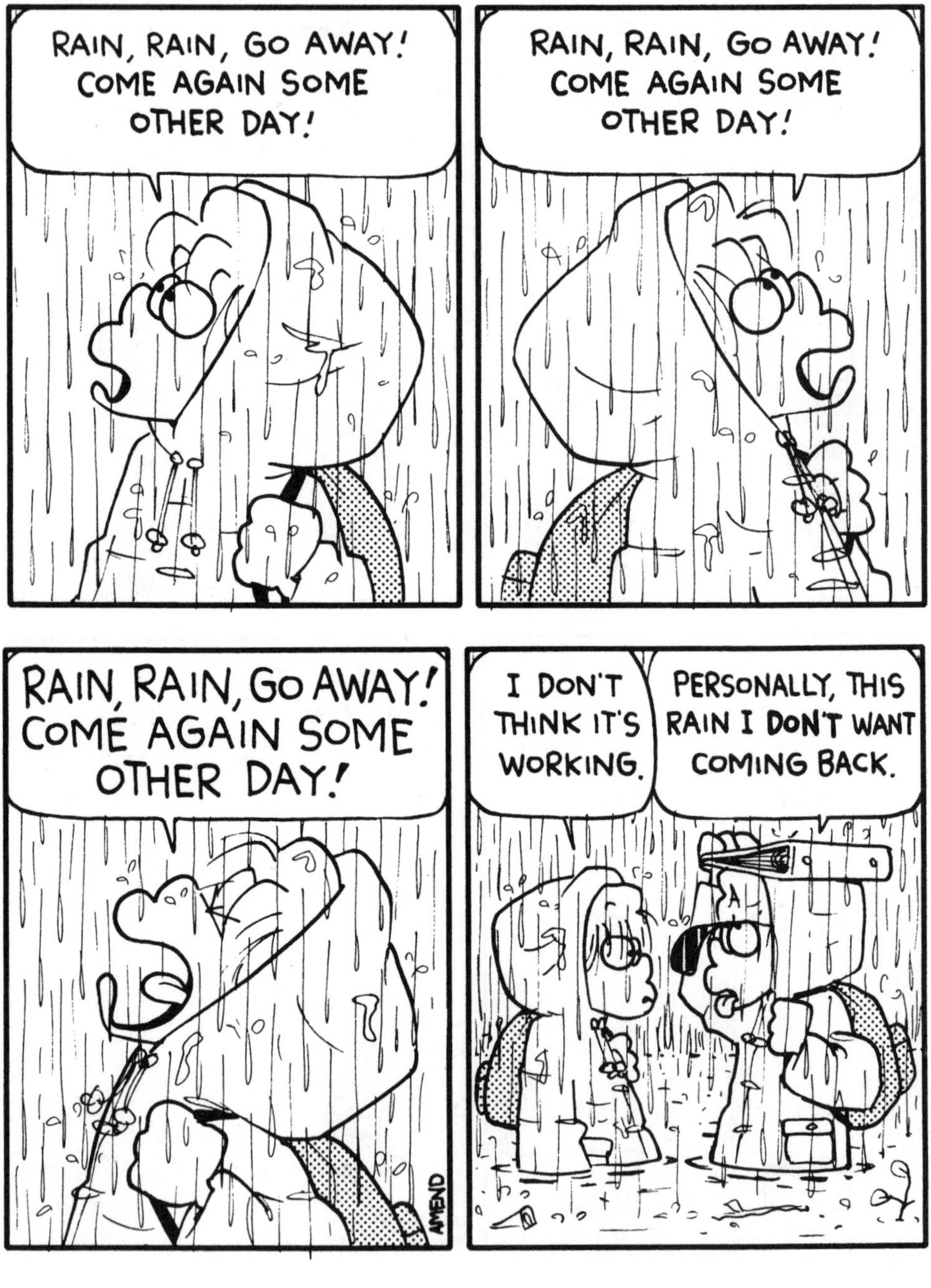
RAIN, RAIN, GO AWAY! COME AGAIN SOME OTHER DAY!
RAIN, RAIN, GO AWAY! COME AGAIN SOME OTHER DAY!
RAIN, RAIN, GO AWAY! COME AGAIN SOME OTHER DAY!
AMEND
I DON'T THINK IT'S WORKING.
PERSONALLY, THIS RAIN I **DON'T** WANT COMING BACK.

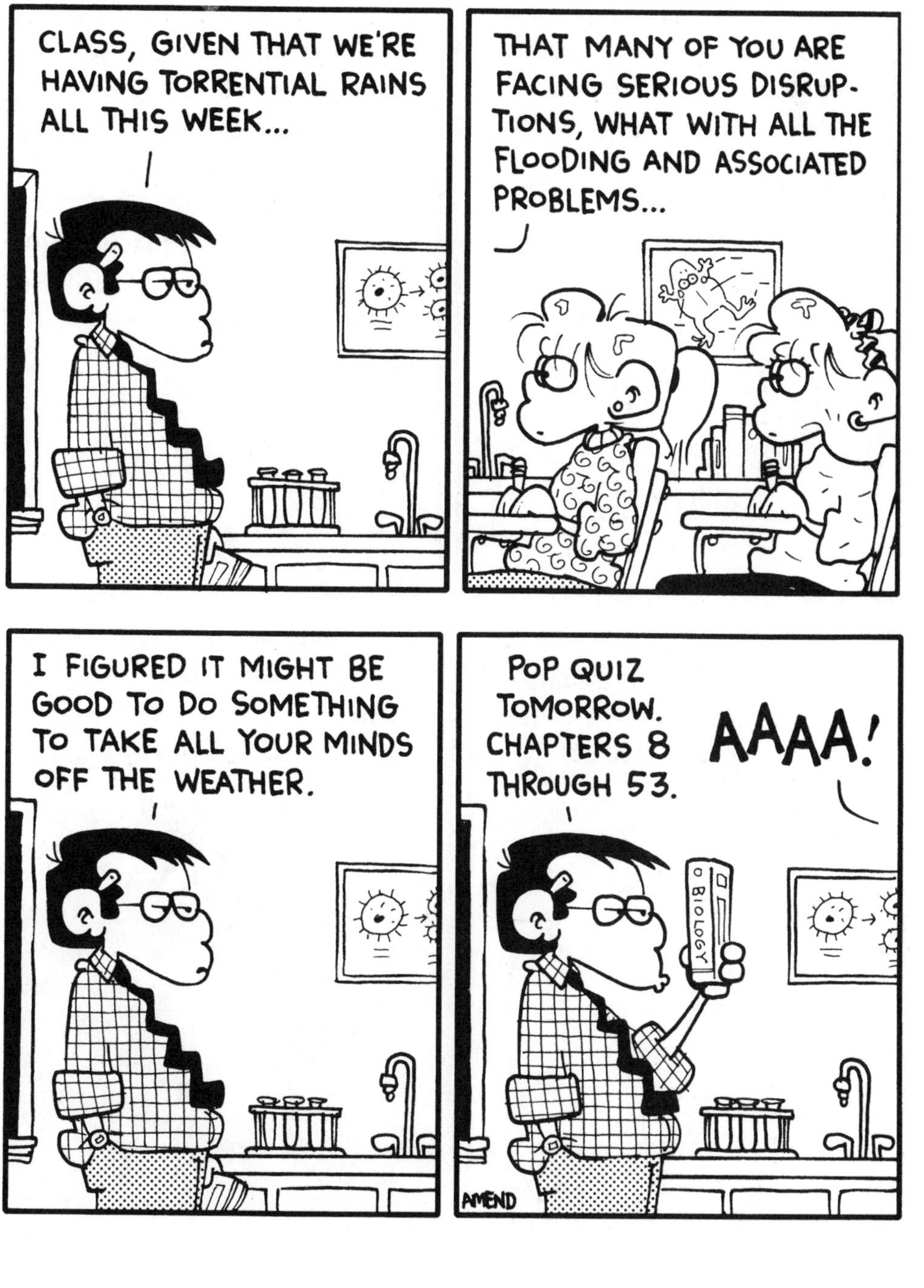
CLASS, GIVEN THAT WE'RE HAVING TORRENTIAL RAINS ALL THIS WEEK...
THAT MANY OF YOU ARE FACING SERIOUS DISRUP-TIONS, WHAT WITH ALL THE FLOODING AND ASSOCIATED PROBLEMS...
I FIGURED IT MIGHT BE GOOD TO DO SOMETHING TO TAKE ALL YOUR MINDS OFF THE WEATHER.
POP QUIZ TOMORROW. CHAPTERS 8 THROUGH 53.
AAAA!
BIOLOGY
AMEND

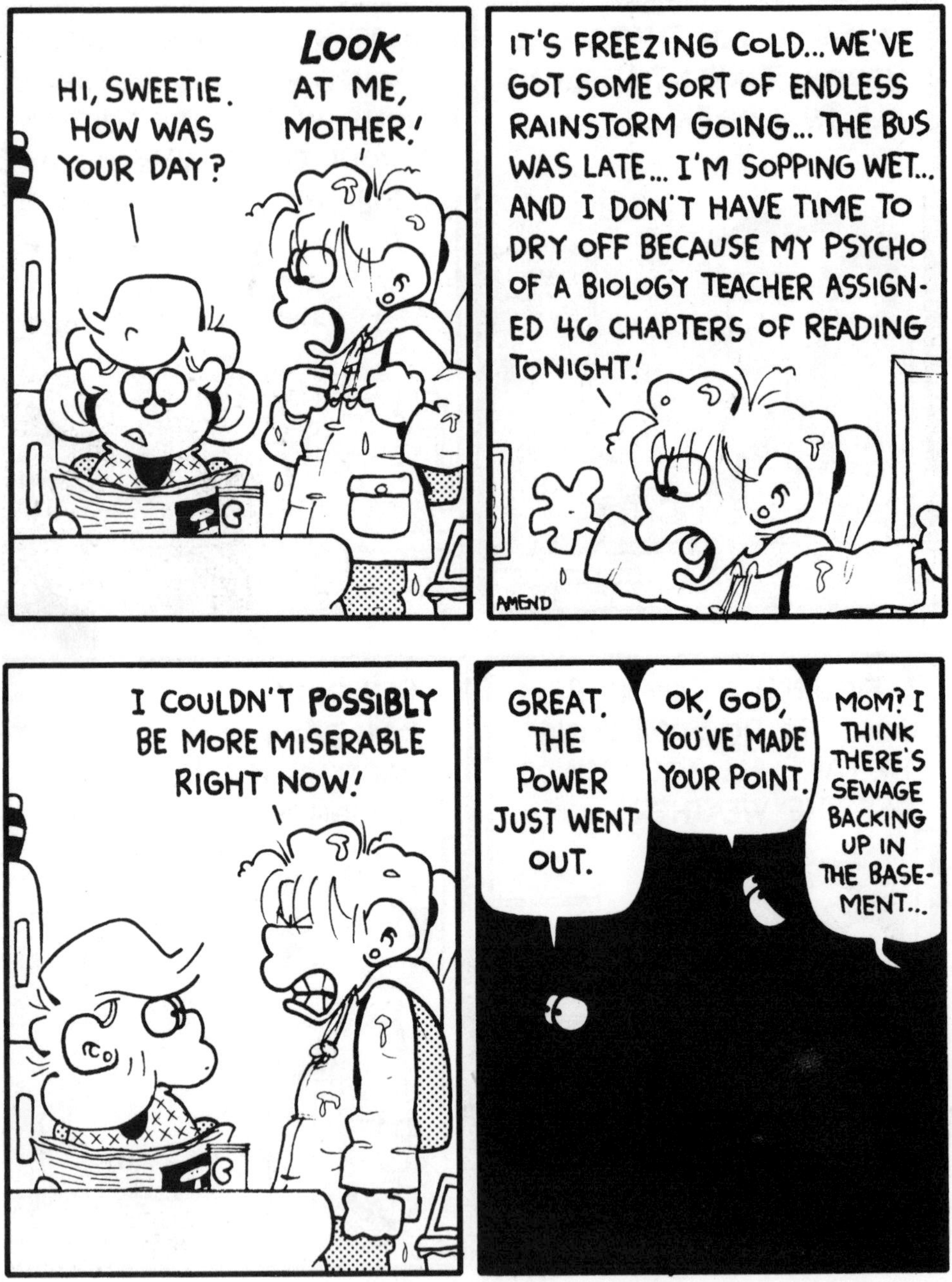
HI, SWEETIE. HOW WAS YOUR DAY?
LOOK AT ME, MOTHER!
IT'S FREEZING COLD... WE'VE GOT SOME SORT OF ENDLESS RAINSTORM GOING... THE BUS WAS LATE... I'M SOPPING WET... AND I DON'T HAVE TIME TO DRY OFF BECAUSE MY PSYCHO OF A BIOLOGY TEACHER ASSIGNED 46 CHAPTERS OF READING TONIGHT!
AMEND
I COULDN'T POSSIBLY BE MORE MISERABLE RIGHT NOW!
GREAT. THE POWER JUST WENT OUT.
OK, GOD, YOU'VE MADE YOUR POINT.
MOM? I THINK THERE'S SEWAGE BACKING UP IN THE BASEMENT...

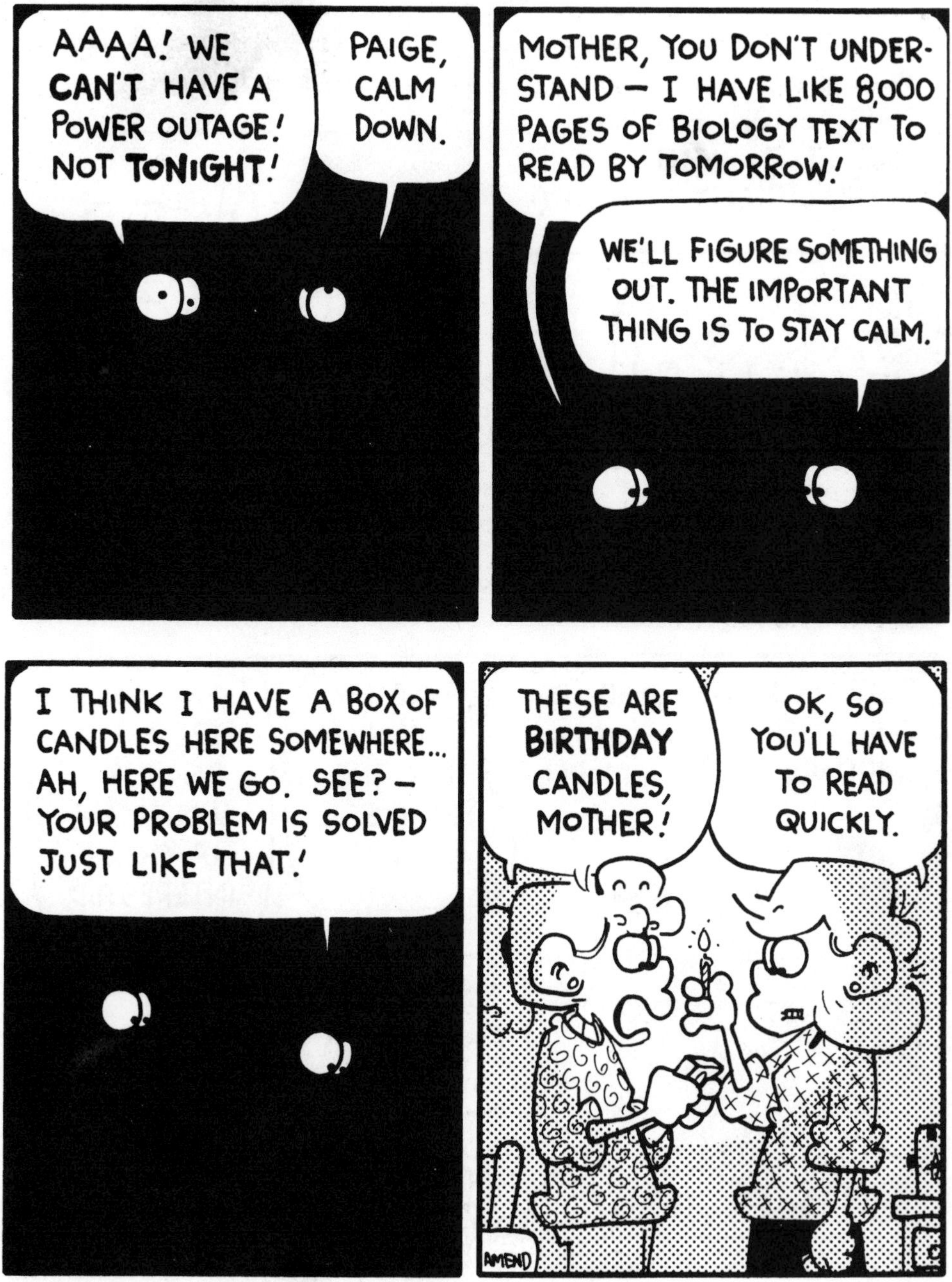
AAAA! WE CAN'T HAVE A POWER OUTAGE! NOT TONIGHT!
PAIGE, CALM DOWN.
MOTHER, YOU DON'T UNDERSTAND — I HAVE LIKE 8,000 PAGES OF BIOLOGY TEXT TO READ BY TOMORROW!
WE'LL FIGURE SOMETHING OUT. THE IMPORTANT THING IS TO STAY CALM.
I THINK I HAVE A BOX OF CANDLES HERE SOMEWHERE... AH, HERE WE GO. SEE? — YOUR PROBLEM IS SOLVED JUST LIKE THAT!
THESE ARE BIRTHDAY CANDLES, MOTHER!
OK, SO YOU'LL HAVE TO READ QUICKLY.
AMEND

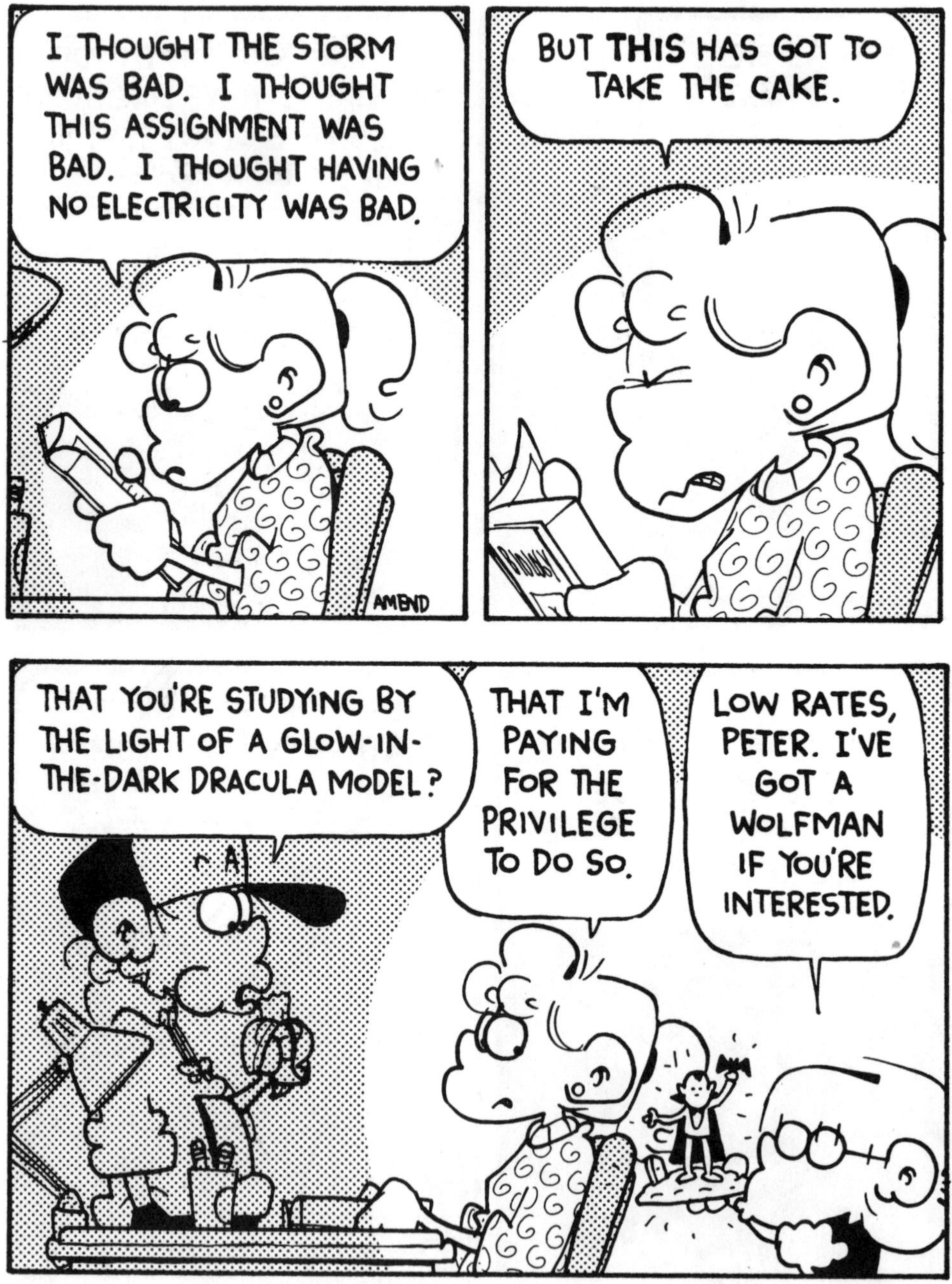
I THOUGHT THE STORM WAS BAD. I THOUGHT THIS ASSIGNMENT WAS BAD. I THOUGHT HAVING NO ELECTRICITY WAS BAD.
AMEND
BUT THIS HAS GOT TO TAKE THE CAKE.
THAT YOU'RE STUDYING BY THE LIGHT OF A GLOW-IN-THE-DARK DRACULA MODEL?
THAT I'M PAYING FOR THE PRIVILEGE TO DO SO.
LOW RATES, PETER. I'VE GOT A WOLFMAN IF YOU'RE INTERESTED.

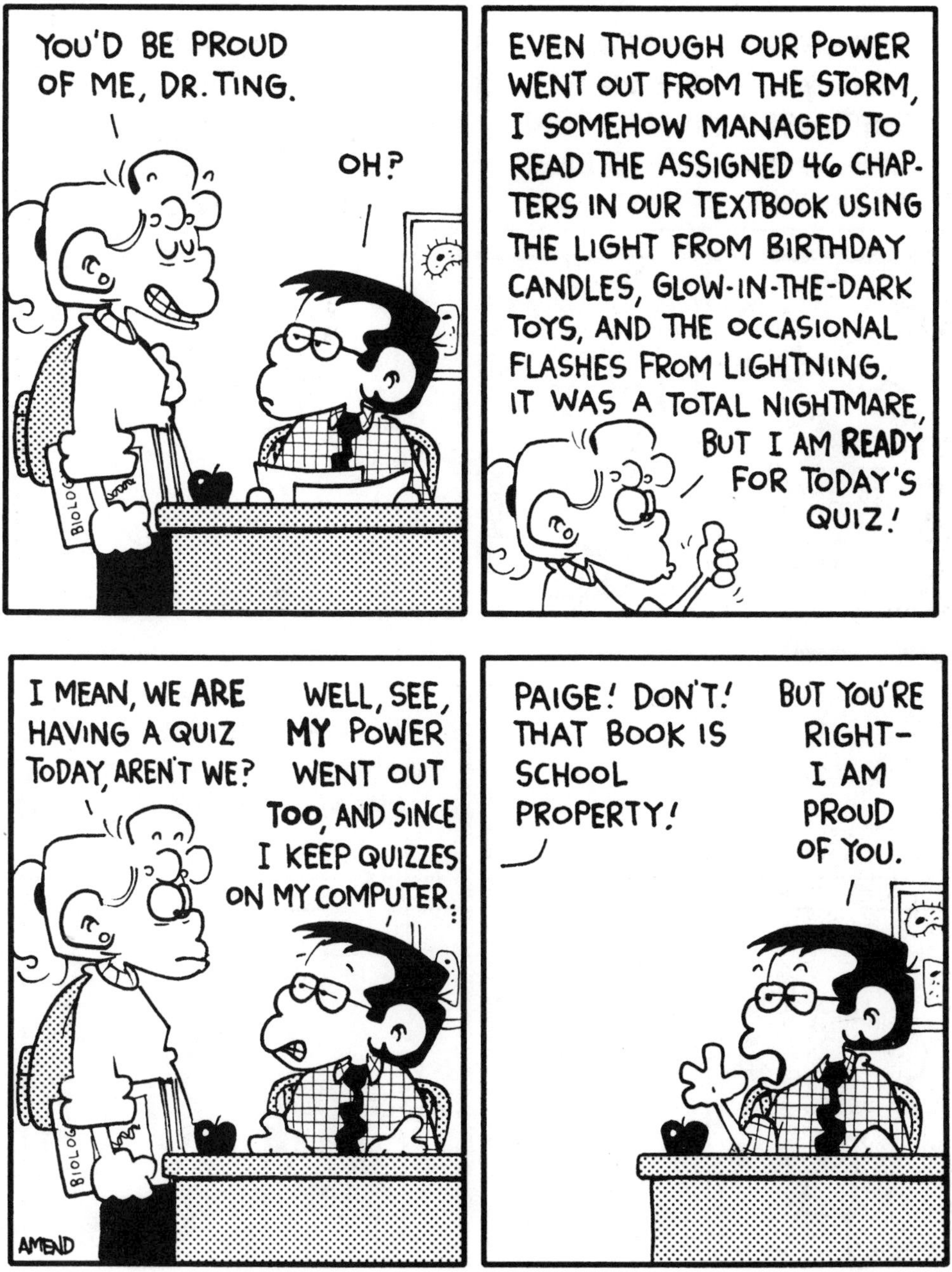
YOU'D BE PROUD OF ME, DR. TING.
OH?
EVEN THOUGH OUR POWER WENT OUT FROM THE STORM, I SOMEHOW MANAGED TO READ THE ASSIGNED 46 CHAPTERS IN OUR TEXTBOOK USING THE LIGHT FROM BIRTHDAY CANDLES, GLOW-IN-THE-DARK TOYS, AND THE OCCASIONAL FLASHES FROM LIGHTNING. IT WAS A TOTAL NIGHTMARE, BUT I AM READY FOR TODAY'S QUIZ!
I MEAN, WE ARE HAVING A QUIZ TODAY, AREN'T WE?
WELL, SEE, MY POWER WENT OUT TOO, AND SINCE I KEEP QUIZZES ON MY COMPUTER...
AMEND
PAIGE! DON'T! THAT BOOK IS SCHOOL PROPERTY!
BUT YOU'RE RIGHT— I AM PROUD OF YOU.

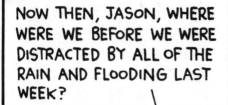

NOW THEN, JASON, WHERE WERE WE BEFORE WE WERE DISTRACTED BY ALL OF THE RAIN AND FLOODING LAST WEEK?

OH, THAT'S RIGHT... YOU HAD JUST LET SLIP THE ADMISSION THAT YOU REALLY DO LIKE ME. SHALL WE PICK UP WHERE WE LEFT OFF?

WHAM! WHAM! WHAM! WHAM!

ACTUALLY, I THINK YOU WERE BEATING YOUR HEAD ON THIS LOCKER OVER HERE.

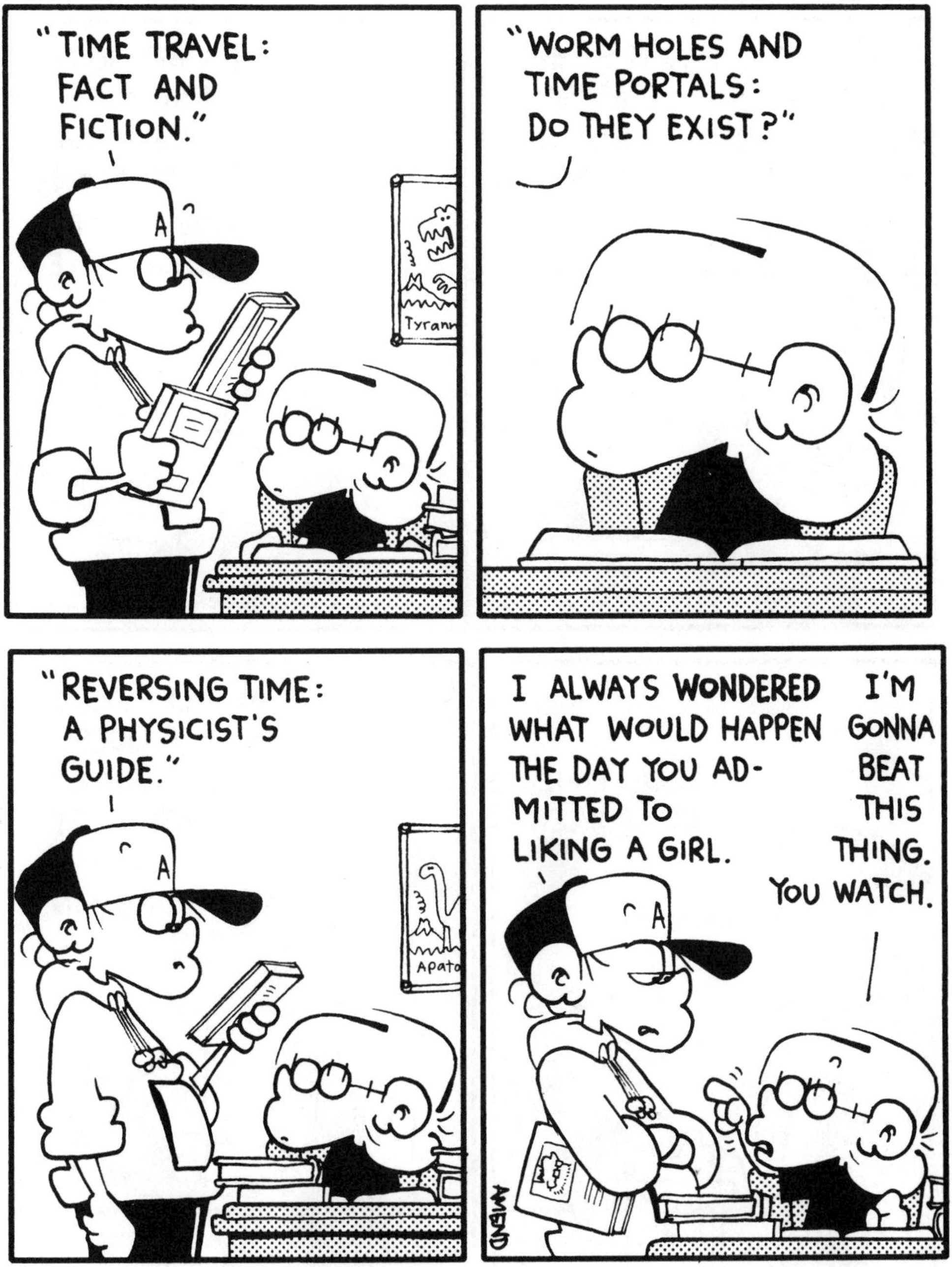
"TIME TRAVEL: FACT AND FICTION."
Tyrann
"WORM HOLES AND TIME PORTALS: DO THEY EXIST?"
"REVERSING TIME: A PHYSICIST'S GUIDE."
Apato
I ALWAYS WONDERED WHAT WOULD HAPPEN THE DAY YOU ADMITTED TO LIKING A GIRL.
I'M GONNA BEAT THIS THING. YOU WATCH.
AMEND

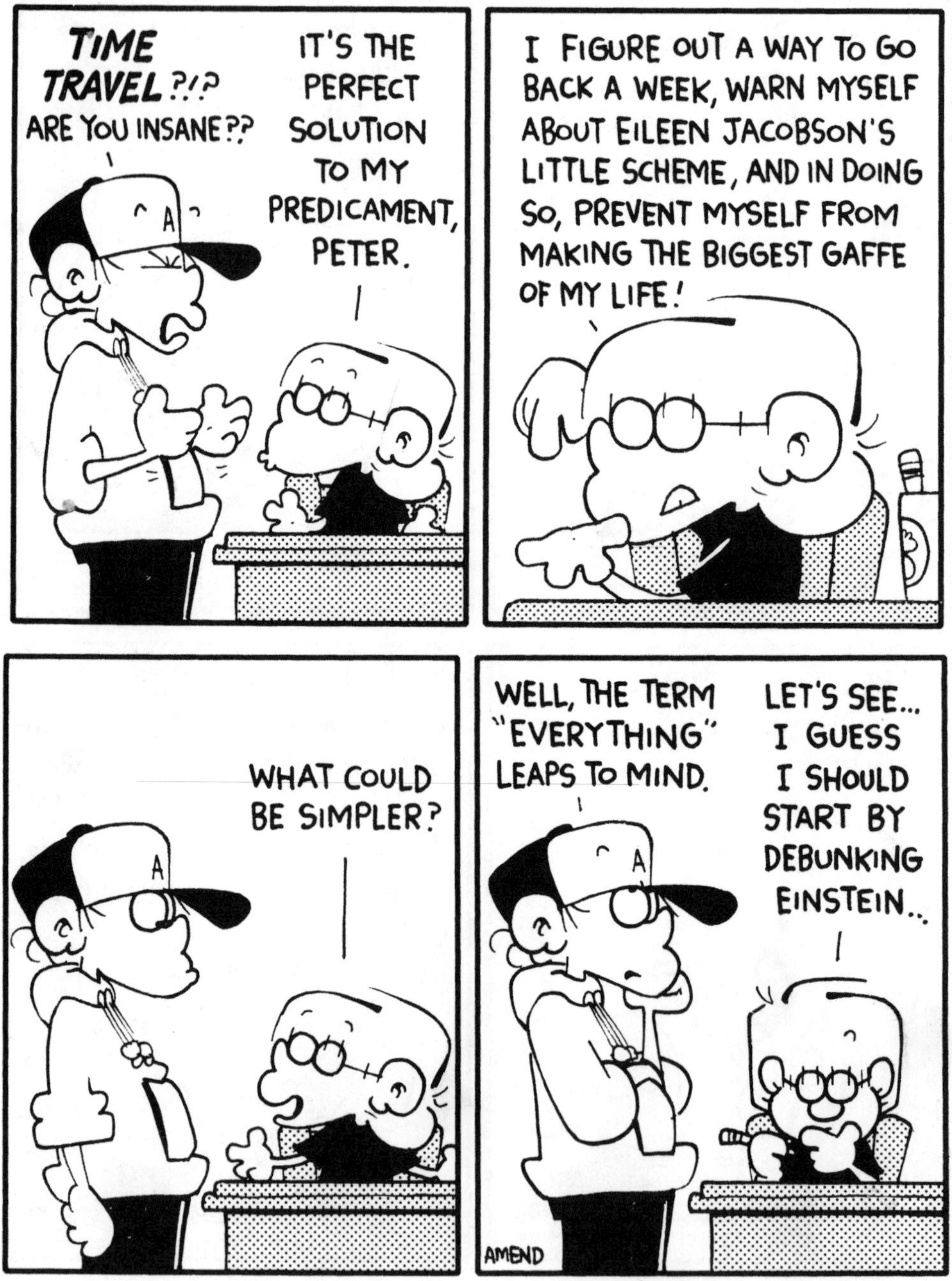
TIME TRAVEL?!? ARE YOU INSANE??
IT'S THE PERFECT SOLUTION TO MY PREDICAMENT, PETER.
I FIGURE OUT A WAY TO GO BACK A WEEK, WARN MYSELF ABOUT EILEEN JACOBSON'S LITTLE SCHEME, AND IN DOING SO, PREVENT MYSELF FROM MAKING THE BIGGEST GAFFE OF MY LIFE!
WHAT COULD BE SIMPLER?
WELL, THE TERM "EVERYTHING" LEAPS TO MIND.
LET'S SEE... I GUESS I SHOULD START BY DEBUNKING EINSTEIN...
AMEND

JASON, YOU HAVEN'T TOUCHED YOUR DINNER AT ALL! SORRY, MOM. I'M ON A SUPER CRASH DIET.

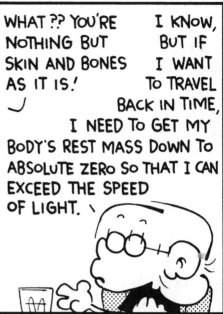

WHAT?? YOU'RE NOTHING BUT SKIN AND BONES AS IT IS! I KNOW, BUT IF I WANT TO TRAVEL BACK IN TIME, I NEED TO GET MY BODY'S REST MASS DOWN TO ABSOLUTE ZERO SO THAT I CAN EXCEED THE SPEED OF LIGHT.

IT'S A PAIN, BUT THAT STUFF I TOLD EILEEN JACOBSON LAST WEEK HAS GOT TO BE UNDONE.

SO THIS CRASH DIET HAS NOTHING TO DO WITH MY SERVING EGGPLANT LOAF TONIGHT? TOTALLY A COINCIDENCE. BUT I APPRECIATE THE HELP.

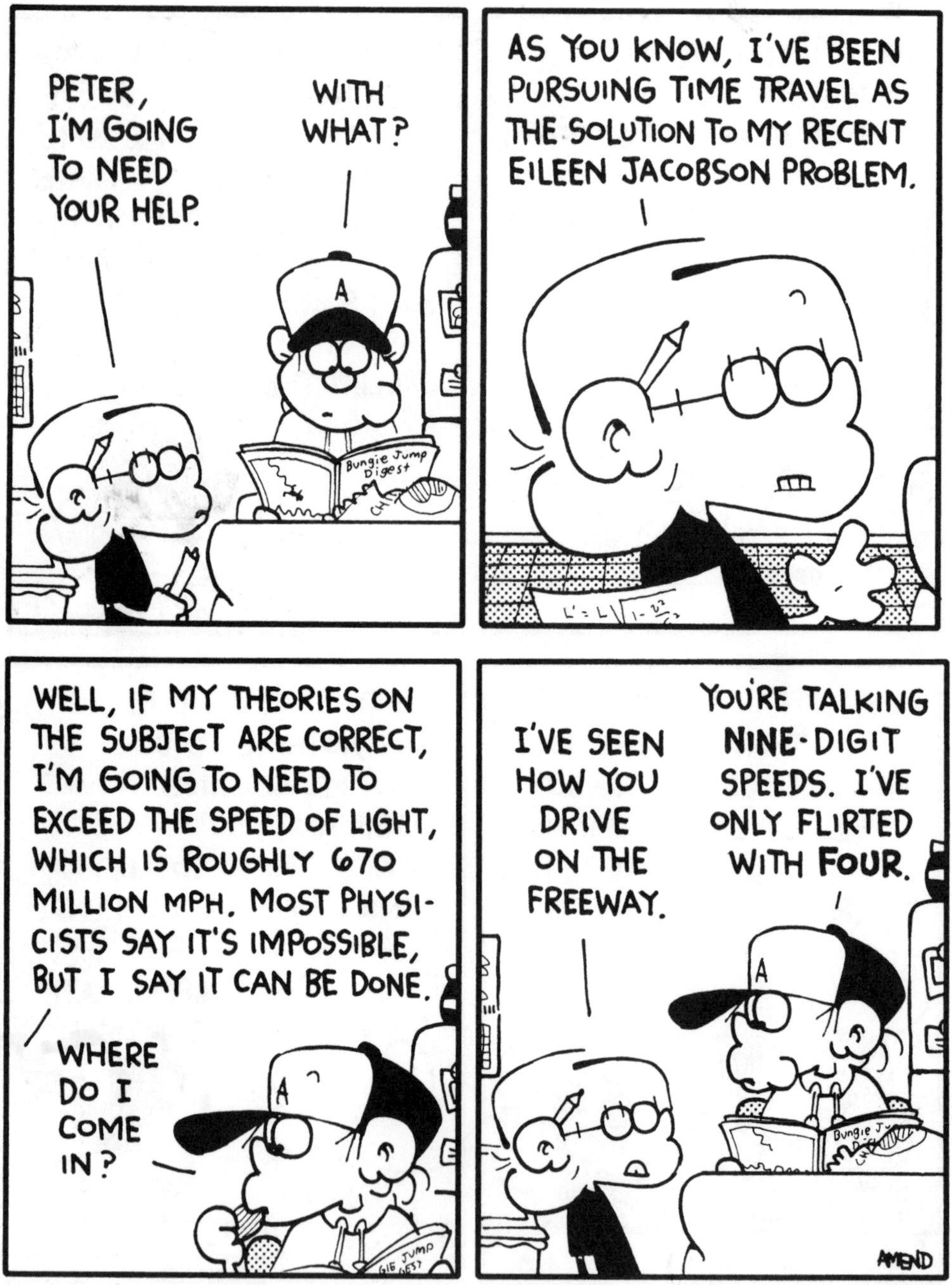
PETER, I'M GOING TO NEED YOUR HELP.
WITH WHAT?
Bungie Jump Digest
AS YOU KNOW, I'VE BEEN PURSUING TIME TRAVEL AS THE SOLUTION TO MY RECENT EILEEN JACOBSON PROBLEM.
WELL, IF MY THEORIES ON THE SUBJECT ARE CORRECT, I'M GOING TO NEED TO EXCEED THE SPEED OF LIGHT, WHICH IS ROUGHLY 670 MILLION MPH. MOST PHYSICISTS SAY IT'S IMPOSSIBLE, BUT I SAY IT CAN BE DONE.
WHERE DO I COME IN?
I'VE SEEN HOW YOU DRIVE ON THE FREEWAY.
YOU'RE TALKING NINE-DIGIT SPEEDS. I'VE ONLY FLIRTED WITH **FOUR**.
AMEND

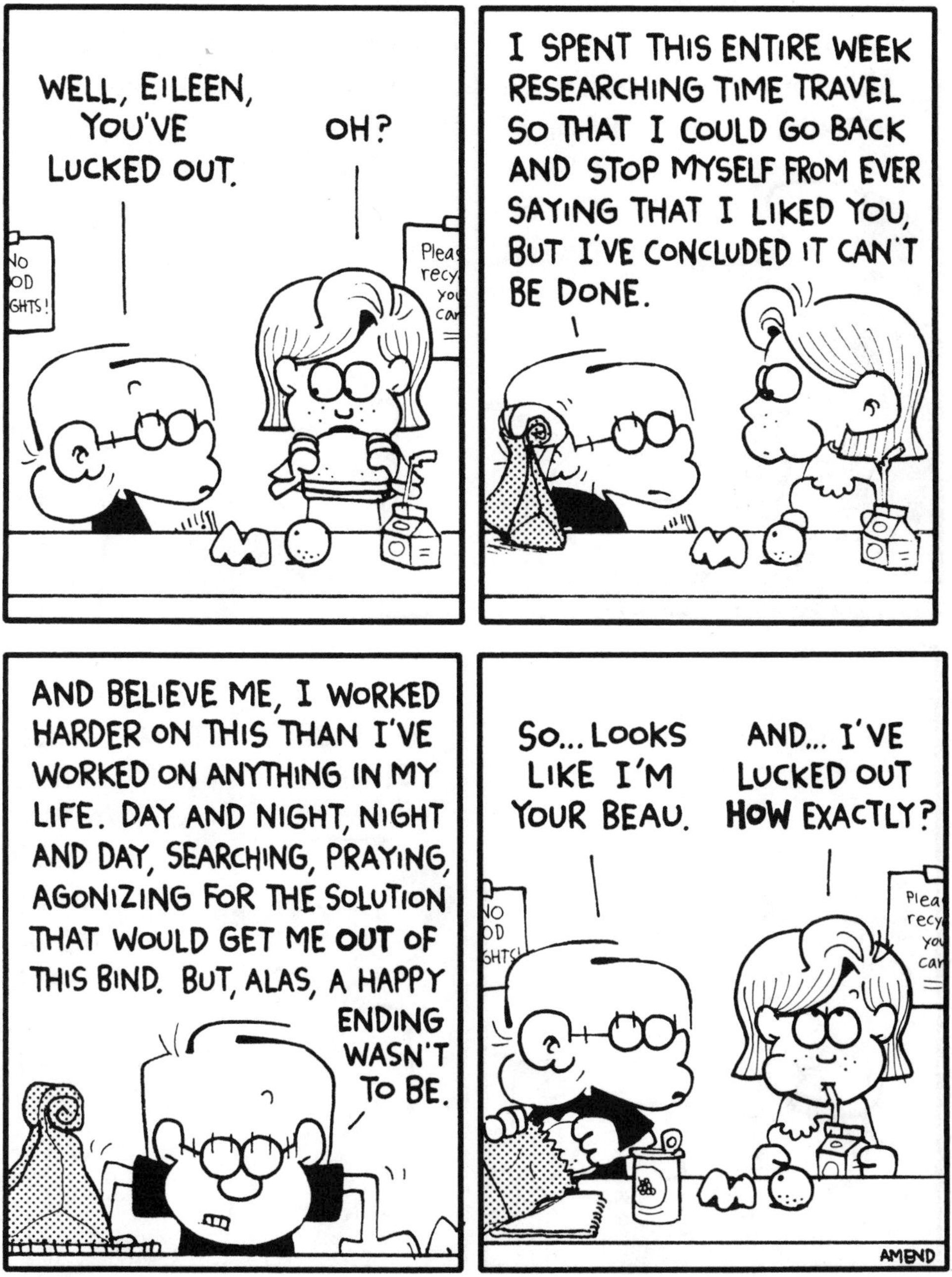
WELL, EILEEN, YOU'VE LUCKED OUT.
OH?
I SPENT THIS ENTIRE WEEK RESEARCHING TIME TRAVEL SO THAT I COULD GO BACK AND STOP MYSELF FROM EVER SAYING THAT I LIKED YOU, BUT I'VE CONCLUDED IT CAN'T BE DONE.
AND BELIEVE ME, I WORKED HARDER ON THIS THAN I'VE WORKED ON ANYTHING IN MY LIFE. DAY AND NIGHT, NIGHT AND DAY, SEARCHING, PRAYING, AGONIZING FOR THE SOLUTION THAT WOULD GET ME OUT OF THIS BIND. BUT, ALAS, A HAPPY ENDING WASN'T TO BE.
SO... LOOKS LIKE I'M YOUR BEAU.
AND... I'VE LUCKED OUT HOW EXACTLY?
AMEND

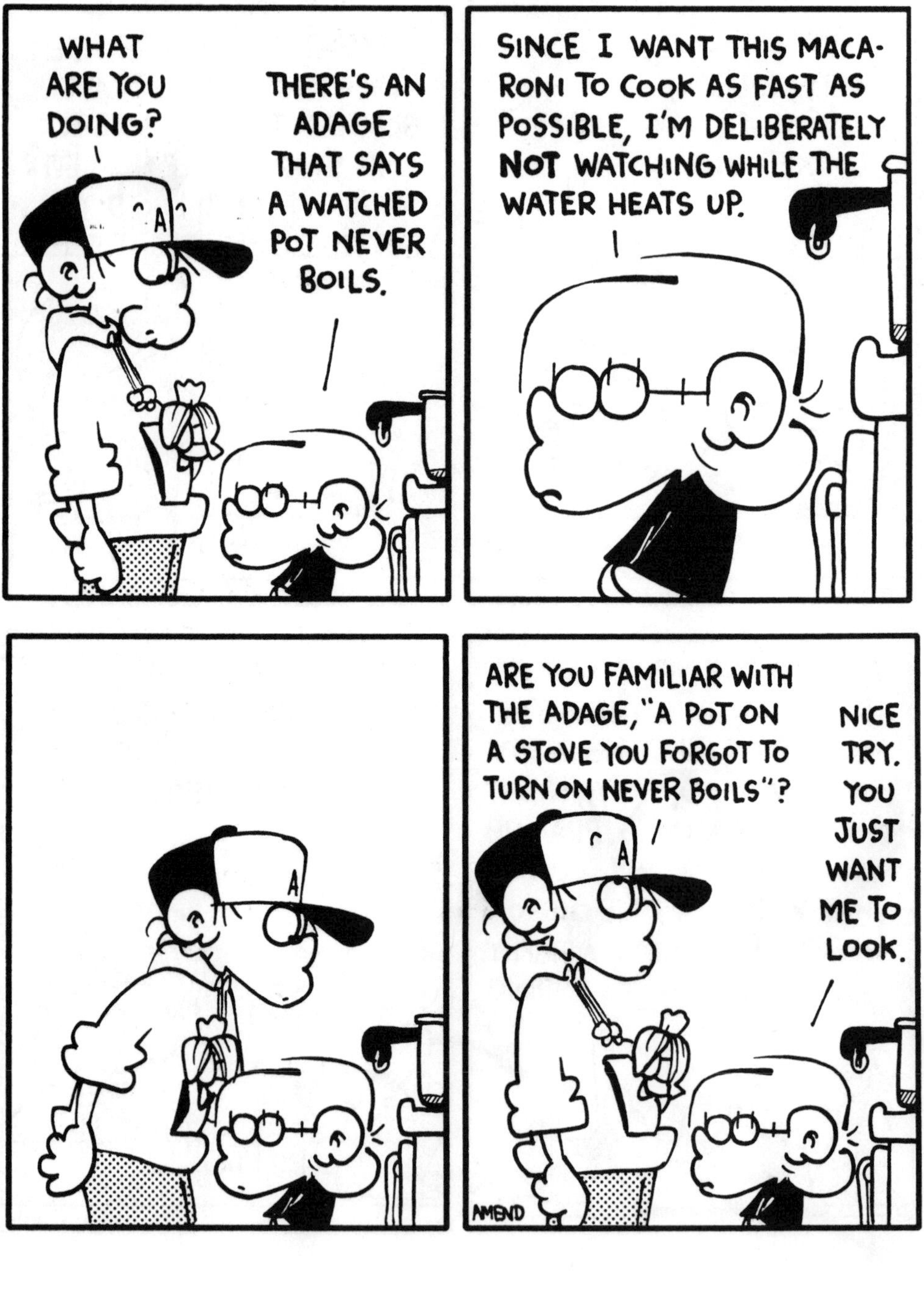
WHAT ARE YOU DOING?
THERE'S AN ADAGE THAT SAYS A WATCHED POT NEVER BOILS.
SINCE I WANT THIS MACARONI TO COOK AS FAST AS POSSIBLE, I'M DELIBERATELY NOT WATCHING WHILE THE WATER HEATS UP.
ARE YOU FAMILIAR WITH THE ADAGE, "A POT ON A STOVE YOU FORGOT TO TURN ON NEVER BOILS"?
NICE TRY. YOU JUST WANT ME TO LOOK.
AMEND

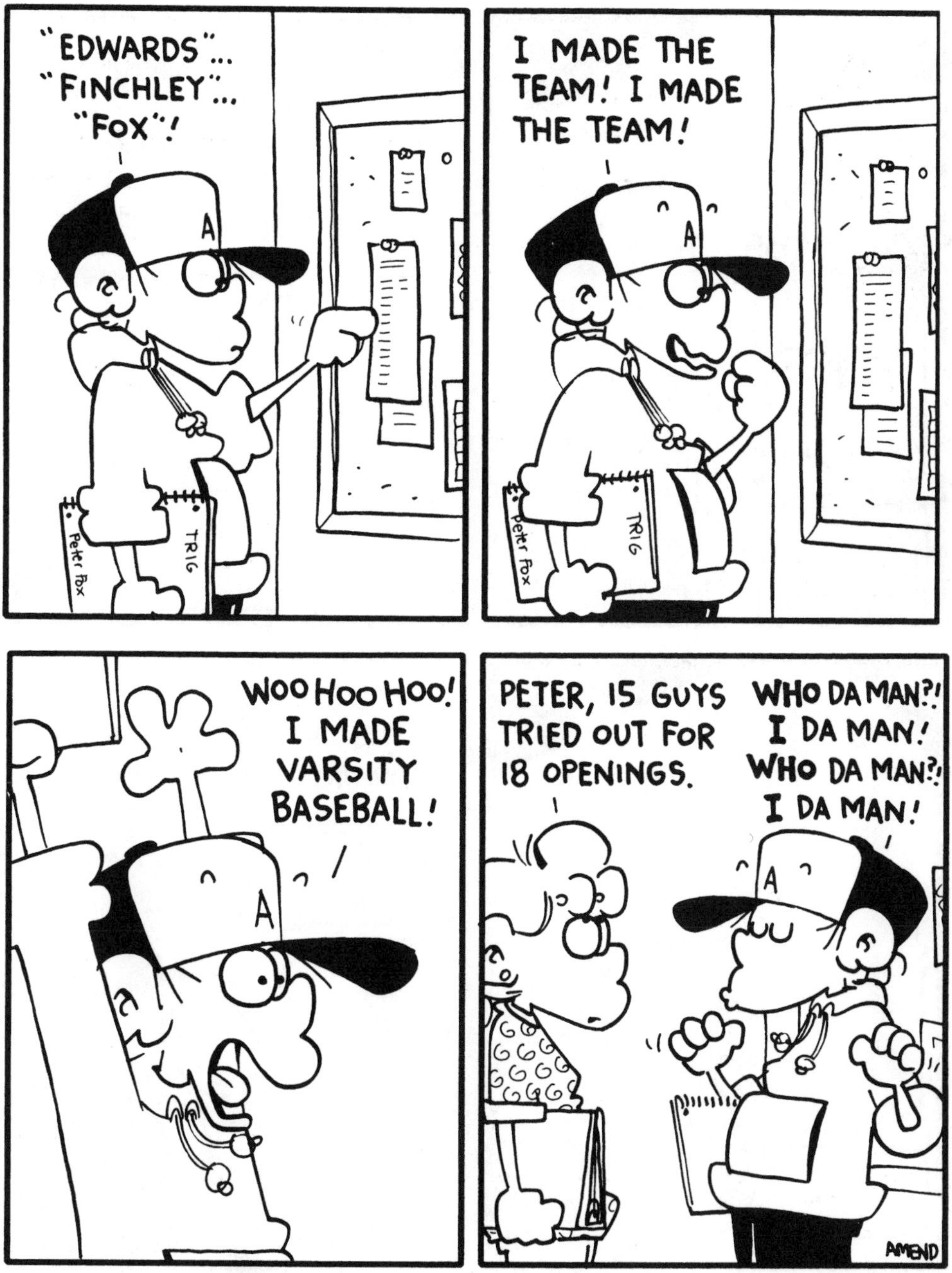
"EDWARDS"... "FINCHLEY"... "FOX"!
Peter Fox
TRIG
I MADE THE TEAM! I MADE THE TEAM!
Peter Fox
TRIG
WOO HOO HOO! I MADE VARSITY BASEBALL!
PETER, 15 GUYS TRIED OUT FOR 18 OPENINGS.
WHO DA MAN?! I DA MAN! WHO DA MAN?! I DA MAN!
AMEND

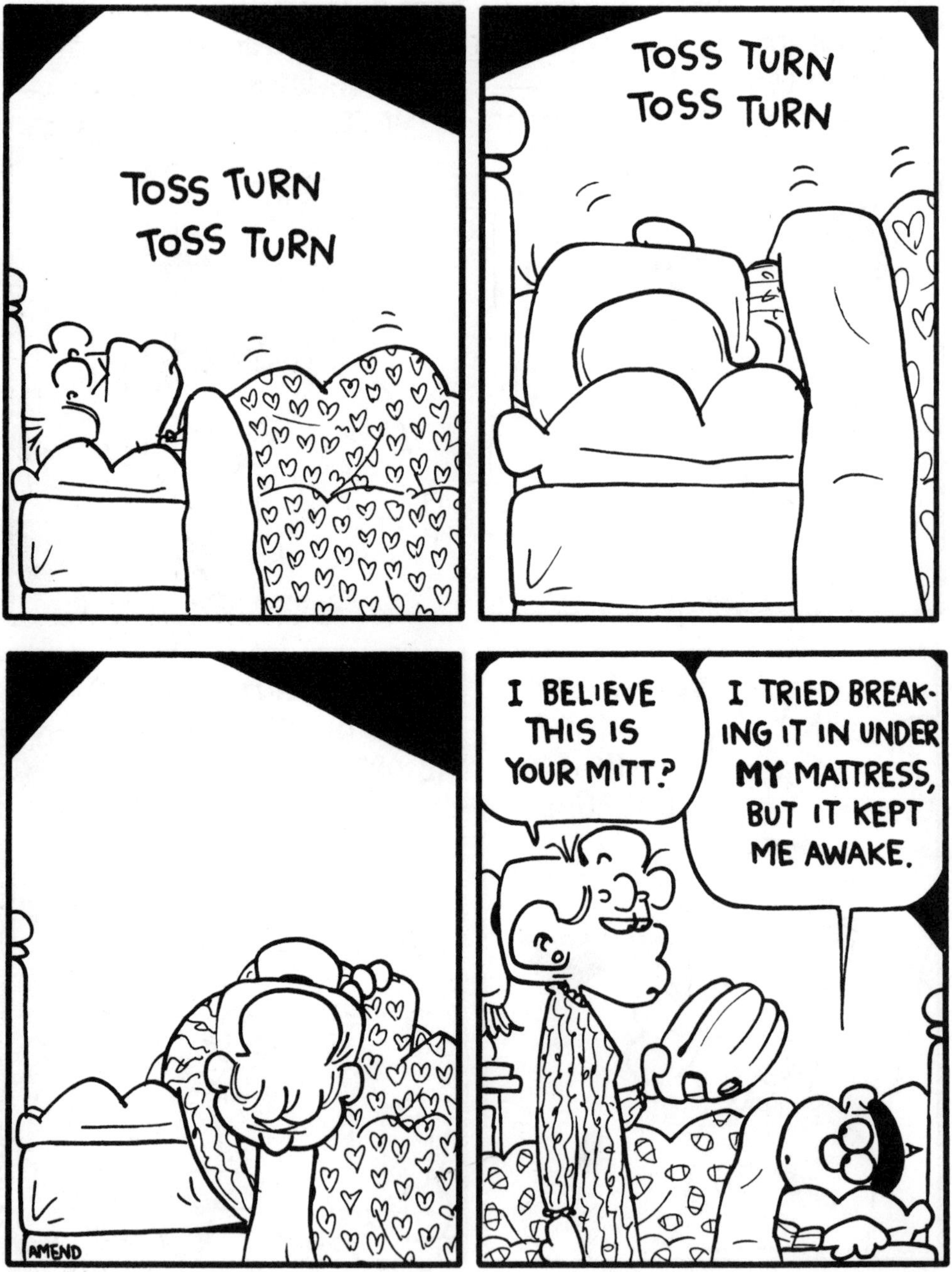
TOSS TURN
TOSS TURN
TOSS TURN
TOSS TURN
I BELIEVE THIS IS YOUR MITT?
I TRIED BREAK-ING IT IN UNDER MY MATTRESS, BUT IT KEPT ME AWAKE.
AMEND

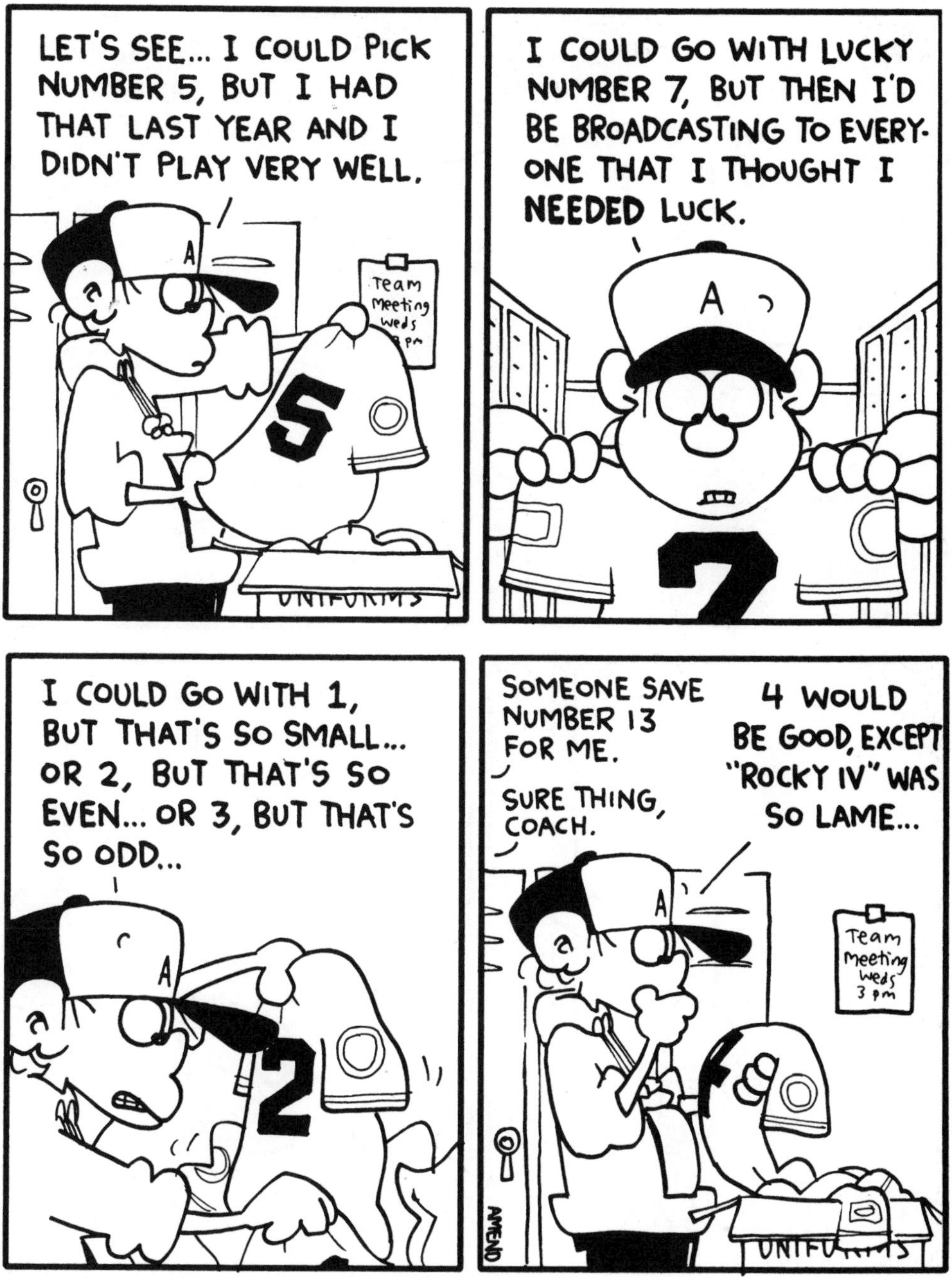
LET'S SEE... I COULD PICK NUMBER 5, BUT I HAD THAT LAST YEAR AND I DIDN'T PLAY VERY WELL.
Team Meeting Weds
UNIFORMS
I COULD GO WITH LUCKY NUMBER 7, BUT THEN I'D BE BROADCASTING TO EVERYONE THAT I THOUGHT I NEEDED LUCK.
I COULD GO WITH 1, BUT THAT'S SO SMALL... OR 2, BUT THAT'S SO EVEN... OR 3, BUT THAT'S SO ODD...
SOMEONE SAVE NUMBER 13 FOR ME.
SURE THING, COACH.
4 WOULD BE GOOD, EXCEPT "ROCKY IV" WAS SO LAME...
Team Meeting Weds 3 pm
UNIFORMS
AMEND

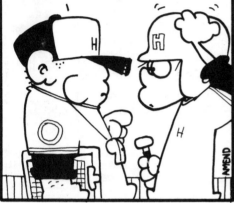

FOX, HOLD ON — DON'T TAKE BATTING PRACTICE YET. MY CAR'S IN THE PARKING LOT WHERE YOUR FOUL BALLS TEND TO LAND.

I WANT TO MOVE IT TO SOME-PLACE WHERE YOU WON'T BE LIKELY TO HIT IT.

WHY'S HE DRIVING IT INTO CENTER FIELD?

FOX, AS YOU'LL RECALL, LAST YEAR I MOVED YOU AROUND QUITE A BIT.
I STARTED YOU AT SECOND BASE, THEN MOVED YOU TO LEFT FIELD, THEN CENTER, THEN RIGHT, THEN BACK TO THE INFIELD, THEN BACK TO THE OUTFIELD...
WELL, THIS YEAR, SON, I WANT TO KEEP YOU IN ONE SPOT FOR THE WHOLE SEASON.
SOUNDS GOOD TO ME, COACH. WHERE?
AMEND
NO SPITTING IN DUGOUT!

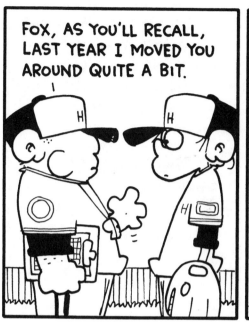

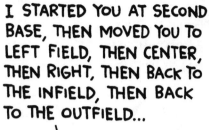

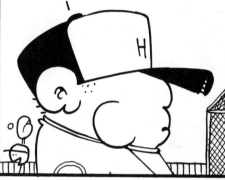

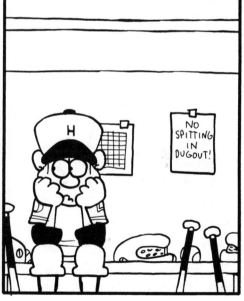

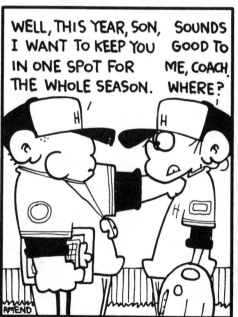

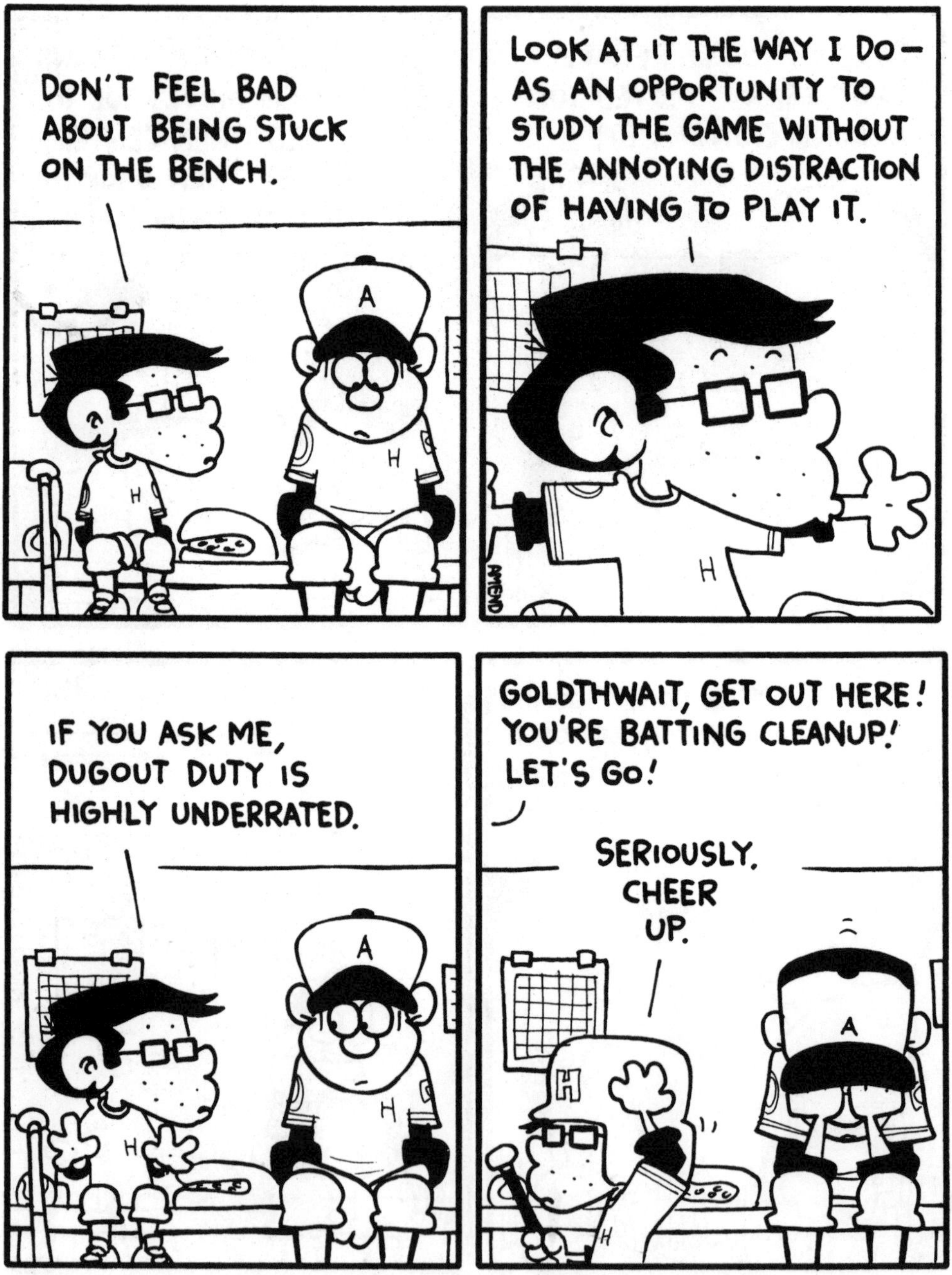
DON'T FEEL BAD ABOUT BEING STUCK ON THE BENCH.
LOOK AT IT THE WAY I DO— AS AN OPPORTUNITY TO STUDY THE GAME WITHOUT THE ANNOYING DISTRACTION OF HAVING TO PLAY IT.
AMEND
IF YOU ASK ME, DUGOUT DUTY IS HIGHLY UNDERRATED.
GOLDTHWAIT, GET OUT HERE! YOU'RE BATTING CLEANUP! LET'S GO!
SERIOUSLY. CHEER UP.

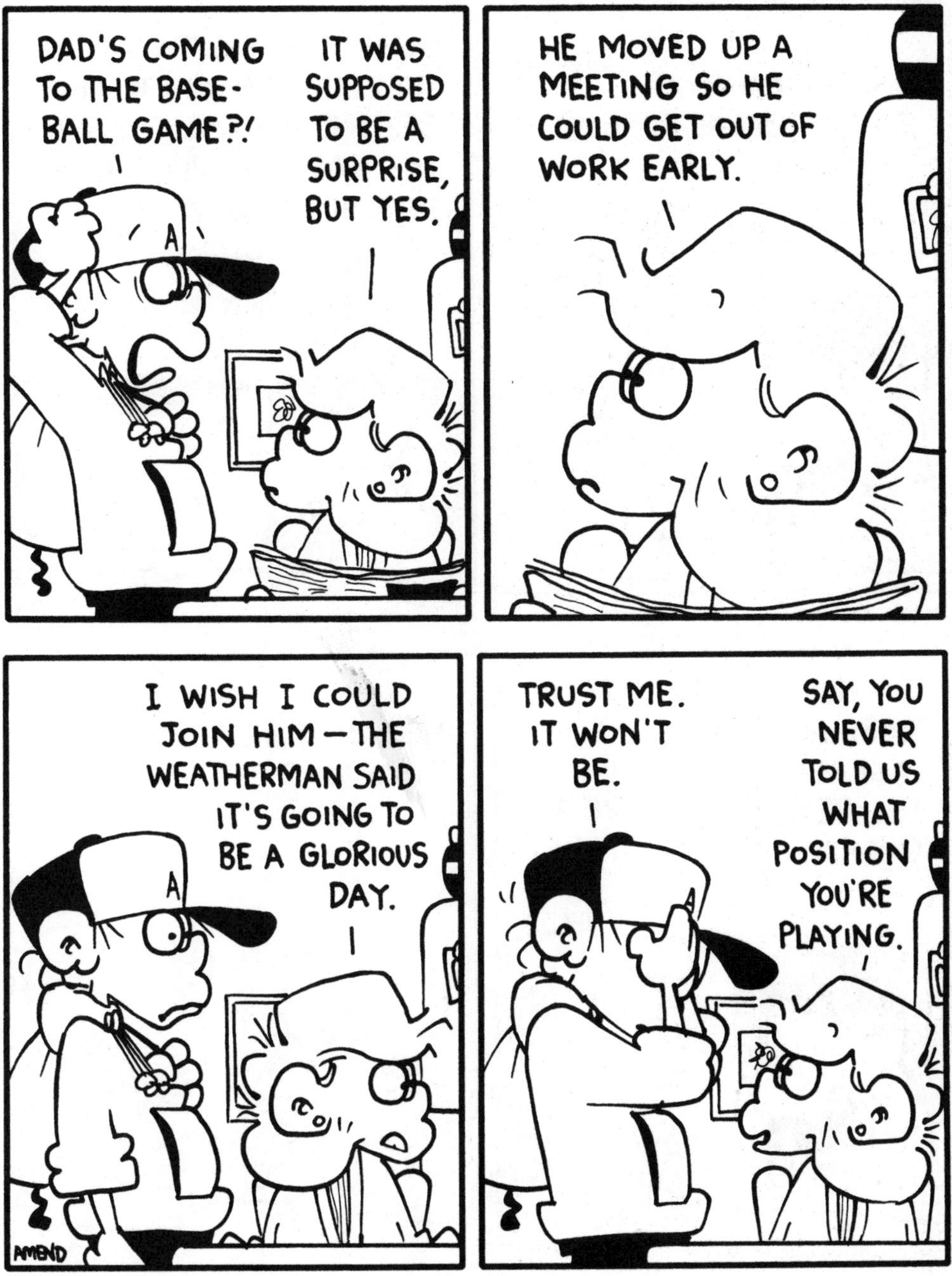
DAD'S COMING TO THE BASE-BALL GAME?!
IT WAS SUPPOSED TO BE A SURPRISE, BUT YES.
HE MOVED UP A MEETING SO HE COULD GET OUT OF WORK EARLY.
I WISH I COULD JOIN HIM—THE WEATHERMAN SAID IT'S GOING TO BE A GLORIOUS DAY.
AMEND
TRUST ME. IT WON'T BE.
SAY, YOU NEVER TOLD US WHAT POSITION YOU'RE PLAYING.

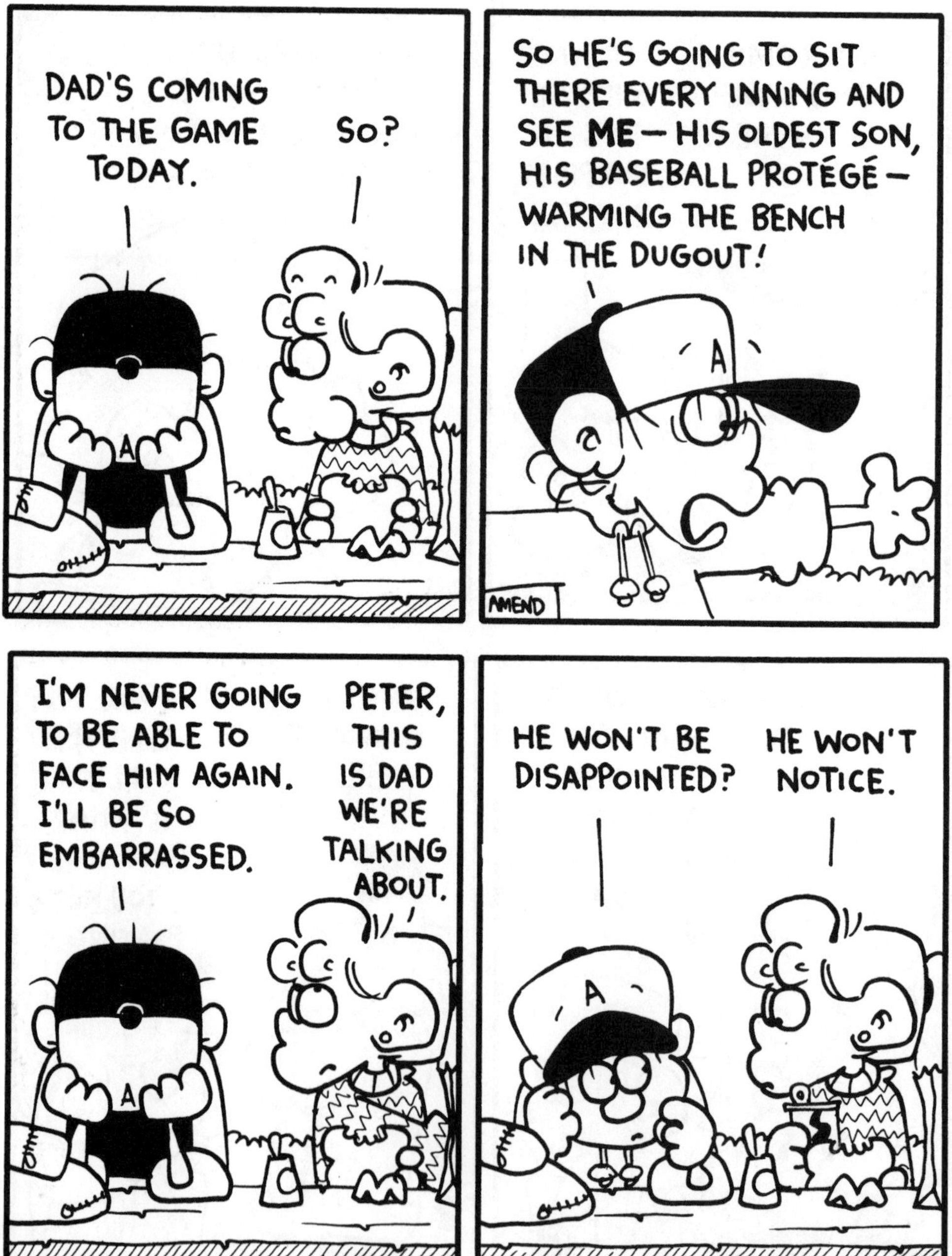
DAD'S COMING TO THE GAME TODAY.
SO?
SO HE'S GOING TO SIT THERE EVERY INNING AND SEE **ME**—HIS OLDEST SON, HIS BASEBALL PROTÉGÉ—WARMING THE BENCH IN THE DUGOUT!
AMEND
I'M NEVER GOING TO BE ABLE TO FACE HIM AGAIN. I'LL BE SO EMBARRASSED.
PETER, THIS IS DAD WE'RE TALKING ABOUT.
HE WON'T BE DISAPPOINTED?
HE WON'T NOTICE.

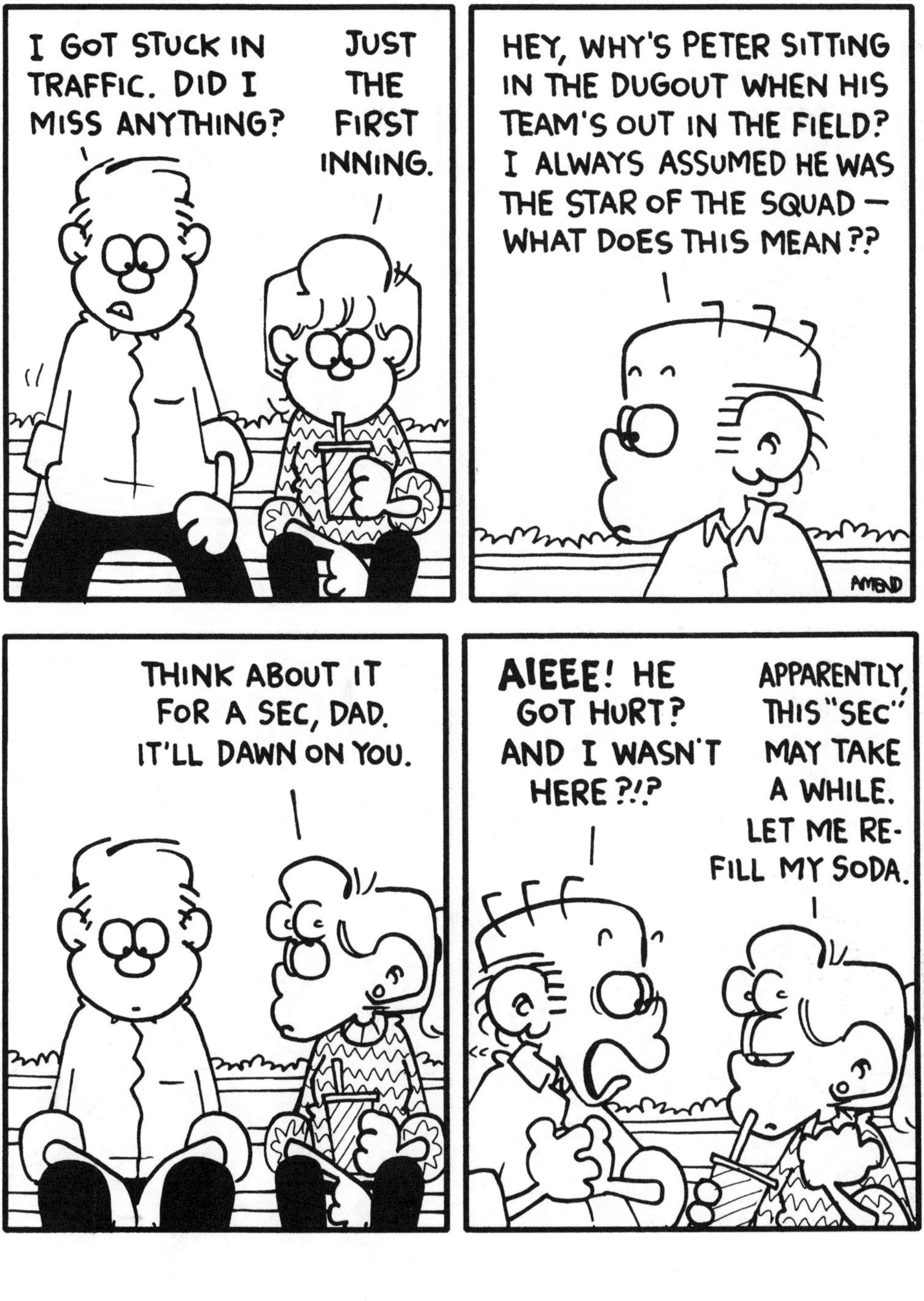
I GOT STUCK IN TRAFFIC. DID I MISS ANYTHING?
JUST THE FIRST INNING.
HEY, WHY'S PETER SITTING IN THE DUGOUT WHEN HIS TEAM'S OUT IN THE FIELD? I ALWAYS ASSUMED HE WAS THE STAR OF THE SQUAD — WHAT DOES THIS MEAN??
AMEND
THINK ABOUT IT FOR A SEC, DAD. IT'LL DAWN ON YOU.
AIEEE! HE GOT HURT? AND I WASN'T HERE?!?
APPARENTLY, THIS "SEC" MAY TAKE A WHILE. LET ME RE-FILL MY SODA.

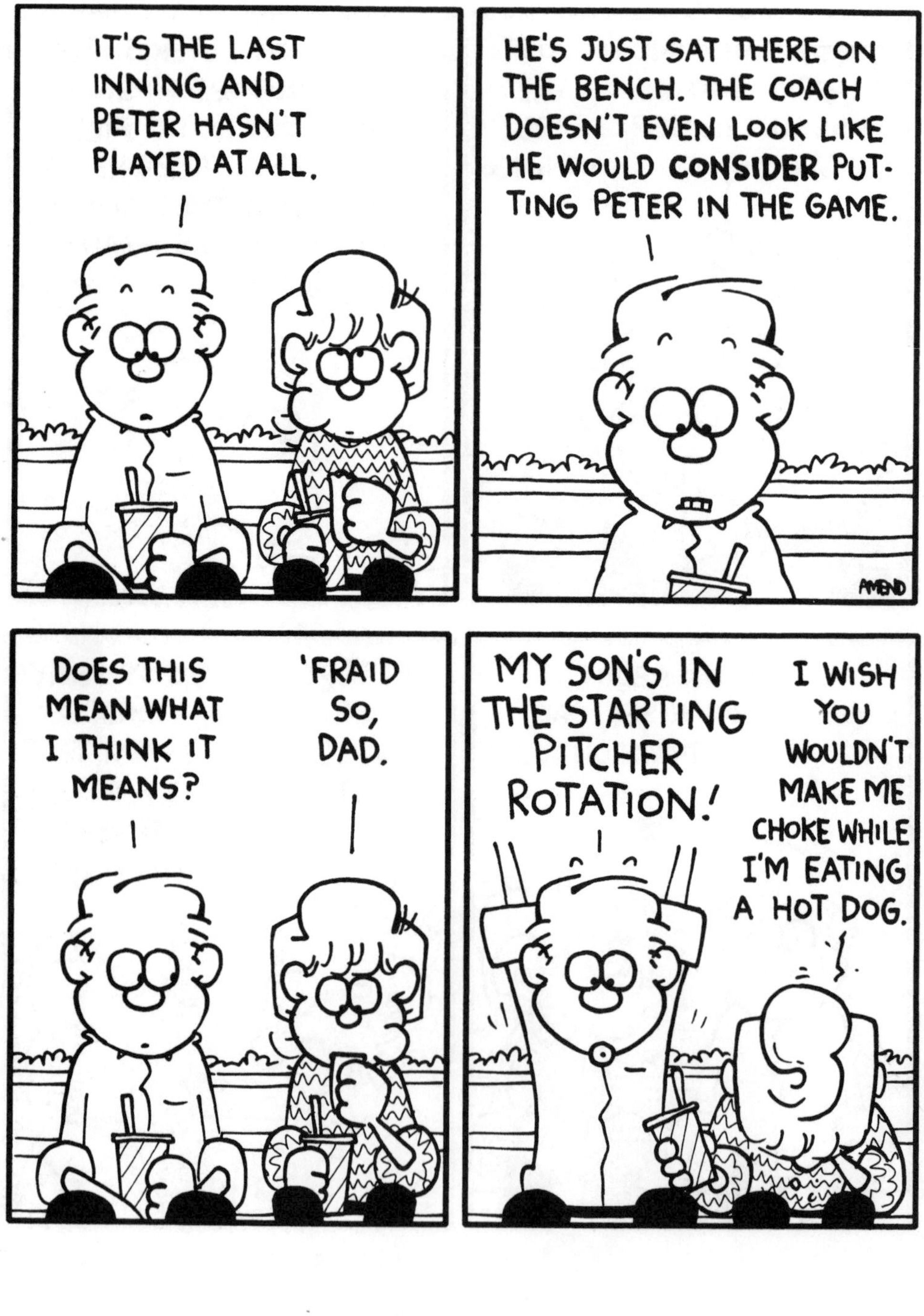
IT'S THE LAST INNING AND PETER HASN'T PLAYED AT ALL.
HE'S JUST SAT THERE ON THE BENCH. THE COACH DOESN'T EVEN LOOK LIKE HE WOULD **CONSIDER** PUTTING PETER IN THE GAME.
AMEND
DOES THIS MEAN WHAT I THINK IT MEANS?
'FRAID SO, DAD.
MY SON'S IN THE STARTING PITCHER ROTATION!
I WISH YOU WOULDN'T MAKE ME CHOKE WHILE I'M EATING A HOT DOG.

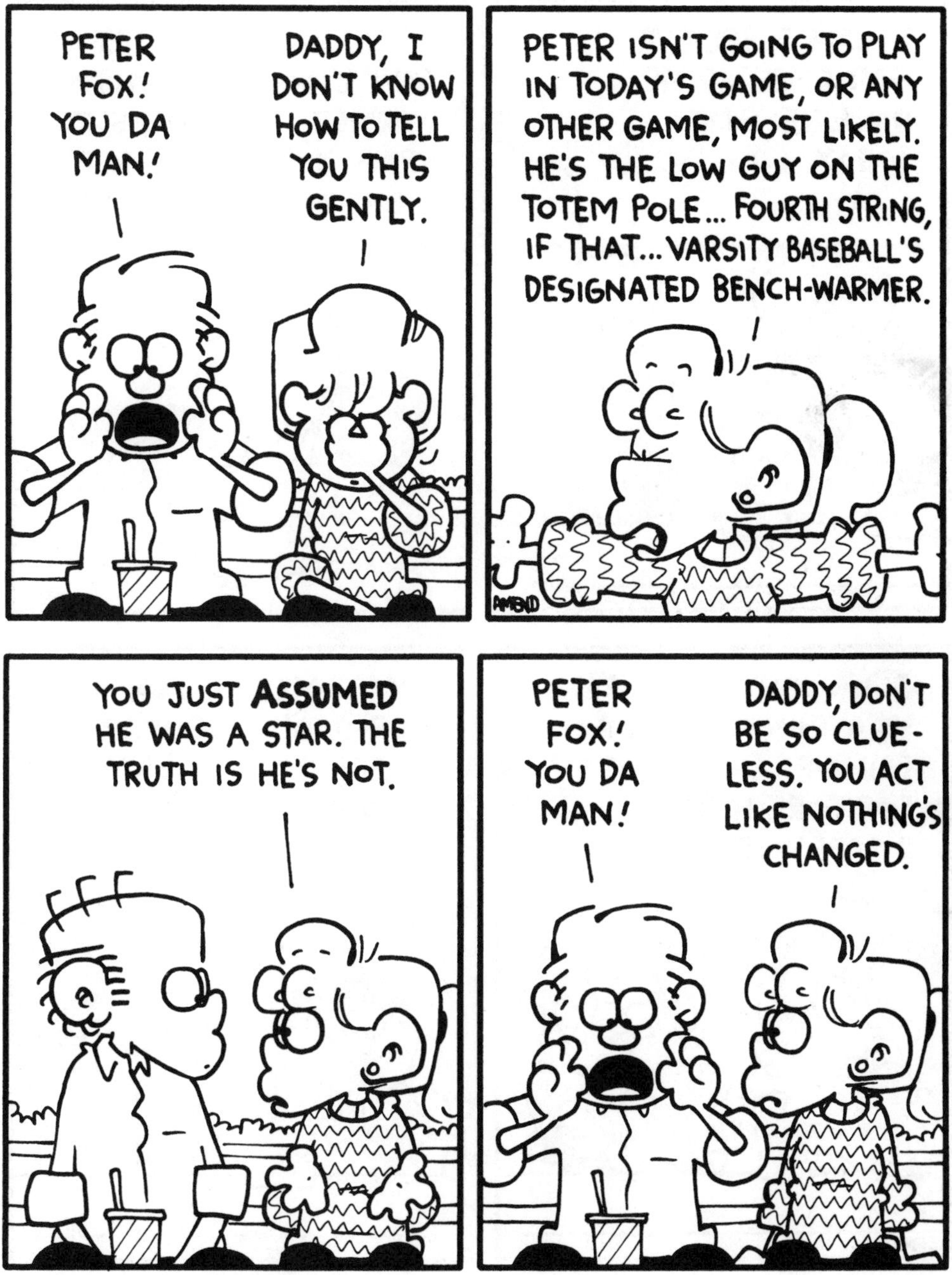
PETER FOX! YOU DA MAN!
DADDY, I DON'T KNOW HOW TO TELL YOU THIS GENTLY.
PETER ISN'T GOING TO PLAY IN TODAY'S GAME, OR ANY OTHER GAME, MOST LIKELY. HE'S THE LOW GUY ON THE TOTEM POLE... FOURTH STRING, IF THAT... VARSITY BASEBALL'S DESIGNATED BENCH-WARMER.
AMEND
YOU JUST **ASSUMED** HE WAS A STAR. THE TRUTH IS HE'S NOT.
PETER FOX! YOU DA MAN!
DADDY, DON'T BE SO CLUE-LESS. YOU ACT LIKE NOTHING'S CHANGED.

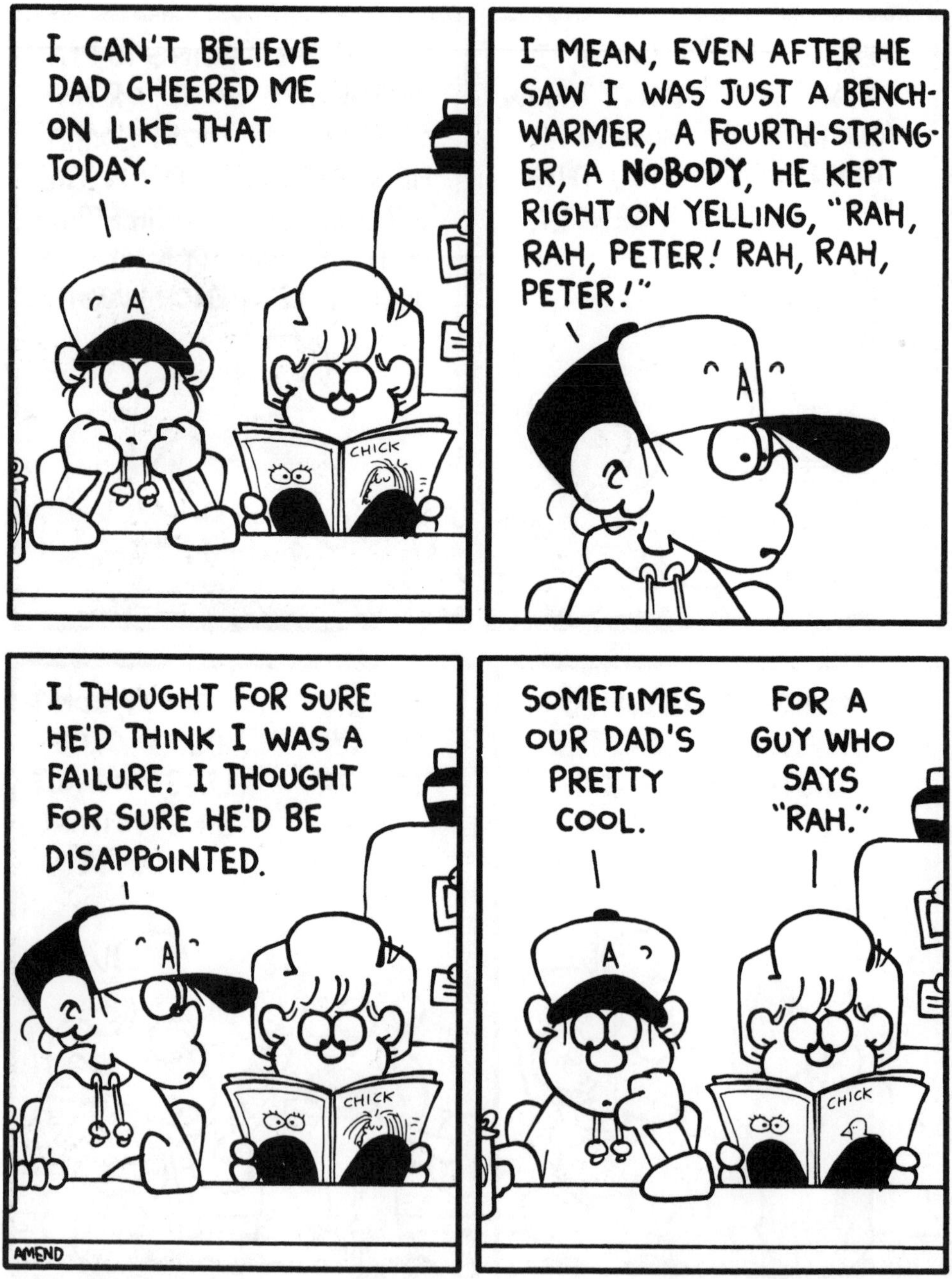
I CAN'T BELIEVE DAD CHEERED ME ON LIKE THAT TODAY.
CHICK
I MEAN, EVEN AFTER HE SAW I WAS JUST A BENCH-WARMER, A FOURTH-STRING-ER, A **NOBODY**, HE KEPT RIGHT ON YELLING, "RAH, RAH, PETER! RAH, RAH, PETER!"
I THOUGHT FOR SURE HE'D THINK I WAS A FAILURE. I THOUGHT FOR SURE HE'D BE DISAPPOINTED.
CHICK
AMEND
SOMETIMES OUR DAD'S PRETTY COOL.
FOR A GUY WHO SAYS "RAH."
CHICK

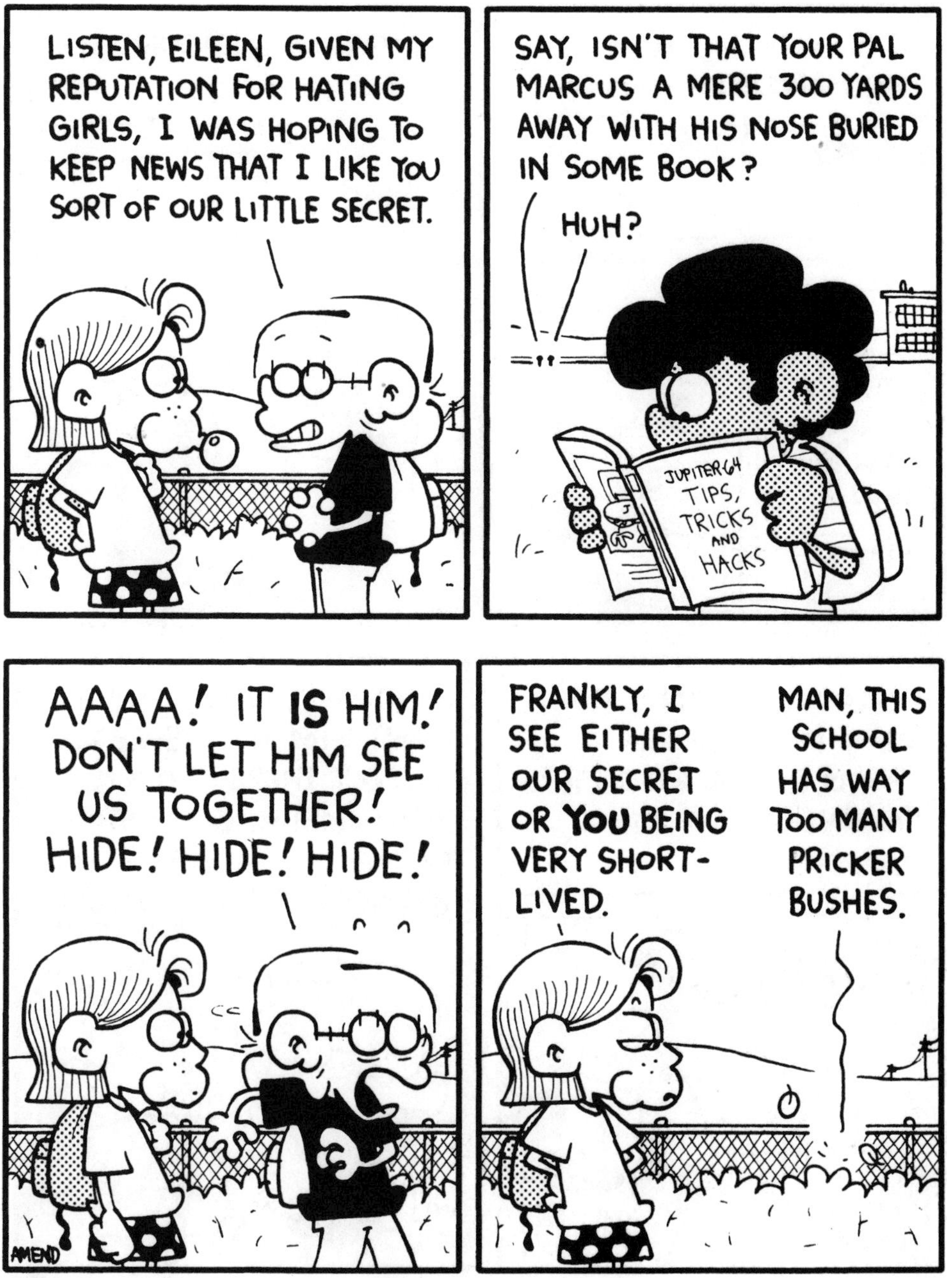
LISTEN, EILEEN, GIVEN MY REPUTATION FOR HATING GIRLS, I WAS HOPING TO KEEP NEWS THAT I LIKE YOU SORT OF OUR LITTLE SECRET.
SAY, ISN'T THAT YOUR PAL MARCUS A MERE 300 YARDS AWAY WITH HIS NOSE BURIED IN SOME BOOK?
HUH?
JUPITER 64 TIPS, TRICKS AND HACKS
AAAA! IT IS HIM! DON'T LET HIM SEE US TOGETHER! HIDE! HIDE! HIDE!
AMEND
FRANKLY, I SEE EITHER OUR SECRET OR YOU BEING VERY SHORT-LIVED.
MAN, THIS SCHOOL HAS WAY TOO MANY PRICKER BUSHES.

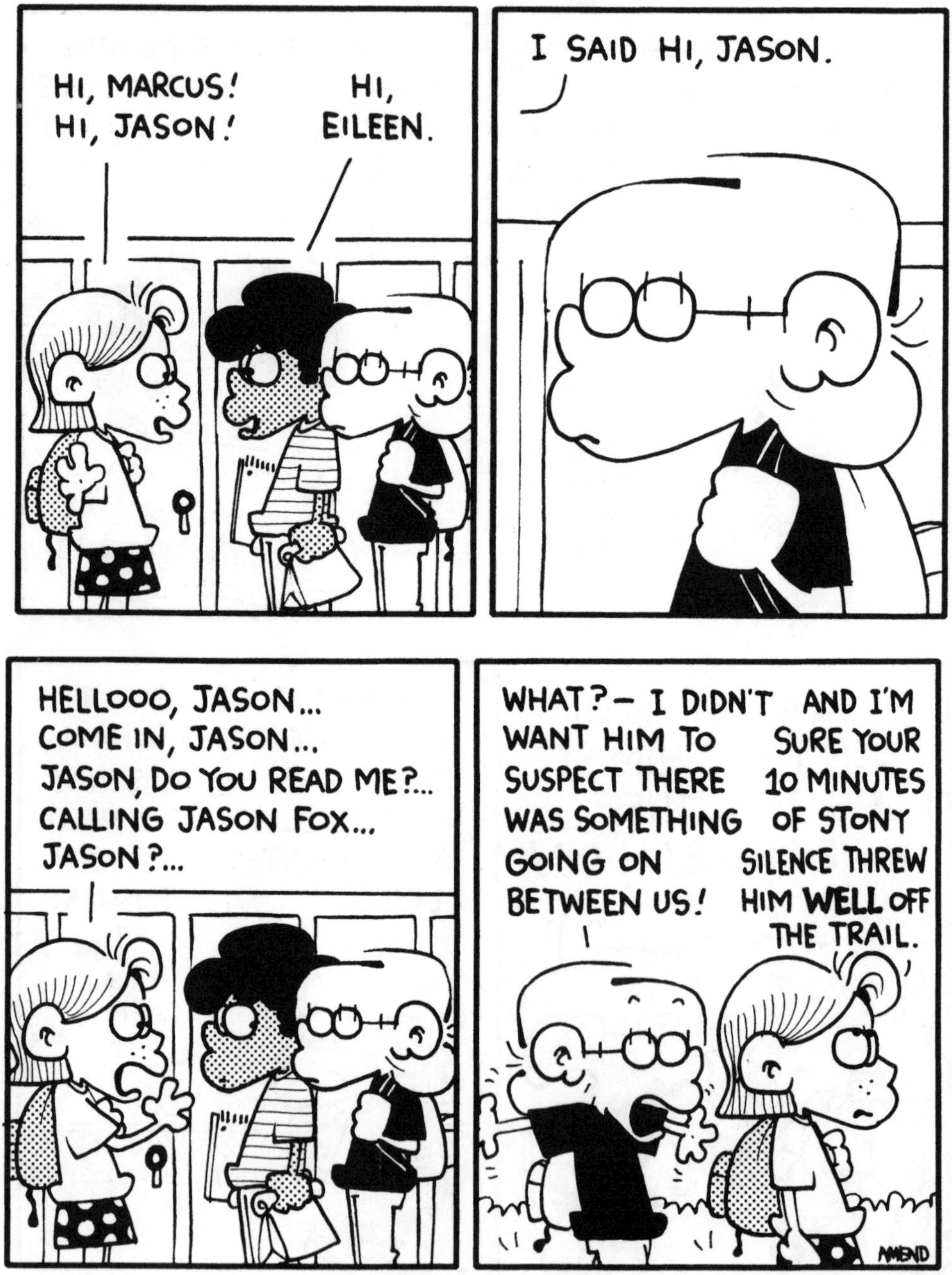
HI, MARCUS!
HI, JASON!
HI, EILEEN.
I SAID HI, JASON.
HELLOOO, JASON... COME IN, JASON... JASON, DO YOU READ ME?... CALLING JASON FOX... JASON?...
WHAT?– I DIDN'T WANT HIM TO SUSPECT THERE WAS SOMETHING GOING ON BETWEEN US!
AND I'M SURE YOUR 10 MINUTES OF STONY SILENCE THREW HIM WELL OFF THE TRAIL.
AMEND

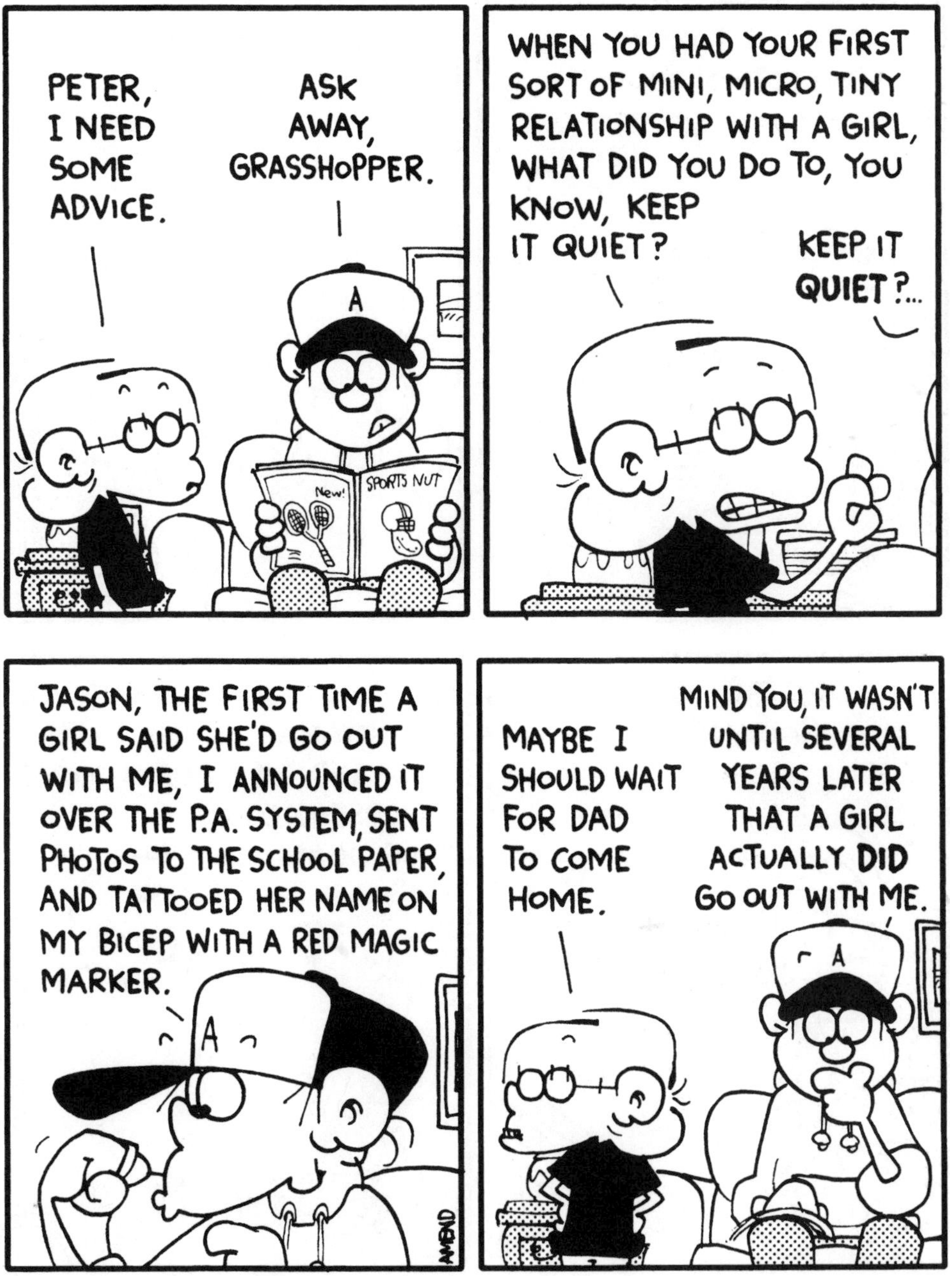
PETER, I NEED SOME ADVICE.
ASK AWAY, GRASSHOPPER.
New!
SPORTS NUT
WHEN YOU HAD YOUR FIRST SORT OF MINI, MICRO, TINY RELATIONSHIP WITH A GIRL, WHAT DID YOU DO TO, YOU KNOW, KEEP IT QUIET?
KEEP IT **QUIET**?...
JASON, THE FIRST TIME A GIRL SAID SHE'D GO OUT WITH ME, I ANNOUNCED IT OVER THE P.A. SYSTEM, SENT PHOTOS TO THE SCHOOL PAPER, AND TATTOOED HER NAME ON MY BICEP WITH A RED MAGIC MARKER.
MAYBE I SHOULD WAIT FOR DAD TO COME HOME.
MIND YOU, IT WASN'T UNTIL SEVERAL YEARS LATER THAT A GIRL ACTUALLY **DID** GO OUT WITH ME.
AMEND

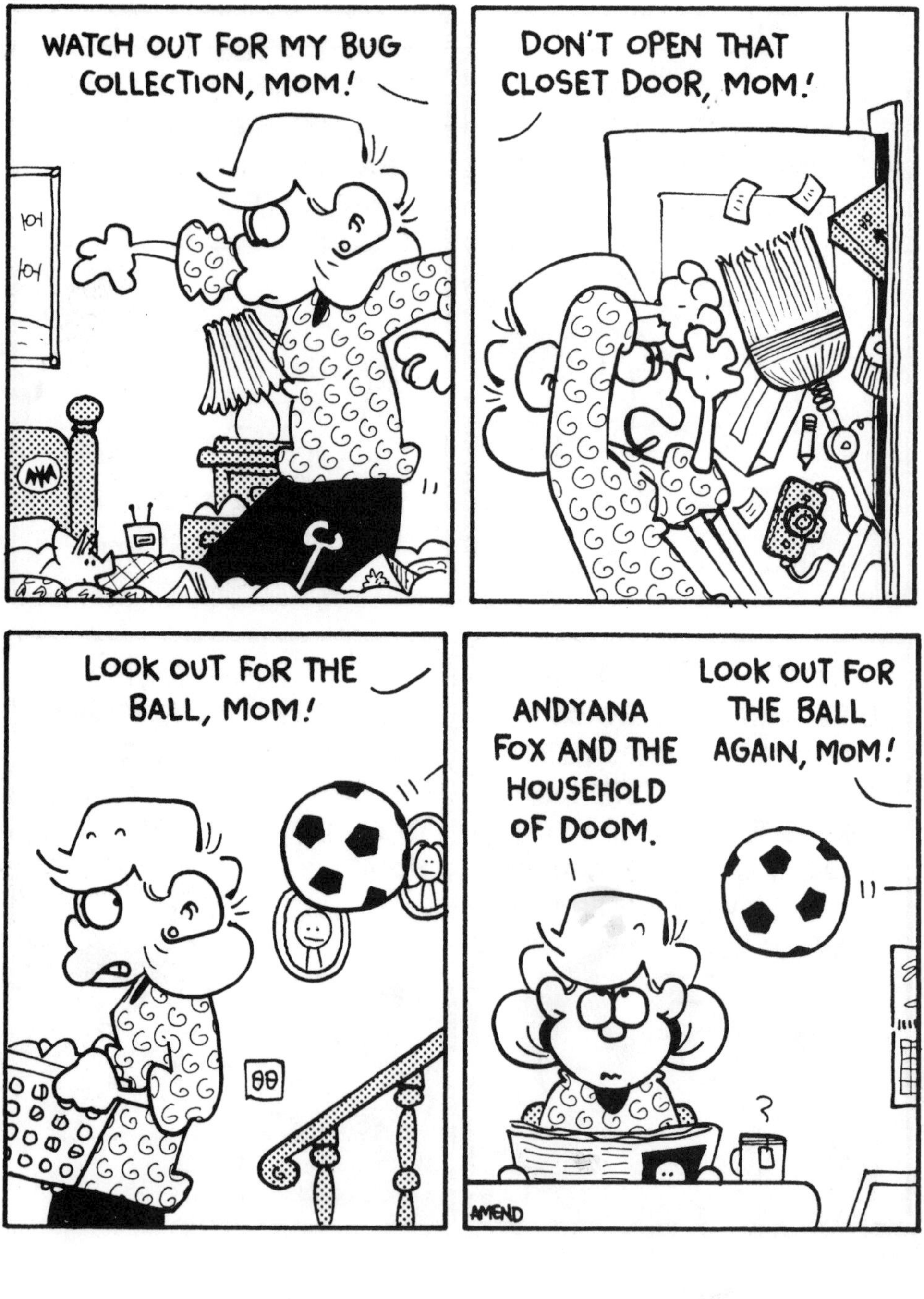
WATCH OUT FOR MY BUG COLLECTION, MOM!
DON'T OPEN THAT CLOSET DOOR, MOM!
LOOK OUT FOR THE BALL, MOM!
LOOK OUT FOR THE BALL AGAIN, MOM!
ANDYANA FOX AND THE HOUSEHOLD OF DOOM.
?
AMEND

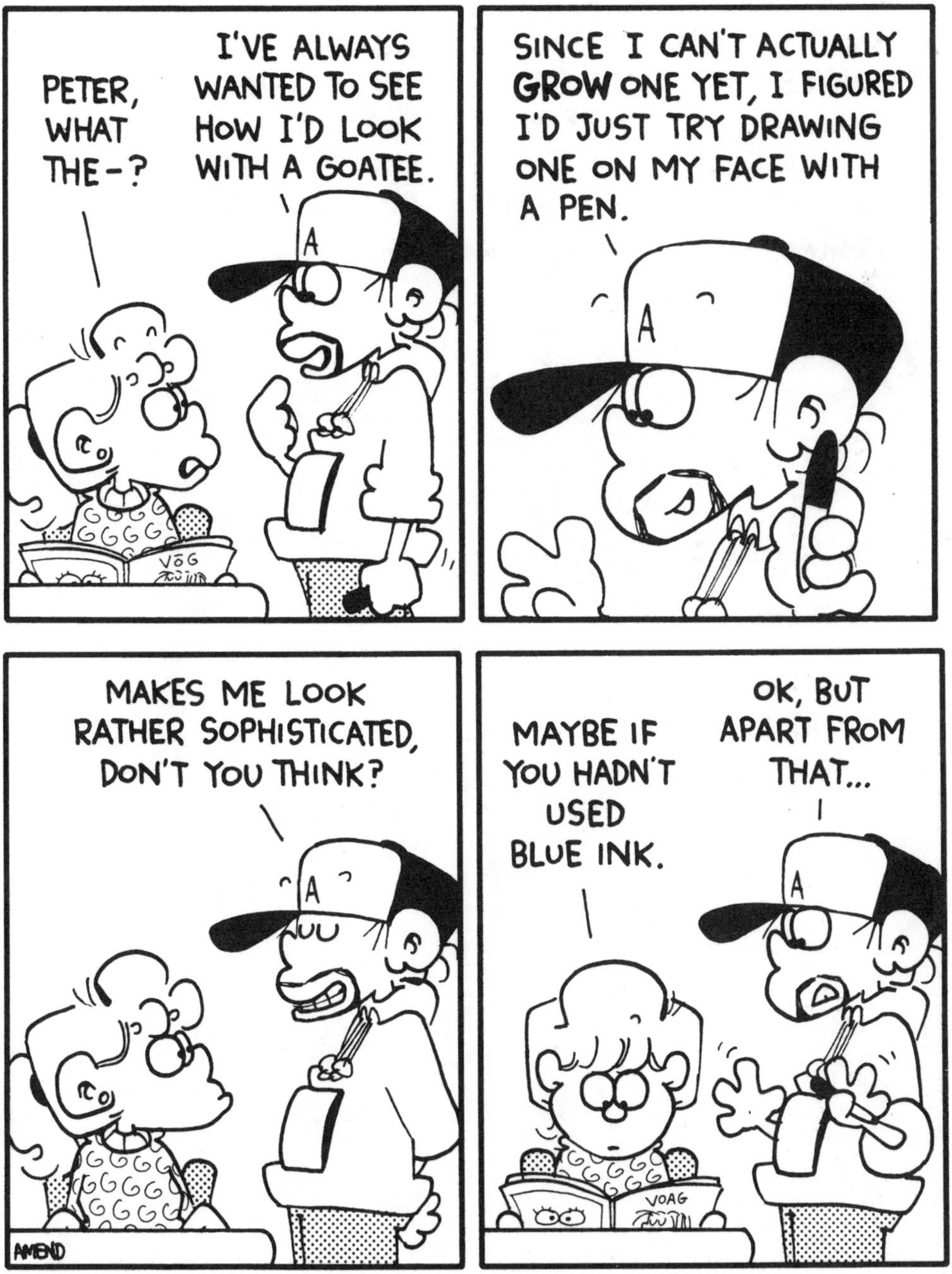
PETER, WHAT THE-?
I'VE ALWAYS WANTED TO SEE HOW I'D LOOK WITH A GOATEE.
VŌG
SINCE I CAN'T ACTUALLY GROW ONE YET, I FIGURED I'D JUST TRY DRAWING ONE ON MY FACE WITH A PEN.
MAKES ME LOOK RATHER SOPHISTICATED, DON'T YOU THINK?
AMEND
MAYBE IF YOU HADN'T USED BLUE INK.
OK, BUT APART FROM THAT...
VOAG

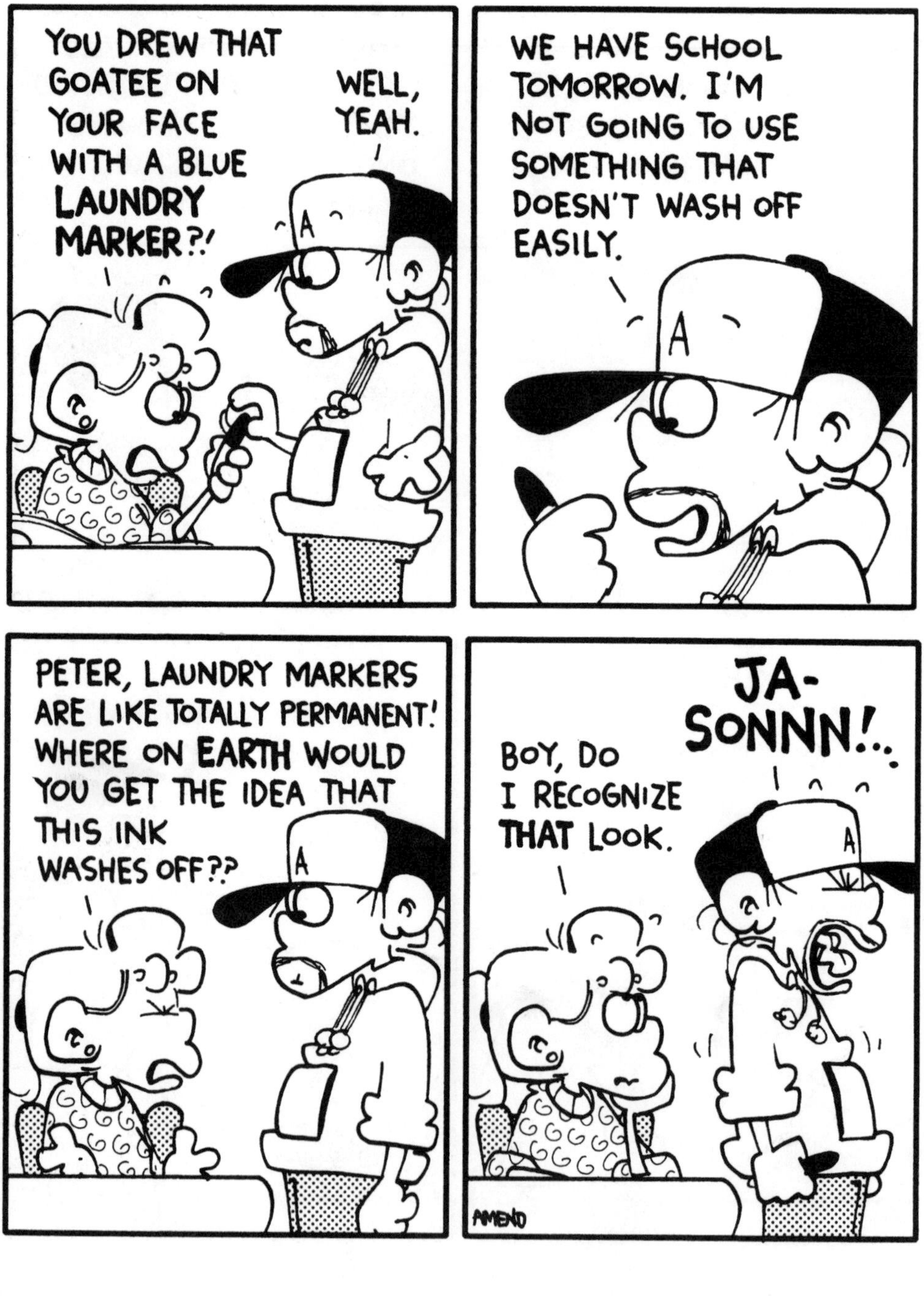
YOU DREW THAT GOATEE ON YOUR FACE WITH A BLUE LAUNDRY MARKER?!
WELL, YEAH.
WE HAVE SCHOOL TOMORROW. I'M NOT GOING TO USE SOMETHING THAT DOESN'T WASH OFF EASILY.
PETER, LAUNDRY MARKERS ARE LIKE TOTALLY PERMANENT! WHERE ON EARTH WOULD YOU GET THE IDEA THAT THIS INK WASHES OFF??
JA-SONNN!..
BOY, DO I RECOGNIZE THAT LOOK.
AMEND

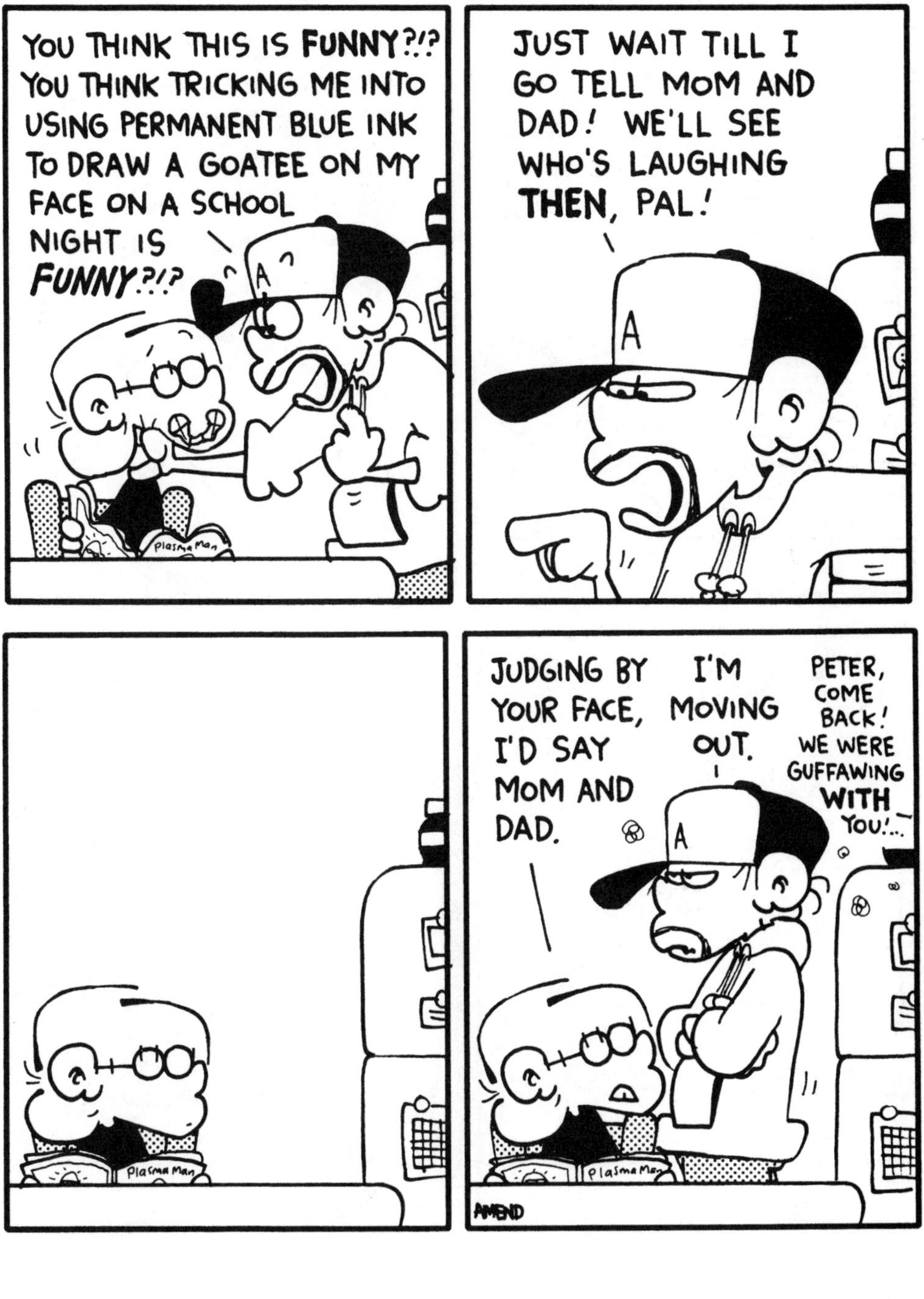
YOU THINK THIS IS FUNNY?!? YOU THINK TRICKING ME INTO USING PERMANENT BLUE INK TO DRAW A GOATEE ON MY FACE ON A SCHOOL NIGHT IS FUNNY?!?
Plasma Man
JUST WAIT TILL I GO TELL MOM AND DAD! WE'LL SEE WHO'S LAUGHING THEN, PAL!
Plasma Man
JUDGING BY YOUR FACE, I'D SAY MOM AND DAD.
I'M MOVING OUT.
PETER, COME BACK! WE WERE GUFFAWING WITH YOU!...
Plasma Man
AMEND

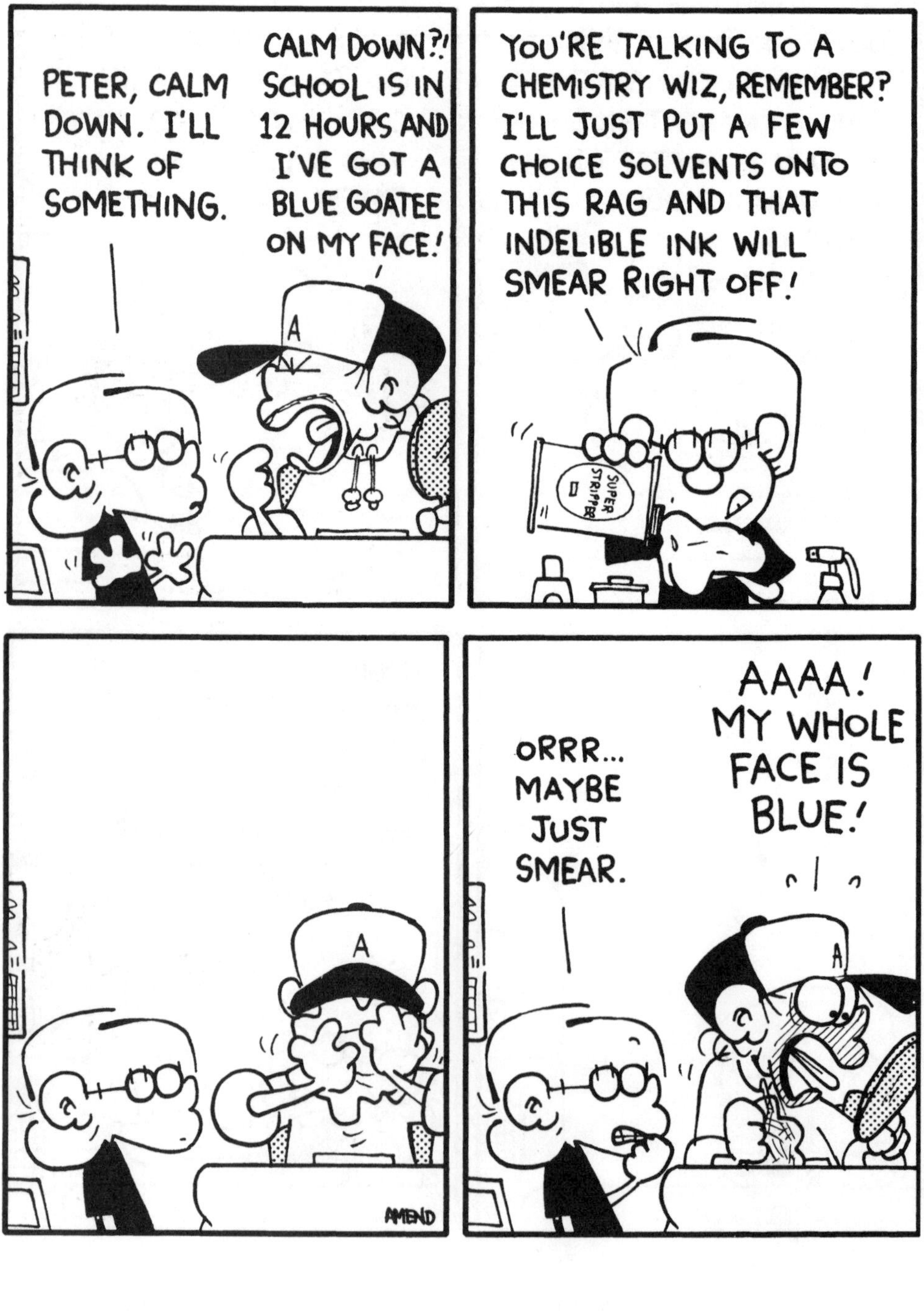
PETER, CALM DOWN. I'LL THINK OF SOMETHING.
CALM DOWN?! SCHOOL IS IN 12 HOURS AND I'VE GOT A BLUE GOATEE ON MY FACE!
YOU'RE TALKING TO A CHEMISTRY WIZ, REMEMBER? I'LL JUST PUT A FEW CHOICE SOLVENTS ONTO THIS RAG AND THAT INDELIBLE INK WILL SMEAR RIGHT OFF!
SUPER STRIPPER
AMEND
ORRR... MAYBE JUST SMEAR.
AAAA! MY WHOLE FACE IS BLUE!

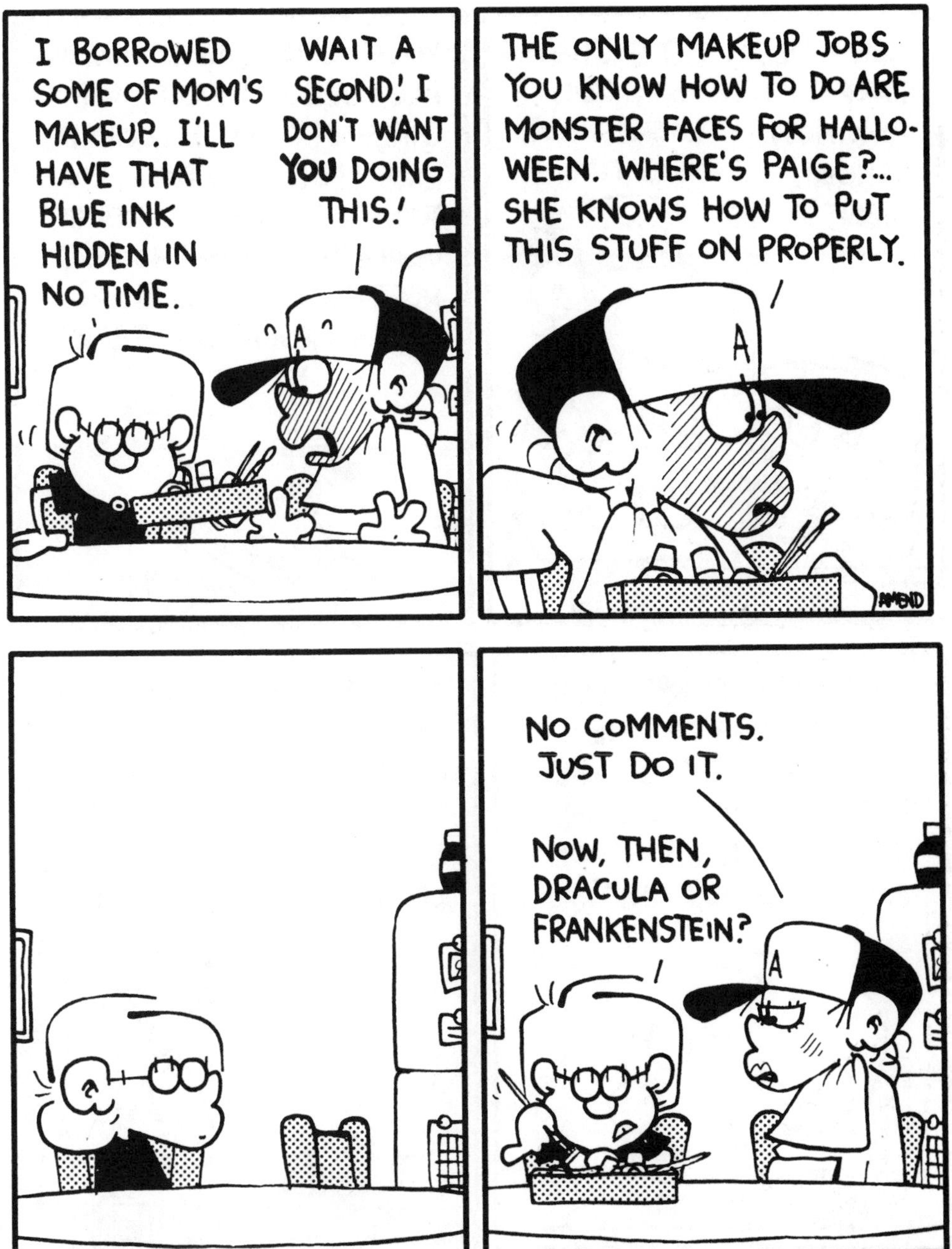
I BORROWED SOME OF MOM'S MAKEUP. I'LL HAVE THAT BLUE INK HIDDEN IN NO TIME.
WAIT A SECOND! I DON'T WANT YOU DOING THIS!
THE ONLY MAKEUP JOBS YOU KNOW HOW TO DO ARE MONSTER FACES FOR HALLO-WEEN. WHERE'S PAIGE?... SHE KNOWS HOW TO PUT THIS STUFF ON PROPERLY.
AMEND
NO COMMENTS. JUST DO IT.
NOW, THEN, DRACULA OR FRANKENSTEIN?

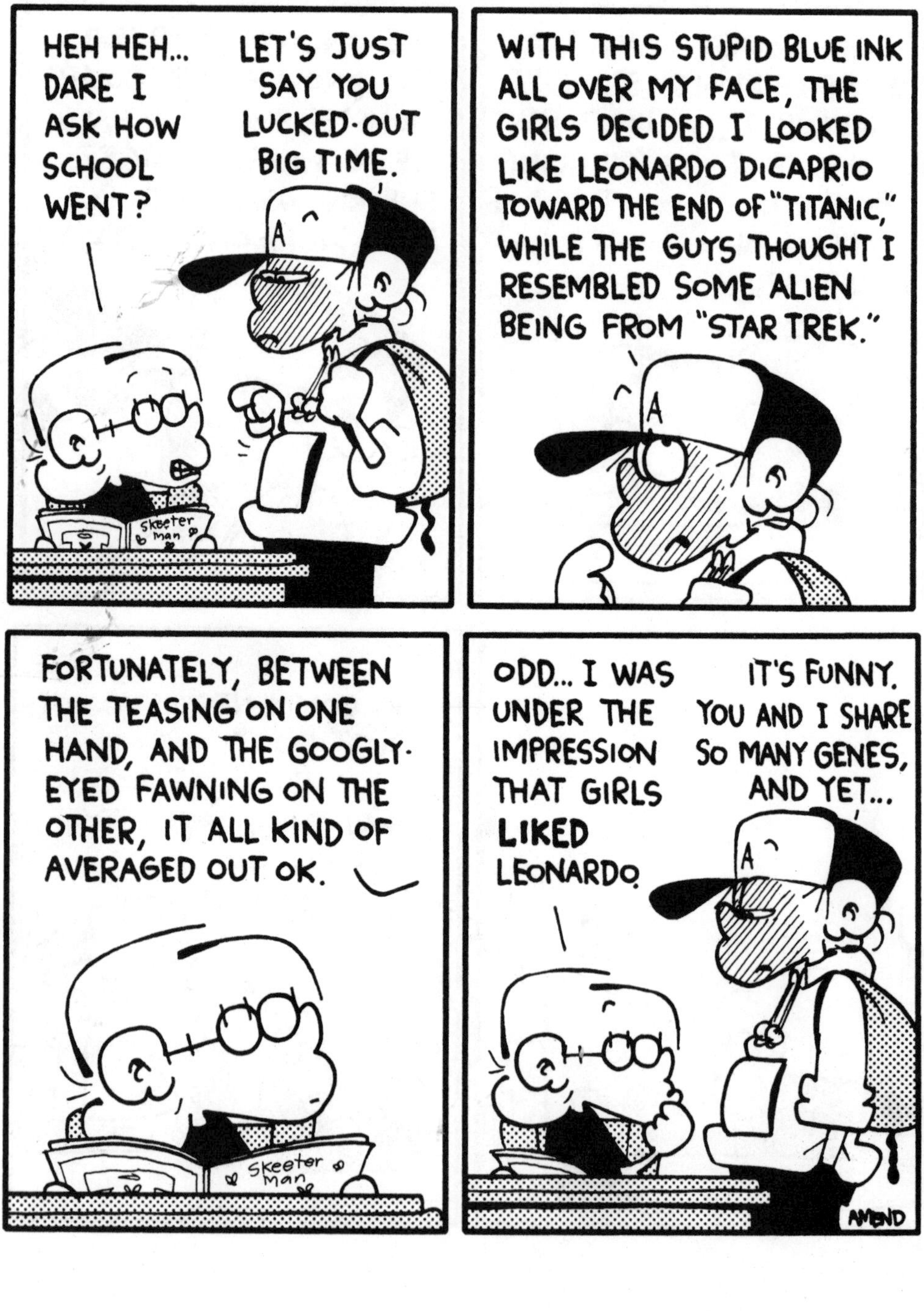
HEH HEH... DARE I ASK HOW SCHOOL WENT?
LET'S JUST SAY YOU LUCKED-OUT BIG TIME.
WITH THIS STUPID BLUE INK ALL OVER MY FACE, THE GIRLS DECIDED I LOOKED LIKE LEONARDO DICAPRIO TOWARD THE END OF "TITANIC," WHILE THE GUYS THOUGHT I RESEMBLED SOME ALIEN BEING FROM "STAR TREK."
FORTUNATELY, BETWEEN THE TEASING ON ONE HAND, AND THE GOOGLY-EYED FAWNING ON THE OTHER, IT ALL KIND OF AVERAGED OUT OK.
ODD... I WAS UNDER THE IMPRESSION THAT GIRLS **LIKED** LEONARDO.
IT'S FUNNY. YOU AND I SHARE SO MANY GENES, AND YET...
AMEND

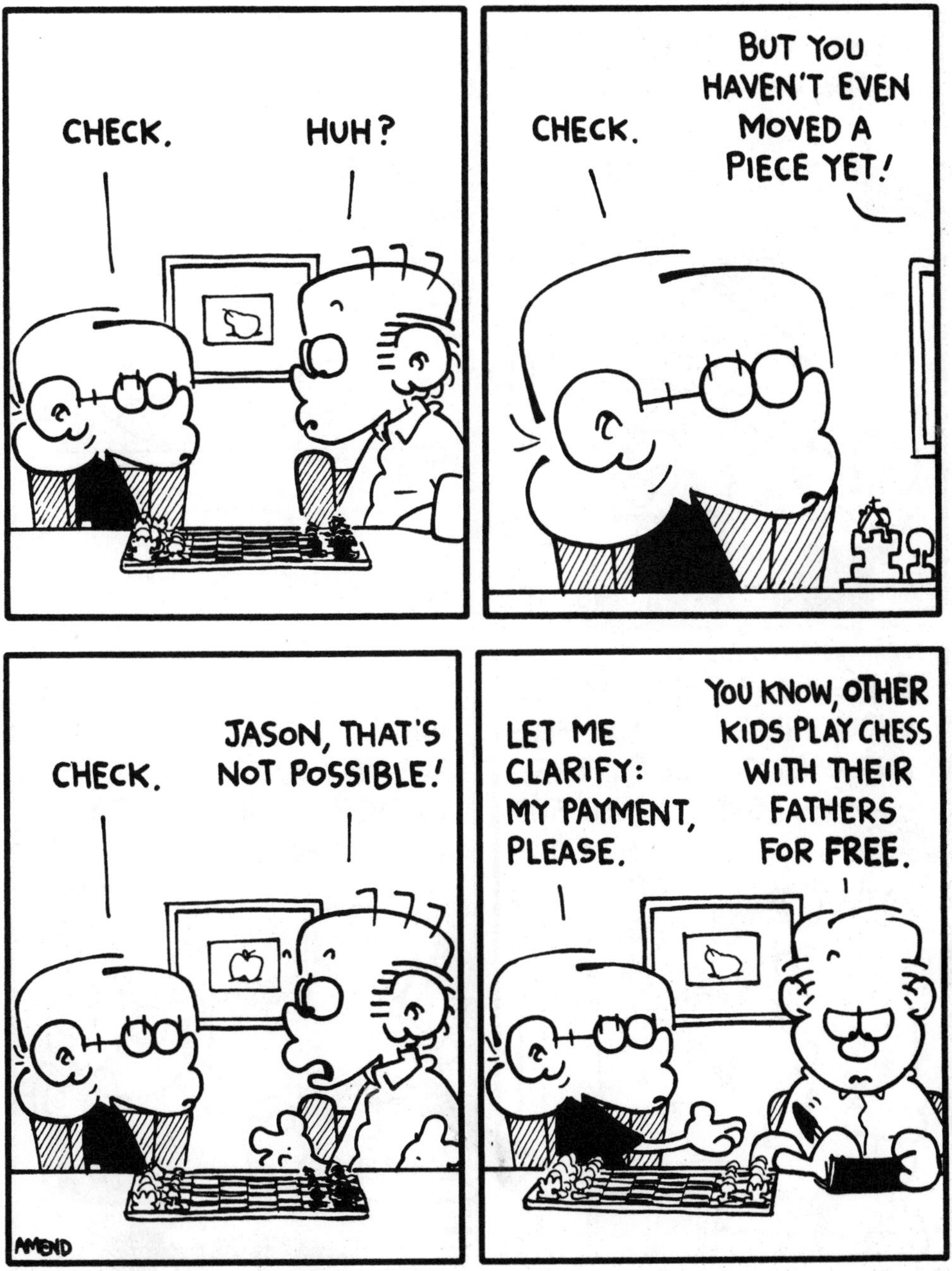

CHECK.
HUH?
CHECK.
BUT YOU HAVEN'T EVEN MOVED A PIECE YET!
CHECK.
JASON, THAT'S NOT POSSIBLE!
LET ME CLARIFY: MY PAYMENT, PLEASE.
YOU KNOW, OTHER KIDS PLAY CHESS WITH THEIR FATHERS FOR FREE.
AMEND

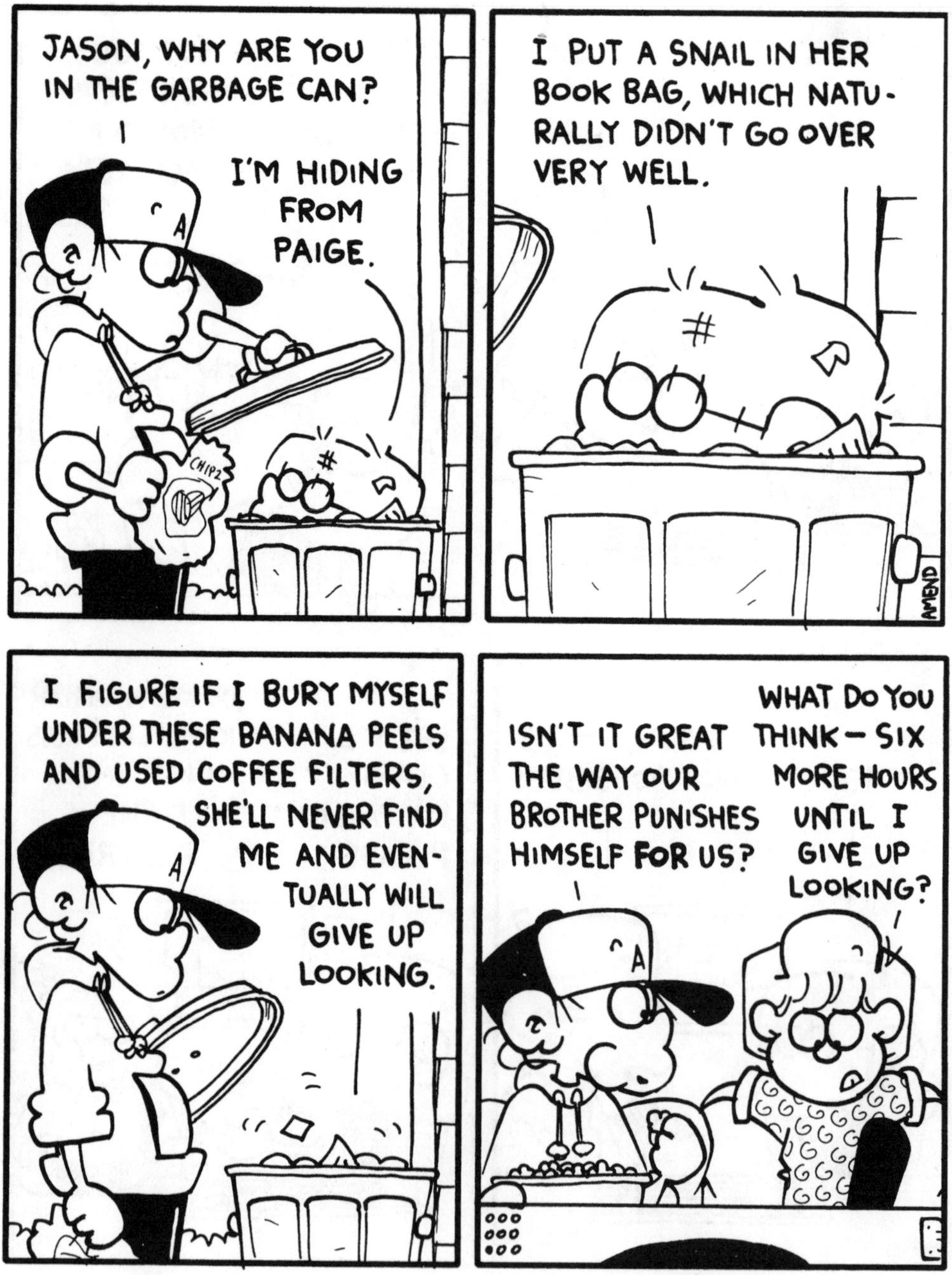
JASON, WHY ARE YOU IN THE GARBAGE CAN?
I'M HIDING FROM PAIGE.
CHIPZ
I PUT A SNAIL IN HER BOOK BAG, WHICH NATU-RALLY DIDN'T GO OVER VERY WELL.
AMEND
I FIGURE IF I BURY MYSELF UNDER THESE BANANA PEELS AND USED COFFEE FILTERS, SHE'LL NEVER FIND ME AND EVENTUALLY WILL GIVE UP LOOKING.
ISN'T IT GREAT THE WAY OUR BROTHER PUNISHES HIMSELF FOR US?
WHAT DO YOU THINK – SIX MORE HOURS UNTIL I GIVE UP LOOKING?

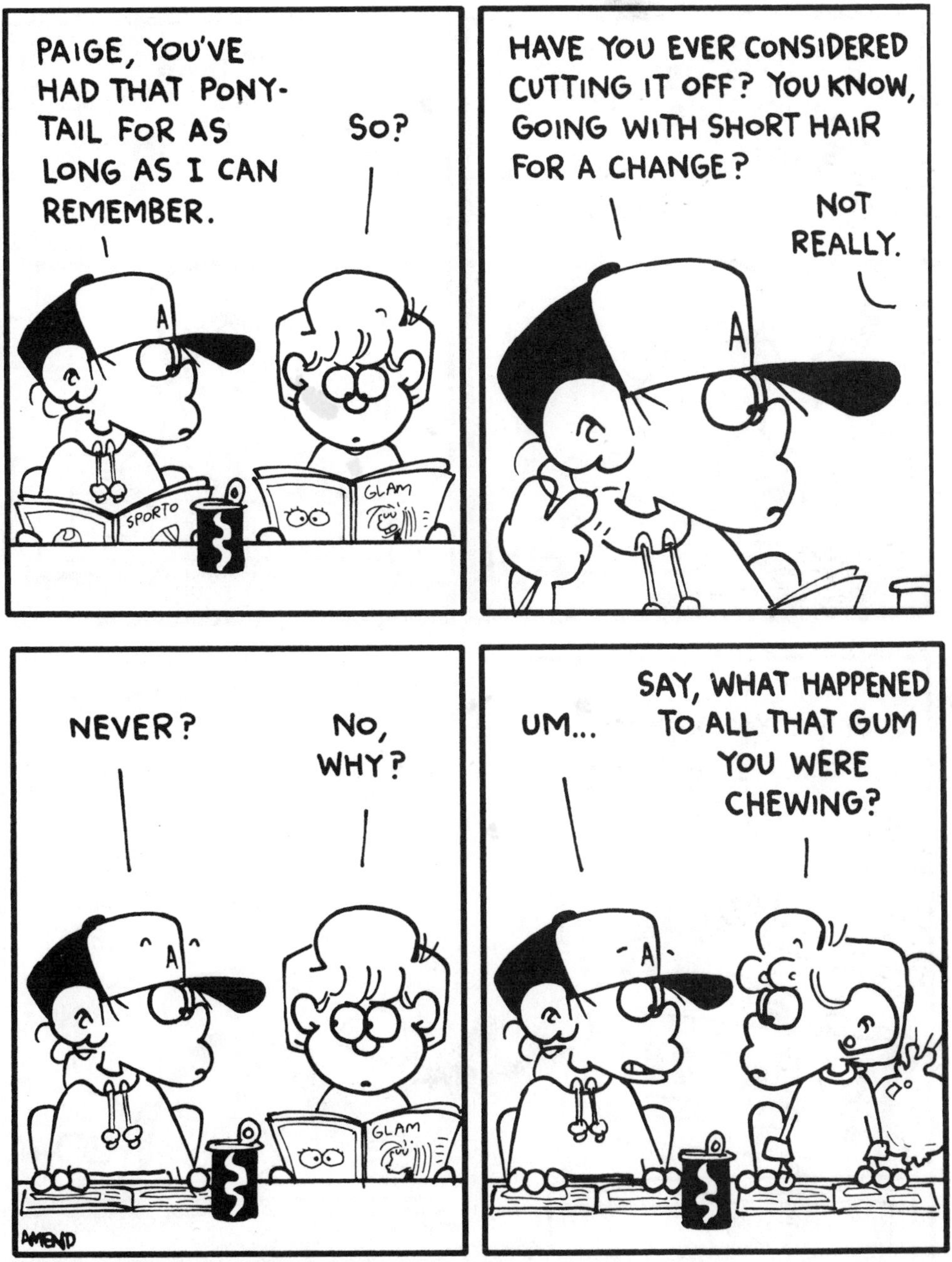
PAIGE, YOU'VE HAD THAT PONY-TAIL FOR AS LONG AS I CAN REMEMBER.
SO?
SPORTO
GLAM
HAVE YOU EVER CONSIDERED CUTTING IT OFF? YOU KNOW, GOING WITH SHORT HAIR FOR A CHANGE?
NOT REALLY.
NEVER?
NO, WHY?
GLAM
AMEND
UM...
SAY, WHAT HAPPENED TO ALL THAT GUM YOU WERE CHEWING?

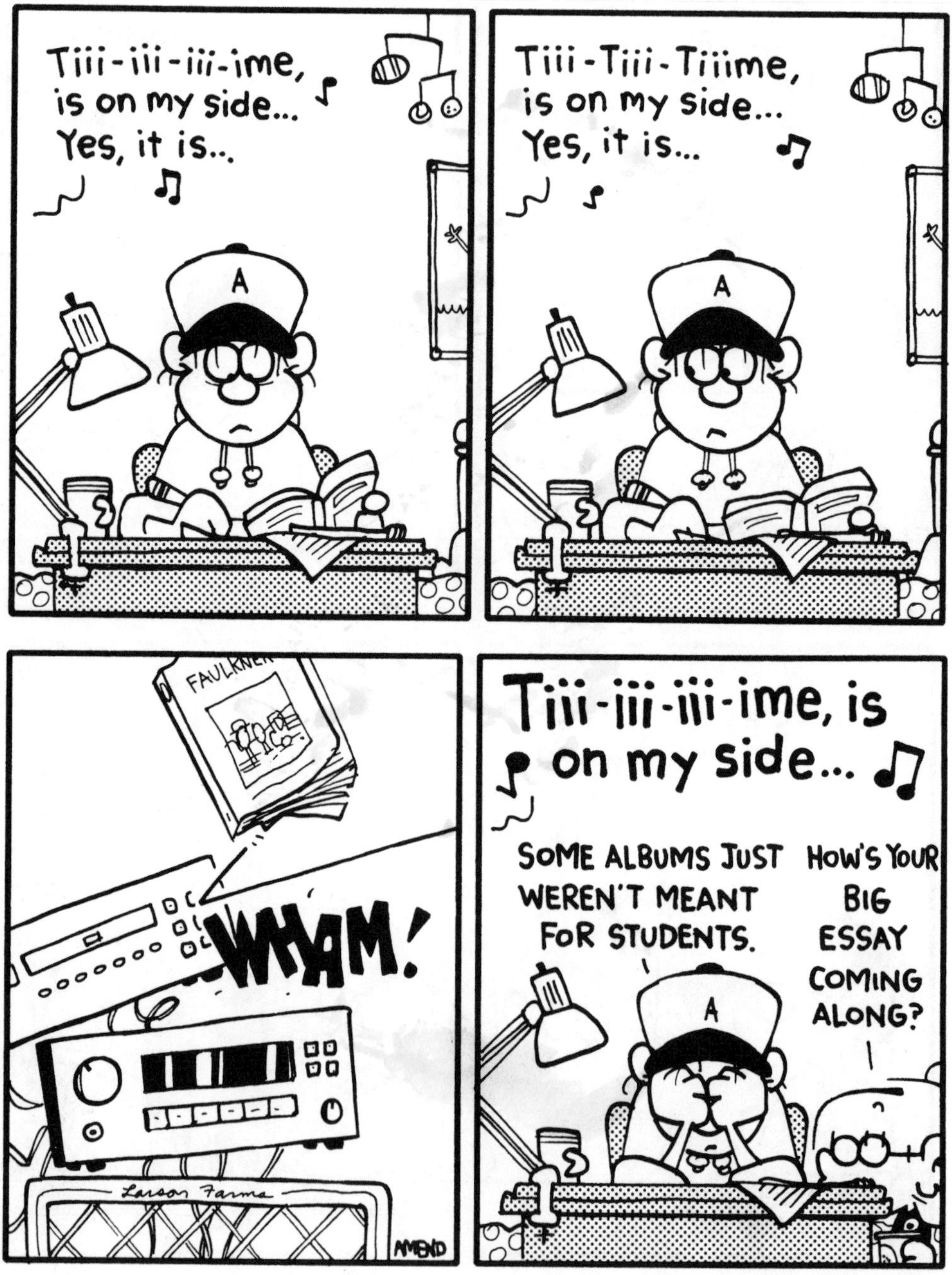
Tiii-iii-iii-ime,
is on my side...
Yes, it is...
Tiii-Tiii-Tiiime,
is on my side...
Yes, it is...
FAULKNER
WHAM!
Larson Farms
AMEND
Tiii-iii-iii-ime, is on my side...
SOME ALBUMS JUST WEREN'T MEANT FOR STUDENTS.
HOW'S YOUR BIG ESSAY COMING ALONG?

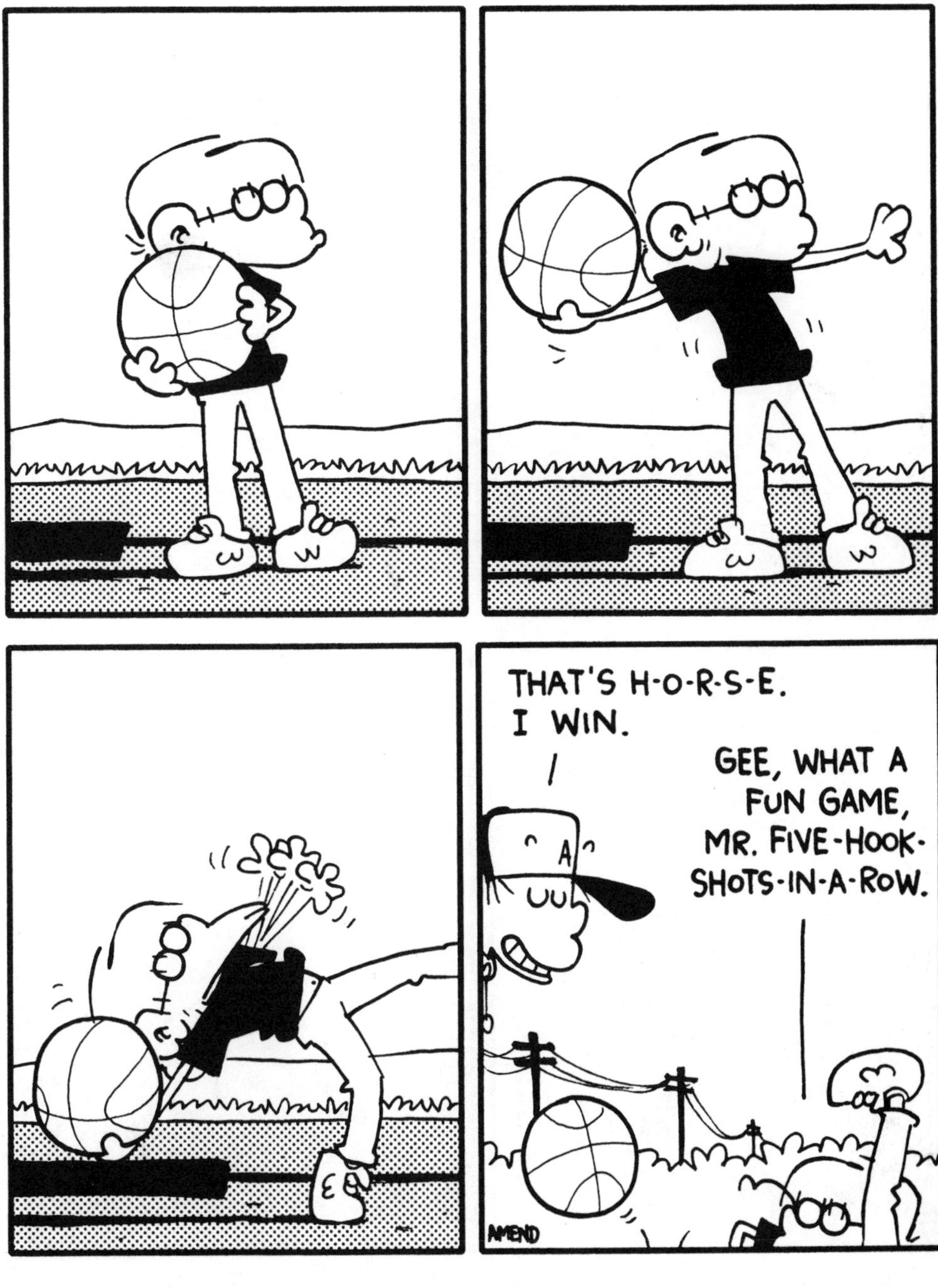
THAT'S H-O-R-S-E.
I WIN.
GEE, WHAT A FUN GAME, MR. FIVE-HOOK-SHOTS-IN-A-ROW.
AMEND

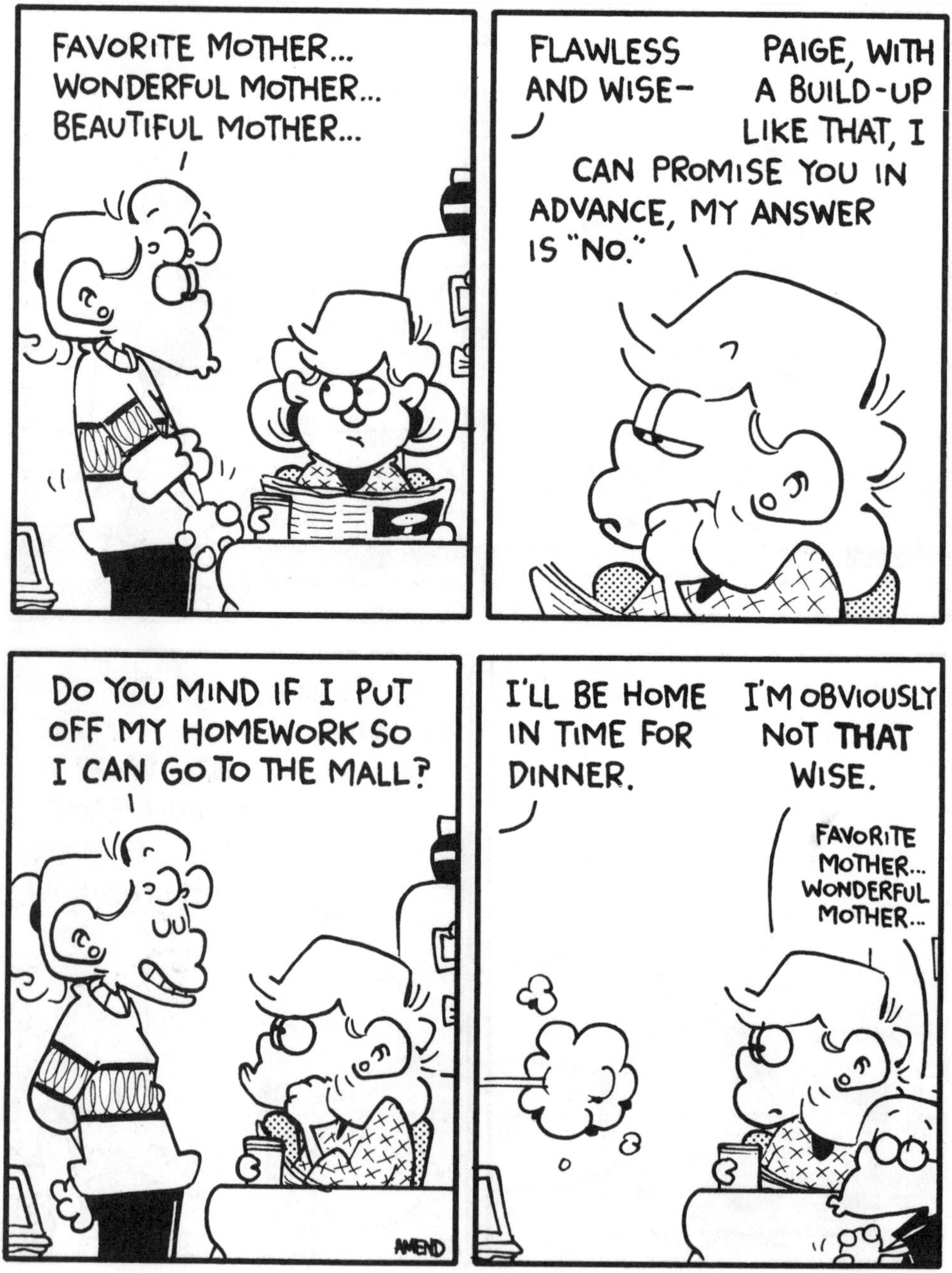
FAVORITE MOTHER... WONDERFUL MOTHER... BEAUTIFUL MOTHER...
FLAWLESS AND WISE-
PAIGE, WITH A BUILD-UP LIKE THAT, I CAN PROMISE YOU IN ADVANCE, MY ANSWER IS "NO."
DO YOU MIND IF I PUT OFF MY HOMEWORK SO I CAN GO TO THE MALL?
AMEND
I'LL BE HOME IN TIME FOR DINNER.
I'M OBVIOUSLY NOT THAT WISE.
FAVORITE MOTHER... WONDERFUL MOTHER...

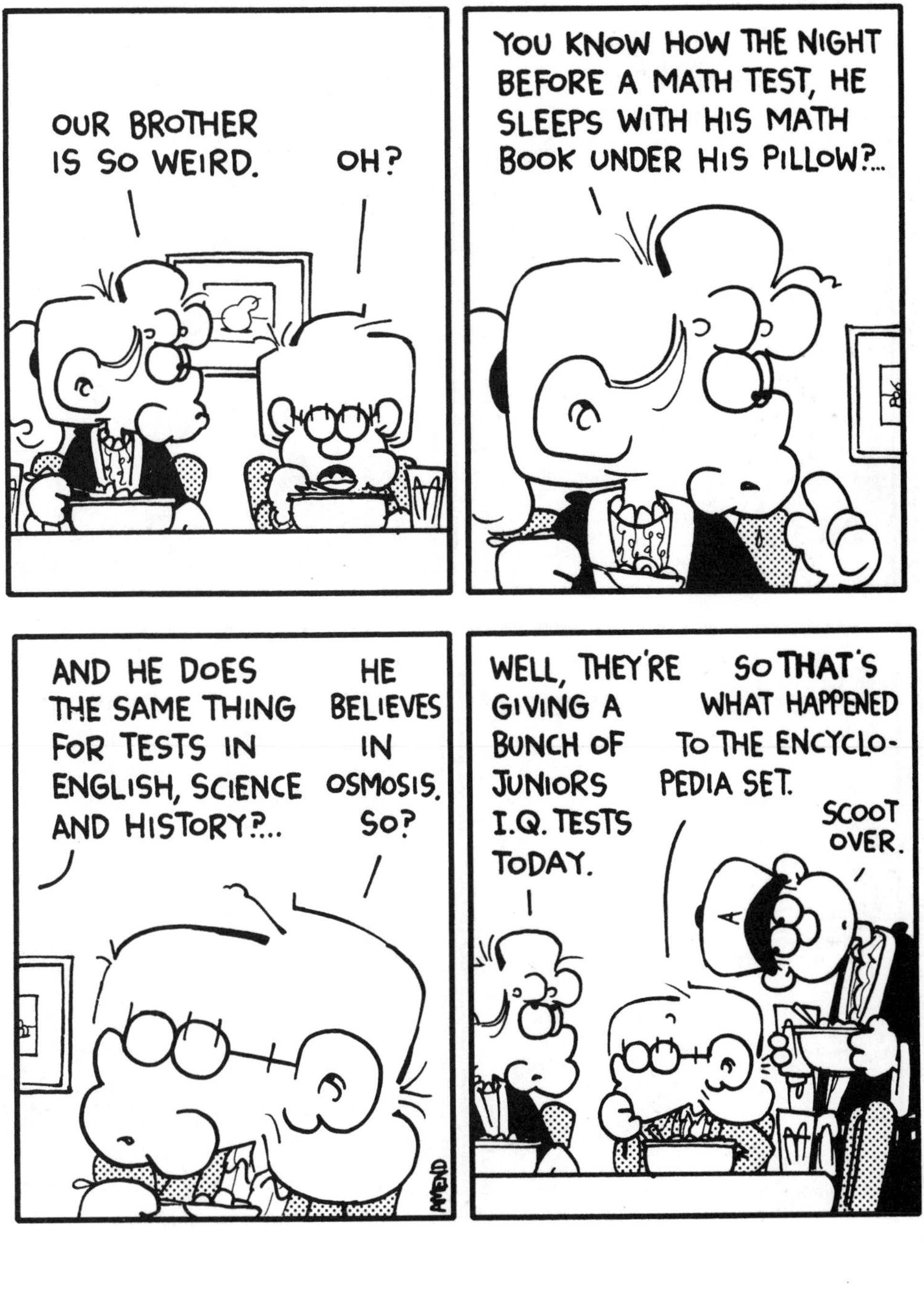
OUR BROTHER IS SO WEIRD.
OH?
YOU KNOW HOW THE NIGHT BEFORE A MATH TEST, HE SLEEPS WITH HIS MATH BOOK UNDER HIS PILLOW?...
AND HE DOES THE SAME THING FOR TESTS IN ENGLISH, SCIENCE AND HISTORY?...
HE BELIEVES IN OSMOSIS. SO?
WELL, THEY'RE GIVING A BUNCH OF JUNIORS I.Q. TESTS TODAY.
SO THAT'S WHAT HAPPENED TO THE ENCYCLOPEDIA SET.
SCOOT OVER.
AMEND

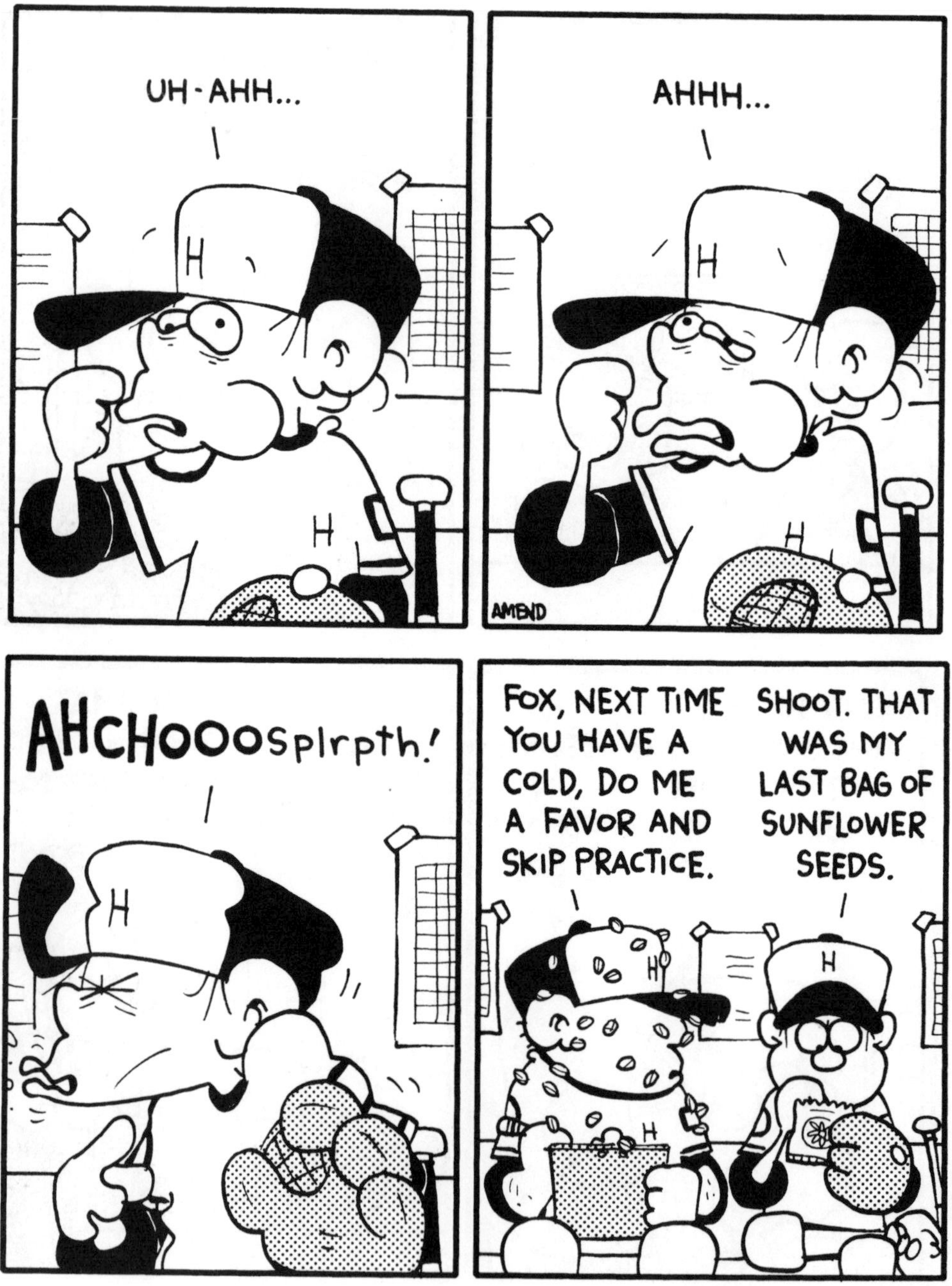
UH-AHH...
AHHH...
AMEND
AHCHOOOsplrpth!
FOX, NEXT TIME YOU HAVE A COLD, DO ME A FAVOR AND SKIP PRACTICE.
SHOOT. THAT WAS MY LAST BAG OF SUNFLOWER SEEDS.

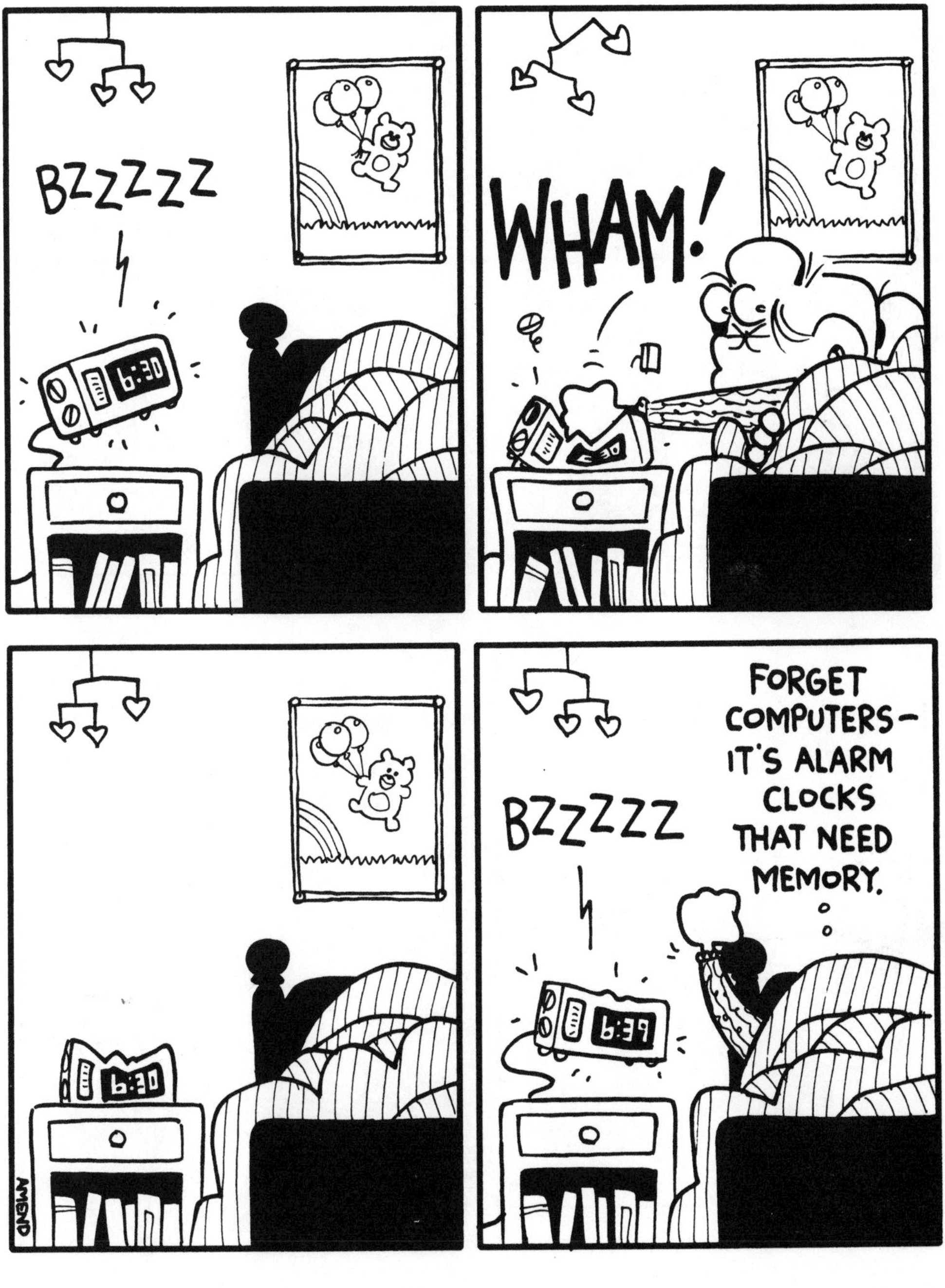
BZZZZZ
6:30
WHAM!
6:30
BZZZZZ
6:39
FORGET COMPUTERS– IT'S ALARM CLOCKS THAT NEED MEMORY.
AMEND

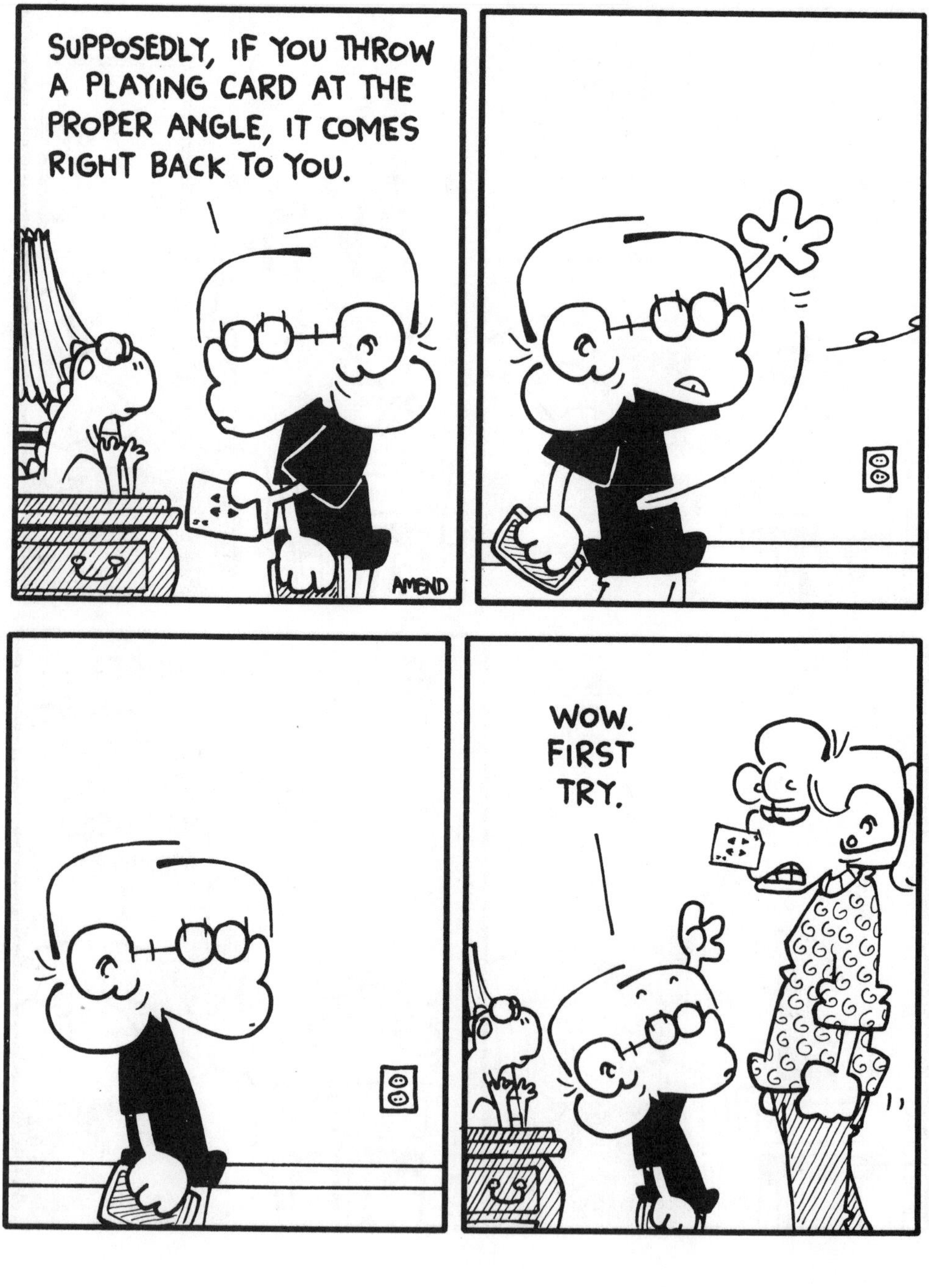
SUPPOSEDLY, IF YOU THROW A PLAYING CARD AT THE PROPER ANGLE, IT COMES RIGHT BACK TO YOU.
AMEND
WOW. FIRST TRY.

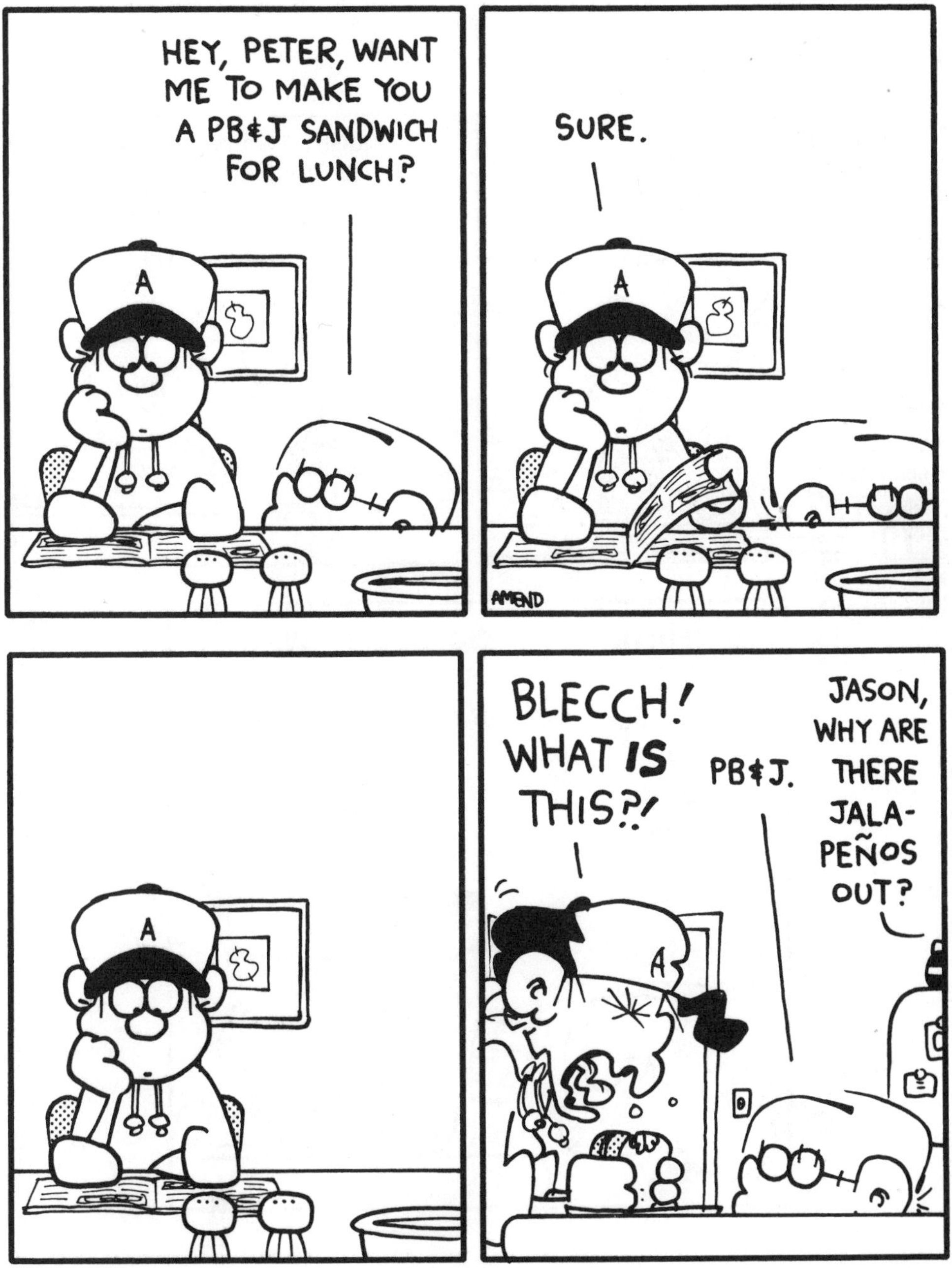

HEY, PETER, WANT ME TO MAKE YOU A PB&J SANDWICH FOR LUNCH?
SURE.
AMEND
BLECCH! WHAT IS THIS?!
PB&J.
JASON, WHY ARE THERE JALAPEÑOS OUT?

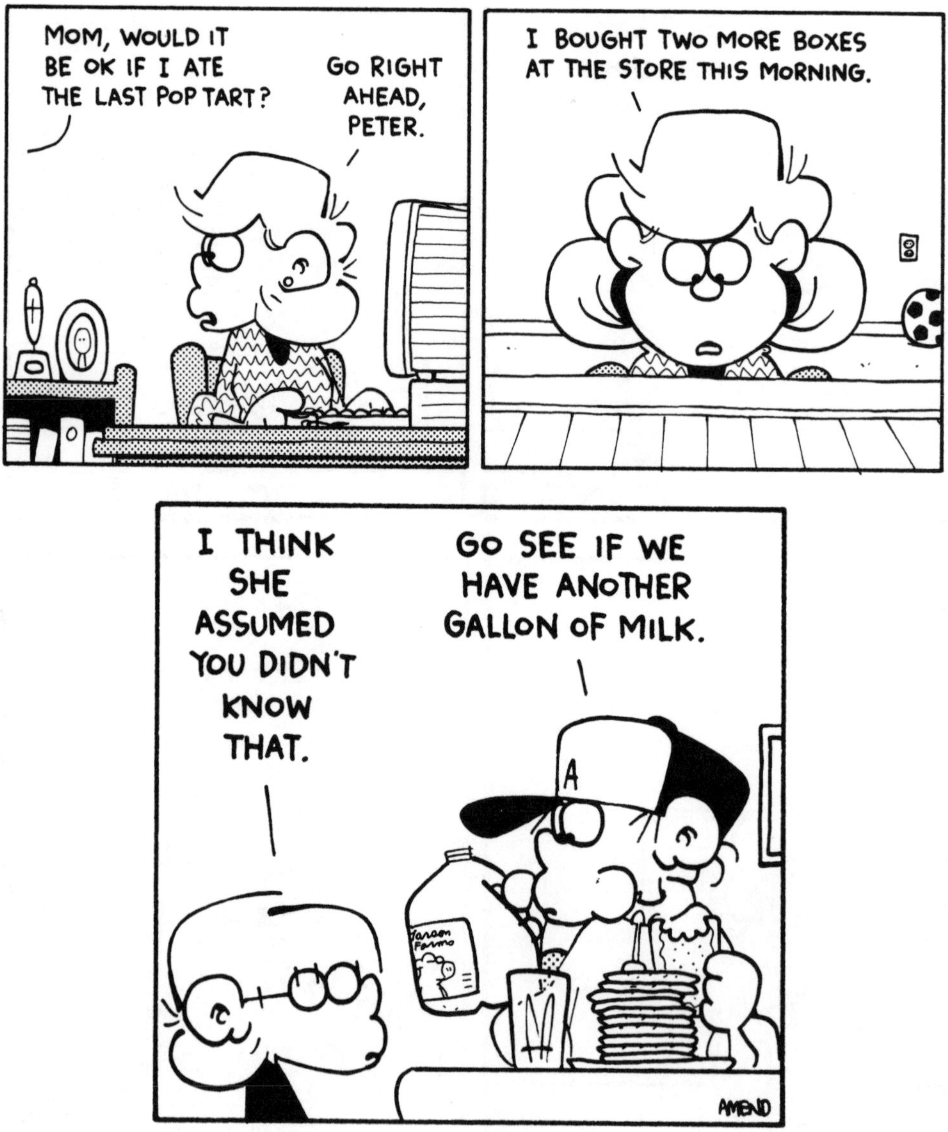

MOM, WOULD IT BE OK IF I ATE THE LAST POP TART?
GO RIGHT AHEAD, PETER.
I BOUGHT TWO MORE BOXES AT THE STORE THIS MORNING.
I THINK SHE ASSUMED YOU DIDN'T KNOW THAT.
GO SEE IF WE HAVE ANOTHER GALLON OF MILK.
AMEND

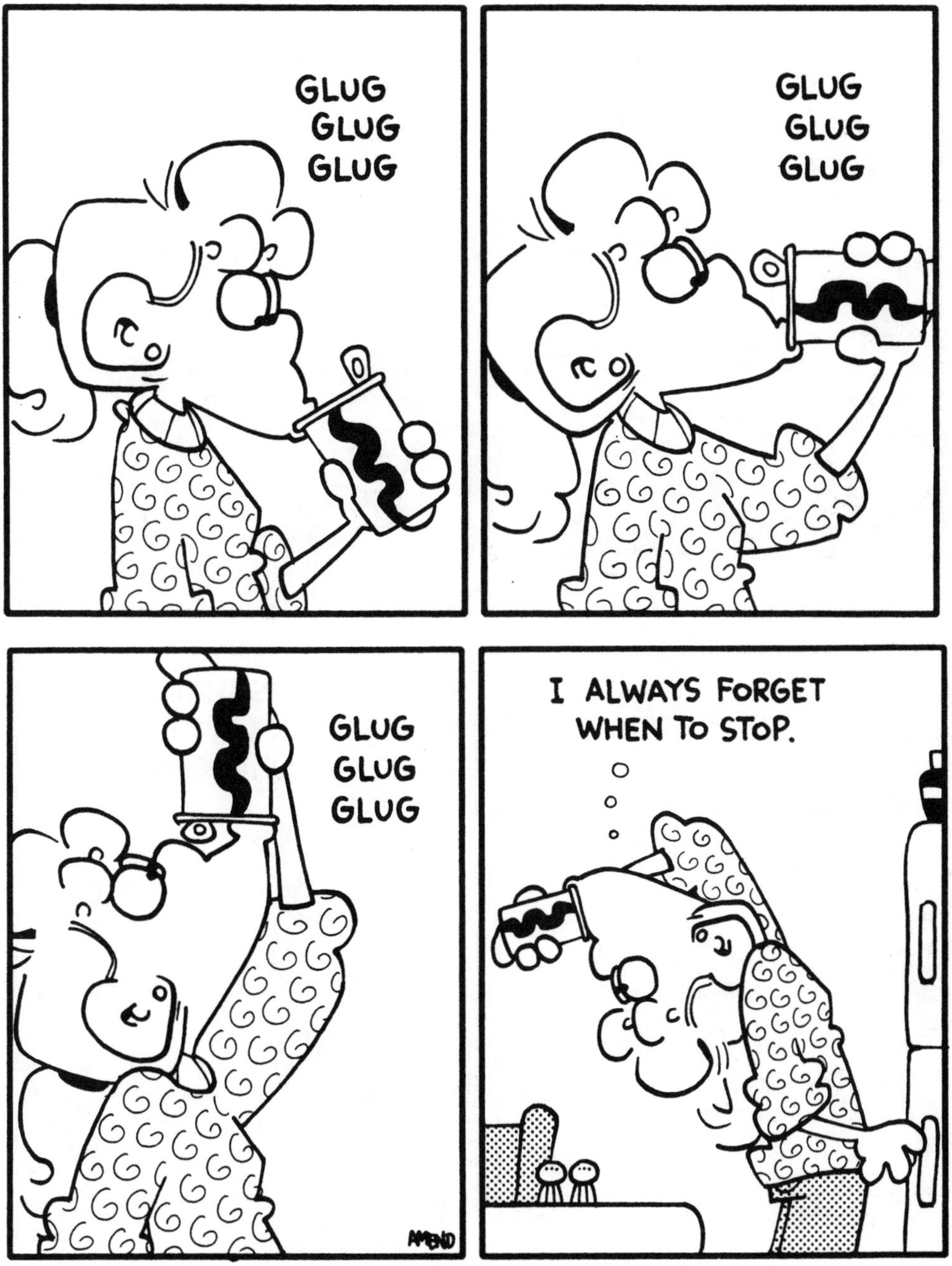
GLUG
GLUG
GLUG
GLUG
GLUG
GLUG
GLUG
GLUG
GLUG
I ALWAYS FORGET WHEN TO STOP.
AMEND

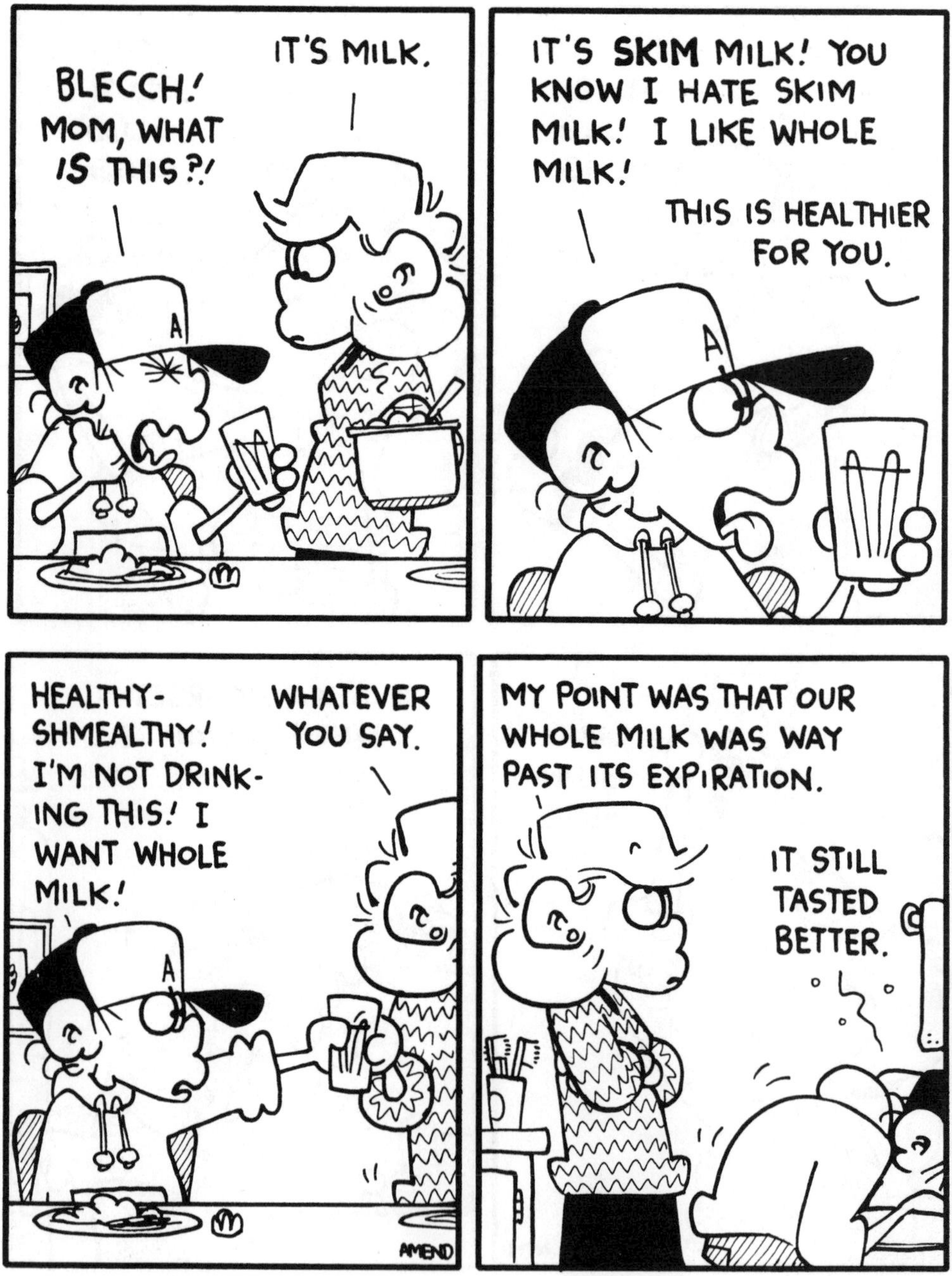
BLECCH! MOM, WHAT IS THIS?!
IT'S MILK.
IT'S SKIM MILK! YOU KNOW I HATE SKIM MILK! I LIKE WHOLE MILK!
THIS IS HEALTHIER FOR YOU.
HEALTHY-SHMEALTHY! I'M NOT DRINKING THIS! I WANT WHOLE MILK!
WHATEVER YOU SAY.
AMEND
MY POINT WAS THAT OUR WHOLE MILK WAS WAY PAST ITS EXPIRATION.
IT STILL TASTED BETTER.

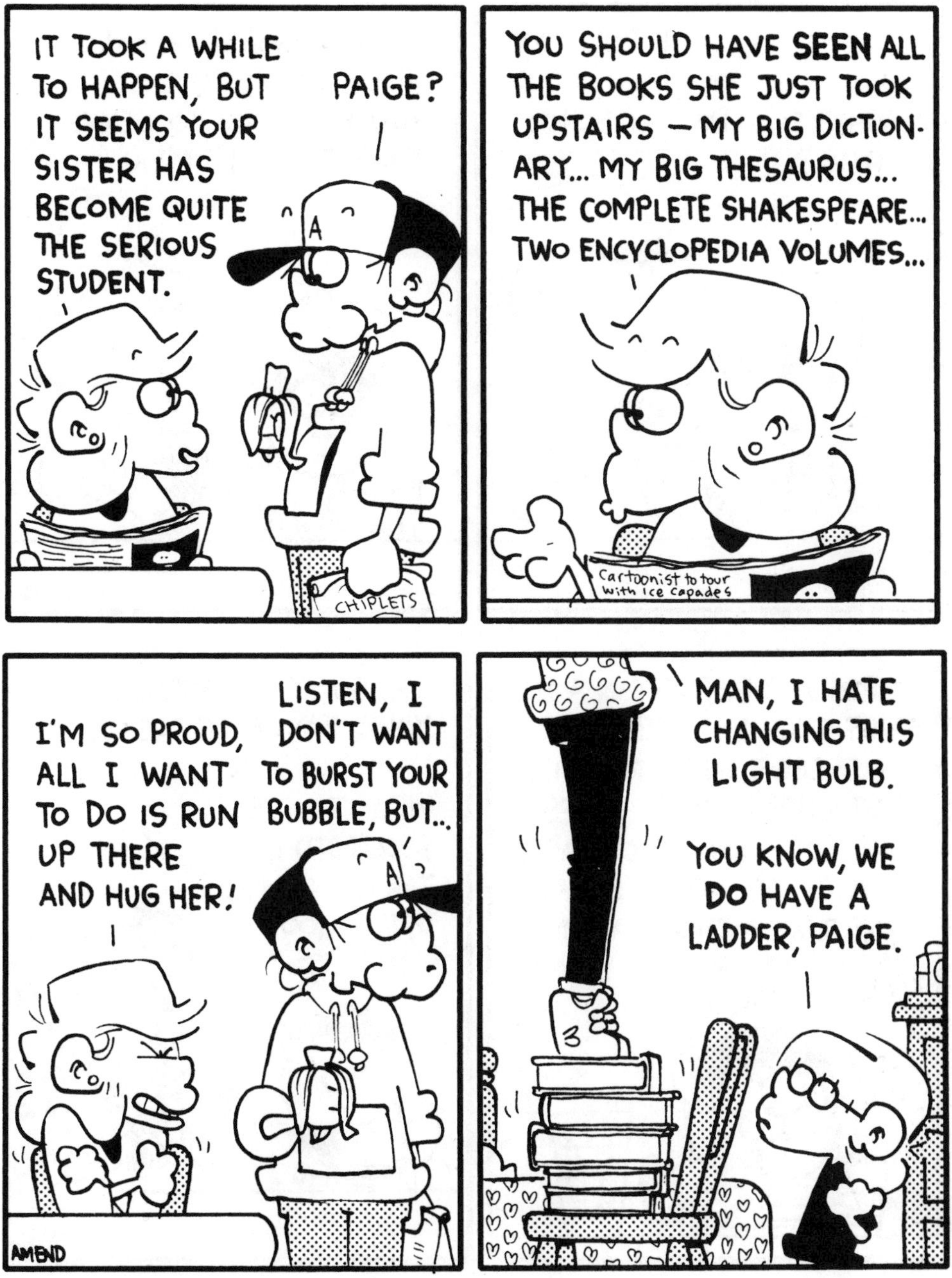
IT TOOK A WHILE TO HAPPEN, BUT IT SEEMS YOUR SISTER HAS BECOME QUITE THE SERIOUS STUDENT.
PAIGE?
CHIPLETS
YOU SHOULD HAVE SEEN ALL THE BOOKS SHE JUST TOOK UPSTAIRS — MY BIG DICTIONARY... MY BIG THESAURUS... THE COMPLETE SHAKESPEARE... TWO ENCYCLOPEDIA VOLUMES...
Cartoonist to tour with Ice Capades
I'M SO PROUD, ALL I WANT TO DO IS RUN UP THERE AND HUG HER!
LISTEN, I DON'T WANT TO BURST YOUR BUBBLE, BUT...
AMEND
MAN, I HATE CHANGING THIS LIGHT BULB.
YOU KNOW, WE DO HAVE A LADDER, PAIGE.

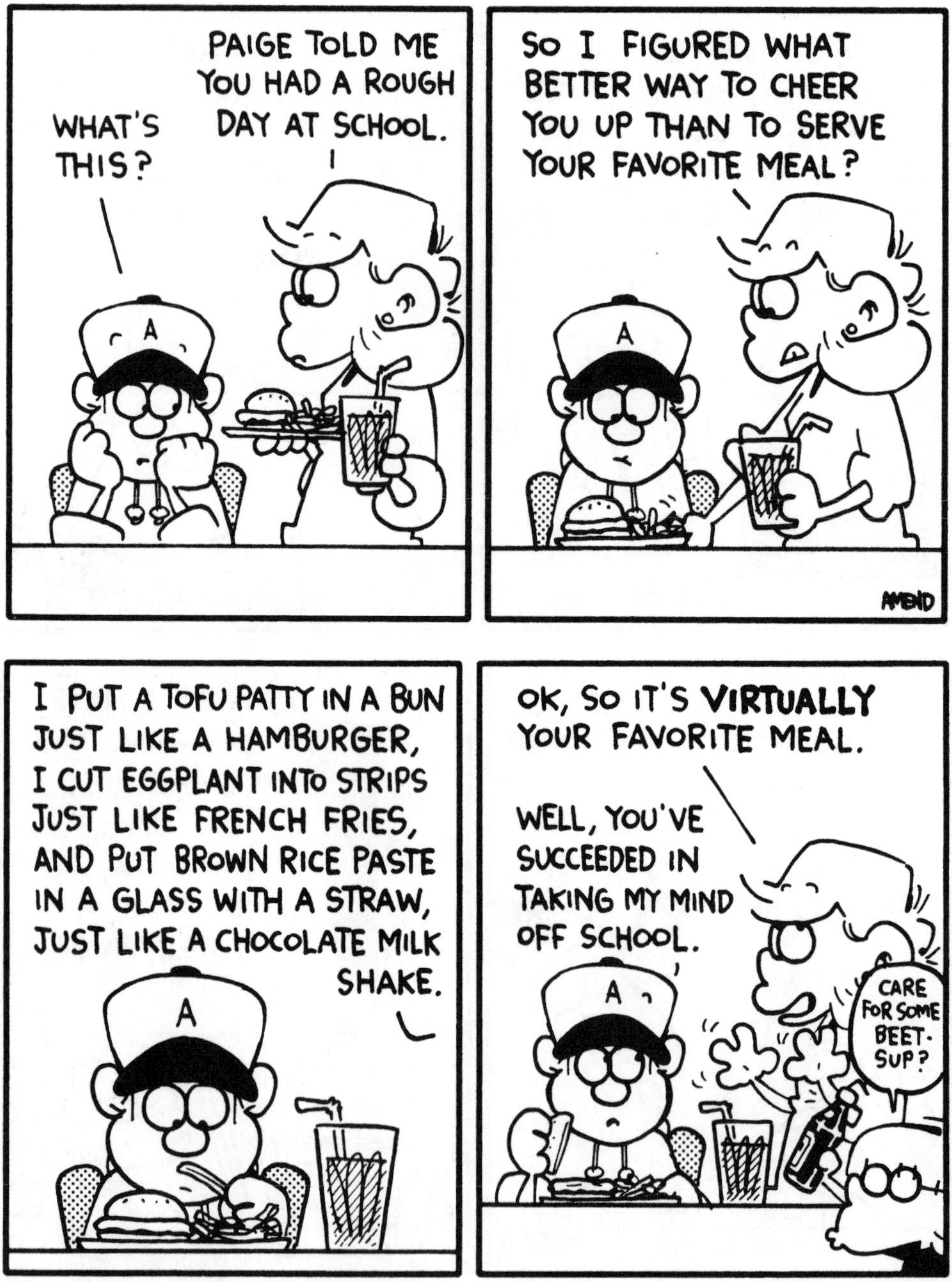
WHAT'S THIS?
PAIGE TOLD ME YOU HAD A ROUGH DAY AT SCHOOL.
SO I FIGURED WHAT BETTER WAY TO CHEER YOU UP THAN TO SERVE YOUR FAVORITE MEAL?
AMEND
I PUT A TOFU PATTY IN A BUN JUST LIKE A HAMBURGER, I CUT EGGPLANT INTO STRIPS JUST LIKE FRENCH FRIES, AND PUT BROWN RICE PASTE IN A GLASS WITH A STRAW, JUST LIKE A CHOCOLATE MILK SHAKE.
OK, SO IT'S **VIRTUALLY** YOUR FAVORITE MEAL.
WELL, YOU'VE SUCCEEDED IN TAKING MY MIND OFF SCHOOL.
CARE FOR SOME BEET-SUP?

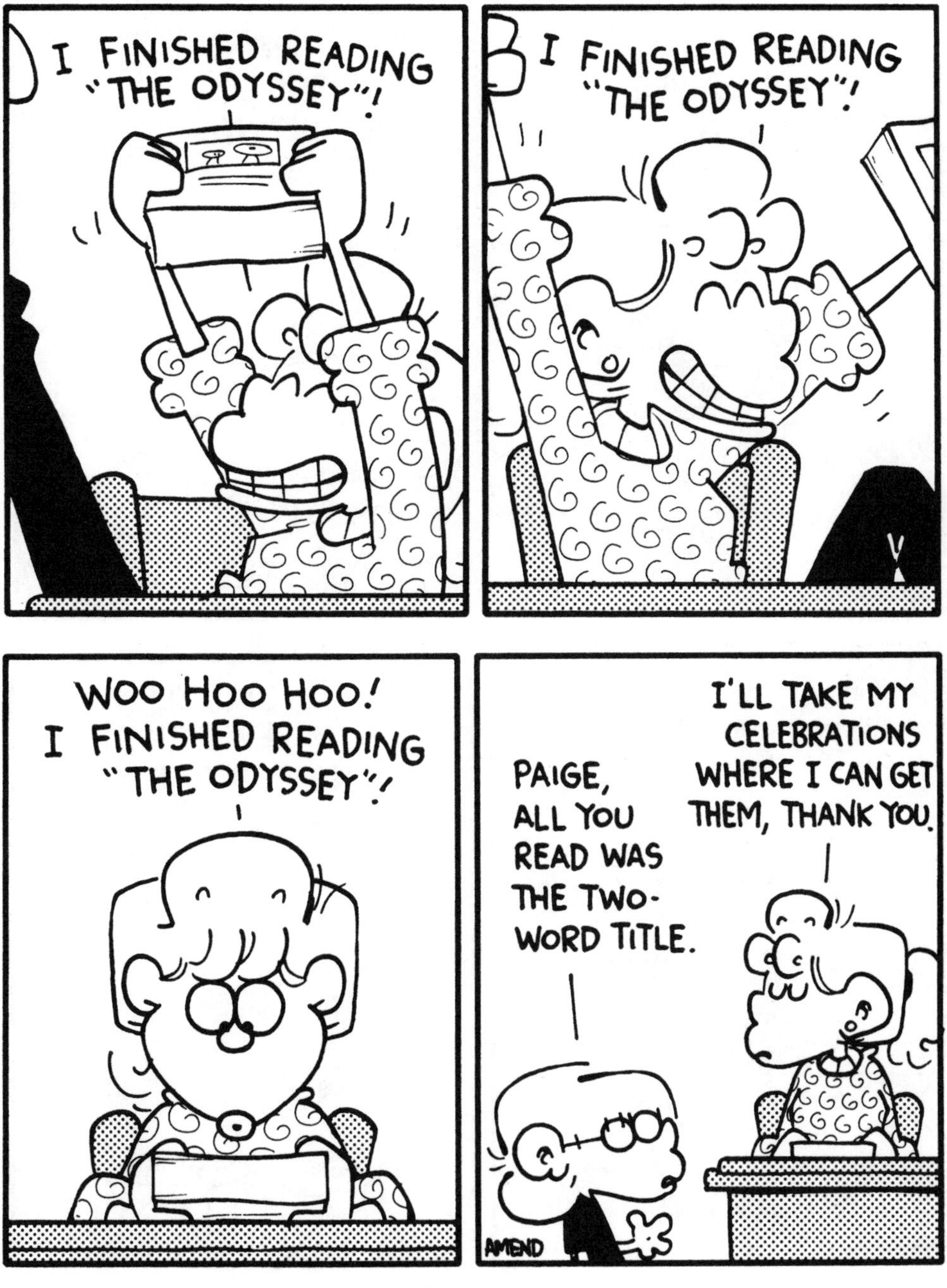
I FINISHED READING "THE ODYSSEY"!
I FINISHED READING "THE ODYSSEY"!
WOO HOO HOO! I FINISHED READING "THE ODYSSEY"!
PAIGE, ALL YOU READ WAS THE TWO-WORD TITLE.
I'LL TAKE MY CELEBRATIONS WHERE I CAN GET THEM, THANK YOU.
AMEND

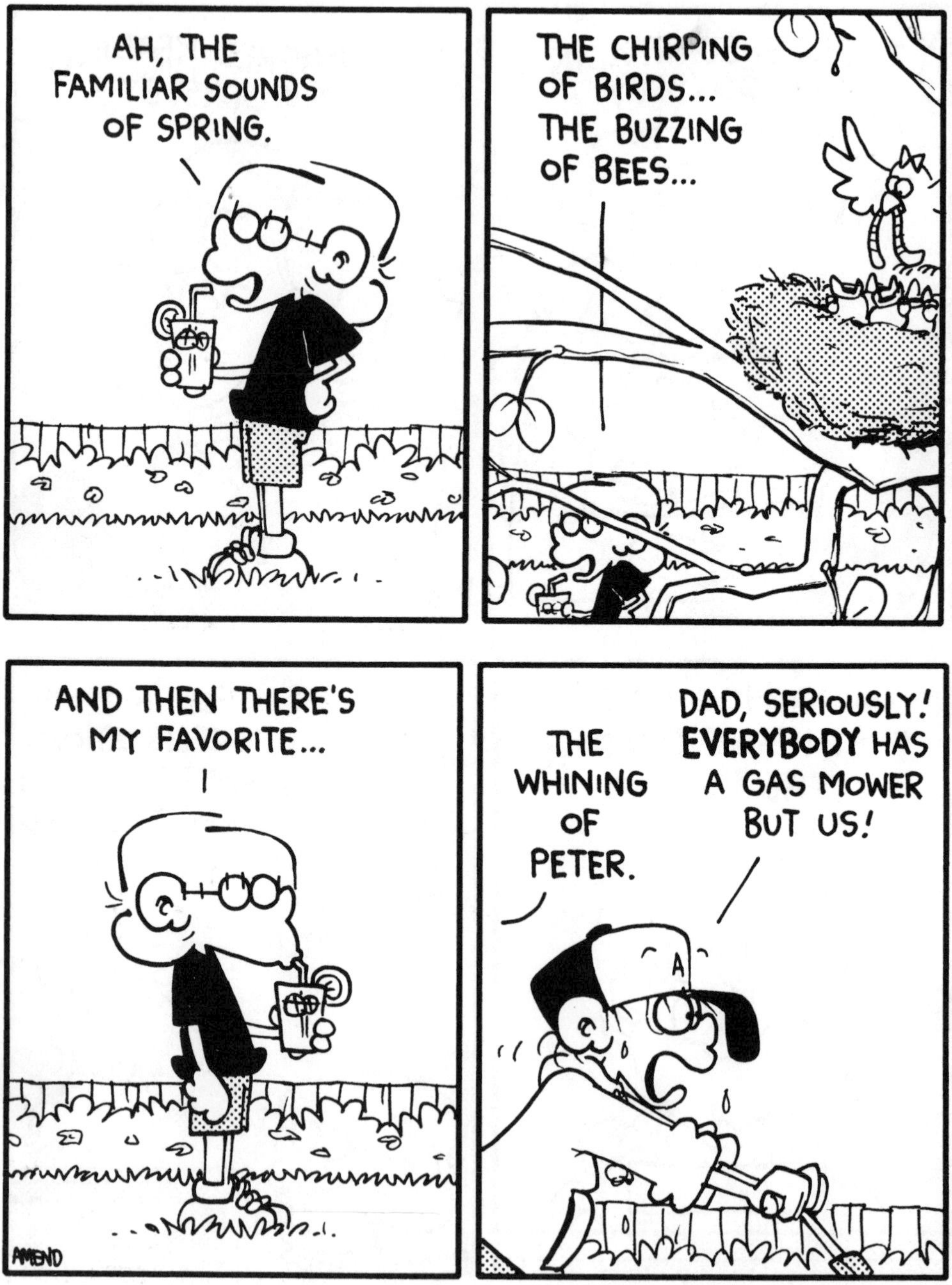
AH, THE FAMILIAR SOUNDS OF SPRING.
THE CHIRPING OF BIRDS... THE BUZZING OF BEES...
AND THEN THERE'S MY FAVORITE...
THE WHINING OF PETER.
DAD, SERIOUSLY! EVERYBODY HAS A GAS MOWER BUT US!
AMEND

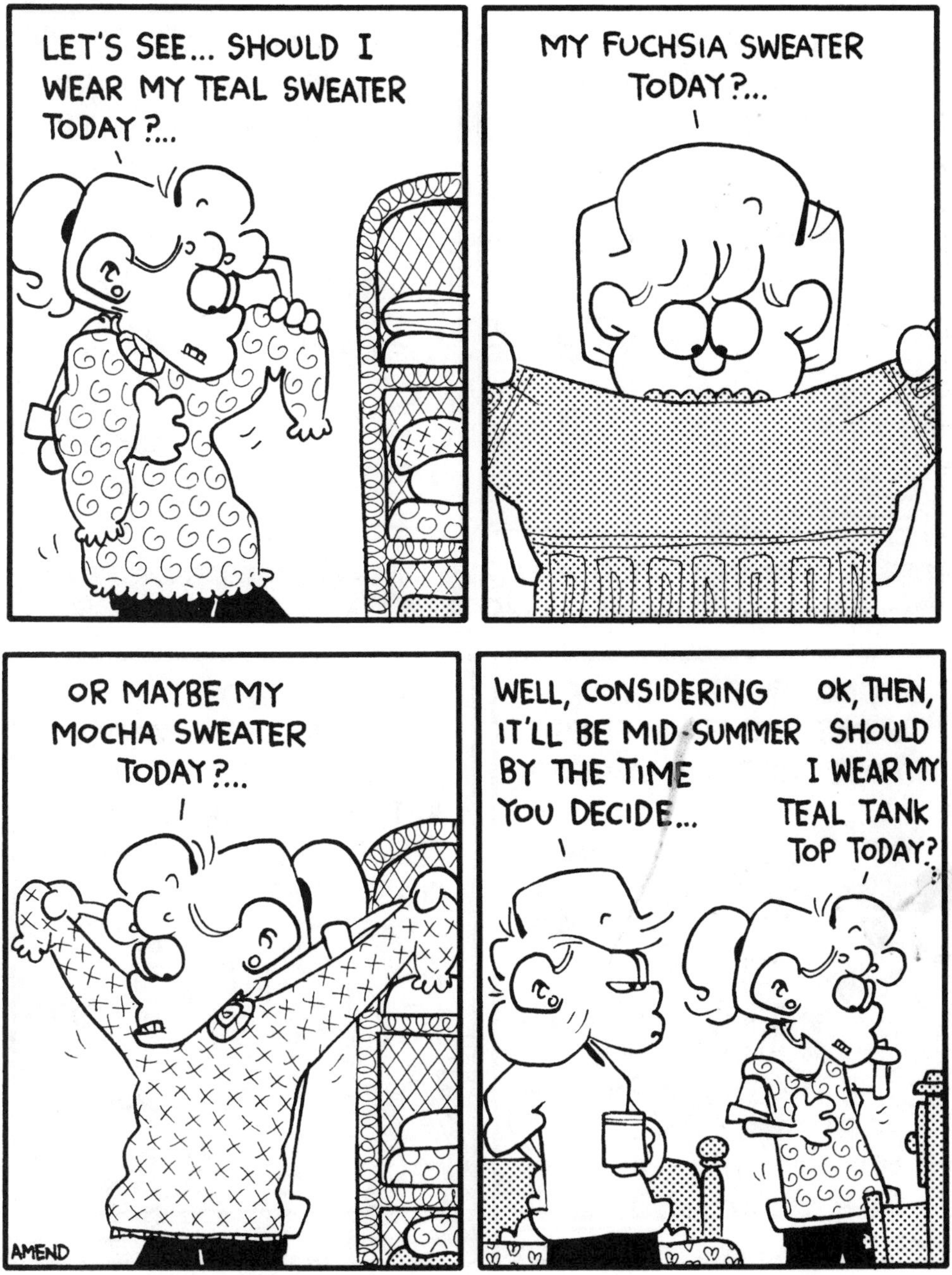
LET'S SEE... SHOULD I WEAR MY TEAL SWEATER TODAY?...
MY FUCHSIA SWEATER TODAY?...
OR MAYBE MY MOCHA SWEATER TODAY?...
AMEND
WELL, CONSIDERING IT'LL BE MID-SUMMER BY THE TIME YOU DECIDE...
OK, THEN, SHOULD I WEAR MY TEAL TANK TOP TODAY?

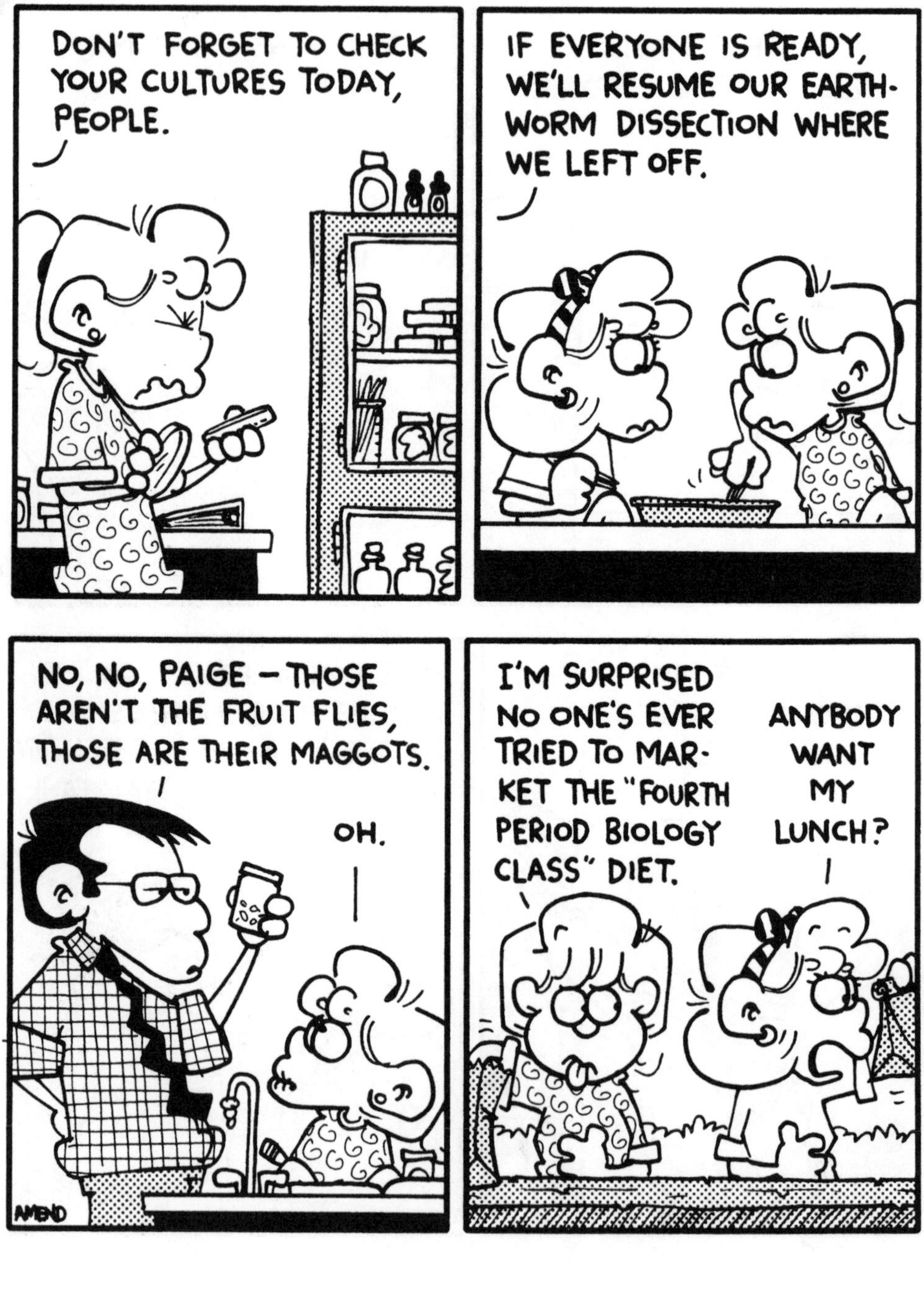
DON'T FORGET TO CHECK YOUR CULTURES TODAY, PEOPLE.
IF EVERYONE IS READY, WE'LL RESUME OUR EARTH-WORM DISSECTION WHERE WE LEFT OFF.
NO, NO, PAIGE – THOSE AREN'T THE FRUIT FLIES, THOSE ARE THEIR MAGGOTS.
OH.
AMEND
I'M SURPRISED NO ONE'S EVER TRIED TO MAR-KET THE "FOURTH PERIOD BIOLOGY CLASS" DIET.
ANYBODY WANT MY LUNCH?

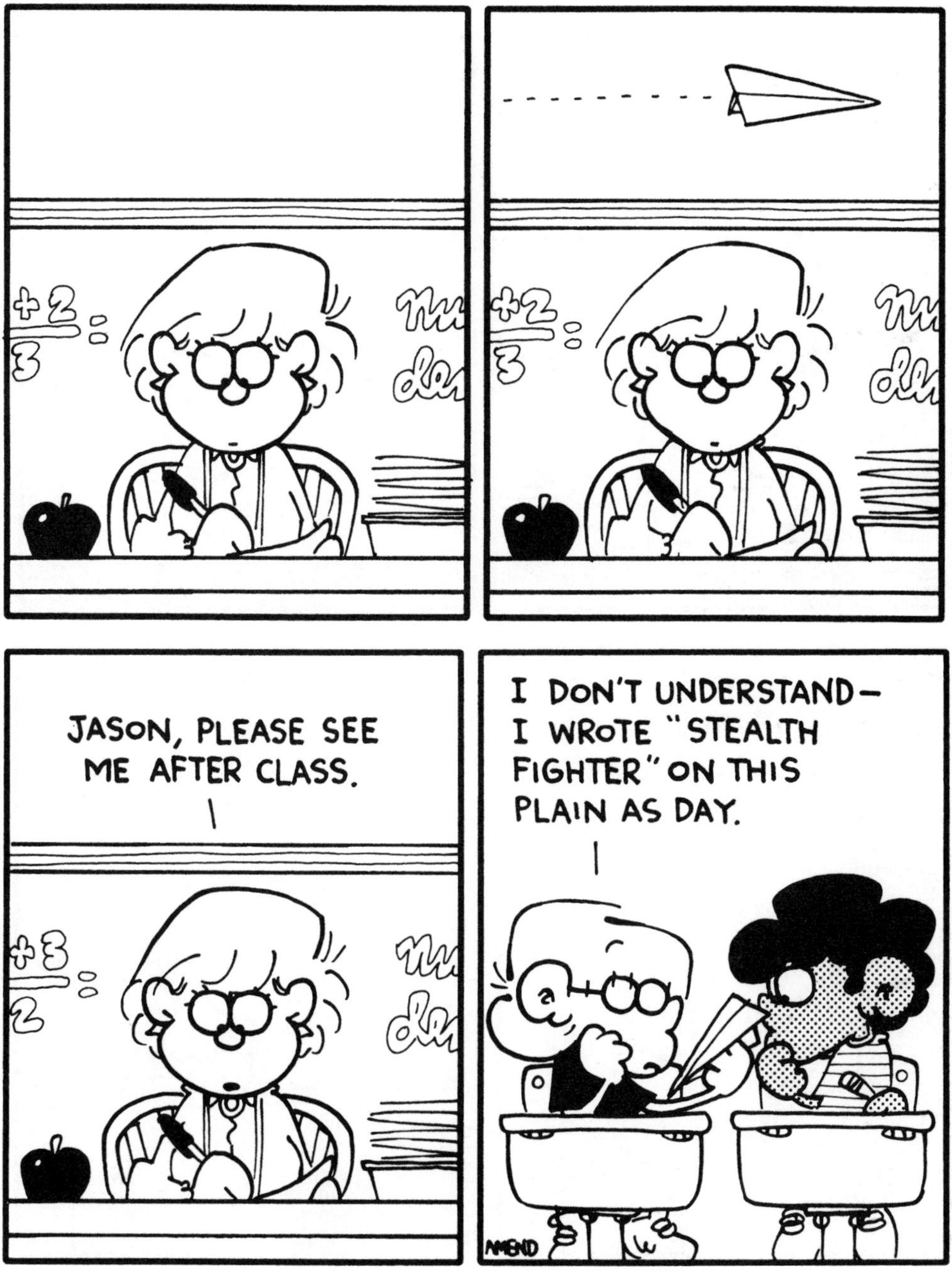

JASON, PLEASE SEE ME AFTER CLASS.
I DON'T UNDERSTAND– I WROTE "STEALTH FIGHTER" ON THIS PLAIN AS DAY.
AMEND

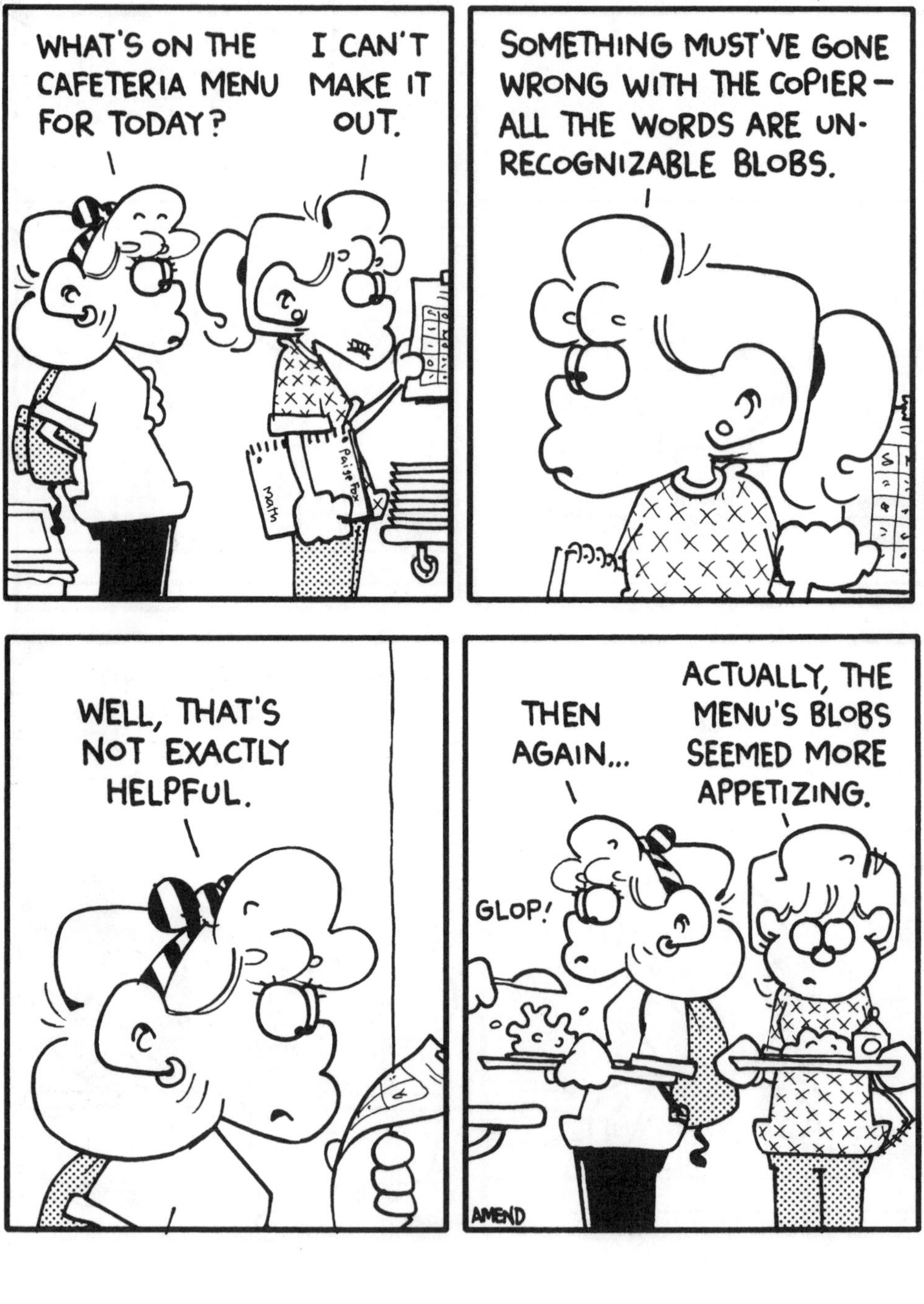
WHAT'S ON THE CAFETERIA MENU FOR TODAY?
I CAN'T MAKE IT OUT.
math
Paige Fox
SOMETHING MUST'VE GONE WRONG WITH THE COPIER – ALL THE WORDS ARE UN-RECOGNIZABLE BLOBS.
WELL, THAT'S NOT EXACTLY HELPFUL.
THEN AGAIN...
ACTUALLY, THE MENU'S BLOBS SEEMED MORE APPETIZING.
GLOP!
AMEND

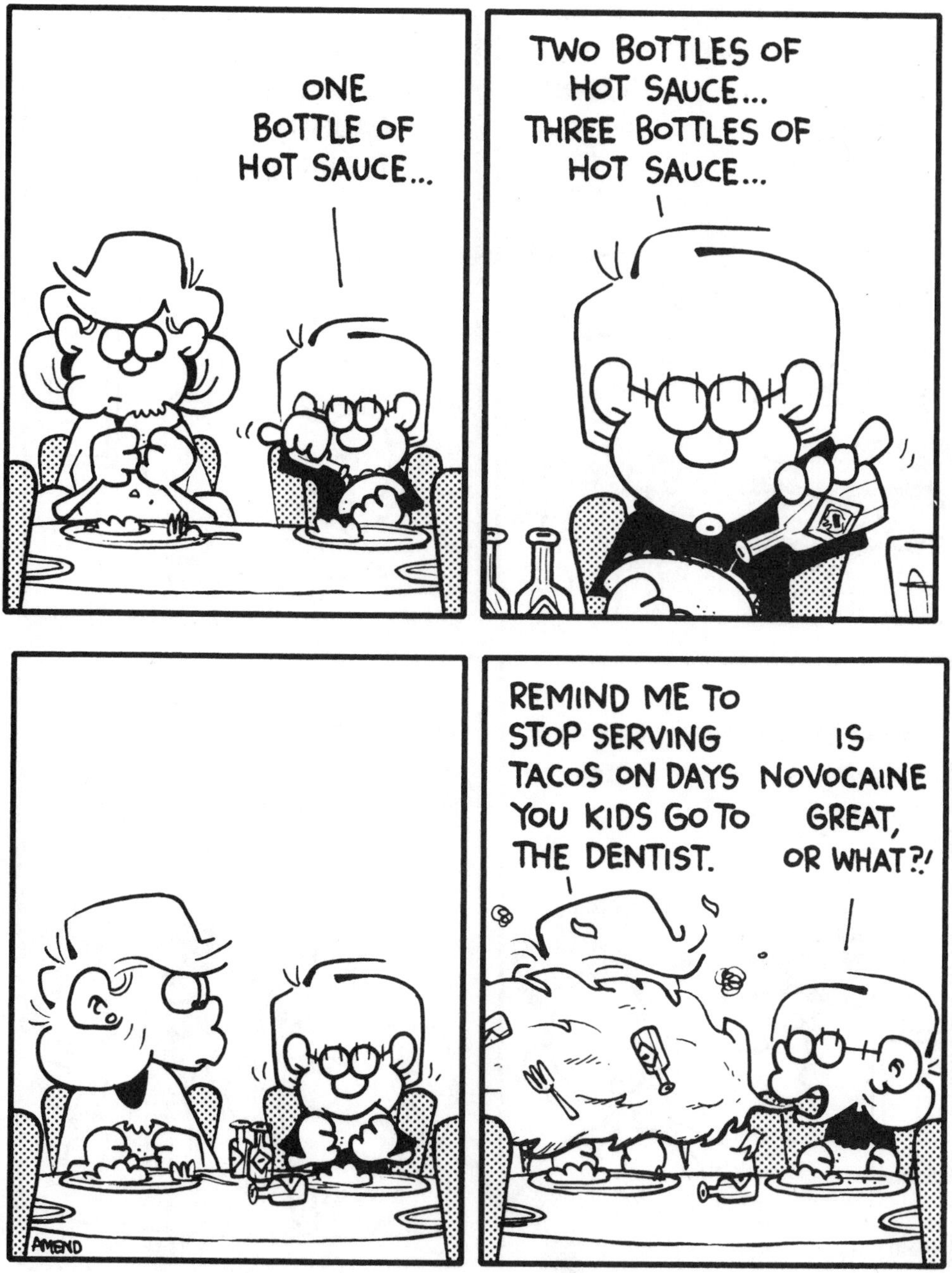
ONE BOTTLE OF HOT SAUCE...
TWO BOTTLES OF HOT SAUCE... THREE BOTTLES OF HOT SAUCE...
AMEND
REMIND ME TO STOP SERVING TACOS ON DAYS YOU KIDS GO TO THE DENTIST.
IS NOVOCAINE GREAT, OR WHAT?!

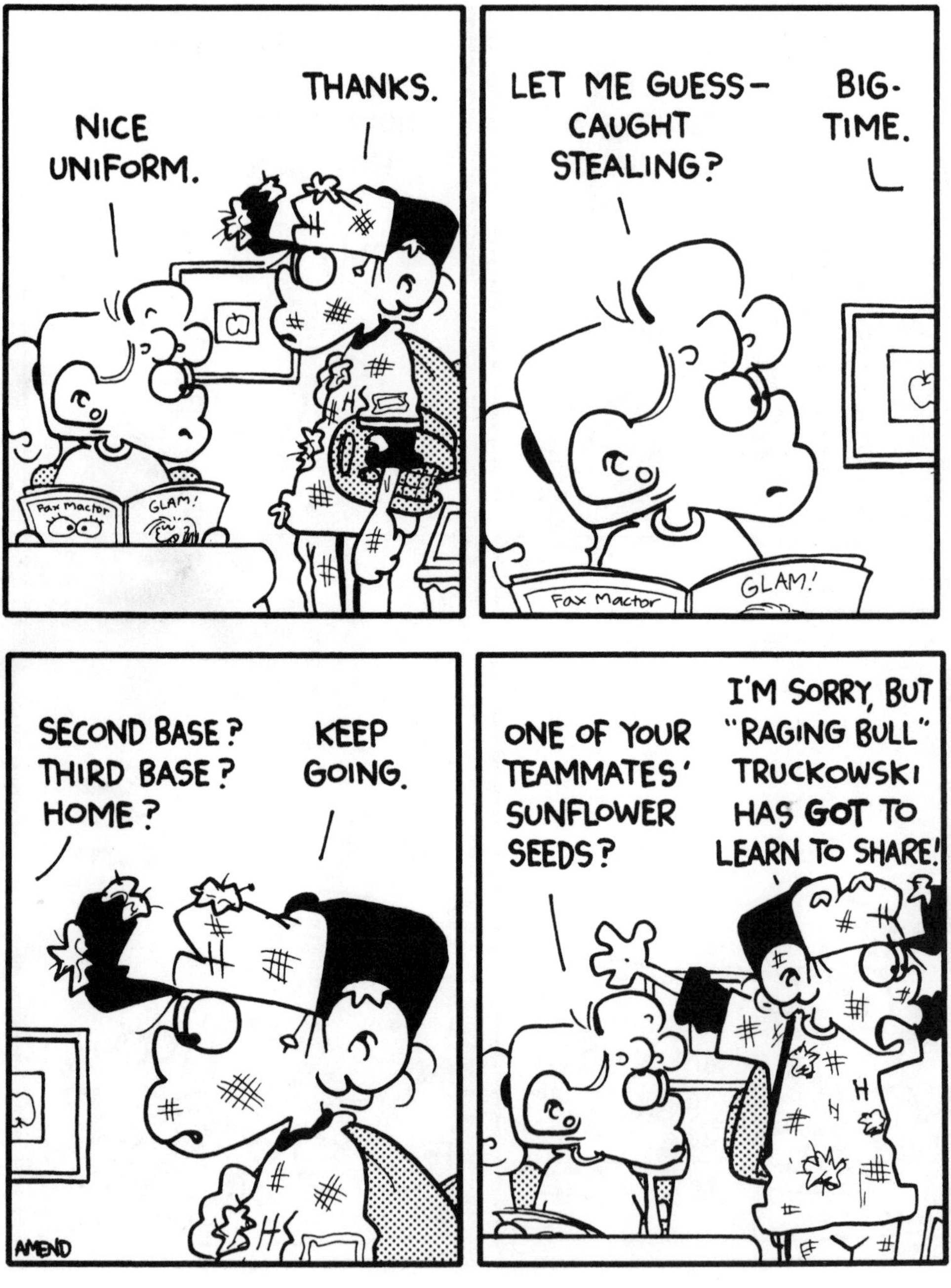
NICE UNIFORM.
THANKS.
LET ME GUESS– CAUGHT STEALING?
BIG-TIME.
SECOND BASE? THIRD BASE? HOME?
KEEP GOING.
ONE OF YOUR TEAMMATES' SUNFLOWER SEEDS?
I'M SORRY, BUT "RAGING BULL" TRUCKOWSKI HAS GOT TO LEARN TO SHARE!
Fax Mactor
GLAM!
AMEND

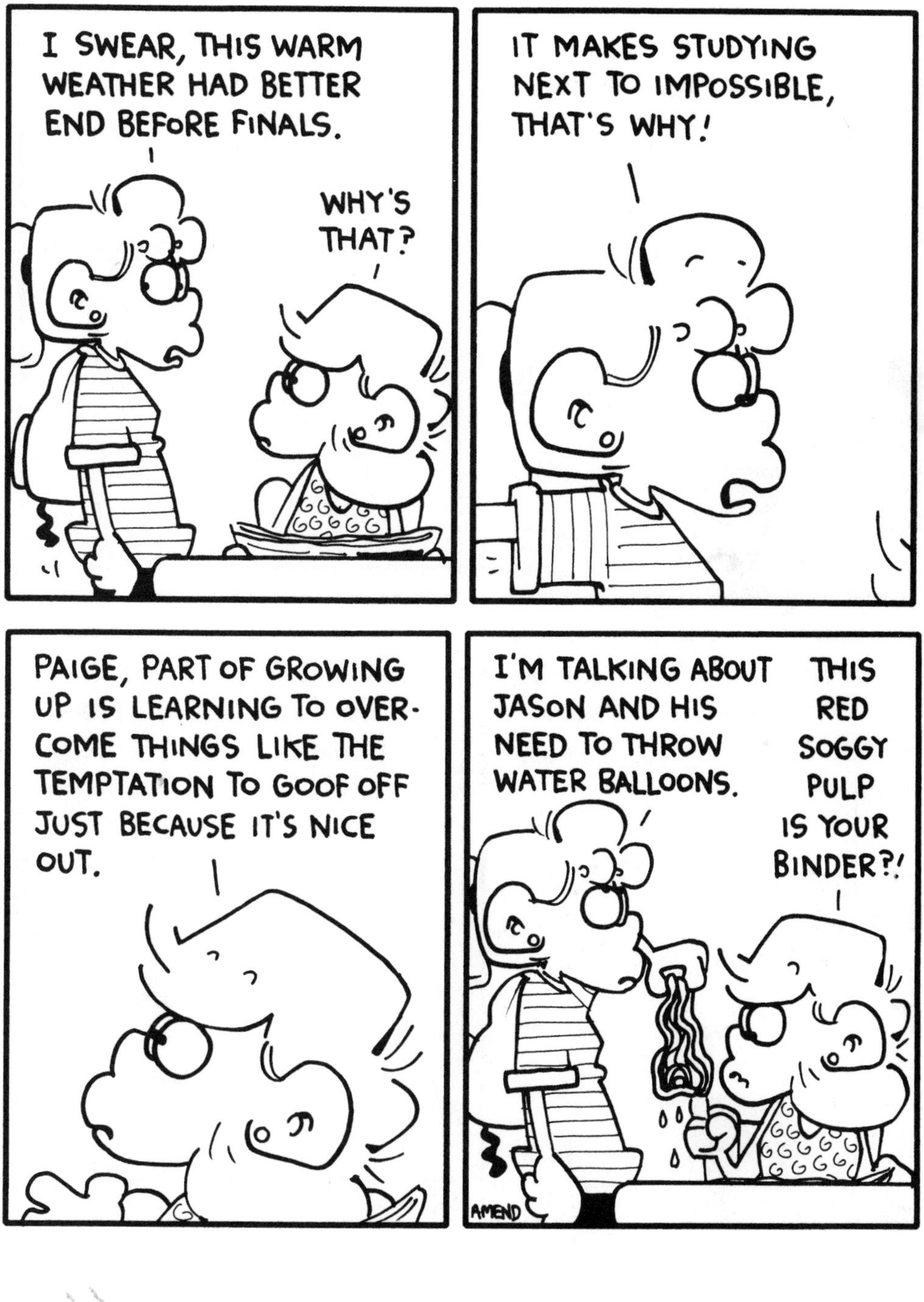
I SWEAR, THIS WARM WEATHER HAD BETTER END BEFORE FINALS.
WHY'S THAT?
IT MAKES STUDYING NEXT TO IMPOSSIBLE, THAT'S WHY!
PAIGE, PART OF GROWING UP IS LEARNING TO OVER-COME THINGS LIKE THE TEMPTATION TO GOOF OFF JUST BECAUSE IT'S NICE OUT.
I'M TALKING ABOUT JASON AND HIS NEED TO THROW WATER BALLOONS.
THIS RED SOGGY PULP IS YOUR BINDER?!
AMEND

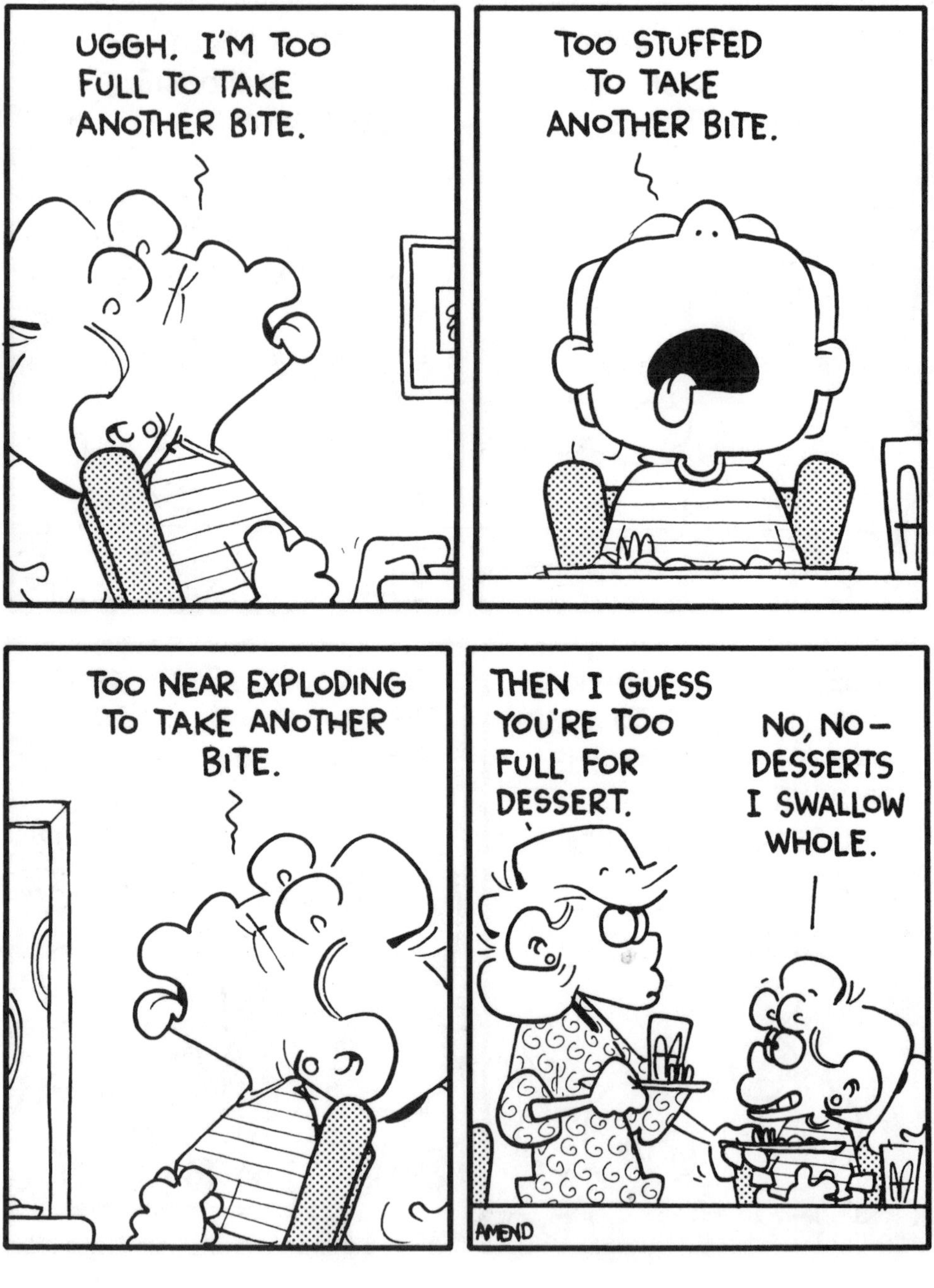
UGGH. I'M TOO FULL TO TAKE ANOTHER BITE.
TOO STUFFED TO TAKE ANOTHER BITE.
TOO NEAR EXPLODING TO TAKE ANOTHER BITE.
THEN I GUESS YOU'RE TOO FULL FOR DESSERT.
NO, NO – DESSERTS I SWALLOW WHOLE.
AMEND

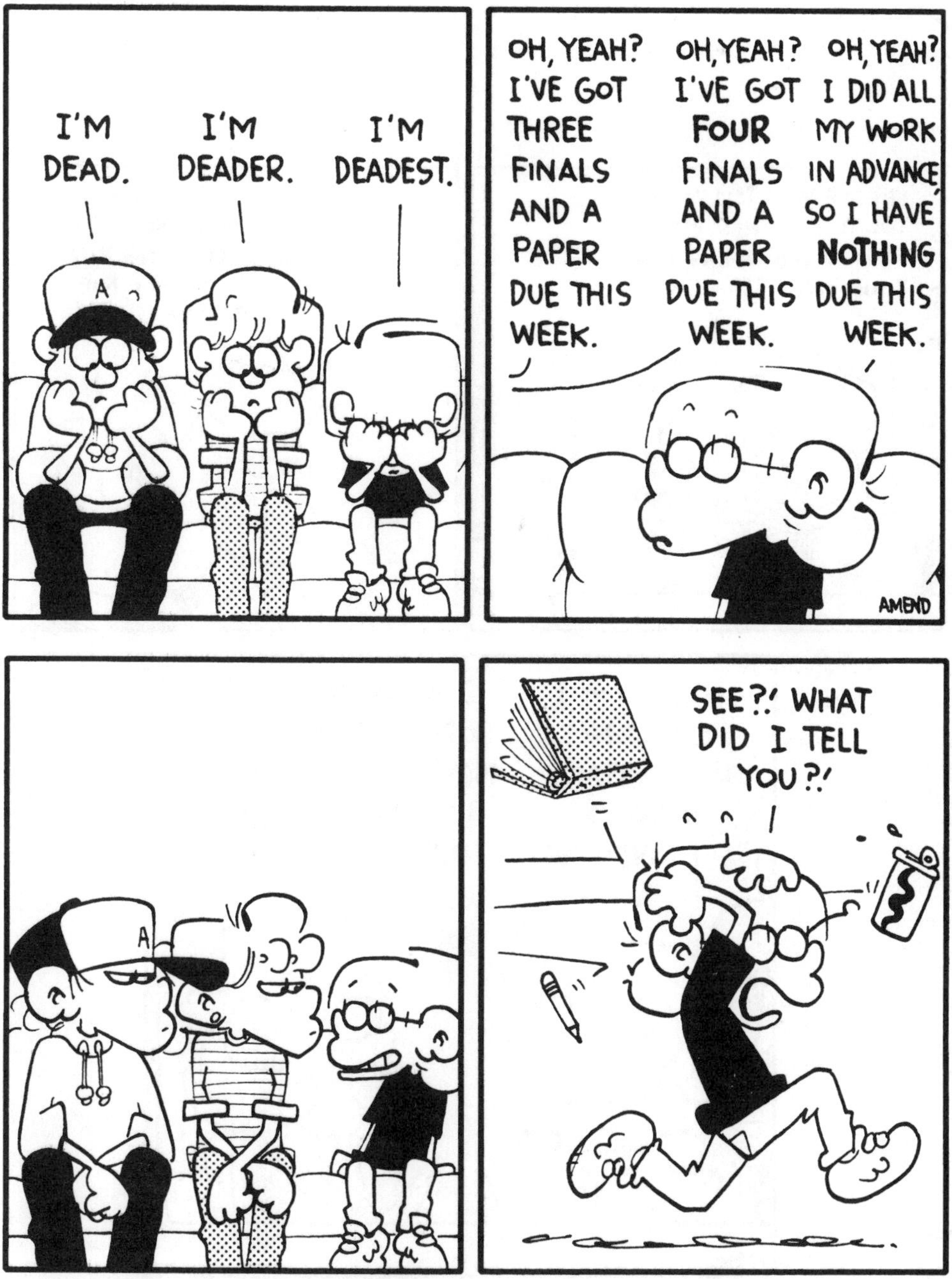
I'M DEAD.
I'M DEADER.
I'M DEADEST.
OH, YEAH? I'VE GOT THREE FINALS AND A PAPER DUE THIS WEEK.
OH, YEAH? I'VE GOT FOUR FINALS AND A PAPER DUE THIS WEEK.
OH, YEAH? I DID ALL MY WORK IN ADVANCE, SO I HAVE NOTHING DUE THIS WEEK.
AMEND
SEE?! WHAT DID I TELL YOU?!

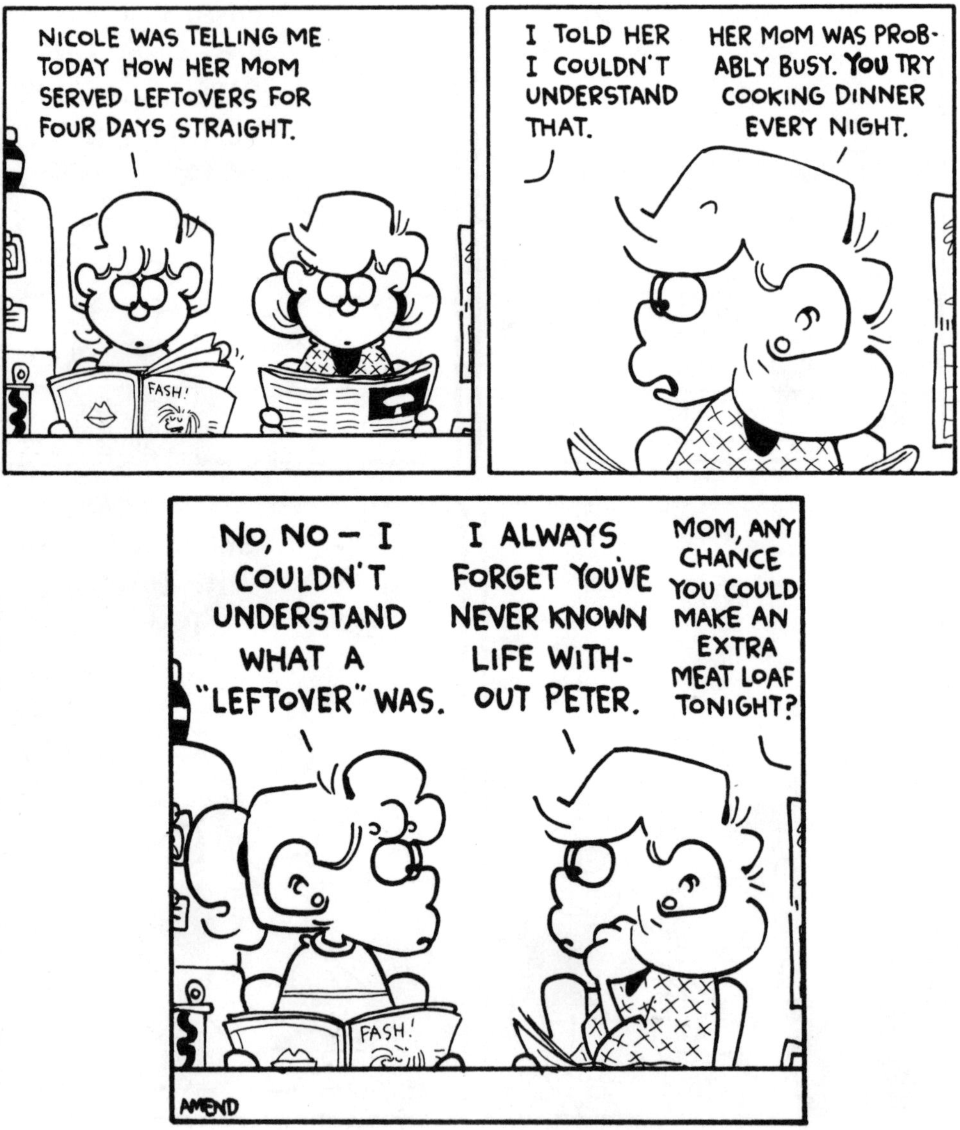
NICOLE WAS TELLING ME TODAY HOW HER MOM SERVED LEFTOVERS FOR FOUR DAYS STRAIGHT.
FASH!
I TOLD HER I COULDN'T UNDERSTAND THAT.
HER MOM WAS PROBABLY BUSY. YOU TRY COOKING DINNER EVERY NIGHT.
NO, NO - I COULDN'T UNDERSTAND WHAT A "LEFTOVER" WAS.
I ALWAYS FORGET YOU'VE NEVER KNOWN LIFE WITHOUT PETER.
MOM, ANY CHANCE YOU COULD MAKE AN EXTRA MEAT LOAF TONIGHT?
FASH!
AMEND

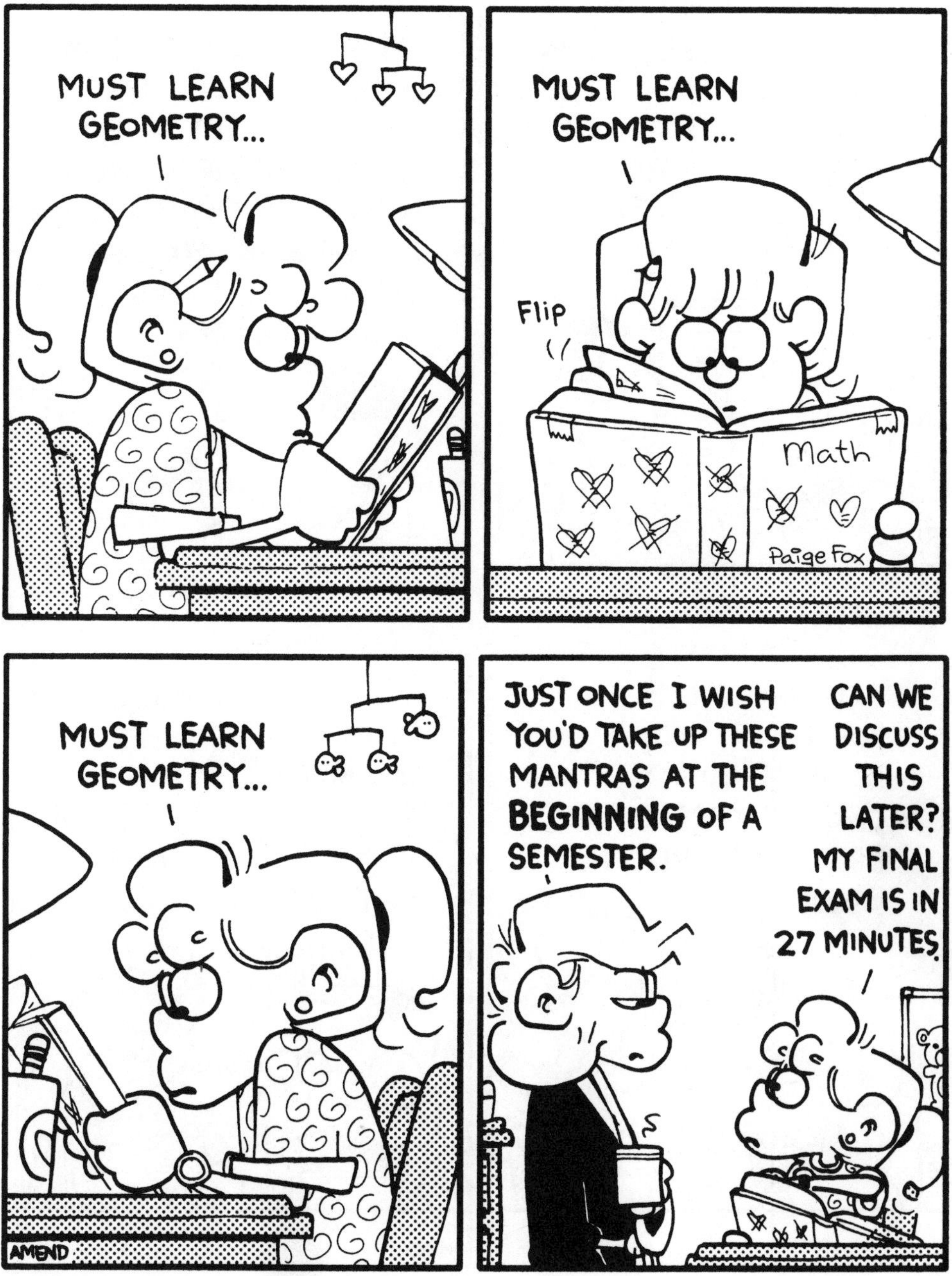
MUST LEARN GEOMETRY...
MUST LEARN GEOMETRY...
Flip
Math
Paige Fox
MUST LEARN GEOMETRY...
AMEND
JUST ONCE I WISH YOU'D TAKE UP THESE MANTRAS AT THE BEGINNING OF A SEMESTER.
CAN WE DISCUSS THIS LATER? MY FINAL EXAM IS IN 27 MINUTES.

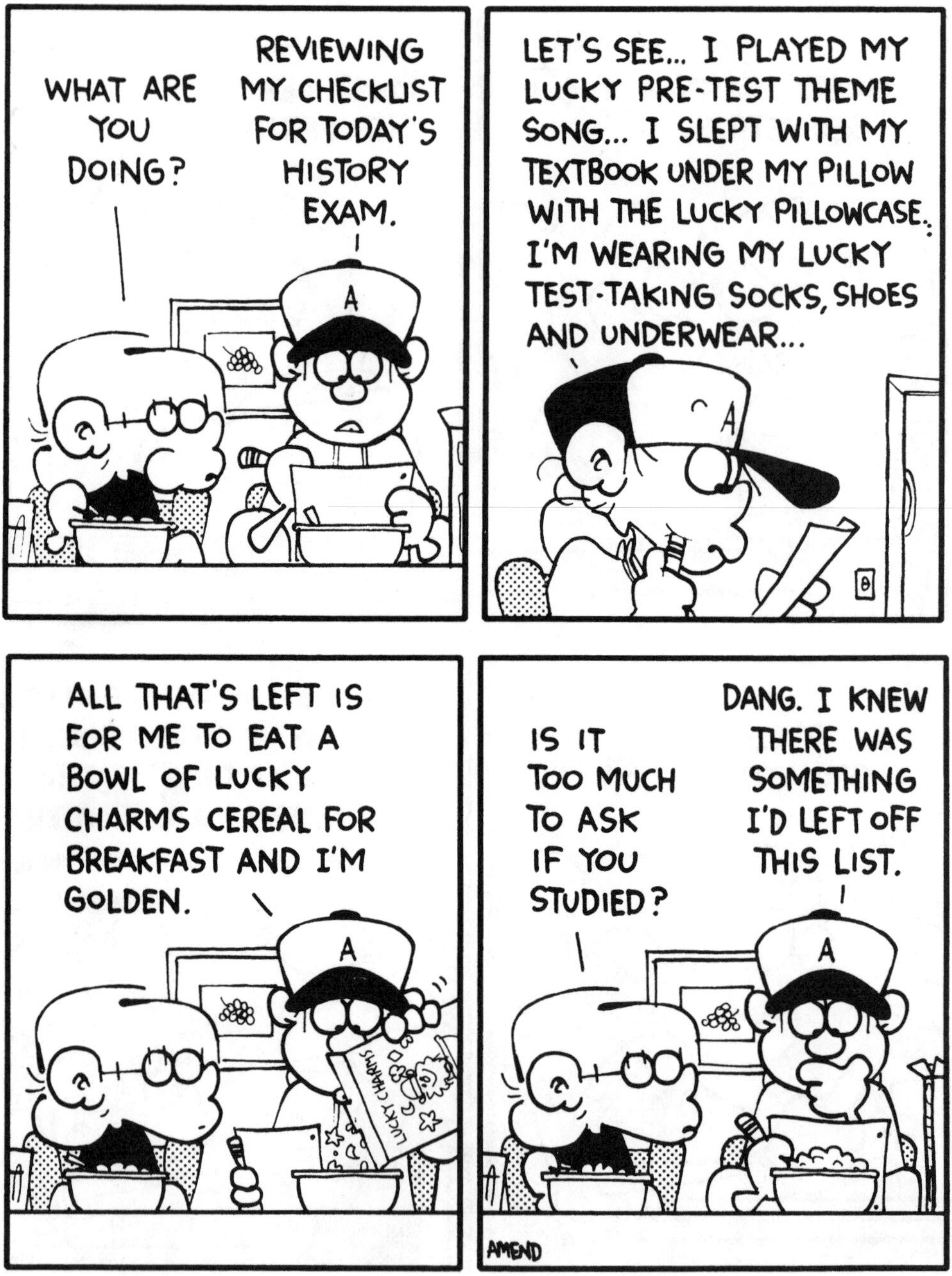
WHAT ARE YOU DOING?
REVIEWING MY CHECKLIST FOR TODAY'S HISTORY EXAM.
A
LET'S SEE... I PLAYED MY LUCKY PRE-TEST THEME SONG... I SLEPT WITH MY TEXTBOOK UNDER MY PILLOW WITH THE LUCKY PILLOWCASE... I'M WEARING MY LUCKY TEST-TAKING SOCKS, SHOES AND UNDERWEAR...
ALL THAT'S LEFT IS FOR ME TO EAT A BOWL OF LUCKY CHARMS CEREAL FOR BREAKFAST AND I'M GOLDEN.
LUCKY CHARMS
IS IT TOO MUCH TO ASK IF YOU STUDIED?
DANG. I KNEW THERE WAS SOMETHING I'D LEFT OFF THIS LIST.
AMEND

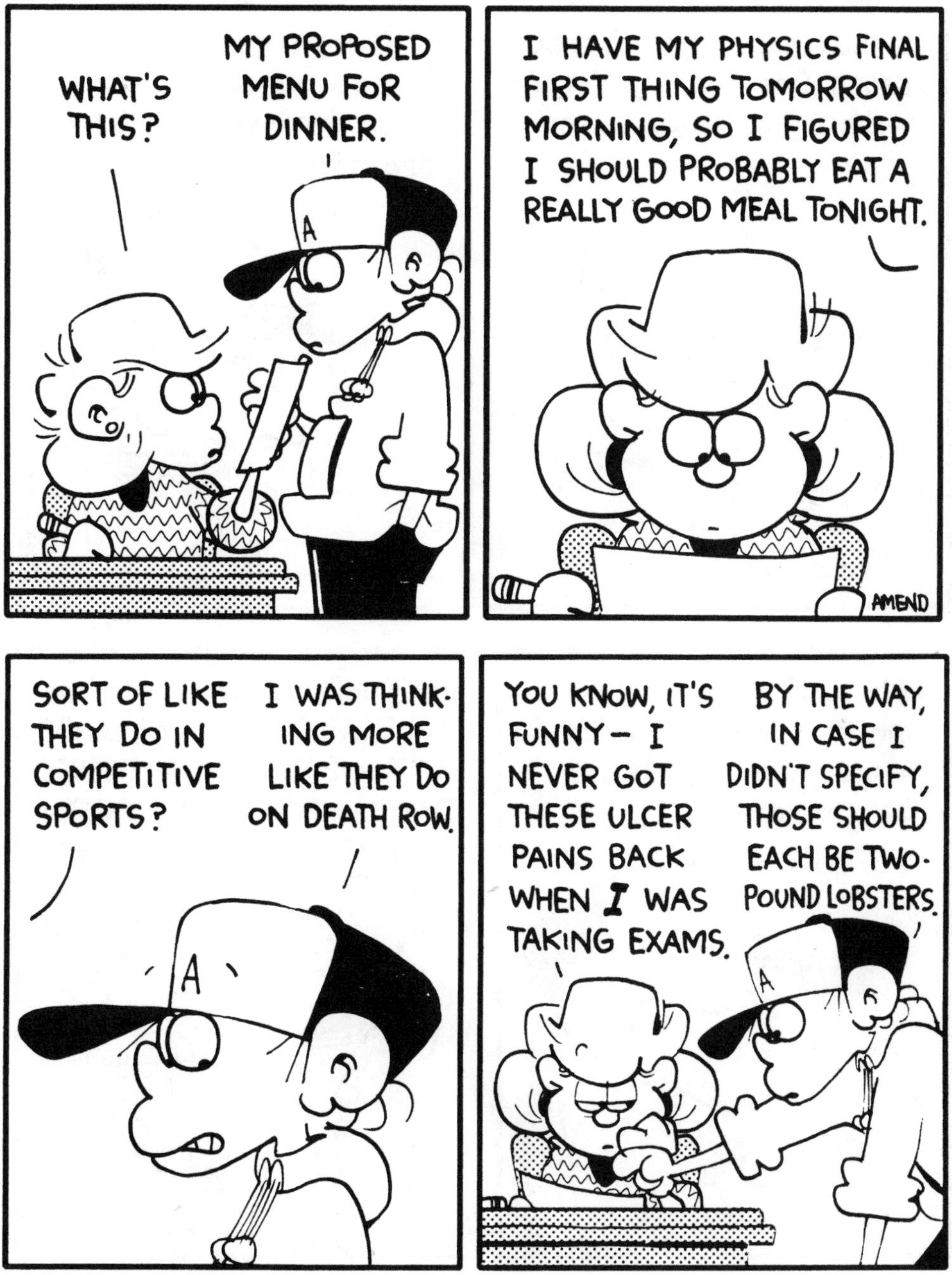
WHAT'S THIS?
MY PROPOSED MENU FOR DINNER.
I HAVE MY PHYSICS FINAL FIRST THING TOMORROW MORNING, SO I FIGURED I SHOULD PROBABLY EAT A REALLY GOOD MEAL TONIGHT.
AMEND
SORT OF LIKE THEY DO IN COMPETITIVE SPORTS?
I WAS THINKING MORE LIKE THEY DO ON DEATH ROW.
YOU KNOW, IT'S FUNNY— I NEVER GOT THESE ULCER PAINS BACK WHEN I WAS TAKING EXAMS.
BY THE WAY, IN CASE I DIDN'T SPECIFY, THOSE SHOULD EACH BE TWO-POUND LOBSTERS.

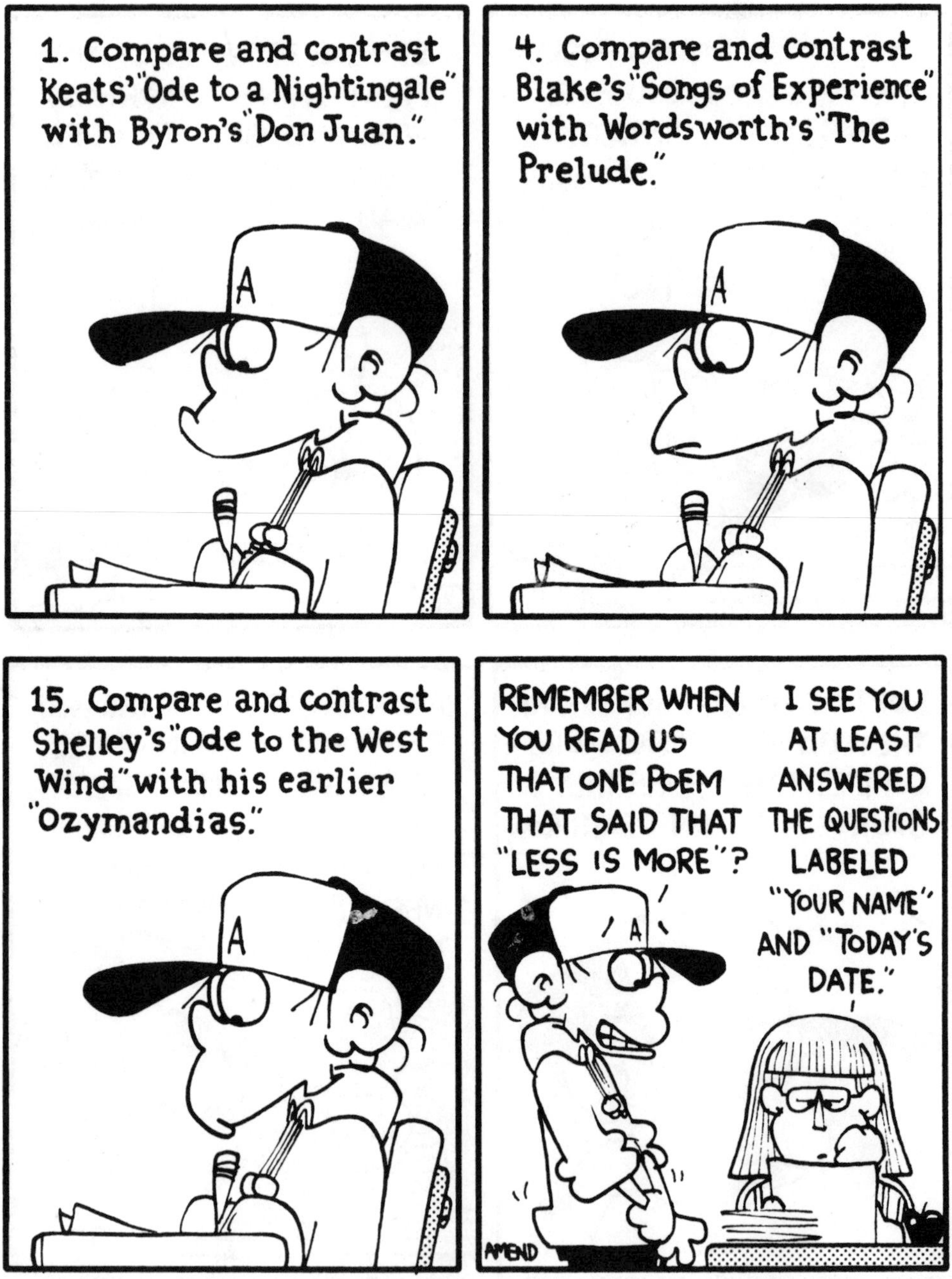
1. Compare and contrast Keats' "Ode to a Nightingale" with Byron's "Don Juan."
4. Compare and contrast Blake's "Songs of Experience" with Wordsworth's "The Prelude."
15. Compare and contrast Shelley's "Ode to the West Wind" with his earlier "Ozymandias."
REMEMBER WHEN YOU READ US THAT ONE POEM THAT SAID THAT "LESS IS MORE"?
I SEE YOU AT LEAST ANSWERED THE QUESTIONS LABELED "YOUR NAME" AND "TODAY'S DATE."
AMEND

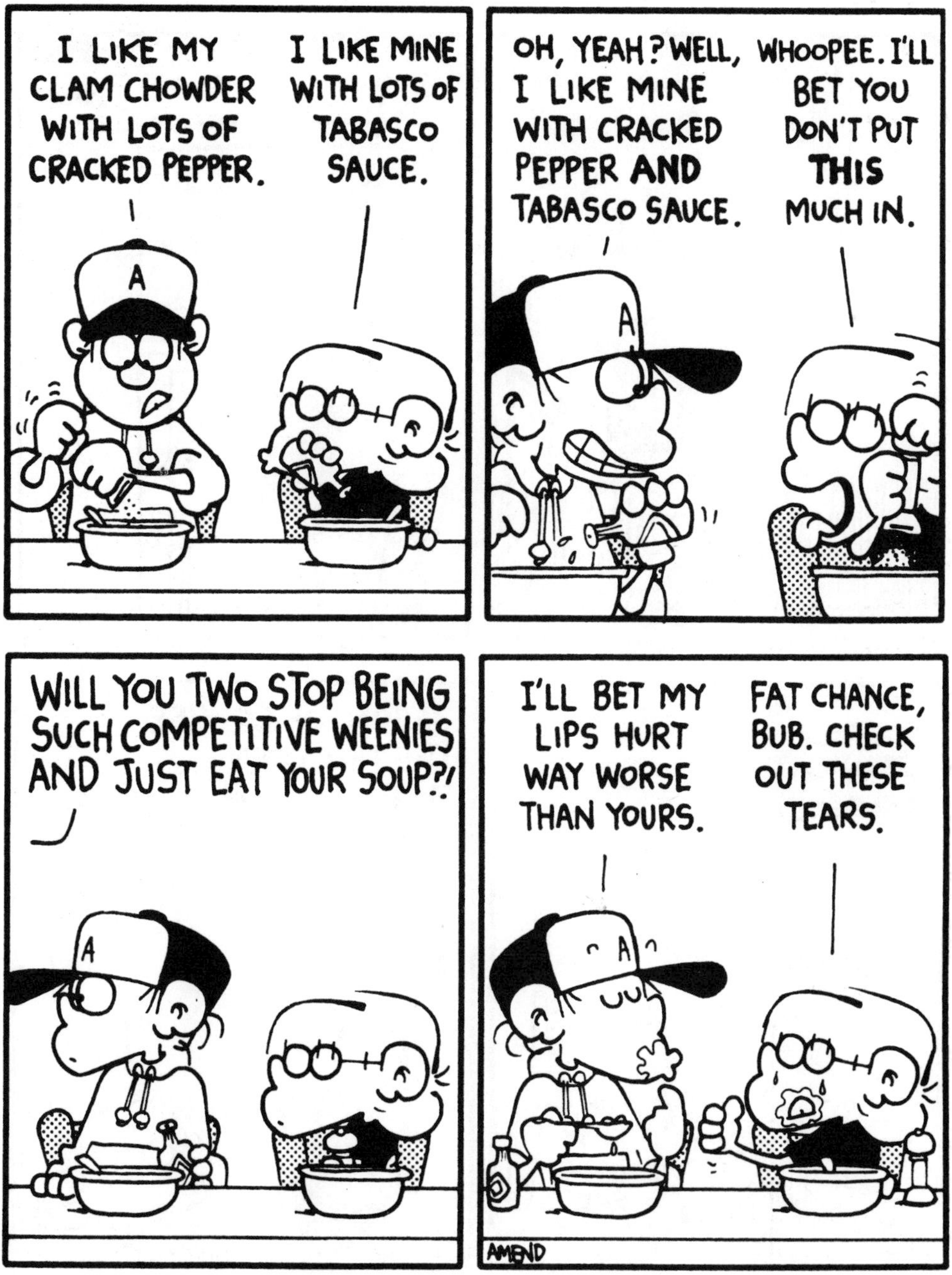
I LIKE MY CLAM CHOWDER WITH LOTS OF CRACKED PEPPER.
I LIKE MINE WITH LOTS OF TABASCO SAUCE.
OH, YEAH? WELL, I LIKE MINE WITH CRACKED PEPPER AND TABASCO SAUCE.
WHOOPEE. I'LL BET YOU DON'T PUT THIS MUCH IN.
WILL YOU TWO STOP BEING SUCH COMPETITIVE WEENIES AND JUST EAT YOUR SOUP?!
I'LL BET MY LIPS HURT WAY WORSE THAN YOURS.
FAT CHANCE, BUB. CHECK OUT THESE TEARS.
AMEND

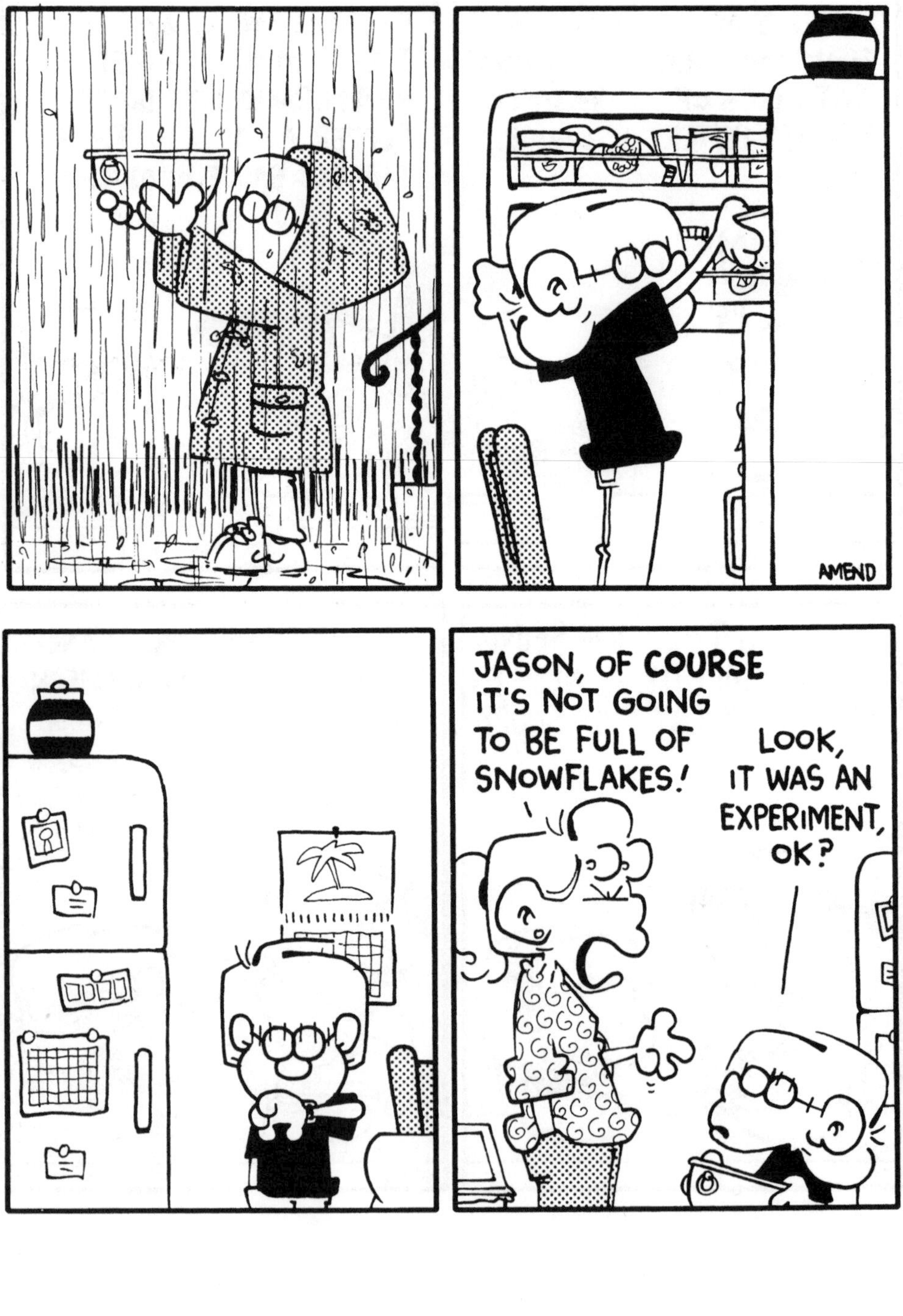
AMEND
JASON, OF COURSE IT'S NOT GOING TO BE FULL OF SNOWFLAKES!
LOOK, IT WAS AN EXPERIMENT, OK?

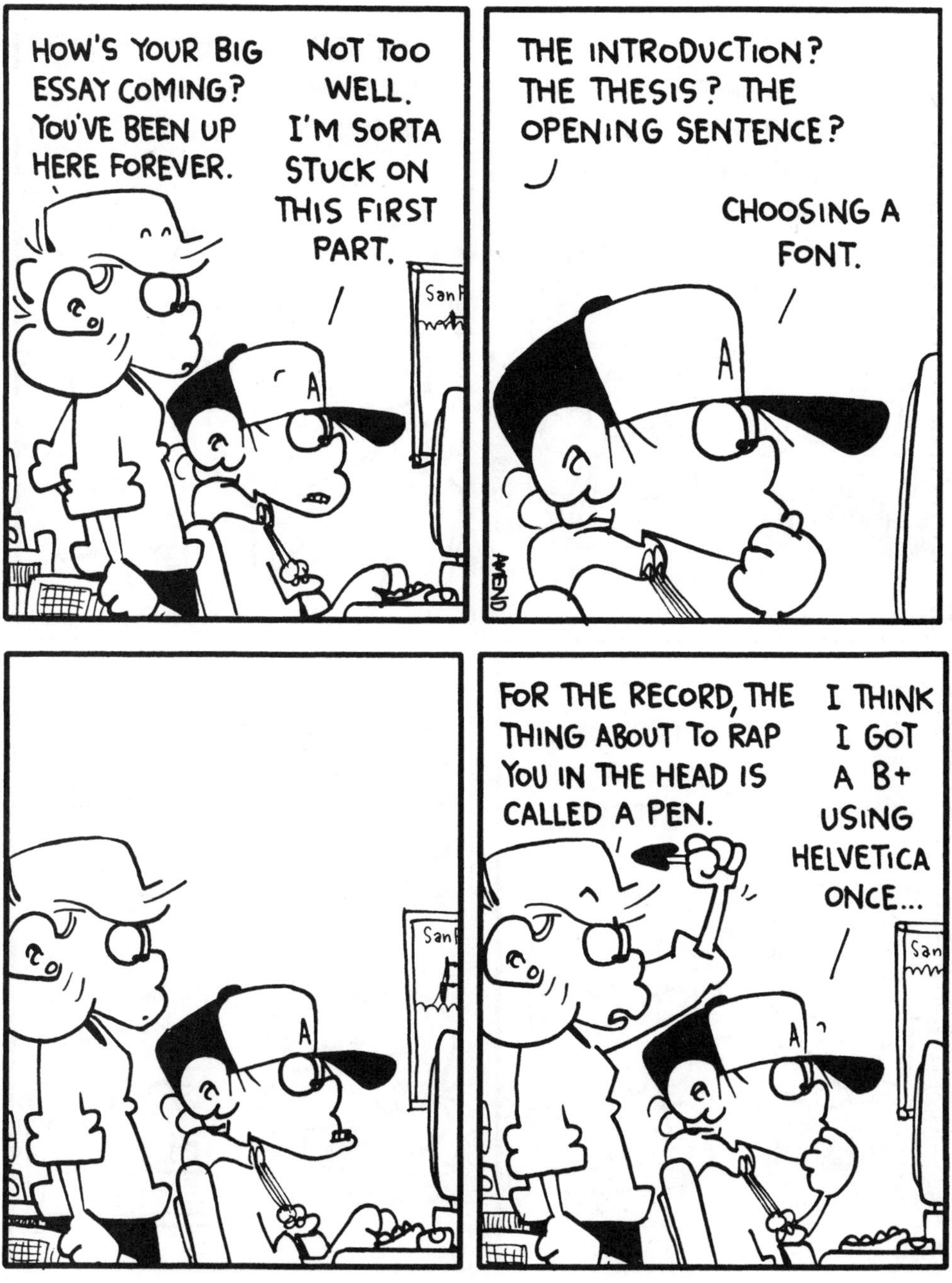
HOW'S YOUR BIG ESSAY COMING? YOU'VE BEEN UP HERE FOREVER.
NOT TOO WELL. I'M SORTA STUCK ON THIS FIRST PART.
THE INTRODUCTION? THE THESIS? THE OPENING SENTENCE?
CHOOSING A FONT.
FOR THE RECORD, THE THING ABOUT TO RAP YOU IN THE HEAD IS CALLED A PEN.
I THINK I GOT A B+ USING HELVETICA ONCE...

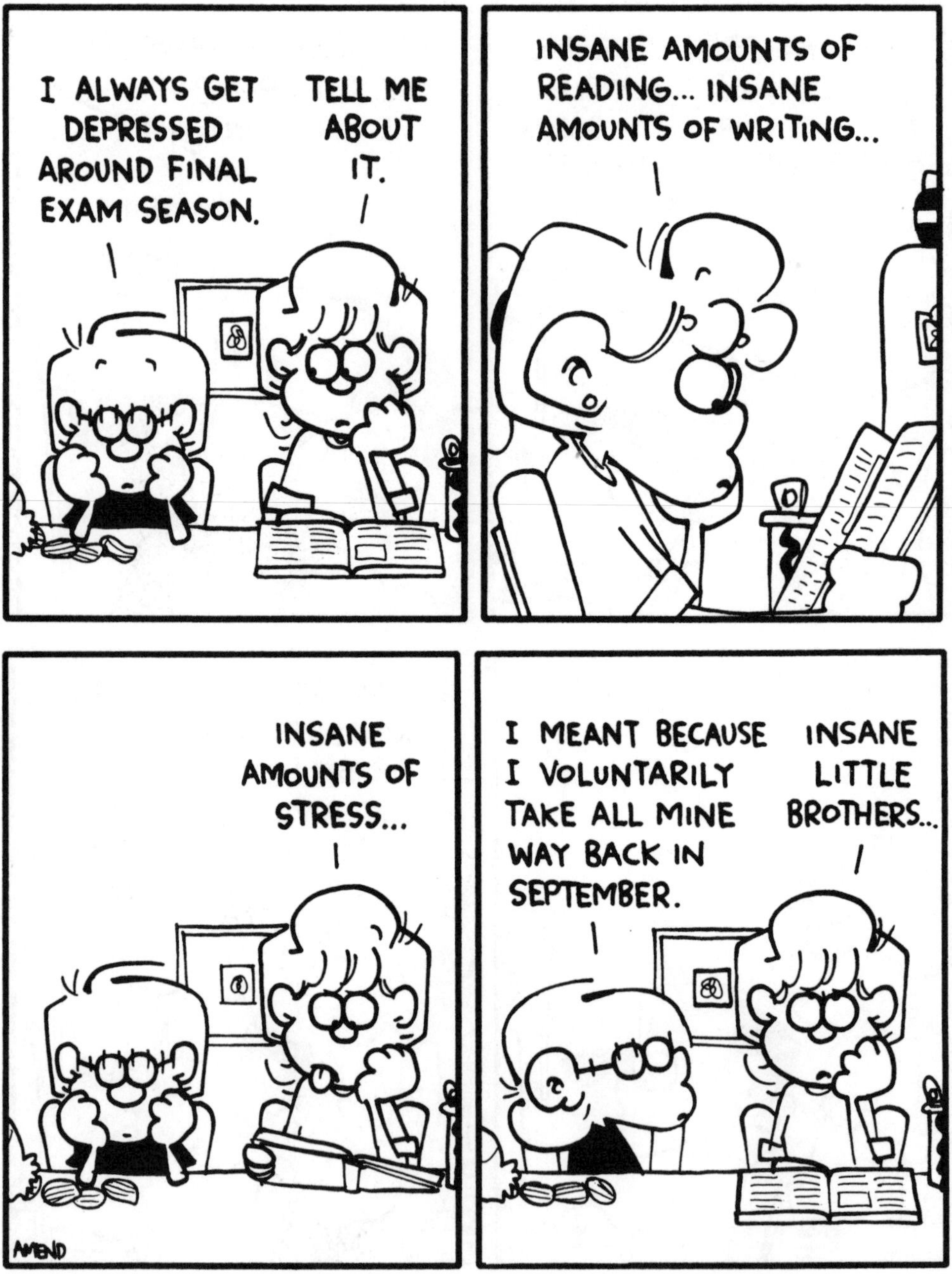
I ALWAYS GET DEPRESSED AROUND FINAL EXAM SEASON.
TELL ME ABOUT IT.
INSANE AMOUNTS OF READING... INSANE AMOUNTS OF WRITING...
INSANE AMOUNTS OF STRESS...
I MEANT BECAUSE I VOLUNTARILY TAKE ALL MINE WAY BACK IN SEPTEMBER.
INSANE LITTLE BROTHERS...
AMEND

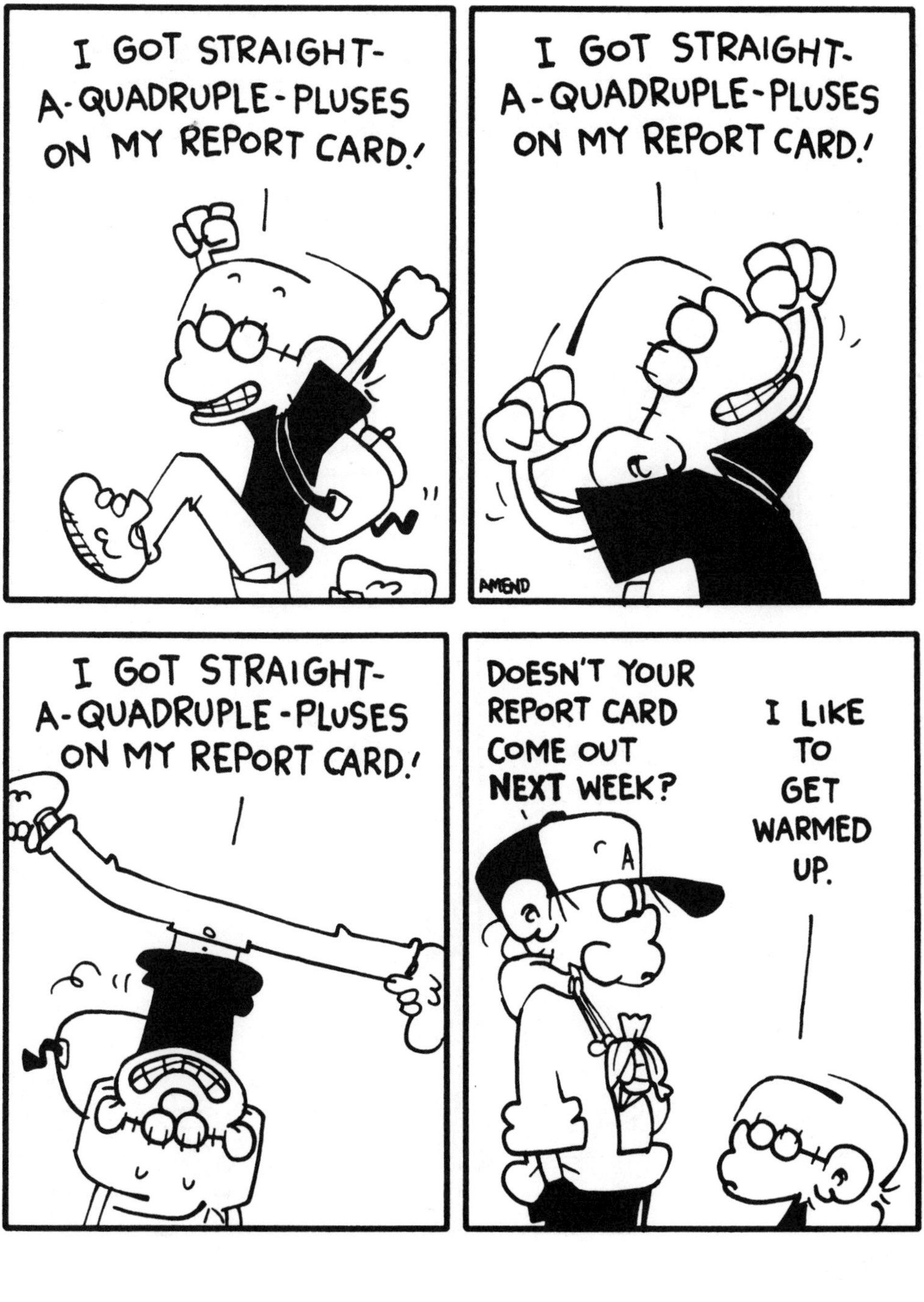
I GOT STRAIGHT-A-QUADRUPLE-PLUSES ON MY REPORT CARD!
I GOT STRAIGHT-A-QUADRUPLE-PLUSES ON MY REPORT CARD!
AMEND
I GOT STRAIGHT-A-QUADRUPLE-PLUSES ON MY REPORT CARD!
DOESN'T YOUR REPORT CARD COME OUT NEXT WEEK?
A
I LIKE TO GET WARMED UP.

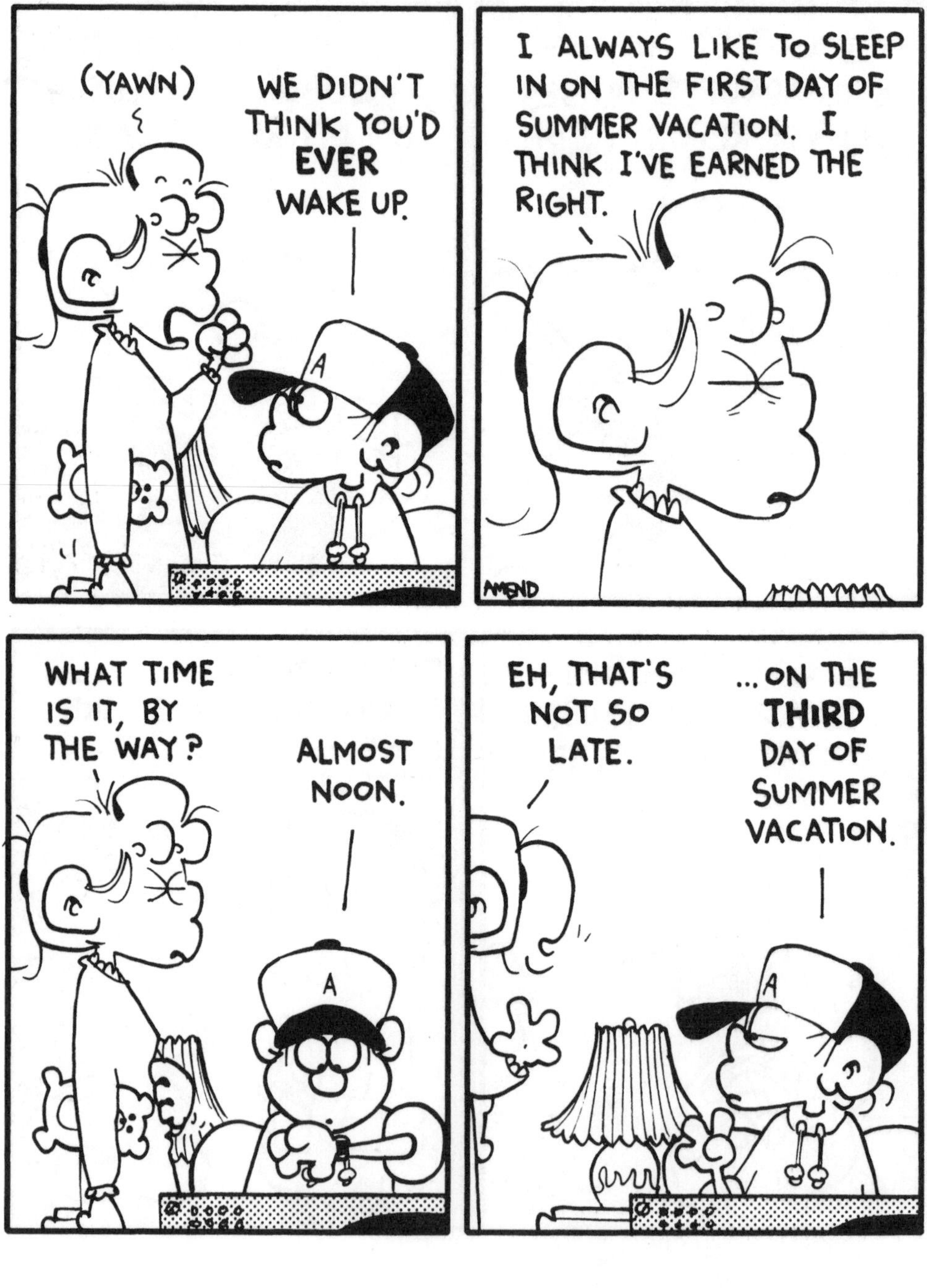
(YAWN)
WE DIDN'T THINK YOU'D EVER WAKE UP.
I ALWAYS LIKE TO SLEEP IN ON THE FIRST DAY OF SUMMER VACATION. I THINK I'VE EARNED THE RIGHT.
AMEND
WHAT TIME IS IT, BY THE WAY?
ALMOST NOON.
EH, THAT'S NOT SO LATE.
...ON THE THIRD DAY OF SUMMER VACATION.

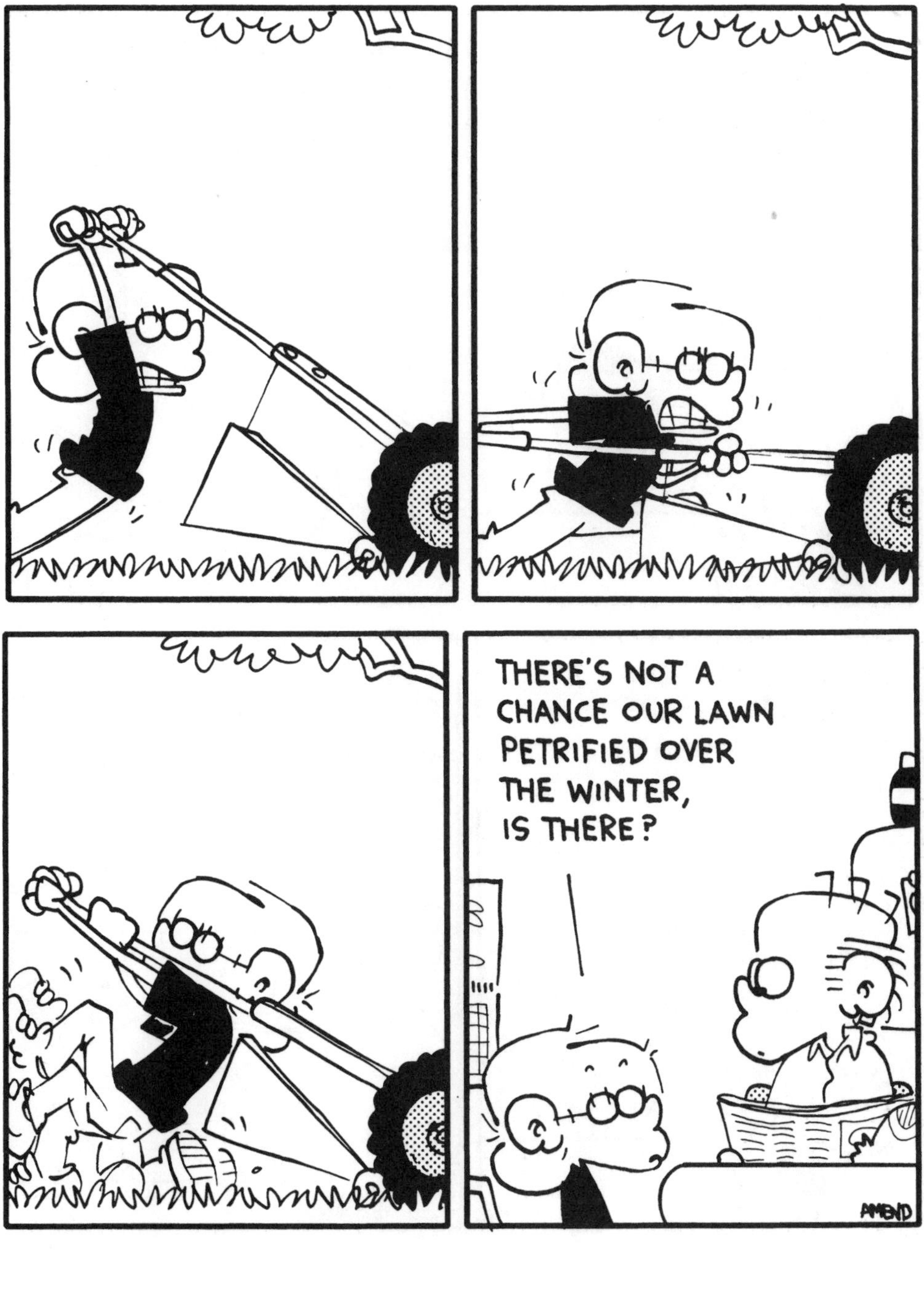
THERE'S NOT A CHANCE OUR LAWN PETRIFIED OVER THE WINTER, IS THERE?
AMEND

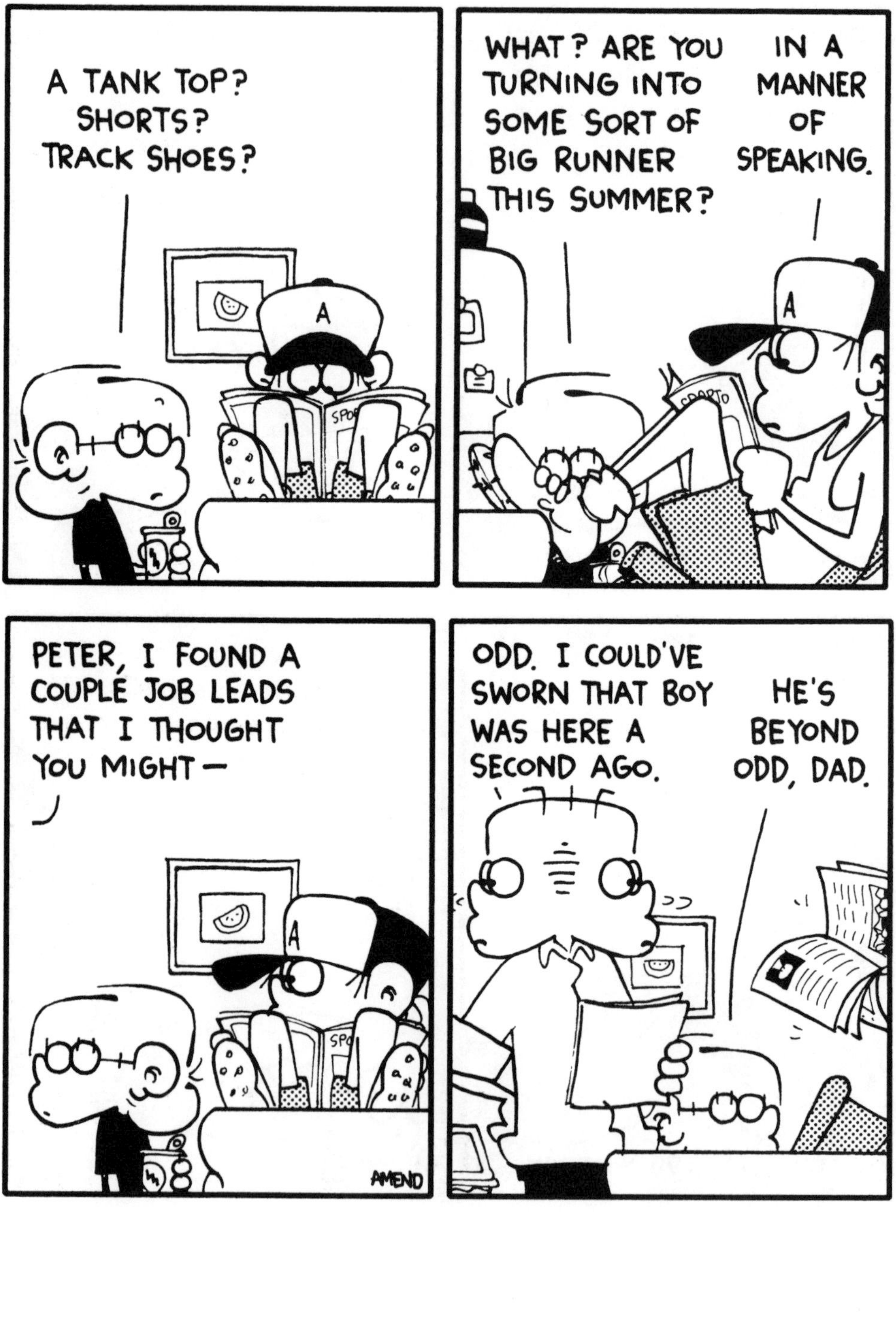
A TANK TOP? SHORTS? TRACK SHOES?
WHAT? ARE YOU TURNING INTO SOME SORT OF BIG RUNNER THIS SUMMER?
IN A MANNER OF SPEAKING.
PETER, I FOUND A COUPLE JOB LEADS THAT I THOUGHT YOU MIGHT—
AMEND
ODD. I COULD'VE SWORN THAT BOY WAS HERE A SECOND AGO.
HE'S BEYOND ODD, DAD.

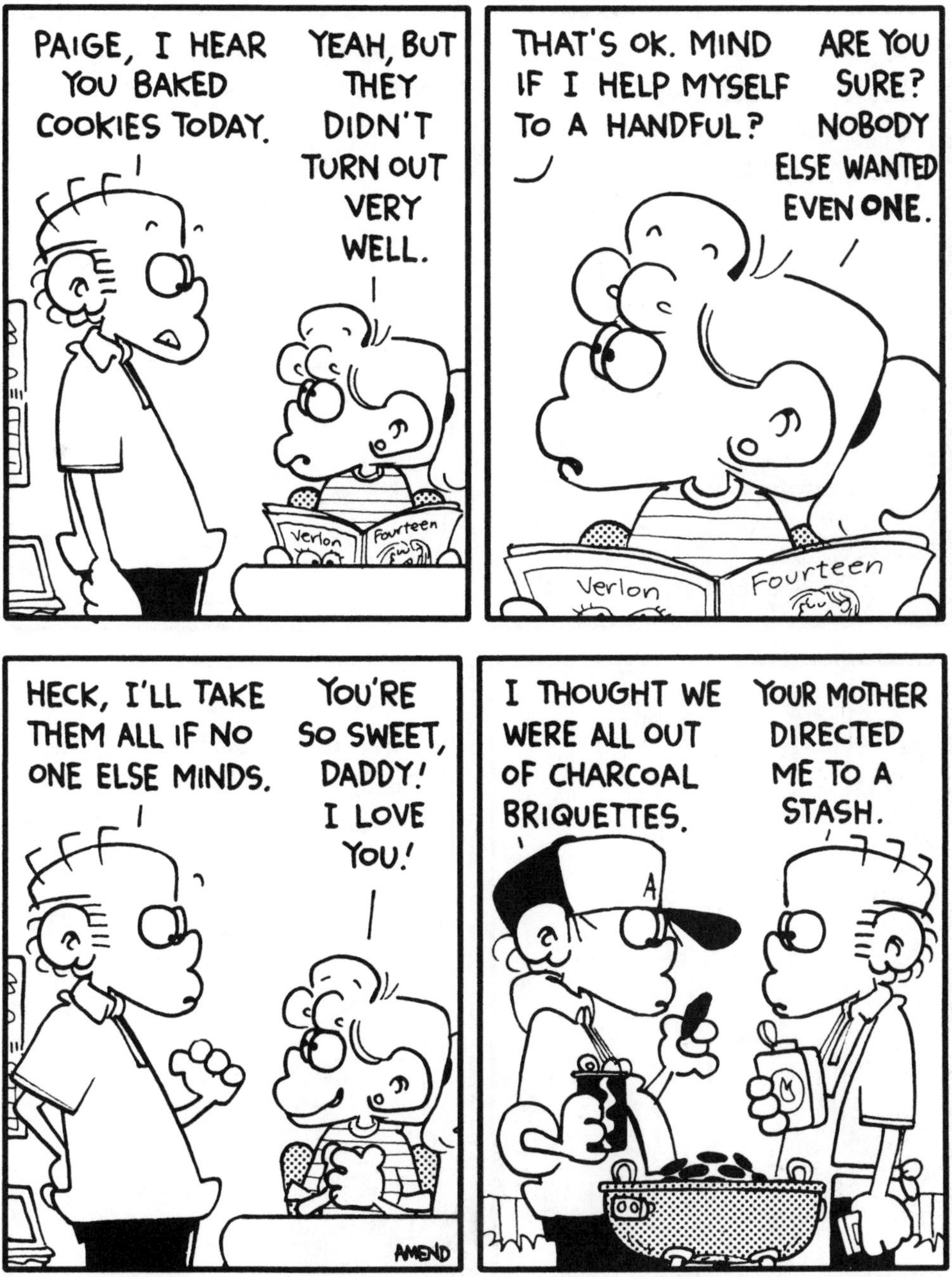
PAIGE, I HEAR YOU BAKED COOKIES TODAY.
YEAH, BUT THEY DIDN'T TURN OUT VERY WELL.
Verlon
Fourteen
THAT'S OK. MIND IF I HELP MYSELF TO A HANDFUL?
ARE YOU SURE? NOBODY ELSE WANTED EVEN ONE.
Verlon
Fourteen
HECK, I'LL TAKE THEM ALL IF NO ONE ELSE MINDS.
YOU'RE SO SWEET, DADDY! I LOVE YOU!
AMEND
I THOUGHT WE WERE ALL OUT OF CHARCOAL BRIQUETTES.
YOUR MOTHER DIRECTED ME TO A STASH.

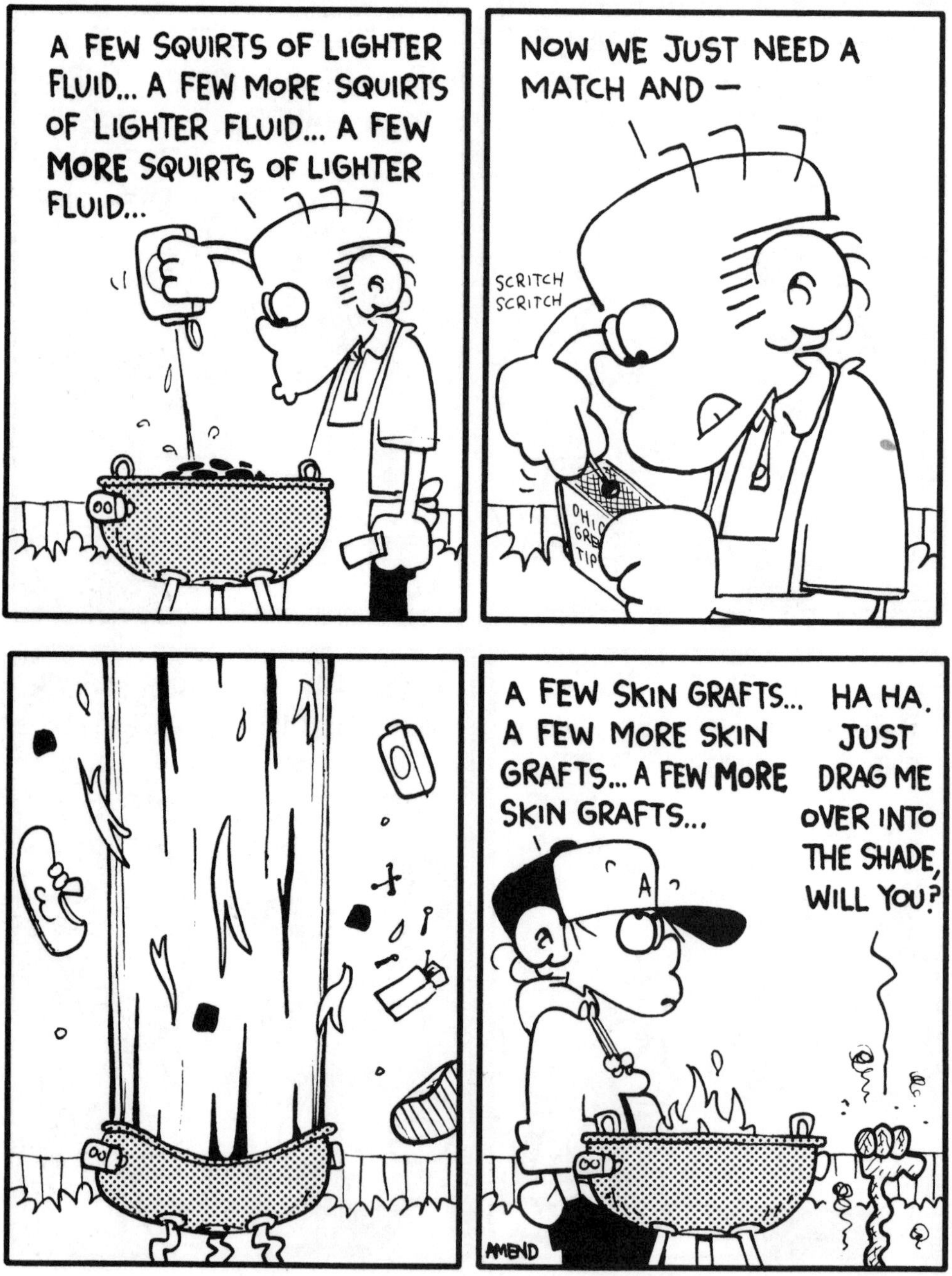
A FEW SQUIRTS OF LIGHTER FLUID... A FEW MORE SQUIRTS OF LIGHTER FLUID... A FEW MORE SQUIRTS OF LIGHTER FLUID...
NOW WE JUST NEED A MATCH AND —
SCRITCH SCRITCH
A FEW SKIN GRAFTS... A FEW MORE SKIN GRAFTS... A FEW MORE SKIN GRAFTS...
HA HA. JUST DRAG ME OVER INTO THE SHADE, WILL YOU?
AMEND

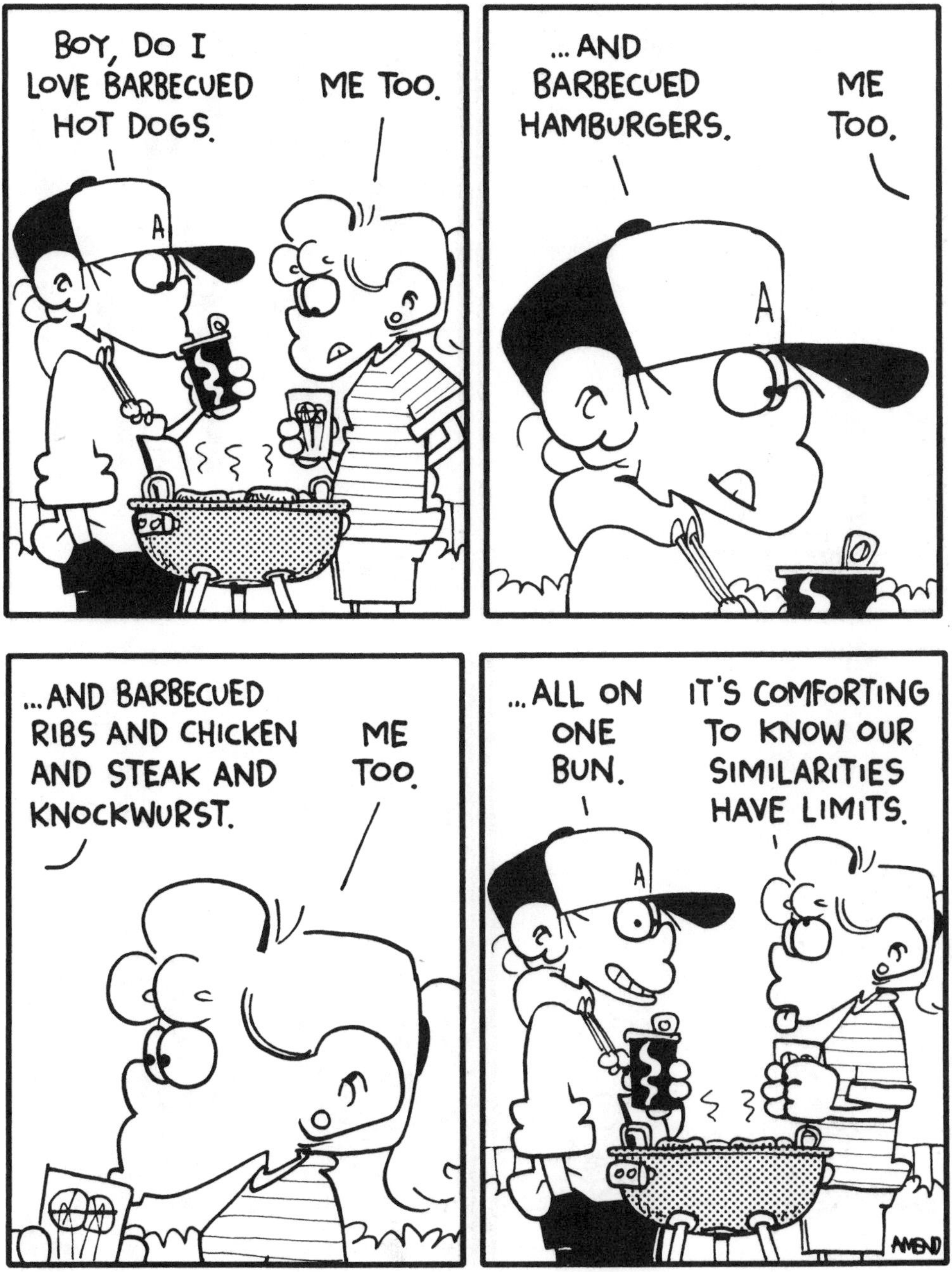
BOY, DO I LOVE BARBECUED HOT DOGS.
ME TOO.
...AND BARBECUED HAMBURGERS.
ME TOO.
...AND BARBECUED RIBS AND CHICKEN AND STEAK AND KNOCKWURST.
ME TOO.
...ALL ON ONE BUN.
IT'S COMFORTING TO KNOW OUR SIMILARITIES HAVE LIMITS.
AMEND

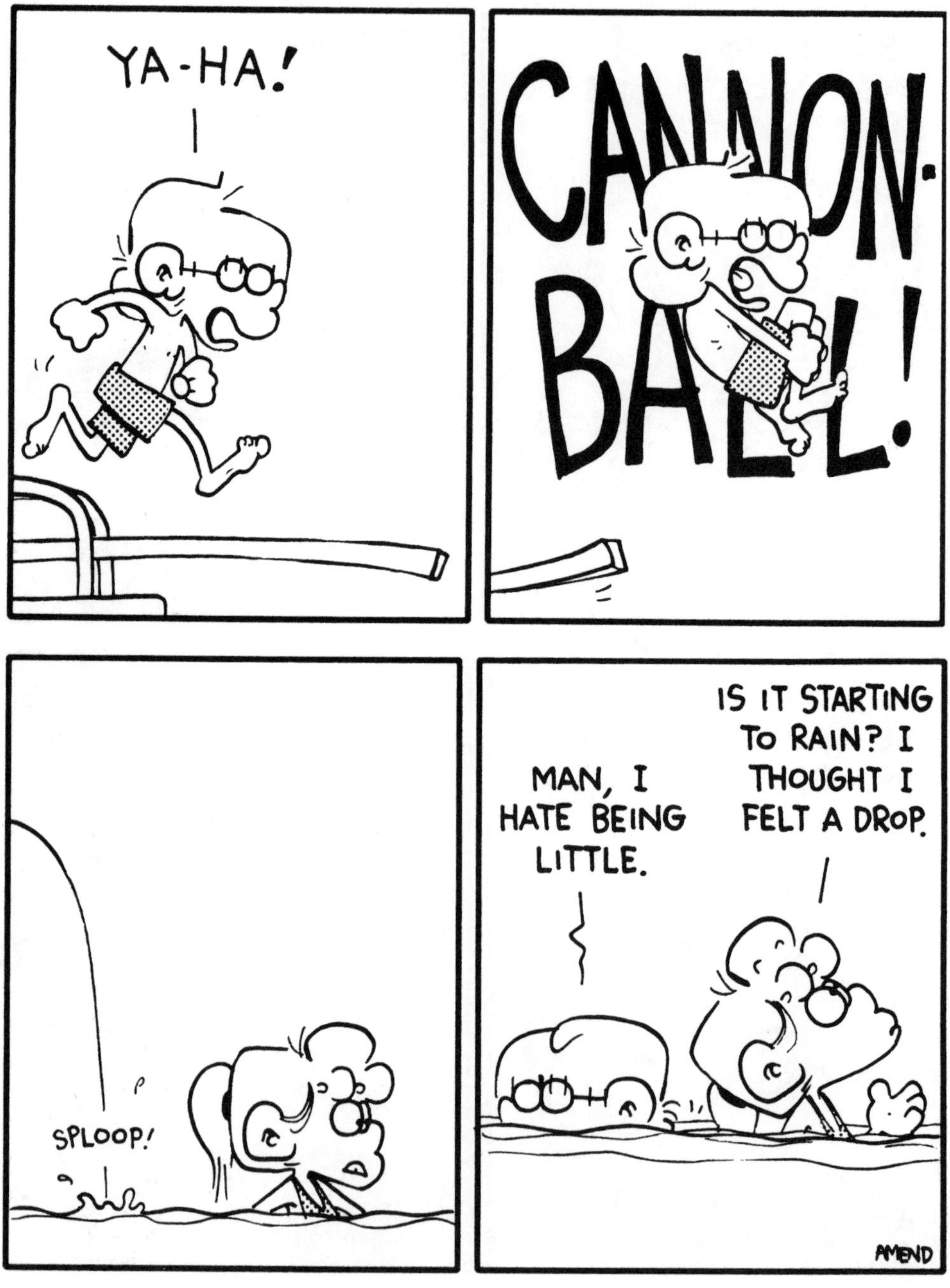
YA-HA!
CANNON-BALL!
SPLOOP!
MAN, I HATE BEING LITTLE.
IS IT STARTING TO RAIN? I THOUGHT I FELT A DROP.
AMEND

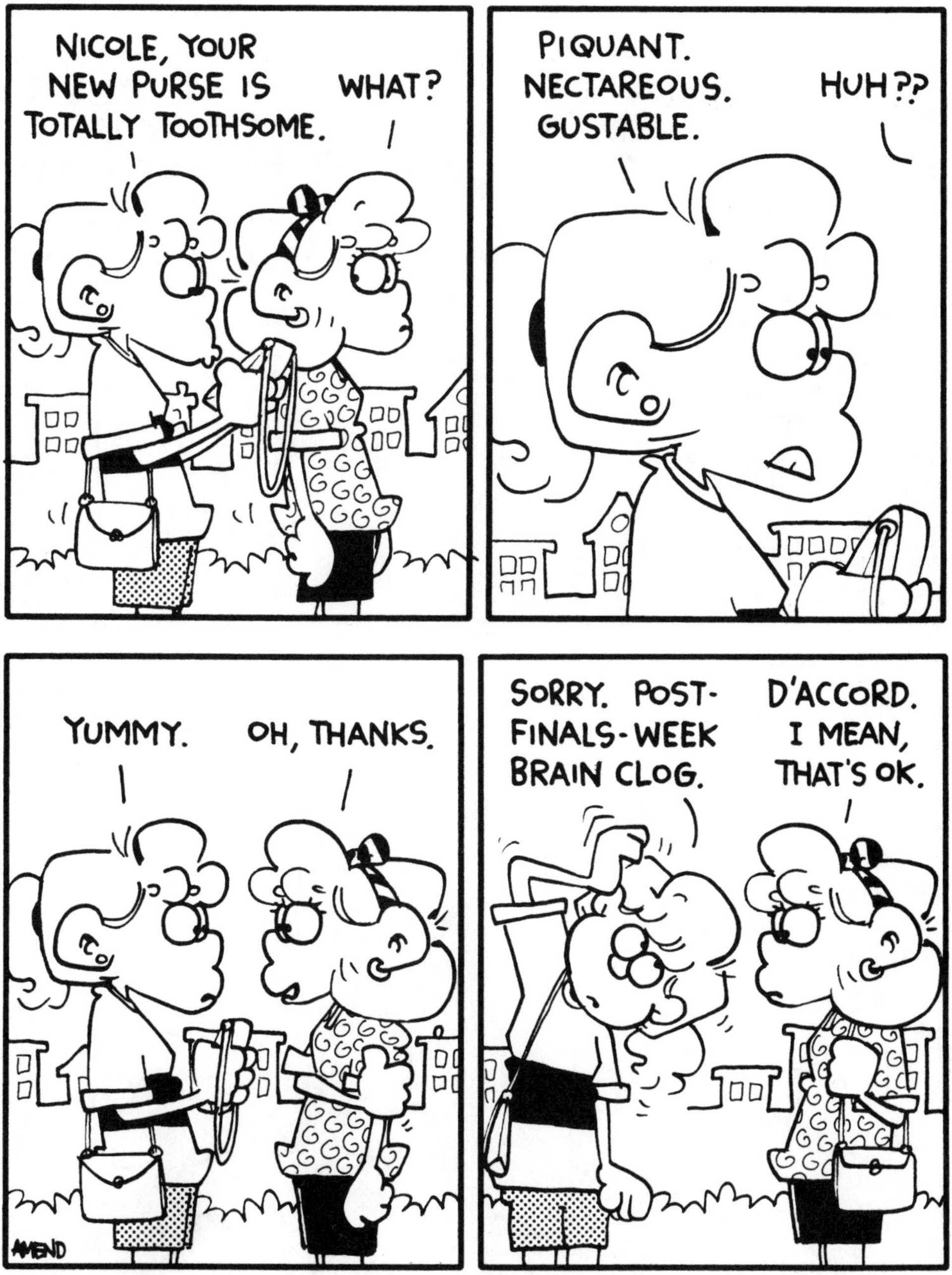
NICOLE, YOUR NEW PURSE IS TOTALLY TOOTHSOME.
WHAT?
PIQUANT. NECTAREOUS. GUSTABLE.
HUH??
YUMMY.
OH, THANKS.
AMEND
SORRY. POST-FINALS-WEEK BRAIN CLOG.
D'ACCORD. I MEAN, THAT'S OK.

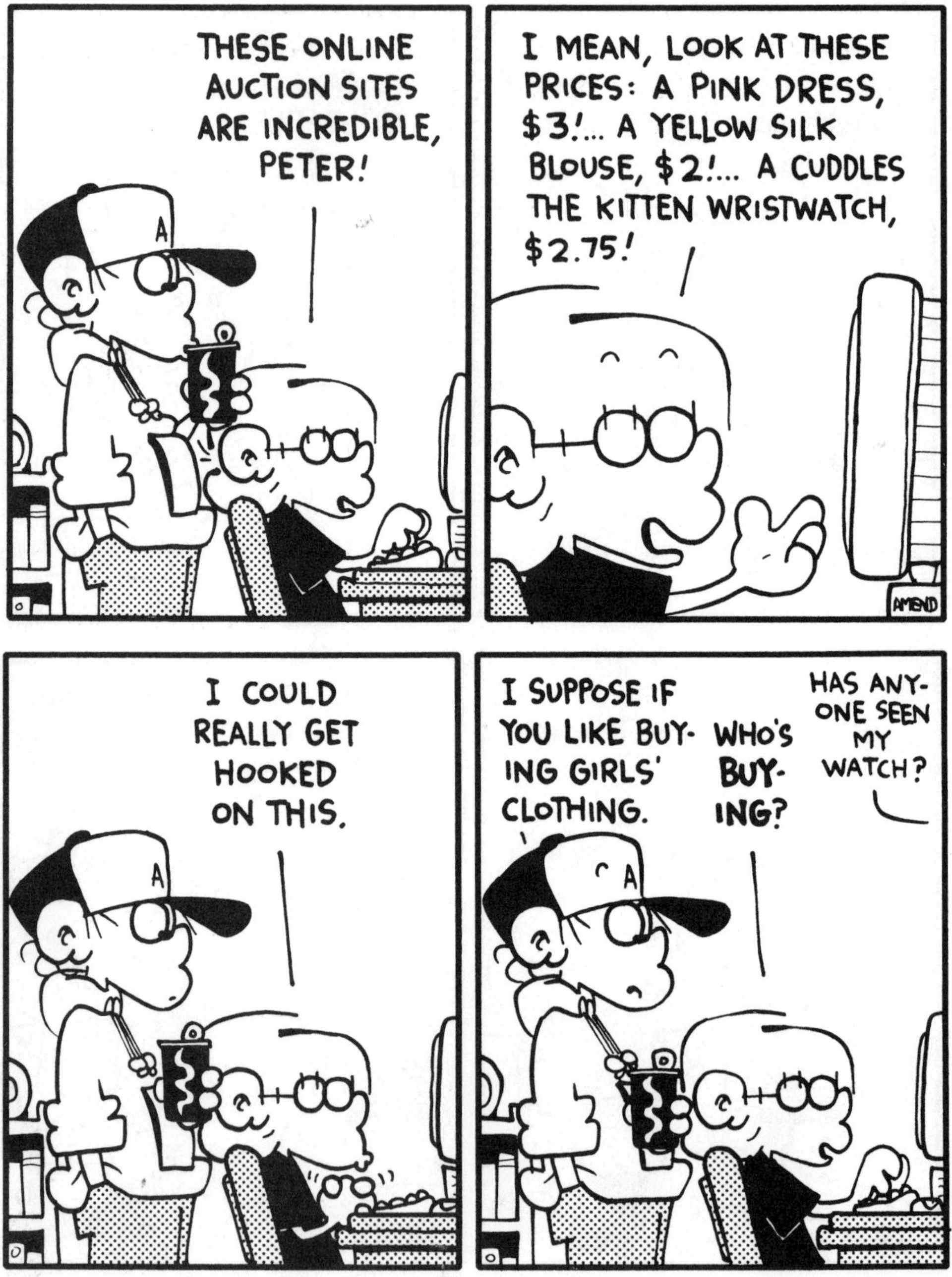
THESE ONLINE AUCTION SITES ARE INCREDIBLE, PETER!
I MEAN, LOOK AT THESE PRICES: A PINK DRESS, $3!... A YELLOW SILK BLOUSE, $2!... A CUDDLES THE KITTEN WRISTWATCH, $2.75!
AMEND
I COULD REALLY GET HOOKED ON THIS.
I SUPPOSE IF YOU LIKE BUY-ING GIRLS' CLOTHING.
WHO'S BUY-ING?
HAS ANY-ONE SEEN MY WATCH?

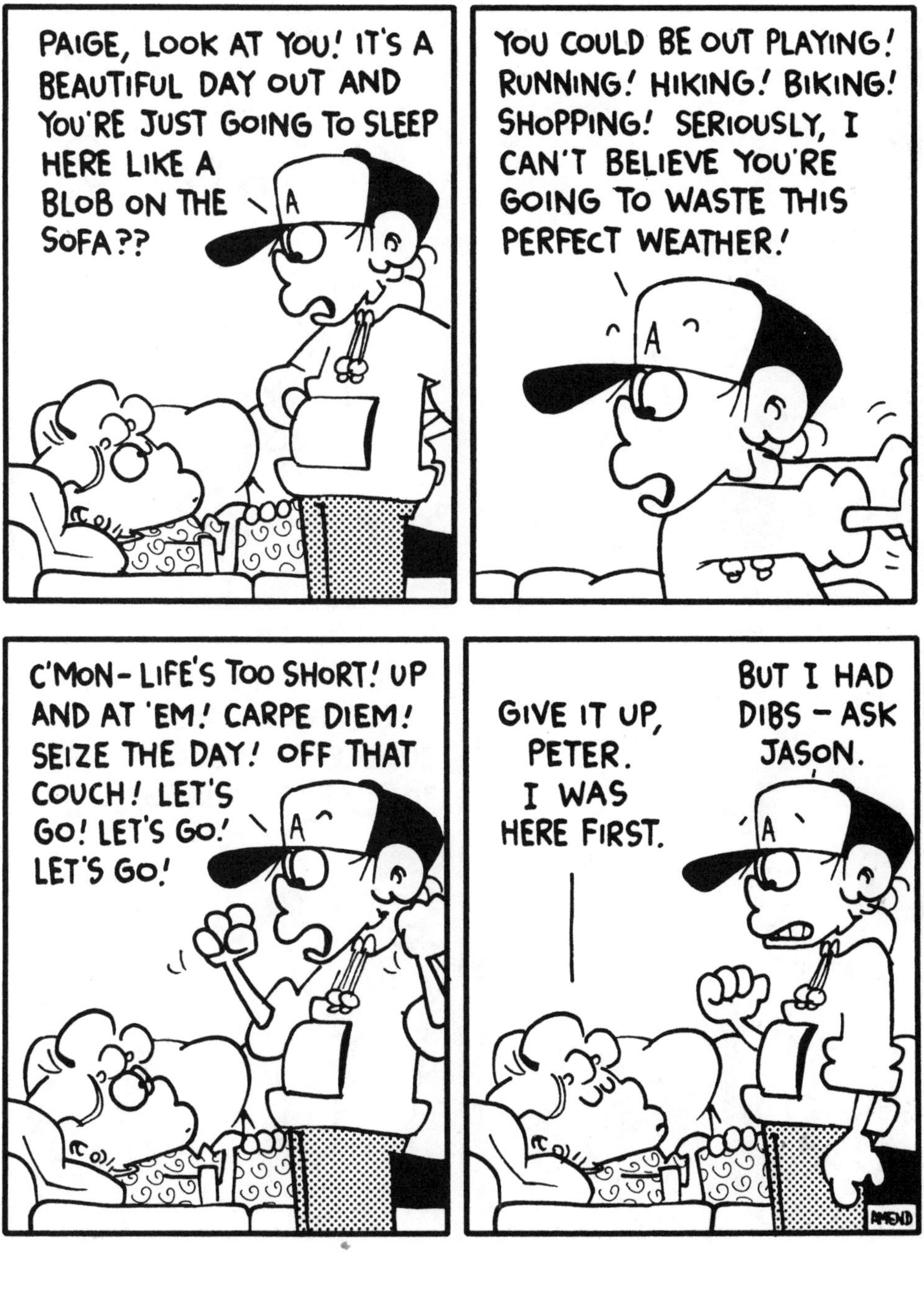
PAIGE, LOOK AT YOU! IT'S A BEAUTIFUL DAY OUT AND YOU'RE JUST GOING TO SLEEP HERE LIKE A BLOB ON THE SOFA??
YOU COULD BE OUT PLAYING! RUNNING! HIKING! BIKING! SHOPPING! SERIOUSLY, I CAN'T BELIEVE YOU'RE GOING TO WASTE THIS PERFECT WEATHER!
C'MON- LIFE'S TOO SHORT! UP AND AT 'EM! CARPE DIEM! SEIZE THE DAY! OFF THAT COUCH! LET'S GO! LET'S GO! LET'S GO!
BUT I HAD DIBS - ASK JASON.
GIVE IT UP, PETER. I WAS HERE FIRST.
AMEND

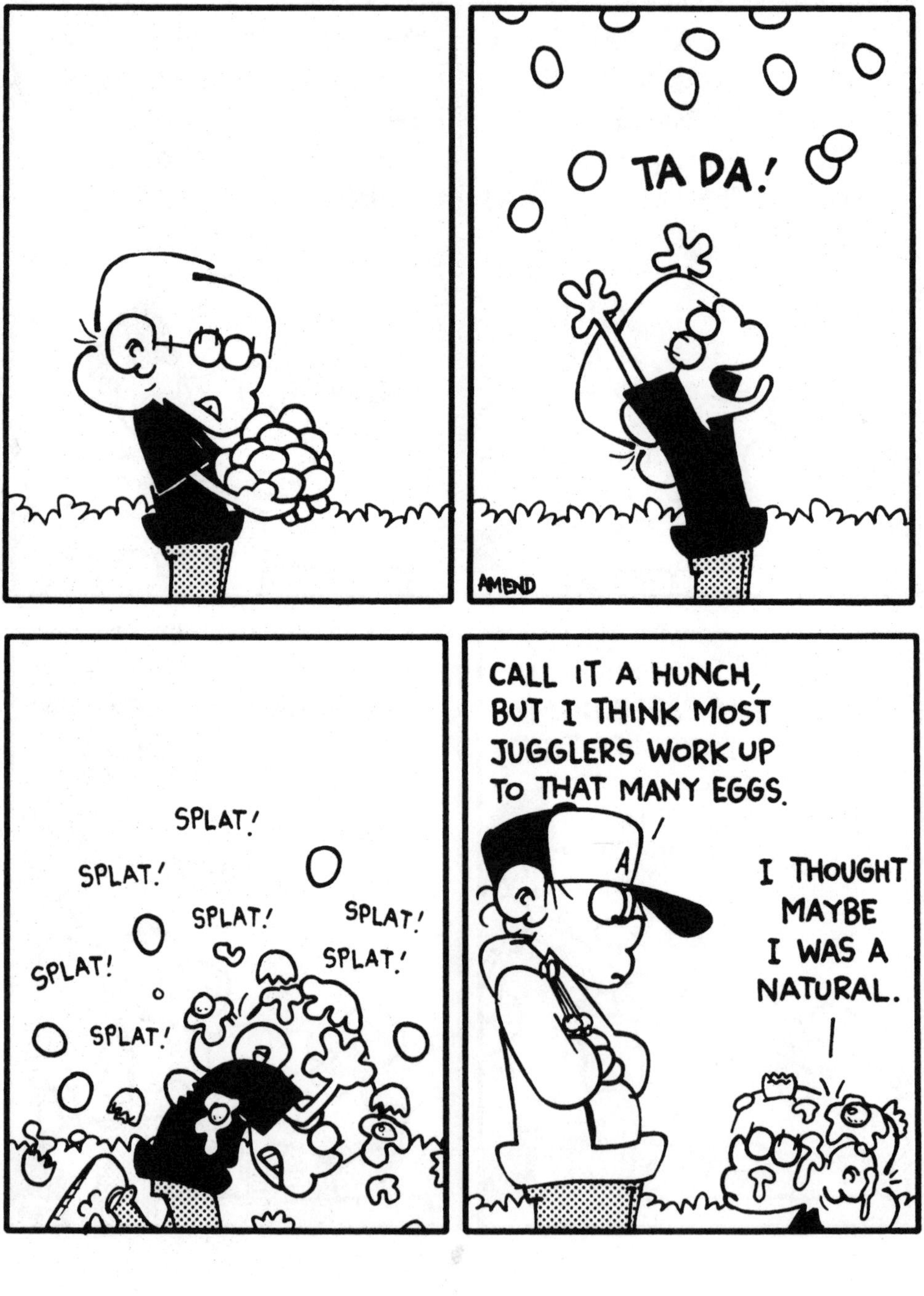
TA DA!
SPLAT!
SPLAT!
SPLAT!
SPLAT!
SPLAT!
SPLAT!
SPLAT!
CALL IT A HUNCH, BUT I THINK MOST JUGGLERS WORK UP TO THAT MANY EGGS.
I THOUGHT MAYBE I WAS A NATURAL.
AMEND

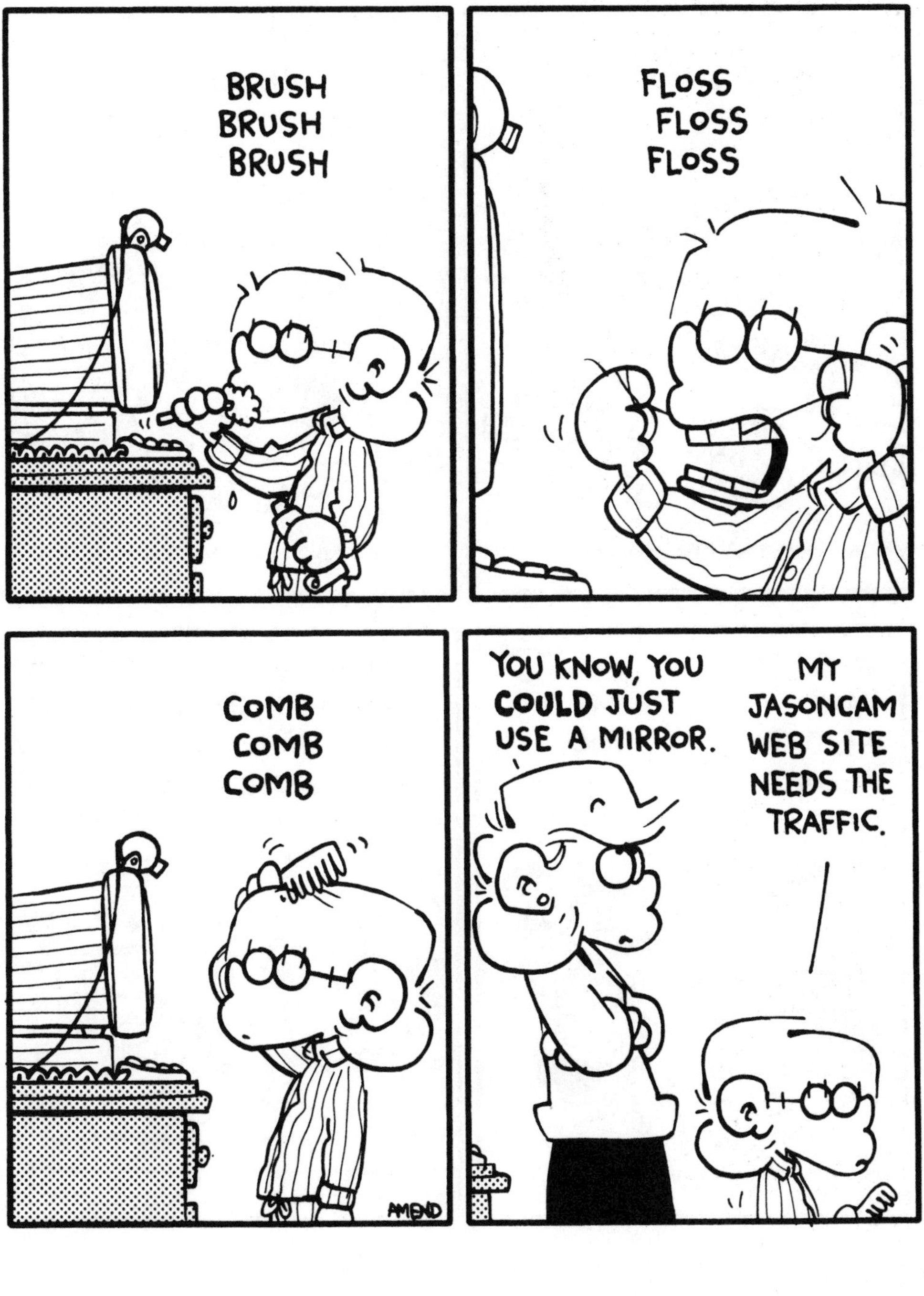
BRUSH BRUSH BRUSH
FLOSS FLOSS FLOSS
COMB COMB COMB
YOU KNOW, YOU COULD JUST USE A MIRROR.
MY JASONCAM WEB SITE NEEDS THE TRAFFIC.
AMEND

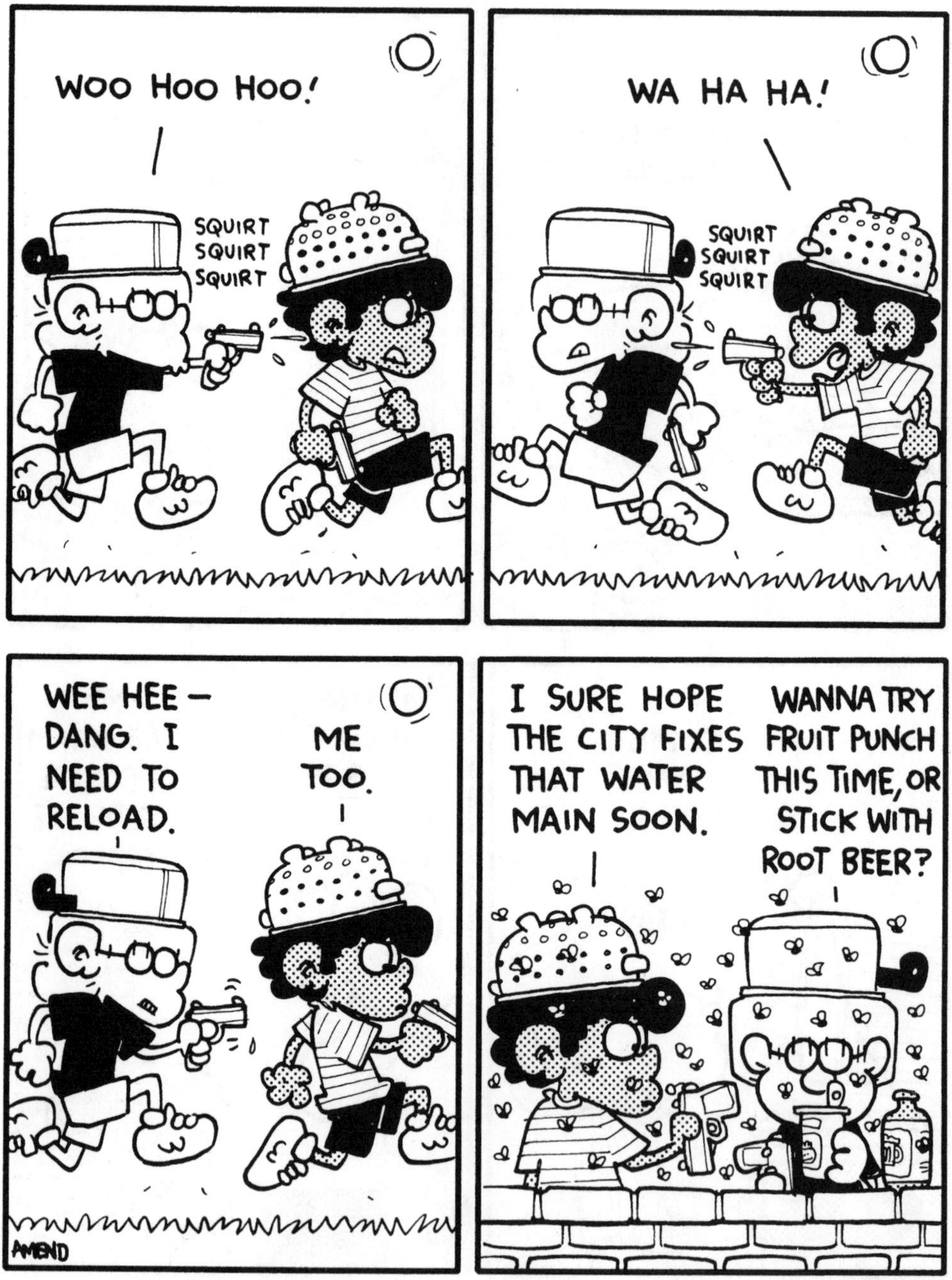
WOO HOO HOO!
SQUIRT SQUIRT SQUIRT
WA HA HA!
SQUIRT SQUIRT SQUIRT
WEE HEE— DANG. I NEED TO RELOAD.
ME TOO.
I SURE HOPE THE CITY FIXES THAT WATER MAIN SOON.
WANNA TRY FRUIT PUNCH THIS TIME, OR STICK WITH ROOT BEER?
AMEND

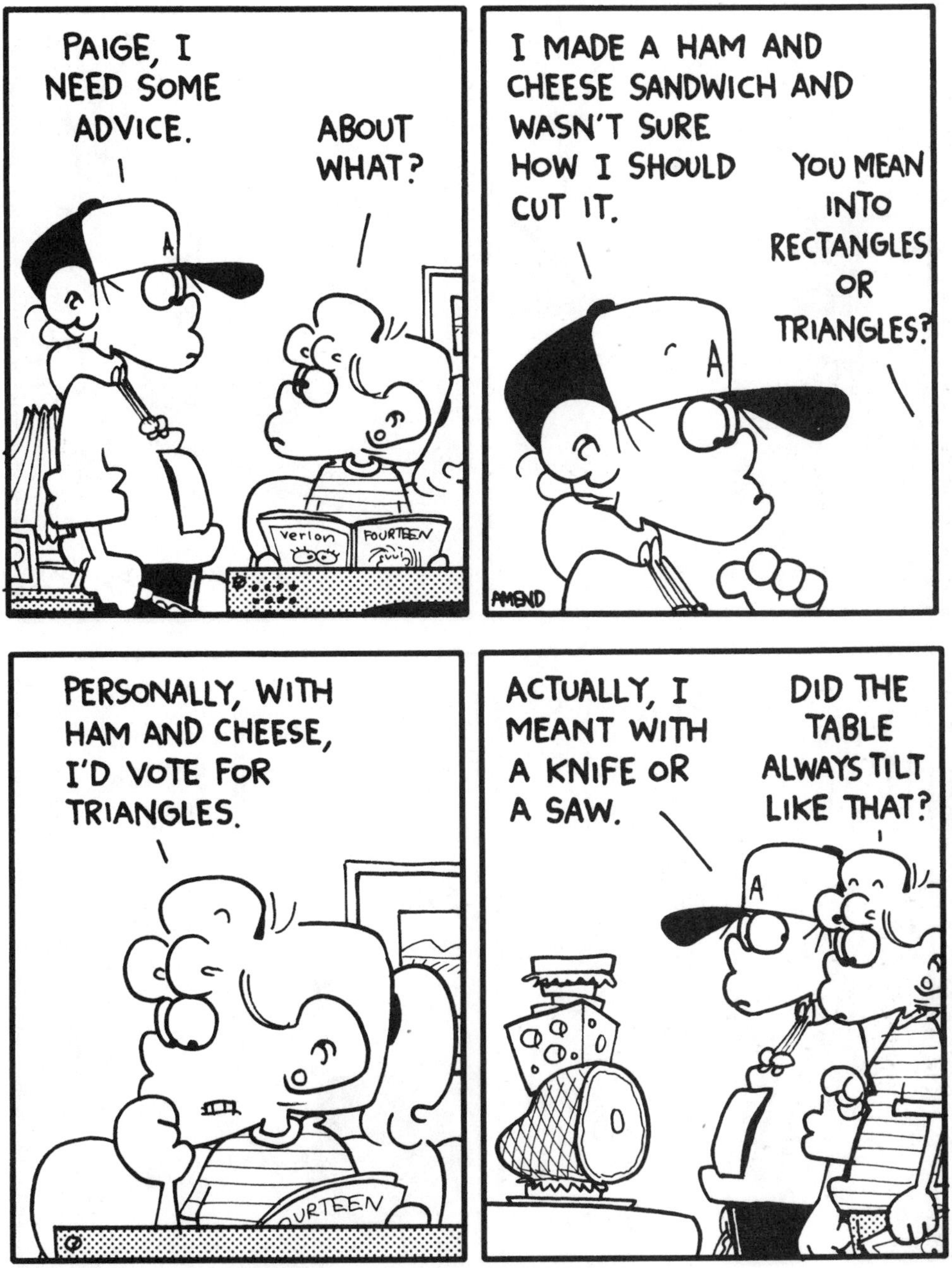
PAIGE, I NEED SOME ADVICE.
ABOUT WHAT?
I MADE A HAM AND CHEESE SANDWICH AND WASN'T SURE HOW I SHOULD CUT IT.
YOU MEAN INTO RECTANGLES OR TRIANGLES?
AMEND
PERSONALLY, WITH HAM AND CHEESE, I'D VOTE FOR TRIANGLES.
ACTUALLY, I MEANT WITH A KNIFE OR A SAW.
DID THE TABLE ALWAYS TILT LIKE THAT?

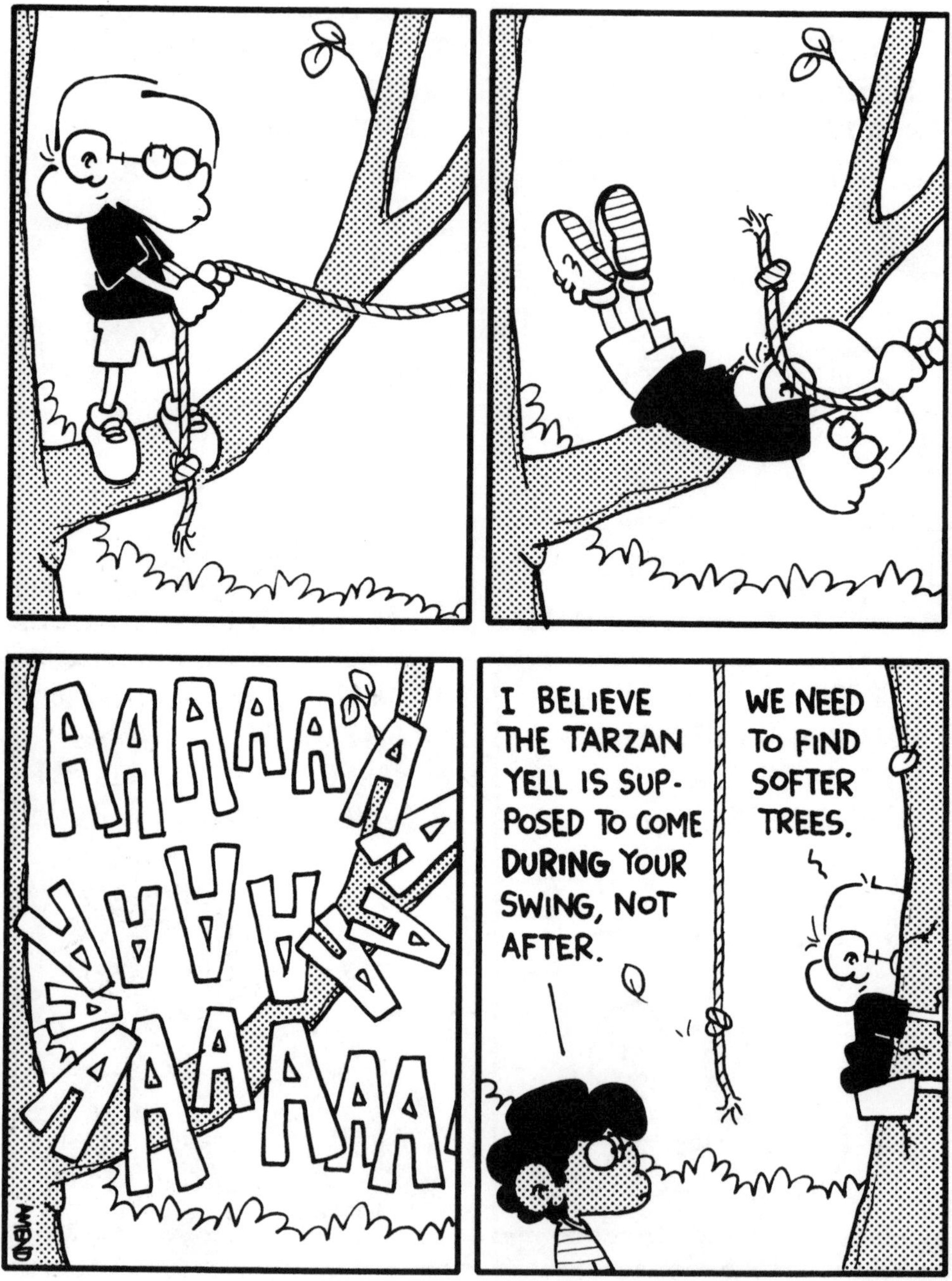
I BELIEVE THE TARZAN YELL IS SUP-POSED TO COME DURING YOUR SWING, NOT AFTER.
WE NEED TO FIND SOFTER TREES.

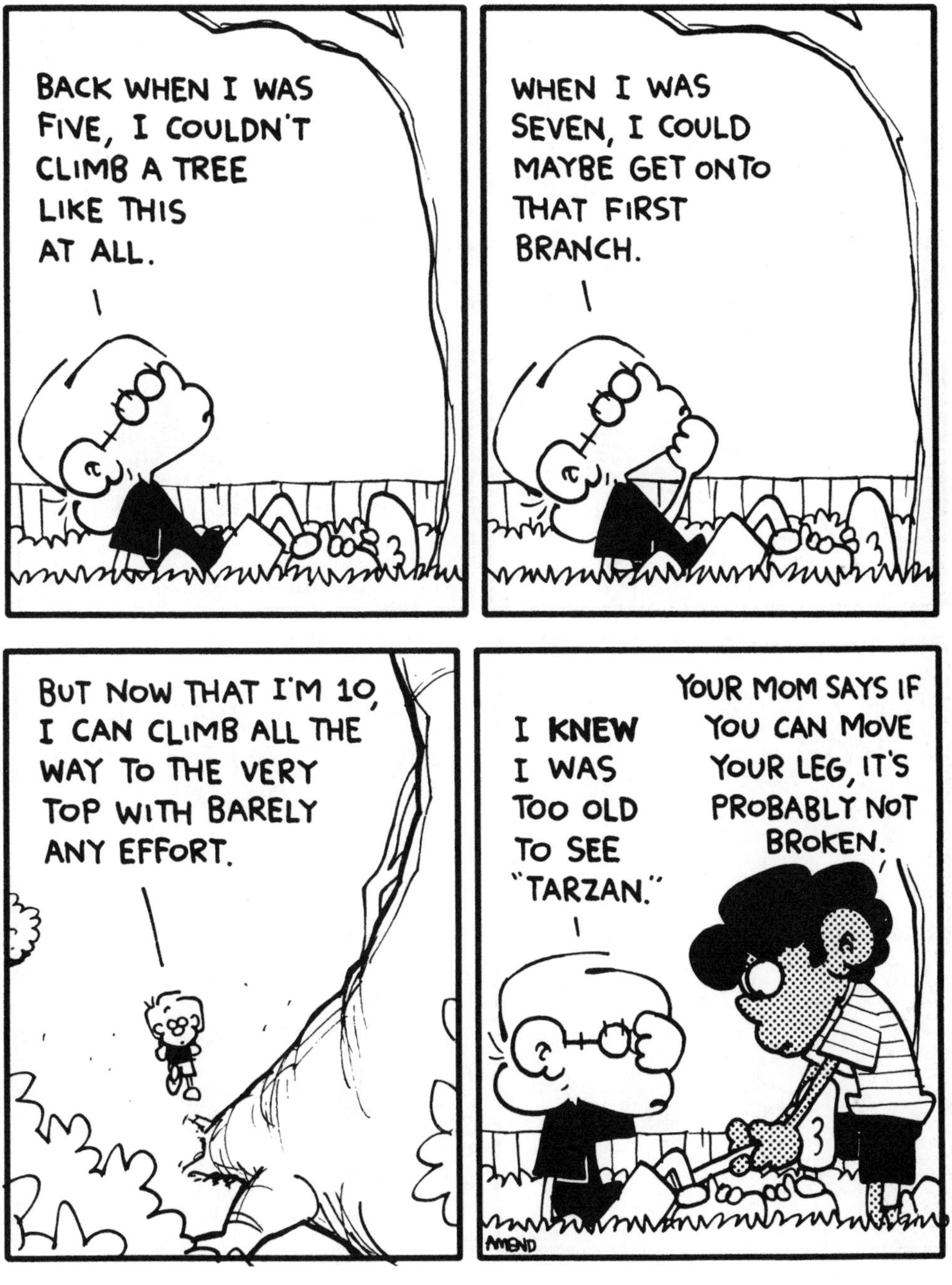
BACK WHEN I WAS FIVE, I COULDN'T CLIMB A TREE LIKE THIS AT ALL.
WHEN I WAS SEVEN, I COULD MAYBE GET ONTO THAT FIRST BRANCH.
BUT NOW THAT I'M 10, I CAN CLIMB ALL THE WAY TO THE VERY TOP WITH BARELY ANY EFFORT.
YOUR MOM SAYS IF YOU CAN MOVE YOUR LEG, IT'S PROBABLY NOT BROKEN.
I KNEW I WAS TOO OLD TO SEE "TARZAN."
AMEND

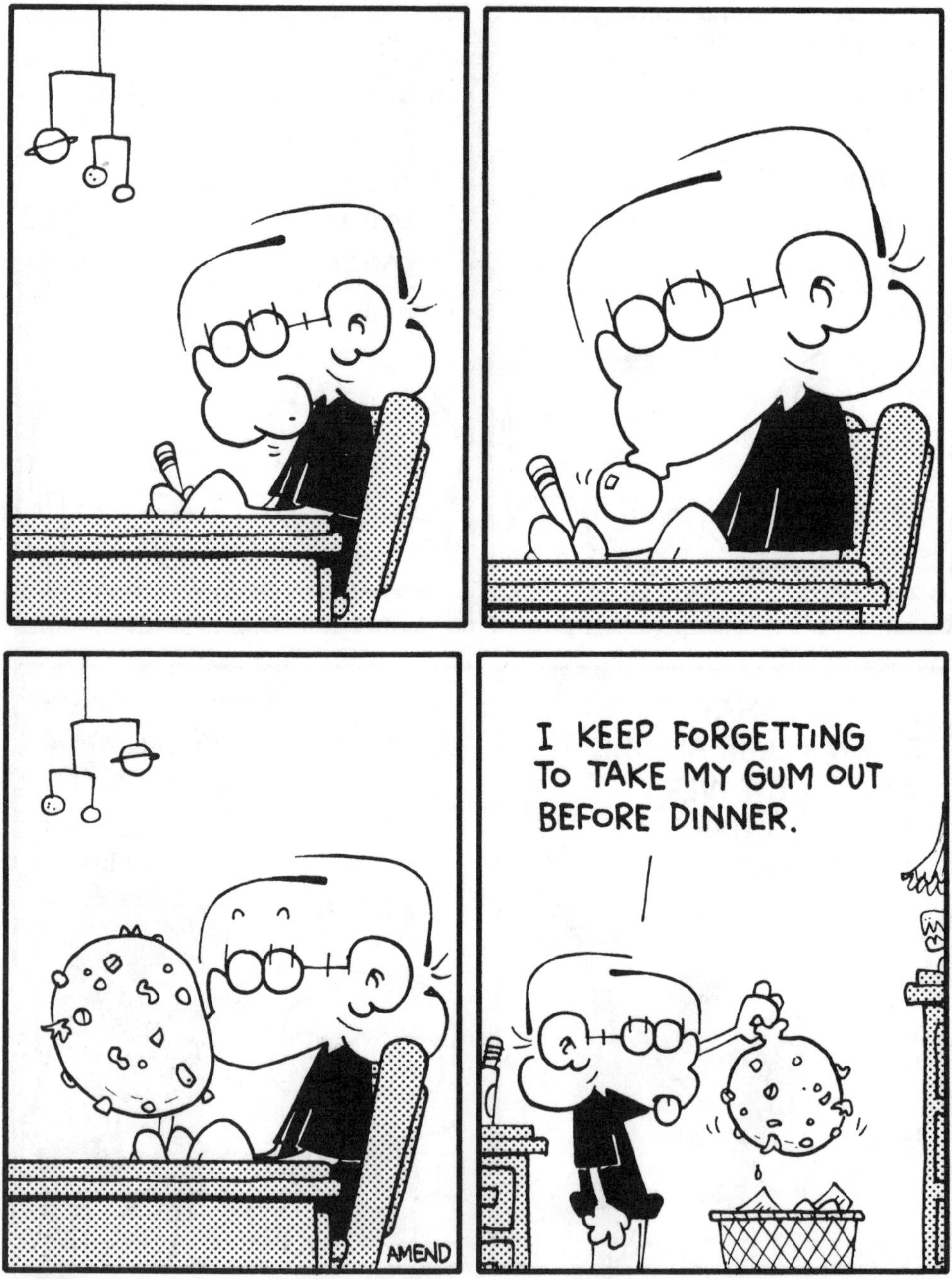
I KEEP FORGETTING TO TAKE MY GUM OUT BEFORE DINNER.
AMEND

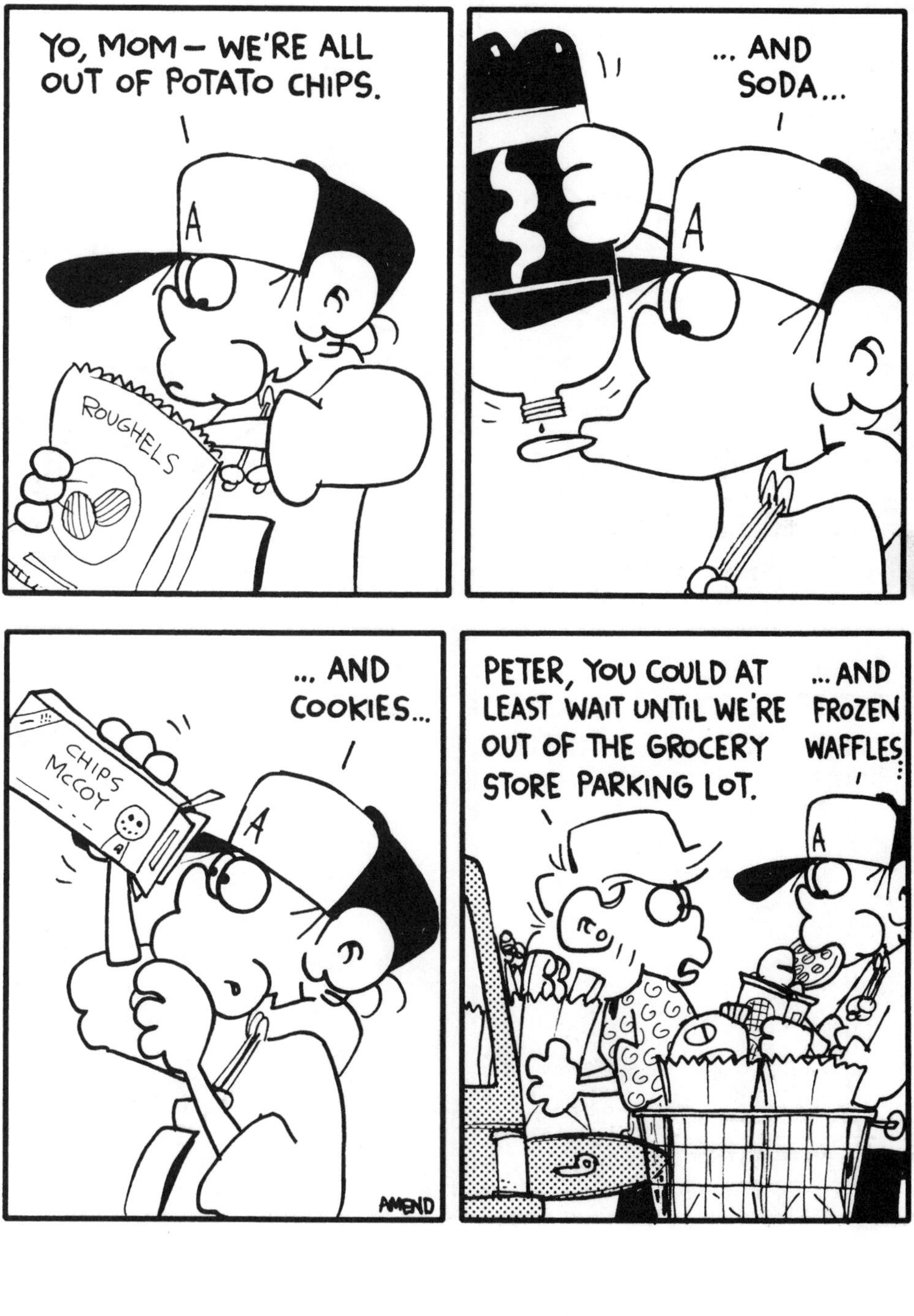
YO, MOM – WE'RE ALL OUT OF POTATO CHIPS.
ROUGHELS
... AND SODA...
... AND COOKIES...
CHIPS McCOY
AMEND
PETER, YOU COULD AT LEAST WAIT UNTIL WE'RE OUT OF THE GROCERY STORE PARKING LOT.
... AND FROZEN WAFFLES

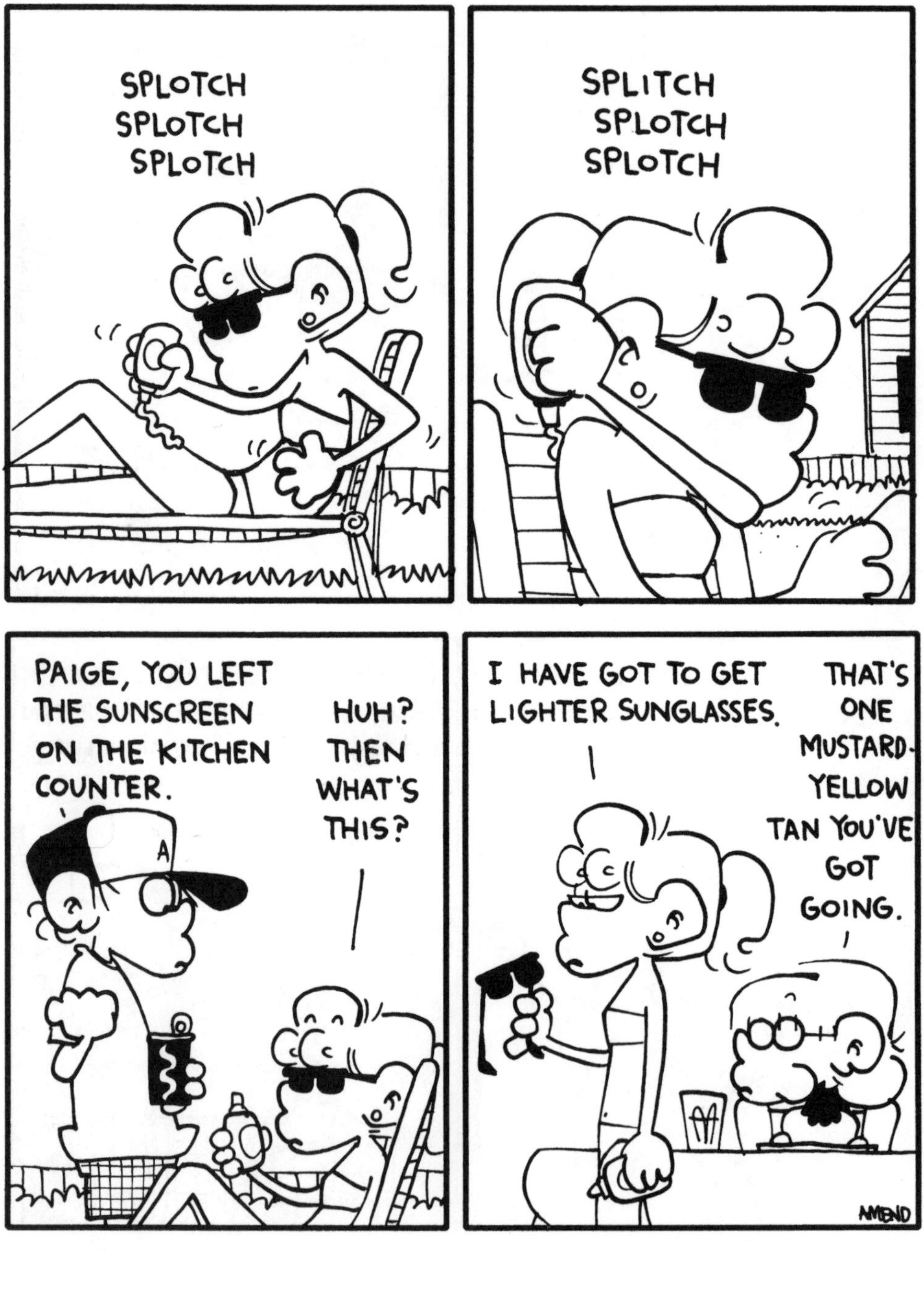
SPLOTCH
SPLOTCH
SPLOTCH
SPLITCH
SPLOTCH
SPLOTCH
PAIGE, YOU LEFT THE SUNSCREEN ON THE KITCHEN COUNTER.
HUH? THEN WHAT'S THIS?
I HAVE GOT TO GET LIGHTER SUNGLASSES.
THAT'S ONE MUSTARD-YELLOW TAN YOU'VE GOT GOING.
AMEND

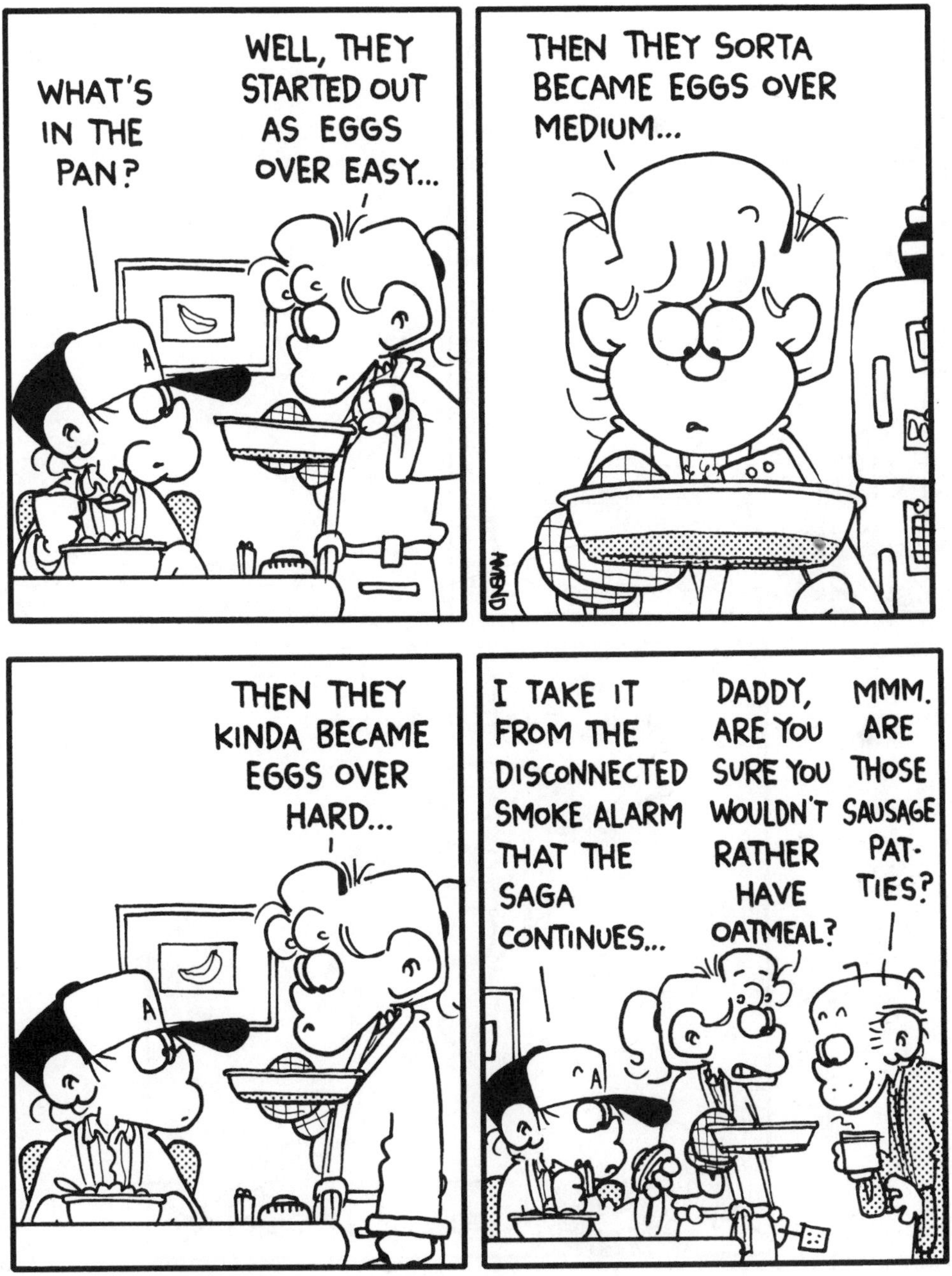
WHAT'S IN THE PAN?
WELL, THEY STARTED OUT AS EGGS OVER EASY...
THEN THEY SORTA BECAME EGGS OVER MEDIUM...
THEN THEY KINDA BECAME EGGS OVER HARD...
I TAKE IT FROM THE DISCONNECTED SMOKE ALARM THAT THE SAGA CONTINUES...
DADDY, ARE YOU SURE YOU WOULDN'T RATHER HAVE OATMEAL?
MMM. ARE THOSE SAUSAGE PAT-TIES?

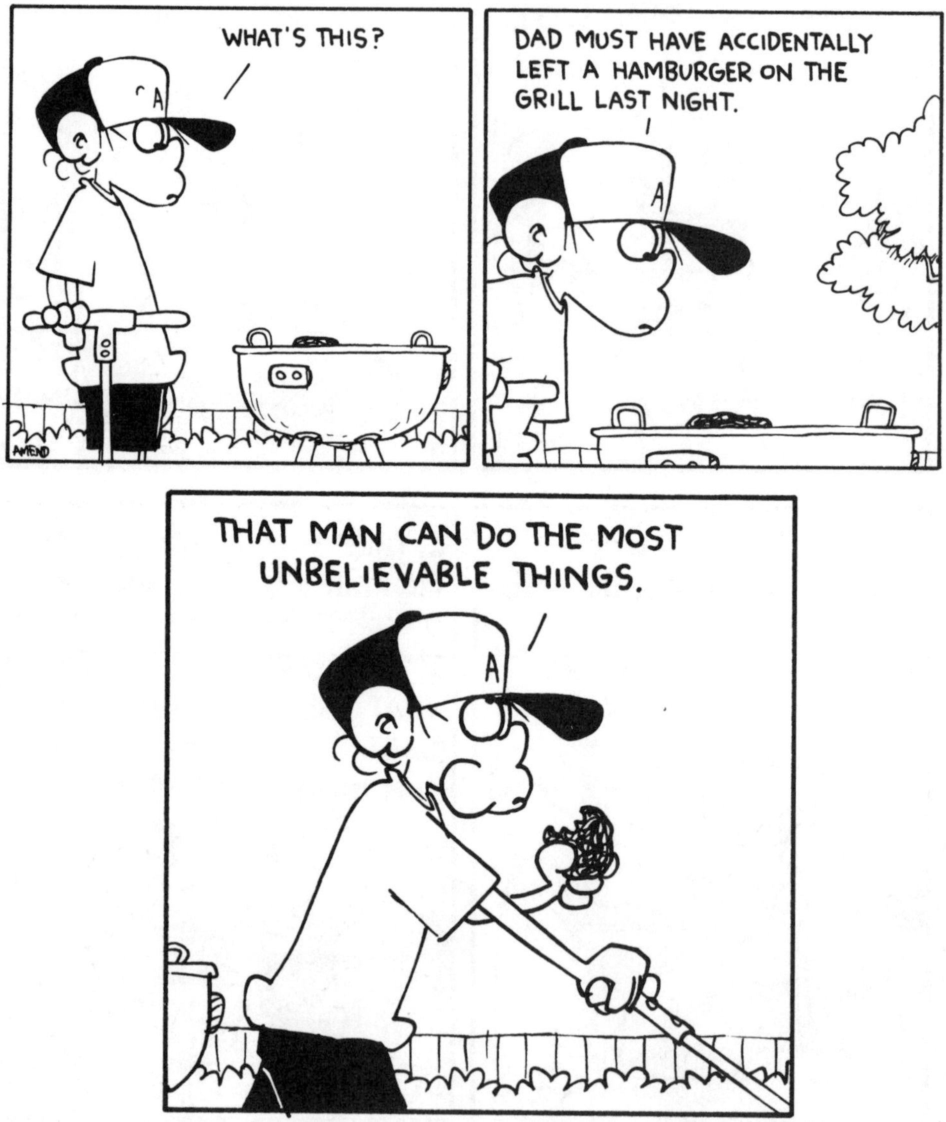
WHAT'S THIS?
DAD MUST HAVE ACCIDENTALLY LEFT A HAMBURGER ON THE GRILL LAST NIGHT.
THAT MAN CAN DO THE MOST UNBELIEVABLE THINGS.
AMEND

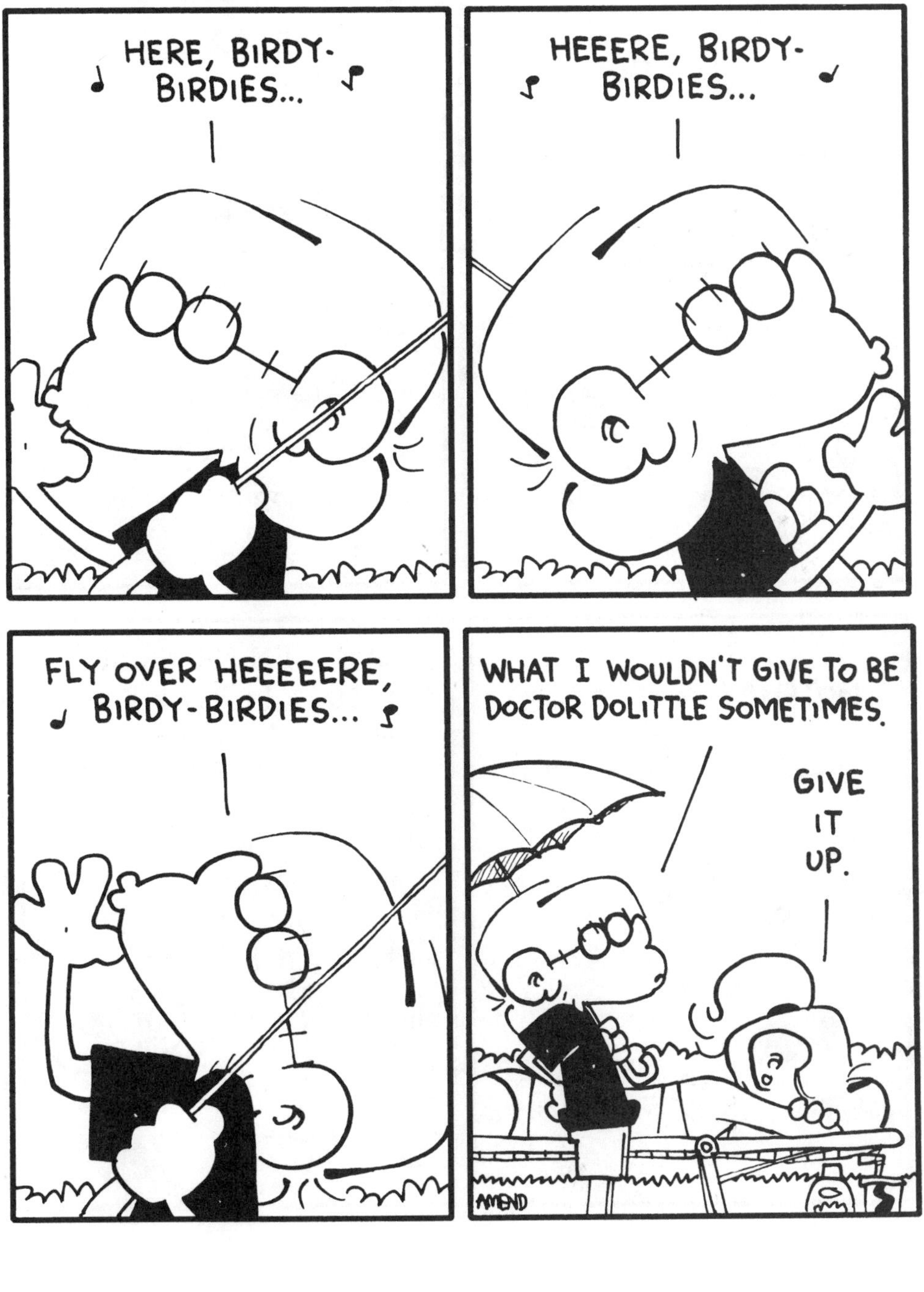
HERE, BIRDY-BIRDIES...
HEEERE, BIRDY-BIRDIES...
FLY OVER HEEEEERE, BIRDY-BIRDIES...
WHAT I WOULDN'T GIVE TO BE DOCTOR DOLITTLE SOMETIMES.
GIVE IT UP.
AMEND

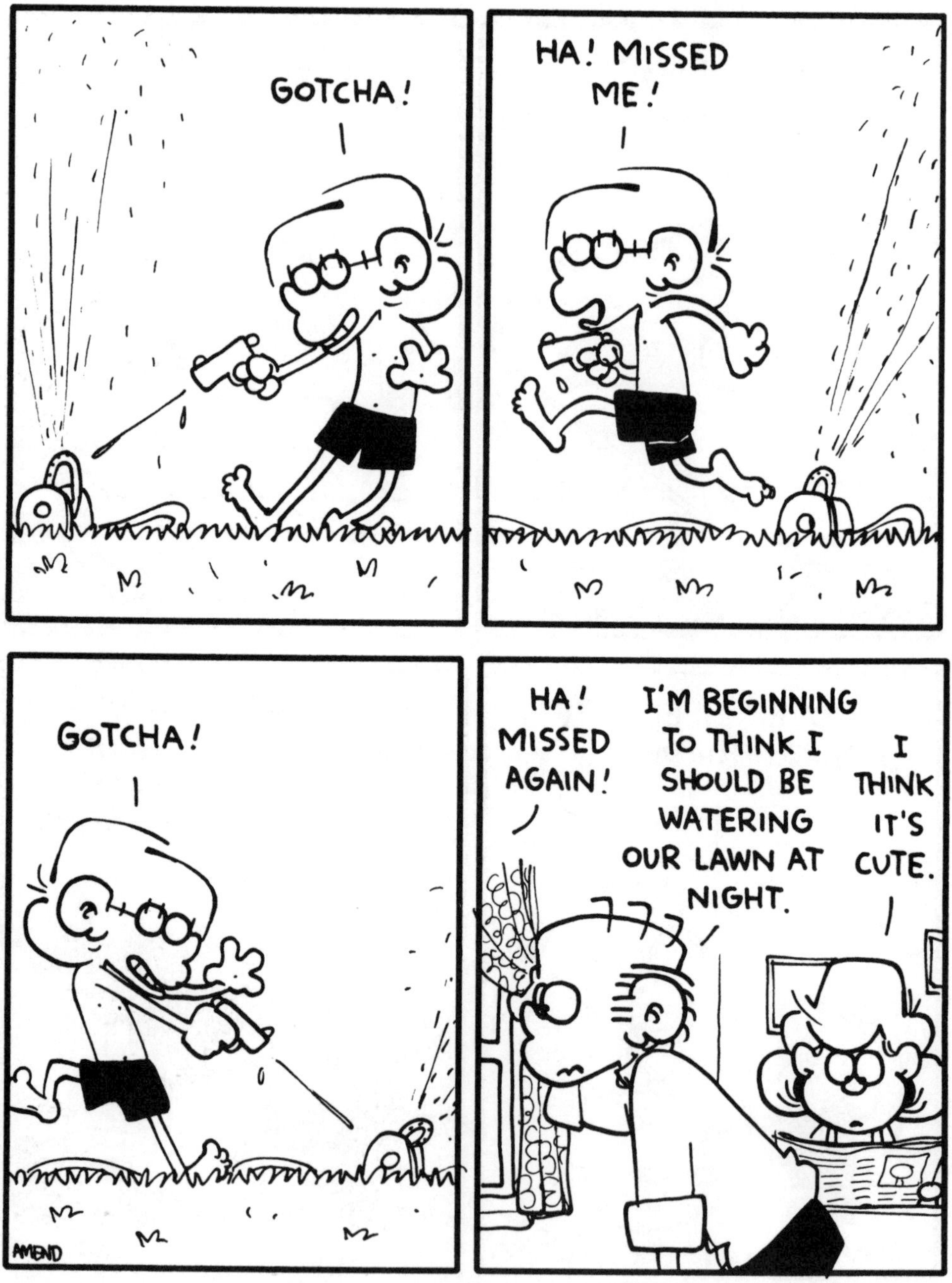
GOTCHA!
HA! MISSED ME!
GOTCHA!
HA! MISSED AGAIN!
I'M BEGINNING TO THINK I SHOULD BE WATERING OUR LAWN AT NIGHT.
I THINK IT'S CUTE.
AMEND

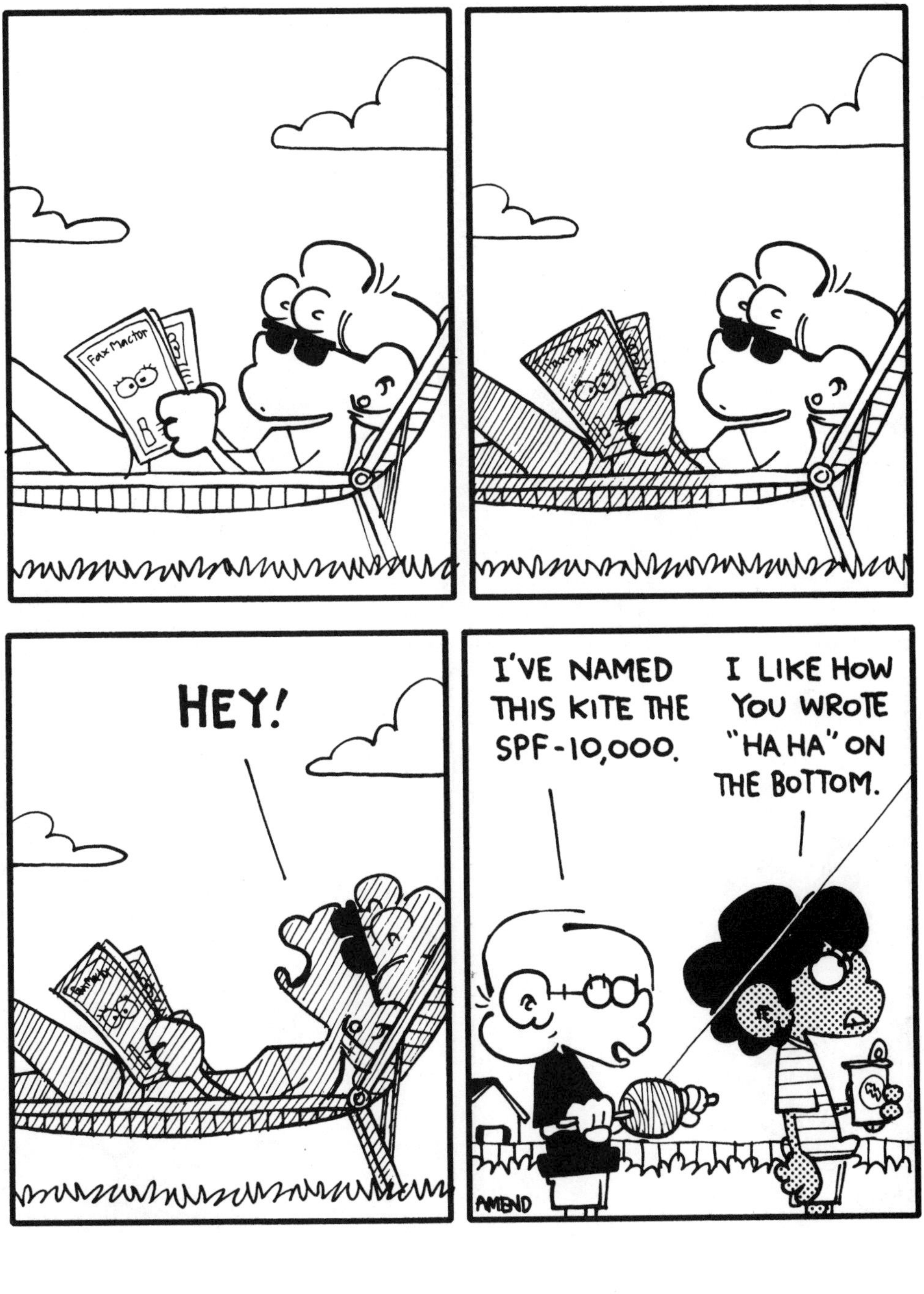
Fax Mactor
HEY!
I'VE NAMED THIS KITE THE SPF-10,000.
I LIKE HOW YOU WROTE "HA HA" ON THE BOTTOM.
AMEND

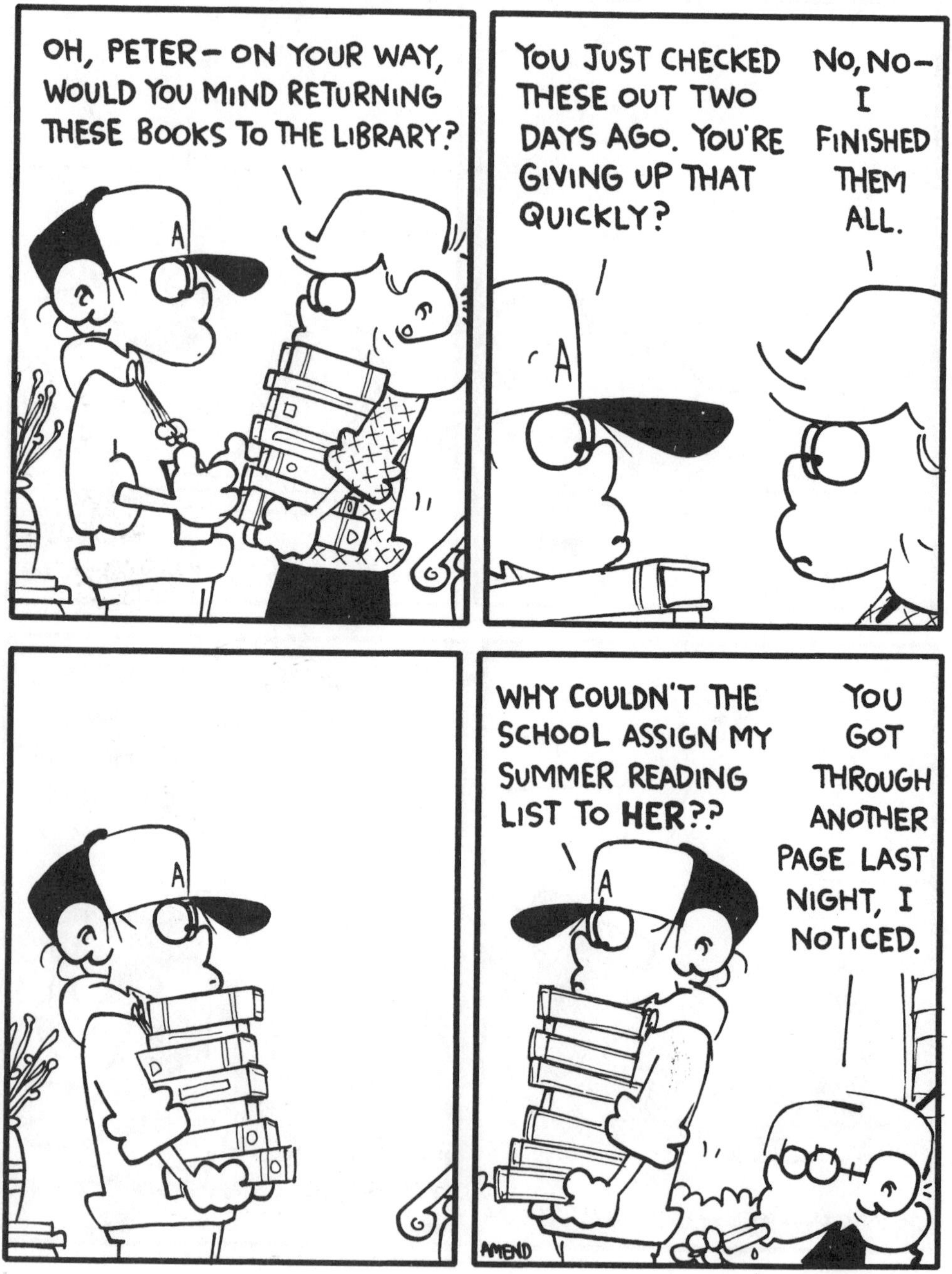
OH, PETER — ON YOUR WAY, WOULD YOU MIND RETURNING THESE BOOKS TO THE LIBRARY?
YOU JUST CHECKED THESE OUT TWO DAYS AGO. YOU'RE GIVING UP THAT QUICKLY?
NO, NO — I FINISHED THEM ALL.
WHY COULDN'T THE SCHOOL ASSIGN MY SUMMER READING LIST TO HER??
YOU GOT THROUGH ANOTHER PAGE LAST NIGHT, I NOTICED.
AMEND

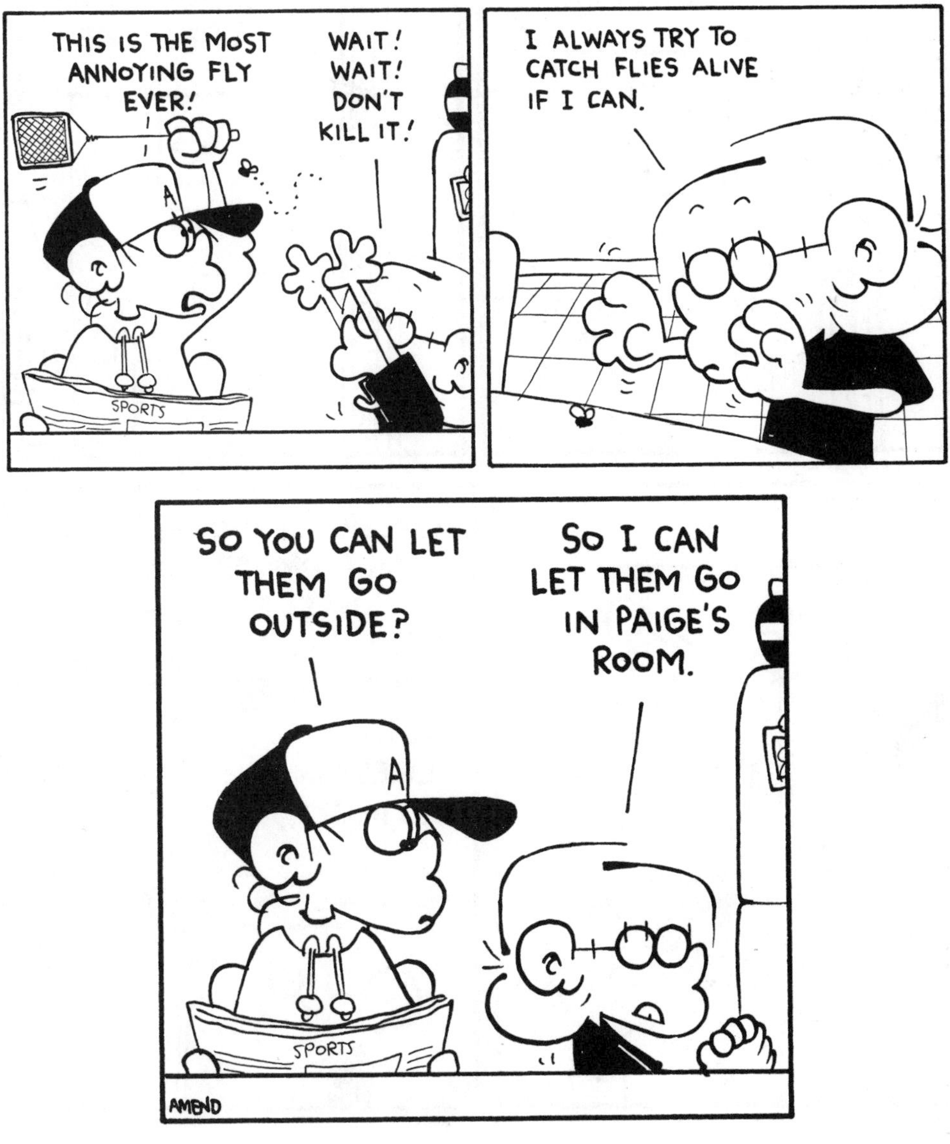
THIS IS THE MOST ANNOYING FLY EVER!
WAIT! WAIT! DON'T KILL IT!
I ALWAYS TRY TO CATCH FLIES ALIVE IF I CAN.
SPORTS
SO YOU CAN LET THEM GO OUTSIDE?
SO I CAN LET THEM GO IN PAIGE'S ROOM.
SPORTS
AMEND

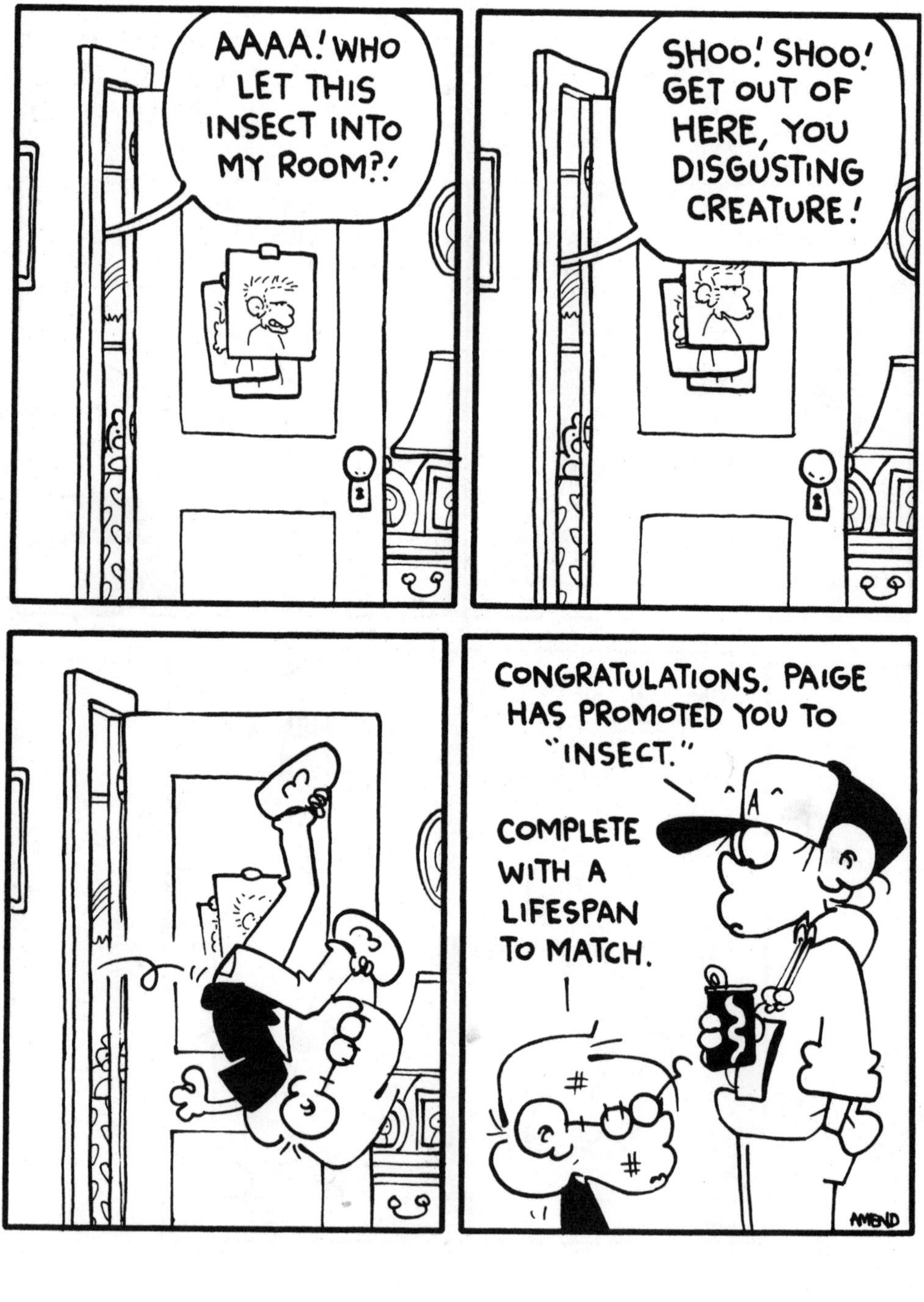
AAAA! WHO LET THIS INSECT INTO MY ROOM?!
SHOO! SHOO! GET OUT OF HERE, YOU DISGUSTING CREATURE!
CONGRATULATIONS. PAIGE HAS PROMOTED YOU TO "INSECT."
COMPLETE WITH A LIFESPAN TO MATCH.
AMEND

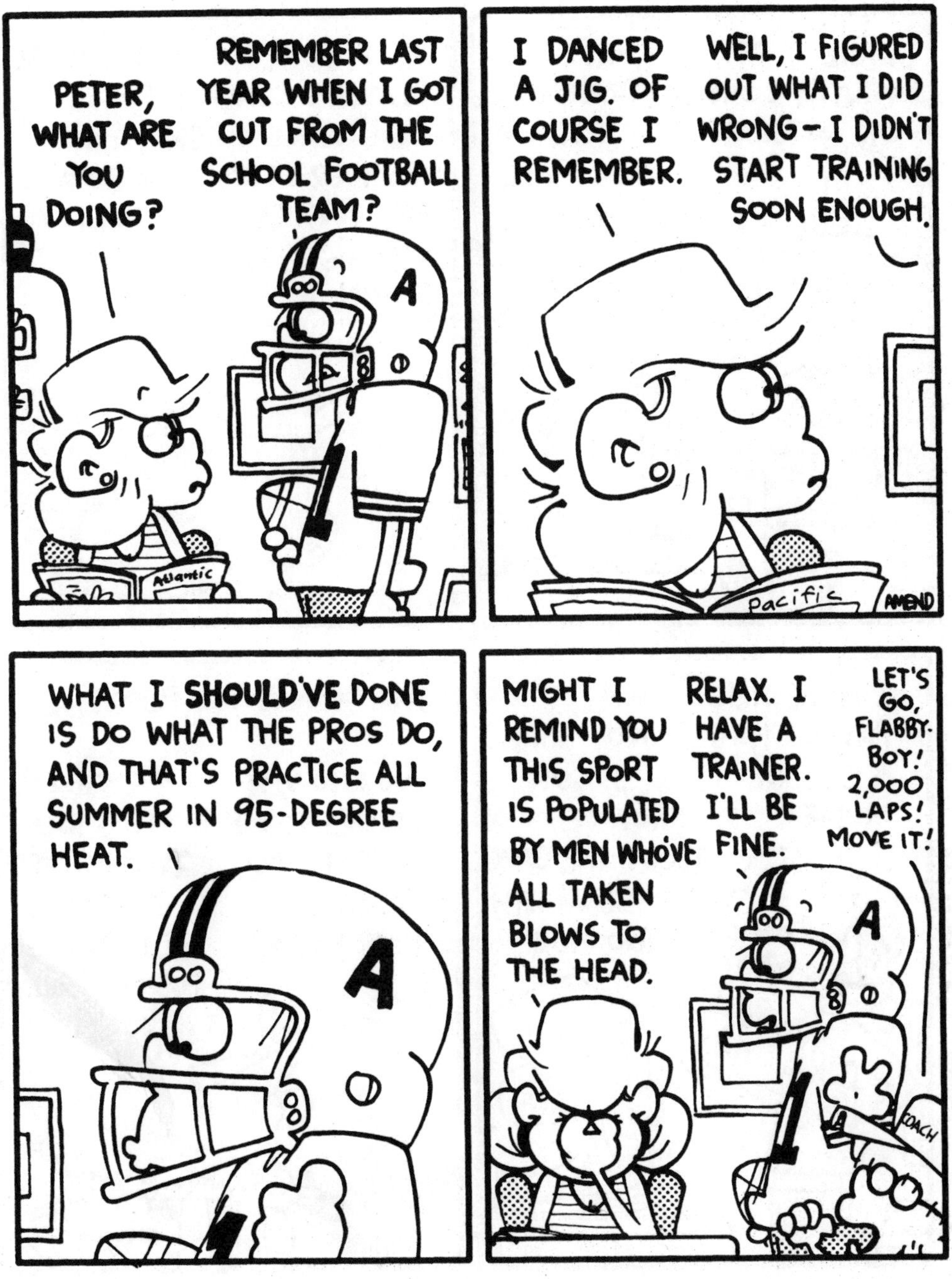
PETER, WHAT ARE YOU DOING?
REMEMBER LAST YEAR WHEN I GOT CUT FROM THE SCHOOL FOOTBALL TEAM?
Atlantic
I DANCED A JIG. OF COURSE I REMEMBER.
WELL, I FIGURED OUT WHAT I DID WRONG – I DIDN'T START TRAINING SOON ENOUGH.
Pacific
AMEND
WHAT I SHOULD'VE DONE IS DO WHAT THE PROS DO, AND THAT'S PRACTICE ALL SUMMER IN 95-DEGREE HEAT.
MIGHT I REMIND YOU THIS SPORT IS POPULATED BY MEN WHO'VE ALL TAKEN BLOWS TO THE HEAD.
RELAX. I HAVE A TRAINER. I'LL BE FINE.
LET'S GO, FLABBY-BOY! 2,000 LAPS! MOVE IT!
COACH

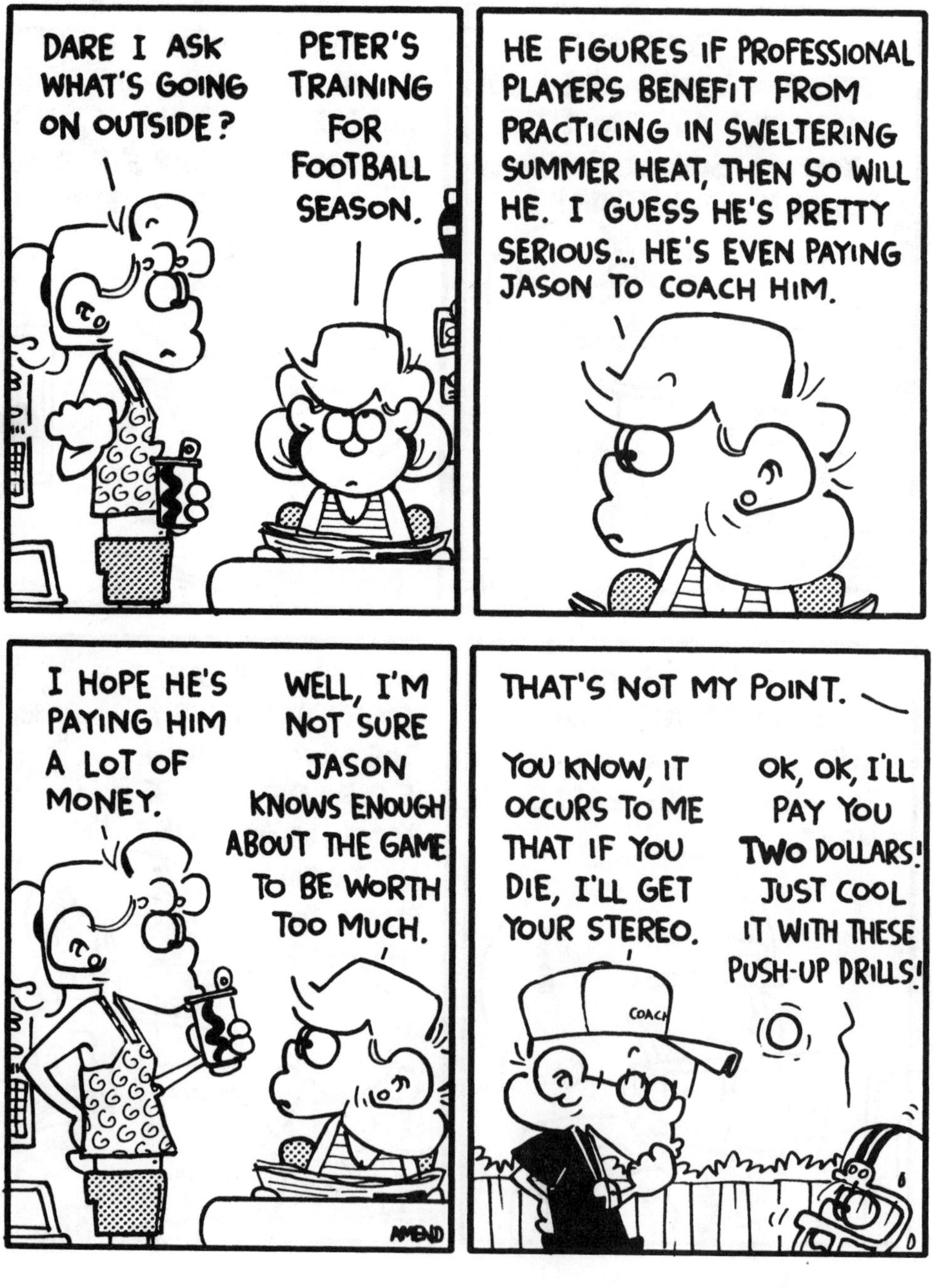
DARE I ASK WHAT'S GOING ON OUTSIDE?
PETER'S TRAINING FOR FOOTBALL SEASON.
HE FIGURES IF PROFESSIONAL PLAYERS BENEFIT FROM PRACTICING IN SWELTERING SUMMER HEAT, THEN SO WILL HE. I GUESS HE'S PRETTY SERIOUS... HE'S EVEN PAYING JASON TO COACH HIM.
I HOPE HE'S PAYING HIM A LOT OF MONEY.
WELL, I'M NOT SURE JASON KNOWS ENOUGH ABOUT THE GAME TO BE WORTH TOO MUCH.
AMEND
THAT'S NOT MY POINT.
YOU KNOW, IT OCCURS TO ME THAT IF YOU DIE, I'LL GET YOUR STEREO.
OK, OK, I'LL PAY YOU TWO DOLLARS! JUST COOL IT WITH THESE PUSH-UP DRILLS!
COACH

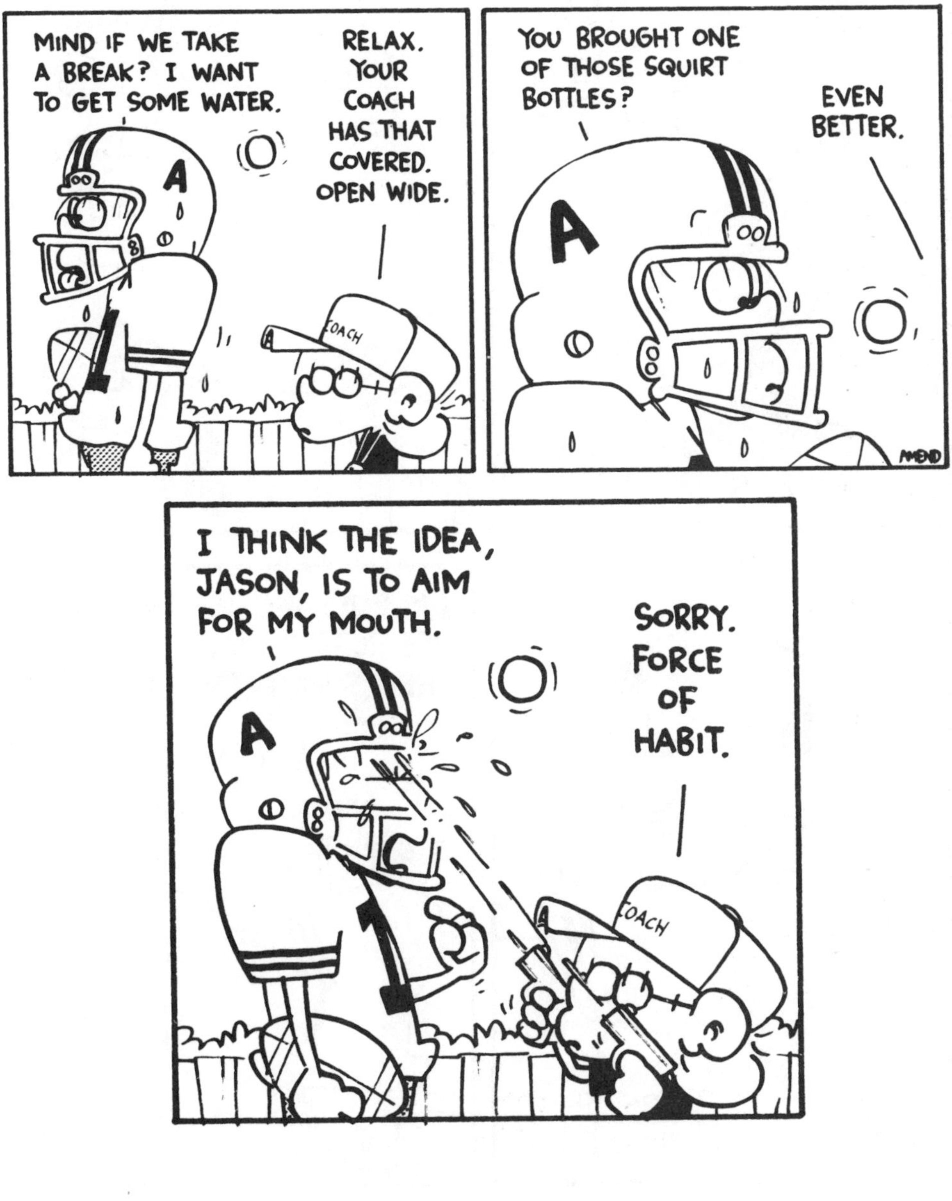
MIND IF WE TAKE A BREAK? I WANT TO GET SOME WATER.
RELAX. YOUR COACH HAS THAT COVERED. OPEN WIDE.
COACH
YOU BROUGHT ONE OF THOSE SQUIRT BOTTLES?
EVEN BETTER.
AMEND
I THINK THE IDEA, JASON, IS TO AIM FOR MY MOUTH.
SORRY. FORCE OF HABIT.
COACH

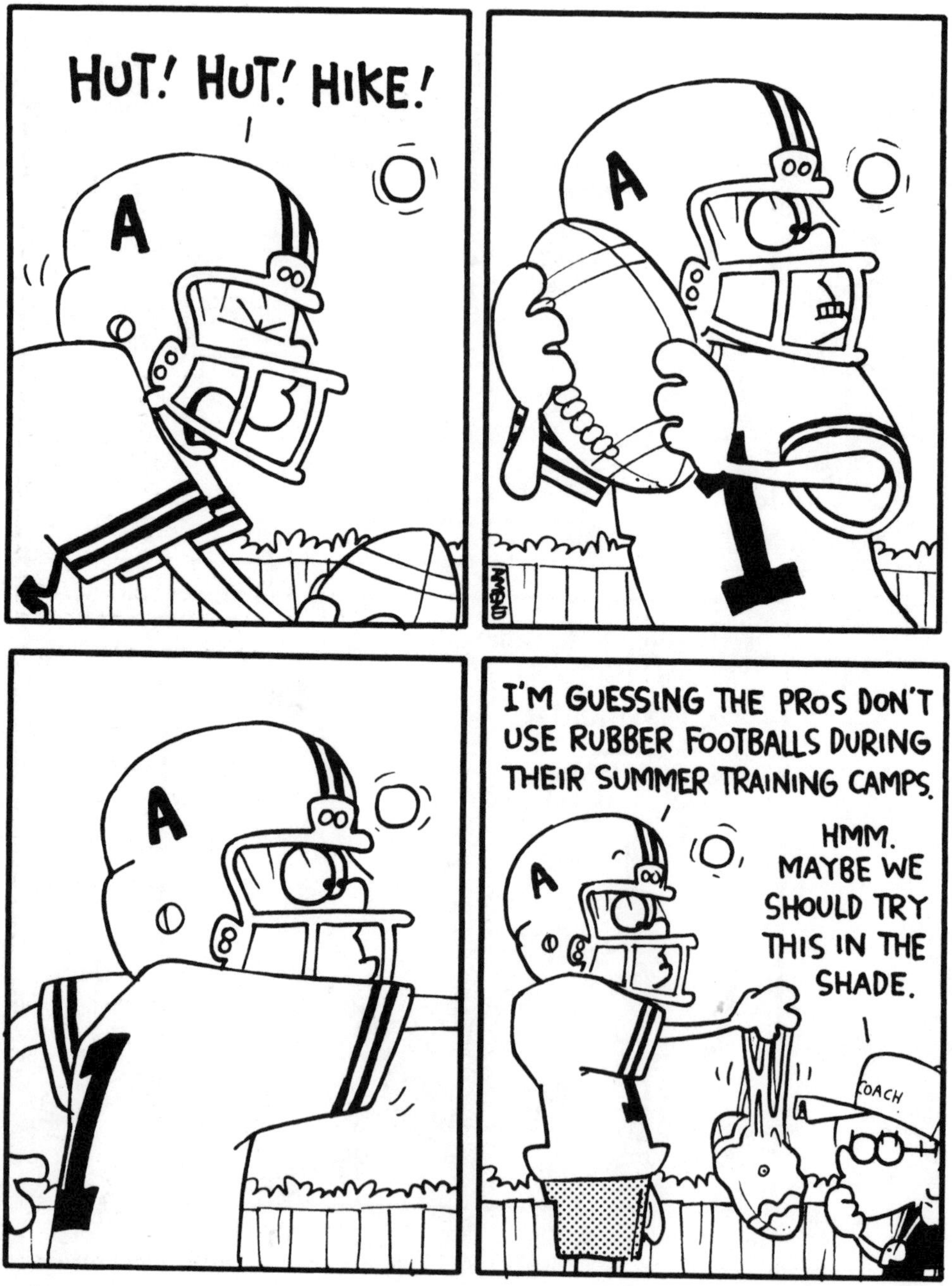
HUT! HUT! HIKE!
AMEND
I'M GUESSING THE PROS DON'T USE RUBBER FOOTBALLS DURING THEIR SUMMER TRAINING CAMPS.
HMM. MAYBE WE SHOULD TRY THIS IN THE SHADE.
COACH

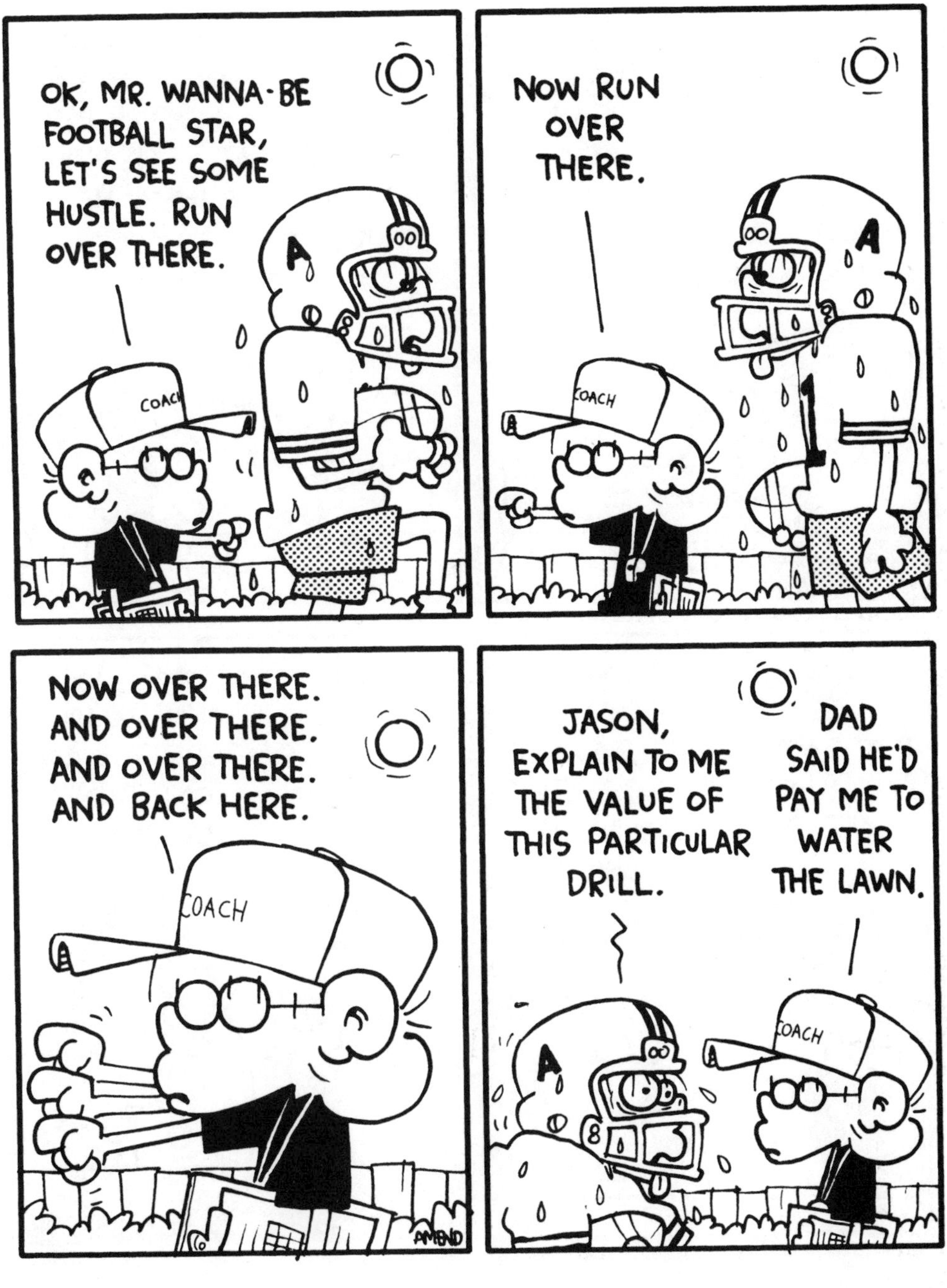
OK, MR. WANNA-BE FOOTBALL STAR, LET'S SEE SOME HUSTLE. RUN OVER THERE.
COACH
A
NOW RUN OVER THERE.
COACH
A
NOW OVER THERE. AND OVER THERE. AND OVER THERE. AND BACK HERE.
COACH
AMEND
JASON, EXPLAIN TO ME THE VALUE OF THIS PARTICULAR DRILL.
DAD SAID HE'D PAY ME TO WATER THE LAWN.
A
COACH

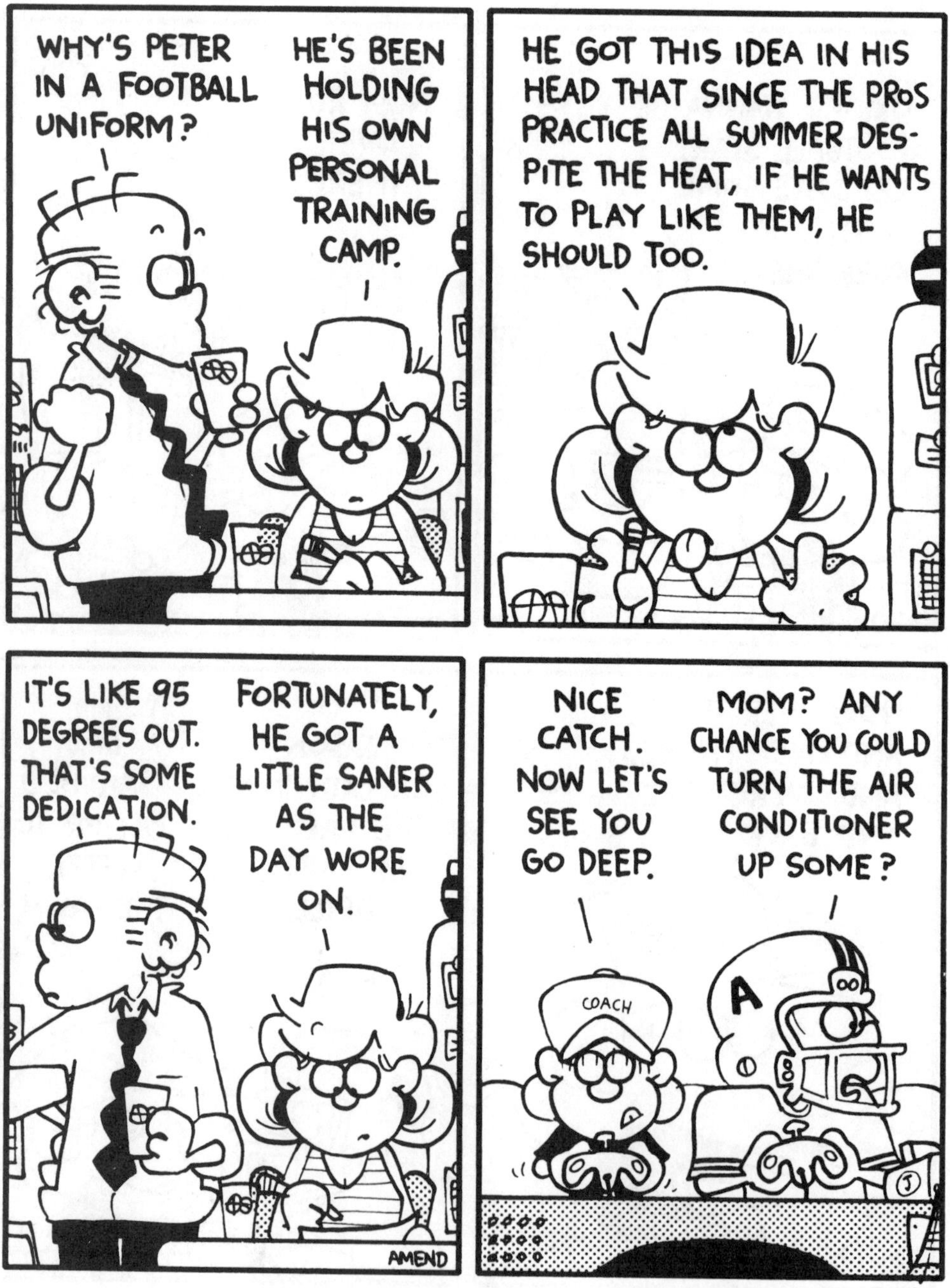
WHY'S PETER IN A FOOTBALL UNIFORM?
HE'S BEEN HOLDING HIS OWN PERSONAL TRAINING CAMP.
HE GOT THIS IDEA IN HIS HEAD THAT SINCE THE PROS PRACTICE ALL SUMMER DES-PITE THE HEAT, IF HE WANTS TO PLAY LIKE THEM, HE SHOULD TOO.
IT'S LIKE 95 DEGREES OUT. THAT'S SOME DEDICATION.
FORTUNATELY, HE GOT A LITTLE SANER AS THE DAY WORE ON.
AMEND
NICE CATCH. NOW LET'S SEE YOU GO DEEP.
MOM? ANY CHANCE YOU COULD TURN THE AIR CONDITIONER UP SOME?
COACH
A

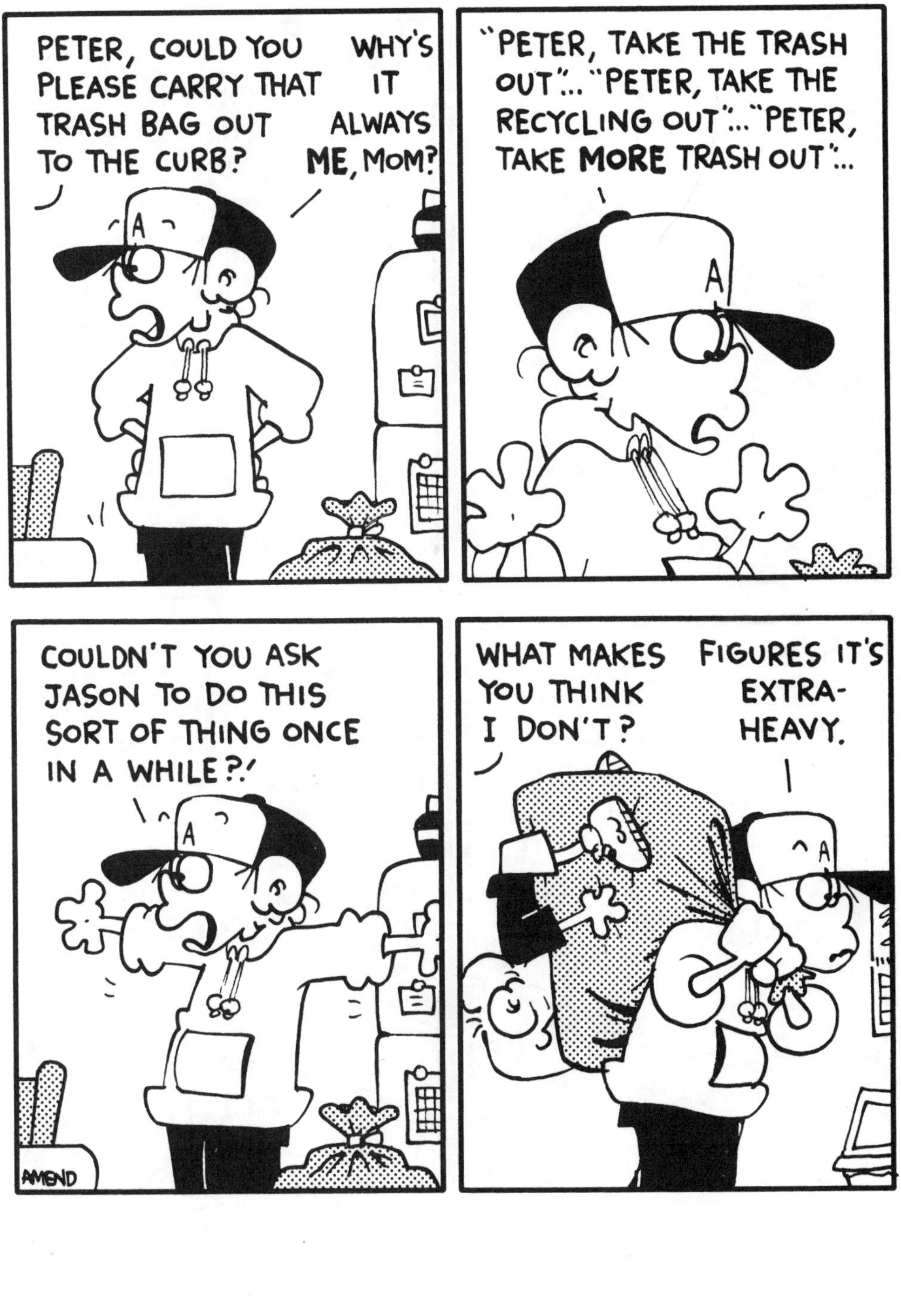
PETER, COULD YOU PLEASE CARRY THAT TRASH BAG OUT TO THE CURB?
WHY'S IT ALWAYS **ME**, MOM?
"PETER, TAKE THE TRASH OUT"... "PETER, TAKE THE RECYCLING OUT"... "PETER, TAKE **MORE** TRASH OUT"...
COULDN'T YOU ASK JASON TO DO THIS SORT OF THING ONCE IN A WHILE?!
WHAT MAKES YOU THINK I DON'T?
FIGURES IT'S EXTRA-HEAVY.
AMEND

DID THE PHONE RING WHILE I WAS OUT? I'M EXPECTING A CALL FROM HOLLYWOOD.

COOL DUDE

DARE I ASK WHY?

WELL, IN CASE YOU HADN'T NOTICED, THEY'VE COME OUT WITH A SEQUEL TO THAT MOVIE ABOUT A DOG THAT PLAYS BASKETBALL. HE PLAYS FOOTBALL IN THIS NEW ONE.

SO IT OCCURRED TO ME THAT IF A STUDIO WILL PAY MILLIONS TO FILM AN ATHLETICALLY GIFTED DOG, JUST IMAGINE WHAT THEY'D PAY FOR AN ATHLETICALLY GIFTED IGUANA!

COOL DUDE

THAT WOULD REQUIRE YOUR **HAVING** AN ATHLETICALLY GIFTED IGUANA.

ACTUALLY, I MEANT TO ASK YOU – IS THERE A SPORT THAT INVOLVES A LOT OF EATING AND SLEEPING?

COOL DUDE

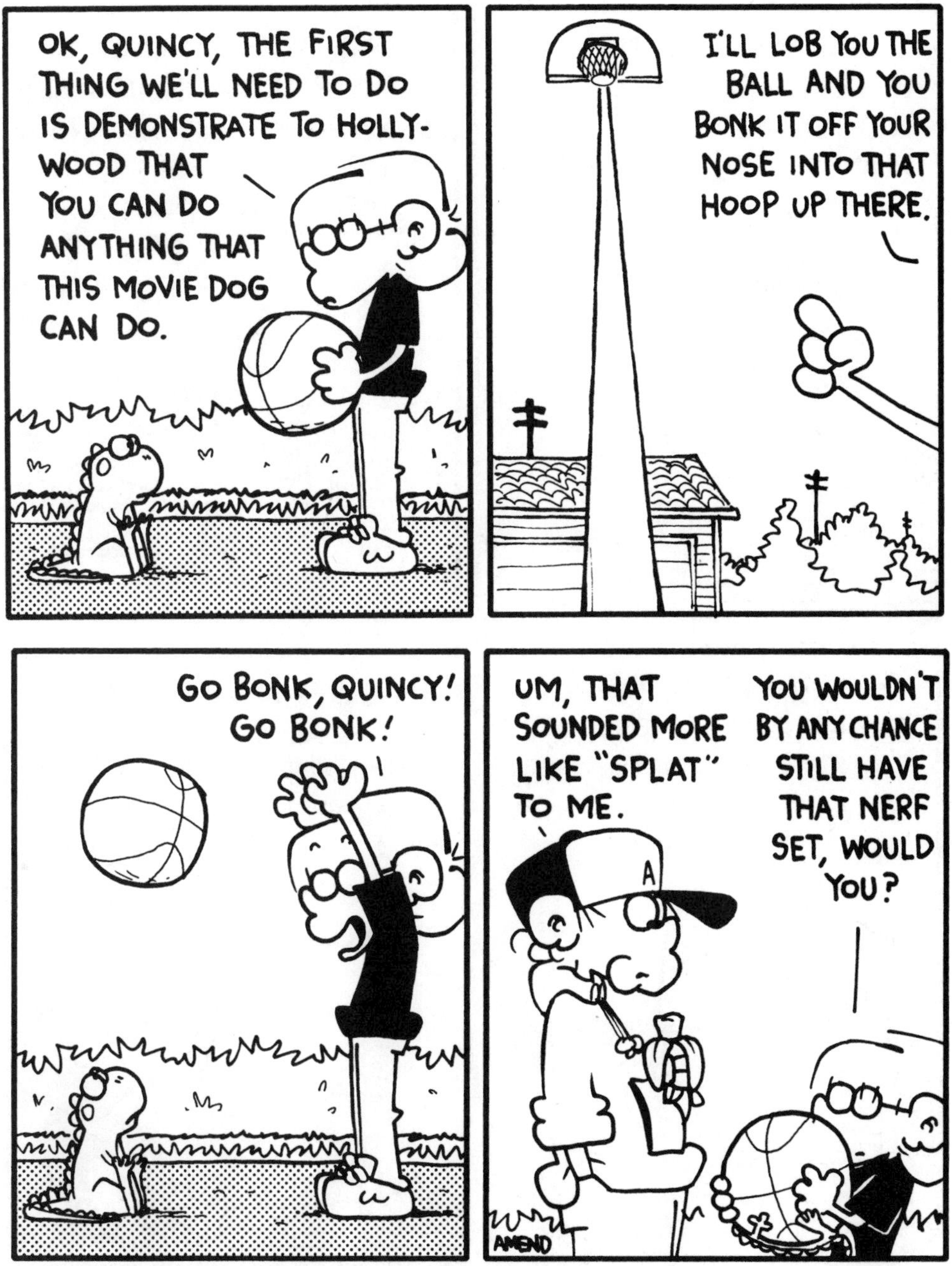
OK, QUINCY, THE FIRST THING WE'LL NEED TO DO IS DEMONSTRATE TO HOLLY-WOOD THAT YOU CAN DO ANYTHING THAT THIS MOVIE DOG CAN DO.
I'LL LOB YOU THE BALL AND YOU BONK IT OFF YOUR NOSE INTO THAT HOOP UP THERE.
GO BONK, QUINCY! GO BONK!
UM, THAT SOUNDED MORE LIKE "SPLAT" TO ME.
YOU WOULDN'T BY ANY CHANCE STILL HAVE THAT NERF SET, WOULD YOU?
A
AMEND

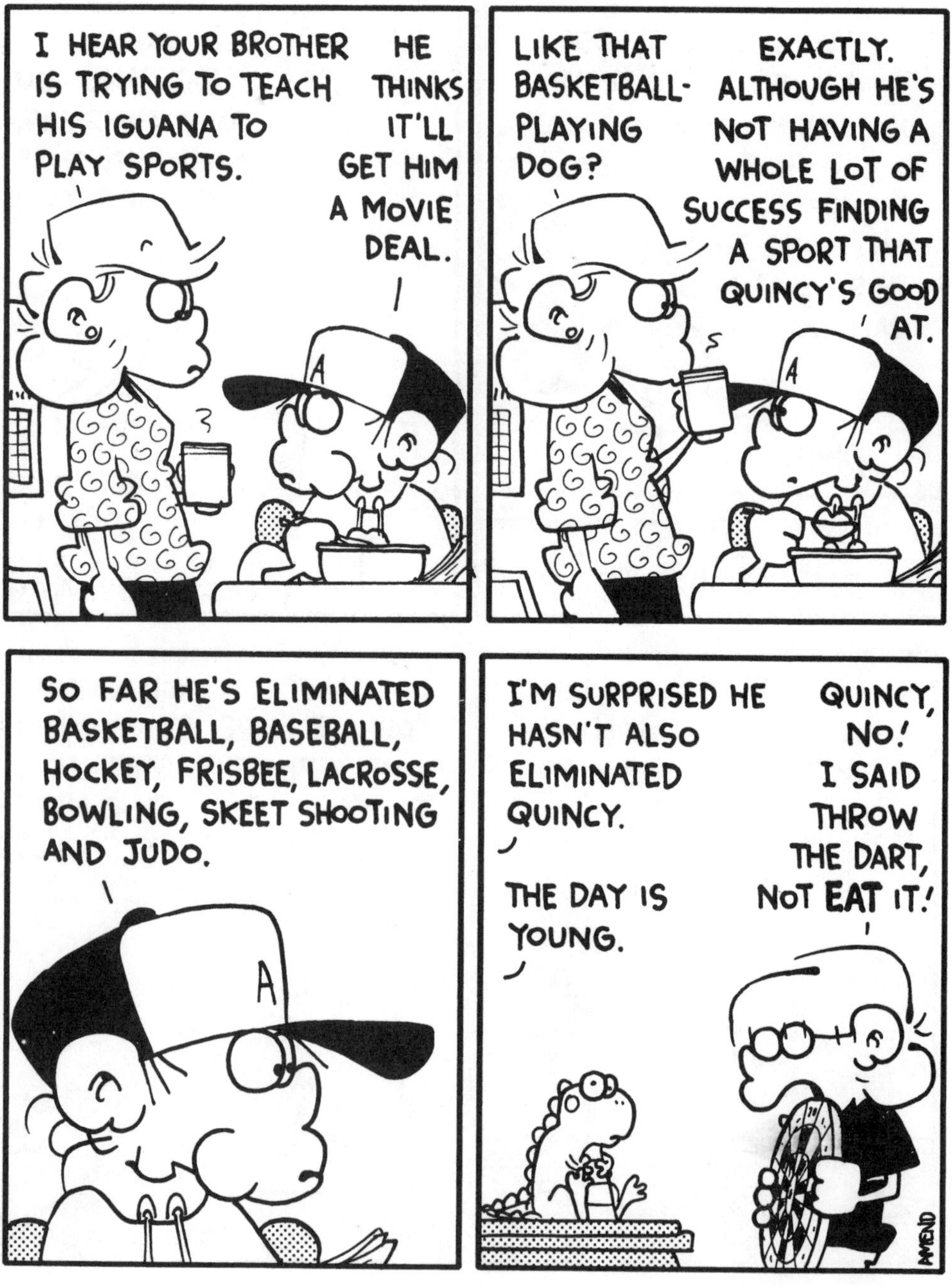
I HEAR YOUR BROTHER IS TRYING TO TEACH HIS IGUANA TO PLAY SPORTS.
HE THINKS IT'LL GET HIM A MOVIE DEAL.
LIKE THAT BASKETBALL-PLAYING DOG?
EXACTLY. ALTHOUGH HE'S NOT HAVING A WHOLE LOT OF SUCCESS FINDING A SPORT THAT QUINCY'S GOOD AT.
SO FAR HE'S ELIMINATED BASKETBALL, BASEBALL, HOCKEY, FRISBEE, LACROSSE, BOWLING, SKEET SHOOTING AND JUDO.
I'M SURPRISED HE HASN'T ALSO ELIMINATED QUINCY.
THE DAY IS YOUNG.
QUINCY, NO! I SAID THROW THE DART, NOT EAT IT!
AMEND

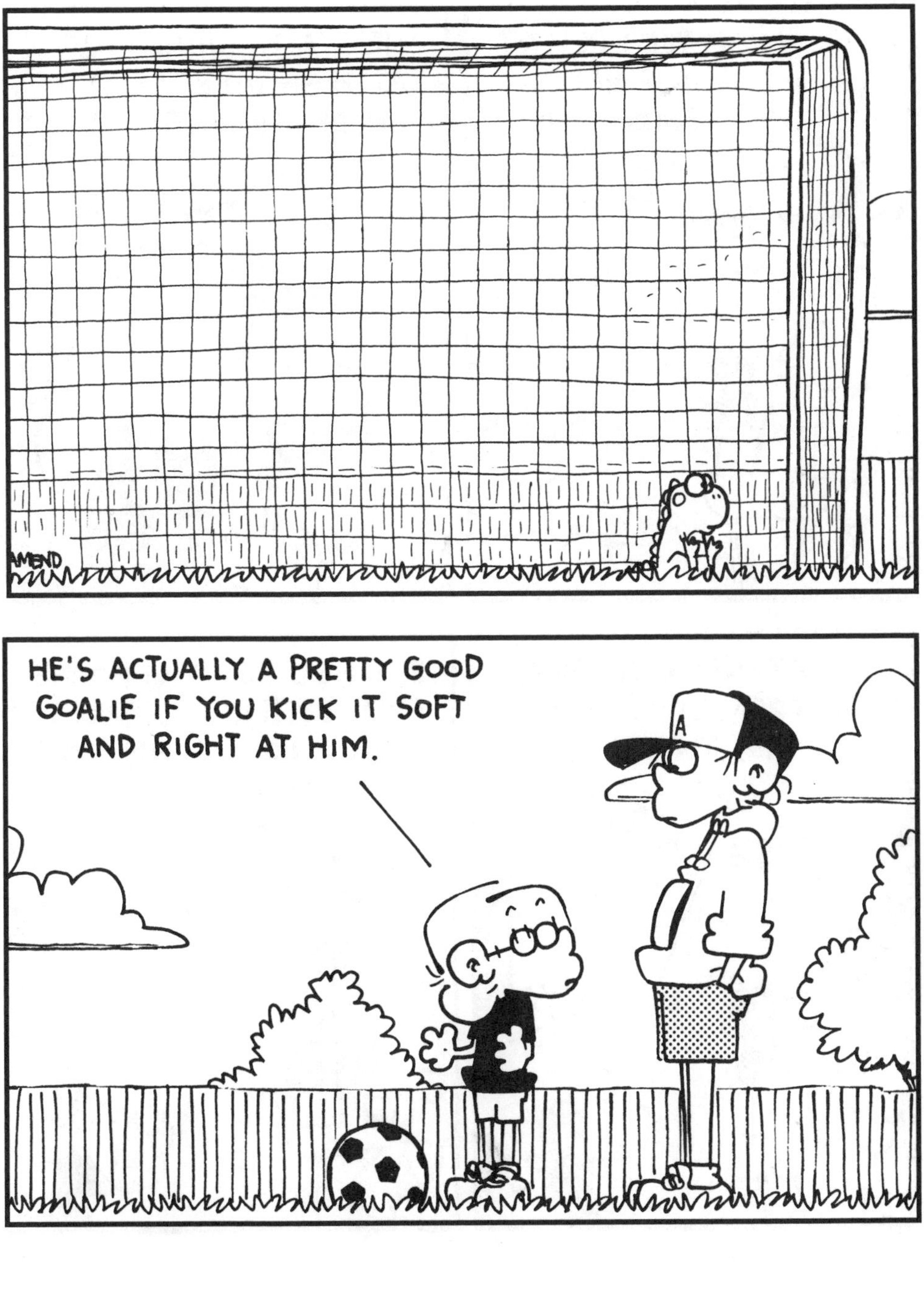
AMEND
HE'S ACTUALLY A PRETTY GOOD GOALIE IF YOU KICK IT SOFT AND RIGHT AT HIM.

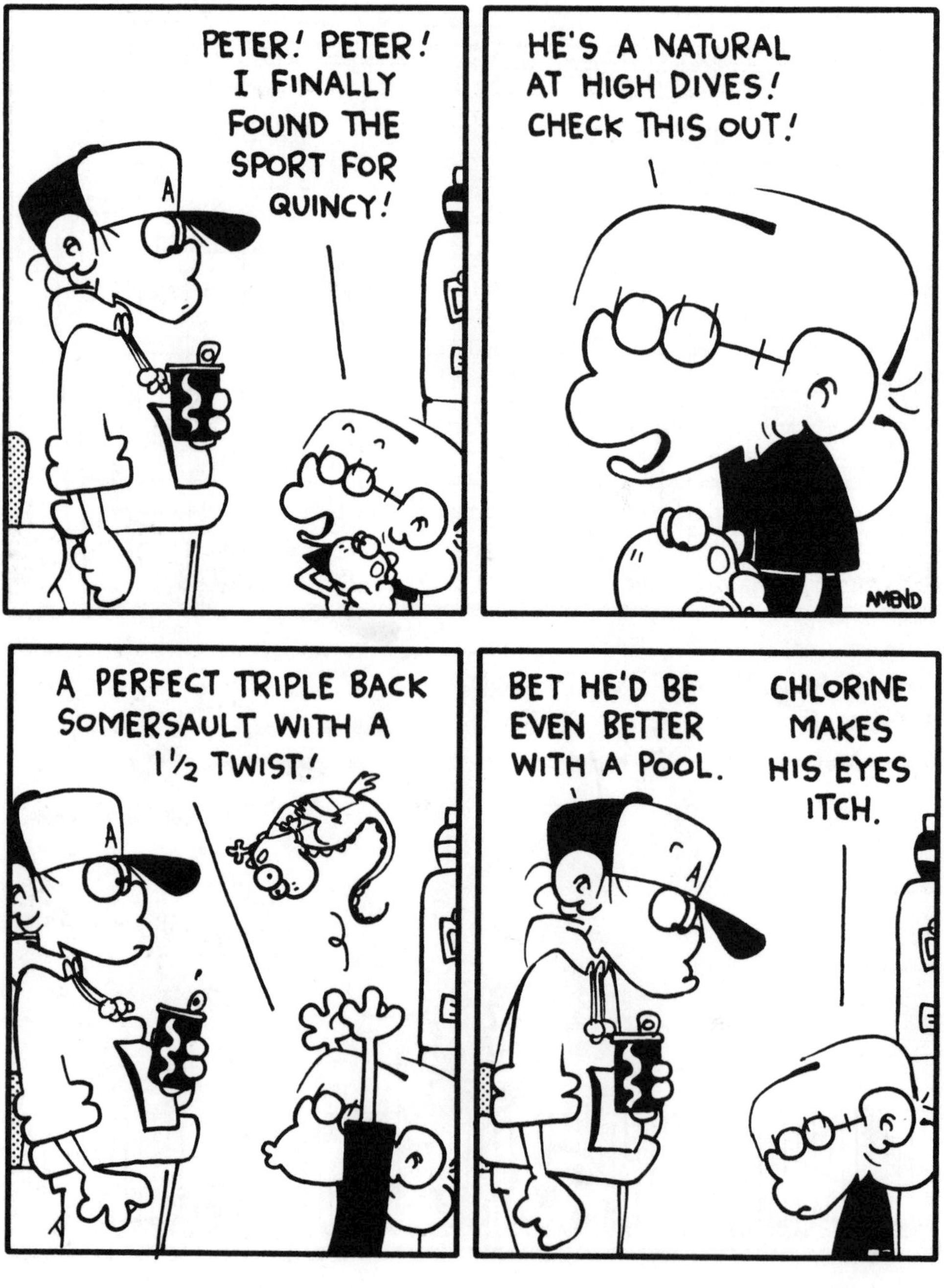
PETER! PETER! I FINALLY FOUND THE SPORT FOR QUINCY!
HE'S A NATURAL AT HIGH DIVES! CHECK THIS OUT!
AMEND
A PERFECT TRIPLE BACK SOMERSAULT WITH A 1½ TWIST!
BET HE'D BE EVEN BETTER WITH A POOL.
CHLORINE MAKES HIS EYES ITCH.

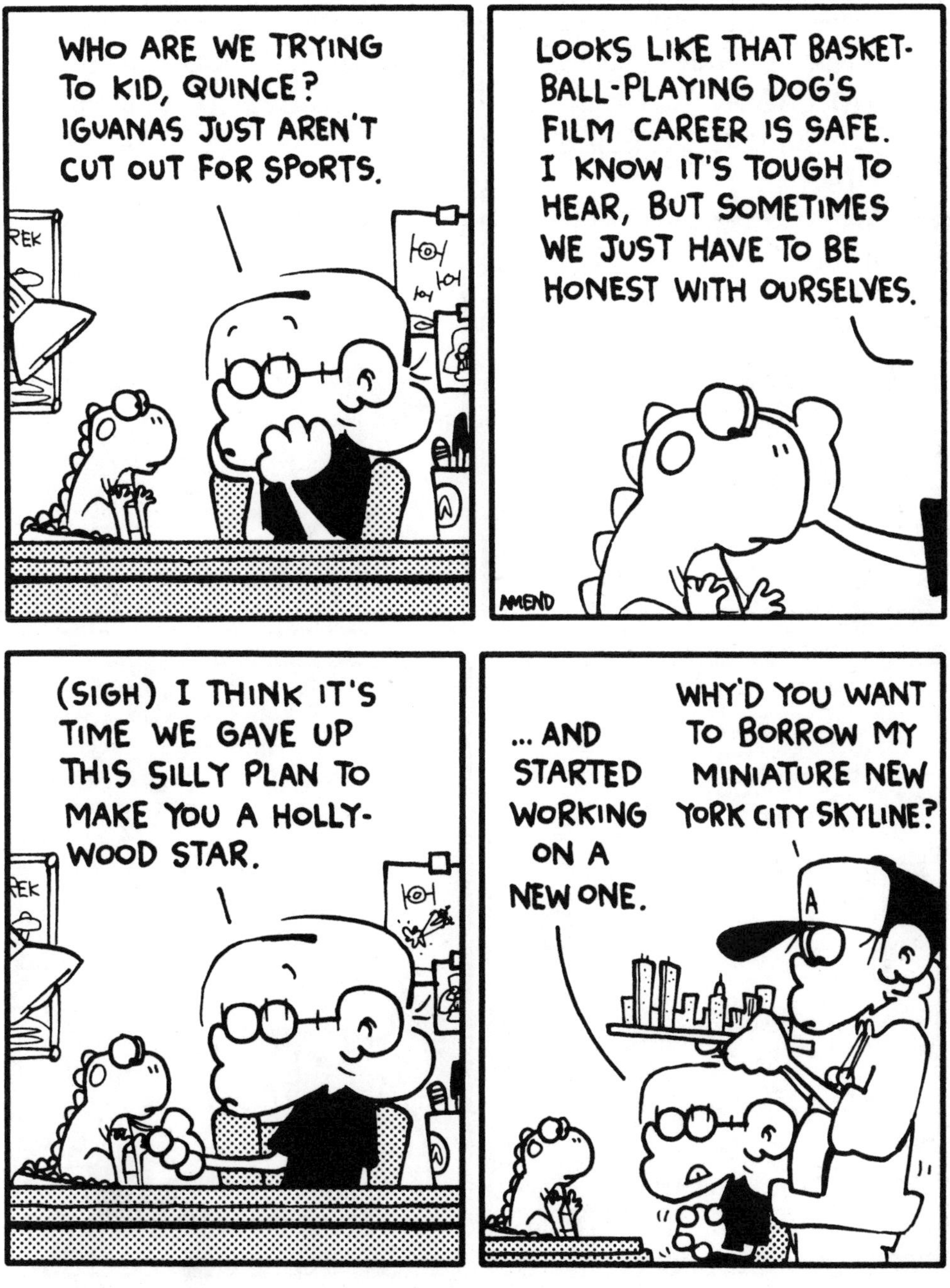
WHO ARE WE TRYING TO KID, QUINCE? IGUANAS JUST AREN'T CUT OUT FOR SPORTS.
LOOKS LIKE THAT BASKET-BALL-PLAYING DOG'S FILM CAREER IS SAFE. I KNOW IT'S TOUGH TO HEAR, BUT SOMETIMES WE JUST HAVE TO BE HONEST WITH OURSELVES.
AMEND
(SIGH) I THINK IT'S TIME WE GAVE UP THIS SILLY PLAN TO MAKE YOU A HOLLY-WOOD STAR.
... AND STARTED WORKING ON A NEW ONE.
WHY'D YOU WANT TO BORROW MY MINIATURE NEW YORK CITY SKYLINE?

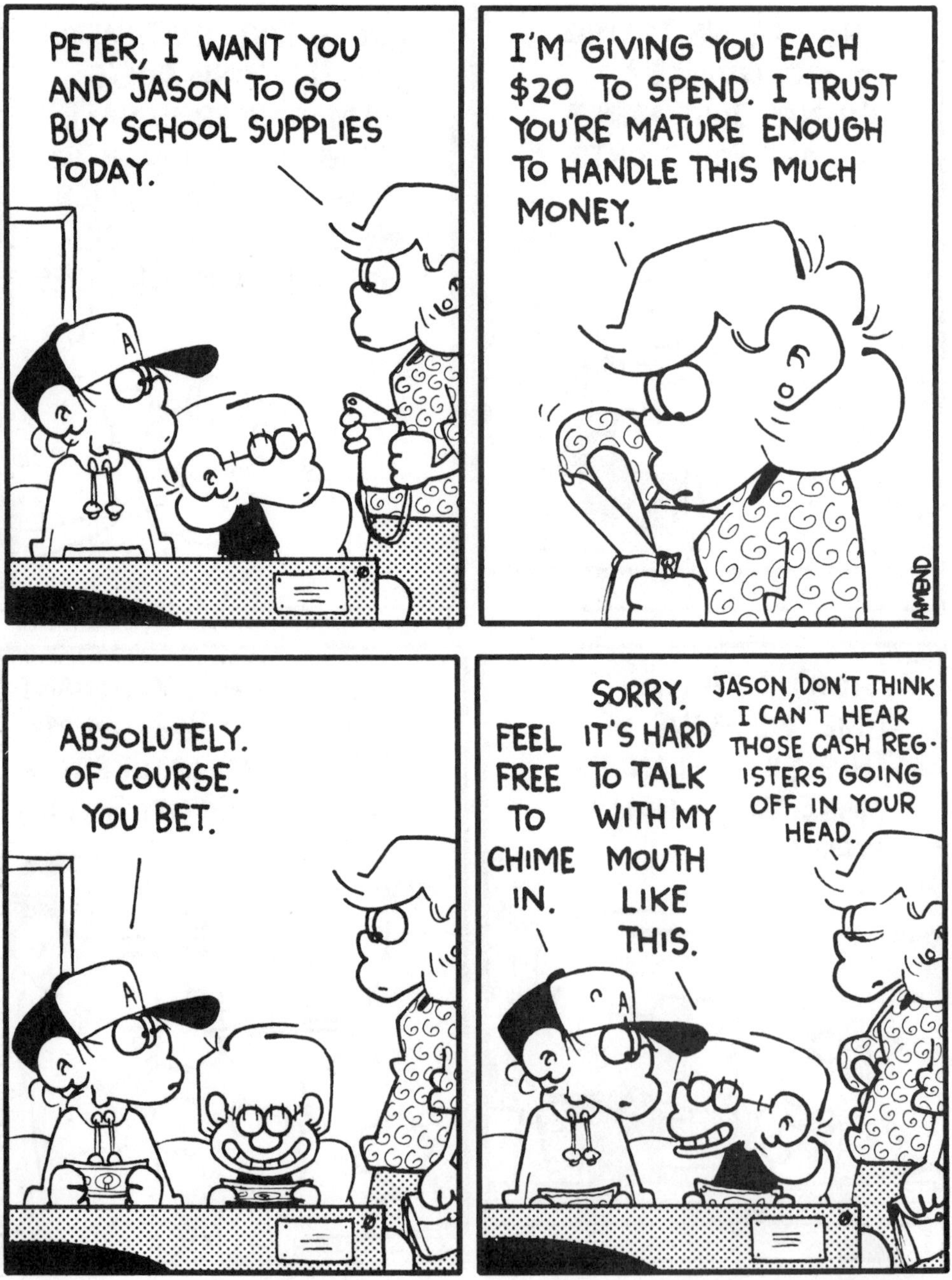
PETER, I WANT YOU AND JASON TO GO BUY SCHOOL SUPPLIES TODAY.
I'M GIVING YOU EACH $20 TO SPEND. I TRUST YOU'RE MATURE ENOUGH TO HANDLE THIS MUCH MONEY.
AMEND
ABSOLUTELY. OF COURSE. YOU BET.
FEEL FREE TO CHIME IN.
SORRY. IT'S HARD TO TALK WITH MY MOUTH LIKE THIS.
JASON, DON'T THINK I CAN'T HEAR THOSE CASH REG-ISTERS GOING OFF IN YOUR HEAD.

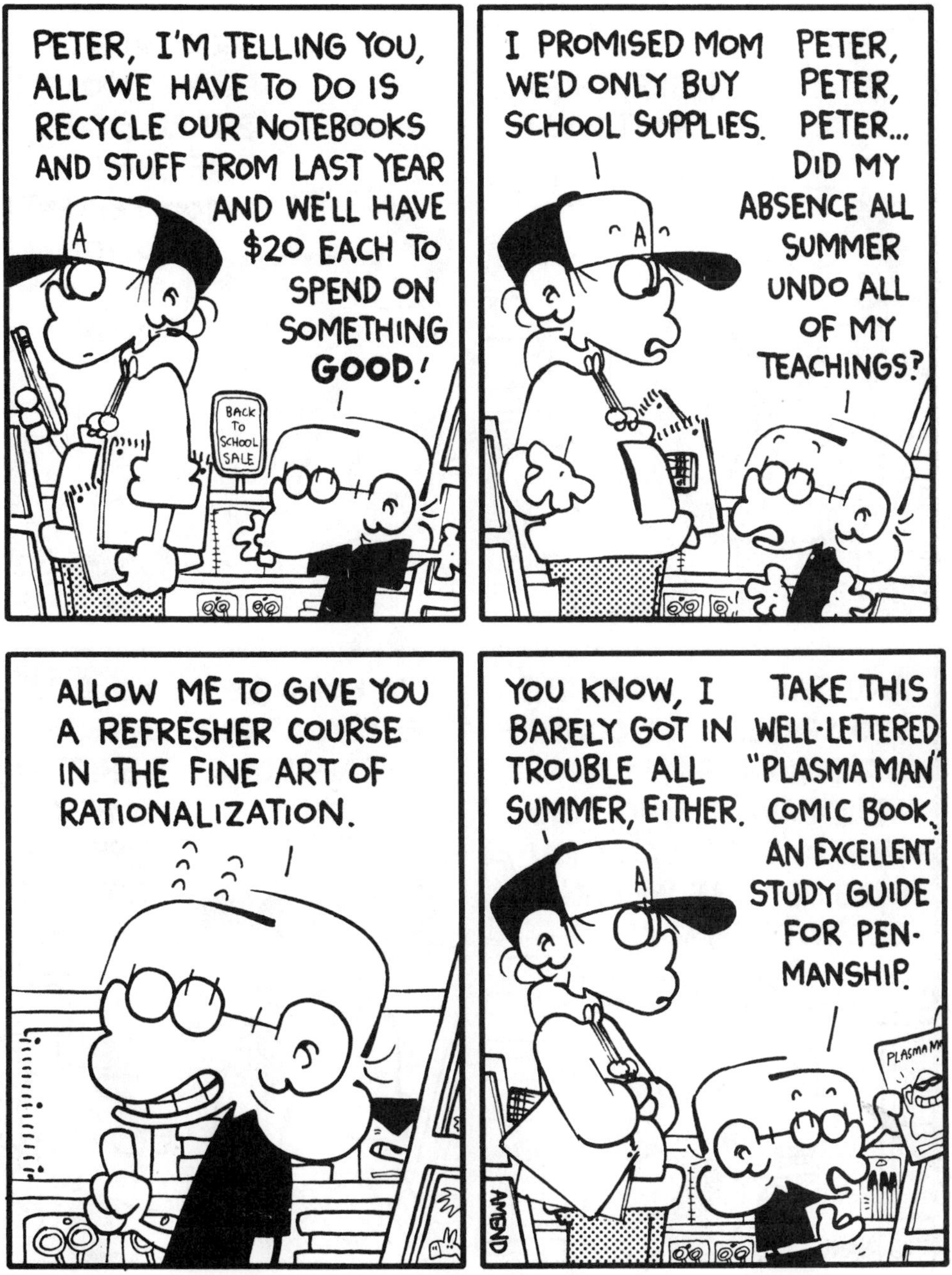
PETER, I'M TELLING YOU, ALL WE HAVE TO DO IS RECYCLE OUR NOTEBOOKS AND STUFF FROM LAST YEAR AND WE'LL HAVE $20 EACH TO SPEND ON SOMETHING GOOD!
BACK TO SCHOOL SALE
I PROMISED MOM WE'D ONLY BUY SCHOOL SUPPLIES.
PETER, PETER, PETER... DID MY ABSENCE ALL SUMMER UNDO ALL OF MY TEACHINGS?
ALLOW ME TO GIVE YOU A REFRESHER COURSE IN THE FINE ART OF RATIONALIZATION.
YOU KNOW, I BARELY GOT IN TROUBLE ALL SUMMER, EITHER.
TAKE THIS WELL-LETTERED "PLASMA MAN" COMIC BOOK... AN EXCELLENT STUDY GUIDE FOR PENMANSHIP.
AMEND

PETER, THINK ABOUT WHAT $20 CAN BUY!

ARMLOADS OF COMIC BOOKS! ENTIRE BOXES OF GUM! A 100 PERCENT COTTON "DUKE QUAKEM" T-SHIRT!

AND THAT'S JUST AT THE $20 LEVEL! IF WE **COMBINE** OUR SCHOOL SUPPLY MONEY, WE'LL HAVE A WHOPPING **$40** TO SPEND! CAN YOU IMAGINE WHAT WE CAN GET WITH **THAT**?!

AMEND

I'M HOPING WE CAN AFFORD A BRAIN SCAN FOR YOU.

TWO "DUKE QUAKEM" T-SHIRTS! MY HEART SKIPPED A BEAT JUST SAYING THAT.

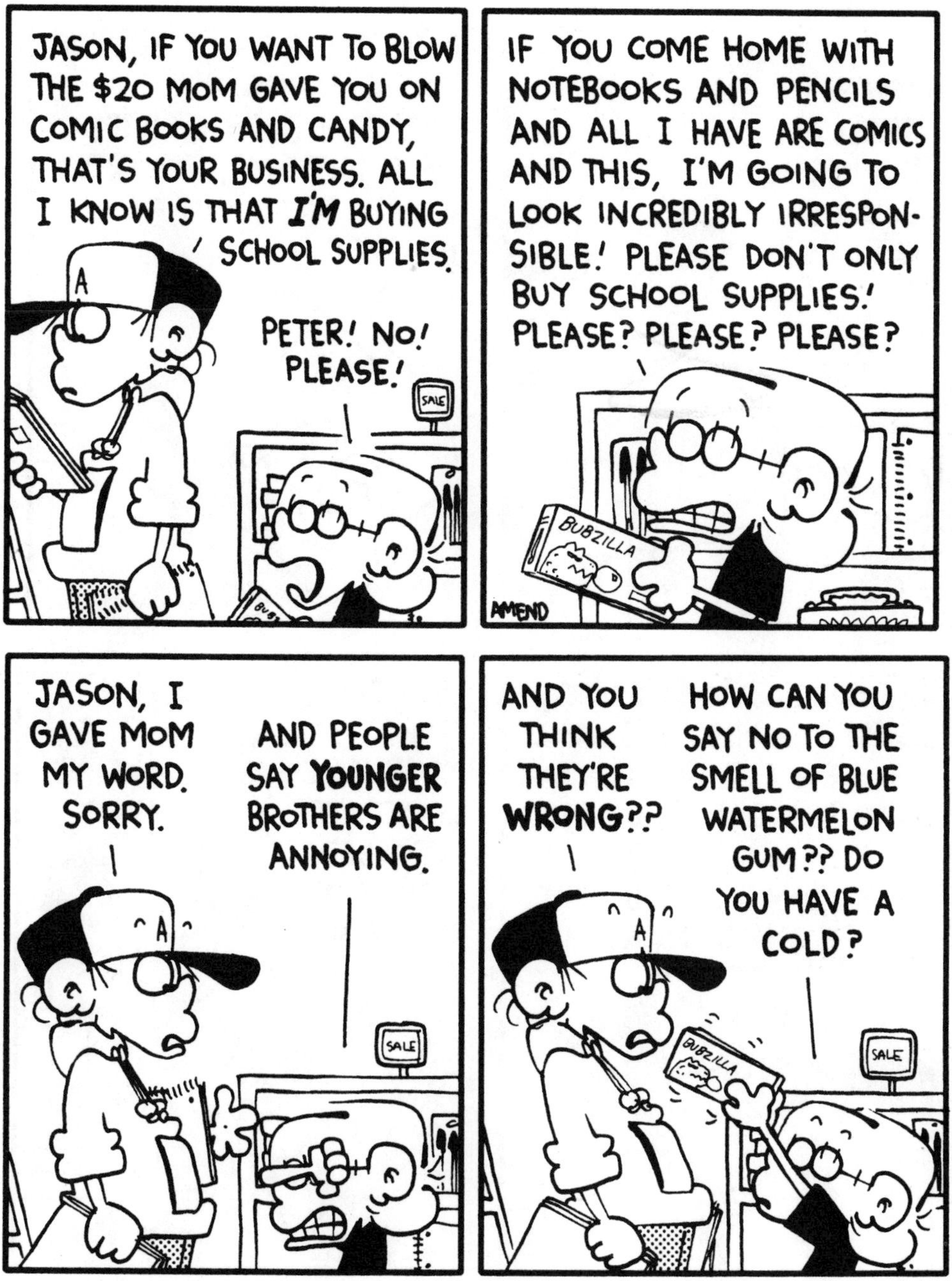
JASON, IF YOU WANT TO BLOW THE $20 MOM GAVE YOU ON COMIC BOOKS AND CANDY, THAT'S YOUR BUSINESS. ALL I KNOW IS THAT I'M BUYING SCHOOL SUPPLIES.
PETER! NO! PLEASE!
SALE
IF YOU COME HOME WITH NOTEBOOKS AND PENCILS AND ALL I HAVE ARE COMICS AND THIS, I'M GOING TO LOOK INCREDIBLY IRRESPONSIBLE! PLEASE DON'T ONLY BUY SCHOOL SUPPLIES! PLEASE? PLEASE? PLEASE?
BUBZILLA
AMEND
JASON, I GAVE MOM MY WORD. SORRY.
AND PEOPLE SAY YOUNGER BROTHERS ARE ANNOYING.
SALE
AND YOU THINK THEY'RE WRONG??
HOW CAN YOU SAY NO TO THE SMELL OF BLUE WATERMELON GUM?? DO YOU HAVE A COLD?
BUBZILLA
SALE

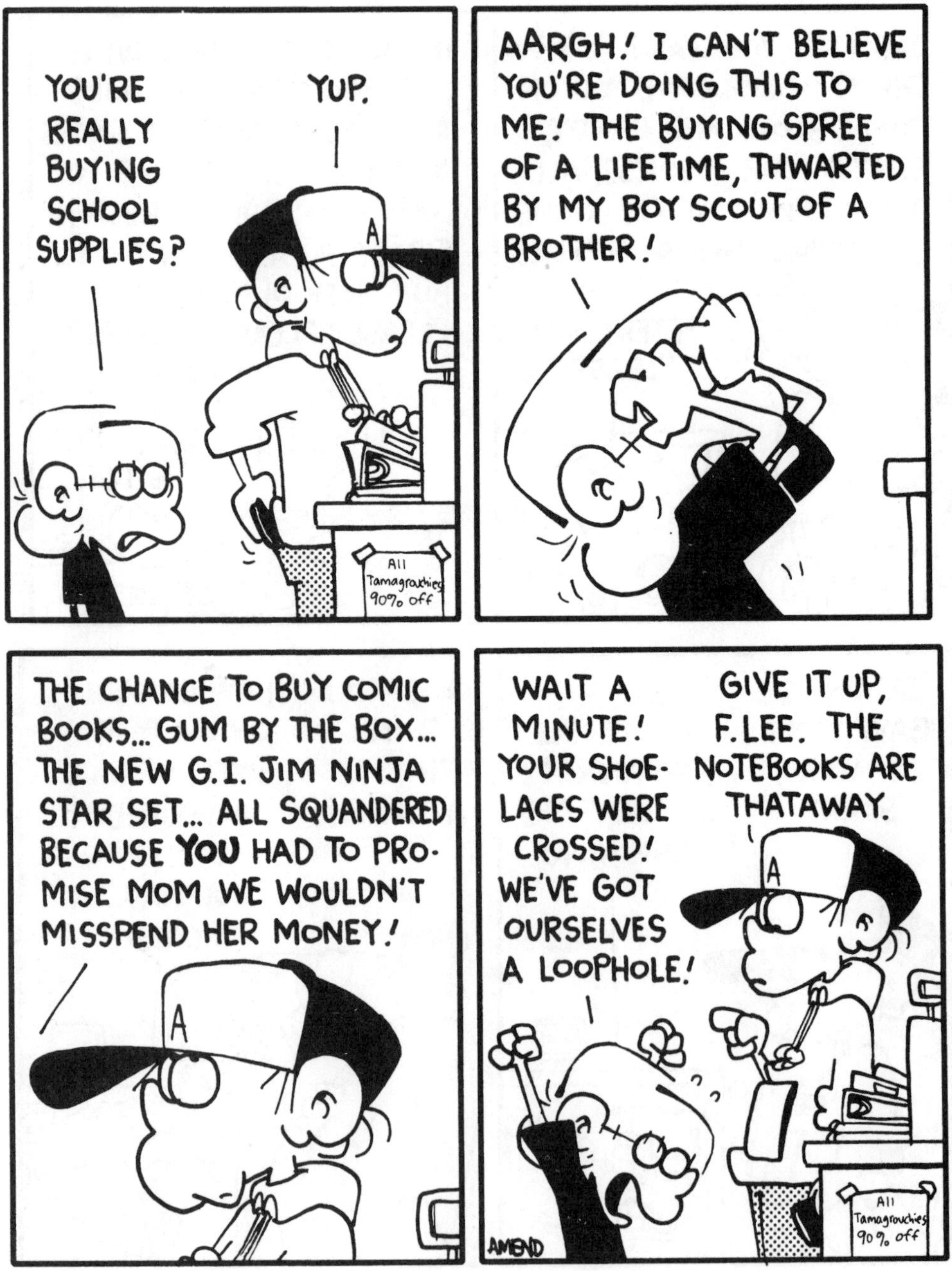
YOU'RE REALLY BUYING SCHOOL SUPPLIES?
YUP.
All Tamagrouchies 90% off
AARGH! I CAN'T BELIEVE YOU'RE DOING THIS TO ME! THE BUYING SPREE OF A LIFETIME, THWARTED BY MY BOY SCOUT OF A BROTHER!
THE CHANCE TO BUY COMIC BOOKS... GUM BY THE BOX... THE NEW G.I. JIM NINJA STAR SET... ALL SQUANDERED BECAUSE YOU HAD TO PRO-MISE MOM WE WOULDN'T MISSPEND HER MONEY!
WAIT A MINUTE! YOUR SHOE-LACES WERE CROSSED! WE'VE GOT OURSELVES A LOOPHOLE!
GIVE IT UP, F.LEE. THE NOTEBOOKS ARE THATAWAY.
All Tamagrouchies 90% off
AMEND

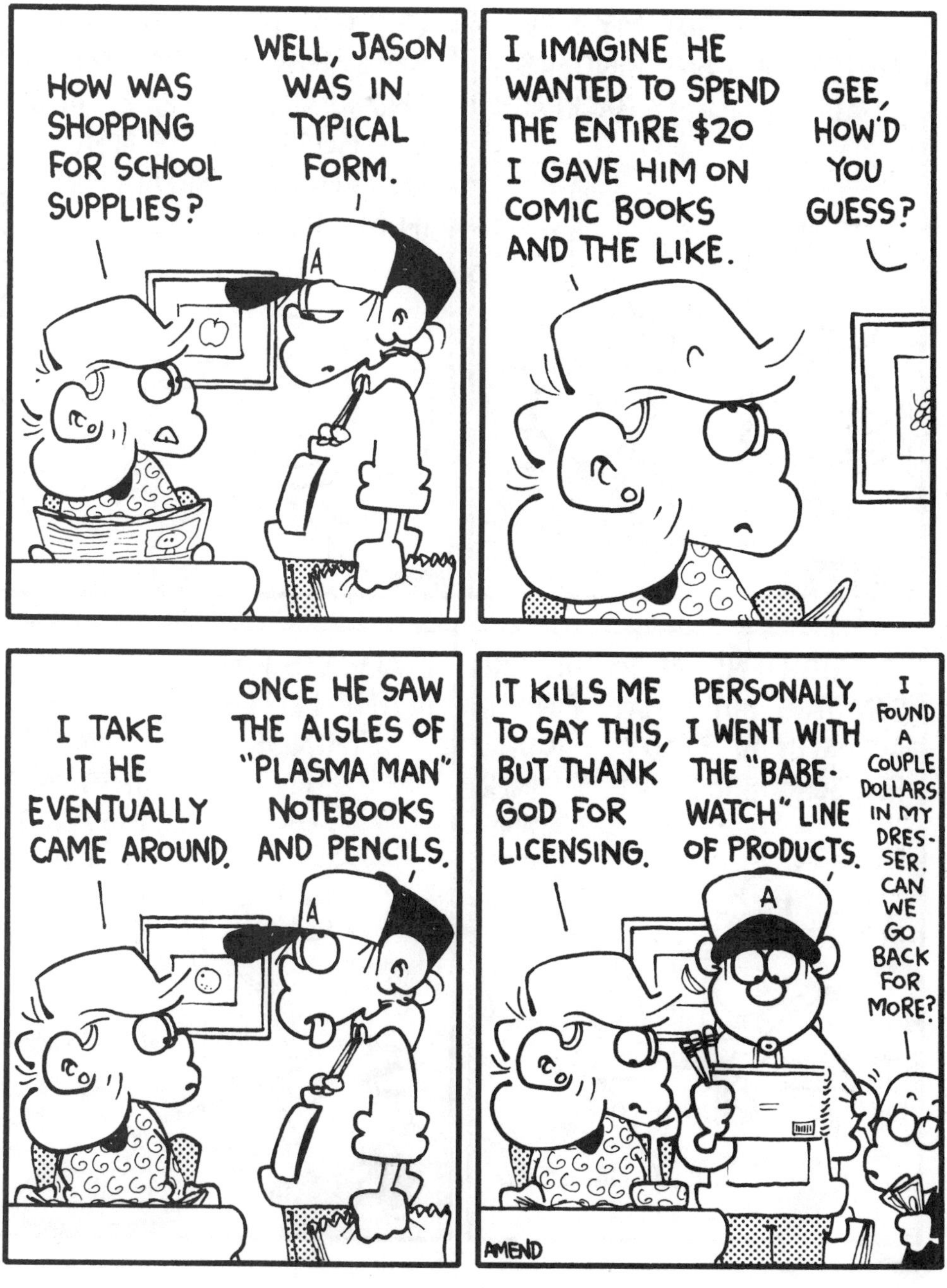
HOW WAS SHOPPING FOR SCHOOL SUPPLIES?
WELL, JASON WAS IN TYPICAL FORM.
I IMAGINE HE WANTED TO SPEND THE ENTIRE $20 I GAVE HIM ON COMIC BOOKS AND THE LIKE.
GEE, HOW'D YOU GUESS?
I TAKE IT HE EVENTUALLY CAME AROUND.
ONCE HE SAW THE AISLES OF "PLASMA MAN" NOTEBOOKS AND PENCILS.
IT KILLS ME TO SAY THIS, BUT THANK GOD FOR LICENSING.
PERSONALLY, I WENT WITH THE "BABE-WATCH" LINE OF PRODUCTS.
I FOUND A COUPLE DOLLARS IN MY DRESSER. CAN WE GO BACK FOR MORE?
AMEND

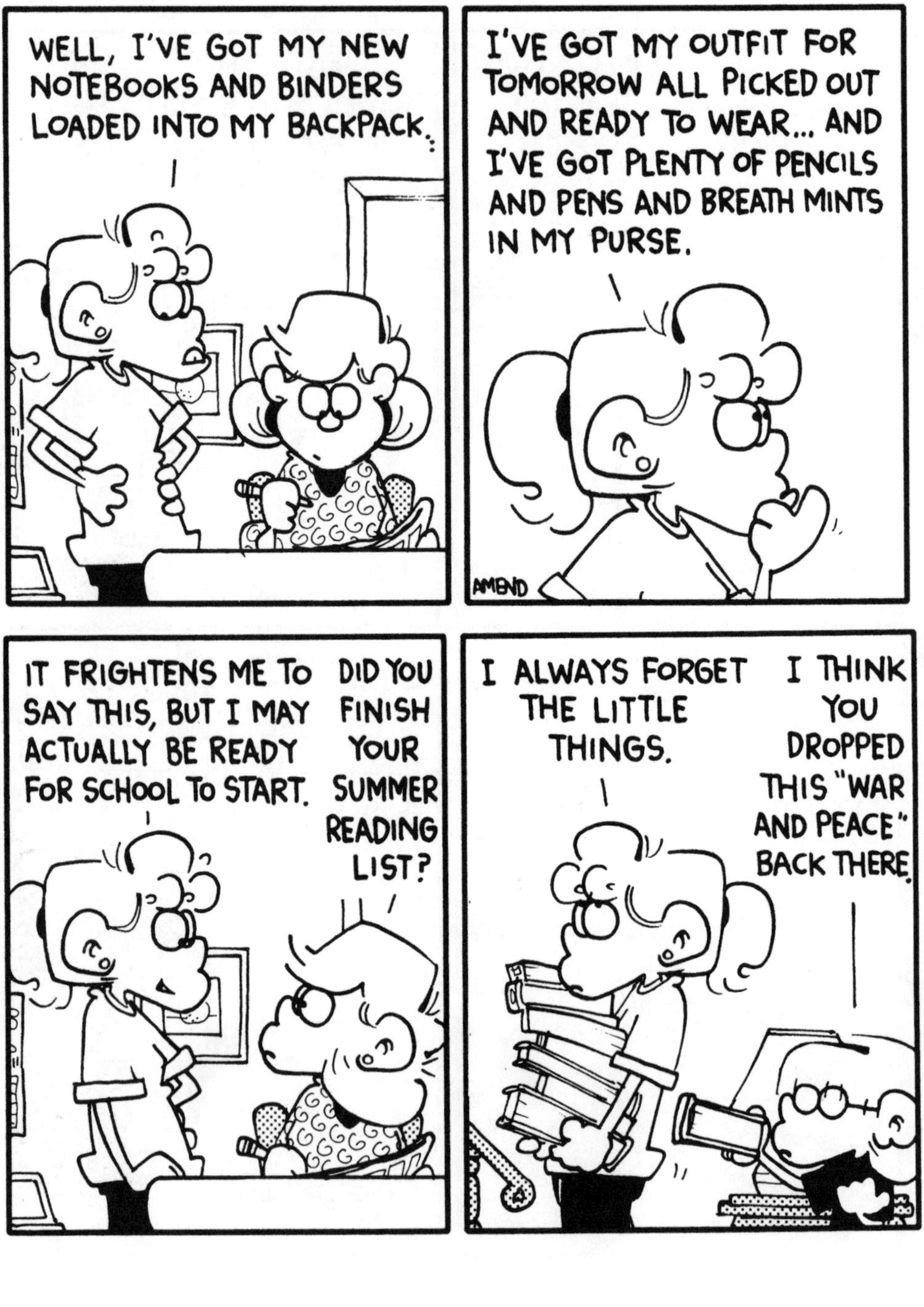
WELL, I'VE GOT MY NEW NOTEBOOKS AND BINDERS LOADED INTO MY BACKPACK.
I'VE GOT MY OUTFIT FOR TOMORROW ALL PICKED OUT AND READY TO WEAR... AND I'VE GOT PLENTY OF PENCILS AND PENS AND BREATH MINTS IN MY PURSE.
AMEND
IT FRIGHTENS ME TO SAY THIS, BUT I MAY ACTUALLY BE READY FOR SCHOOL TO START.
DID YOU FINISH YOUR SUMMER READING LIST?
I ALWAYS FORGET THE LITTLE THINGS.
I THINK YOU DROPPED THIS "WAR AND PEACE" BACK THERE.

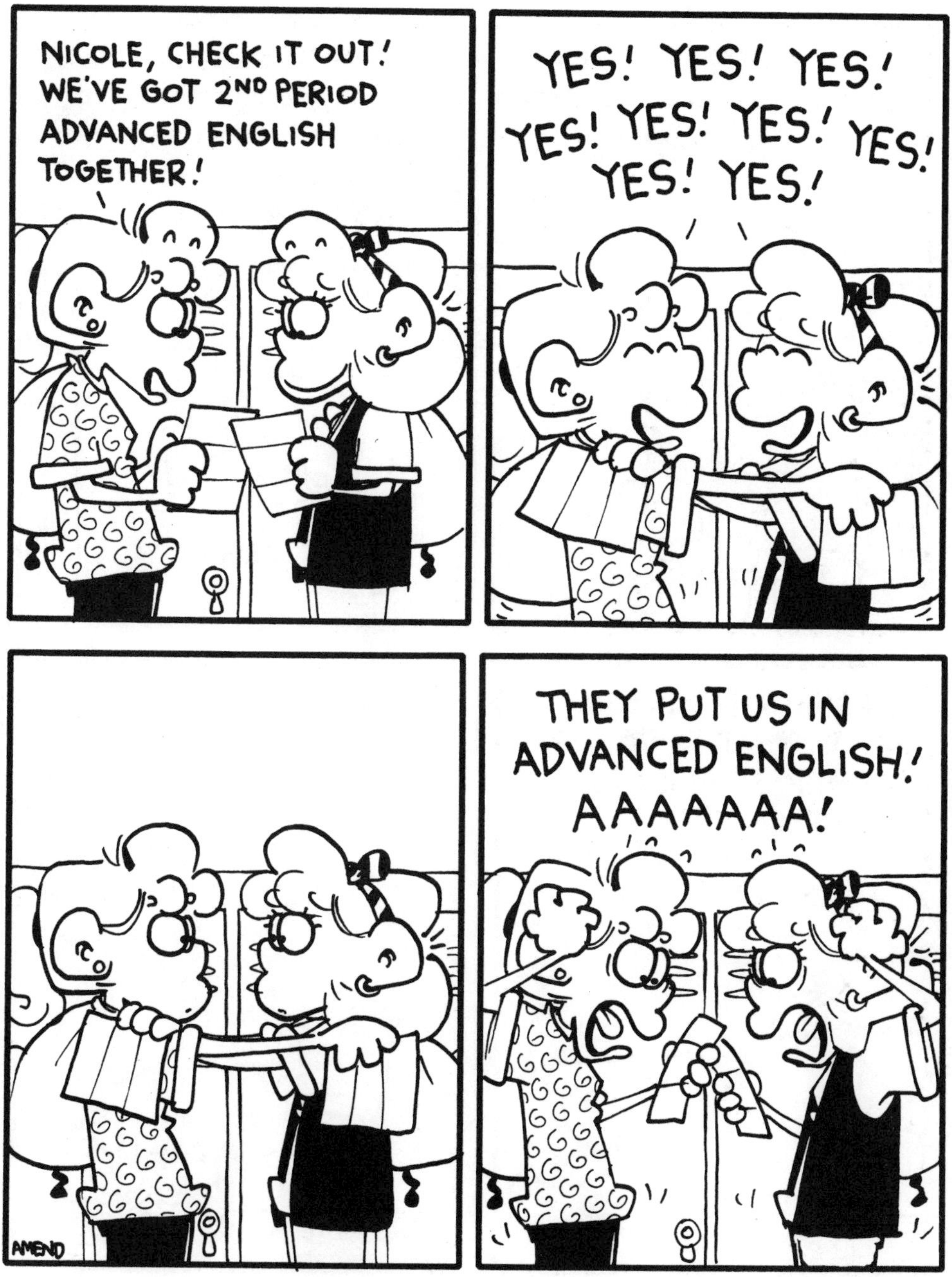
NICOLE, CHECK IT OUT! WE'VE GOT 2ND PERIOD ADVANCED ENGLISH TOGETHER!
YES! YES! YES! YES! YES! YES! YES! YES! YES!
THEY PUT US IN ADVANCED ENGLISH! AAAAAAA!
AMEND

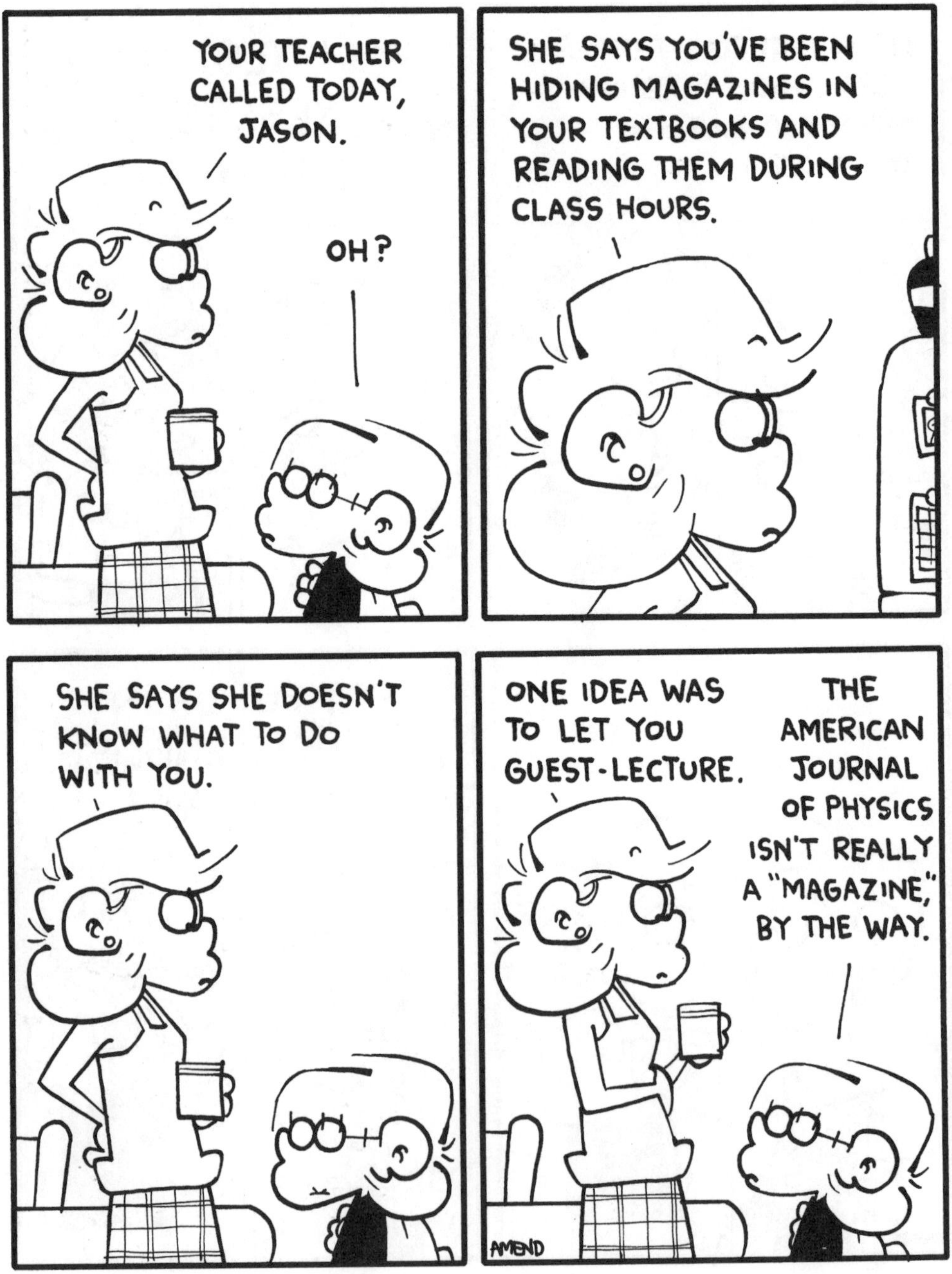
YOUR TEACHER CALLED TODAY, JASON.
OH?
SHE SAYS YOU'VE BEEN HIDING MAGAZINES IN YOUR TEXTBOOKS AND READING THEM DURING CLASS HOURS.
SHE SAYS SHE DOESN'T KNOW WHAT TO DO WITH YOU.
ONE IDEA WAS TO LET YOU GUEST-LECTURE.
THE AMERICAN JOURNAL OF PHYSICS ISN'T REALLY A "MAGAZINE," BY THE WAY.
AMEND

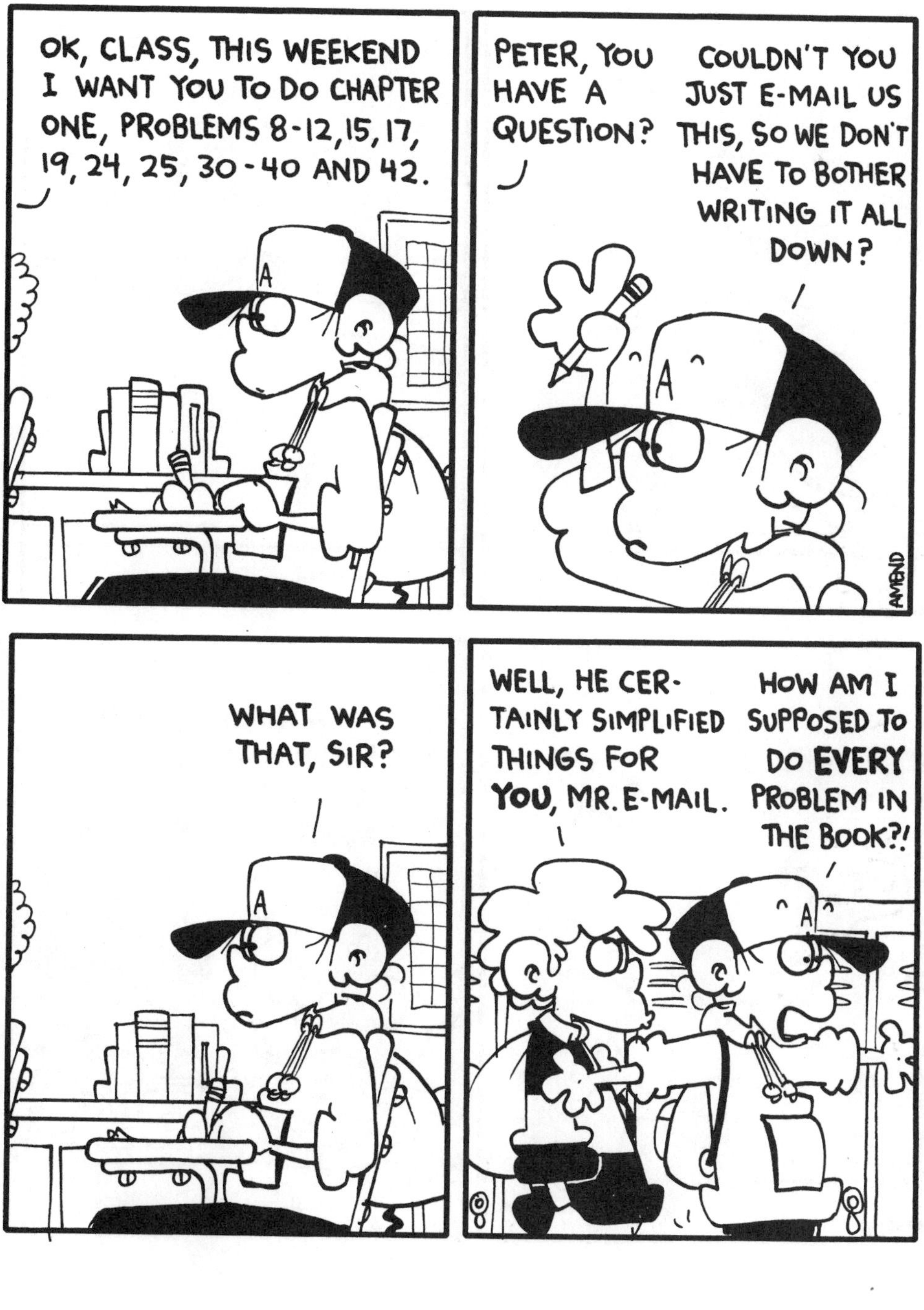
OK, CLASS, THIS WEEKEND I WANT YOU TO DO CHAPTER ONE, PROBLEMS 8-12, 15, 17, 19, 24, 25, 30-40 AND 42.
PETER, YOU HAVE A QUESTION?
COULDN'T YOU JUST E-MAIL US THIS, SO WE DON'T HAVE TO BOTHER WRITING IT ALL DOWN?
AMEND
WHAT WAS THAT, SIR?
WELL, HE CER-TAINLY SIMPLIFIED THINGS FOR **YOU**, MR. E-MAIL.
HOW AM I SUPPOSED TO DO **EVERY** PROBLEM IN THE BOOK?!

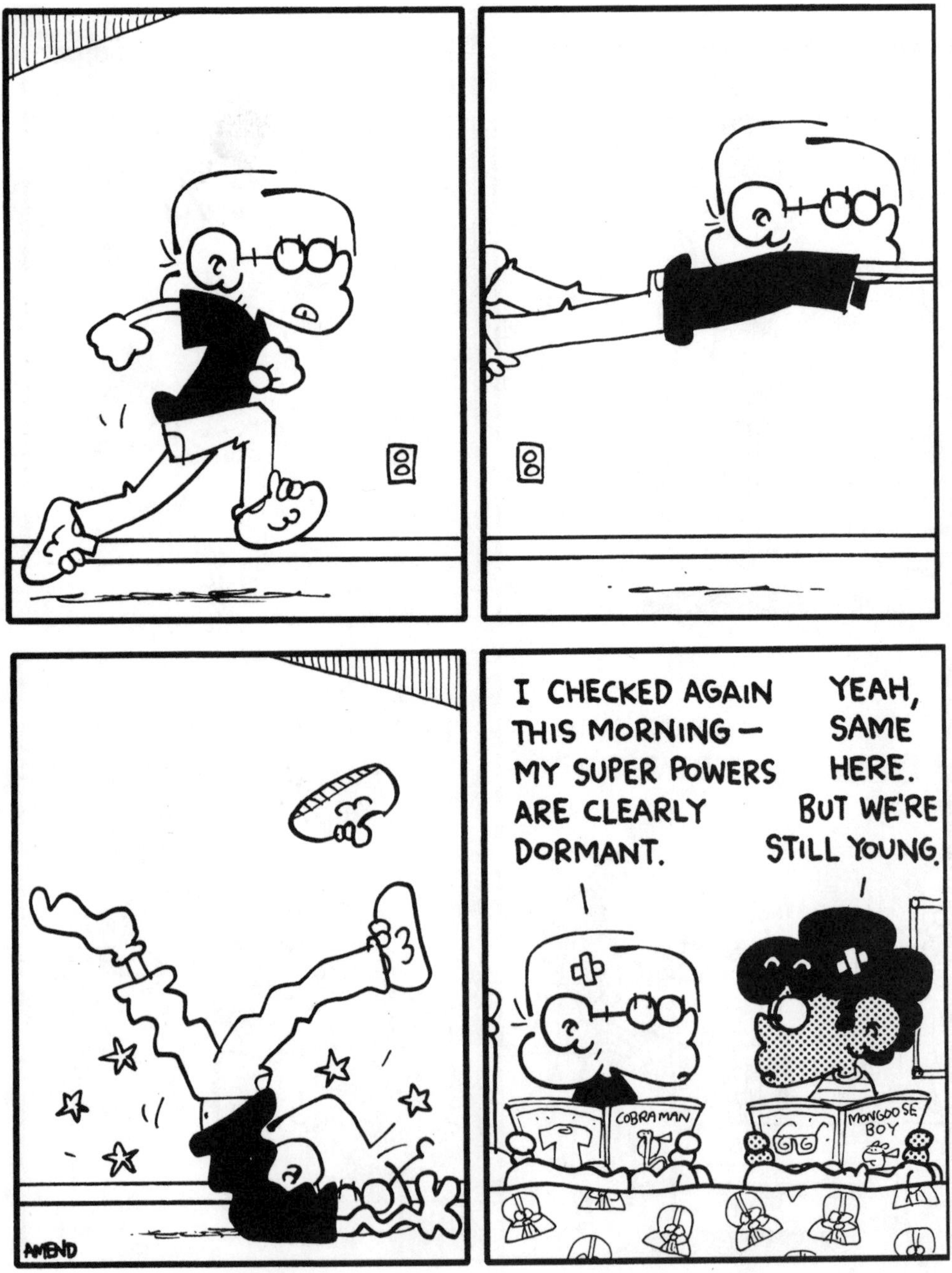
I CHECKED AGAIN THIS MORNING – MY SUPER POWERS ARE CLEARLY DORMANT.
YEAH, SAME HERE. BUT WE'RE STILL YOUNG.
COBRAMAN
MONGOOSE BOY
AMEND

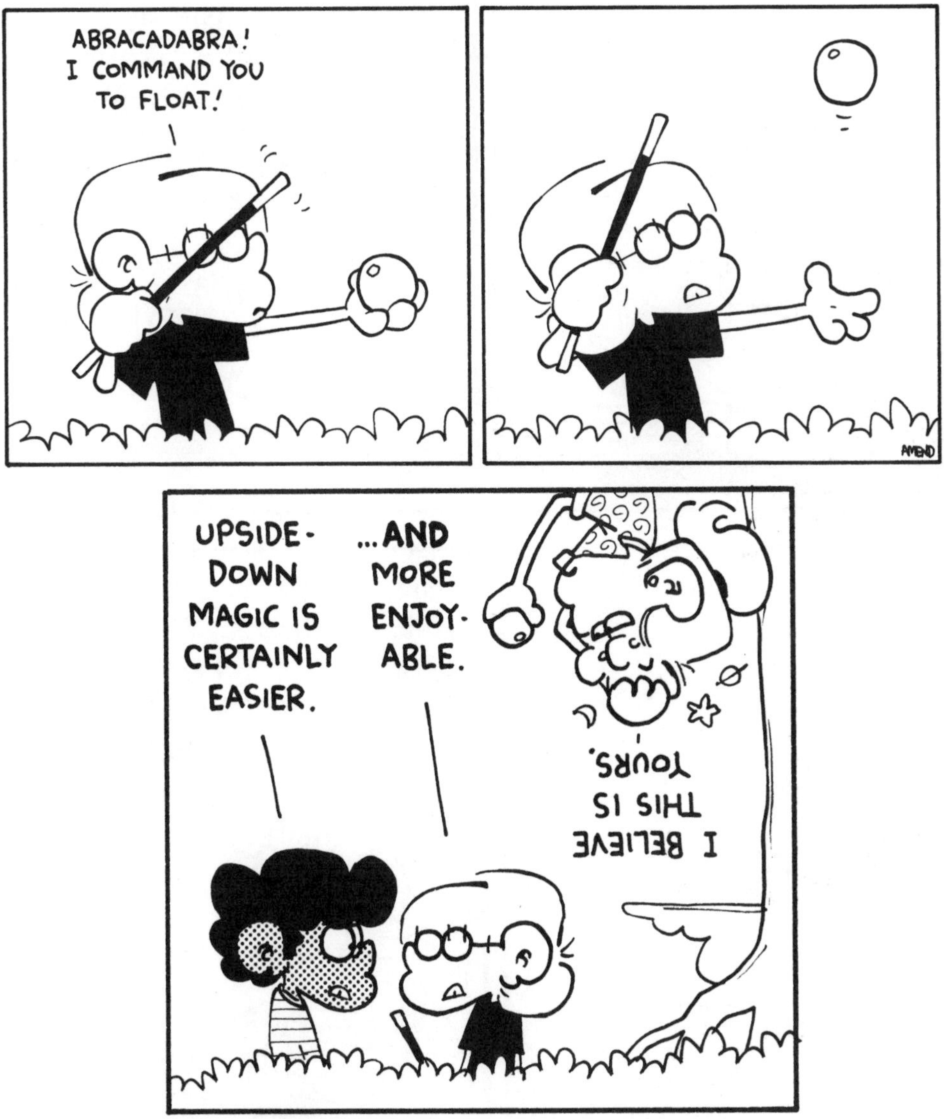
ABRACADABRA! I COMMAND YOU TO FLOAT!
UPSIDE-DOWN MAGIC IS CERTAINLY EASIER.
...AND MORE ENJOY-ABLE.
I BELIEVE THIS IS YOURS.
AMEND

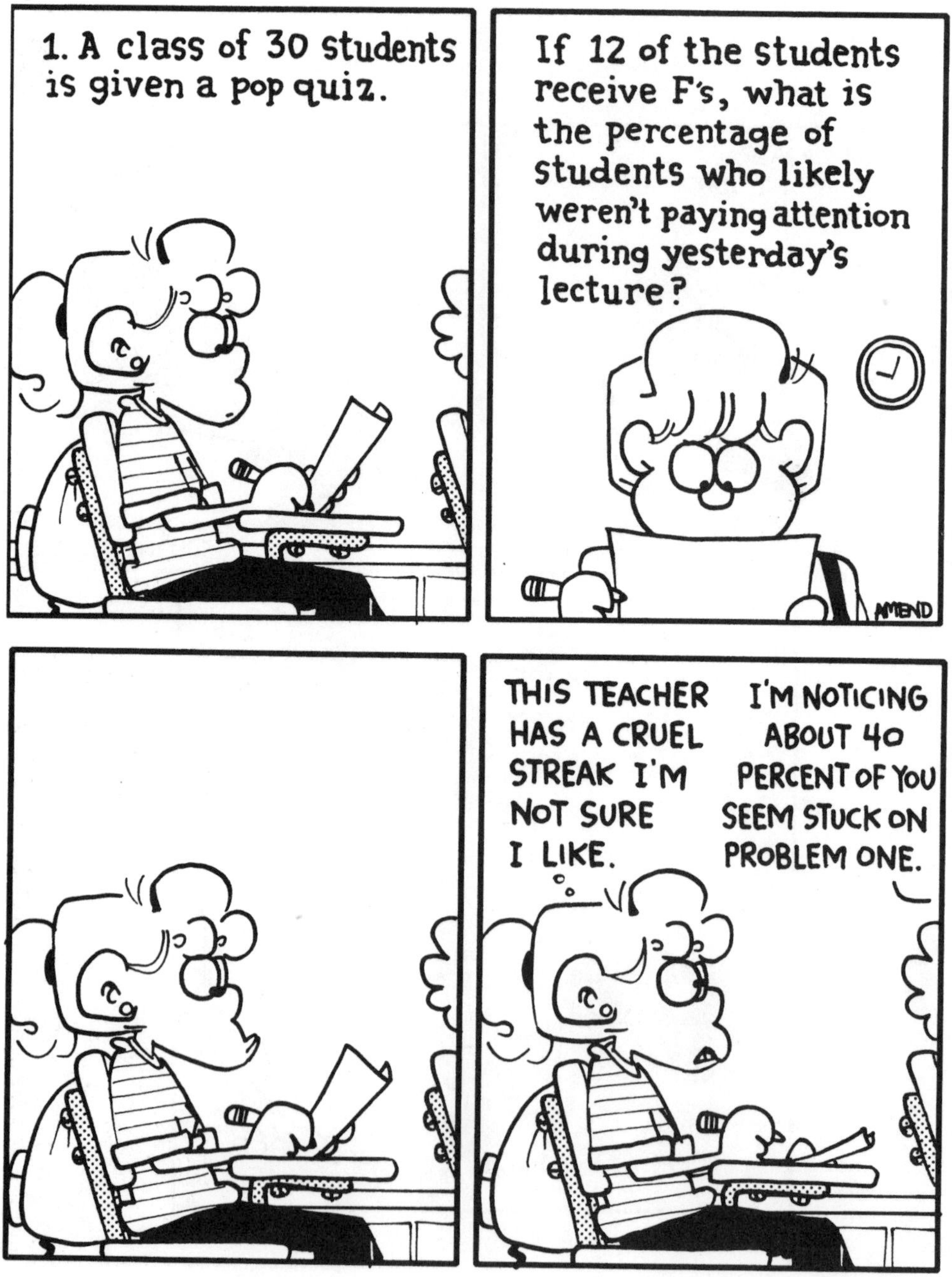
1. A class of 30 students is given a pop quiz.
If 12 of the students receive F's, what is the percentage of students who likely weren't paying attention during yesterday's lecture?
AMEND
THIS TEACHER HAS A CRUEL STREAK I'M NOT SURE I LIKE.
I'M NOTICING ABOUT 40 PERCENT OF YOU SEEM STUCK ON PROBLEM ONE.

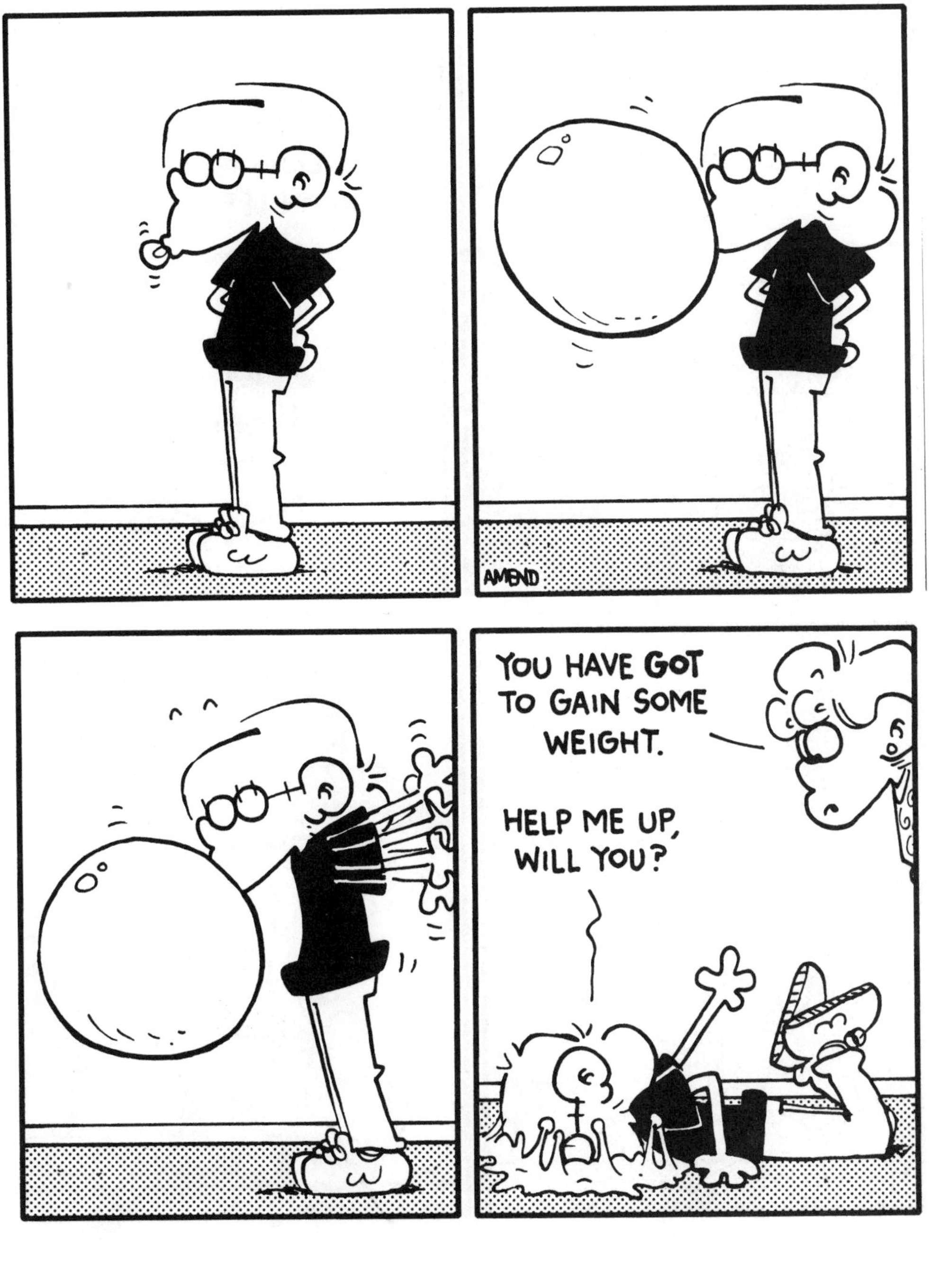
AMEND
YOU HAVE GOT TO GAIN SOME WEIGHT.
HELP ME UP, WILL YOU?

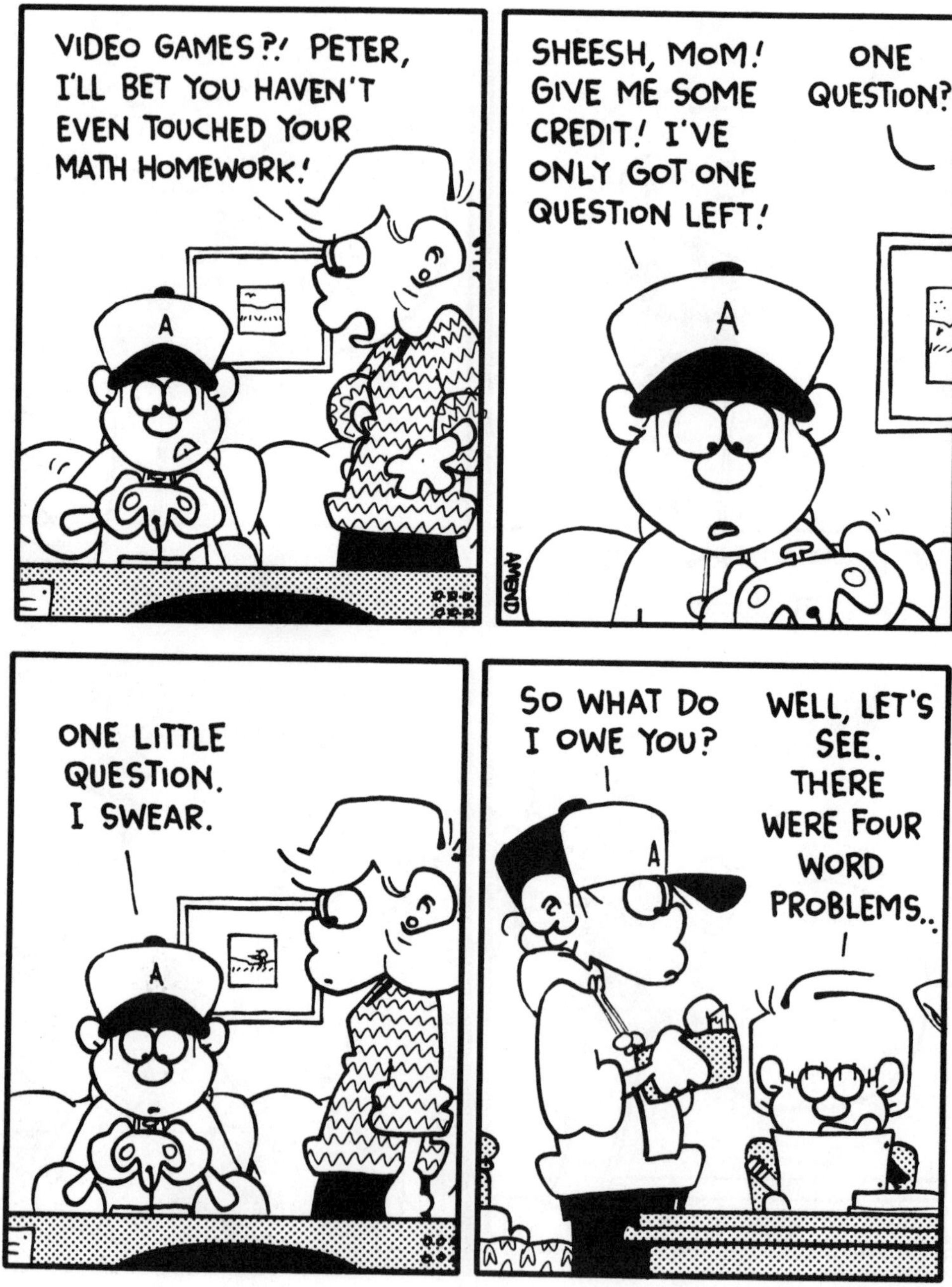
VIDEO GAMES?! PETER, I'LL BET YOU HAVEN'T EVEN TOUCHED YOUR MATH HOMEWORK!
SHEESH, MOM! GIVE ME SOME CREDIT! I'VE ONLY GOT ONE QUESTION LEFT!
ONE QUESTION?
AMEND
ONE LITTLE QUESTION. I SWEAR.
SO WHAT DO I OWE YOU?
WELL, LET'S SEE. THERE WERE FOUR WORD PROBLEMS..

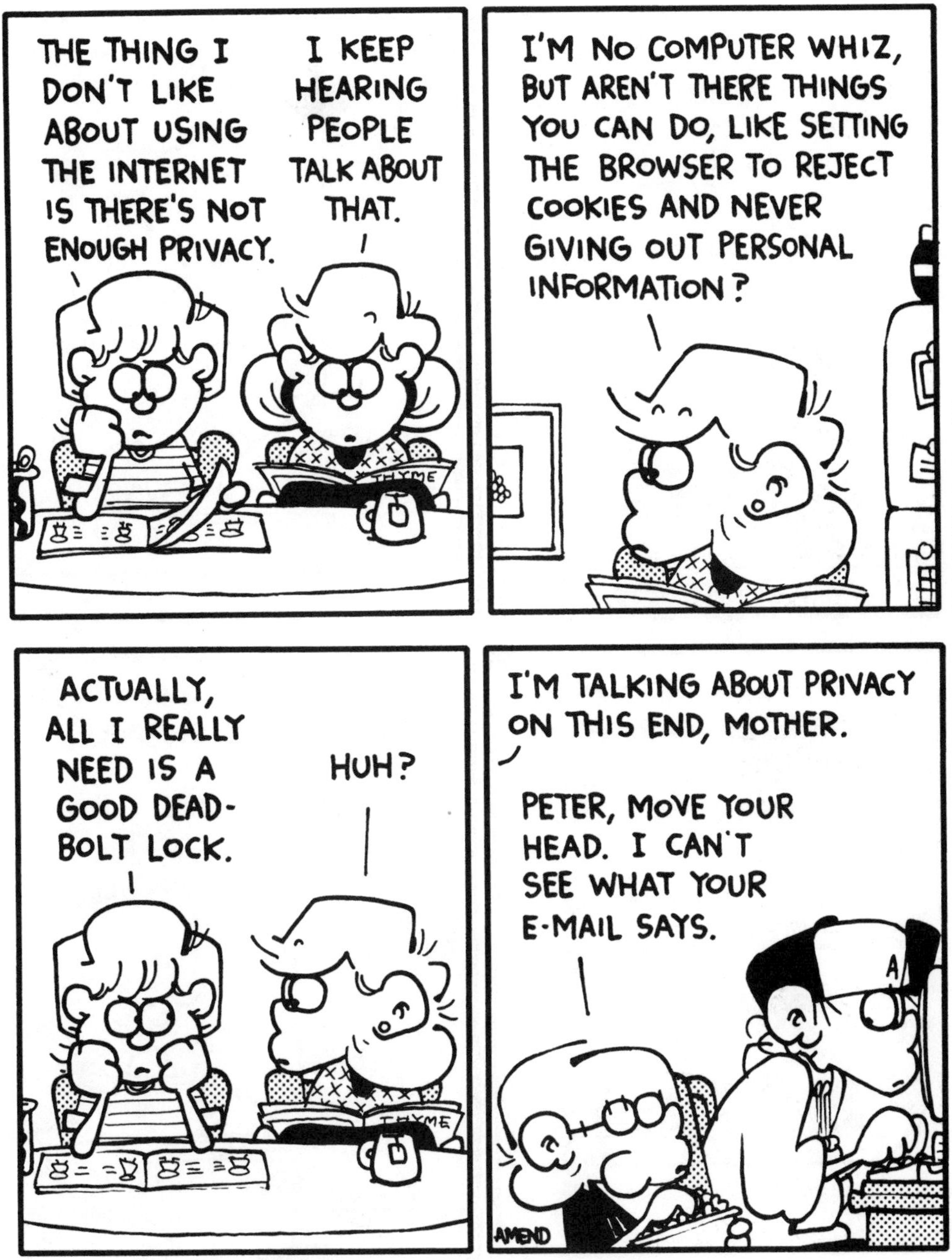
THE THING I DON'T LIKE ABOUT USING THE INTERNET IS THERE'S NOT ENOUGH PRIVACY.
I KEEP HEARING PEOPLE TALK ABOUT THAT.
THYME
I'M NO COMPUTER WHIZ, BUT AREN'T THERE THINGS YOU CAN DO, LIKE SETTING THE BROWSER TO REJECT COOKIES AND NEVER GIVING OUT PERSONAL INFORMATION?
ACTUALLY, ALL I REALLY NEED IS A GOOD DEAD-BOLT LOCK.
HUH?
THYME
I'M TALKING ABOUT PRIVACY ON THIS END, MOTHER.
PETER, MOVE YOUR HEAD. I CAN'T SEE WHAT YOUR E-MAIL SAYS.
AMEND

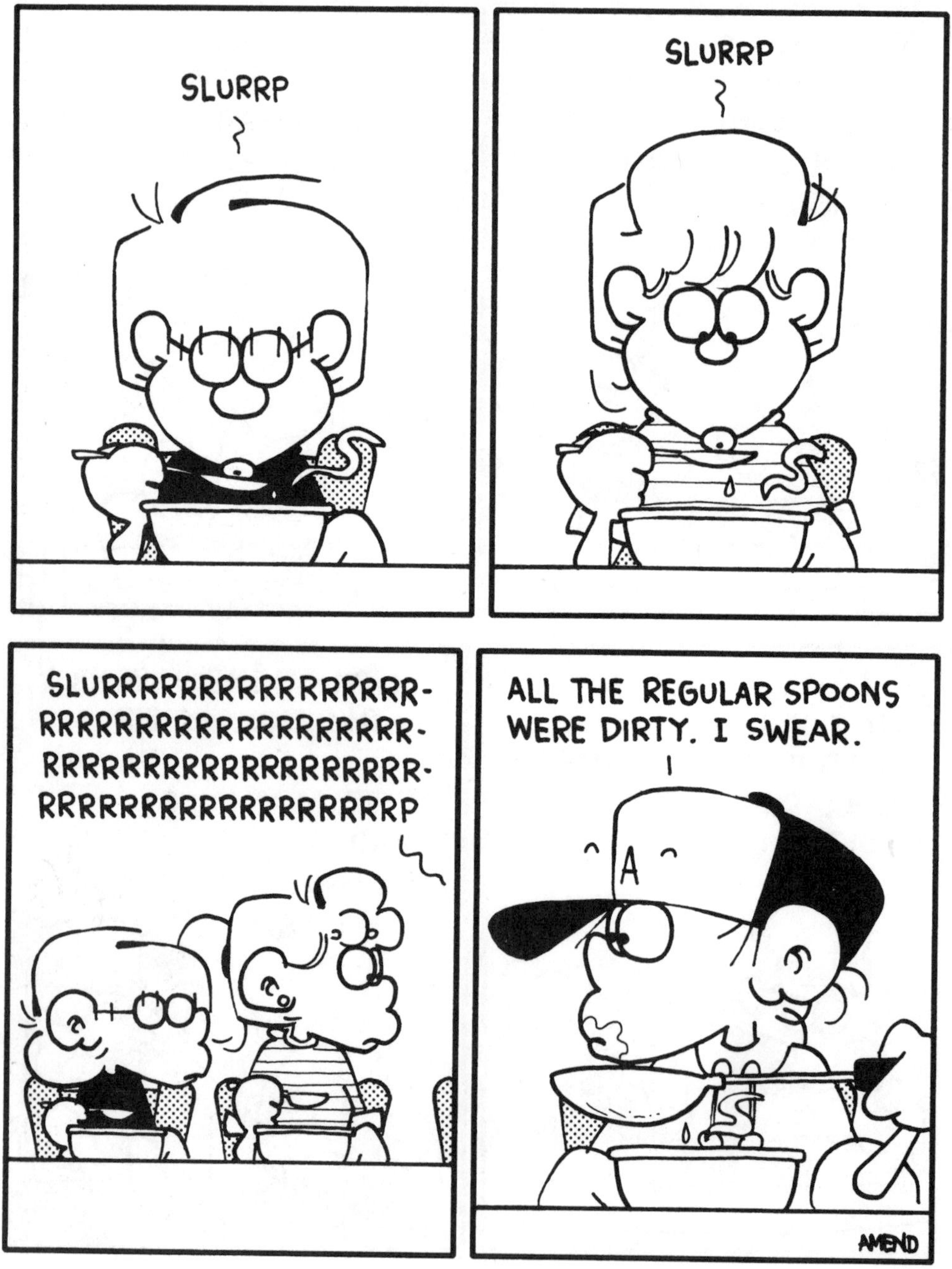
SLURRP
SLURRP
SLURRRRRRRRRRRRRRRR-RRRRRRRRRRRRRRRRRRR-RRRRRRRRRRRRRRRRRRR-RRRRRRRRRRRRRRRRRRP
ALL THE REGULAR SPOONS WERE DIRTY. I SWEAR.
AMEND

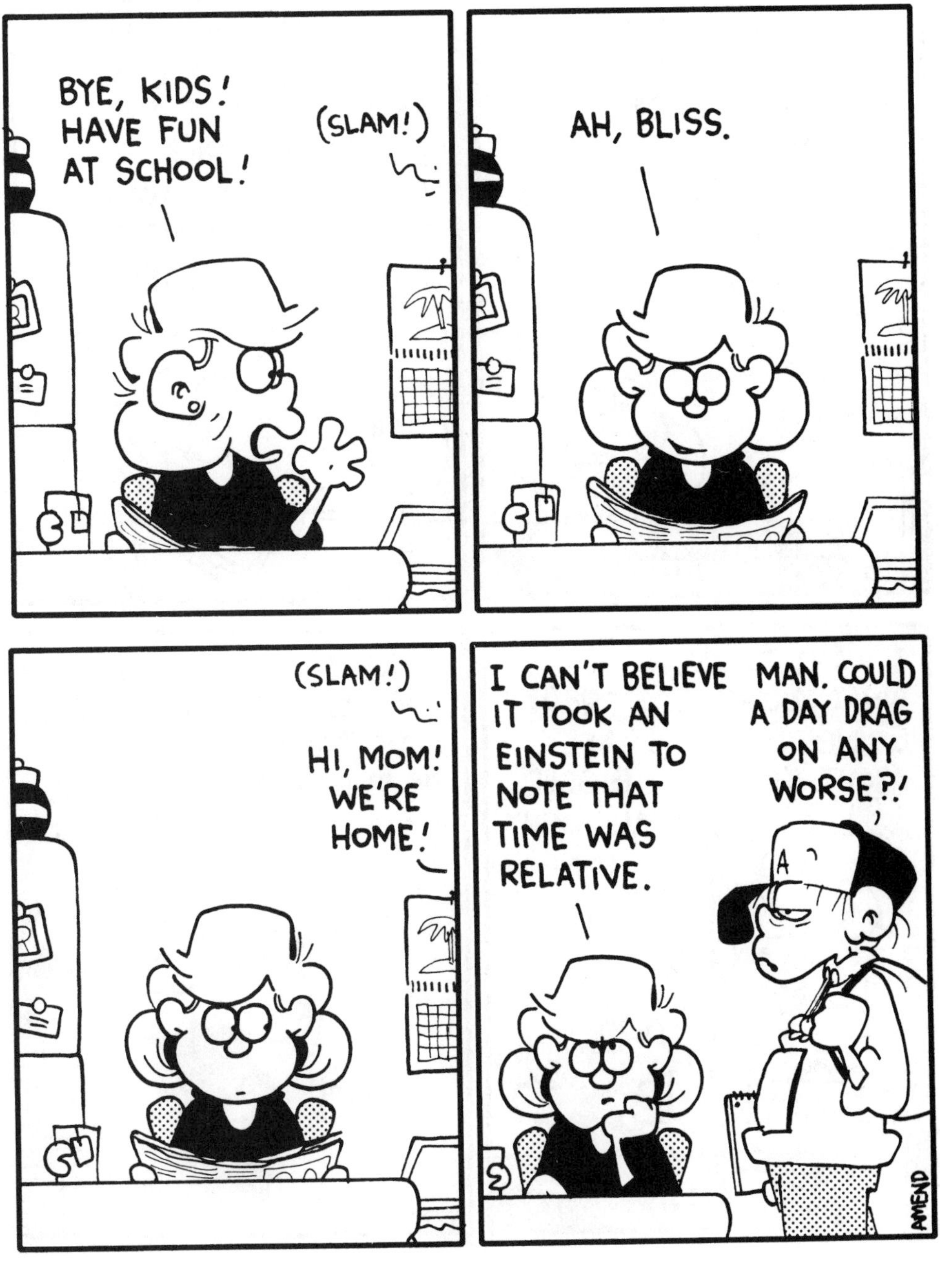
BYE, KIDS! HAVE FUN AT SCHOOL!
(SLAM!)
AH, BLISS.
(SLAM!)
HI, MOM! WE'RE HOME!
I CAN'T BELIEVE IT TOOK AN EINSTEIN TO NOTE THAT TIME WAS RELATIVE.
MAN. COULD A DAY DRAG ON ANY WORSE?!
AMEND

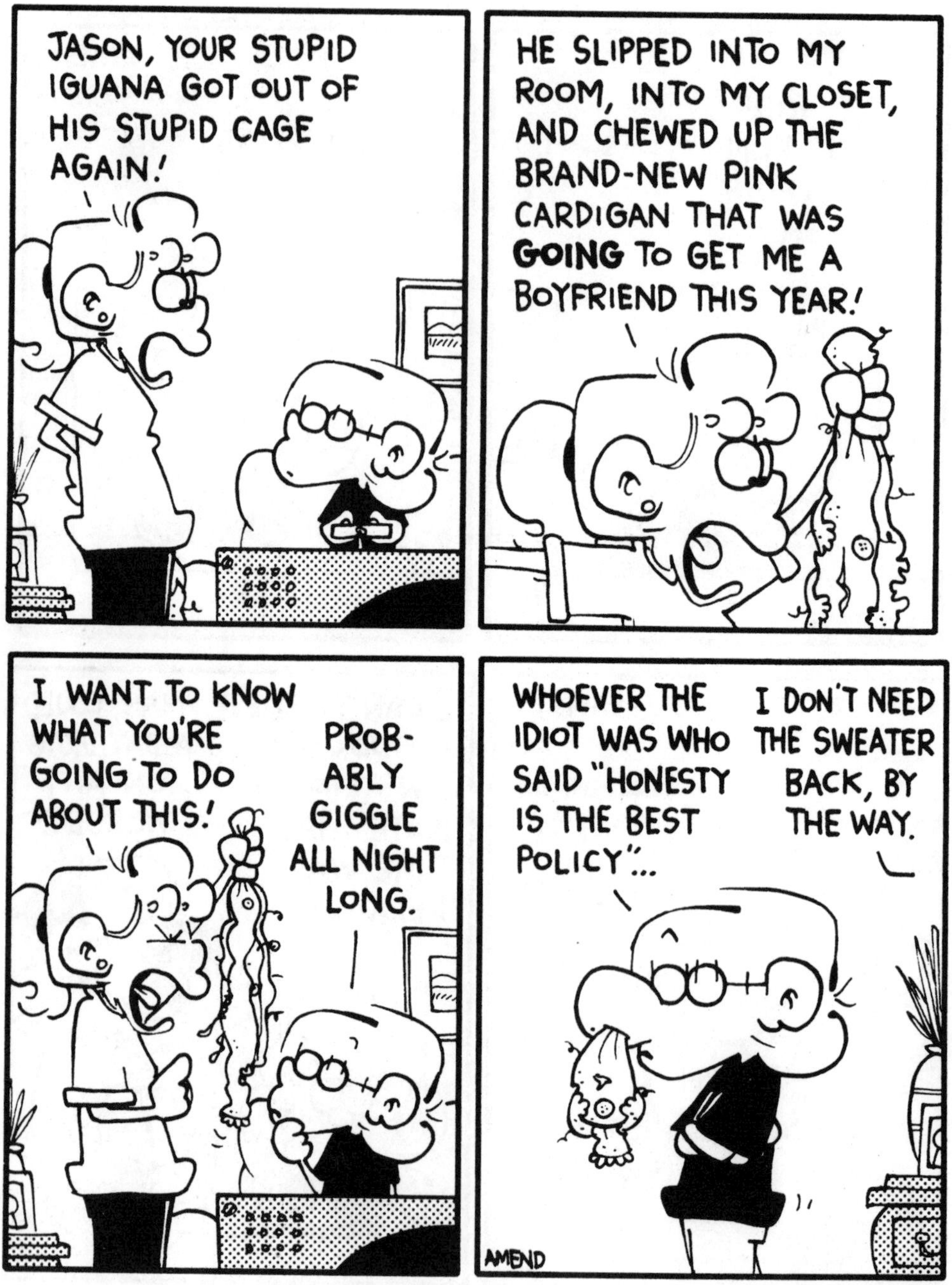
JASON, YOUR STUPID IGUANA GOT OUT OF HIS STUPID CAGE AGAIN!
HE SLIPPED INTO MY ROOM, INTO MY CLOSET, AND CHEWED UP THE BRAND-NEW PINK CARDIGAN THAT WAS GOING TO GET ME A BOYFRIEND THIS YEAR!
I WANT TO KNOW WHAT YOU'RE GOING TO DO ABOUT THIS!
PROB-ABLY GIGGLE ALL NIGHT LONG.
WHOEVER THE IDIOT WAS WHO SAID "HONESTY IS THE BEST POLICY"...
I DON'T NEED THE SWEATER BACK, BY THE WAY.
AMEND

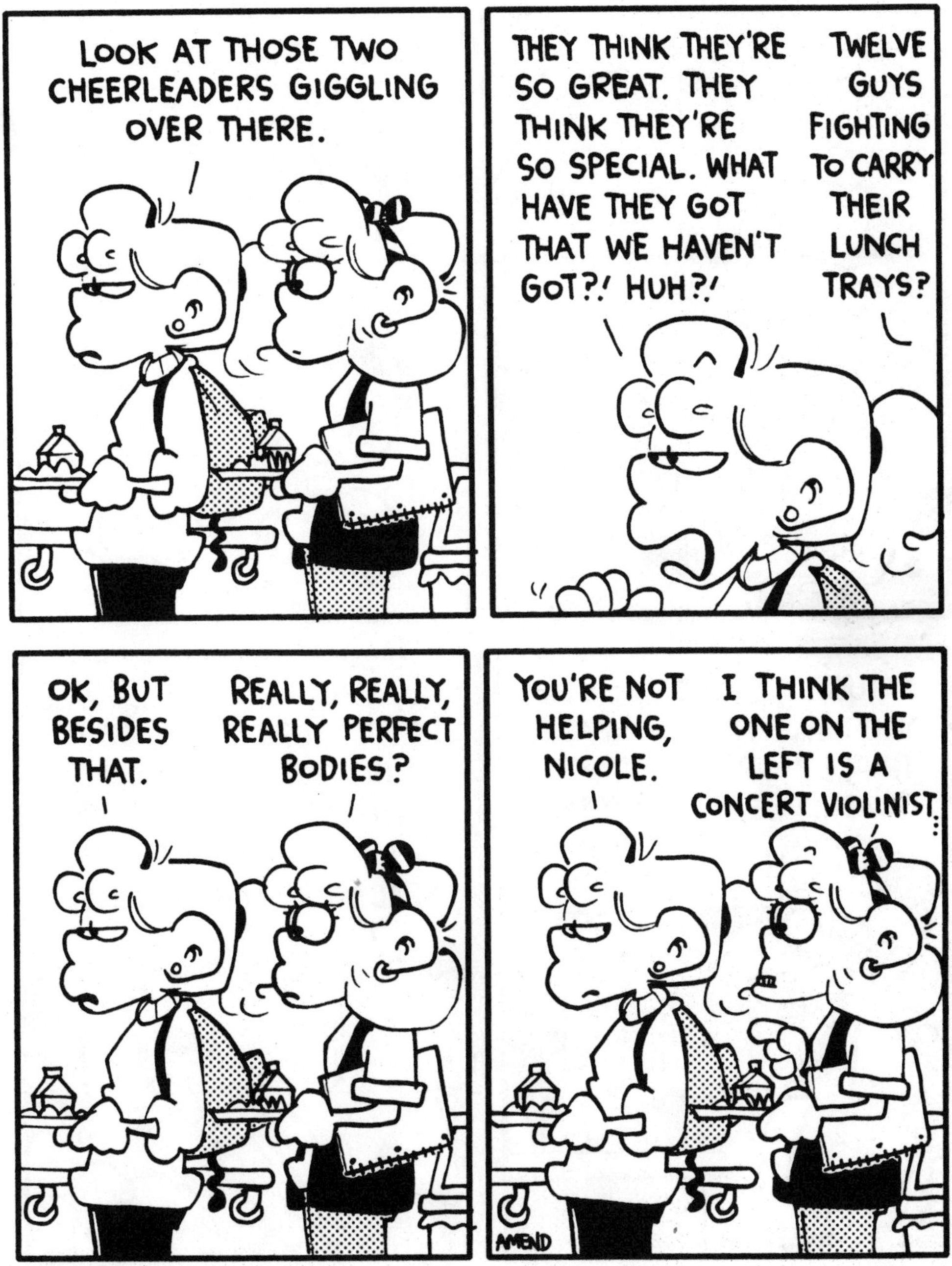
LOOK AT THOSE TWO CHEERLEADERS GIGGLING OVER THERE.
THEY THINK THEY'RE SO GREAT. THEY THINK THEY'RE SO SPECIAL. WHAT HAVE THEY GOT THAT WE HAVEN'T GOT?! HUH?!
TWELVE GUYS FIGHTING TO CARRY THEIR LUNCH TRAYS?
OK, BUT BESIDES THAT.
REALLY, REALLY, REALLY PERFECT BODIES?
YOU'RE NOT HELPING, NICOLE.
I THINK THE ONE ON THE LEFT IS A CONCERT VIOLINIST.
AMEND

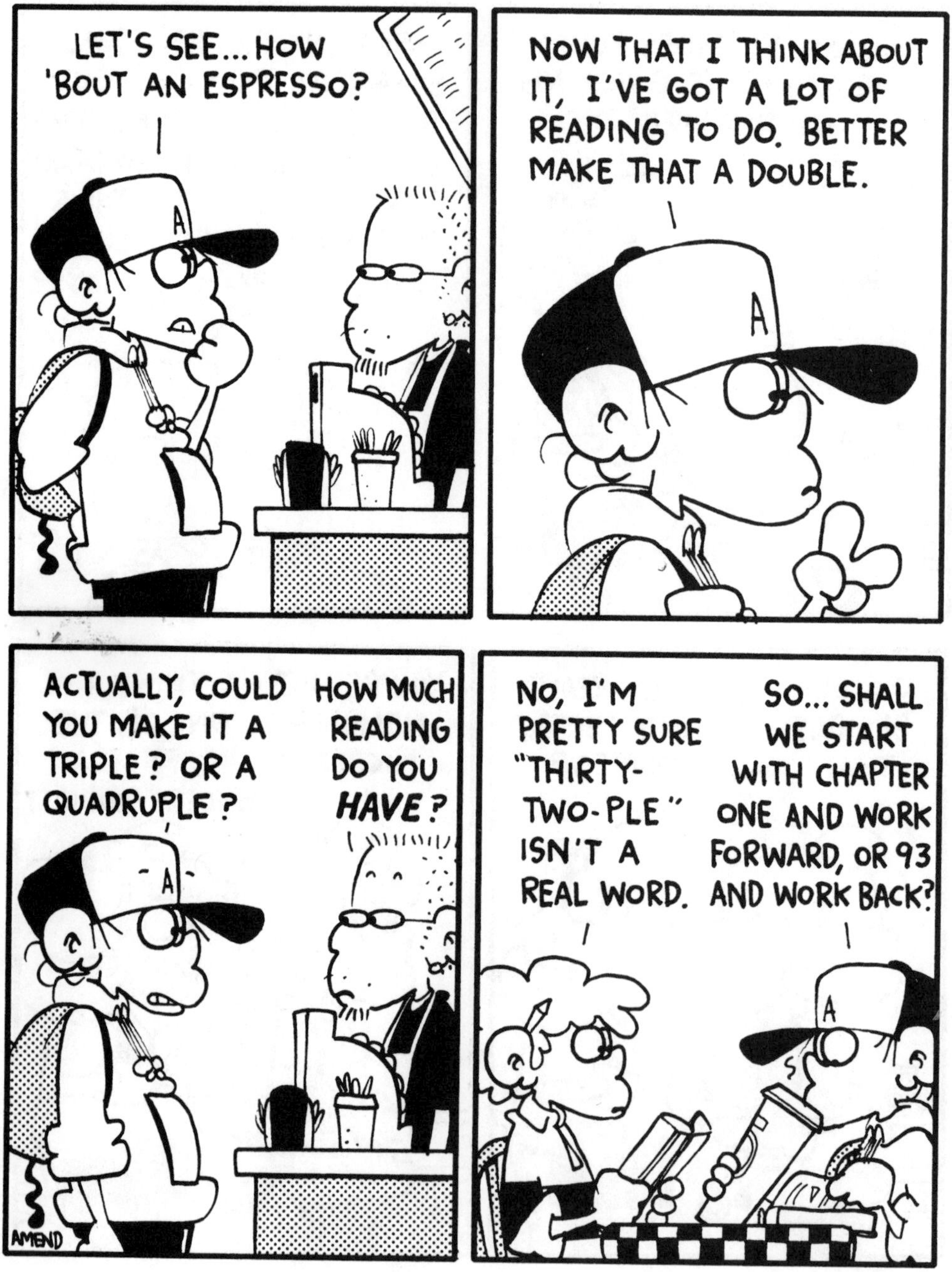
LET'S SEE... HOW 'BOUT AN ESPRESSO?
NOW THAT I THINK ABOUT IT, I'VE GOT A LOT OF READING TO DO. BETTER MAKE THAT A DOUBLE.
ACTUALLY, COULD YOU MAKE IT A TRIPLE? OR A QUADRUPLE?
HOW MUCH READING DO YOU *HAVE*?
NO, I'M PRETTY SURE "THIRTY-TWO-PLE" ISN'T A REAL WORD.
SO... SHALL WE START WITH CHAPTER ONE AND WORK FORWARD, OR 93 AND WORK BACK?
AMEND

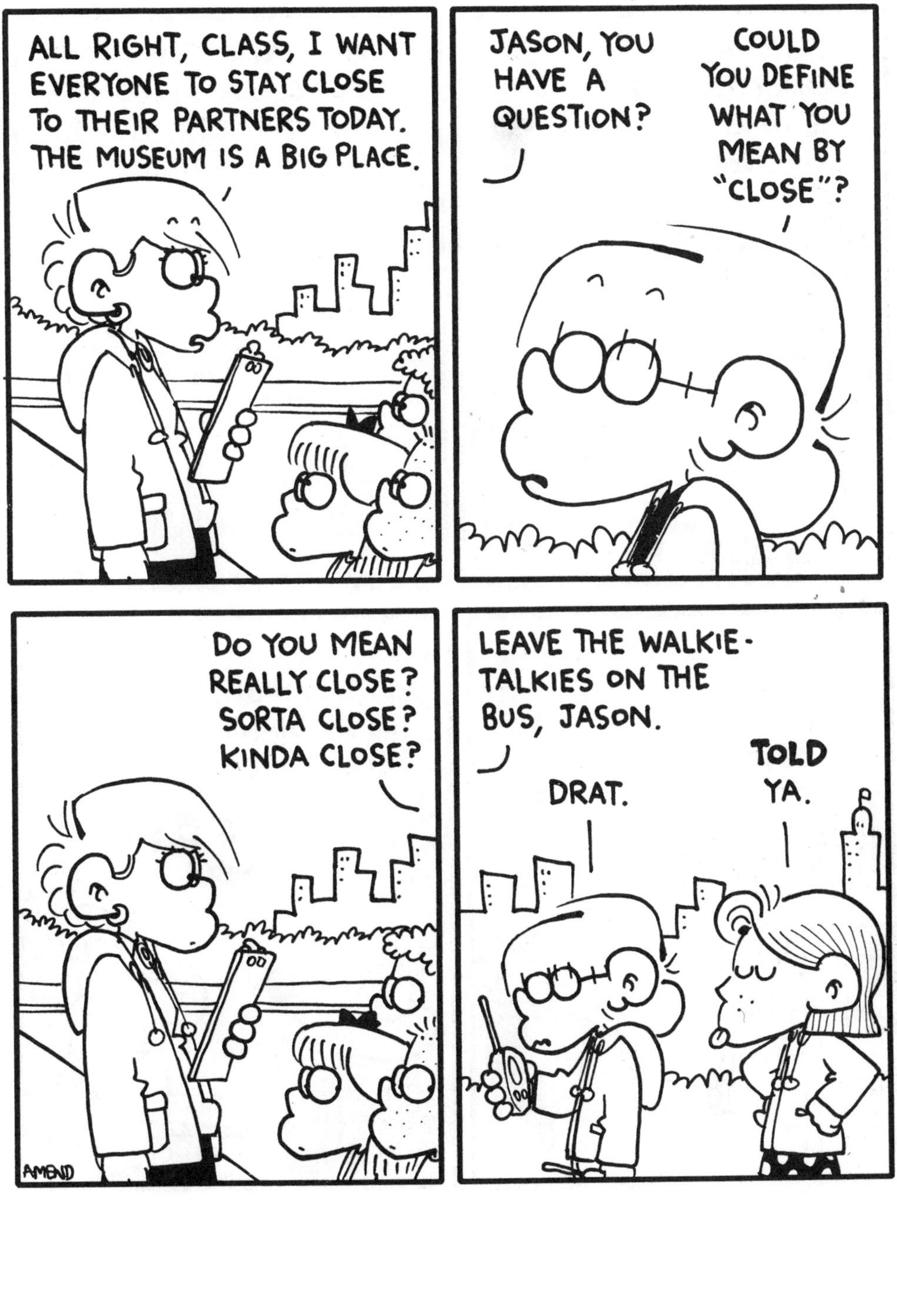
ALL RIGHT, CLASS, I WANT EVERYONE TO STAY CLOSE TO THEIR PARTNERS TODAY. THE MUSEUM IS A BIG PLACE.
JASON, YOU HAVE A QUESTION?
COULD YOU DEFINE WHAT YOU MEAN BY "CLOSE"?
DO YOU MEAN REALLY CLOSE? SORTA CLOSE? KINDA CLOSE?
AMEND
LEAVE THE WALKIE-TALKIES ON THE BUS, JASON.
DRAT.
TOLD YA.

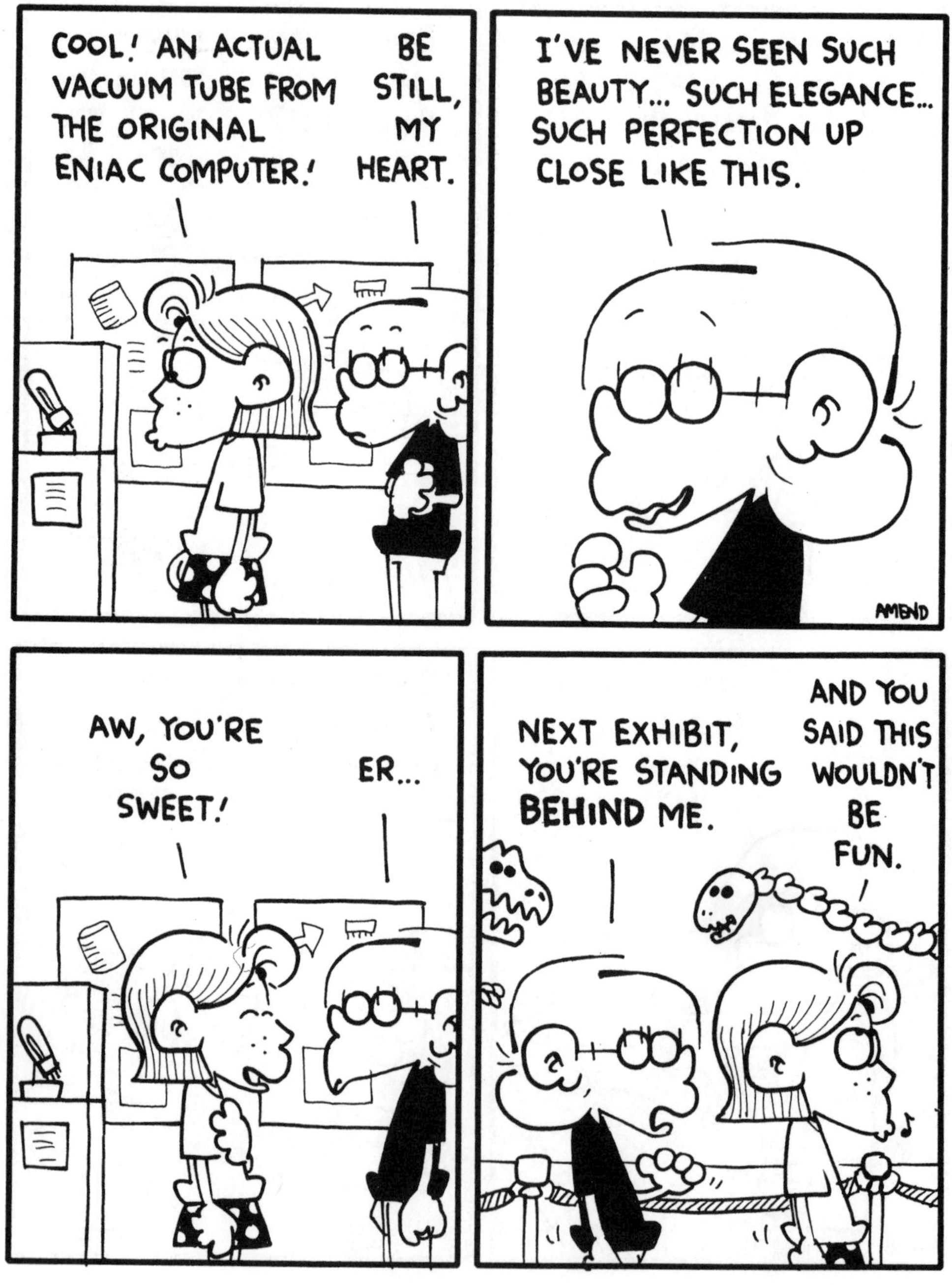
COOL! AN ACTUAL VACUUM TUBE FROM THE ORIGINAL ENIAC COMPUTER!
BE STILL, MY HEART.
I'VE NEVER SEEN SUCH BEAUTY... SUCH ELEGANCE... SUCH PERFECTION UP CLOSE LIKE THIS.
AMEND
AW, YOU'RE SO SWEET!
ER...
NEXT EXHIBIT, YOU'RE STANDING BEHIND ME.
AND YOU SAID THIS WOULDN'T BE FUN.

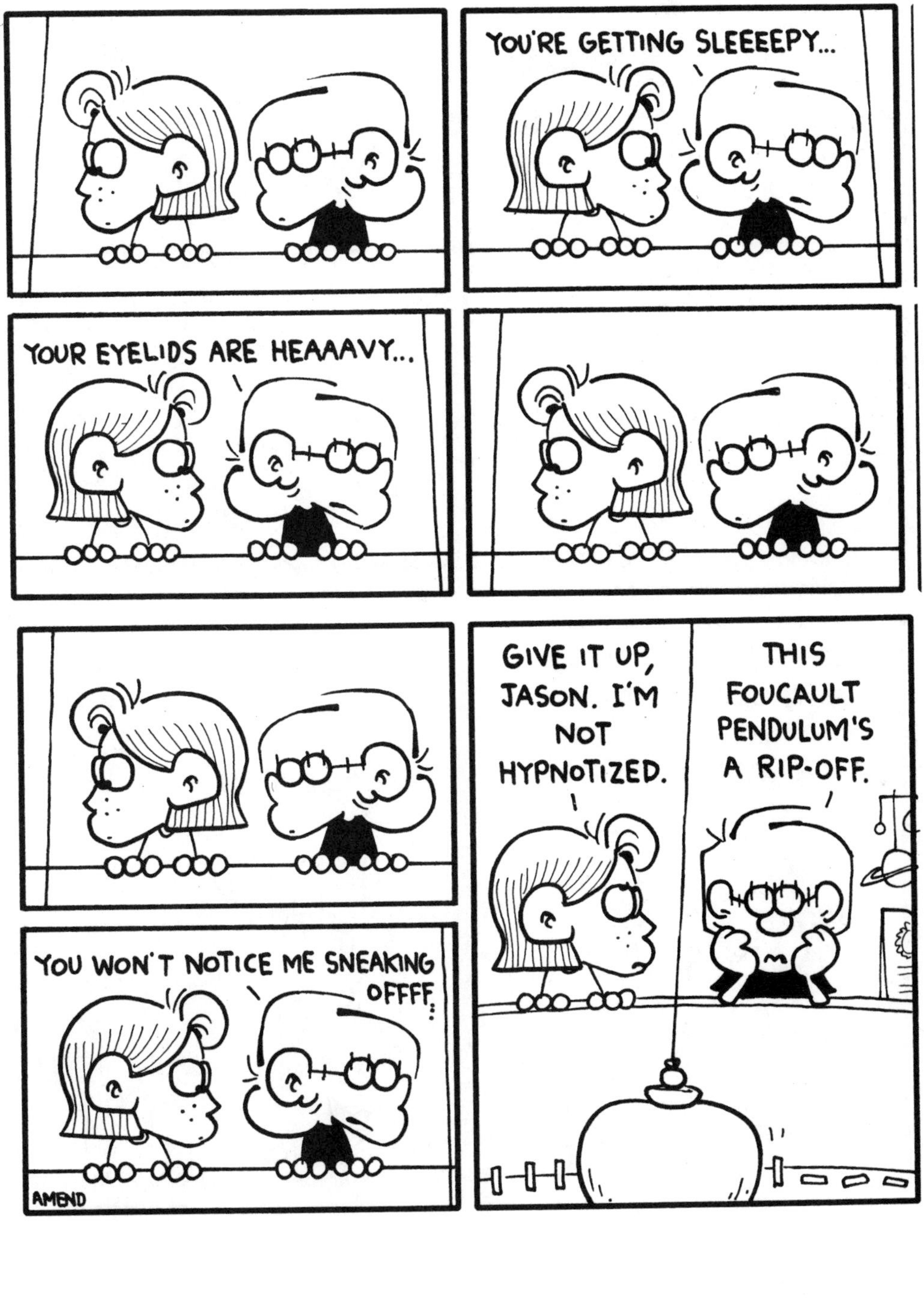
YOU'RE GETTING SLEEEEPY...
YOUR EYELIDS ARE HEAAAVY...
YOU WON'T NOTICE ME SNEAKING OFFFF...
AMEND
GIVE IT UP, JASON. I'M NOT HYPNOTIZED.
THIS FOUCAULT PENDULUM'S A RIP-OFF.

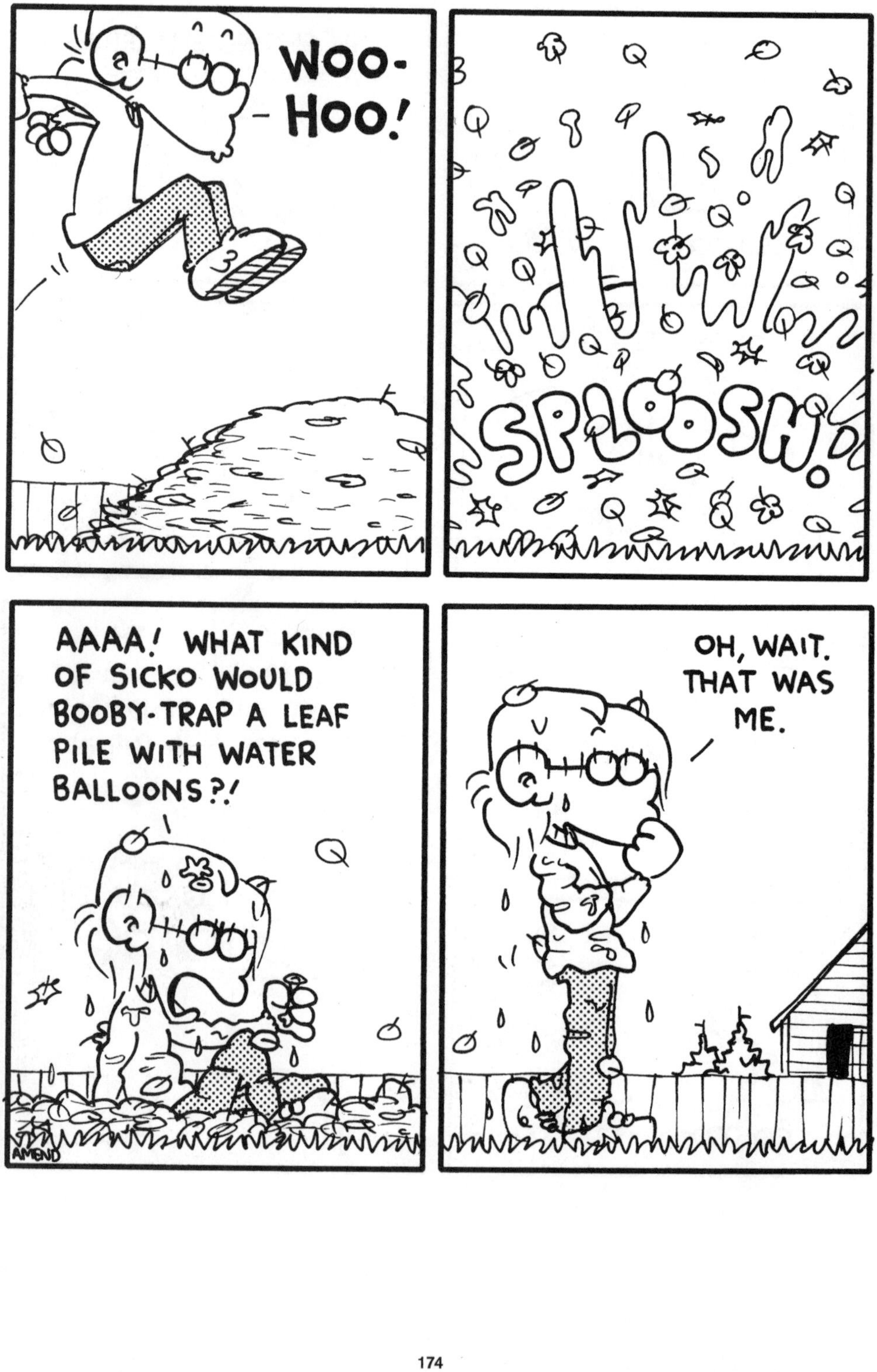
WOO-
-HOO!
SPLOOSH!
AAAA! WHAT KIND OF SICKO WOULD BOOBY-TRAP A LEAF PILE WITH WATER BALLOONS?!
AMEND
OH, WAIT. THAT WAS ME.

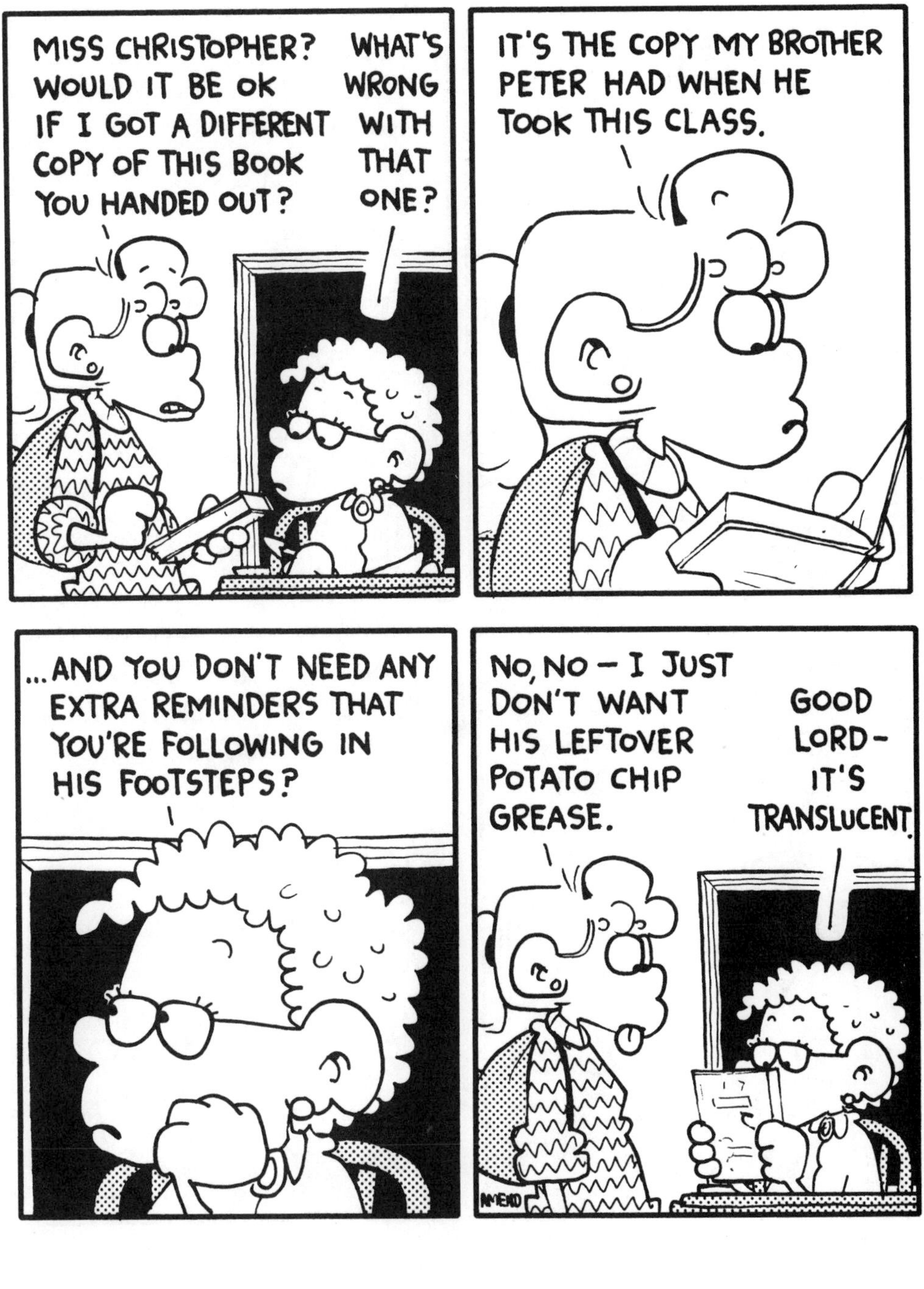
MISS CHRISTOPHER? WOULD IT BE OK IF I GOT A DIFFERENT COPY OF THIS BOOK YOU HANDED OUT?
WHAT'S WRONG WITH THAT ONE?
IT'S THE COPY MY BROTHER PETER HAD WHEN HE TOOK THIS CLASS.
...AND YOU DON'T NEED ANY EXTRA REMINDERS THAT YOU'RE FOLLOWING IN HIS FOOTSTEPS?
NO, NO – I JUST DON'T WANT HIS LEFTOVER POTATO CHIP GREASE.
GOOD LORD – IT'S TRANSLUCENT.
AMEND

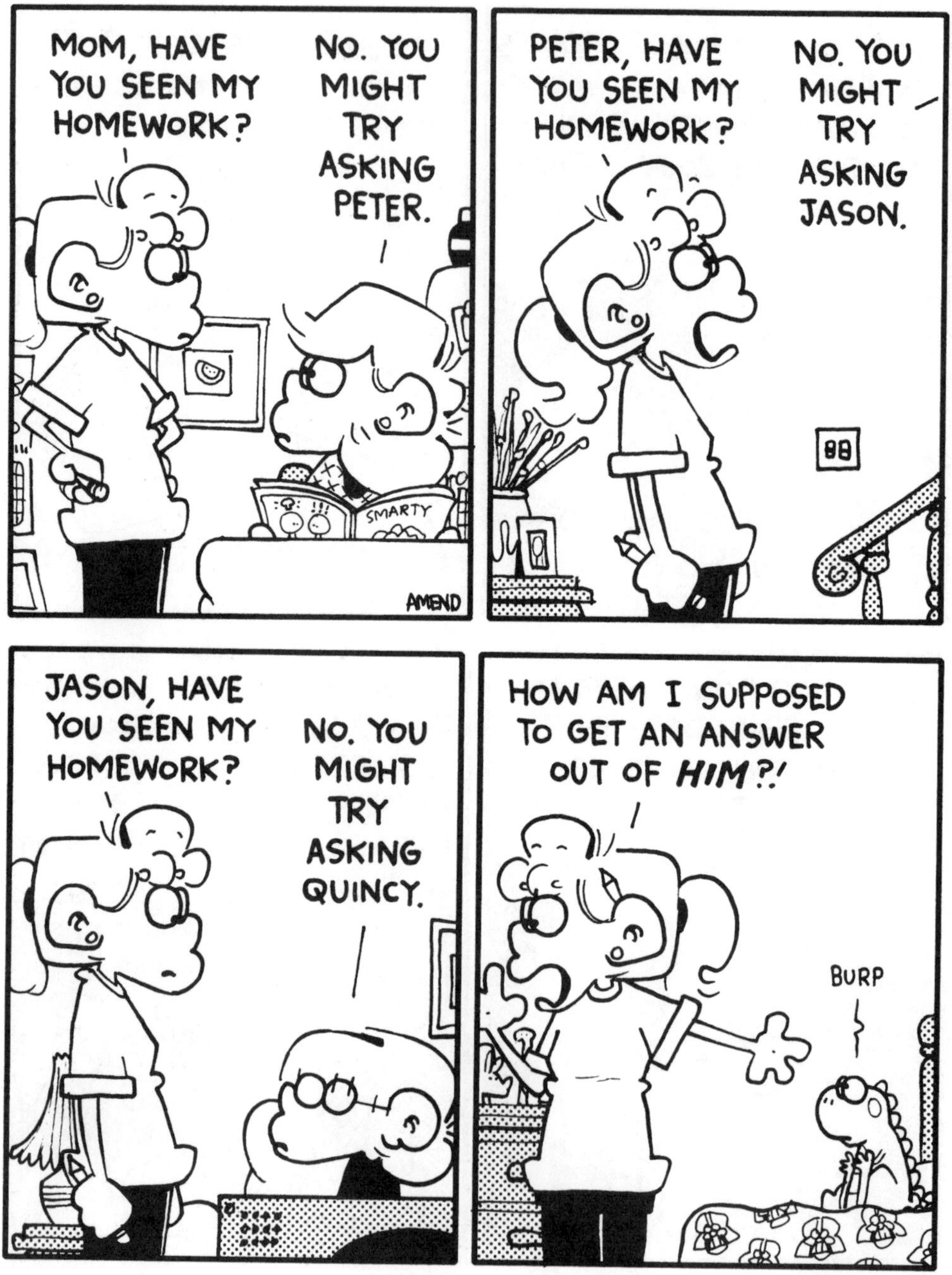

MOM, HAVE YOU SEEN MY HOMEWORK?
NO. YOU MIGHT TRY ASKING PETER.
AMEND
PETER, HAVE YOU SEEN MY HOMEWORK?
NO. YOU MIGHT TRY ASKING JASON.
JASON, HAVE YOU SEEN MY HOMEWORK?
NO. YOU MIGHT TRY ASKING QUINCY.
HOW AM I SUPPOSED TO GET AN ANSWER OUT OF *HIM*?!
BURP

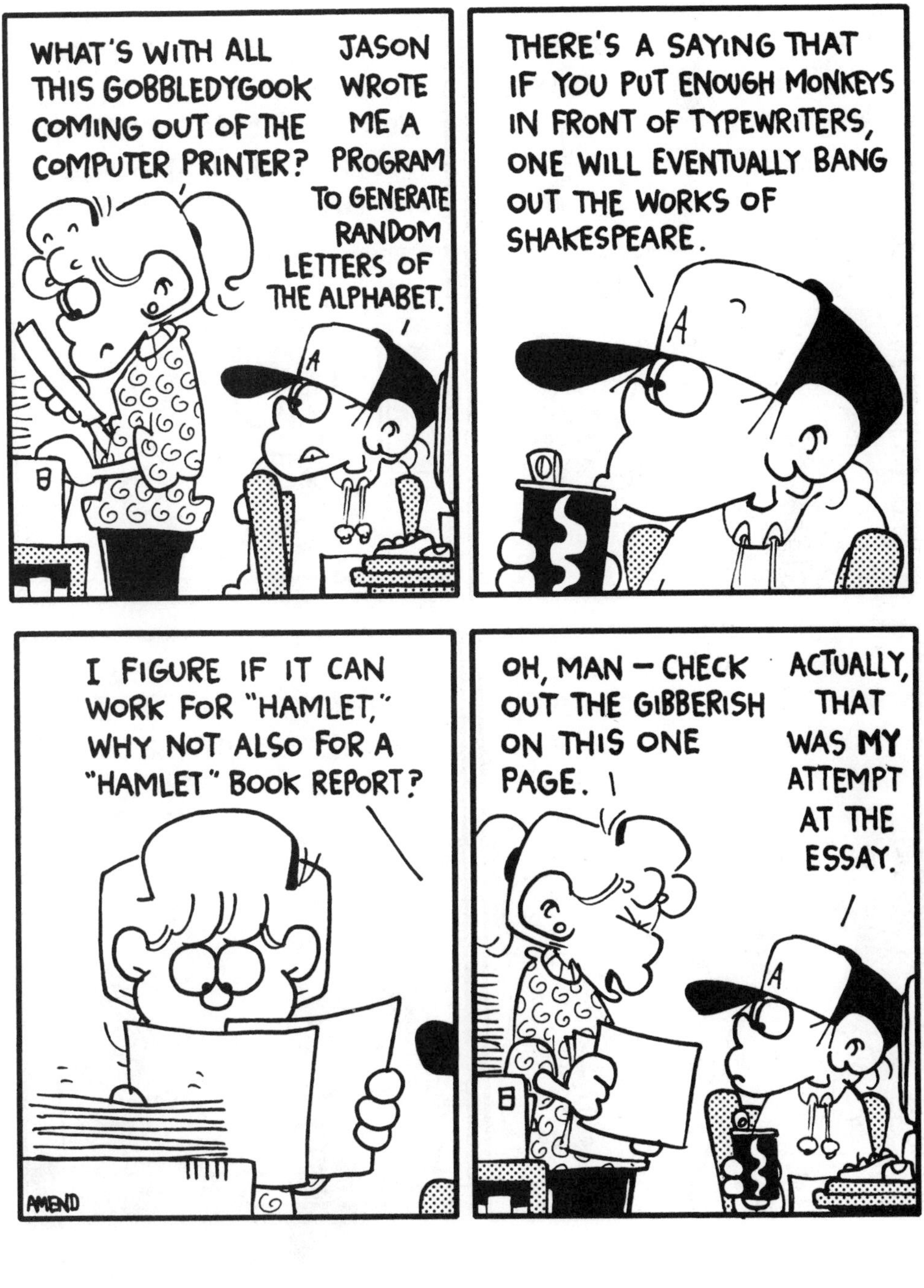
WHAT'S WITH ALL THIS GOBBLEDYGOOK COMING OUT OF THE COMPUTER PRINTER?
JASON WROTE ME A PROGRAM TO GENERATE RANDOM LETTERS OF THE ALPHABET.
THERE'S A SAYING THAT IF YOU PUT ENOUGH MONKEYS IN FRONT OF TYPEWRITERS, ONE WILL EVENTUALLY BANG OUT THE WORKS OF SHAKESPEARE.
I FIGURE IF IT CAN WORK FOR "HAMLET," WHY NOT ALSO FOR A "HAMLET" BOOK REPORT?
AMEND
OH, MAN – CHECK OUT THE GIBBERISH ON THIS ONE PAGE.
ACTUALLY, THAT WAS MY ATTEMPT AT THE ESSAY.

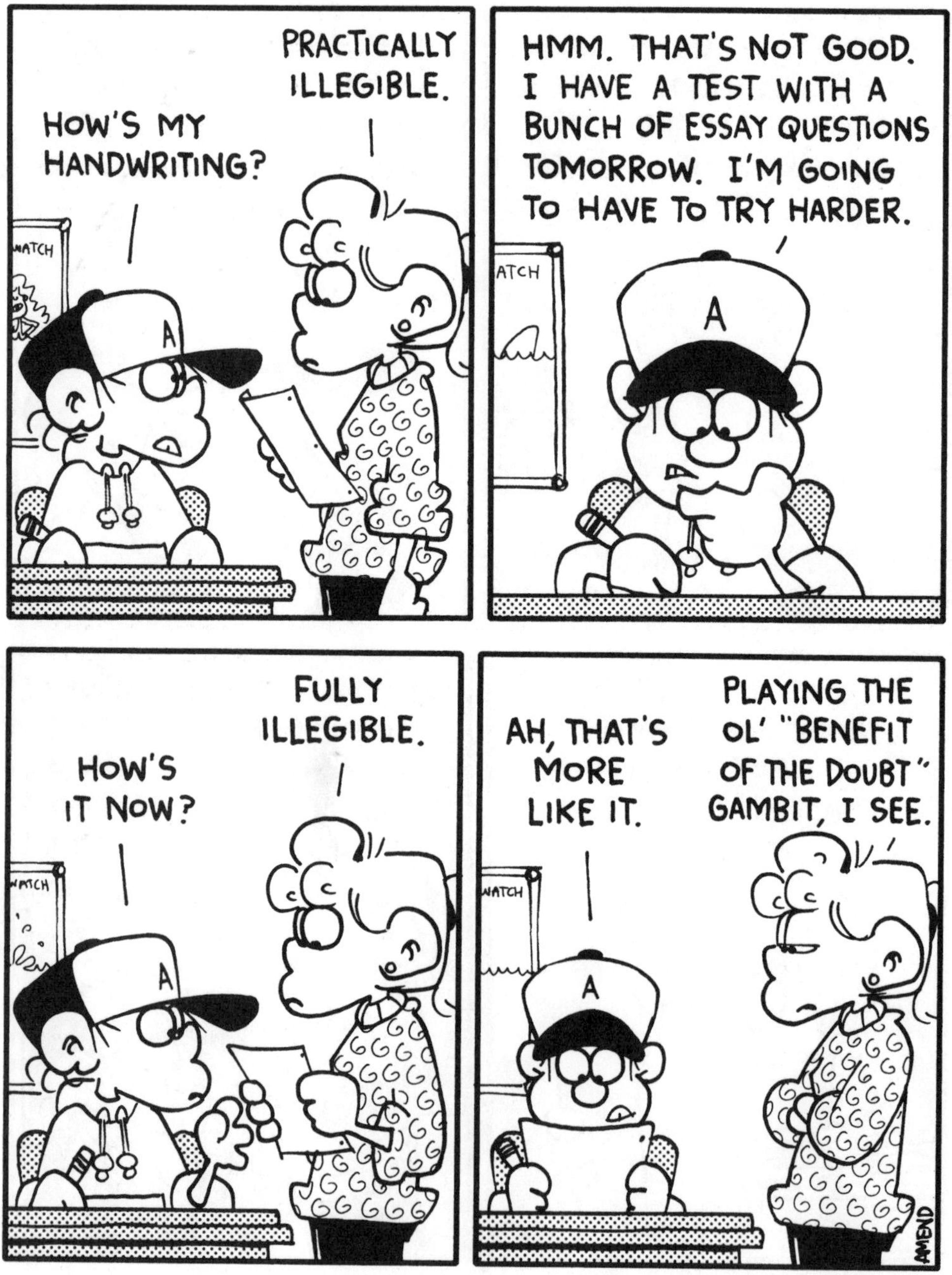
HOW'S MY HANDWRITING?
PRACTICALLY ILLEGIBLE.
HMM. THAT'S NOT GOOD. I HAVE A TEST WITH A BUNCH OF ESSAY QUESTIONS TOMORROW. I'M GOING TO HAVE TO TRY HARDER.
HOW'S IT NOW?
FULLY ILLEGIBLE.
AH, THAT'S MORE LIKE IT.
PLAYING THE OL' "BENEFIT OF THE DOUBT" GAMBIT, I SEE.
AMEND

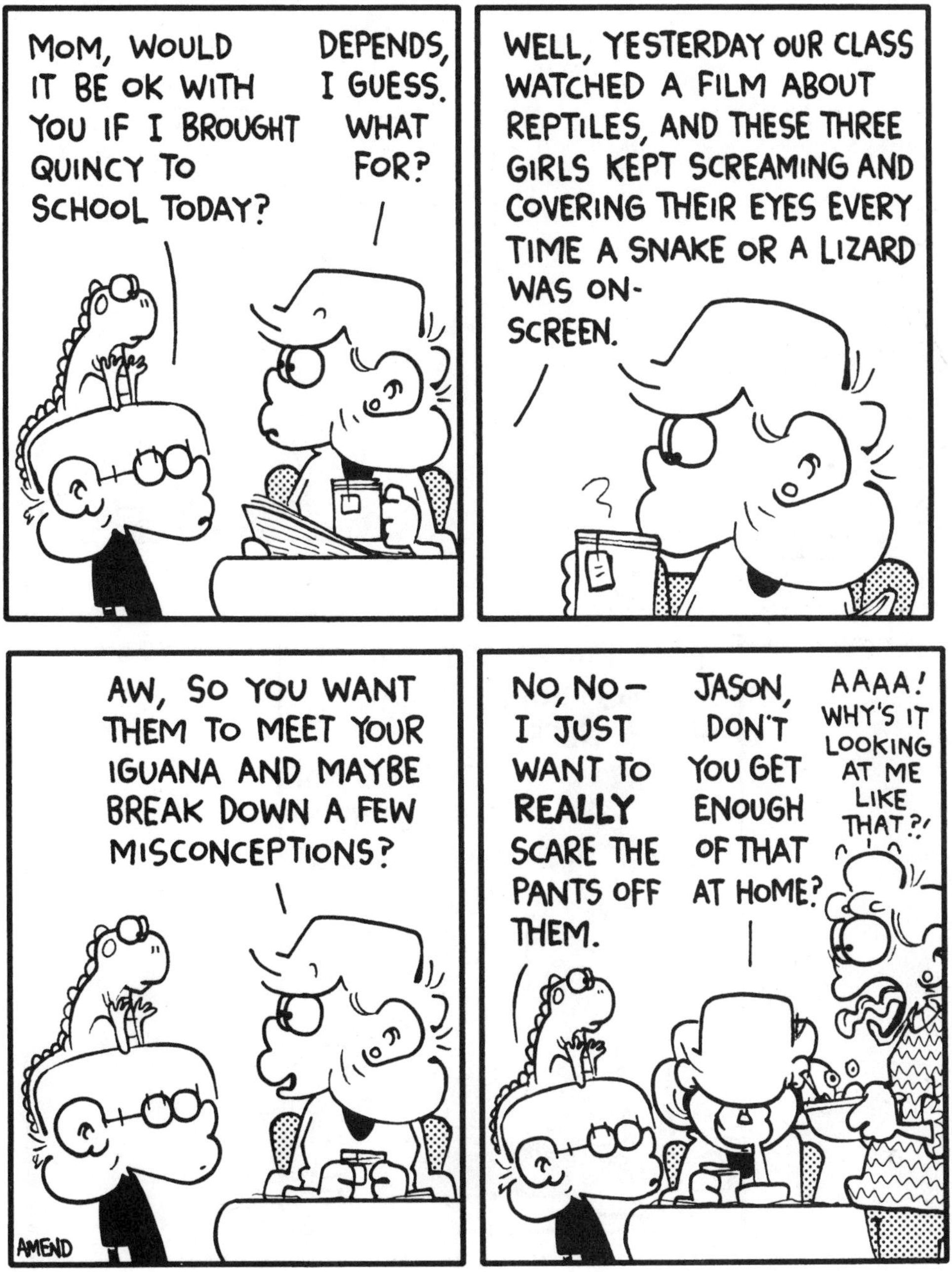
MOM, WOULD IT BE OK WITH YOU IF I BROUGHT QUINCY TO SCHOOL TODAY?
DEPENDS, I GUESS. WHAT FOR?
WELL, YESTERDAY OUR CLASS WATCHED A FILM ABOUT REPTILES, AND THESE THREE GIRLS KEPT SCREAMING AND COVERING THEIR EYES EVERY TIME A SNAKE OR A LIZARD WAS ON-SCREEN.
AW, SO YOU WANT THEM TO MEET YOUR IGUANA AND MAYBE BREAK DOWN A FEW MISCONCEPTIONS?
AMEND
NO, NO— I JUST WANT TO **REALLY** SCARE THE PANTS OFF THEM.
JASON, DON'T YOU GET ENOUGH OF THAT AT HOME?
AAAA! WHY'S IT LOOKING AT ME LIKE THAT?!

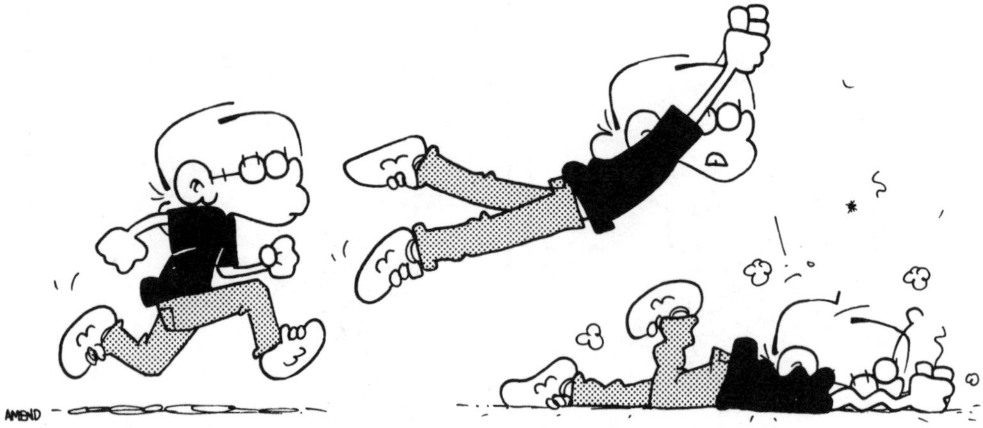
AMEND

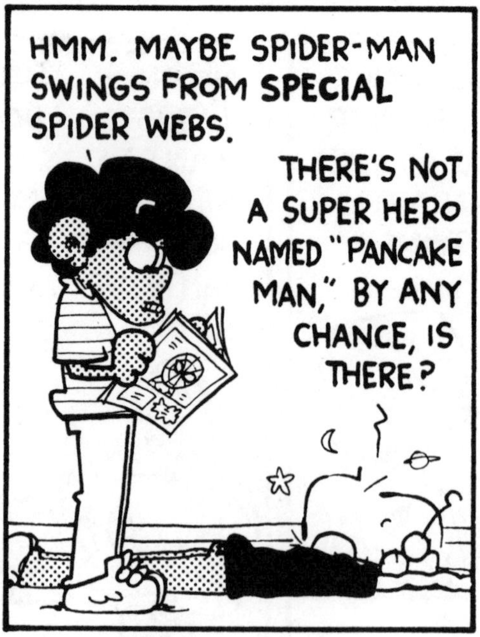
HMM. MAYBE SPIDER-MAN SWINGS FROM **SPECIAL** SPIDER WEBS.
THERE'S NOT A SUPER HERO NAMED "PANCAKE MAN," BY ANY CHANCE, IS THERE?

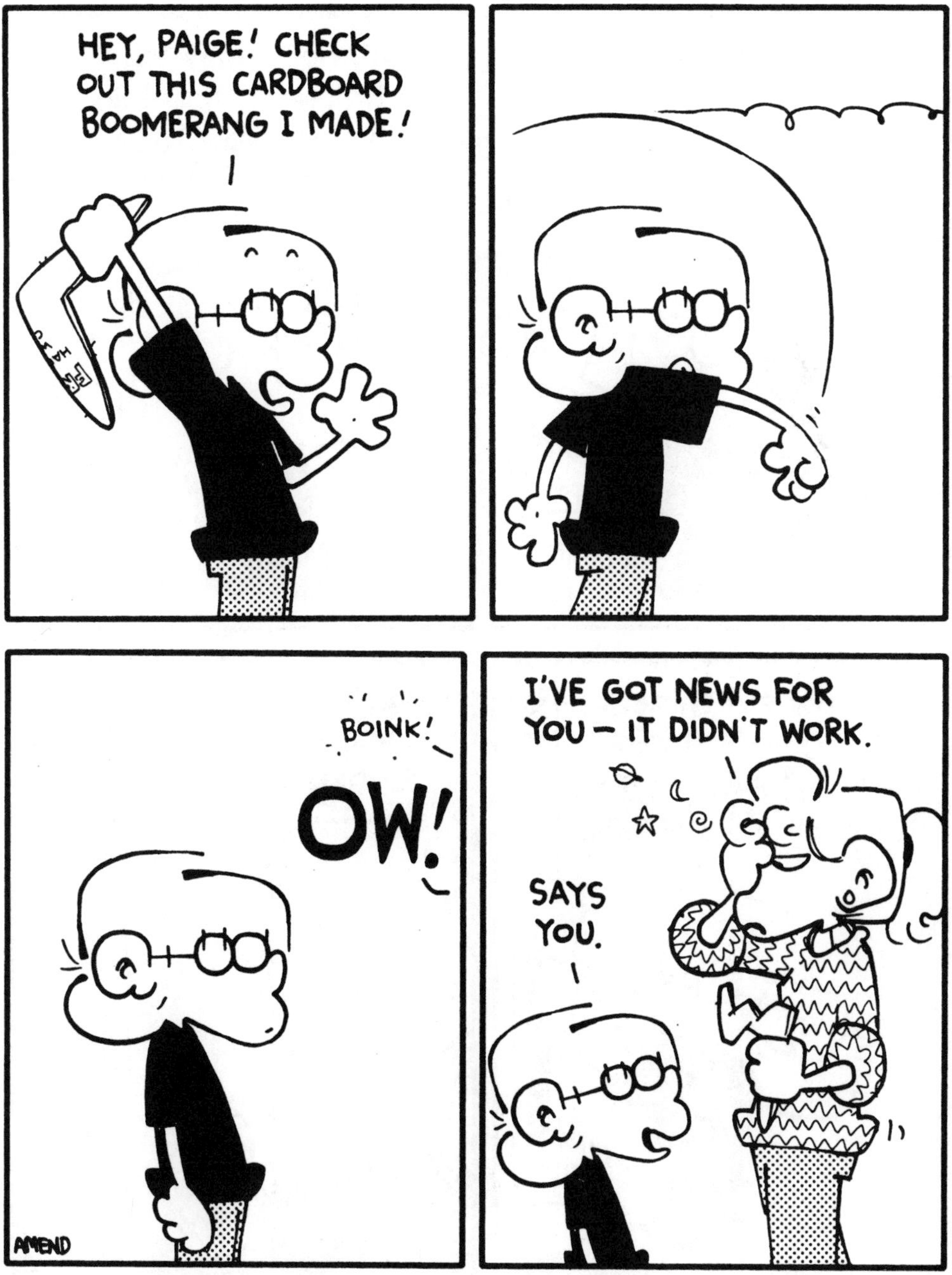
HEY, PAIGE! CHECK OUT THIS CARDBOARD BOOMERANG I MADE!
BOINK!
OW!
AMEND
I'VE GOT NEWS FOR YOU – IT DIDN'T WORK.
SAYS YOU.

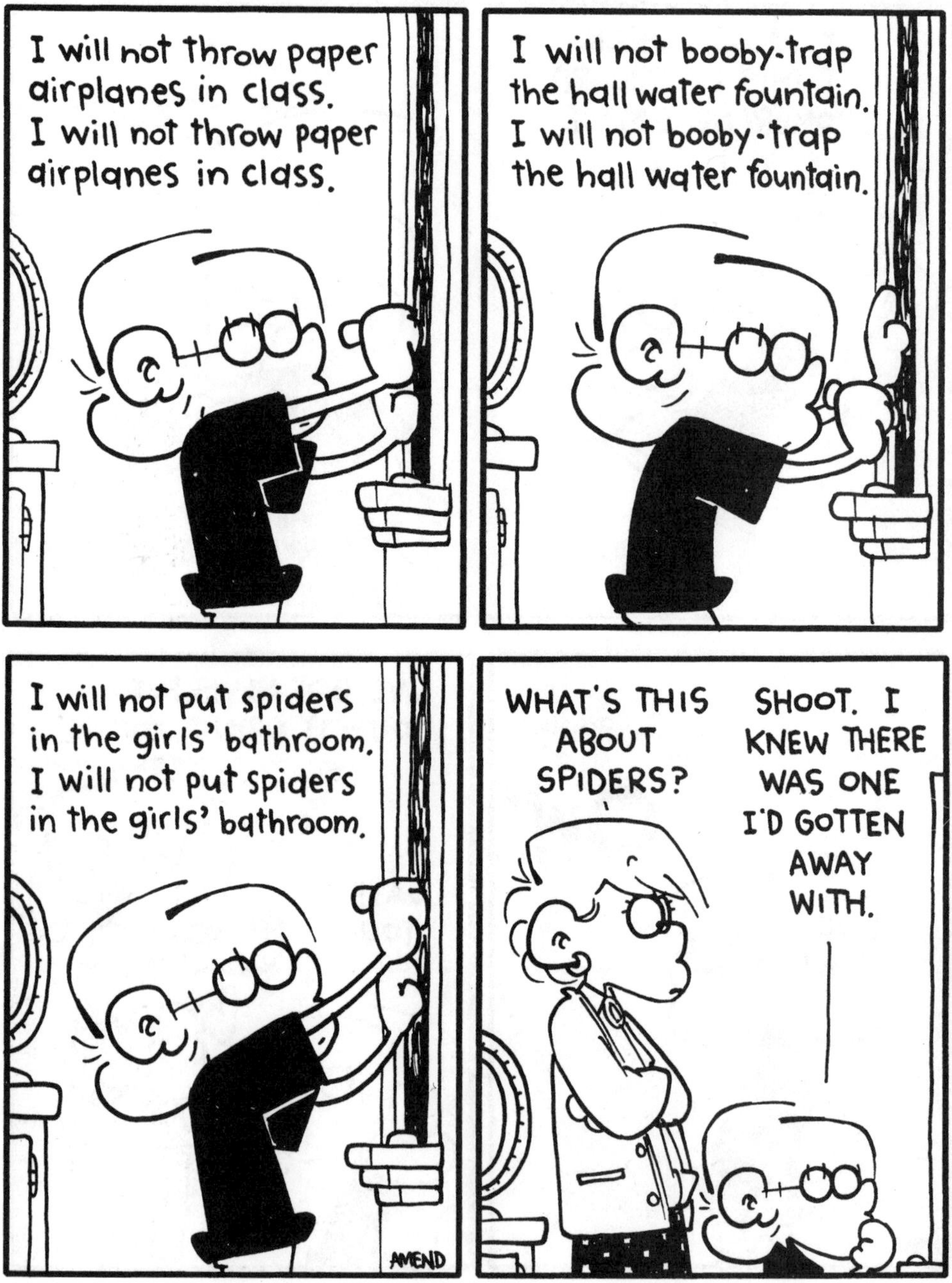
I will not throw paper airplanes in class. I will not throw paper airplanes in class.
I will not booby-trap the hall water fountain. I will not booby-trap the hall water fountain.
I will not put spiders in the girls' bathroom. I will not put spiders in the girls' bathroom.
AMEND
WHAT'S THIS ABOUT SPIDERS?
SHOOT. I KNEW THERE WAS ONE I'D GOTTEN AWAY WITH.

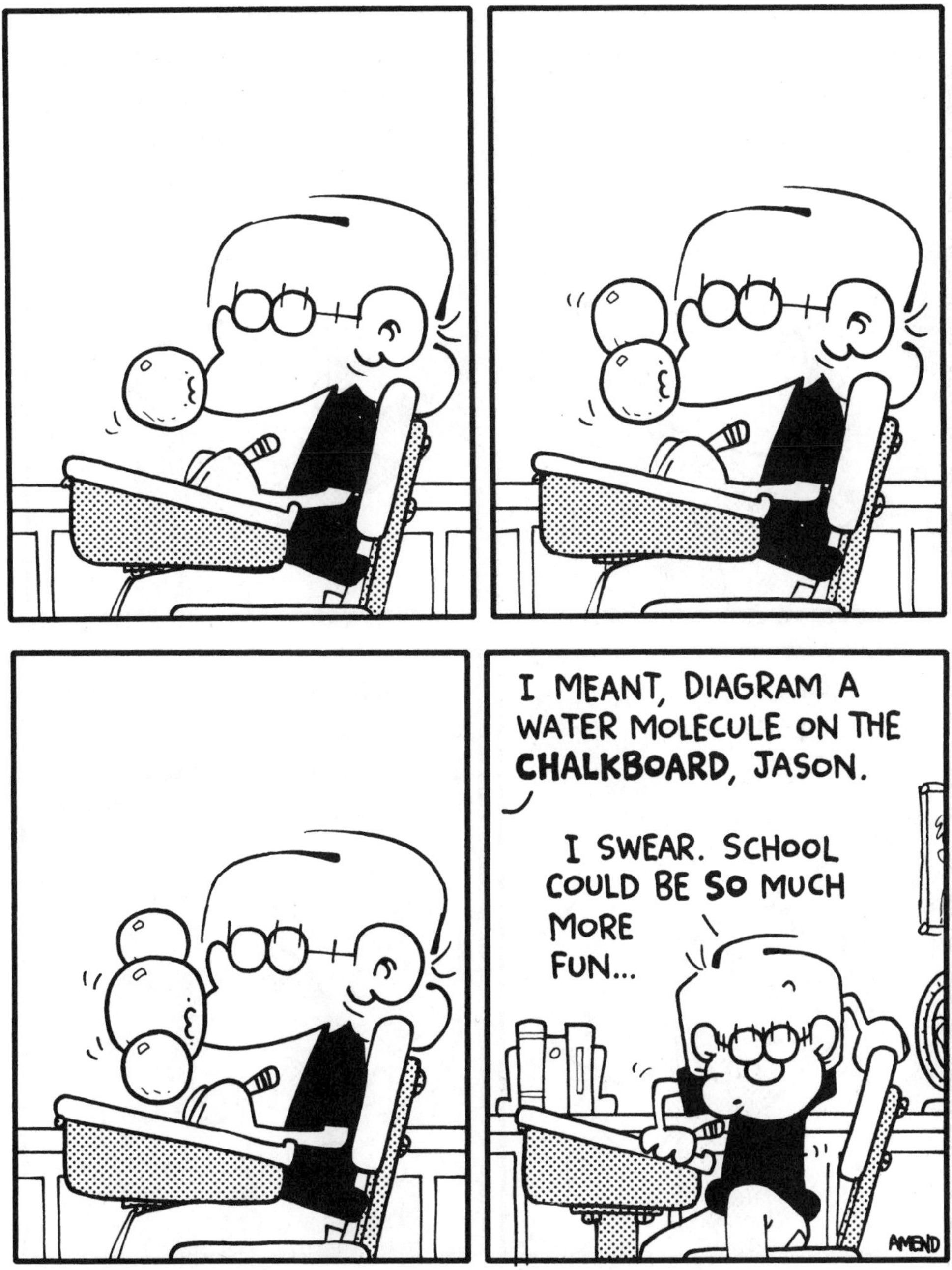
I MEANT, DIAGRAM A WATER MOLECULE ON THE CHALKBOARD, JASON.
I SWEAR. SCHOOL COULD BE SO MUCH MORE FUN...
AMEND

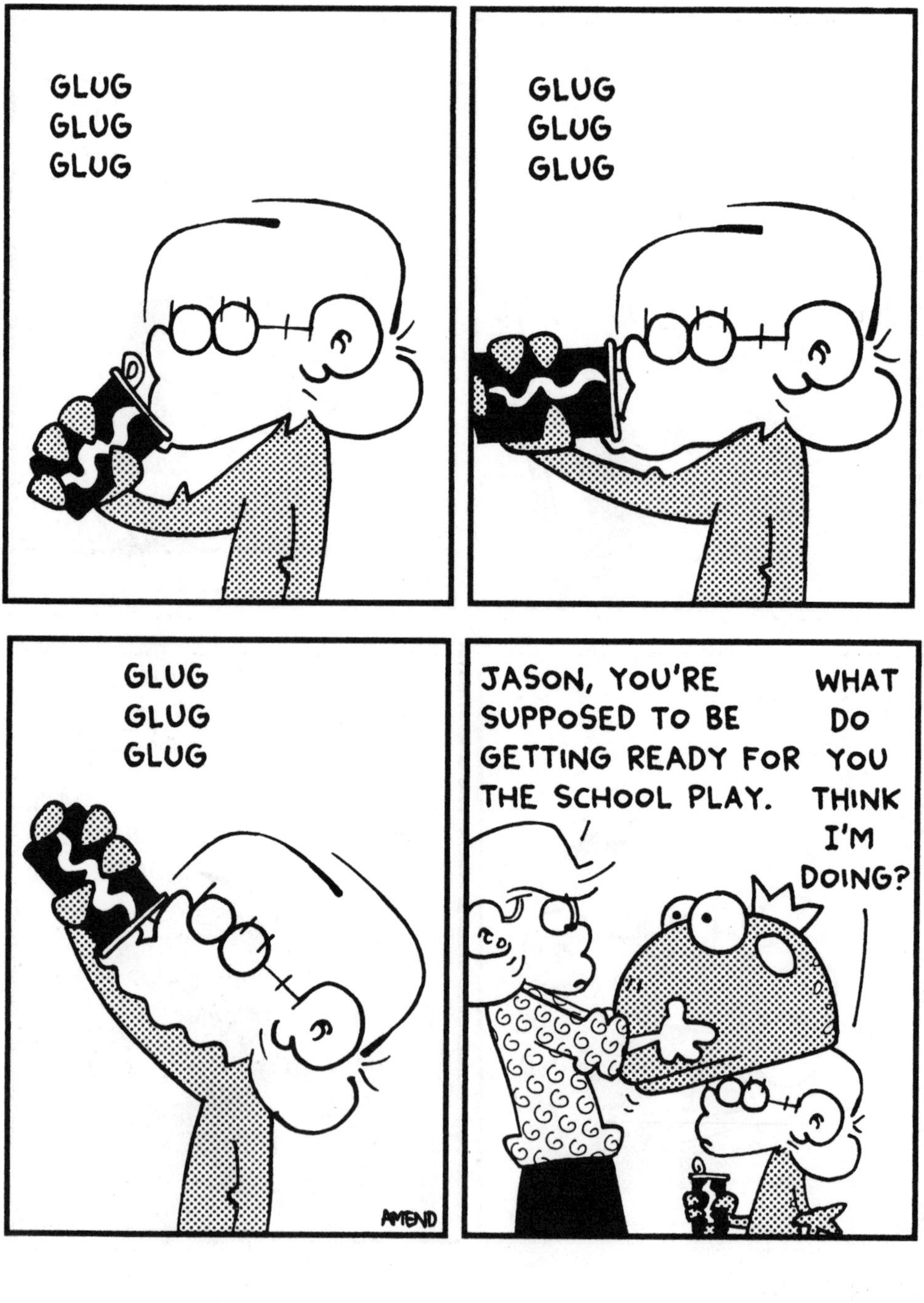
GLUG
GLUG
GLUG
GLUG
GLUG
GLUG
GLUG
GLUG
GLUG
AMEND
JASON, YOU'RE SUPPOSED TO BE GETTING READY FOR THE SCHOOL PLAY.
WHAT DO YOU THINK I'M DOING?

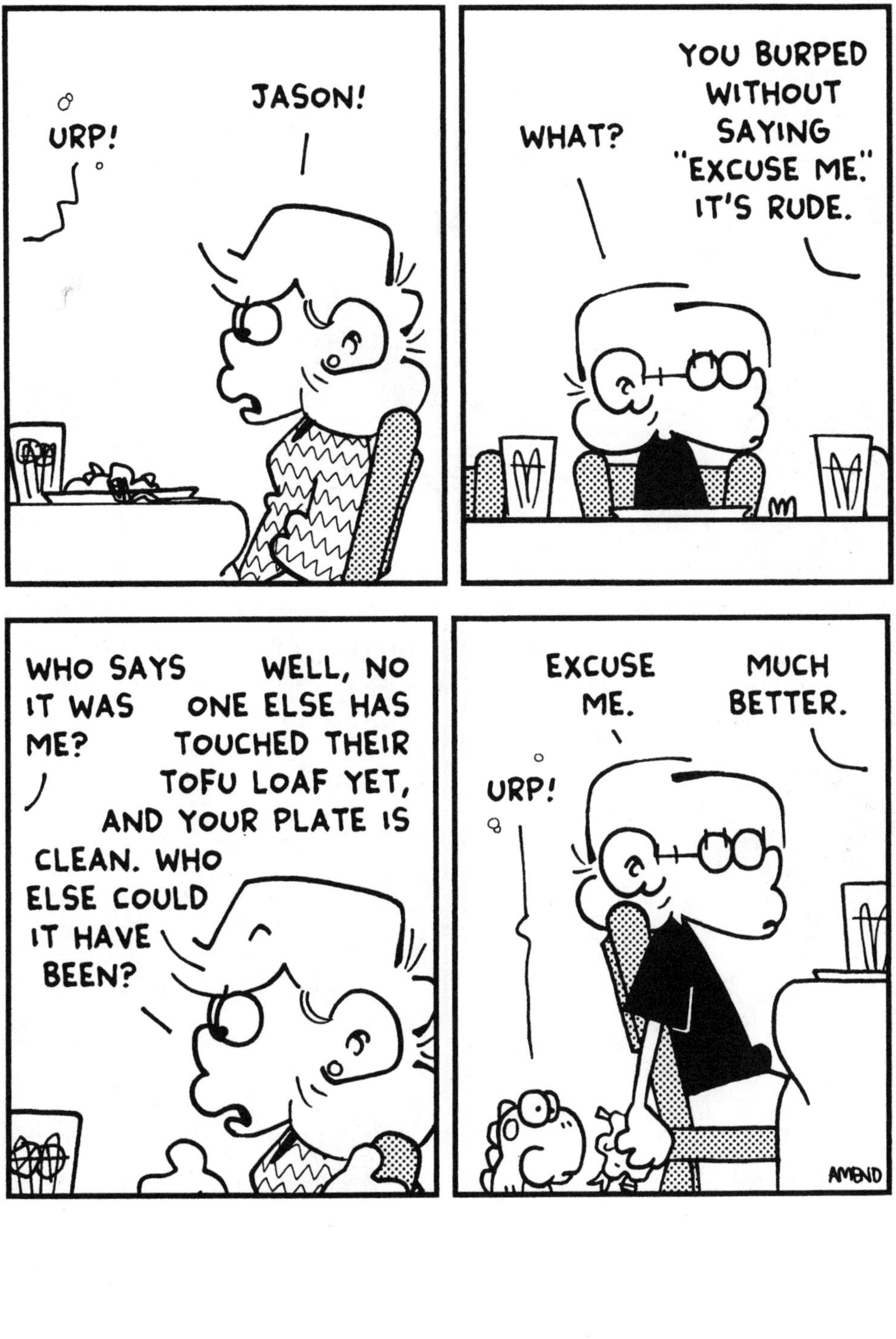
URP!
JASON!
WHAT?
YOU BURPED WITHOUT SAYING "EXCUSE ME." IT'S RUDE.
WHO SAYS IT WAS ME?
WELL, NO ONE ELSE HAS TOUCHED THEIR TOFU LOAF YET, AND YOUR PLATE IS CLEAN. WHO ELSE COULD IT HAVE BEEN?
EXCUSE ME.
MUCH BETTER.
URP!
AMEND

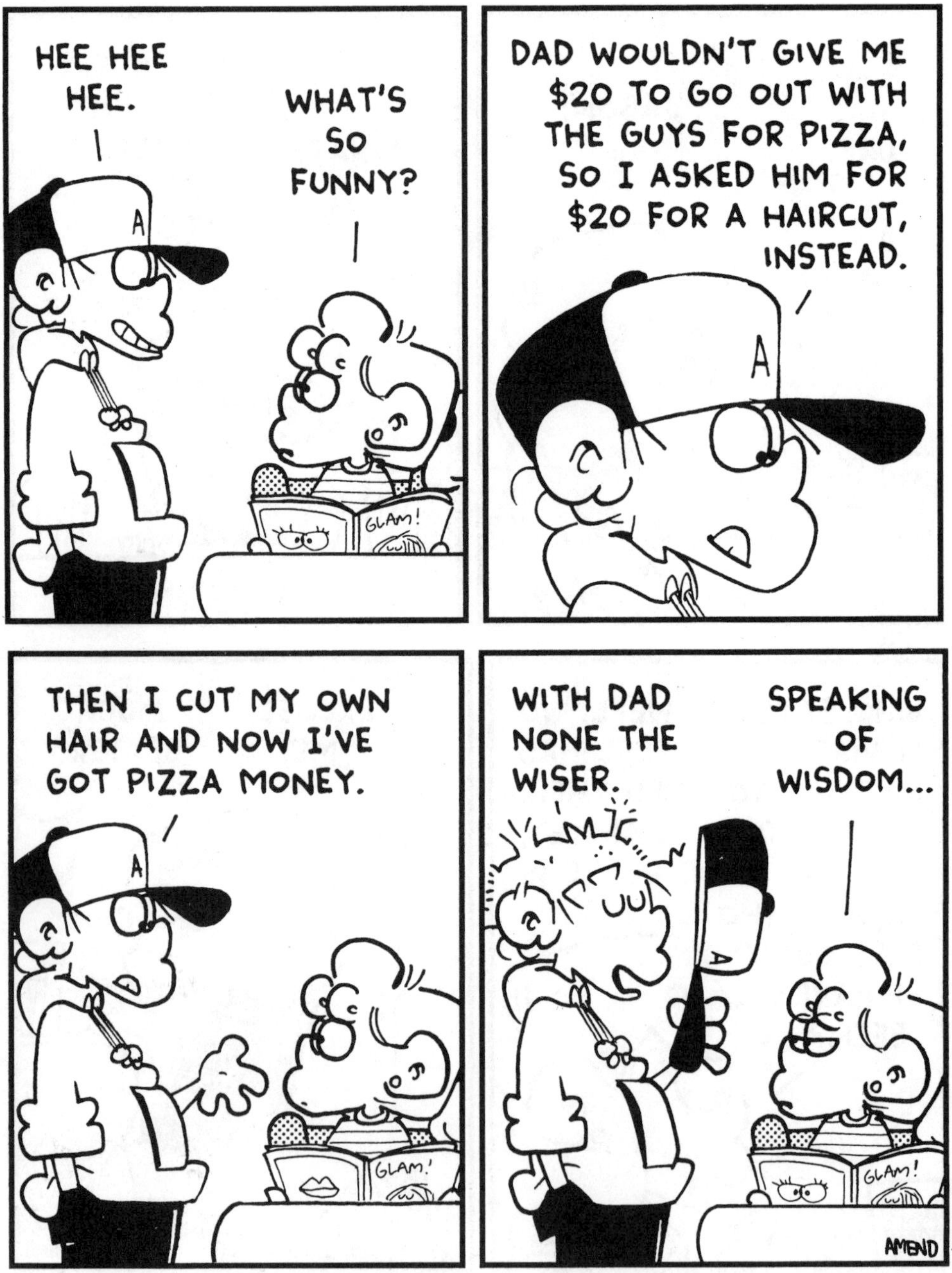
HEE HEE HEE.
WHAT'S SO FUNNY?
DAD WOULDN'T GIVE ME $20 TO GO OUT WITH THE GUYS FOR PIZZA, SO I ASKED HIM FOR $20 FOR A HAIRCUT, INSTEAD.
THEN I CUT MY OWN HAIR AND NOW I'VE GOT PIZZA MONEY.
WITH DAD NONE THE WISER.
SPEAKING OF WISDOM...
GLAM!
AMEND

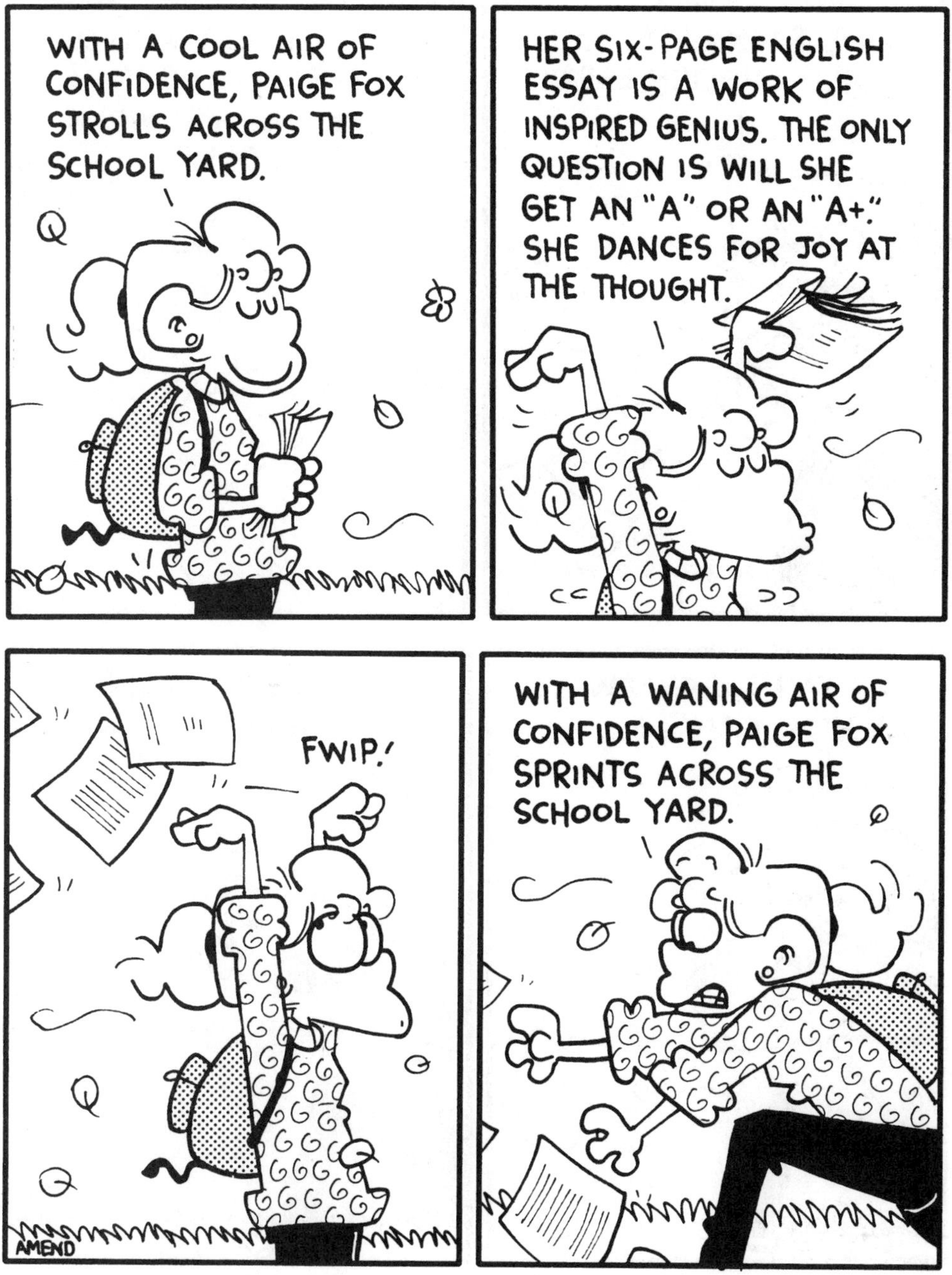
WITH A COOL AIR OF CONFIDENCE, PAIGE FOX STROLLS ACROSS THE SCHOOL YARD.
HER SIX-PAGE ENGLISH ESSAY IS A WORK OF INSPIRED GENIUS. THE ONLY QUESTION IS WILL SHE GET AN "A" OR AN "A+." SHE DANCES FOR JOY AT THE THOUGHT.
FWIP!
AMEND
WITH A WANING AIR OF CONFIDENCE, PAIGE FOX SPRINTS ACROSS THE SCHOOL YARD.

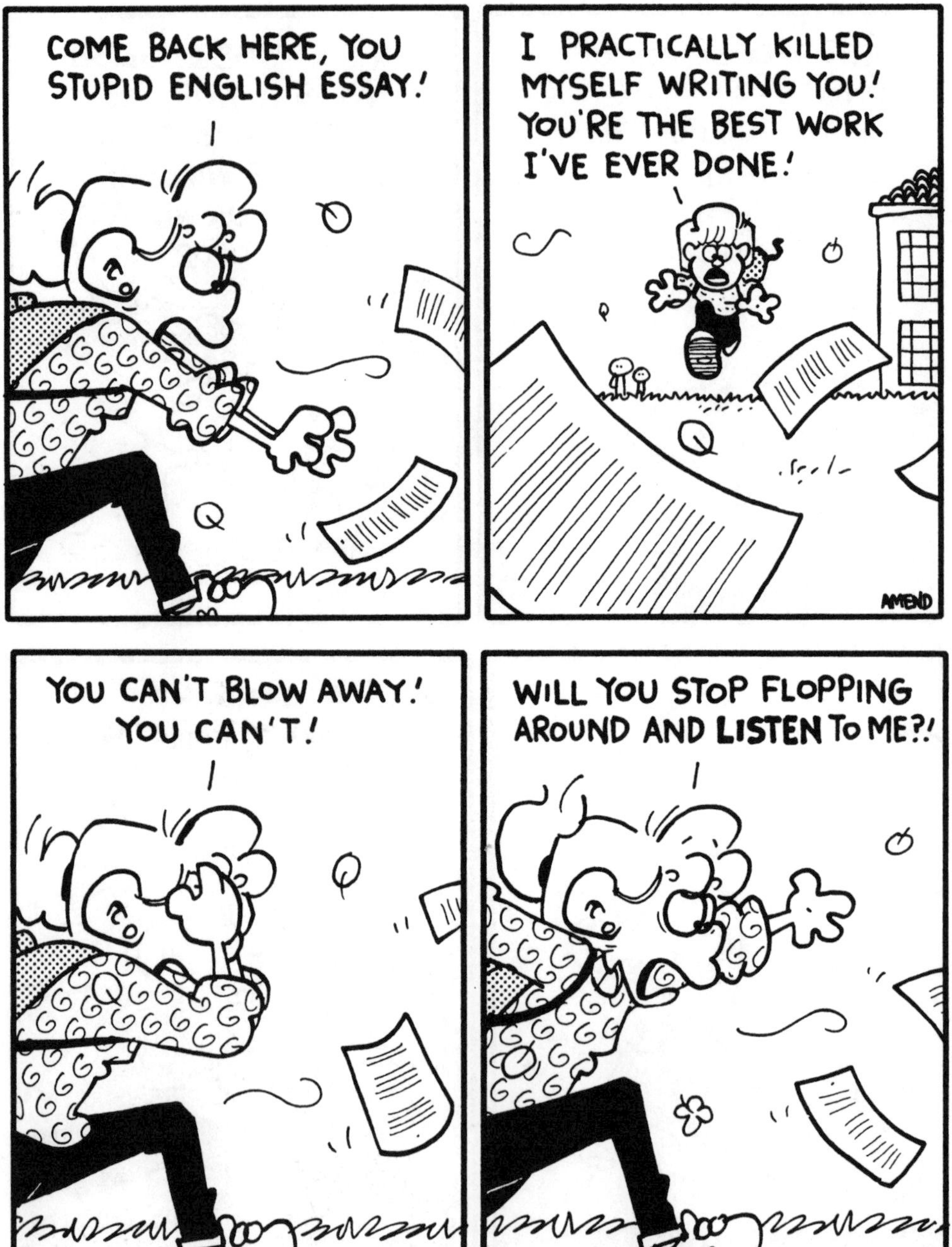
COME BACK HERE, YOU STUPID ENGLISH ESSAY!
I PRACTICALLY KILLED MYSELF WRITING YOU! YOU'RE THE BEST WORK I'VE EVER DONE!
AMEND
YOU CAN'T BLOW AWAY! YOU CAN'T!
WILL YOU STOP FLOPPING AROUND AND LISTEN TO ME?!

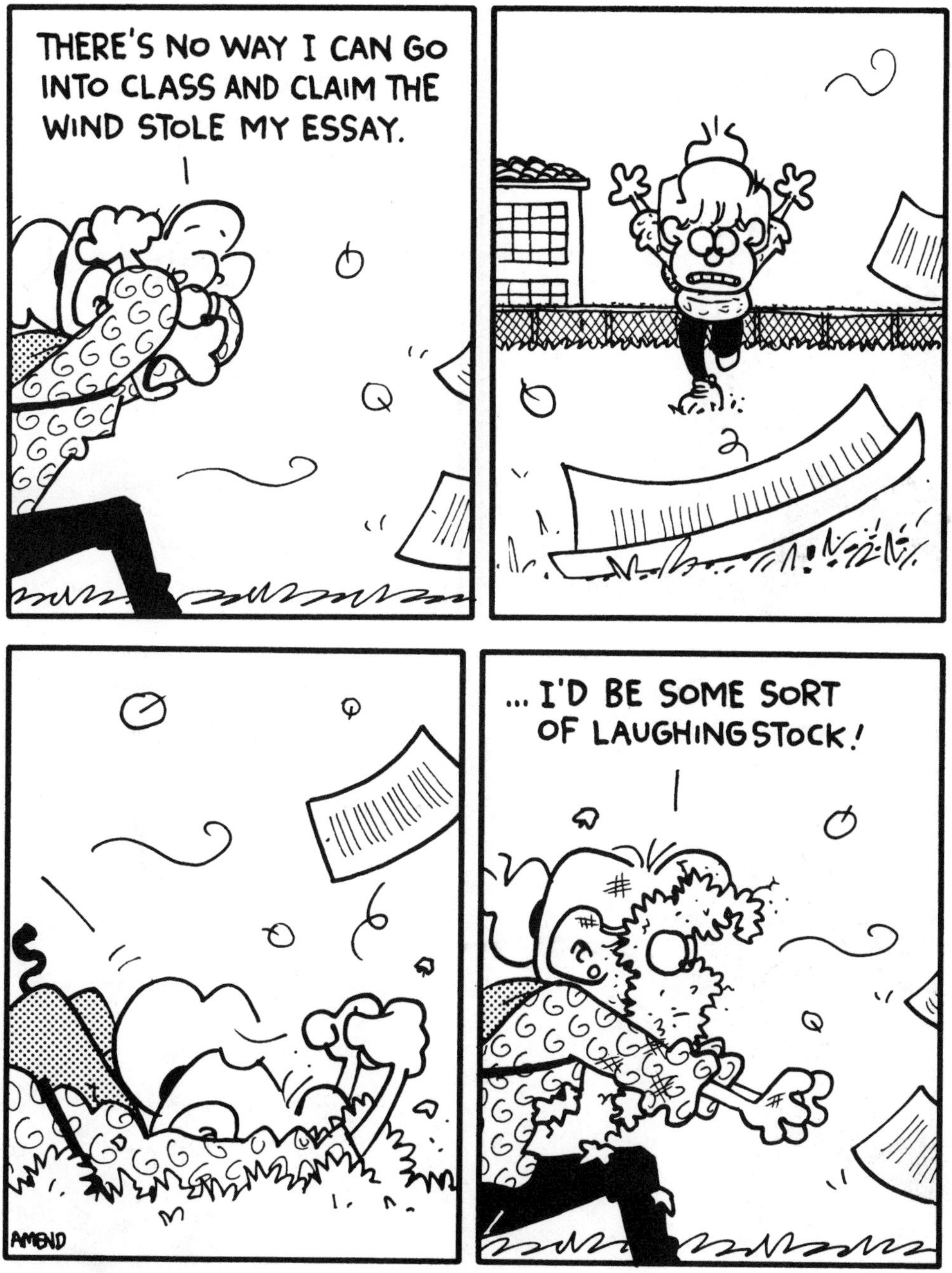
THERE'S NO WAY I CAN GO INTO CLASS AND CLAIM THE WIND STOLE MY ESSAY.
... I'D BE SOME SORT OF LAUGHINGSTOCK!
AMEND

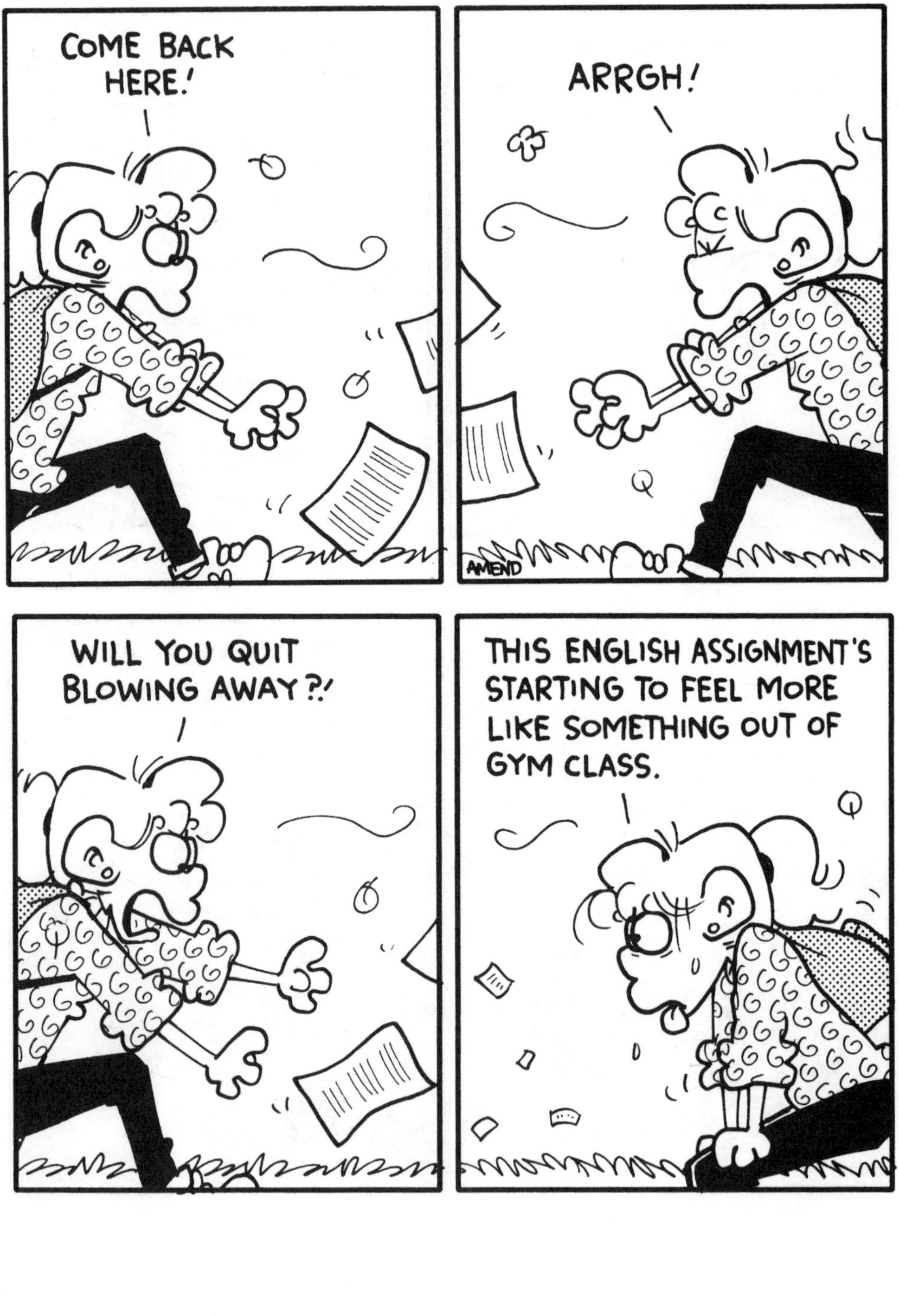

COME BACK HERE!
ARRGH!
AMEND
WILL YOU QUIT BLOWING AWAY?!
THIS ENGLISH ASSIGNMENT'S STARTING TO FEEL MORE LIKE SOMETHING OUT OF GYM CLASS.

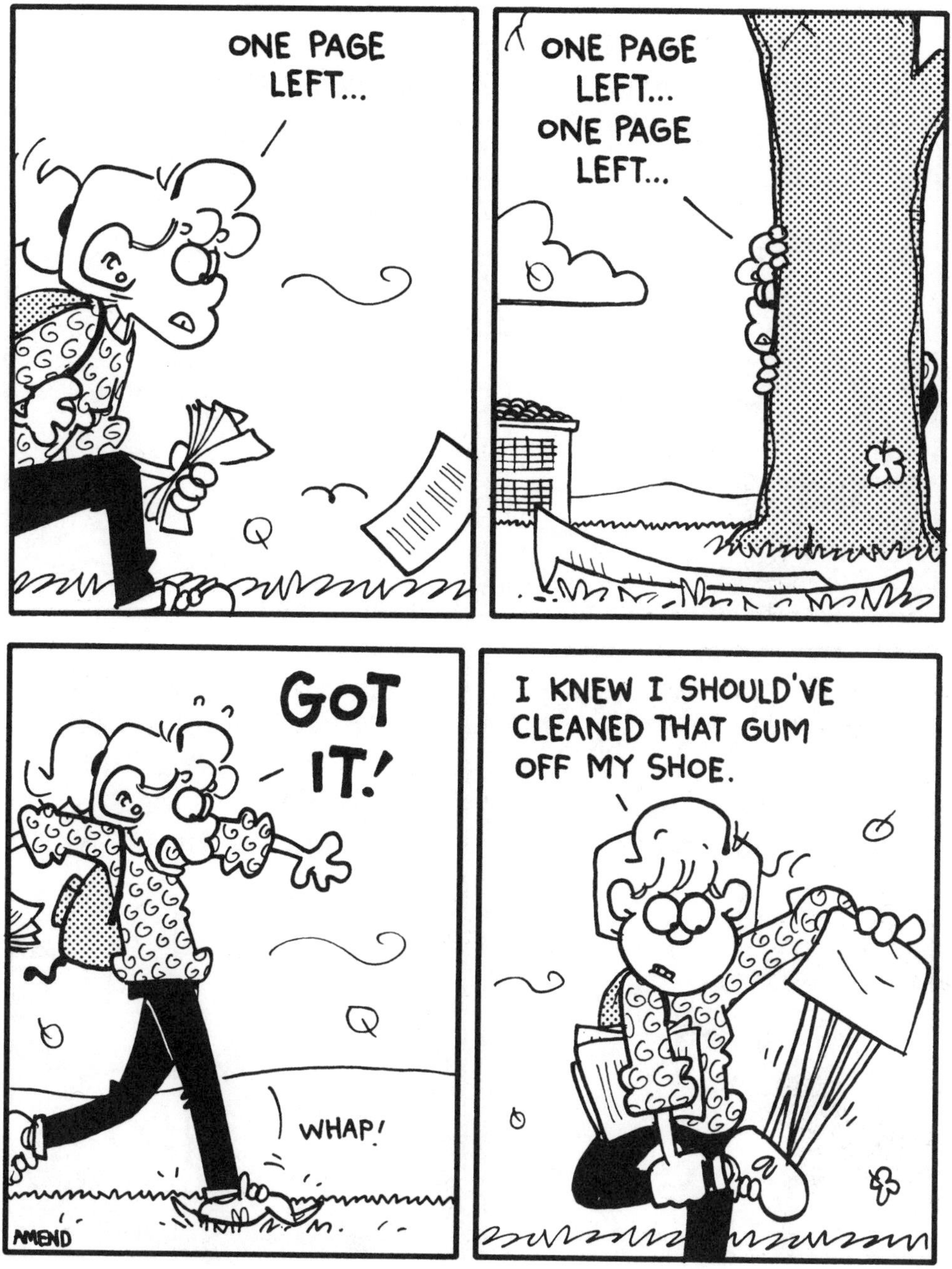
ONE PAGE LEFT...
ONE PAGE LEFT... ONE PAGE LEFT...
GOT IT!
WHAP!
AMEND
I KNEW I SHOULD'VE CLEANED THAT GUM OFF MY SHOE.

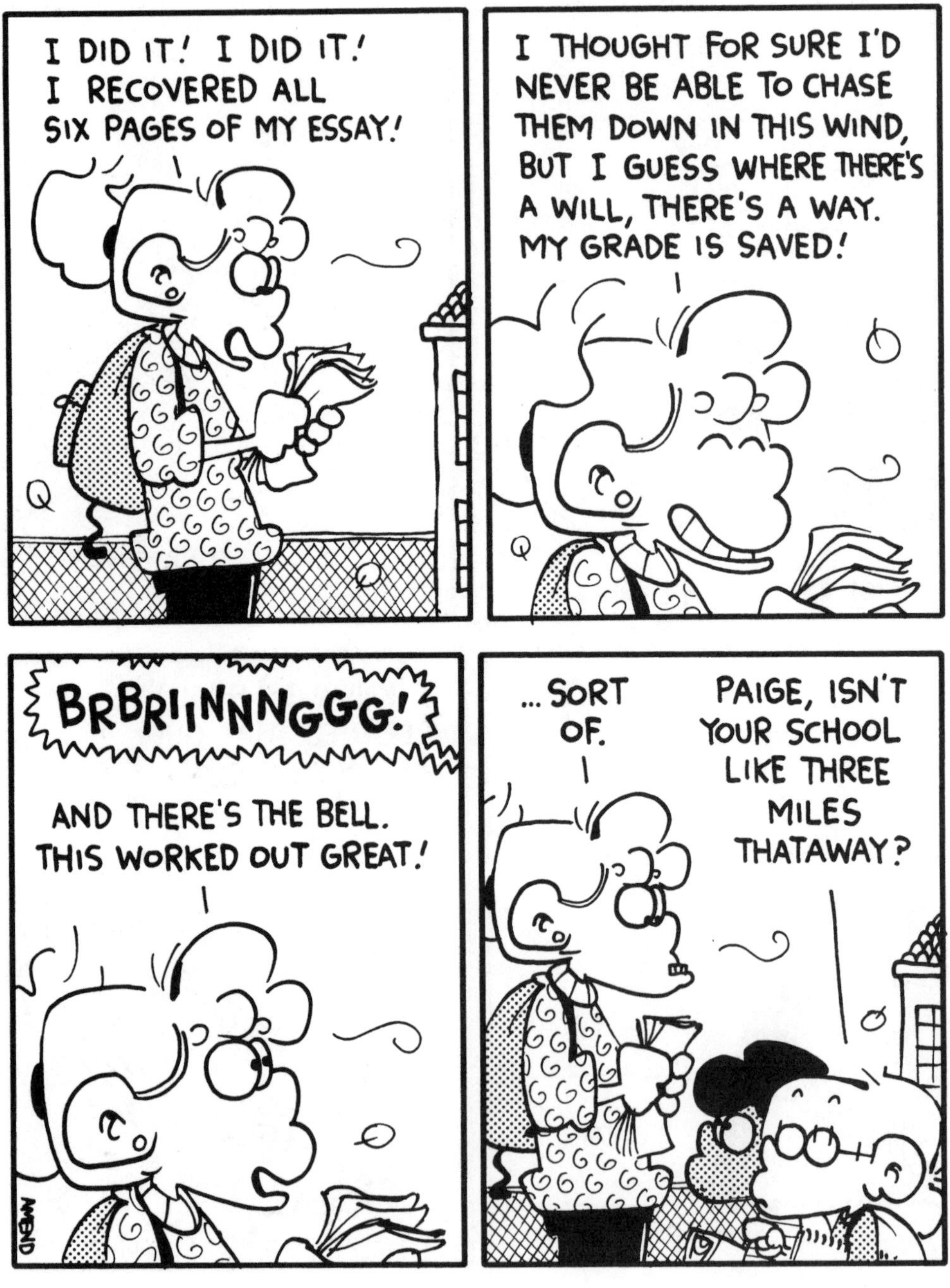
I DID IT! I DID IT! I RECOVERED ALL SIX PAGES OF MY ESSAY!
I THOUGHT FOR SURE I'D NEVER BE ABLE TO CHASE THEM DOWN IN THIS WIND, BUT I GUESS WHERE THERE'S A WILL, THERE'S A WAY. MY GRADE IS SAVED!
BRBRIINNNGGG!
AND THERE'S THE BELL. THIS WORKED OUT GREAT!
AMEND
...SORT OF.
PAIGE, ISN'T YOUR SCHOOL LIKE THREE MILES THATAWAY?

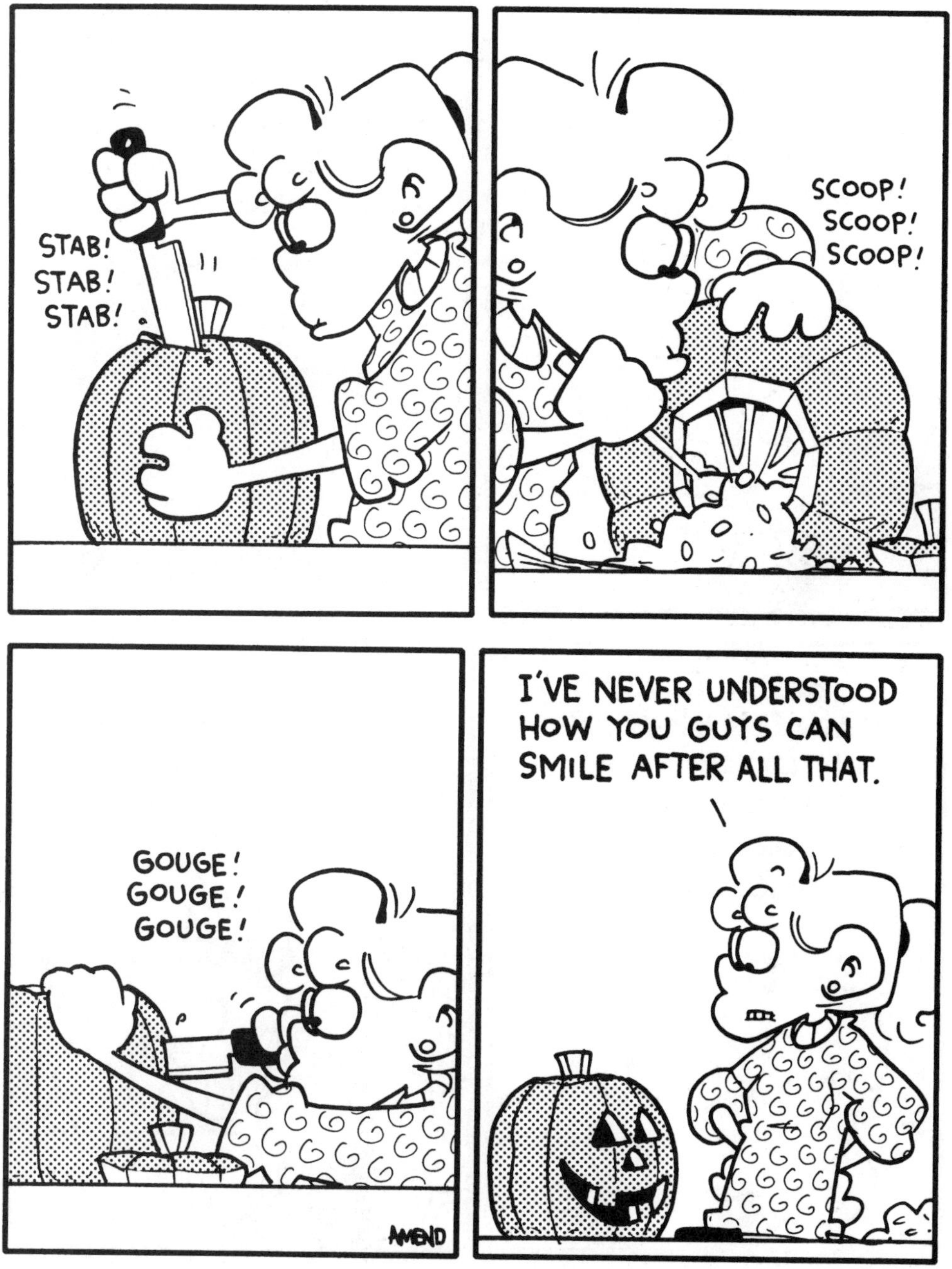
STAB! STAB! STAB!
SCOOP! SCOOP! SCOOP!
GOUGE! GOUGE! GOUGE!
AMEND
I'VE NEVER UNDERSTOOD HOW YOU GUYS CAN SMILE AFTER ALL THAT.

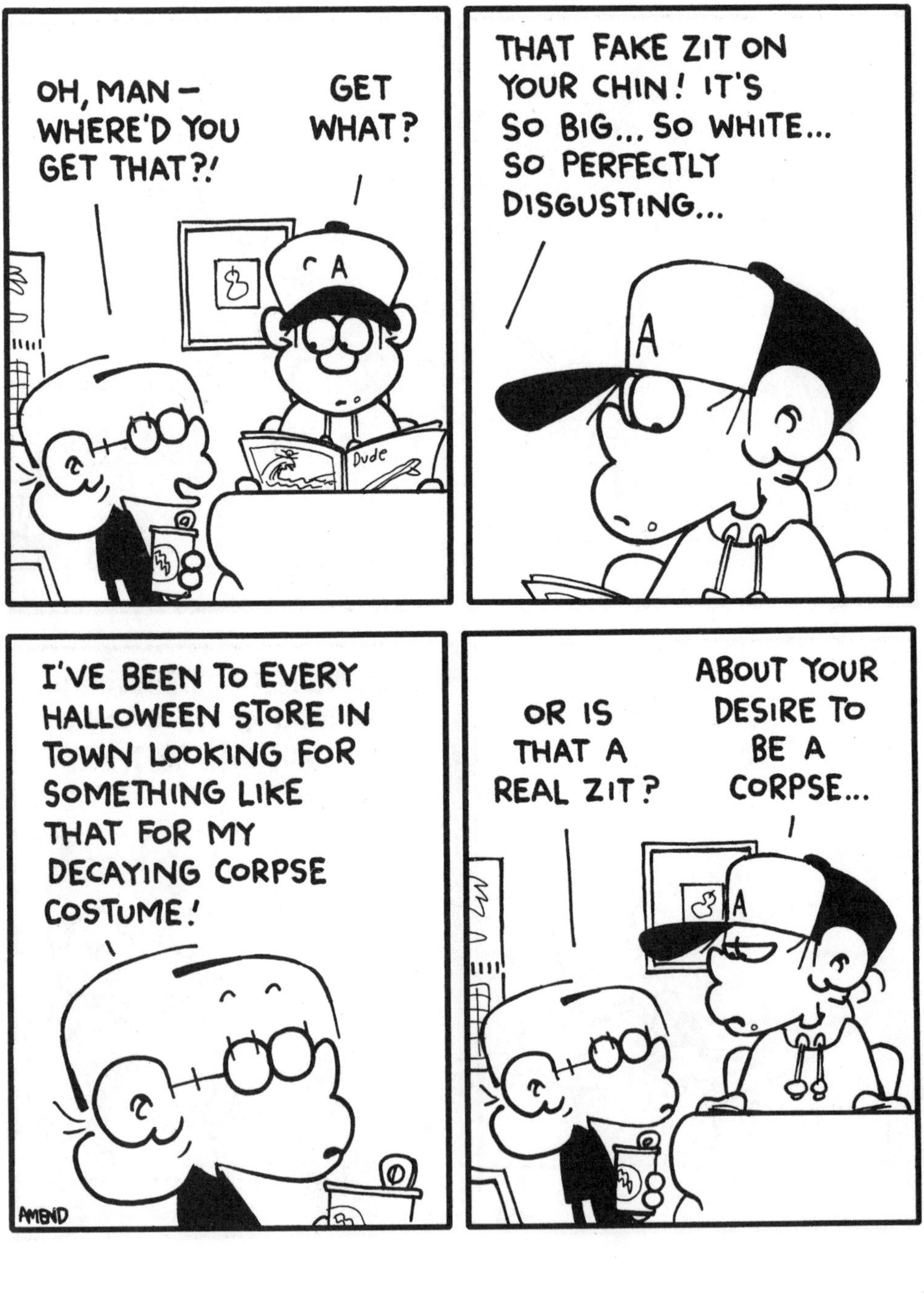
OH, MAN— WHERE'D YOU GET THAT?!
GET WHAT?
THAT FAKE ZIT ON YOUR CHIN! IT'S SO BIG... SO WHITE... SO PERFECTLY DISGUSTING...
Dude
I'VE BEEN TO EVERY HALLOWEEN STORE IN TOWN LOOKING FOR SOMETHING LIKE THAT FOR MY DECAYING CORPSE COSTUME!
AMEND
OR IS THAT A REAL ZIT?
ABOUT YOUR DESIRE TO BE A CORPSE...

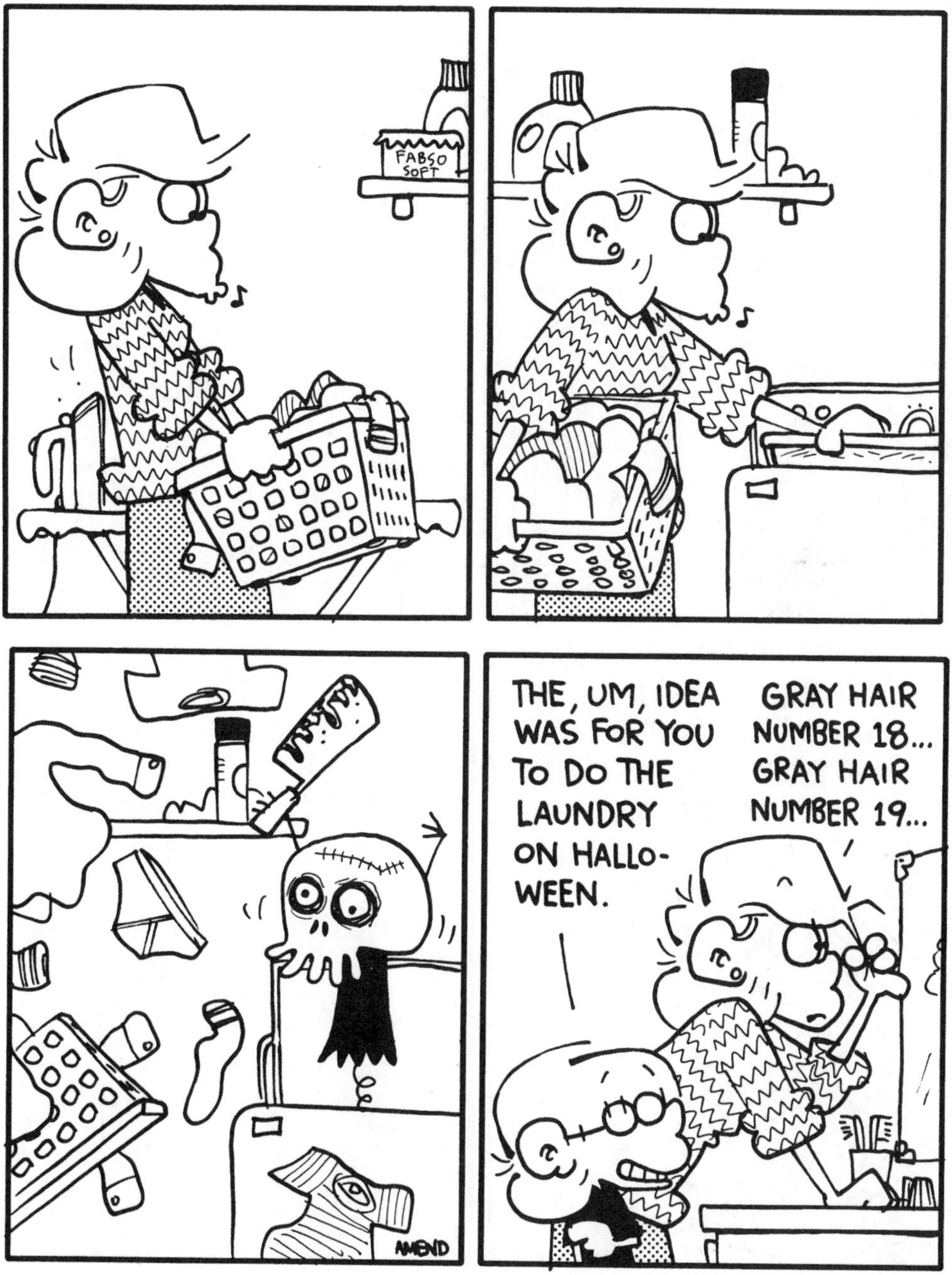
FABSO SOFT
THE, UM, IDEA WAS FOR YOU TO DO THE LAUNDRY ON HALLO-WEEN.
GRAY HAIR NUMBER 18... GRAY HAIR NUMBER 19...
AMEND

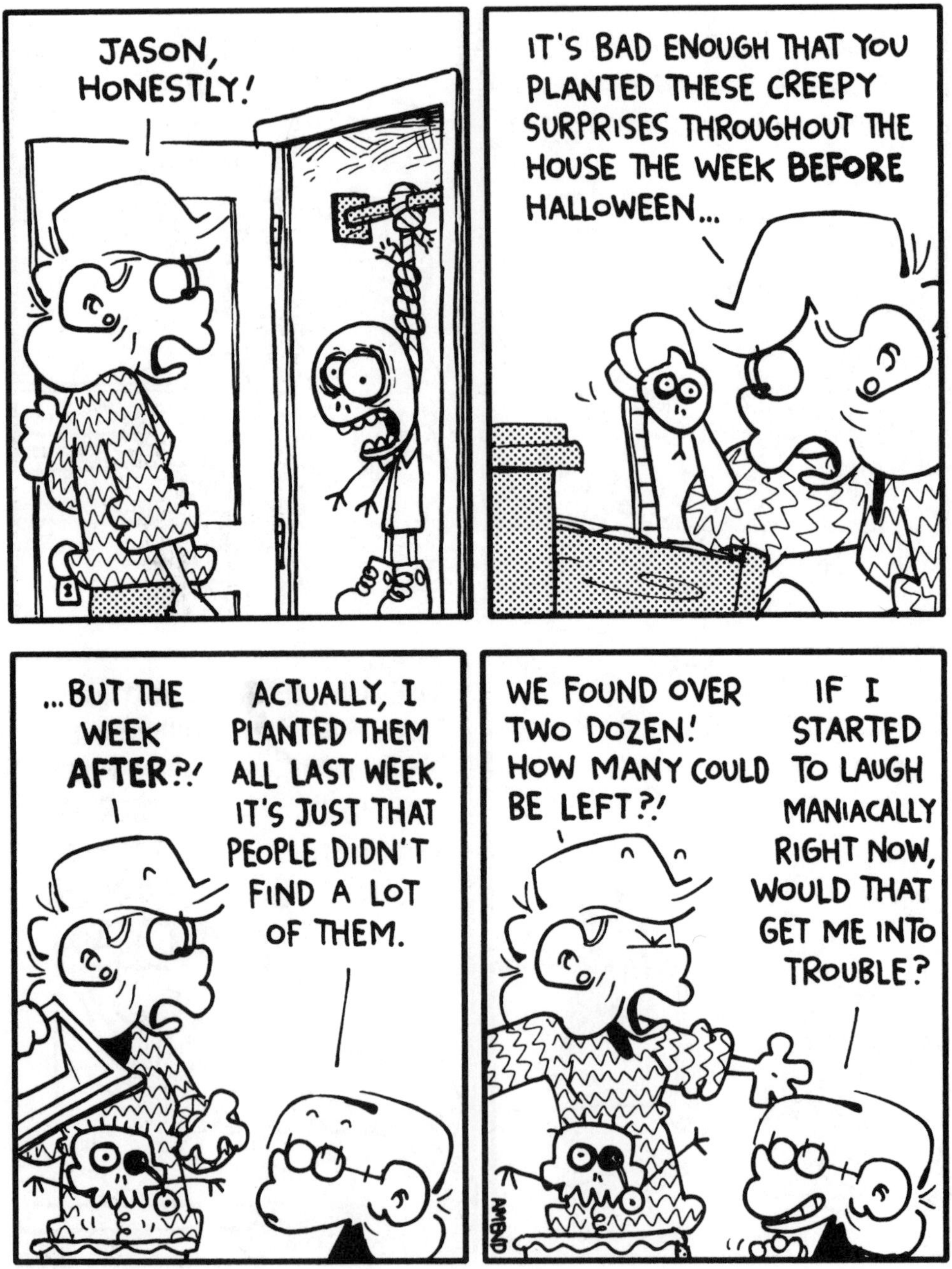
JASON, HONESTLY!
IT'S BAD ENOUGH THAT YOU PLANTED THESE CREEPY SURPRISES THROUGHOUT THE HOUSE THE WEEK BEFORE HALLOWEEN...
...BUT THE WEEK AFTER?!
ACTUALLY, I PLANTED THEM ALL LAST WEEK. IT'S JUST THAT PEOPLE DIDN'T FIND A LOT OF THEM.
WE FOUND OVER TWO DOZEN! HOW MANY COULD BE LEFT?!
IF I STARTED TO LAUGH MANIACALLY RIGHT NOW, WOULD THAT GET ME INTO TROUBLE?
AMEND

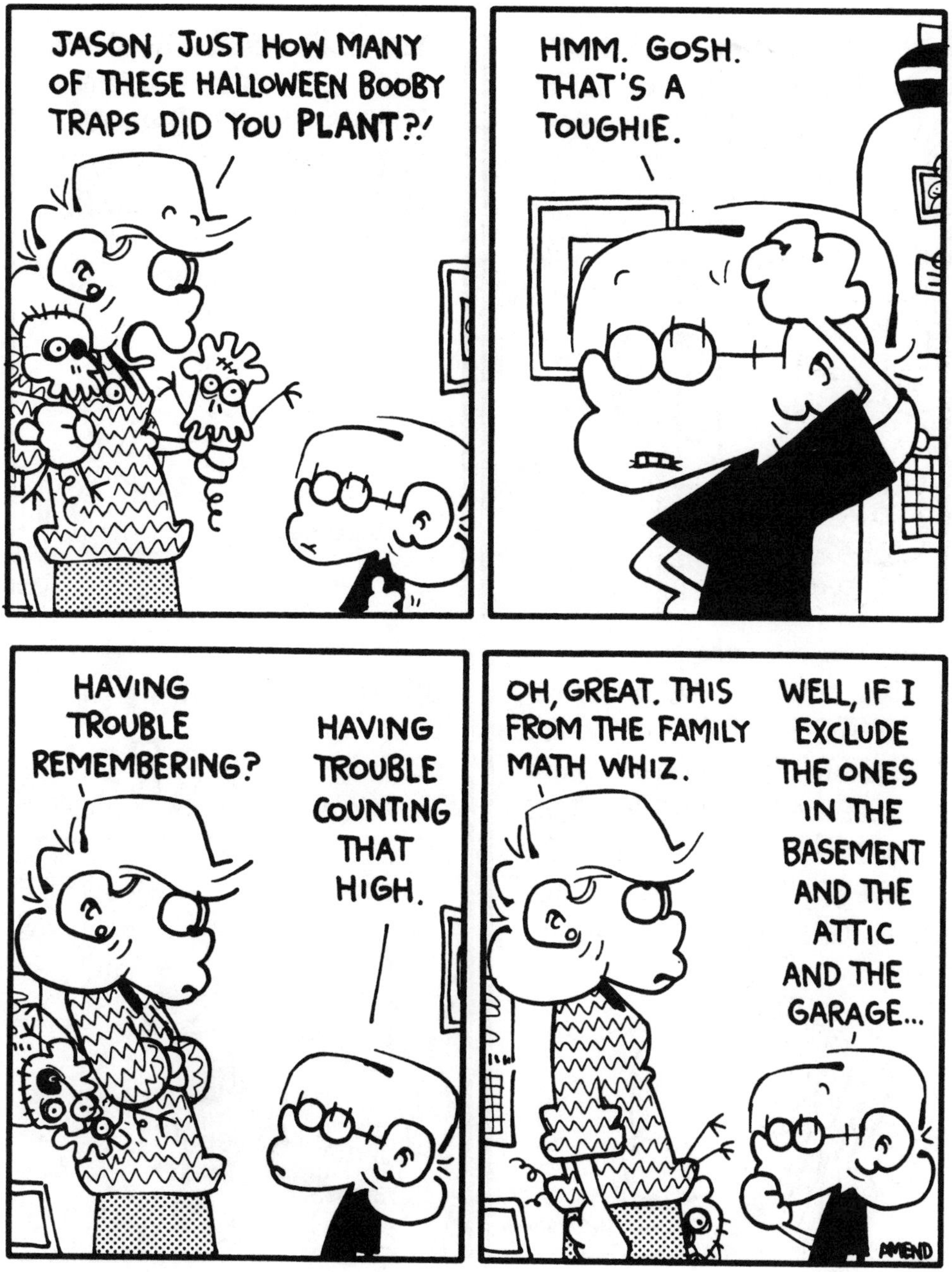
JASON, JUST HOW MANY OF THESE HALLOWEEN BOOBY TRAPS DID YOU PLANT?!
HMM. GOSH. THAT'S A TOUGHIE.
HAVING TROUBLE REMEMBERING?
HAVING TROUBLE COUNTING THAT HIGH.
OH, GREAT. THIS FROM THE FAMILY MATH WHIZ.
WELL, IF I EXCLUDE THE ONES IN THE BASEMENT AND THE ATTIC AND THE GARAGE...
AMEND

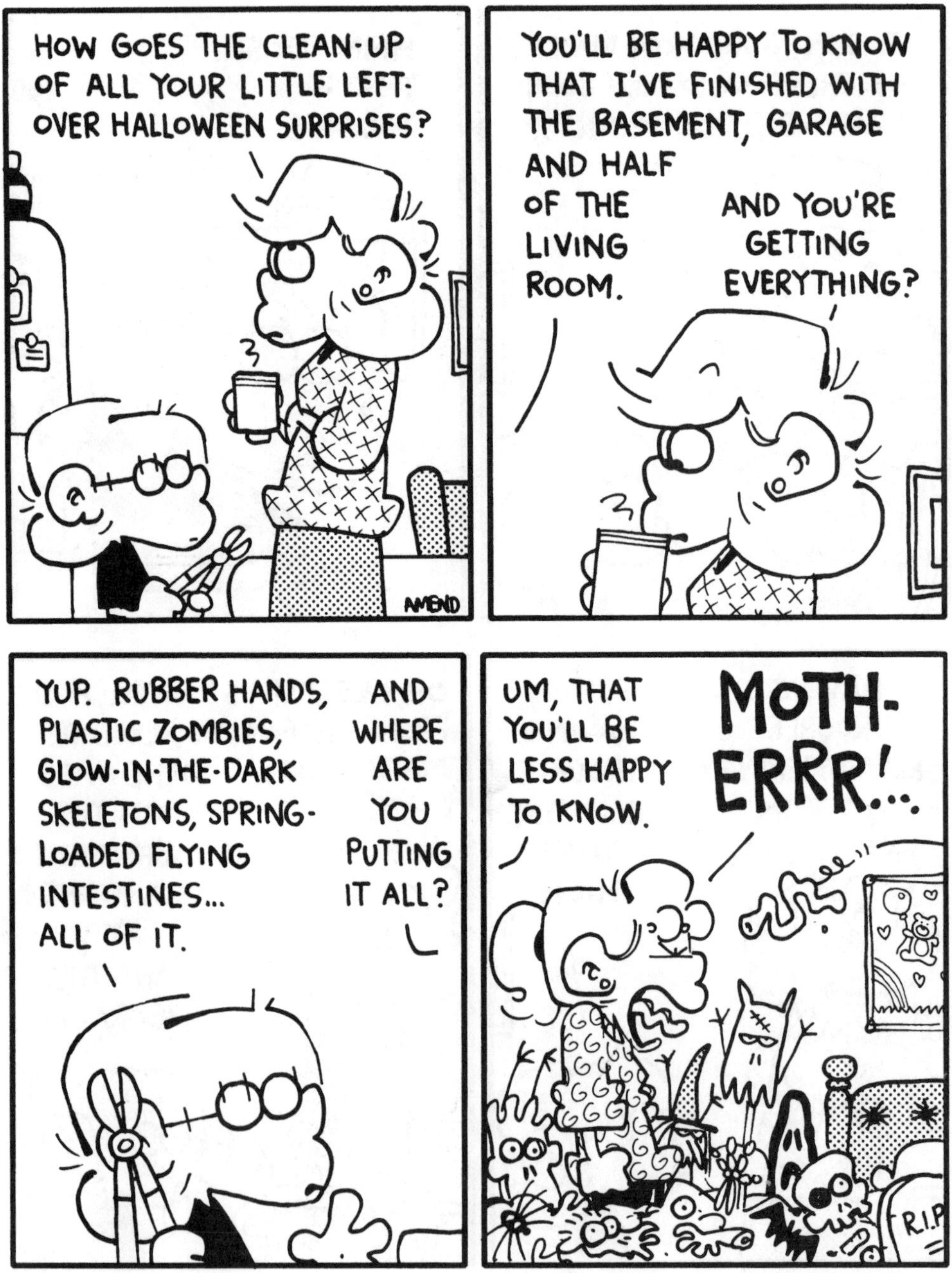
HOW GOES THE CLEAN-UP OF ALL YOUR LITTLE LEFT-OVER HALLOWEEN SURPRISES?
AMEND
YOU'LL BE HAPPY TO KNOW THAT I'VE FINISHED WITH THE BASEMENT, GARAGE AND HALF OF THE LIVING ROOM.
AND YOU'RE GETTING EVERYTHING?
YUP. RUBBER HANDS, PLASTIC ZOMBIES, GLOW-IN-THE-DARK SKELETONS, SPRING-LOADED FLYING INTESTINES... ALL OF IT.
AND WHERE ARE YOU PUTTING IT ALL?
UM, THAT YOU'LL BE LESS HAPPY TO KNOW.
MOTH-ERRR!...
R.I.P

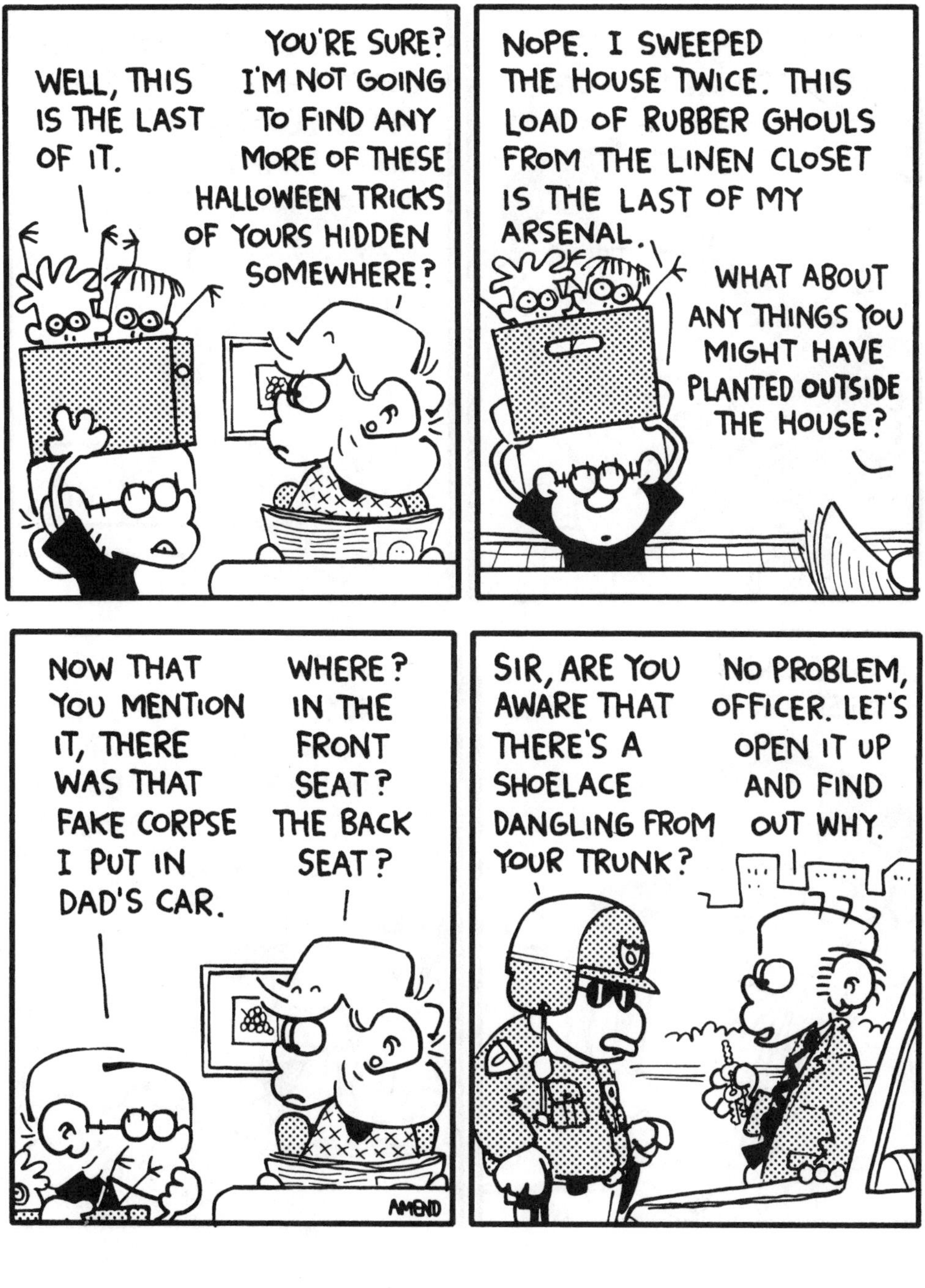
WELL, THIS IS THE LAST OF IT.
YOU'RE SURE? I'M NOT GOING TO FIND ANY MORE OF THESE HALLOWEEN TRICKS OF YOURS HIDDEN SOMEWHERE?
NOPE. I SWEEPED THE HOUSE TWICE. THIS LOAD OF RUBBER GHOULS FROM THE LINEN CLOSET IS THE LAST OF MY ARSENAL.
WHAT ABOUT ANY THINGS YOU MIGHT HAVE PLANTED OUTSIDE THE HOUSE?
NOW THAT YOU MENTION IT, THERE WAS THAT FAKE CORPSE I PUT IN DAD'S CAR.
WHERE? IN THE FRONT SEAT? THE BACK SEAT?
AMEND
SIR, ARE YOU AWARE THAT THERE'S A SHOELACE DANGLING FROM YOUR TRUNK?
NO PROBLEM, OFFICER. LET'S OPEN IT UP AND FIND OUT WHY.

GHASTLY EYEBALLS PAINTED ON THE EGGS...

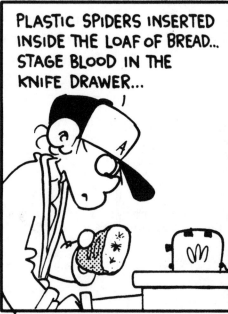

PLASTIC SPIDERS INSERTED INSIDE THE LOAF OF BREAD... STAGE BLOOD IN THE KNIFE DRAWER...

FAKE GREEN MOLD ALL OVER THE BACON STRIPS...

JASON, PROMISE ME NEXT YEAR YOU WON'T GO SO HALLOWEEN GOOFY.

WHAT WAS THAT PART ABOUT MOLD?

CRUNCH
CRUNCH
CRUNCH

AMEND

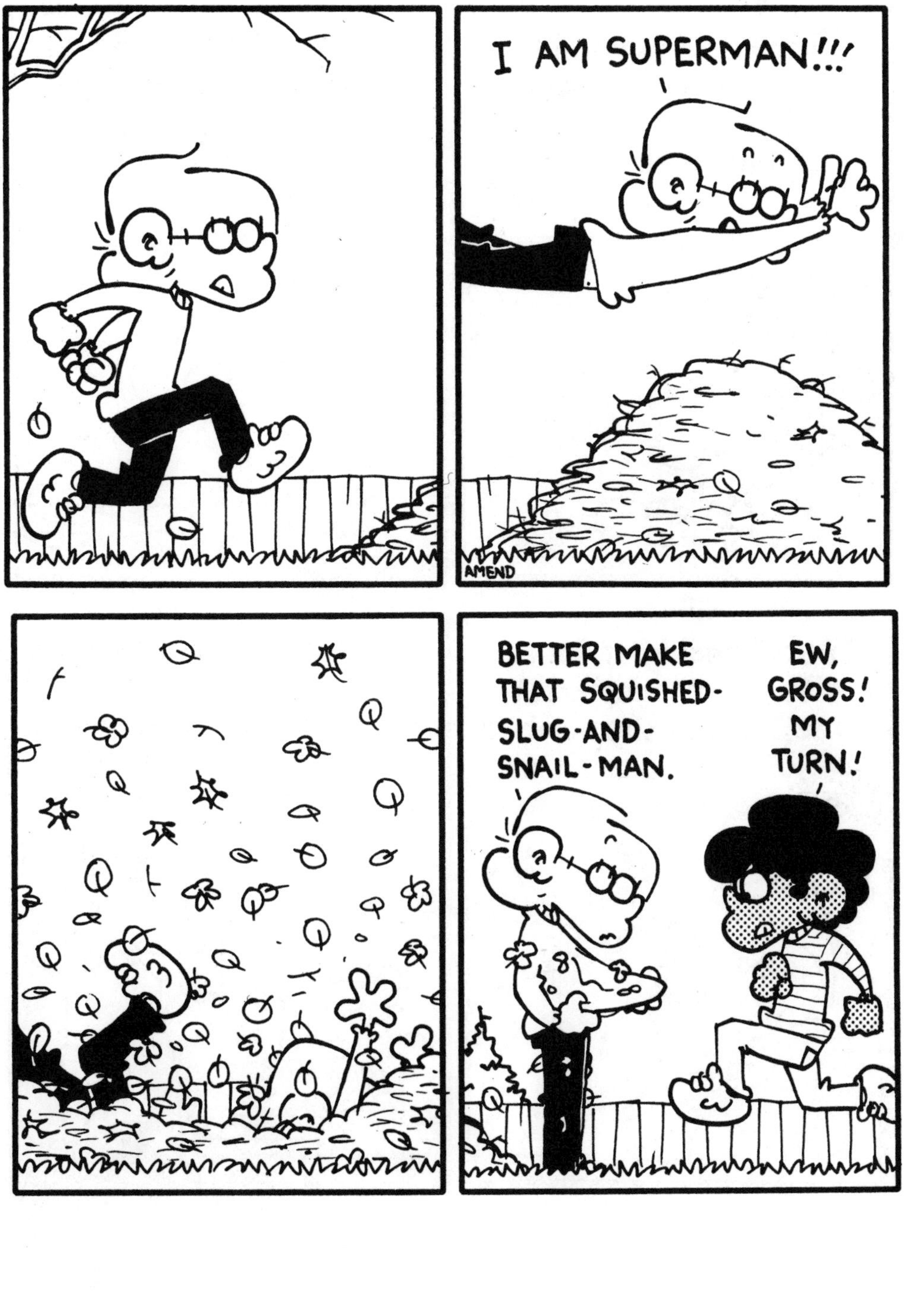
I AM SUPERMAN!!!
AMEND
BETTER MAKE THAT SQUISHED-SLUG-AND-SNAIL-MAN.
EW, GROSS! MY TURN!

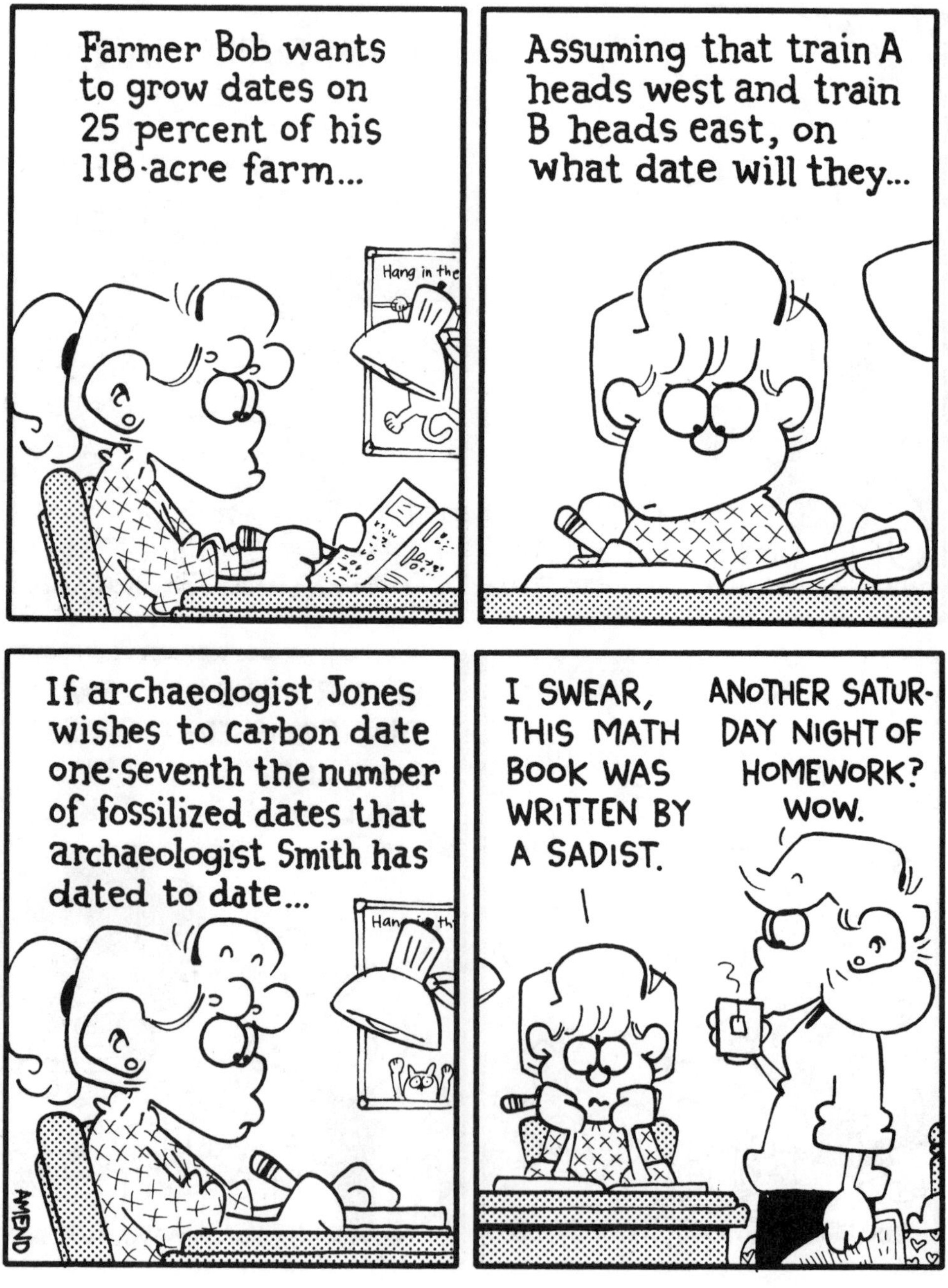
Farmer Bob wants to grow dates on 25 percent of his 118-acre farm...
Hang in the
Assuming that train A heads west and train B heads east, on what date will they...
If archaeologist Jones wishes to carbon date one-seventh the number of fossilized dates that archaeologist Smith has dated to date...
AMEND
I SWEAR, THIS MATH BOOK WAS WRITTEN BY A SADIST.
ANOTHER SATURDAY NIGHT OF HOMEWORK? WOW.

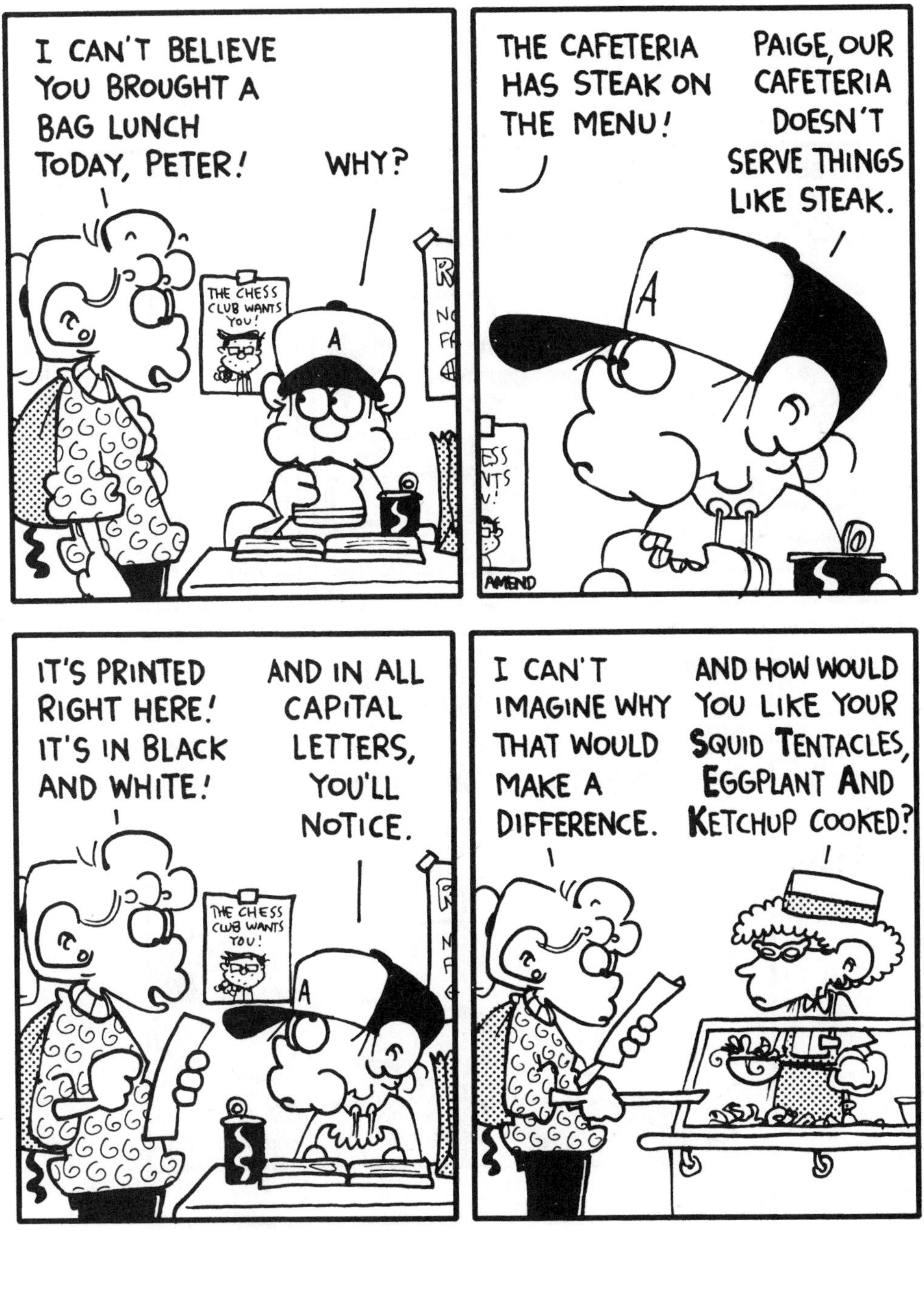
I CAN'T BELIEVE YOU BROUGHT A BAG LUNCH TODAY, PETER!
WHY?
THE CHESS CLUB WANTS YOU!
THE CAFETERIA HAS STEAK ON THE MENU!
PAIGE, OUR CAFETERIA DOESN'T SERVE THINGS LIKE STEAK.
AMEND
IT'S PRINTED RIGHT HERE! IT'S IN BLACK AND WHITE!
AND IN ALL CAPITAL LETTERS, YOU'LL NOTICE.
THE CHESS CLUB WANTS YOU!
I CAN'T IMAGINE WHY THAT WOULD MAKE A DIFFERENCE.
AND HOW WOULD YOU LIKE YOUR SQUID TENTACLES, EGGPLANT AND KETCHUP COOKED?

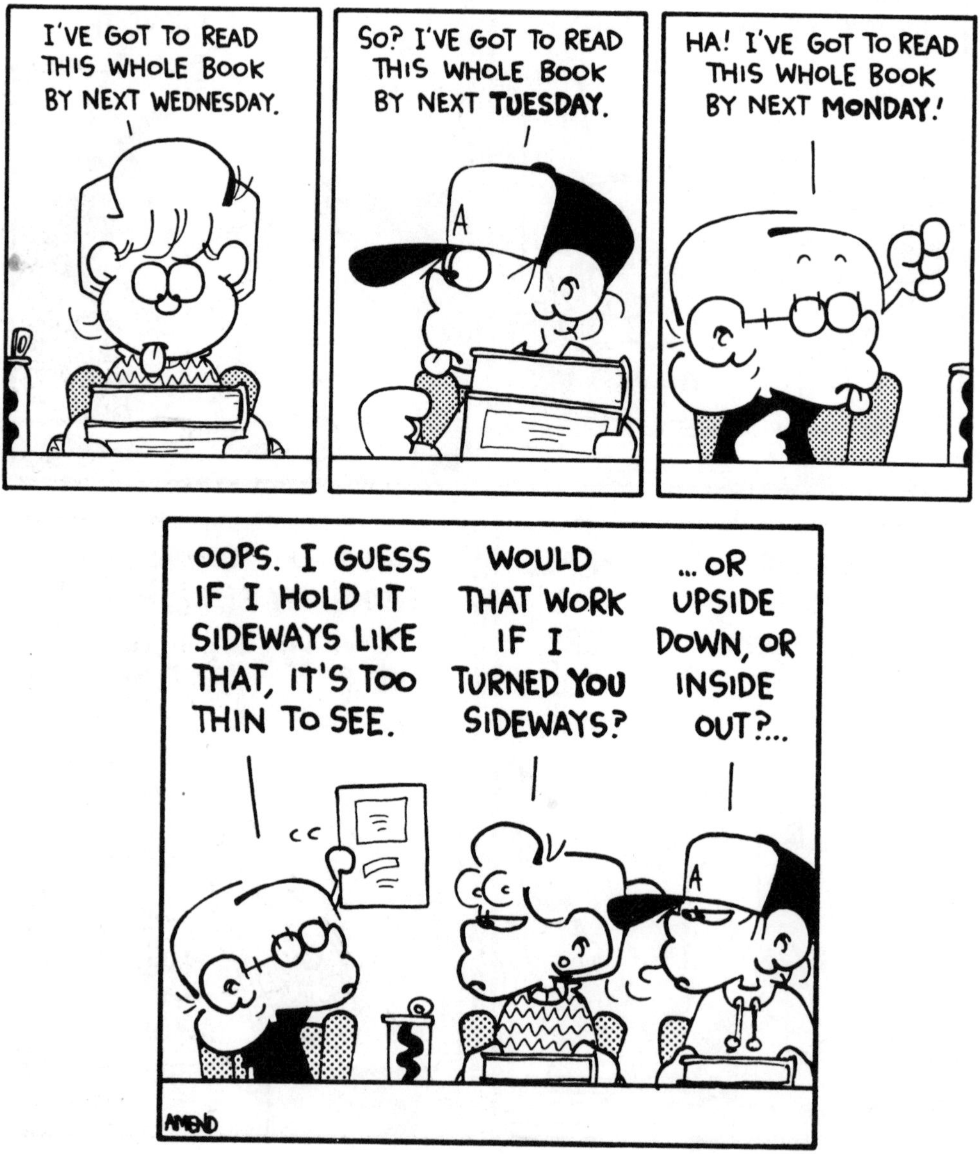
I'VE GOT TO READ THIS WHOLE BOOK BY NEXT WEDNESDAY.
SO? I'VE GOT TO READ THIS WHOLE BOOK BY NEXT **TUESDAY**.
HA! I'VE GOT TO READ THIS WHOLE BOOK BY NEXT **MONDAY**!
OOPS. I GUESS IF I HOLD IT SIDEWAYS LIKE THAT, IT'S TOO THIN TO SEE.
WOULD THAT WORK IF I TURNED **YOU** SIDEWAYS?
... OR UPSIDE DOWN, OR INSIDE OUT?...
AMEND

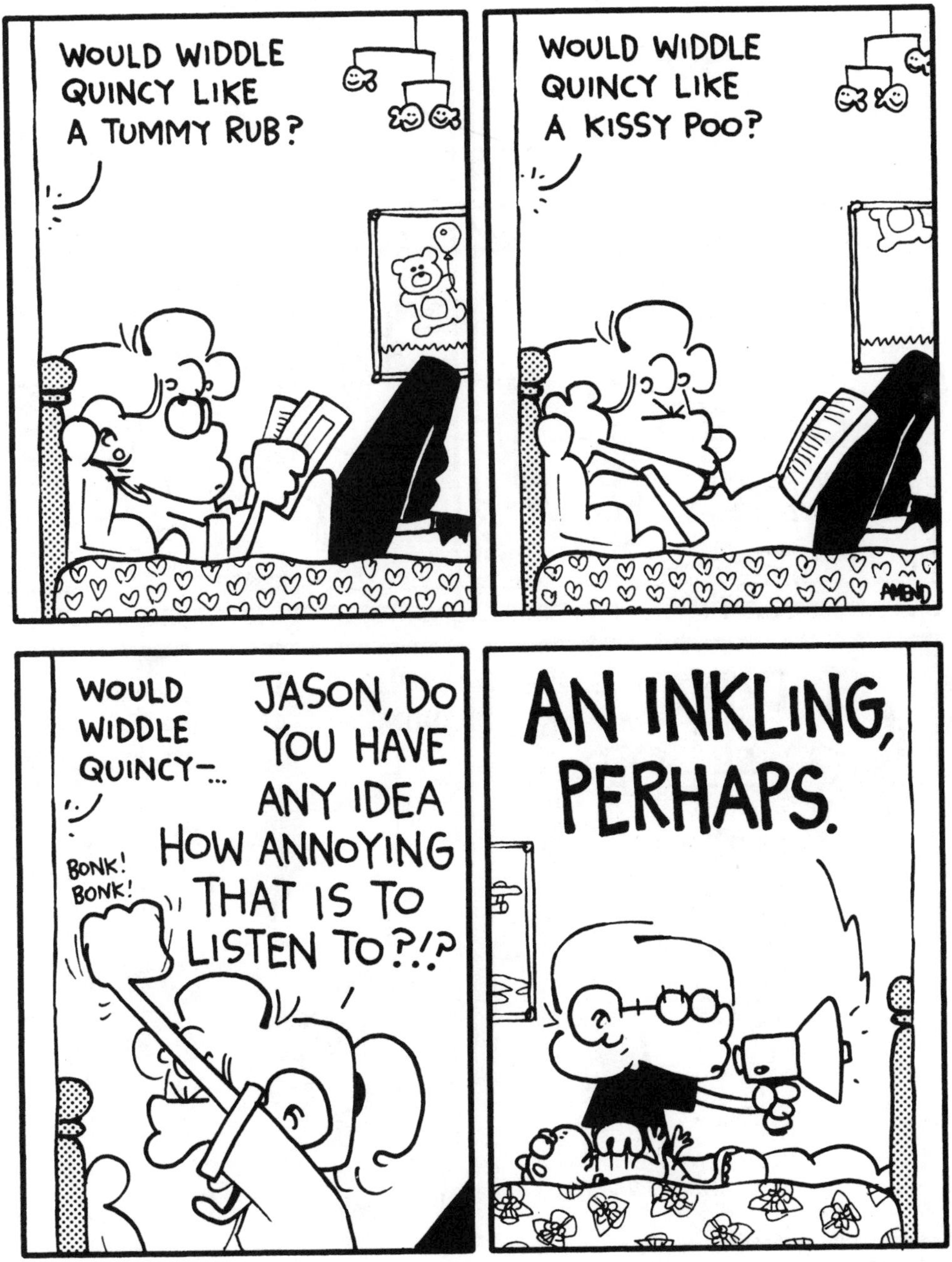
WOULD WIDDLE QUINCY LIKE A TUMMY RUB?
WOULD WIDDLE QUINCY LIKE A KISSY POO?
AMEND
WOULD WIDDLE QUINCY-...
JASON, DO YOU HAVE ANY IDEA HOW ANNOYING THAT IS TO LISTEN TO?!?
BONK! BONK!
AN INKLING, PERHAPS.

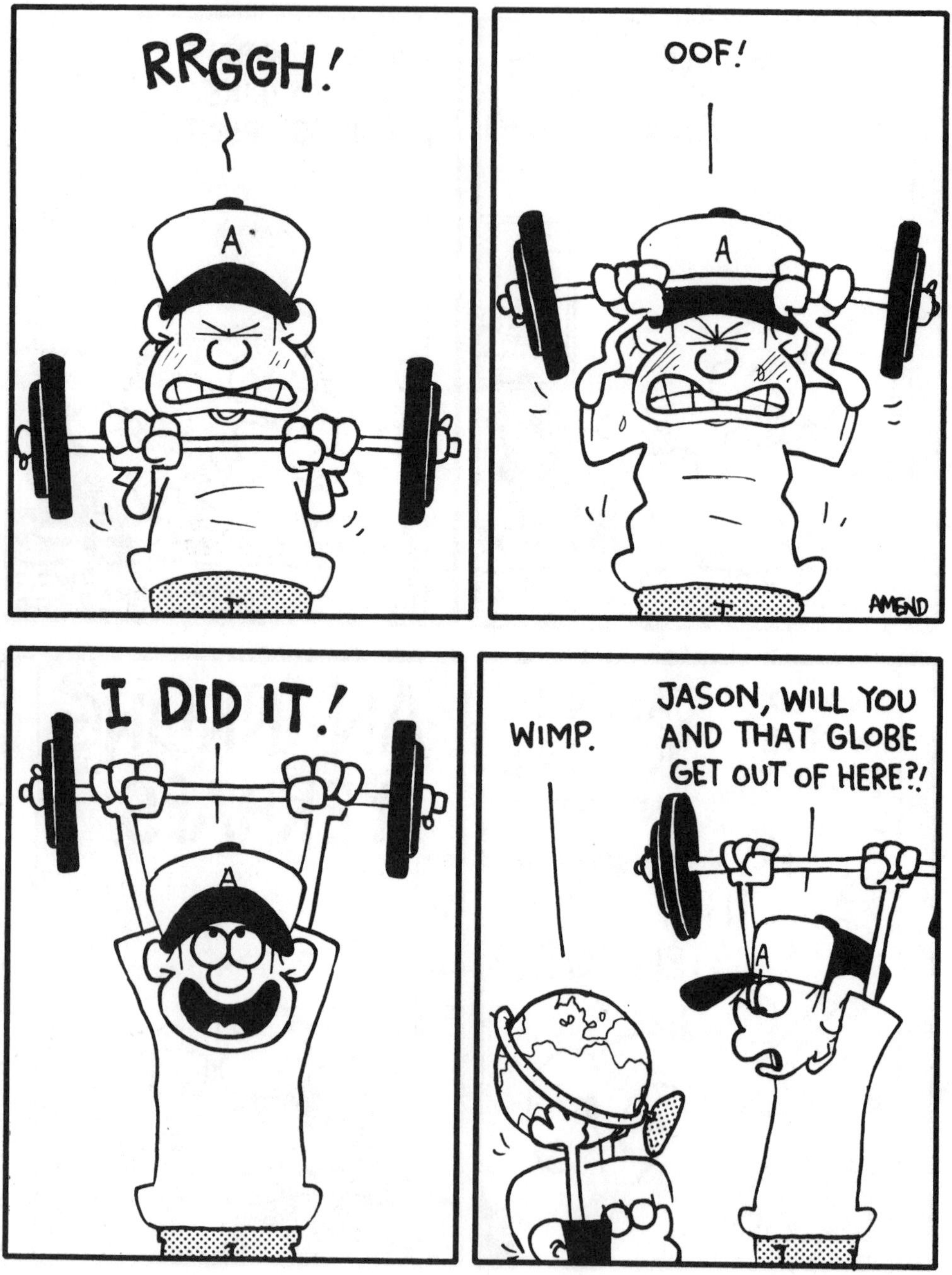
RRGGH!
OOF!
AMEND
I DID IT!
WIMP.
JASON, WILL YOU AND THAT GLOBE GET OUT OF HERE?!

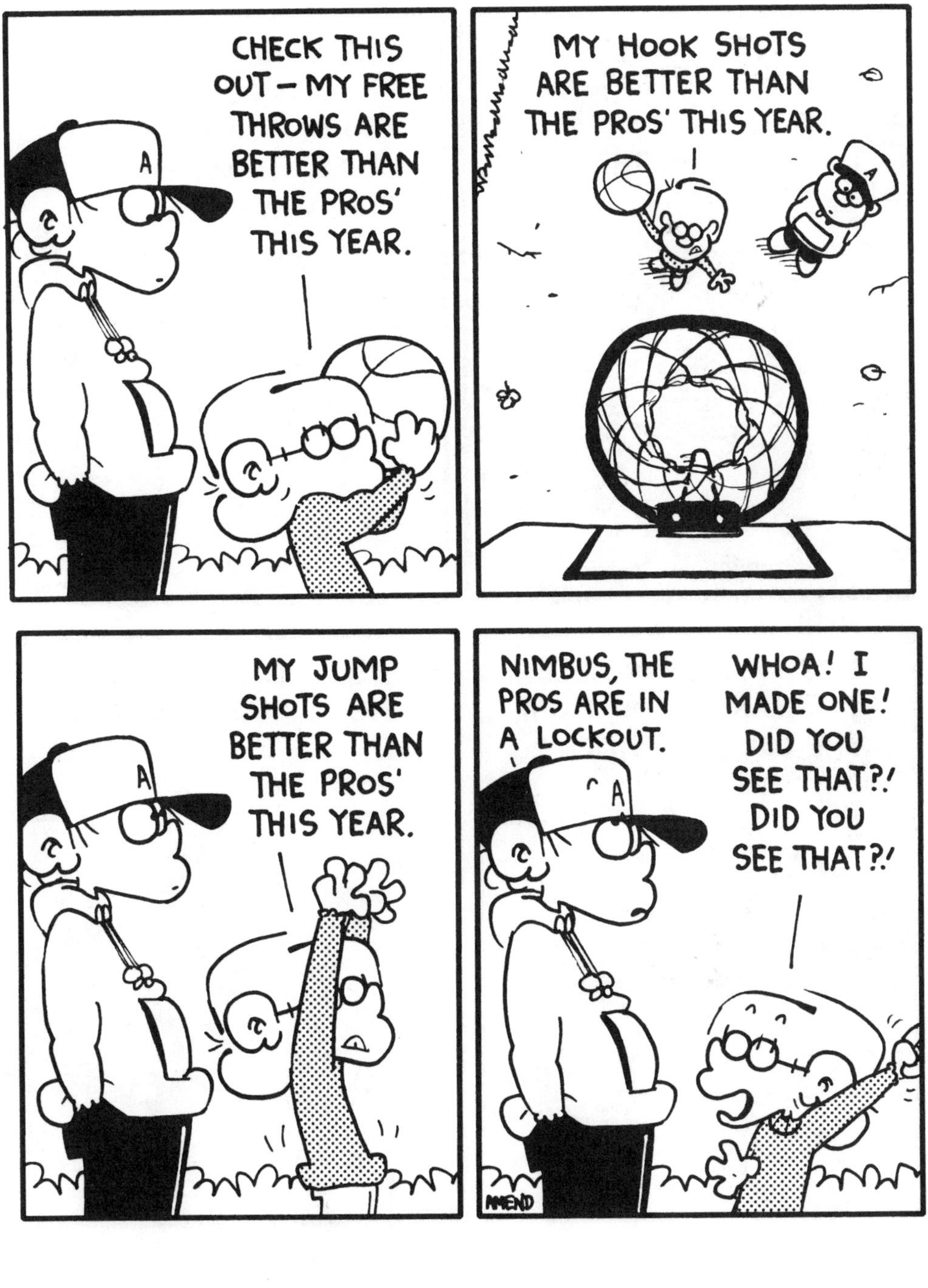
CHECK THIS OUT – MY FREE THROWS ARE BETTER THAN THE PROS' THIS YEAR.
MY HOOK SHOTS ARE BETTER THAN THE PROS' THIS YEAR.
MY JUMP SHOTS ARE BETTER THAN THE PROS' THIS YEAR.
NIMBUS, THE PROS ARE IN A LOCKOUT.
WHOA! I MADE ONE! DID YOU SEE THAT?! DID YOU SEE THAT?!
AMEND

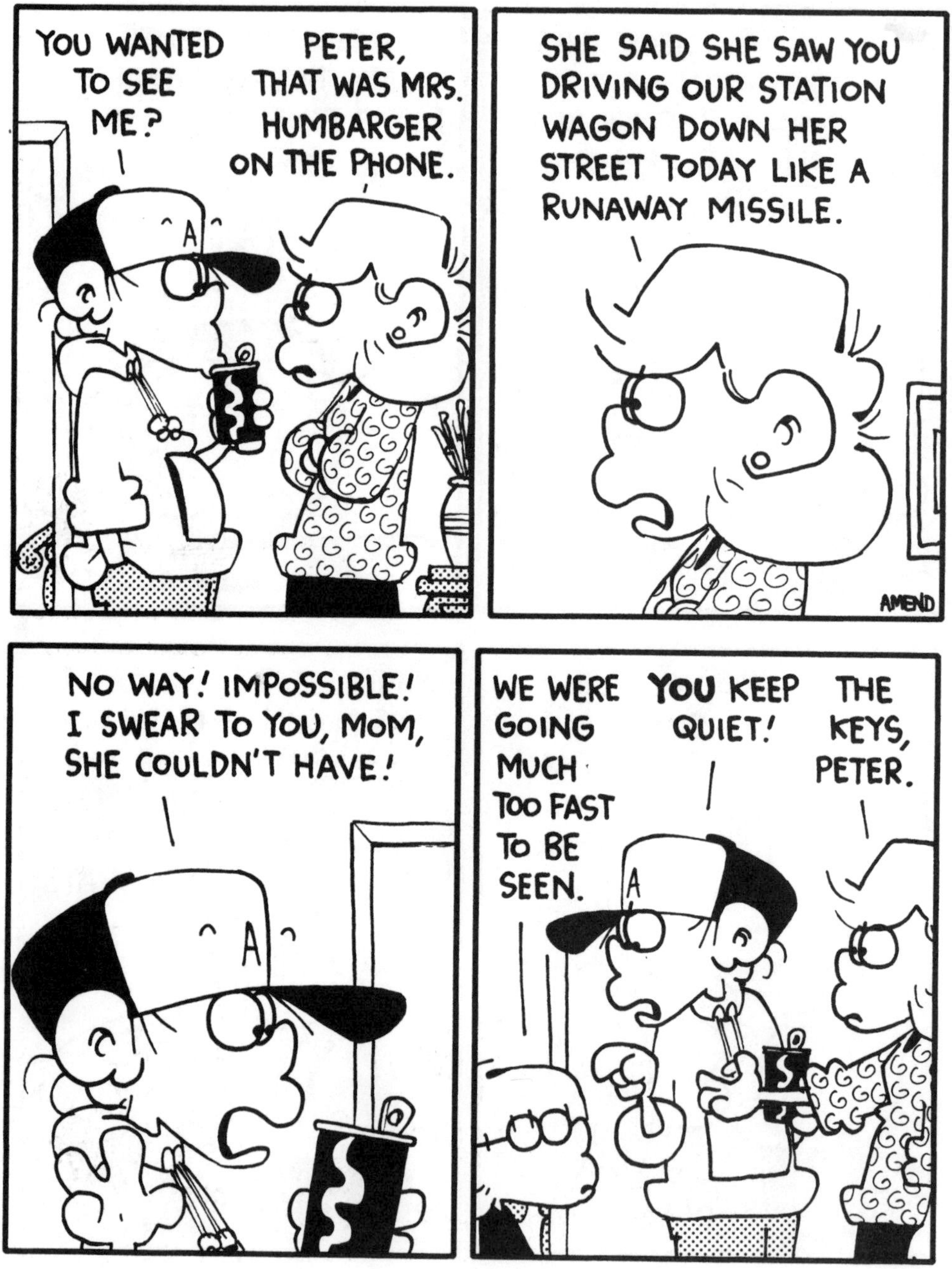
YOU WANTED TO SEE ME?
PETER, THAT WAS MRS. HUMBARGER ON THE PHONE.
SHE SAID SHE SAW YOU DRIVING OUR STATION WAGON DOWN HER STREET TODAY LIKE A RUNAWAY MISSILE.
AMEND
NO WAY! IMPOSSIBLE! I SWEAR TO YOU, MOM, SHE COULDN'T HAVE!
WE WERE GOING MUCH TOO FAST TO BE SEEN.
YOU KEEP QUIET!
THE KEYS, PETER.

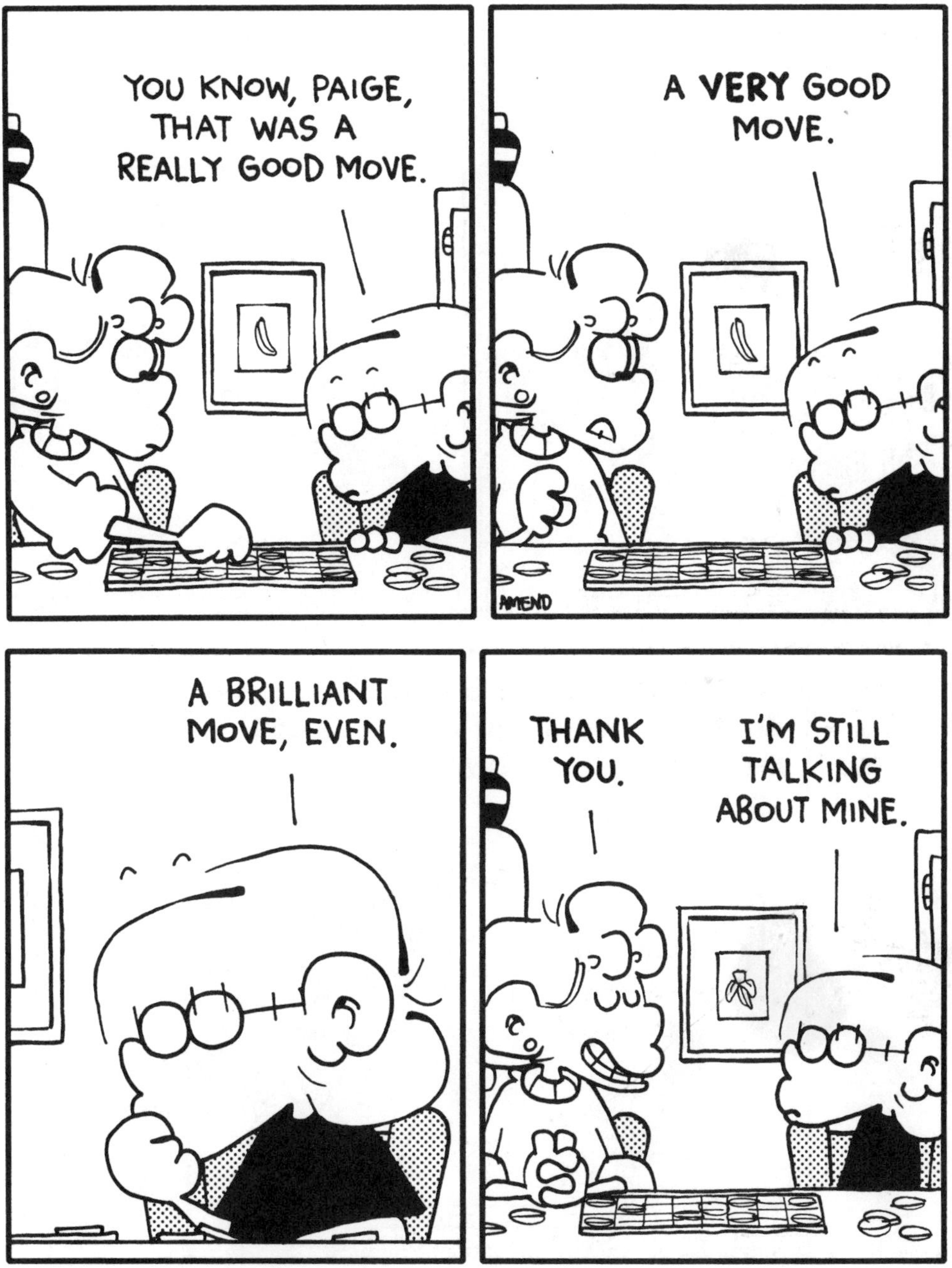
YOU KNOW, PAIGE, THAT WAS A REALLY GOOD MOVE.
A VERY GOOD MOVE.
AMEND
A BRILLIANT MOVE, EVEN.
THANK YOU.
I'M STILL TALKING ABOUT MINE.

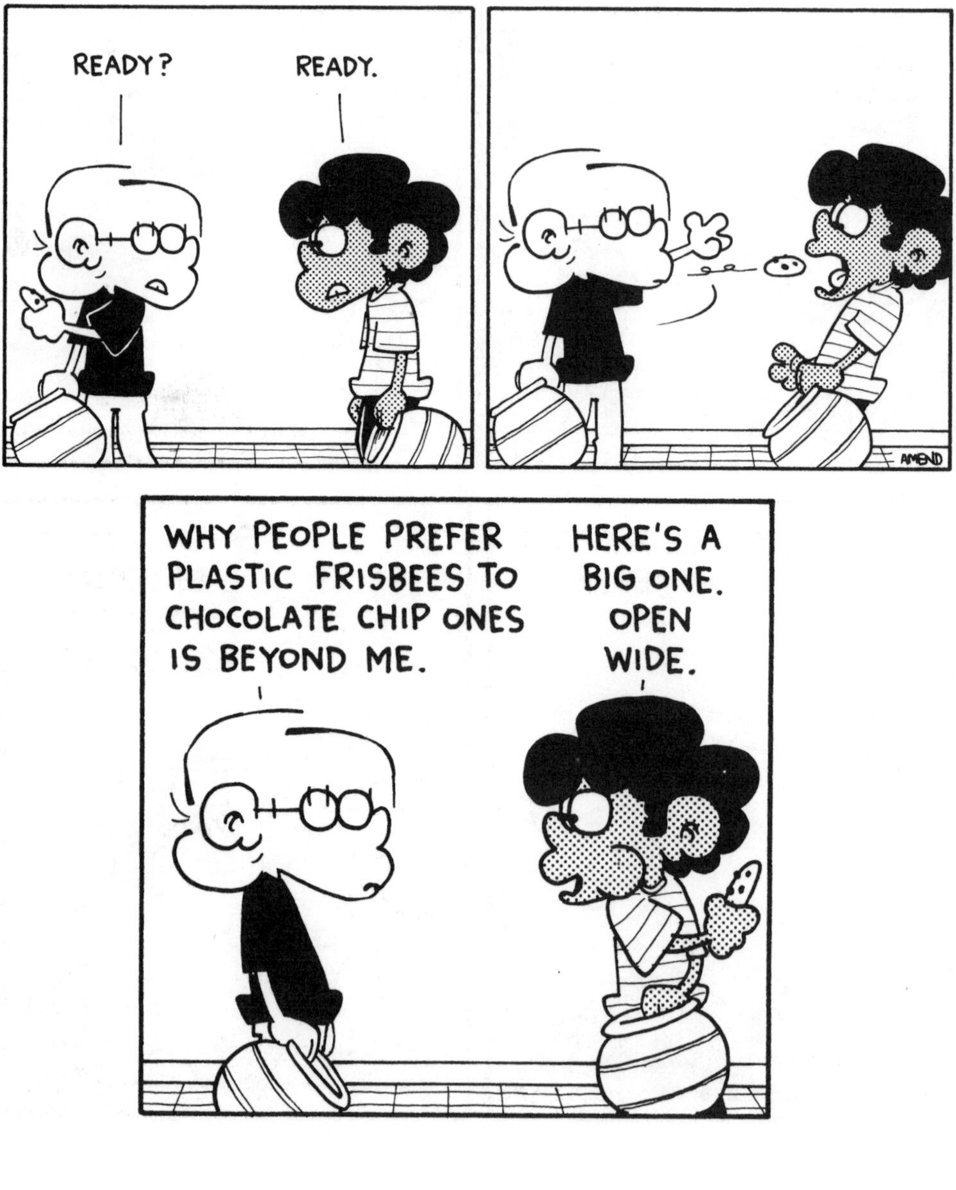
READY?
READY.
AMEND
WHY PEOPLE PREFER PLASTIC FRISBEES TO CHOCOLATE CHIP ONES IS BEYOND ME.
HERE'S A BIG ONE. OPEN WIDE.

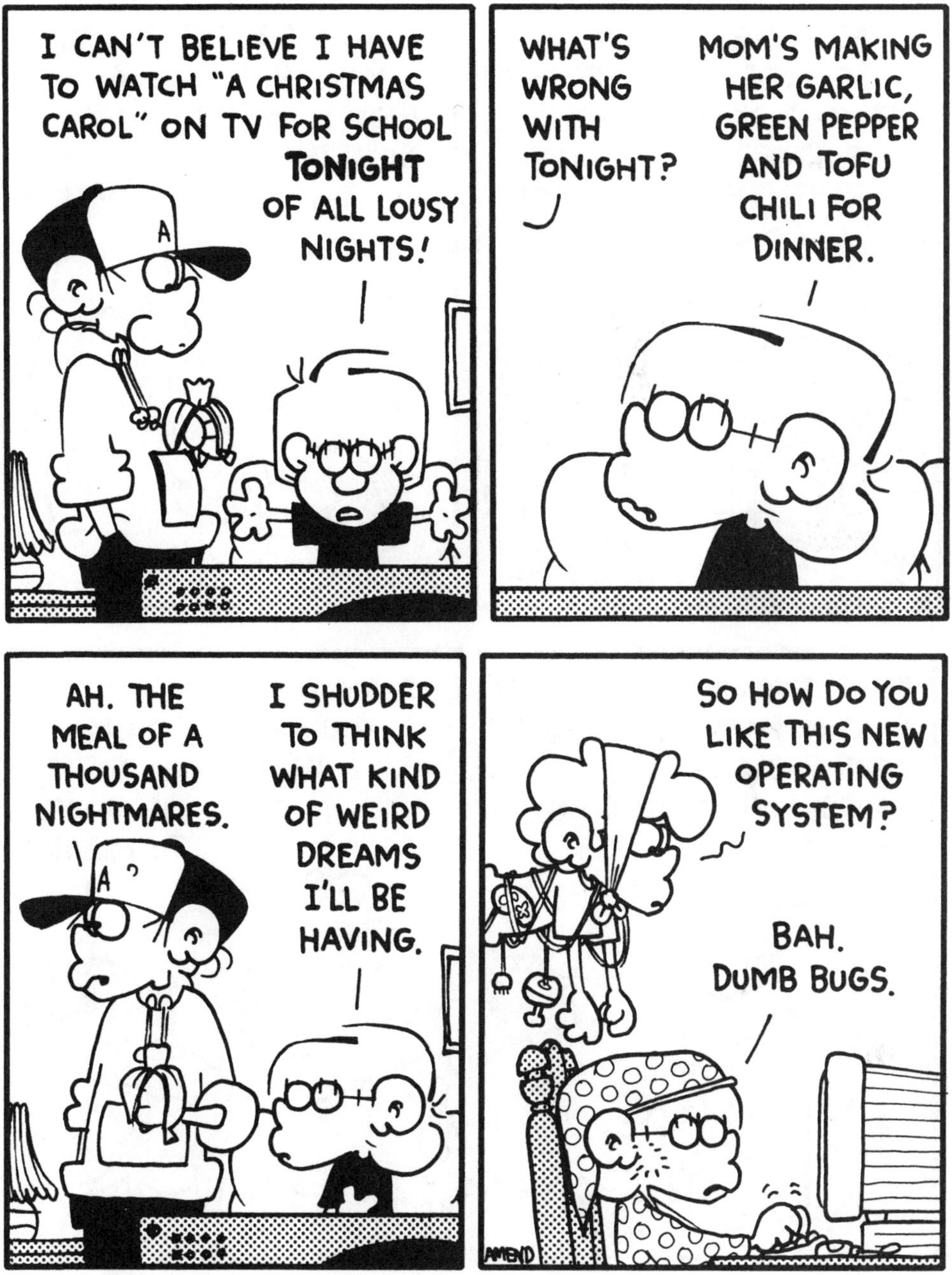
I CAN'T BELIEVE I HAVE TO WATCH "A CHRISTMAS CAROL" ON TV FOR SCHOOL **TONIGHT** OF ALL LOUSY NIGHTS!
WHAT'S WRONG WITH TONIGHT?
MOM'S MAKING HER GARLIC, GREEN PEPPER AND TOFU CHILI FOR DINNER.
AH. THE MEAL OF A THOUSAND NIGHTMARES.
I SHUDDER TO THINK WHAT KIND OF WEIRD DREAMS I'LL BE HAVING.
SO HOW DO YOU LIKE THIS NEW OPERATING SYSTEM?
BAH. DUMB BUGS.
AMEND

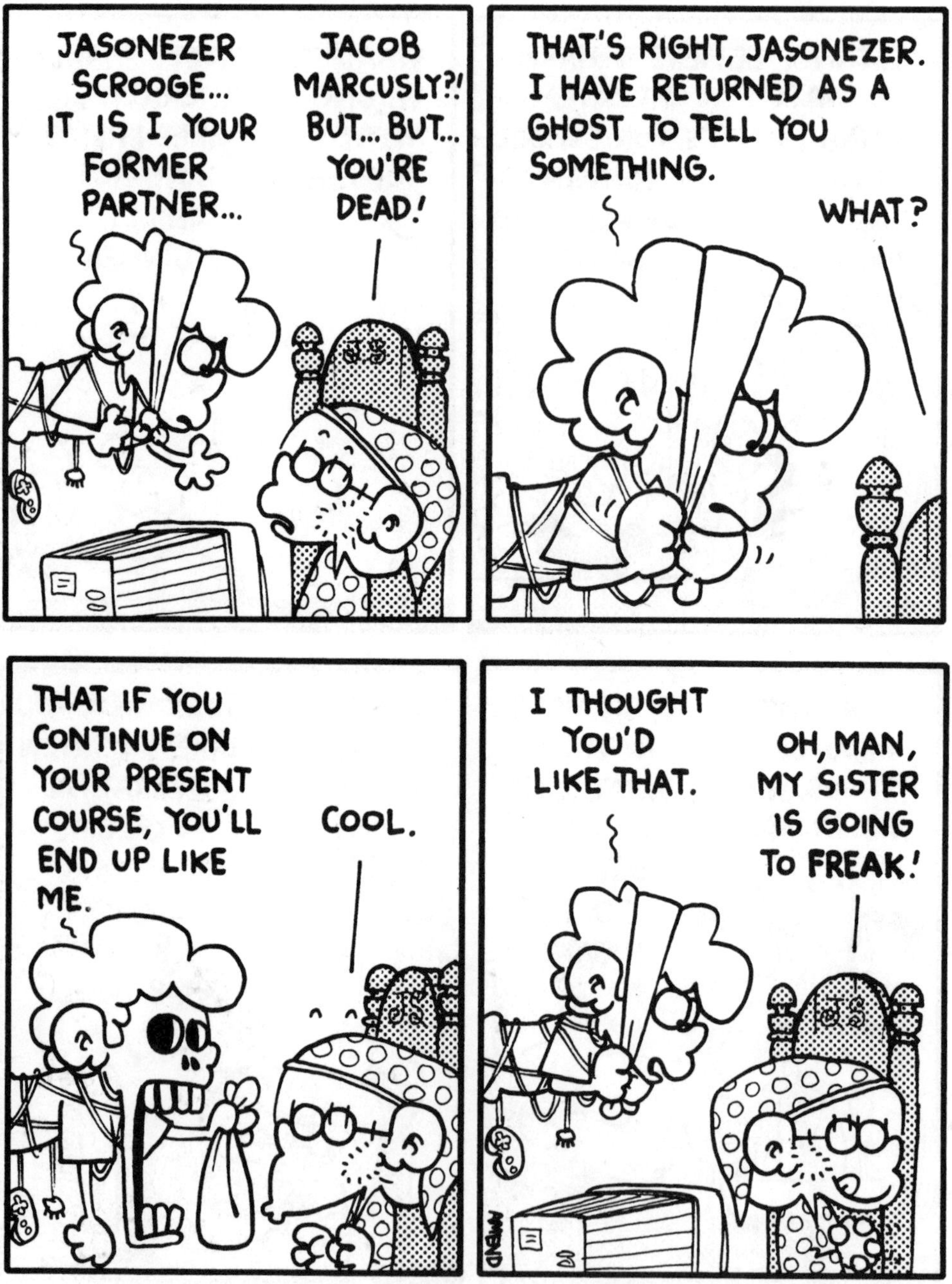
JASONEZER SCROOGE... IT IS I, YOUR FORMER PARTNER...
JACOB MARCUSLY?! BUT... BUT... YOU'RE DEAD!
THAT'S RIGHT, JASONEZER. I HAVE RETURNED AS A GHOST TO TELL YOU SOMETHING.
WHAT?
THAT IF YOU CONTINUE ON YOUR PRESENT COURSE, YOU'LL END UP LIKE ME.
COOL.
I THOUGHT YOU'D LIKE THAT.
OH, MAN, MY SISTER IS GOING TO FREAK!

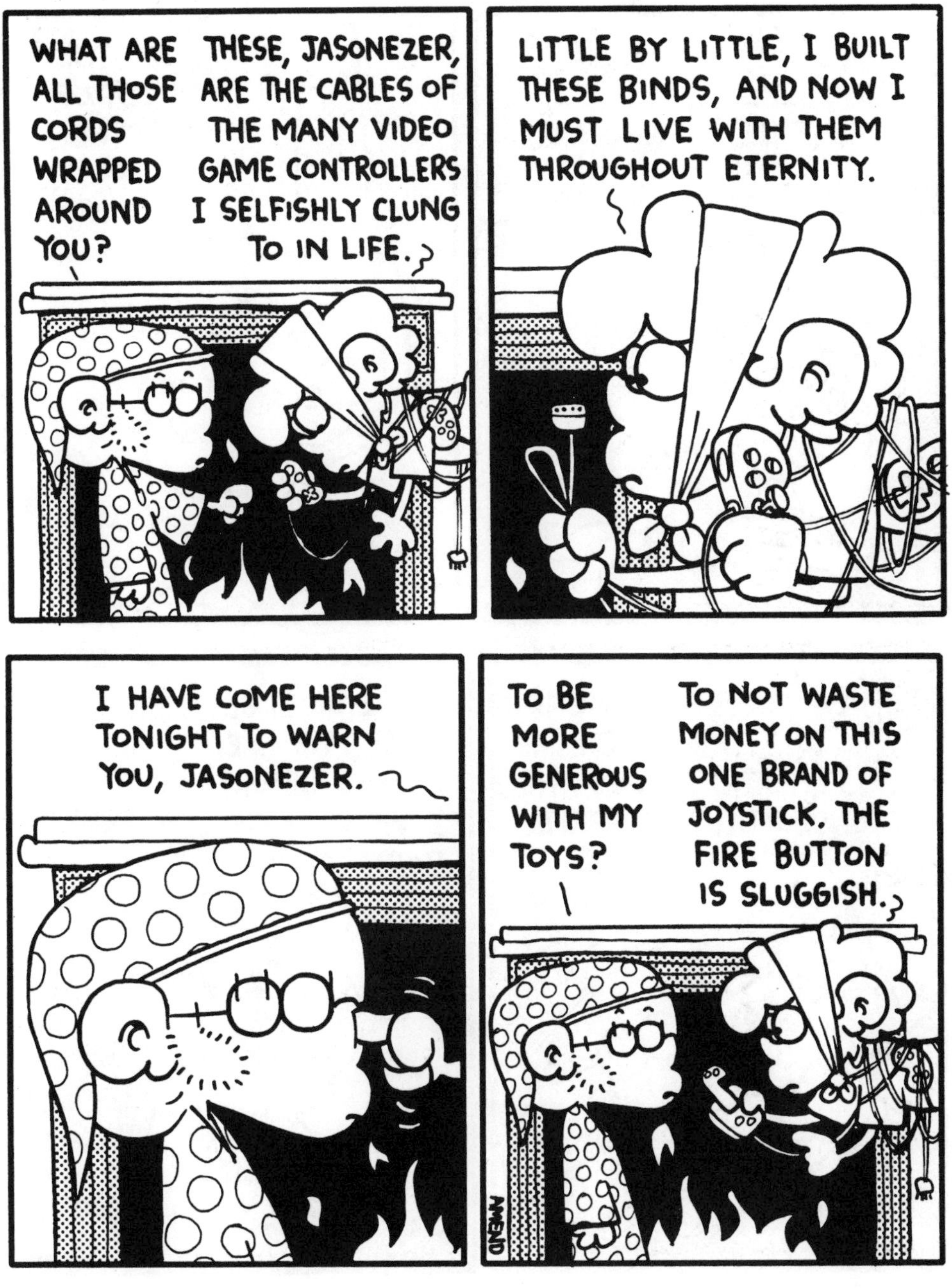
WHAT ARE ALL THOSE CORDS WRAPPED AROUND YOU?
THESE, JASONEZER, ARE THE CABLES OF THE MANY VIDEO GAME CONTROLLERS I SELFISHLY CLUNG TO IN LIFE.
LITTLE BY LITTLE, I BUILT THESE BINDS, AND NOW I MUST LIVE WITH THEM THROUGHOUT ETERNITY.
I HAVE COME HERE TONIGHT TO WARN YOU, JASONEZER.
TO BE MORE GENEROUS WITH MY TOYS?
TO NOT WASTE MONEY ON THIS ONE BRAND OF JOYSTICK. THE FIRE BUTTON IS SLUGGISH.
AMEND

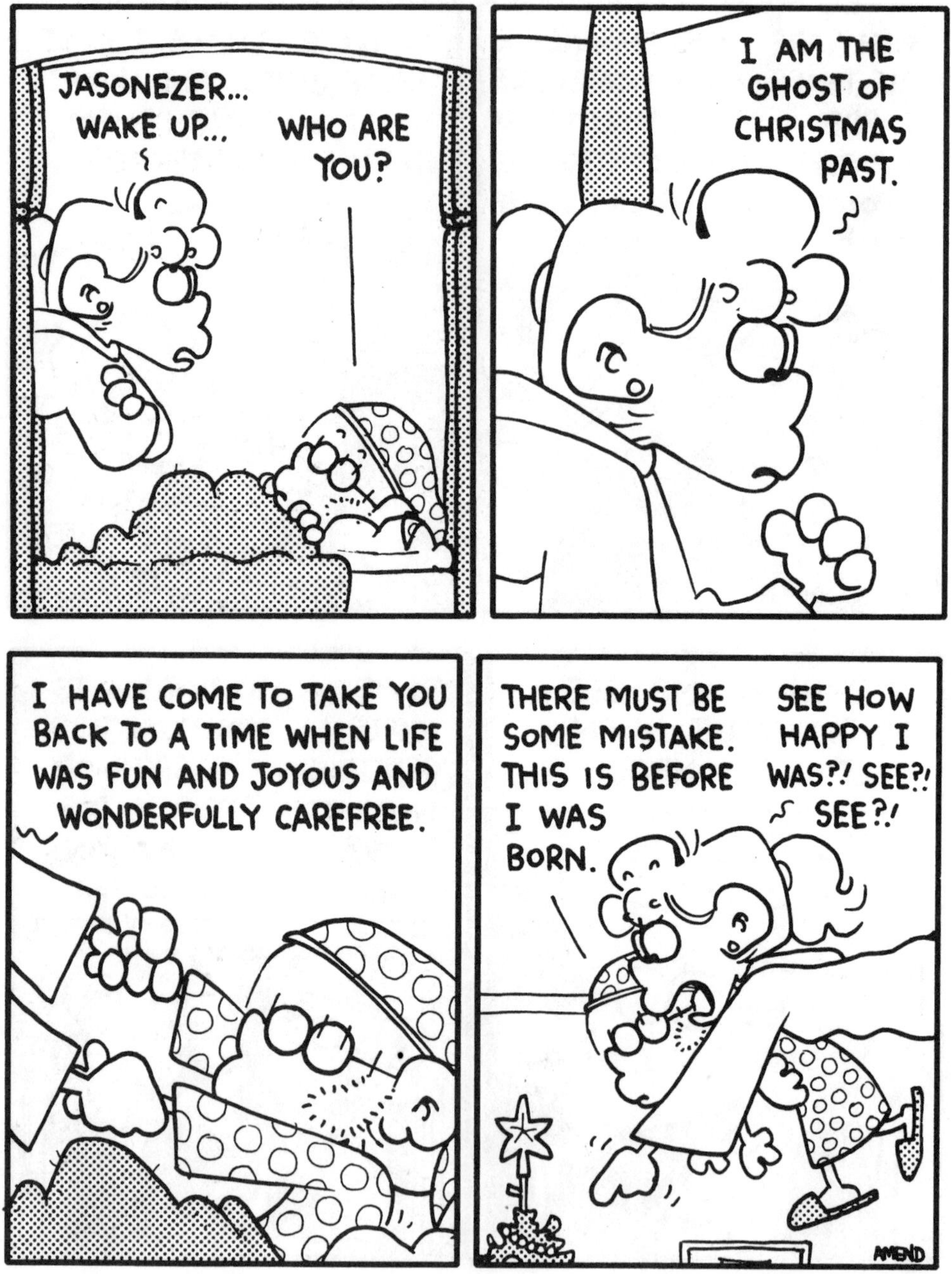
JASONEZER...
WAKE UP...
WHO ARE YOU?
I AM THE GHOST OF CHRISTMAS PAST.
I HAVE COME TO TAKE YOU BACK TO A TIME WHEN LIFE WAS FUN AND JOYOUS AND WONDERFULLY CAREFREE.
THERE MUST BE SOME MISTAKE. THIS IS BEFORE I WAS BORN.
SEE HOW HAPPY I WAS?! SEE?! SEE?!
AMEND

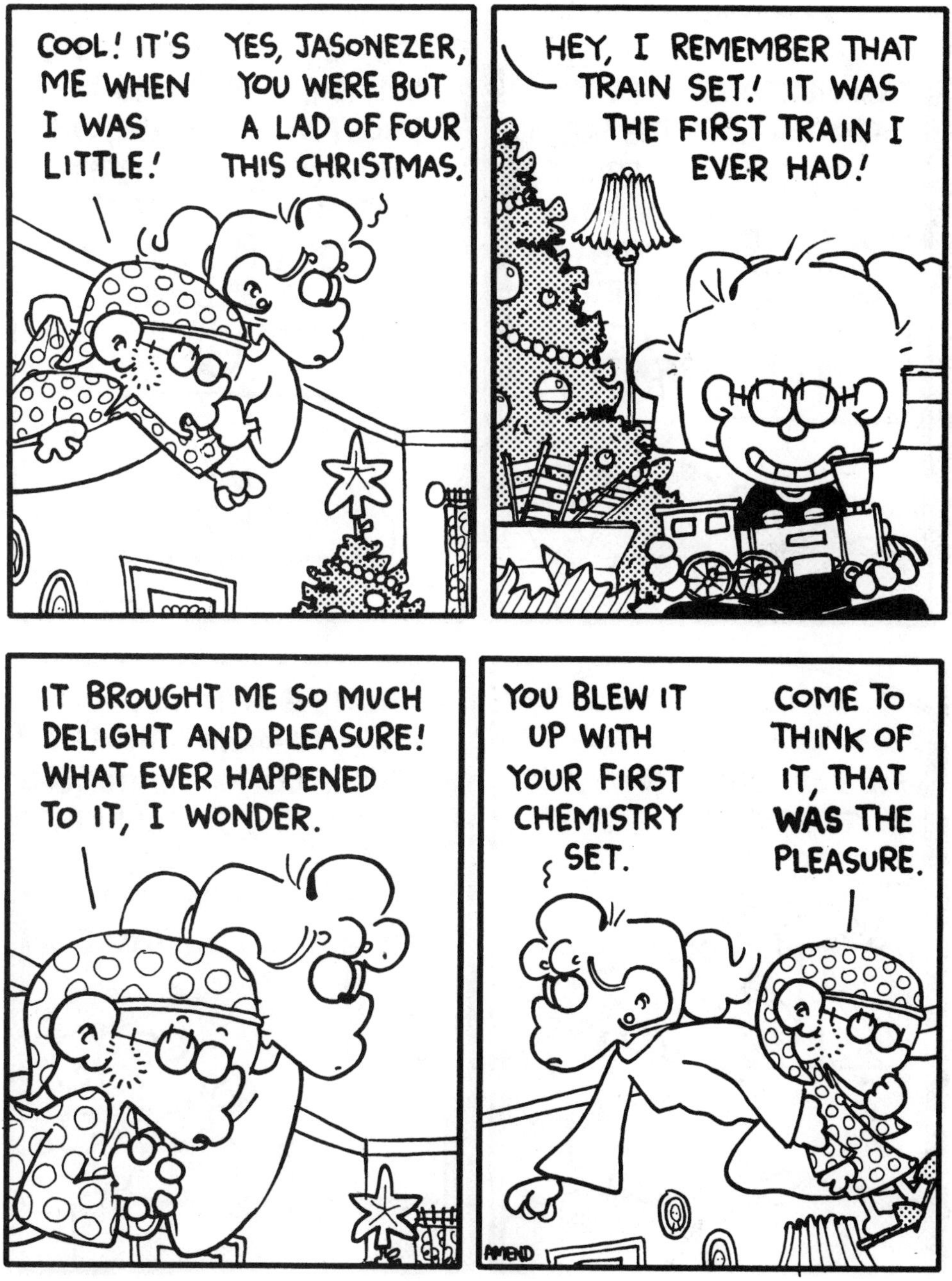
COOL! IT'S ME WHEN I WAS LITTLE!
YES, JASONEZER, YOU WERE BUT A LAD OF FOUR THIS CHRISTMAS.
HEY, I REMEMBER THAT TRAIN SET! IT WAS THE FIRST TRAIN I EVER HAD!
IT BROUGHT ME SO MUCH DELIGHT AND PLEASURE! WHAT EVER HAPPENED TO IT, I WONDER.
YOU BLEW IT UP WITH YOUR FIRST CHEMISTRY SET.
COME TO THINK OF IT, THAT WAS THE PLEASURE.
AMEND

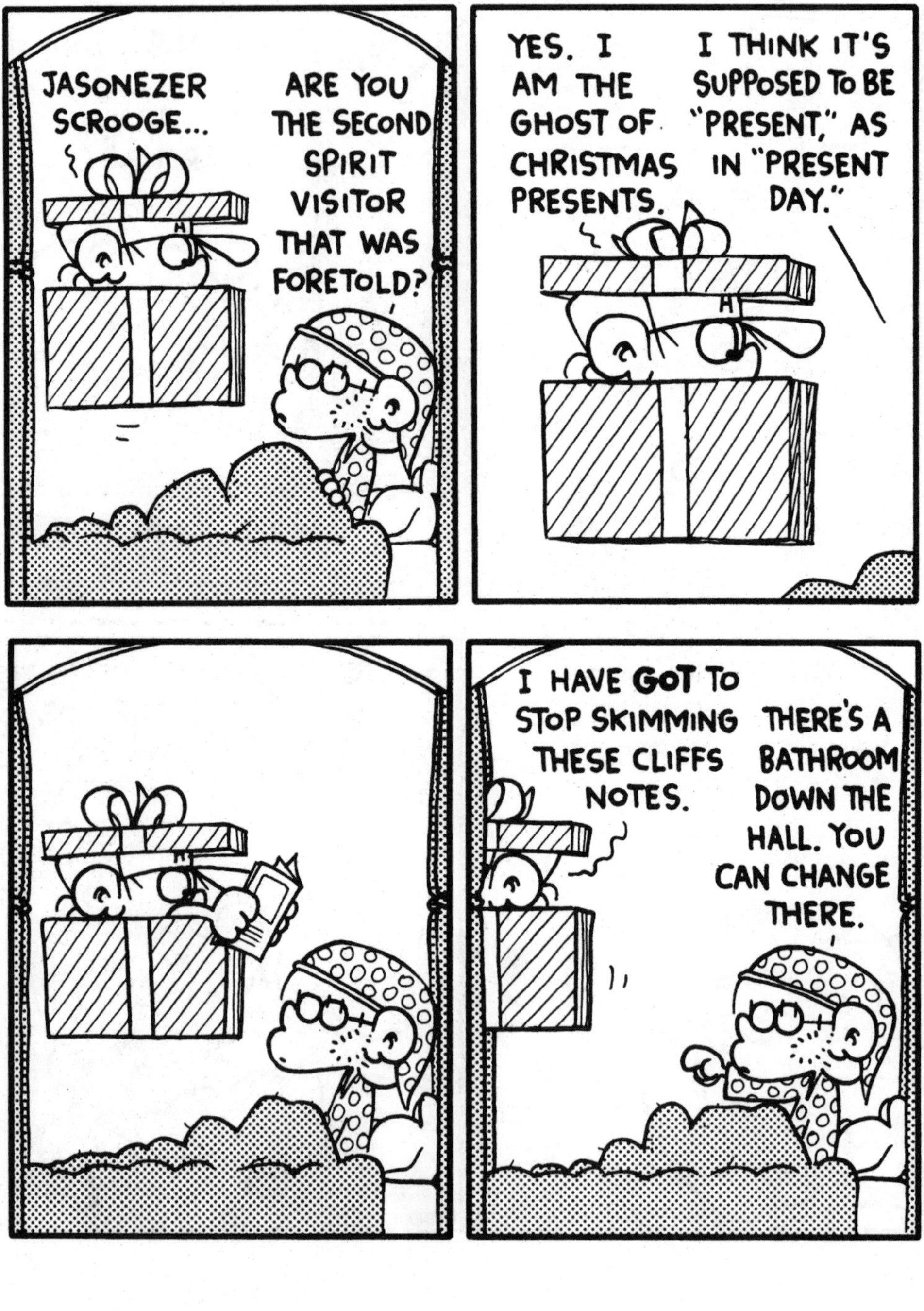
JASONEZER SCROOGE...
ARE YOU THE SECOND SPIRIT VISITOR THAT WAS FORETOLD?
YES. I AM THE GHOST OF CHRISTMAS PRESENTS.
I THINK IT'S SUPPOSED TO BE "PRESENT," AS IN "PRESENT DAY."
I HAVE GOT TO STOP SKIMMING THESE CLIFFS NOTES.
THERE'S A BATHROOM DOWN THE HALL. YOU CAN CHANGE THERE.

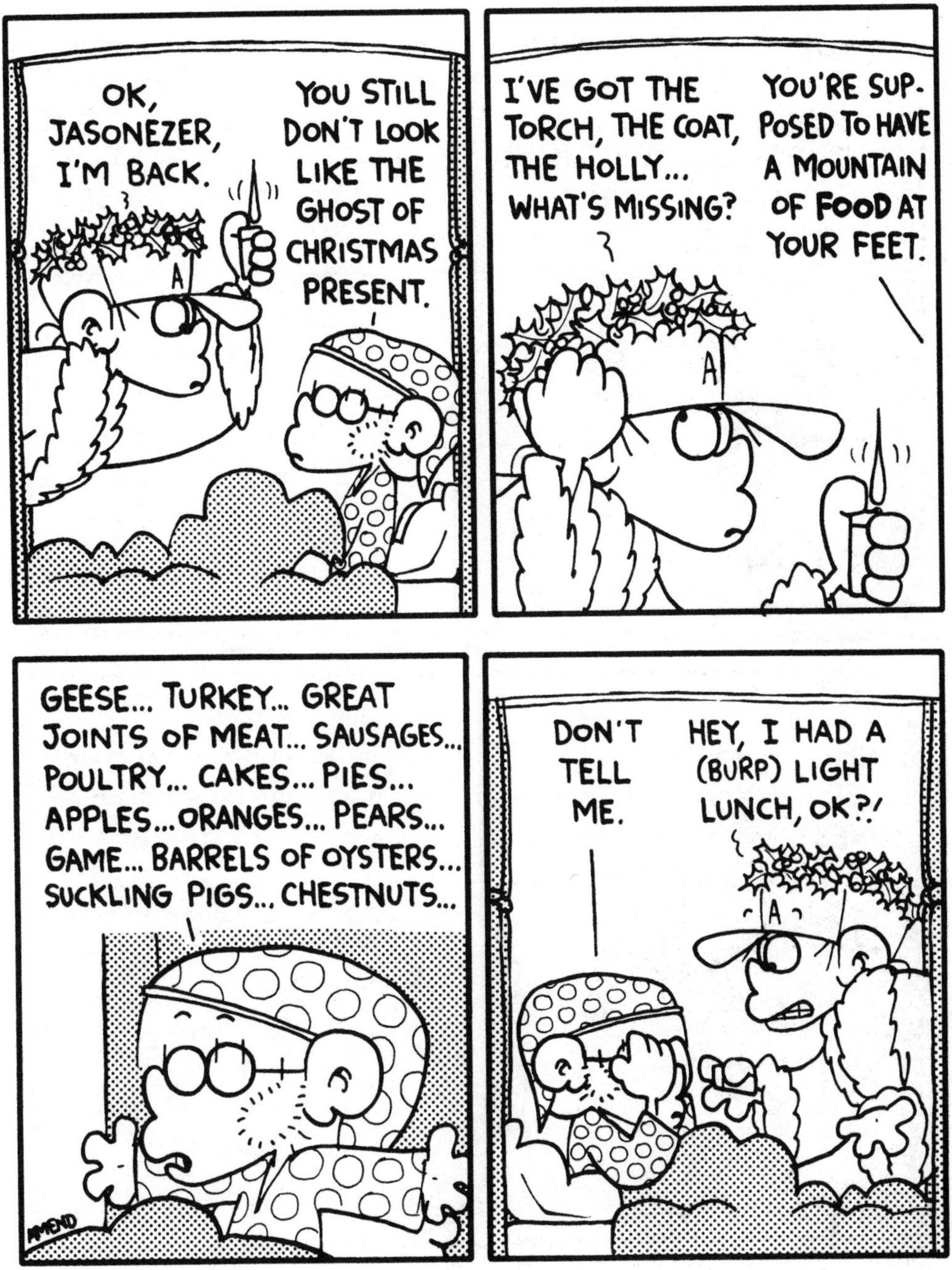
OK, JASONEZER, I'M BACK.
YOU STILL DON'T LOOK LIKE THE GHOST OF CHRISTMAS PRESENT.
I'VE GOT THE TORCH, THE COAT, THE HOLLY... WHAT'S MISSING?
YOU'RE SUPPOSED TO HAVE A MOUNTAIN OF FOOD AT YOUR FEET.
GEESE... TURKEY... GREAT JOINTS OF MEAT... SAUSAGES... POULTRY... CAKES... PIES... APPLES...ORANGES... PEARS... GAME... BARRELS OF OYSTERS... SUCKLING PIGS... CHESTNUTS...
AMEND
DON'T TELL ME.
HEY, I HAD A (BURP) LIGHT LUNCH, OK?!

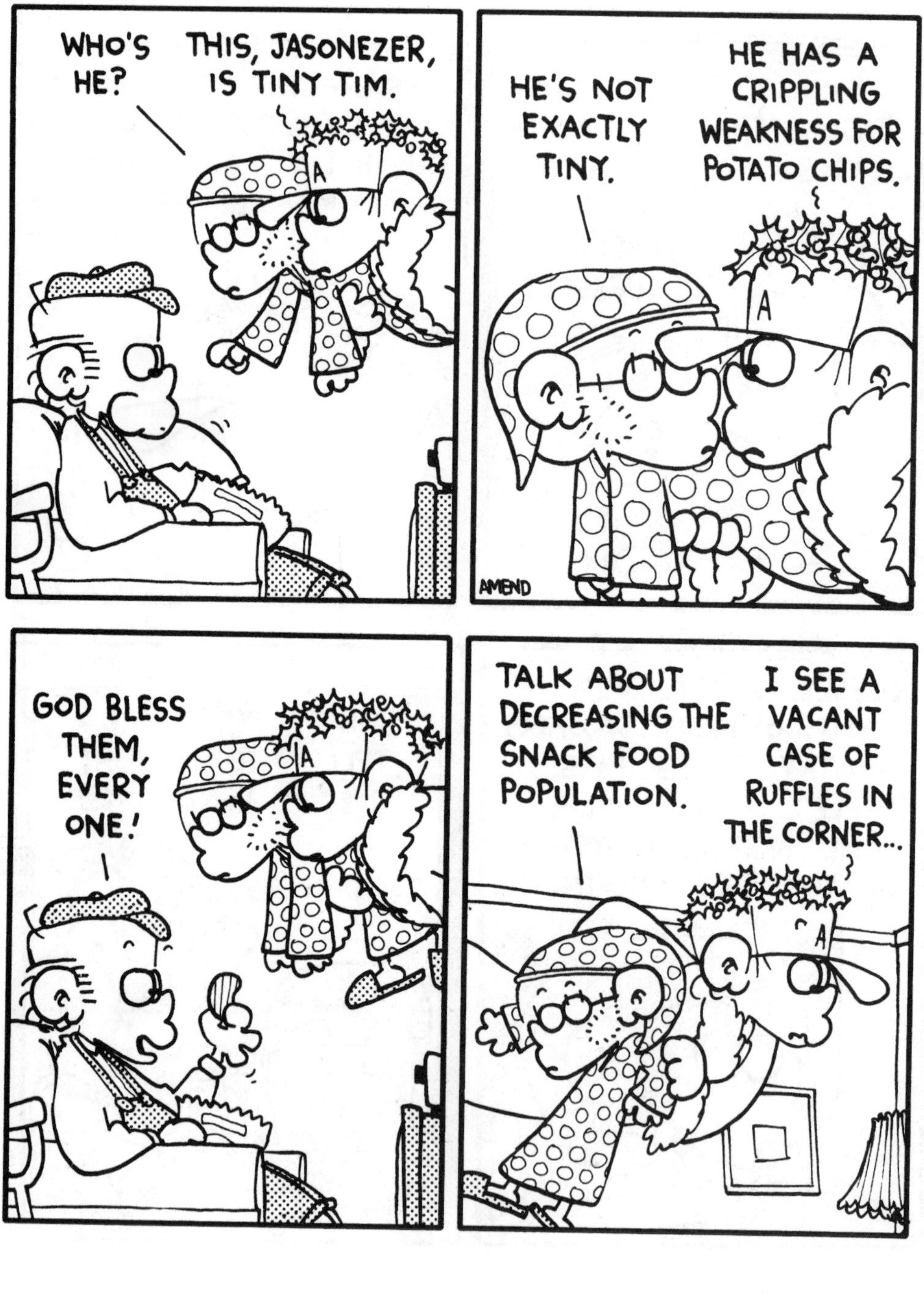
WHO'S HE?
THIS, JASONEZER, IS TINY TIM.
HE'S NOT EXACTLY TINY.
HE HAS A CRIPPLING WEAKNESS FOR POTATO CHIPS.
AMEND
GOD BLESS THEM, EVERY ONE!
TALK ABOUT DECREASING THE SNACK FOOD POPULATION.
I SEE A VACANT CASE OF RUFFLES IN THE CORNER...

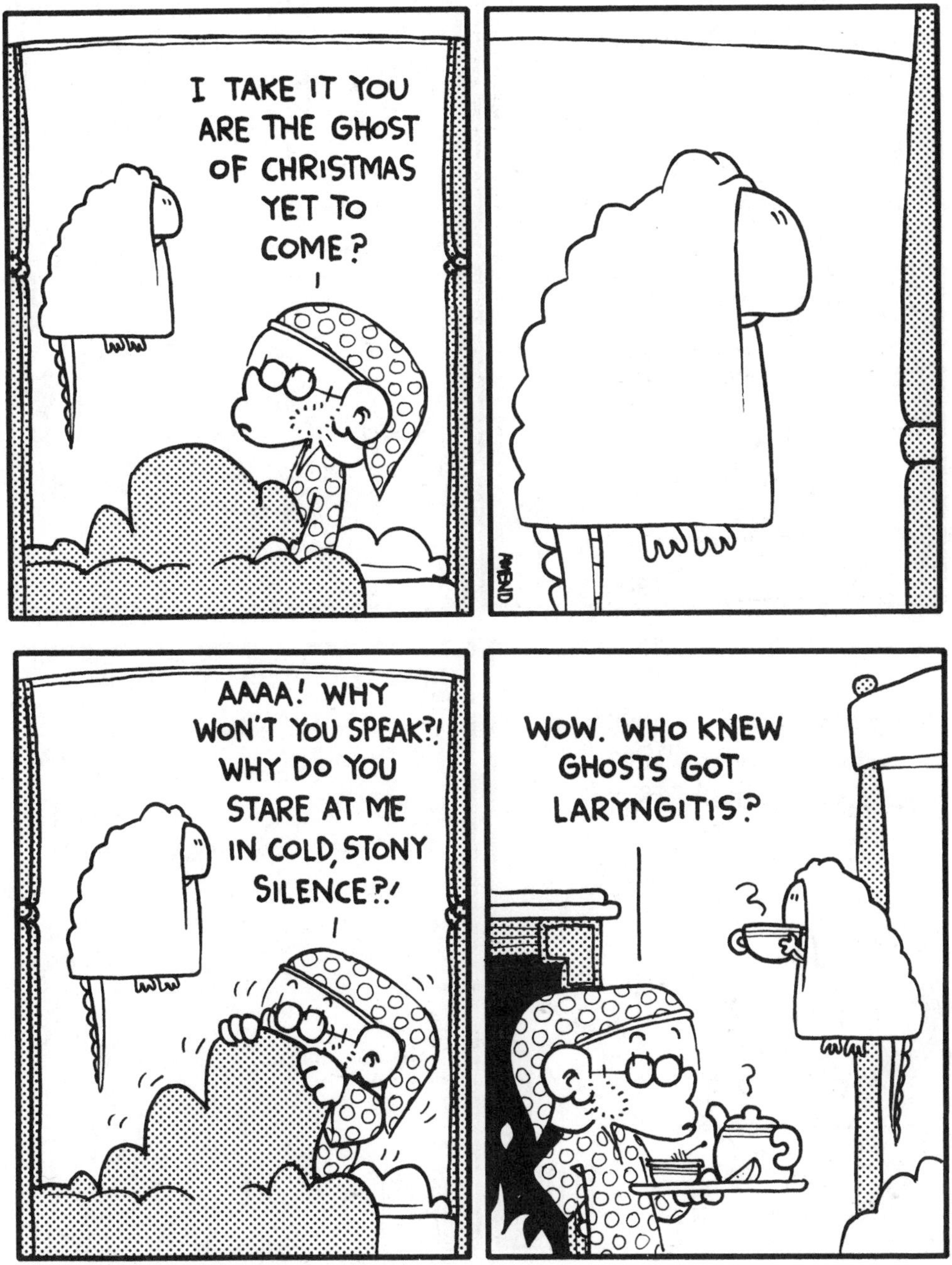
I TAKE IT YOU ARE THE GHOST OF CHRISTMAS YET TO COME?
MEND
AAAA! WHY WON'T YOU SPEAK?! WHY DO YOU STARE AT ME IN COLD, STONY SILENCE?!
WOW. WHO KNEW GHOSTS GOT LARYNGITIS?

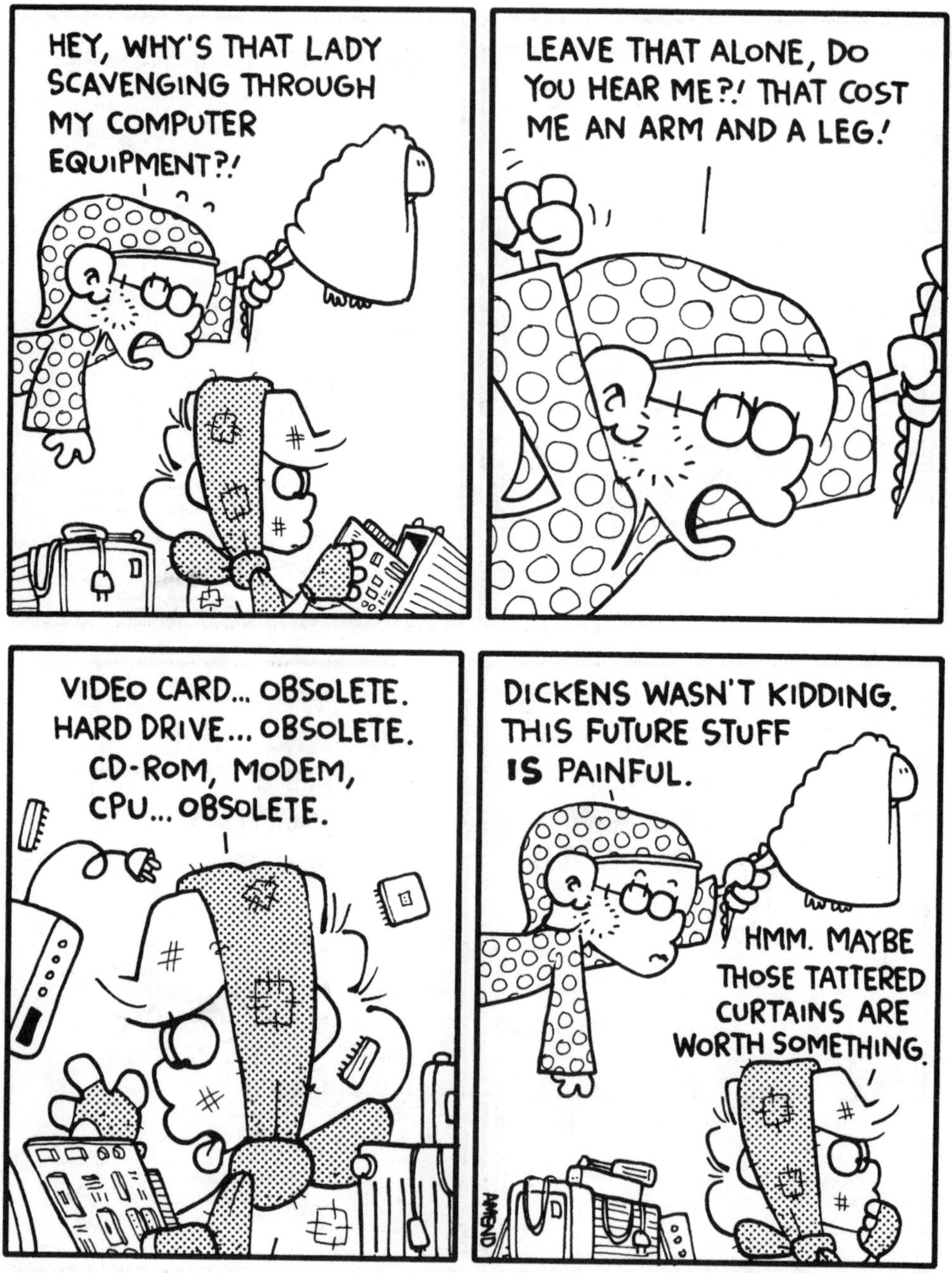
HEY, WHY'S THAT LADY SCAVENGING THROUGH MY COMPUTER EQUIPMENT?!
LEAVE THAT ALONE, DO YOU HEAR ME?! THAT COST ME AN ARM AND A LEG!
VIDEO CARD... OBSOLETE. HARD DRIVE... OBSOLETE. CD-ROM, MODEM, CPU... OBSOLETE.
DICKENS WASN'T KIDDING. THIS FUTURE STUFF IS PAINFUL.
HMM. MAYBE THOSE TATTERED CURTAINS ARE WORTH SOMETHING.
AMEND

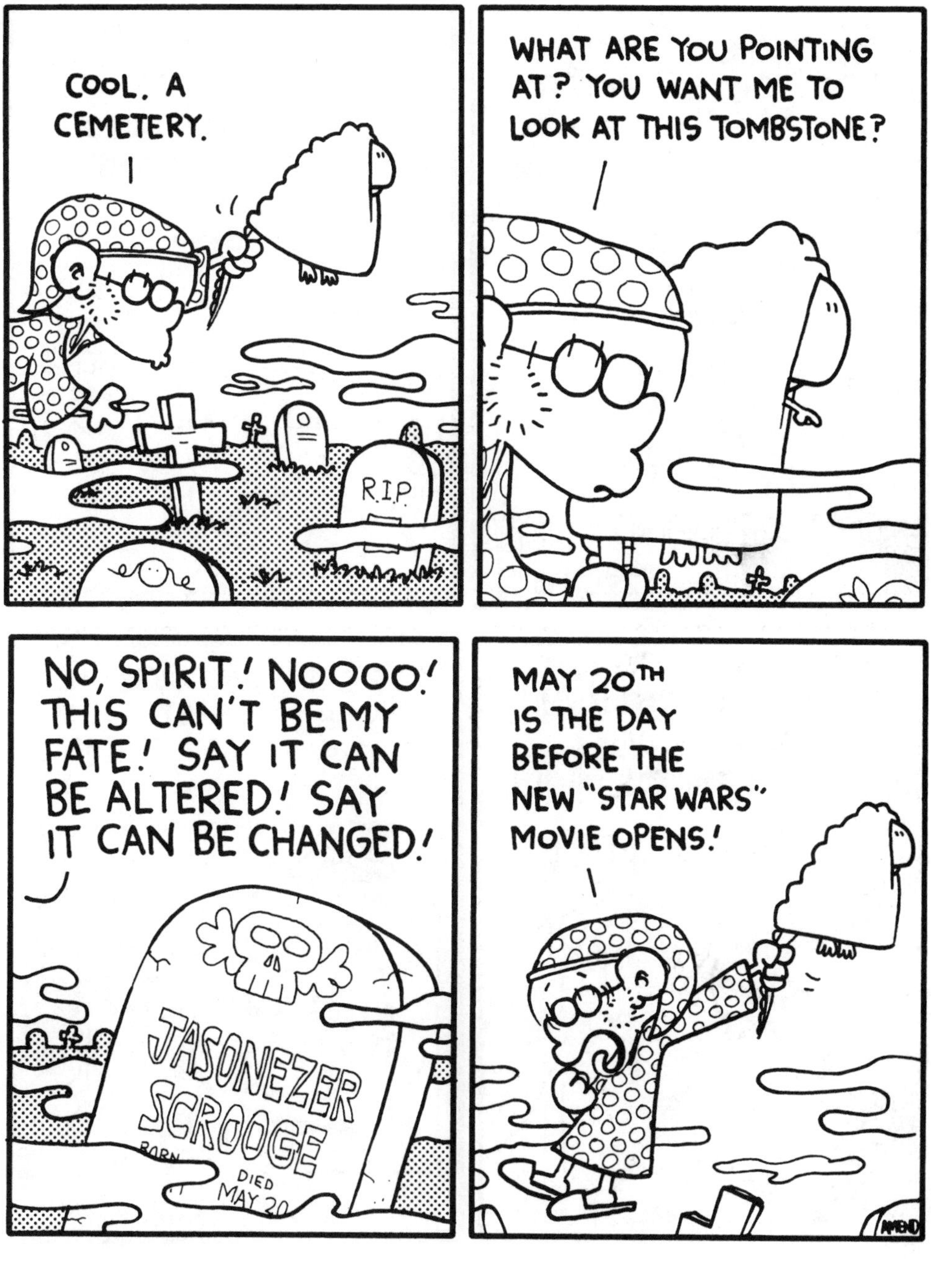
COOL. A CEMETERY.
R.I.P.
WHAT ARE YOU POINTING AT? YOU WANT ME TO LOOK AT THIS TOMBSTONE?
NO, SPIRIT! NOOOO! THIS CAN'T BE MY FATE! SAY IT CAN BE ALTERED! SAY IT CAN BE CHANGED!
JASONEZER SCROOGE
BORN
DIED MAY 20
MAY 20TH IS THE DAY BEFORE THE NEW "STAR WARS" MOVIE OPENS!
AMEND

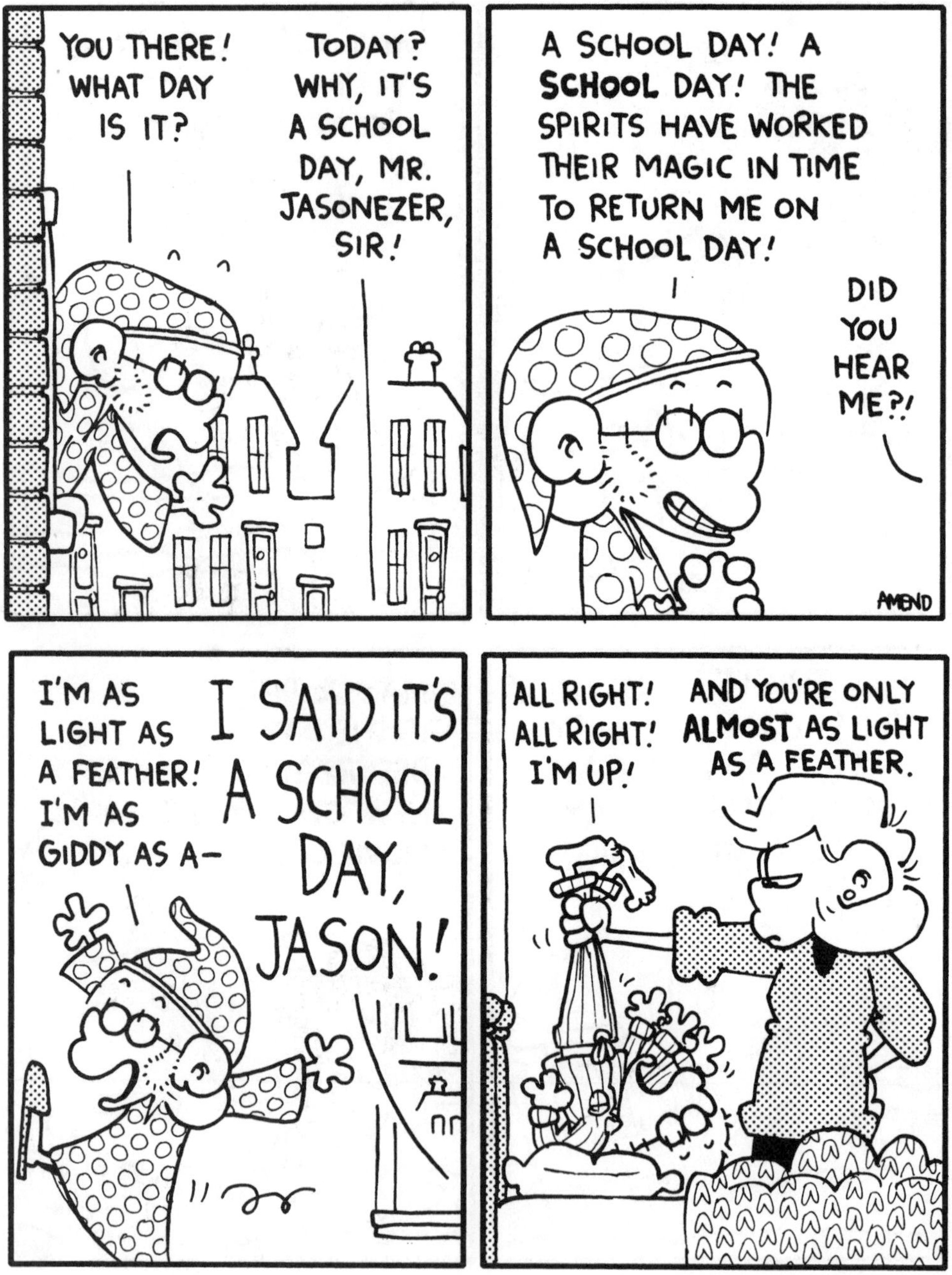
YOU THERE! WHAT DAY IS IT?
TODAY? WHY, IT'S A SCHOOL DAY, MR. JASONEZER, SIR!
A SCHOOL DAY! A SCHOOL DAY! THE SPIRITS HAVE WORKED THEIR MAGIC IN TIME TO RETURN ME ON A SCHOOL DAY!
DID YOU HEAR ME?!
AMEND
I'M AS LIGHT AS A FEATHER! I'M AS GIDDY AS A-
I SAID IT'S A SCHOOL DAY, JASON!
ALL RIGHT! ALL RIGHT! I'M UP!
AND YOU'RE ONLY ALMOST AS LIGHT AS A FEATHER.

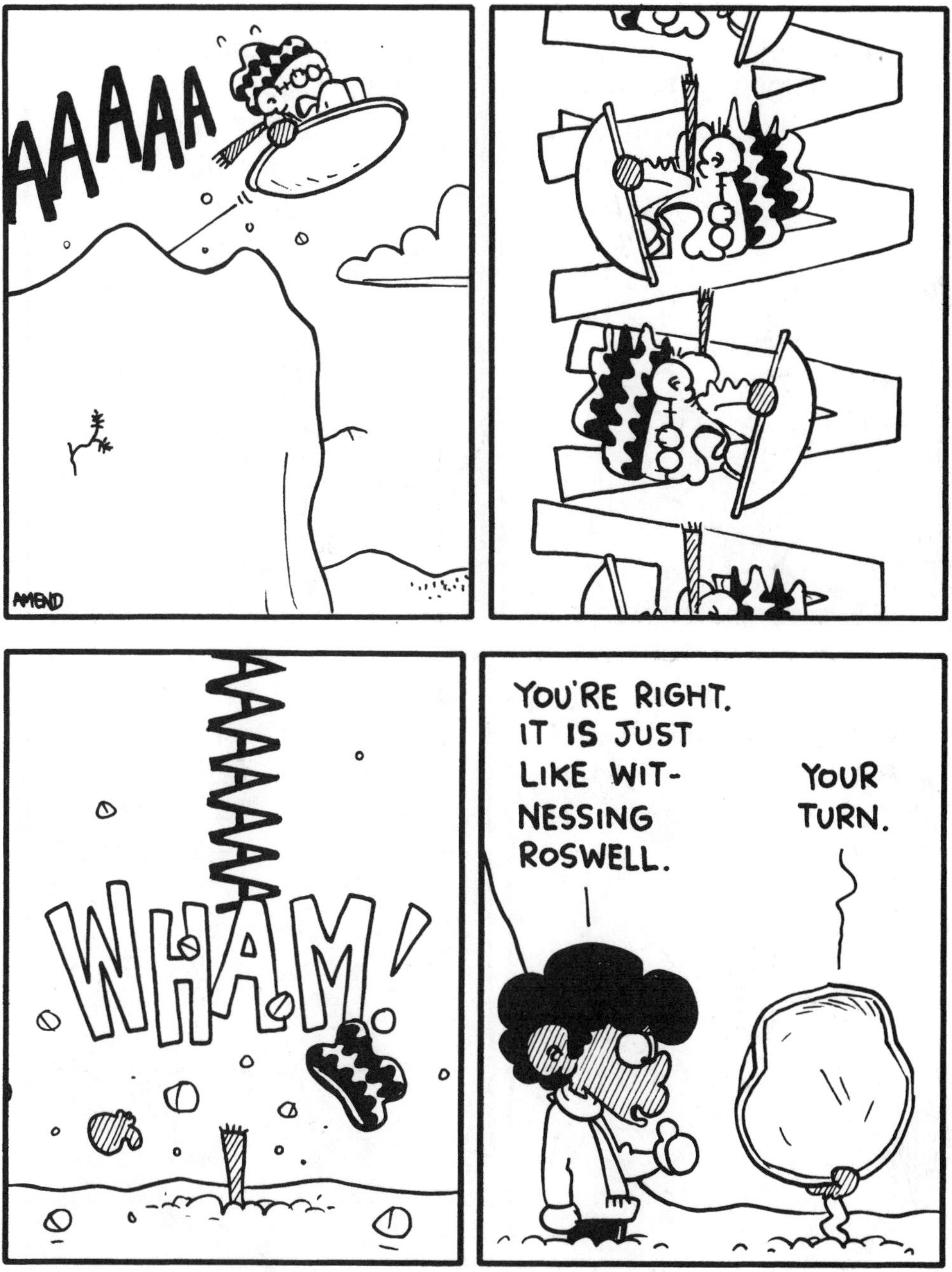
AAAAA
AMEND
WHAM!
YOU'RE RIGHT. IT IS JUST LIKE WIT- NESSING ROSWELL.
YOUR TURN.

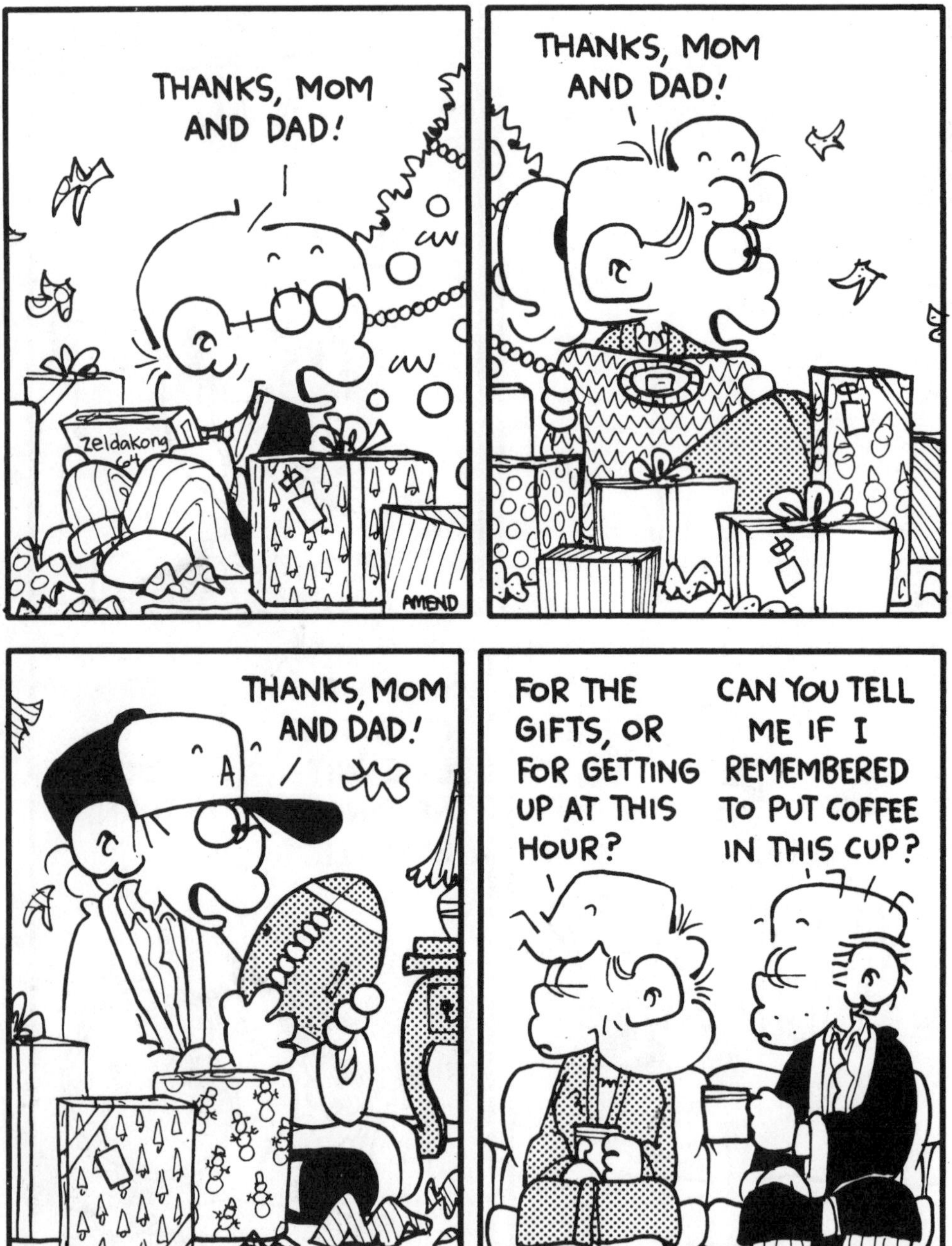
THANKS, MOM AND DAD!
Zeldakong 64
AMEND
THANKS, MOM AND DAD!
THANKS, MOM AND DAD!
FOR THE GIFTS, OR FOR GETTING UP AT THIS HOUR?
CAN YOU TELL ME IF I REMEMBERED TO PUT COFFEE IN THIS CUP?